THE
MOUNTAIN
SHADOW

Also by Gregory David Roberts

Shantaram

THE
MOUNTAIN
SHADOW

GREGORY DAVID
ROBERTS

Grove Press
New York

Published simultaneously in Canada
Printed in the United States of America

FIRST GROVE PRESS EDITION, October 2015

FIRST PAPERBACK EDITION, September 2016

ISBN 978-0-8021-2555-2

Grove Press
an imprint of Grove Atlantic
154 West 14th Street
New York, NY 10011

Distributed by Publishers Group West

groveatlantic.com

16 17 18 19   10 9 8 7 6 5 4 3 2 1

for the Goddess

PART ONE

CHAPTER ONE

THE SOURCE OF ALL THINGS, THE LUMINESCENCE, has more forms than heaven's stars, sure. And one good thought is all it takes to make it shine. But a single mistake can burn down a forest in your heart, hiding all the stars, in all the skies. And while a mistake's still burning, ruined love or lost faith can make you think you're done, and you can't go on. But it's not true. It's never true. No matter what you do, no matter where you're lost, the luminescence never leaves you. Any good thing that dies inside can rise again, if you want it hard enough. The heart doesn't know how to quit, because it doesn't know how to lie. You lift your eyes from the page, fall into the smile of a perfect stranger, and the searching starts all over again. It's not what it was. It's always different. It's always something else. But the new forest that grows back in a scarred heart is sometimes wilder and stronger than it was before the fire. And if you stay there, in that shine within yourself, that new place for the light, forgiving everything and never giving up, sooner or later you'll always find yourself right back there where love and beauty made the world: at the beginning. The beginning. The beginning.

'Hey, Lin, what a beginning to my day!' Vikram shouted from somewhere in the dark, humid room. 'How did you find me? When did you get back?'

'Just now,' I answered, standing at the wide French doors that opened onto the street-front veranda of the room. 'One of the boys told me you were here. Come out for a minute.'

'No, no, come on *in*, man!' Vikram laughed. 'Meet the *guys*!'

I hesitated. My eyes, bright with sky, couldn't see more than lumps of shadow in the dark room. All I could see clearly were two swords of sunlight, stabbing through closed shutters, piercing swirling clouds scented by aromatic hashish and the burnt vanilla of brown heroin.

3

Remembering that day, the drug-smell and the shadows and the burning light cutting across the room, I've asked myself if it was intuition that held me there at the threshold, and stopped me from going in. I've asked myself how different my life might've been if I'd turned and walked away.

The choices we make are branches in the tree of possibility. For three monsoons after that day, Vikram and the strangers in that room were new branches in a forest we shared for a while: an urban woodland of love, death and resurrection.

What I remember clearly, from that flinch of hesitation, that moment I didn't think was important at all at the time, is that when Vikram stepped from the darkness and grabbed my arm, dragging me inside, I shivered at the touch of his sweating hand.

A huge bed, extending three metres from the left-hand wall, dominated the big rectangular room. There was a man, or a dead body, it seemed, dressed in silver pyjamas and stretched out on the bed, with both hands folded across his chest.

His chest, so far as I could tell, didn't rise or fall. Two men, one on the left of the still figure, one on the right, sat on the bed and prepared chillum pipes.

On the wall above, directly over the head of the dead or deeply sleeping man, was a huge painting of Zoroaster, the prophet of the Parsi faith.

As my eyes adjusted to the darkness I saw three large chairs, separated by two heavy antique chests of drawers set against the far wall opposite the veranda, with a man sitting in each of them.

There was a very large, expensive Persian carpet on the floor, and various photographs of figures wearing traditional Parsi dress. To my right, opposite the bed, a hi-fi system rested on a marble-topped dresser. Two ceiling fans rotated just slowly enough not to irritate the clouds of smoke in the room.

Vikram led me past the bed to meet the man sitting in the first of the three chairs. He was a foreigner, like myself, but taller: his long body and even longer legs sprawled in the chair as if he was floating in a bath. I guessed him to be about thirty-five years old.

'This is Concannon,' Vikram said, urging me forward. 'He's in the IRA.'

The hand that shook mine was warm and dry and very strong.

'*Fock* the IRA!' he said, pronouncing the first word in the accent of Northern Ireland. 'I'm an Ulster man, UVF, but I can't expect a heathen cunt like Vikram to understand that, can I?'

I liked the confident gleam in his eye. I didn't like the confident words in his mouth. I withdrew my hand, nodding to him.

'Don't listen to him,' Vikram said. 'He talks a lot of weird shit, but he knows how to party like no foreigner I ever met, let me tell you.'

He pulled me toward the second man in the row of chairs. Just as I approached him, the young man puffed alight a hashish chillum, lit by the man from the third chair. As the flame from the matches was sucked into the pipe, a sudden burst of fire leaped from the bowl of the chillum and flared above the young man's head.

'*Bom shankar!*' Vikram shouted, reaching out for the pipe. 'Lin, this is Naveen Adair. He's a private detective. Honest to God. And Naveen, this is Lin, the guy I've been telling you about. He's a doctor, in the slum.'

The young man stood to shake my hand.

'You know,' he said with a wry smile, 'I'm not much of a detective, yet.'

'That's okay,' I smiled back at him. 'I'm not much of a doctor, period.'

The third man, who'd lit the chillum, took a puff and offered me the pipe. I smiled it away, and he passed it instead to one of the men on the bed.

'I'm Vinson,' he said, with a handshake like a big, happy puppy. 'Stuart Vinson. I've heard, like, a lot about you, man.'

'*Every* cunt has heard about Lin,' Concannon said, accepting a pipe from one of the men on the bed. 'Vikram goes on and on about you, like a fuckin' groupie. Lin this, Lin that, and Lin the other fuckin' thing. Tell me, have you sucked his cock yet, Vikram? Was he any good, or is it all talk?'

'Jesus, Concannon!' Vinson said.

'What?' Concannon asked, eyes wide. '*What?* I'm only askin' the man a question. India's still a free country, isn't it? At least, the parts where they speak English.'

'Don't mind him,' Vinson said to me, shrugging an apology. 'He can't help it. He has, like, Asshole Tourette's or something.'

Stuart Vinson, an American, had a strong physique, wide, clear features and a thick shock of wind-strewn blonde hair, which gave him the look of a sea adventurer, a solo yachtsman. In fact, he was a drug dealer, and a pretty successful one. I'd heard about him, just as he'd heard about me.

'This is Jamal,' Vikram said, ignoring Vinson and Concannon and introducing me to the man sitting on the left of the bed. 'He imports it, rubs it, rolls it and smokes it. He's a One Man Show.'

'One Man Show,' Jamal repeated.

He was thin, chameleon-eyed, and covered in religious amulets. I started counting them, hypnotised by holiness, and got to five major faiths before my eyes strayed into his smile.

'One Man Show,' I said.

'One Man Show,' he repeated.

'One Man Show,' I said.

'One Man Show,' he repeated.

I would've said it again, but Vikram stopped me.

'This is Billy Bhasu,' Vikram said, gesturing toward the small, very slight, cream-skinned man sitting on the other side of the still figure. Billy Bhasu put his palms together in a greeting, and continued to clean one of the chillums.

'Billy Bhasu is a bringer,' Vikram announced. 'He'll bring whatever you want. Anything at all, from a girl to an ice cream. Test him. It's true. Ask him to fetch you an ice cream. He'll bring it, right now. Ask him!'

'I don't want —'

'Billy, go get Lin an ice cream!'

'At once,' Billy replied, putting the chillum aside.

'No, Billy,' I said, raising a palm. 'I don't want an ice cream.'

'But you *love* ice cream,' Vikram observed.

'Not enough to send somebody for it, Vikram. Settle down, man.'

'If he's gonna bring somethin',' Concannon called from the shadows, 'my vote's for the ice cream *and* the girl. Two girls. And he should fuckin' get on with it.'

'You hear that, Billy?' Vikram urged.

He stepped closer to Billy, and began to drag him from the bed for the ice cream, but a voice, deep and resonant, came from the prone figure on the bed, and Vikram froze as if he was facing a gun.

'Vikram,' the voice said. 'You're killing my *high*, man.'

'Oh, shit! Oh, shit! Oh, shit! *Sorry*, Dennis,' Vikram stuttered. 'I was just introducing Lin around, to all the guys, and –'

'Lin,' the figure on the bed said, opening his eyes to stare at me.

They were surprisingly light, grey-coloured eyes, with a velvet radiance.

'My name's Dennis. I'm glad to meet you. Make yourself at home. *Mi casa, es su casa.*'

I stepped forward, shook the limp bird's wing that Dennis raised for me, and stepped back again to the foot of the bed. Dennis followed me with his eyes. His mouth settled into a gentle smile of benediction.

'Wow!' Vinson said softly, coming to stand beside me. 'Dennis, man! Good to see you back! Like, how was it on the other side?'

'Quiet,' Dennis intoned, still smiling at me. 'Very quiet. Until a few moments ago.'

Concannon and Naveen Adair, the young detective, joined us. Everyone was staring at Dennis.

'This is a big honour, Lin,' Vikram said. 'Dennis is looking at you.'

There was a little silence. Concannon broke it.

'That's nice, *that* is!' he growled, through a toothy smile. 'I sit here for six fuckin' months, share my wit and wisdom, smokin' your dope and drinkin' your whiskey, and you only open your eyes twice. Lin walks in the door and you're staring at him like he was on fuckin' fire. What am I, Dennis, a total *cunt?*'

'Like, totally, man,' Vinson said quietly.

Concannon laughed hard. Dennis winced.

'Concannon,' he whispered, 'I love you like a friendly ghost, but you're killing my high.'

'Sorry, Dennis lad,' Concannon grinned.

'Lin,' Dennis murmured, his head and body perfectly still, 'please don't think me rude. I'll have to rest now. It was a pleasure to meet you.'

He turned his head one degree toward Vikram.

'Vikram,' he murmured, in that sonorous, rumbling basso. 'Please keep it down. You're killing my high, man. I'd appreciate it if you'd stop.'

'Of course, Dennis. Sorry.'

'Billy Bhasu?' Dennis said softly.

'Yes, Dennis?'

7

'Fuck the ice cream.'

'Fuck the ice cream, Dennis?'

'Fuck the ice cream. Nobody gets ice cream. Not today.'

'Yes, Dennis.'

'Are we clear on the ice cream?'

'Fuck the ice cream, Dennis.'

'I don't want to hear the words *ice cream* for at least three months.'

'Yes, Dennis.'

'Good. Now, Jamal, please make me another chillum. A big, strong one. A gigantic one. A legendary one. It would be an act of compassion, not far from a miracle. Goodbye, all and everyone, here and there.'

Dennis folded his hands across his chest, closed his eyes and settled into his resting state: death-like rigidity at five breaths a minute.

No-one moved or spoke. Jamal, lip-lock urgent, prepared a legendary chillum. The room stared at Dennis. I seized Vikram by the shirt.

'Come on, we're outta here,' I said, pulling Vikram with me out of the room. 'Goodbye, all and everyone, here and there.'

'Hey, wait for me!' Naveen called after us, rushing out through the French doors.

Back on the street, fresh air stirred Vikram and Naveen awake. Their steps quickened, matching mine.

The breeze driven through a shaded corridor of three-storey buildings and leafy plane trees brought with it the strong, working scent of the fishing fleet at nearby Sassoon Dock.

Pools of sunlight spilled through gaps between the trees. As I passed from shade to light, splashing into each new pool of white heat, I felt the sun flooding into me and then draining away with the shadow tide, beneath the trees.

The sky was haze-blue: glass washed up from the sea. Crows rode on the rooftops of buses to cooler parts of the city. The cries of handcart pullers were confident and fierce.

It was the kind of clear Bombay day that makes Bombay people, Mumbaikars, sing out loud, and as I passed a man walking in the opposite direction, I noticed that we were both humming the same Hindi love song.

'That's funny,' Naveen remarked. 'You were both on the same song, man.'

I smiled, and was about to sing a few more lines, as we do on blue glass Bombay days, when Vikram cut across us with a question.

'So, how did it go? Did you get it?'

One of the reasons why I don't go to Goa very often is that every time I go to Goa, someone asks me to do something down there. When I'd told Vikram, three weeks earlier, that I had a mission in Goa, he'd asked me to do something for him.

He'd left one of his mother's wedding jewels with a loan shark, as collateral for a cash loan. It was a necklace inset with small rubies. Vikram repaid the debt, but the shark refused to return the necklace. He told him to collect it in Goa, in person. Knowing that the shark respected the Sanjay Company mafia gang I worked for, Vikram asked me to visit him.

I'd done it, and I'd retrieved the necklace, but Vikram had over-estimated the loan shark's respect for the mafia Company. He kept me waiting for a week of wasted time, ducking out of one meeting after another, leaving offensive messages about me and the Sanjay Company until finally agreeing to hand the necklace over.

By then, it was too late. He was a shark, and the mafia Company he'd insulted was a shark boat. I called in four local guys who worked for the Sanjay Company. We beat the gangsters that stood between him and us until they ran.

We confronted the shark. He handed over the necklace. Then one of the local guys beat him, in a fair fight, and kept on beating him, in an unfair fight, until the wider point about respect was made.

'Well?' Vikram asked. 'Did you get it, or not?'

'Here,' I said, taking the necklace from my jacket pocket and handing it to Vikram.

'Wow! You got it! I knew I could count on you. Did Danny give you any trouble?'

'Scratch that source of loans from your list, Vikram.'

'*Thik*,' he said. *Okay*.

He poured the jewelled necklace from its blue silk pouch. The rubies, fired with sunlight, bled into his cupped palms.

'Listen, I'm . . . I'm gonna take this home to my Mom. Right now. Can I give you guys a lift in my cab?'

'You're going the other way,' I said, as Vikram flagged down a passing cab. 'I'm gonna walk back to my bike, at Leopold's.'

'If you don't mind,' Naveen asked softly, 'I'd like to walk some of the way with you.'

'Suit yourself,' I replied, watching Vikram put the silk pouch inside his shirt for safekeeping.

He was about to step into the taxi but I stopped him, leaning in close to speak quietly.

'What are you doing?'

'What do you mean?'

'You can't lie to me about drugs, Vik.'

'What *lying*?' he protested. 'Shit, I just had a few little puffs of brown sugar, that's all. So what? It's Concannon's stuff, anyway. He paid for it. I —'

'Take it easy.'

'I always take it easy. You know me.'

'Some people can snap out of a habit, Vikram. Concannon might be one of them. You're not one of them. You know that.'

He smiled, and for a few seconds the old Vikram was there: the Vikram who would've gone to Goa for the necklace without any help from me, or anyone else; the Vikram who wouldn't have left a piece of his mother's wedding jewellery with a loan shark in the first place.

The smile folded from his eyes as he got into the taxi. I watched him away, worried for the danger in what he was: an optimist, ruined by love.

I started walking again, and Naveen fell in beside me.

'He talks about that girl, the English girl, a lot,' Naveen said.

'It's one of those things that should've worked out, but rarely do.'

'He talks about you a lot, too,' Naveen said.

'He talks too much.'

'He talks about Karla and Didier and Lisa. But mostly he talks about you.'

'He talks too much.'

'He told me you escaped from prison,' he said. 'And that you're on the run.'

I stopped walking.

'Now *you're* talking too much. What is this, an epidemic?'

'No, let me explain. You helped a friend of mine, Aslan . . . '

'What?'

'A friend of mine —'

'What are you talking about?'

'It was near Ballard Pier one night, late, a couple of weeks ago. You helped him out of a tight spot.'

A young man, running toward me through Ballard Estate after midnight, the wide street a merchant's bluff of locked buildings on both sides, no escape when the others came, and the young man stopping, streetlights throwing tree shadows on the road, the young man standing to fight them alone, and then not alone.

'What about it?'

'He died. Three days ago. I've been trying to find you, but you were in Goa. I'm taking my chance to tell you now.'

'Tell me what?'

He flinched. I was hard-faced on him, because he'd talked about the prison break, and I wanted him to get to the point.

'He was my friend, in college,' he said evenly. 'He liked roaming, at night, in dangerous places. Like I do. Like *you* do, or else you wouldn't have been there, to help him out that night. I thought, maybe, you'd like to know.'

'Are you kidding?'

We were standing in thin shade. We were inches apart, while the churn of the causeway wound around us.

'What do you mean?'

'You put prison escape on the table, just so you can bring me the sad tidings of Aslan's demise? Is that what you're telling me? Are you nuts, or are you really that nice?'

'I guess,' he said, hurt and getting angry, 'I'm really that nice. Too nice to think you'd take what I'm saying for anything but what it is. I regret that I troubled you. It's the last thing I would want to do. I apologise. I'll take my leave.'

I stopped him.

'Wait!' I said. 'Wait.'

Everything about him was right: the honest stare, the confident stance, and the light in his smile. Instinct chooses her own children. My instincts liked the kid, the young man standing in front of me looking so brave and hurt. Everything about him was right, and you don't see that often.

'Okay, my fault,' I said, raising a hand.

'No problem,' he replied, relaxing again.

11

'So, let's go back to Vikram telling you about a prison break. See, that's the kind of information that *might* raise Interpol's interest, and *always* raises *my* interest. You see that, right?'

It wasn't a question, and he knew it.

'Fuck Interpol.'

'You're a detective.'

'Fuck detectives, too. This is the kind of information about a friend that you don't hide from a friend, when you come to know it. Didn't anybody ever teach you that? I grew up on these streets, right here, and I know that.'

'But we're not friends.'

'Not yet,' Naveen smiled.

I looked at him for a while.

'You like walking?'

'I like walking and talking,' he said, falling into step with me in the serpent lines of people traffic.

'Fuck Interpol,' he said again, after a while.

'You really do like talking, don't you?'

'And walking.'

'Okay, so tell me three very short walking stories.'

'Sure. Fine. Walking story number one?'

'Dennis.'

'You know,' Naveen laughed, dodging a woman carrying a huge bundle of scrap papers on her head, 'that was my first time there, too. Other than what you saw with your own eyes, I can only tell you what I've heard.'

'So heard me.'

'His parents died. Hit him pretty hard, they say. They were loaded. They had the patent for something, and it was worth a lot. Sixty million, to Dennis.'

'That's not a sixty-million-dollar room back there.'

'His money's in trust,' he replied, 'while he's in his trance.'

'While he's lying down, you mean?'

'It's more than lying down. Dennis is in a state of Samadhi when he sleeps. His heartbeat and his breathing slow down until they approach zero. Quite often, he's technically dead.'

'You're fuckin' with me, detective.'

'No,' he laughed. 'Several doctors have signed death certificates in

12

the last year, but Dennis always woke up again. Jamal, the One Man Show, has a collection of them.'

'Okay, so Dennis is occasionally technically dead. That must be tough on his priest, and his accountant.'

'While he's in his trance, Dennis's estate is managed in trust, leaving him enough to buy the apartment we just visited, and maintain himself in a manner suitable to the parameters of his trance states.'

'Did you hear all this, or detective it?'

'Bit of both.'

'Well,' I said, pausing a while to let a car reverse in front of us. 'Whatever his gig, I can truly say I never saw anyone lie down better in my life.'

'No contest,' Naveen grinned.

We both thought about it for a while.

'Second story?' Naveen asked.

'Concannon,' I said, moving on.

'He boxes at my gym. I don't know a lot about him, but I can tell you two things.'

'Which are?'

'He has a mean left hook that bangs a gong, but it leaves him dipping if it misses.'

'Uh-huh?'

'Every time. He jabs with the left, punches with the right, and always brings the left hook straight over the top of it, leaving himself wide open if he doesn't connect. But he's quick, and he doesn't miss often. He's pretty good.'

'And?'

'Second, I can say he's the only guy I met who got me through the door to see Dennis. Dennis loves him. He stayed awake longer for him than anybody else. I heard that he wants to legally adopt Concannon. It's difficult, because Concannon is older than Dennis, and I don't know if there's a legal precedent for an Indian adopting a white man.'

'What do you mean, he got you *through the door*?'

'There's thousands of people who'd like to have an audience with Dennis, while he's in his trance. They believe that while he's *temporarily* dead, he can communicate with the *permanently* dead. Almost nobody can get in.'

'Unless you walk up, and knock on the door.'

13

'You don't get it. Nobody would *dare* to walk up and knock on the door, while Dennis is in his trance.'

'Come on.'

'Nobody, that is, until you did.'

'We already covered Dennis,' I said, pausing to let a four-man hand-cart pass. 'Back to Concannon.'

'Like I said, he boxes at my gym. He's a street fighter. I don't know much about him. He seems like a party guy. He loves a party.'

'He's got a mouth on him. You don't keep a mouth like that to his age without having something to back it up.'

'Are you saying I should watch him?'

'Only the wrong side of him.'

'And the third story?' he asked.

I left the road where we'd been walking, and straddled the hand-width footpath for a few steps.

'Where are we going?' he asked, following me.

'I'm going to get a juice.'

'A juice?'

'It's a hot day. What's the matter with you?'

'Oh, nothing. Cool. I love juice.'

Thirty-nine degrees in Bombay, chilled watermelon juice, fans too close to your head turned up to three: bliss.

'So . . . what's with the *private detective* thing? Is that for real?'

'Yeah. It started by accident, kind of, but I've been doing it for almost a year now.'

'What kind of accident turns someone into a detective?'

'I was doing a law degree,' he smiled. 'Got most of the way there. In my final year, I was researching a paper on private detectives, and how they impact the court system. Pretty soon, the only thing that interested me was the detective part of it, and I dropped out, to give it a shot.'

'How's it working out?'

He laughed.

'Divorce is healthier than the stock exchange, and way more predictable. I did a few divorce cases, but I stopped. I was with another guy. He was teaching me the ropes. He's been scoping divorce for thirty-five years, and still loves it. I didn't. It was always unique for the married men, having the affairs. It was always the same sad movie for me.'

'And since you left the lush pastures of divorce?'

14

'I've found two missing pets, a missing husband, and a missing casserole dish so far,' he said. 'It seems that all of my clients, God bless them, are people too lazy or polite to do it for themselves.'

'But you like it, the detective thing. You get a rush, right?'

'You know, I think at this end of the story you get the truth. As a lawyer you're only ever allowed a version of the truth. This is the real thing, even if it's just a stolen heirloom casserole dish. It's the real story, before everybody lies about it.'

'Are you gonna stick with it?'

'I don't know,' he smiled, looking away again. 'Depends on how good I am, I guess.'

'Or how bad you are.'

'Or how bad I am.'

'We're already on story number three,' I said. 'Naveen Adair, Indian–Irish private detective.'

He laughed, white teeth foaming in the wake of it, but the wave faded quickly.

'Not much to it, really.'

'Naveen Adair,' I pronounced. 'Which part kicked you in the arse more, the Indian part, or the Irish part?'

'Too Anglo for the Indians,' he laughed, 'and too Indian for the Anglos. My father . . .'

Jagged peaks and lost valleys, for too many of us, are the lands called father. Climbing one of those peaks beside him, I waited until he crested the conversation again.

'We lived on the footpath, after he abandoned my Mother. We were on the street, until I was five, but I don't really remember it much.'

'What happened?'

He raised his gaze to the street, eyes floating on the tide of colour and emotion, moving back and forth.

'He had tuberculosis,' the young detective said. 'He made a will, naming my Mother, and it turned out that he'd made a lot of money, somehow, so we were suddenly rich, and . . .'

'Everything changed.'

He looked at me as if he'd told me too much.

The fan, only inches from my head, was giving me an ice-cream headache. I gestured to the waiter, and asked him to turn it down a notch.

'You're cold?' he scoffed, his hand on the switch. 'Let me show you cold.'

He turned the fan to blizzard five. I felt my cheeks beginning to freeze. We paid the bill and left, hearing his goodbye.

'Table two, free again!'

'I love that place,' Naveen said as we left.

'You do?'

'Yeah. Great juice, nasty waiters. Perfect.'

'You and I might get along, detective. We might just get along.'

CHAPTER TWO

THE PAST, BELOVED ENEMY, HAS BAD TIMING. Those Bombay days come back to me so vividly and suddenly that sometimes I'm shaken from the hour I'm in, and lost to the task. A smile, a song, and I'm back there, sleeping sunny mornings away, riding a motorcycle on a mountain road, or tied and beaten and begging Fate for an even break. And I love every minute of it, every minute of friend or foe, of flight and forgiveness: every minute of life. But the past has a way of taking you to the right place at the wrong time, and that can be a storm inside.

I should be bitter, I guess, after some of the things I've done, and had done to me. People tell me I should be bitter. A con once said, *You'd be a top bloke, if you just had a little spite in you.* But I was born without it, and I've never known spite or bitterness. I got angry and I got desperate and did bad things too often, until I stopped, but I never hated anyone, or consciously wished anyone harm, not even men who tortured me. And while a small measure of bitterness might've protected me from time to time, as it sometimes does, I've learned that sweet memories don't walk through cynical doors. And I love my memories, even when they have bad timing: remembered minutes of sunlight staking out patches on tree-lined Bombay streets, of fearless girls flashing through traffic on scooters, of handcart pullers straining under the load but smiling, and those first memories of a young Indian-Irish detective named Naveen Adair.

We walked on the road silently for a while, passing between cars and streams of people, swaying back and forth between the bicycles and handcarts in the dance of the street.

In the wide doorway of the Fire Brigade building, a group of men in heavy navy-blue uniforms chatted and laughed. Inside the firehouse there were two large fire trucks, shimmering sunlight from every polished red or chrome surface.

An extravagantly decorated Hanuman shrine was fixed to one wall, and beside it a sign said:

IF YOU CAN'T STAND THE HEAT,
GET OUT OF THE BURNING BUILDING.

Further along, we entered the shopping district, spilling out from the Colaba market. Glass merchants, picture framers, timber and hardware stores, electrical goods, and plumbers' supplies gradually gave way to clothing, jewellery and food stores.

At the wide entrance to the market itself we had to stop, as several heavy trucks made their way out into the maul of traffic on the main road.

'Listen,' he said as we waited. 'You were right, about Vikram talking too much. But it ends with me. I'll never talk about it to anyone else but you. Never. And if you ever need me, hey, man, I'm there. That's all I'm trying to say. For Aslan, and what you did that night, if you don't want it to be for you.'

It wasn't the first time that I looked out from the red exile my life had become, into eyes alight with fires, burning on cliff-tops of the word *escape*. In my fugitive years, I sometimes found fast friendship in the song of rebellion: in the loyalty others pledged to my escape from the system, as much as to me.

They wanted me to stay free, in part, because they wanted *someone* to escape and stay free. I smiled at Naveen. It wasn't the first or last time I went with the river inside.

'How do you do,' I said, offering my hand. 'I'm Lin. I'm not a doctor in the slum.'

'Pleased to meet you,' Naveen replied, shaking my hand. 'I'm Naveen, and thank you. It's always good to know who's not the doctor.'

'And who's not the police,' I added. 'How about a drink?'

'Don't mind if we do,' he replied graciously.

Just at that moment I had the sense of someone standing too close to my back. I turned hard.

'Hang about!' Gemini George protested. 'Easy does it with the shirt, mate. That's fifty per cent of my wardrobe, I'll have you know!'

18

I could feel the bones of his thin body against my knuckles as I released my grip.

'Sorry, man,' I said, straightening the front of his shirt. 'Creepin' up on people like that. Should know better, Gemini. It'll end in tears one day.'

'My fault, mate,' Gemini George apologised, looking around nervously. 'Got a bit of a problem like, y'know?'

I put my hand in my pocket, but Gemini stopped me.

'Not that sort of problem, mate. Well, to be honest, that *is* a problem, but it's such a constant problem, you know, bein' broke, that it's become more of a *meta-cultural statement*, sort of a grim but compelling penury soundtrack, know what I mean?'

'No, man,' I said, handing him some money. 'What's the problem?'

'Can you wait? I'll just get Scorpio.'

'Sure.'

Gemini looked left and right.

'You'll wait?'

I nodded and he ducked away past a nearby stall that offered small marble figures of gods for sale.

'Mind if I hang with you?' Naveen asked.

'No problem,' I said. 'No secrets are safe with Gemini and Scorpio, especially their own. They could have their own radio station. I'd listen, if they did.'

Moments later Gemini reappeared, dragging the reluctant Scorpio with him.

The Zodiac Georges, one George from south London and the other from Canada, were inseparable street guys. They were mildly addicted to seven drugs, and completely addicted to one another. They slept in a relatively comfortable warehouse doorway, and made a living running errands, sourcing drugs for foreign customers, and occasionally selling information to gangsters.

They bickered and fought from the first yawn to the last stumble into sleep, but they loved each other, and were so constant in their friendship that everyone who knew them loved the Zodiac Georges for it: Gemini George from London, and Scorpio George from Canada.

'Sorry, Lin,' Scorpio mumbled, when Gemini dragged him close. 'I was under cover, like. It's this trouble with the CIA. You must've heard about it.'

'The CIA? Can't say I have. But I've been in Goa. What's up?'

'There's this geezer,' Gemini cut in, while his taller friend nodded quickly. 'Snow-white hair, but not an old guy, with a dark blue suit and tie, a businessman type —'

'Or the CIA,' Scorpio cut in, leaning close to whisper.

'For Chrissakes, Scorpio!' Gemini spluttered. 'What the *fuck* would the CIA want with the likes of *us*?'

'They have these machines that can read our minds,' Scorpio whispered, 'even through walls.'

'If they can read our minds, there's no point whisperin', is there?' Gemini demanded.

'Maybe they already programmed us to whisper, while they read our minds.'

'If they read *your* mind, they'll run screamin' through the streets, you fuckin' twat. It's a wonder *I* don't run screamin' through the streets n'all, innit?'

There was no reliable map of the sidetracks the Zodiac Georges took when argument meandered, and no time limit. I usually liked it, but not always.

'Tell me about the white-haired guy in the suit.'

'We don't know who he is, Lin,' Gemini said, returning to the moment. 'But he's been askin' about Scorpio at Leopold's and other places for the last two days.'

'It's the CIA,' Scorpio repeated, his eyes looking for somewhere to hide.

Gemini looked at me, his face crying why-was-I-born. He tried to be patient. He took a breath. It didn't work.

'If it's the CIA, and they can read our minds,' he shouted at Scorpio through clenched teeth, 'they'd hardly be goin' round askin' *questions* about us, would they? They'd just walk right up, tap us on the shoulder and say *Hey! We just read your mind, old son, with our mind-reading machine, and we didn't have to ask questions about you, or follow you around, because we have mind-reading machines that read people's minds, because we're the fucking CIA, wouldn't they? Wouldn't they?*'

'Well . . . '

'Was he asking after you by name?' Naveen asked, his young face serious. 'And is he asking after both of you, or just Scorpio?'

Both men looked at Naveen.

'This is Naveen Adair,' I said. 'He's a private detective.'

There was a pause.

'Fuckin' hell,' Gemini muttered. 'Not very private, is it, goin' round announcin' it, right here in the fruit and vegetable market? That's more like a *public* detective, innit?'

Naveen laughed.

'You didn't answer my questions,' he said.

There was another pause.

'What . . . *kind* of detective is he?' Scorpio asked suspiciously.

'He's a *detective*,' I said. 'It's like a priest, you pay once. Answer the questions, Scorpio.'

'You know,' Scorpio said, looking at Naveen thoughtfully, 'come to think of it, the guy *has* only been asking after *me*, not Gemini.'

'Where's he staying?' Naveen asked.

'We don't know yet,' Gemini said. 'We didn't take it seriously, at first. But now, it's been two days. It's startin' to get a bit spooky for Scorpio, and he's spooked enough, know what I mean? One of the street boys has been followin' the white-haired geezer today, and we should know where he's stayin' pretty soon.'

'If you want, I'll look into it,' Naveen said softly.

Gemini and Scorpio looked at me. I shrugged.

'Yeah,' Scorpio agreed quickly. 'Hell, yeah. Please try to find out who this guy is, if you can.'

'We've gotta get to the bottom of this,' Gemini added fervently. 'Scorpio's got me so aggravated, I woke up with me hands around me own neck, this mornin'. It's come to a pretty pass, when a man strangles himself in his own sleep.'

'What should we do now?' Scorpio asked.

'Stay out of sight, as much as possible,' Naveen said. 'Let Lin know, if you find out where the guy's staying. Or leave a message for me at the Natraj building, on Merewether. Naveen Adair.'

There was a little silence while the Zodiac Georges looked at one another, then at Naveen, then back at me.

'Sounds like a plan,' I said, shaking hands with Gemini.

The money I'd given him was enough for at least two of their favourite drugs, a few soft days in a rough hotel, clean clothes from their frequently unpaid laundry man, and a diet of the Bengali desserts they loved.

They wriggled into the camouflage of the crowded street, Scorpio stooping to put his head beside the Londoner's as they walked.

'What do you make of it?' I asked Naveen.

'I'm smelling lawyer,' he replied carefully. 'I'll see what pops up from the toaster. I can't guarantee a result. I'm an amateur, remember.'

'An amateur is anyone who hasn't learned how *not* to do it,' I said.

'Not bad. Is that a quote?'

'It is.'

'Who said it?'

'A woman I know. What's it to you?'

'Can I meet her?'

'No.'

'Please.'

'What is it with you and meeting hard-to-meet people?'

'It *was* Karla, wasn't it? An amateur is anyone who hasn't learned how *not* to do it. Nice.'

I stopped, standing close to him.

'Let's make a deal,' I said. 'You don't mention Karla again, to me.'

'That's not a deal,' he said, smiling easily.

'Glad you understand. We were not minding if we do have a drink, remember?'

We walked into Leopold's beer-and-curry-scented cave. It was late afternoon, the lull before the storm of tourists, drug dealers, black marketers, racketeers, actors, students, gangsters, and good girls with an eye for bad boys squalled in through the wide arches to shout, eat, drink and chance their souls on the wet roulette of Leopold's thirty restaurant tables.

It was Didier's favourite time in the bar, nudging out second place, which was every other hour that the bar was open, and I found him sitting alone at his regular table, set against the back wall, with a clear view of all three entrances.

He was reading a newspaper, holding the pages at arm's length.

'Holy shit, Didier! A newspaper! You should warn people about a shock like that.'

I turned to the waiter, uneponymously named Sweetie, who was loitering with intent, his pink nametag loitering sideways on his jacket.

'What's the matter with you, Sweetie? You should've put a sign outside, or something.'

'Fuck you very much,' Sweetie replied, shifting a match from one side of his mouth to the other with his tongue.

Didier tossed the newspaper aside, and hugged me.

'You wear the sun well,' he said.

He held me for a moment, examining me with forensic thoroughness.

'You look like the *stand-out*. That is the expression? Not the *star* actor, but the one who takes all the punishment.'

'The expression is stand-*in*, but I'll take stand-out. Say hello to another stand-out, Naveen Adair.'

'Ah, the detective!' Didier said, shaking hands warmly, and running a professional eye over Naveen's tall, athletic frame. 'I've heard all about you, from my journalist friend, Kavita Singh.'

'She covered you, too,' Naveen replied with a smile. 'And may I say, it's an honour to meet the man behind all the stories.'

'I did not expect a young man of such impeccable manners,' Didier responded quickly, gesturing toward the chairs, and signalling to Sweetie. 'What will you have? Beers? Sweetie! Three very chilled beers, please!'

'Fuck you very much,' Sweetie mumbled, his end-of-shift slippers dragging to the kitchen.

'He's a repellent brute,' Didier said, watching Sweetie leave. 'But I feel myself strangely drawn to the effortlessness of his misery.'

We were three men at the table, but we all sat in a line with our backs to the wall, facing across the scatter of tables to the wide arches, open to the street. Didier let his eyes rove around the restaurant: a castaway, scanning the horizon.

'*Well*,' he said, inclining his head toward me. 'The adventure in Goa?'

I took a small package of letters wrapped in blue ribbons from my pocket, and handed it across. Didier took the bundle and cradled it in his palms for a moment, as if it were an injured bird.

'Did you . . . did you have to *beat* him for them?' he asked me, still staring at the letters.

'No.'

'Oh,' he sighed, looking up quickly.

'Should I have?'

'No, of course, not,' Didier explained, sniffing back a tear. 'Didier could not pay for such a thing.'

'You didn't pay me at all.'

'Technically, in paying *nothing*, I am still paying. Am I right, Naveen?'

'I have no idea what you're talking about,' Naveen replied. 'So, of course, I agree with everything.'

'It's just,' Didier sniffed, looking at the letters, 'I rather thought he might have put up some little *fight*, perhaps, to keep my love letters. Some . . . some show of lingering affection.'

I recalled the look of simian hatred on the face of Gustavo, Didier's ex-lover, as he screamed curses on Didier's genitals, and hurled the little bundle of letters into a rubbish pit below the back window of his bungalow.

I had to pierce his ear with my thumbnail to make him climb into the pit, retrieve the letters, wipe them clean and hand them to me.

'No,' I said. 'Affection has moved on.'

'Well, thank you, Lin,' Didier sighed, putting the letters in his lap as the beers arrived. 'I would have gone down there myself to get the letters, but for that little matter of the outstanding arrest warrant in my name, in Goa.'

'You've gotta keep track of these warrants, Didier,' I said. 'I can't keep up. You could paper a room with my fake yellow slips. It's wearing me out, clearing you of all charges.'

'But there are only four outstanding arrest warrants in all of India, Lin.'

'*Only* four?'

'At one time, it was nine. I think it must be that I am becoming . . . *reformed*,' Didier puffed, curling his lips at the distasteful word.

'A slander,' Naveen observed.

'Why, thank you. You . . . are a very agreeable young man. Do you like guns?'

'I'm not good with relationships,' Naveen answered, finishing his beer and standing. 'I can only bond with the gun in my hand.'

'I can help you with that,' Didier laughed.

'I'll bet you can,' Naveen laughed back. 'Lin, that guy in the suit, the one following the Zodiac Georges, I'll look into it, and get back to you here.'

'Be careful. We don't know what this is, yet.'

'It's cool,' he smiled, all fearless, immortal youth. 'I'll take my leave. Didier, it has been a pleasure and an honour. Goodbye.'

We watched him out into the early evening haze. Didier's brows edged together.

'What?' I asked him.

'Nothing!' he protested.

'What, Didier?'

'I said nothing!'

'I know, but I also know that look.'

'What *look?*' he demanded, as if I'd accused him of stealing my drink.

Didier Levy was in his mid-forties. The first powder snow of winter wove spirals through his dark, curly hair. Soft, brilliantly blue irises hovered in the anemone patchwork of red veins filling the whites of his eyes, making him seem young and dissolute in the same smile: the mischievous boy still hiding inside the ruining man.

He drank any kind of alcohol, at any time of the day or night, dressed like a dandy, long after other dandies melted in the heat, smoked tailor-made joints from a bespoke cigarette case, was a professional at most crimes, the master of a few, and was openly gay, in a city where that was still an oxymoron.

I'd known him for five years, through struggles against enemies, within and without. He was brave: the kind of man who'll face a gun with you and never run, no matter what the fall.

He was authentic. He expressed the uniqueness when what we are, is what we're free to become. I'd known him through lost loves, alarming lust, and kneeling epiphanies, his and mine. And I'd spent enough of those long, lonely wolf nights with him to love him.

'*That* look,' I repeated. 'The look that says you know something that everybody else should know. The look that says *I told you so*, before you tell me anything at all. So *tell* me, before you *told* me so.'

Didier's outraged expression crumbled in smiles, and fell into a laugh.

'It is more of a told *me* so,' he said. 'I like that boy very much. More than I expected to. And more than I should, because this Naveen Adair, he has a reputation.'

'If reputations were votes, we'd be presidents of somewhere.'

'True,' he replied. 'But this boy's reputation carries a warning. A *word to the wise*, isn't that the expression?'

'It is, but I've always wondered why the wise need a word.'

'It is said that he is very, very good with his fists. He was a boxing champion at his university. He could have been the champion of India. His fists are deadly weapons. And as I have heard, he is very quick, too quick perhaps, to provoke into using them.'

'You're no slouch in the provoking department, Didier. And it doesn't take a stick through the bars to get me going.'

'Many men have already fallen to their knees before that young life. It is not a good thing, in a man so young, to see so much submission. There is a lot of blood behind that charming young smile.'

'There's a lot of blood behind *your* charming smile, my friend.'

'Thank you,' he nodded, accepting the compliment with a little toss of the greying curls. 'I'm simply saying that from what I have heard, I would very much prefer to shoot that handsome young fellow than to fight him.'

'Then it's a lucky thing you carry a gun.'

'I'm ... if you'll excuse the lapse ... being *serious*, Lin, and you know how much contempt I have for serious things.'

'I'll keep it in mind. Promise. I'd better go.'

'You're leaving me here to drink alone, and you're going home to *her*?' Didier mocked. 'You think she's waiting for you, after almost three weeks in Goa? What makes you think she hasn't left you for some *greener pastures*, as the English say, with such charming provincialism.'

'I love you, too, brother,' I said, shaking his hand.

I walked out into the breathing street, turning once to see him holding up the little bundle of love letters I'd retrieved for him, and waving goodbye.

It stopped me. I felt, as I too often did, that I was abandoning him. It was foolish, I knew: Didier was arguably the most self-sufficient contrabandist in the city. He was one of the last independent gangsters, owing nothing, not even fear, to the mafia Companies, cops and street gangs that controlled his illegal world.

But there are some people, some loves, that worry every goodbye, and leaving them is like leaving the country of your birth.

Didier, my old friend, Naveen, my new friend, and Bombay, my Island City, for so long as she'd have me: each of us dangerous, in our different ways.

The man I was, when I arrived in Bombay years before, was a stranger in a new jungle. The man I became looked out at strangers, from the cover of the jungle street. I was at home. I knew my way around.

And I was harder, maybe, because something inside me was missing: something that should've been there, next to my heart.

I escaped from prison, Didier escaped from persecution, Naveen escaped from the street, and the southern city escaped from the sea, hurled into its island existence by working men and women, one stone at a time.

I waved goodbye, and Didier smiled, touching the love letters to his forehead. I smiled back, and it was okay: okay to leave him.

No smile would work, no goodbye would pray, no kindness would save, if the truth inside us wasn't beautiful. And the true heart of us, our human kind, is that we're connected, at our best, by purities of love found in no other creature.

CHAPTER THREE

I T WAS A SHORT RIDE FROM LEOPOLD'S to my apartment. I left the busy tourist causeway, crossed the road past the Colaba police station, and cruised on to the corner known to every taxi driver in Bombay as Electric House.

A right turn down the leafy street beside the police station gave me a view into a corner of the cellblock. I'd spent time in those cells.

My rebel eyes found the high, barred windows as I rode by slowly. A little cascade, memories, the stink of open latrines, the mass of men fighting for a slightly cleaner place near the gate bullied through my mind.

At the next corner I turned through the gate that gave access to the courtyard of the Beaumont Villa building, and parked my bike. Nodding to the watchman, I took the stairs three at a time to the third-floor apartment.

I entered, ringing the bell a few times. I walked through the living room to the kitchen, dropping my bag and keys on the table as I passed. Not finding her there or in the bedroom, I moved back into the living room.

'Hi, honey,' I called out, in an American accent. 'I'm home.'

Her laugh rippled from behind the swirling curtains on the terrace. When I shoved the curtains aside I found her kneeling, with her hands in the earth of a garden about the size of an open suitcase. A little flock of pigeons crowded around her, pecking for crumbs, and pestering one another fussily.

'You go to all the trouble of making a garden out here, girl,' I said, 'and then you let the birds walk all over it.'

'You don't get it,' Lisa replied, turning aquamarine eyes on me. 'I made the garden to bring the birds. It's the birds I wanted in the first place.'

28

'You're my flock of birds,' I said, when she stood to kiss me.

'Oh, great,' she mocked. 'The writer's home again.'

'And so damn pleased to see you,' I smiled, beginning to drag her with me toward the bedroom.

'My hands are dirty!' she protested.

'I hope so.'

'No, really,' she laughed, breaking away. 'We've gotta take a shower —'

'I hope so.'

'*You've* gotta take a shower,' she persisted, circling away from me, 'and change your clothes, right away.'

'Clothes?' I mocked back at her. 'We don't need no stinking clothes.'

'Yes, we do. We're going out.'

'Lisa, I just got back. Two weeks.'

'Nearly *three* weeks,' she corrected me. 'And there'll be plenty of time to say hello, before we say goodnight. I promise.'

'*Hello* is sounding a lot like *goodbye*.'

'Hello is always the first part of goodbye. Go get wet.'

'Where are we going?'

'You'll love it.'

'That means I'm gonna hate it, aren't I?'

'An art gallery.'

'Oh. Great.'

'Fuck you,' she laughed. 'These guys are good. They're on the edge, Lin. They're real-deal artists. You're gonna love them. And it's a really important show. And if we don't hurry, we'll be late. And I'm so glad you got back in time.'

I frowned.

'Come on, Lin,' she laughed. 'Without art, what is there?'

'Sex,' I replied. 'And food. And more sex.'

'There'll be plenty of food at the gallery,' she said, shoving me toward the shower. 'And just think how grateful your *little flock of birds* will be when you come home from the art gallery that she *really*, *really*, *really* wants you to take her to, and that we'll miss, if you don't hit the shower *right now*!'

I was pulling my shirt off over my head in the stall. She turned on the shower behind me. Water crashed onto my back and my jeans.

'Hey!' I shouted. 'These are my best jeans!'

'And you've been in them for weeks,' she called back from the kitchen. 'Second-best jeans tonight, please.'

'And I've still got your present,' I shouted. 'Right here, in the pocket of these jeans you just got soaking wet!'

She was at the door.

'You got me a present?' she asked.

'Of course.'

'Good. Very sweet. Let's look at it later.'

She slipped out of sight again.

'Yeah,' I called back. 'Let's do that. After all that fun at the gallery.'

As I finished the shower, I heard her humming, a song from a Hindi movie. By chance, or by the synchronicities that curl within the spiral chambers of love, it was the same song that I'd been singing on the street, walking with Vikram and Naveen only hours before.

And later, as we gathered our things for the ride, we hummed and sang the song together.

Bombay traffic is a system designed by acrobats for small elephants. Twenty minutes of motorcycle fun got us to Cumballa Hill, a money belt district hitched to the hips of South Bombay's most prestigious mountain.

I pulled my motorcycle into a parking area opposite the fashionably controversial Backbeat Gallery, at the commencement of fashionably orthodox Carmichael Road. Expensive imported cars and expensive local personalities drew up outside the gallery.

Lisa led us inside, working her way through the densely packed crowd. The long room held perhaps twice the safety limit of one hundred and fifty persons, a number that was conspicuously displayed on a fire-safety sign near the entrance.

If you can't stand the heat, get out of the burning building.

She found one of her friends at last, and pulled me into an anatomically close introduction.

'This is Rosanna,' Lisa said, squeezed in beside a short girl who wore a large, ornate gold crucifix, with the nailed feet of the Saviour nestled between her breasts. 'This is Lin. He just got back from Goa.'

'We meet at last,' Rosanna said, her chest pressing against mine as she raised a hand to run it through her short, spiked hair.

Her accent was American, but with Indian vowels.

'What took you to Goa?'

'Love letters and rubies,' I said.

Rosanna glanced quickly at Lisa.

'Don't look at *me*,' Lisa sighed, shrugging her shoulders.

'You are *so* fucking *weird*, man!' Rosanna cried out, in a voice like a parrot's panic warning. 'Come with *me*! You've got to meet Taj. Weird is his favourite thing, yaar.'

Wriggling her way through the crowd, Rosanna took us to meet a tall, handsome young man with shoulder-length hair that was sleek with perfumed oil. He was standing in front of a large stone sculpture, some three metres tall, of a wild man-creature.

The plaque beside the sculpture pronounced its name: ENKIDU. The artist greeted Lisa with a kiss on the cheek, and then offered his hand to me.

'Taj,' he said, giving me a smile of open curiosity. 'You must be Lin. Lisa's told me a lot about you.'

I shook his hand, allowed my eyes to search his for a moment, and then shifted my gaze to the huge sculpture behind him. He turned his head slightly, following my eyes.

'What do you think?'

'I like him,' I said. 'If the ceiling in my apartment was a little higher, and the floor a little stronger, I'd buy him.'

'Thanks,' he laughed.

He reached upwards to put a hand on the chest of the stone warrior.

'I really don't know what he is. I just had a compulsion to see him, standing in front of me. It's not any more complicated than that. No metaphor or psychology or anything.'

'Goethe said that all things are metaphors.'

'That's pretty good,' he said, laughing again, the soft bark-brown eyes swimming with light. 'Can I quote that? I might print it out, and put it beside my friend here. It might help me to sell him.'

'Of course. Writers never really die, until people stop quoting them.'

'That's quite enough for this corner,' Rosanna interrupted, seizing my arm. 'Now, come see some of my work.'

She guided Lisa and me through the smoking, drinking, laughing, shouting crowd to the wall opposite the tall sculpture. Spanning half the long wall at eye level was a series of plaster reliefs. The panels had been painted to mimic a classical bronze finish, and told a story in consecutive panels.

'It's about the Sapna killings,' Rosanna explained, shouting into my ear. 'You remember? A couple of years ago? This crazy guy was telling servants to rise up against their rich masters, and kill them. You remember? It was in all the papers.'

I remembered the Sapna killings. And I knew the truth of the story better than Rosanna did, and better than most in the Island City of Bombay. I walked slowly from panel to panel, examining the long tableaux depicting figures from the public story of Sapna.

I felt light-headed and off balance. They were stories of men I'd known: men who'd killed, and died, and had finally become tiny figures fixed in an artist's frieze.

Lisa pulled on my sleeve.

'What is it, Lisa?'

'Let's go to the green room!' she shouted.

'Okay. Okay.'

We followed Rosanna through a leafy hedge of kisses and outstretched arms as she hooted and screeched her way to the back of the gallery. She tapped on the door with a little rhythmic signal.

When the door opened she pushed us through into a dark room illuminated by red motorcycle lights strung on heavy cables.

The room held about twenty people, sitting on chairs, couches and the floor. It was much quieter there. The girl who approached me, offering a joint, spoke in a throaty whisper that ran a hand through my short hair.

'You wanna get fucked up?' she asked rhetorically, offering the joint in her supernaturally long fingers.

'You're too late,' Lisa cut in quickly, taking the joint. 'Fate beat you to it, Anush.'

She puffed the joint and passed it back to the girl.

'This is Anushka,' Lisa said.

As we shook hands, Anushka's long fingers closed all the way around my palm.

'Anushka's a performance artist,' Lisa said.

'You don't say,' I did say.

Anushka leaned in close to kiss me softly on the neck, the fingers of one hand cupping the back of my head.

'Tell me when to stop,' she whispered.

As she kissed my neck, I slowly turned my head until my eyes met Lisa's.

'You know, Lisa, you were right. I *do* like your friends. And I *am* having fun at the gallery, even though I thought I wouldn't.'

'Okay,' Lisa said, pulling Anushka away. 'Show's over.'

'Encore!' I tried.

'No encores,' Lisa said, bringing me to sit on the floor beside a man in his thirties.

His head was shaved to a bright polish, and he wore a burnt-orange kurta pyjama set.

'This is Rish. He mounted the exhibition, and he's exhibiting work as well. Rish, this is Lin.'

'Hey, man,' Rish said, shaking hands. 'How do you like the show?'

'The performance art is outstanding,' I replied, looking around to see Anushka leaning in to bite an unresisting victim.

Lisa slapped me hard on the arm.

'I'm kidding. It's all good. And you got a big crowd. Congratulations.'

'Hope they're in a buying mood,' Lisa said, thinking out loud.

'If they're not, Anushka could convince them.'

Lisa slapped me on the arm again.

'Or you could always get Lisa to slap them.'

'We were lucky,' Rish smiled, offering me the joint.

'No thanks. Never when I've got a passenger. Lucky how?'

'It almost didn't happen. Did you see the big Ram painting? The orange one?'

The large, mainly orange-coloured painting was hanging next to the stone sculpture of Enkidu. I hadn't immediately realised that the striking central figure was a representation of the Hindu God.

'The moral police from the lunatic religious right,' Rish said, 'the Spear of Karma, they call themselves, they heard about the painting and tried to shut us down. We got in touch with Taj's dad. He's a top lawyer, and connected to the Chief Minister. He got a court order, allowing us to put the show on.'

'Who painted it?'

'I did,' Rish said. 'Why?'

'What made you want to paint it in the first place?'

'Are you saying that there are things I shouldn't paint?'

'I'm asking you why you chose to do it.'

'For the freedom of art,' Rish said.

'Viva la revolution,' Anushka purred, sitting down beside Rish and leaning into his lap.

'Whose freedom?' I asked. 'Yours, or theirs?'

'Spear of Karma?' Rosanna sneered. 'Crazy fascist fuckers, all of them. They're nothing. Just a fringe group. Nobody listens to them.'

'The fringe usually works its way to the centre that ignores or insults it.'

'What?' Rosanna spluttered.

'That's true, Lin,' Rish agreed, 'and they've done some violent stuff. No doubt. But they're mainly in the regional centres and the villages. Beating up priests, and burning down a church here and there, that's their thing. They'll never get a big following in Bombay.'

'Vicious fucking fanatics!' a bearded young man wearing a pink shirt spat out viciously. 'They're the stupidest people in the world!'

'I don't think you can say that,' I said softly.

'I just did!' the young man shot back. 'So fuck you. I just said it. So I *can* say it.'

'Okay. I meant that you can't say it with any *validity*. Sure, you can say it. You can say that the moon is a Diwali decoration, but it wouldn't have any validity. It's simply not valid to say that all the people who oppose you are stupid.'

'Then what are they?' Rish asked.

'I think you probably know them and their way of thinking better than I do.'

'No, really, make your point, please.'

'Okay, I think they're devout. And not just devout, but *fervently* devout. I think they're in love with God, *infatuated* with God, actually, and when their God is depicted without faith, it's felt as an insult to the faith inside themselves.'

'So, you're saying I shouldn't have been allowed to put on this show?' Rish pressed.

'I didn't say that.'

'Who the fuck is this guy?' the bearded youth asked no-one.

'Please,' Rish continued. 'Tell me what you *did* say.'

'I stand for your right to create and present art, but I think that rights come with responsibilities, and that we, as artists, have a responsibility not to cause feelings of hurt and injury in the name of art. In the name of truth, maybe. In the name of justice and freedom. But not in the name of art.'

'Why not?'

'We stand on tall shoulders, when we express ourselves as artists, and we have to stay true to the best in the artists who came before us. It's a duty.'

'Who the fuck is this guy?' the bearded youth asked the string of red motorcycle lights.

'So, if those people are offended, it's *my* fault?' Rish asked softly and earnestly.

I was beginning to like him.

'I repeat,' the bearded youth demanded, 'who the fuck is *this* guy?'

I already didn't like the bearded youth.

'I'm the guy who's gonna rearrange your grammar,' I said quietly, 'if you address me in the third person again.'

'He's a *writer*,' Anushka yawned. 'They argue, because —'

'Because they can,' Lisa interjected, tugging at my arm to lift me to my feet. 'C'mon, Lin. Time to dance.'

Loud music thumped from heavy floor-mounted speakers.

'I *love* this song!' Anushka growled, jumping up and pulling Rish to his feet. 'Dance with me, Rish!'

I held Lisa for a moment, and kissed her neck.

'Go ahead,' I smiled. 'Dance your brains out. I'm gonna take another look at the exhibition. I'll meet you outside.'

Lisa kissed me and joined the dancing crowd. I moved through the dancers, resisting the tidal roll of the music.

In the gallery room I stood before the bronze plaster reliefs that purported to tell the story of the Sapna killings. I tried to decide whether it was the artist's nightmare, or mine.

I lost it all. I lost the custody of my daughter. I sleepwalked into heroin addiction and armed robbery. When I was caught, I was sentenced to serve ten years at hard labour, in a maximum-security prison.

I could tell you I was beaten during the first two and a half years of that sentence. I could give you half a dozen other sane reasons for escaping from an insane prison, but the truth of it's simply that one day, freedom was more important to me than my life. And I refused, that day, to be caged. *Not today. Not any more.* I escaped, and became a wanted man.

The fugitive life took me from Australia, through New Zealand, to India. Six months in a remote village in Maharashtra gave me the language of farmers. Eighteen months in a city slum gave me the language of the street.

I went to prison again, in Bombay, as you do sometimes, when you're on the run. The man who paid my freedom-ransom to the authorities was a mafia boss, Khaderbhai. He had a use for me. He had a use for everyone. And when I worked for him, no cop persecuted me in Bombay, and no prison offered hospitality.

Counterfeiting passports, smuggling, black market gold, illegal currency trading, protection rackets, gang wars, Afghanistan, vendettas: one way or another, the mafia life filled the months and years. And none of it mattered much to me, because the bridge to the past, to my family and friends, to my name and my nation and whatever I'd been before Bombay was gone, like the dead men prowling through Rosanna's bronze-coloured frieze.

I left the gallery, made my way through the thinning crowd, and went outside to sit on my motorcycle. I was across the street from the entrance.

A crowd of people had gathered on the footpath, near my bike. Most of them were local people from servants' quarters in the surrounding streets. They'd gathered in the cool nightfall to admire the fine cars and elegantly dressed guests entering and leaving the exhibition.

I heard people speaking in Marathi and Hindi. They commented on the cars and jewellery and dresses with genuine admiration and pleasure. No voice spoke with jealousy or resentment. They were poor people, living the hard, fear-streaked life crushed into the little word *poor*, but they admired the jewels and silks of the rich guests with joyful, unenvious innocence.

When a well-known industrialist and his movie-star wife emerged from the gallery, a little chorus of admiring sighs rose from the group. She wore a bejewelled yellow and white sari. I turned my head to look at the people, smiling and murmuring their appreciation, as if the woman were one of their own neighbours, and I noticed three men standing apart from the group.

Their stone-silent stares were grim. Malevolence rippled outward from their dark, staring eyes: waves so intense that it seemed I could feel them settle on my skin, like misted rain.

And then, as if they sensed my awareness of them, they turned as one and stared directly into my eyes, with clear, unreasoning hatred.

We held the stare, while the happy crowd cooed and murmured their pleasure, while limousines drew up in front of us, and cameras flashed.

I thought of Lisa, still inside the gallery. The men stared, willing darkness at me. My hands moved slowly toward the two knives fixed in canvas scabbards in the small of my back.

'Hey!' Rosanna said, slapping me on the shoulder.

Reflex sent my hand whipping around to grab her wrist, while the other hand shoved her backwards a step.

'Whoa! Take it easy!' she said, her eyes wide with surprise.

'I'm sorry.' I frowned, releasing her wrist.

I turned quickly to search for the hate-filled eyes. The three men were gone.

'Are you okay?' Rosanna asked.

'Sure,' I said, turning to face her again. 'Sure. Sorry. Is it about done in there?'

'Just about,' she said. 'When the big stars leave, the lights go out. Lisa says you're not a Goa fan. Why not? I'm *from* there, you know.'

'I guessed.'

'So, what have you got against Goa?'

'Nothing. It's just that every time I go there, somebody asks me to pick up their dirty laundry.'

'That's not *my* Goa,' she countered.

It wasn't defensive. It was simply a statement of fact.

'Maybe not,' I smiled. 'And Goa's a big place. I only know a couple of beaches and towns.'

She was studying my face.

'What did you say it was?' she asked. 'Rubies and *what*?'

'Rubies and love letters.'

'But you weren't in Goa just for that, were you?'

'Sure,' I lied.

'If I said you were down there for black market business, would I be close to the mark?'

I'd gone to Goa to collect ten handguns. I'd dropped them off with my mafia contact in Bombay, before searching for Vikram to return the necklace. Black market business was close to the mark.

'Look, Rosanna —'

'Has it occurred to you that *you're* the problem here? People like you, who come to India and bring trouble we don't need?'

37

'There was a lotta trouble here before I came, and there'll be plenty left when I'm gone.'

'We're talking about *you*, not India.'

She was right: the two knives pressing against the small of my back made the point.

'You're right,' I conceded.

'I am?'

'Yeah. I'm trouble, alright. And so are you, at the moment, if you don't mind me saying it.'

'Lisa doesn't need trouble from you,' she said, frowning hard.

'No,' I said evenly. 'Nobody needs trouble.'

She studied my face a little longer, her brown eyes searching for something wide enough or deep enough to give the conversation a context. Finally she laughed, and looked away, running a ringed hand through her spiked hair.

'How many days does the show run?' I asked.

'We're supposed to have another week of this,' she remarked, looking at the last guests leaving the exhibition. 'If the crazies don't close us down, that is.'

'If I were you, I'd pay for some security. I'd put a couple of big, sharp guys on the door. Moonlight a few guys from one of the five-star hotels. They're pretty good, some of those guys, and the ones who aren't still *look* good enough.'

'You know something about the show?'

'Not really. I saw some men out here before. Seriously unhappy men. I think they're seriously unhappy with your show.'

'I *hate* those fucking fanatics!' she hissed.

'I think it's mutual.'

I glanced toward the gallery to see Lisa kissing Rish and Taj goodbye.

'Here's Lisa.'

I swung a leg over the bike, and kick-started the engine. It growled to life, settling into a low, bubbling throb. Lisa came to hug Rosanna, and took her place on the back of my bike.

'*Phir milenge,*' I said. *Until we meet again.*

'Not if I see you first.'

We rode down the long slope to the sea, but when we stopped at a traffic signal, a black van pulled up beside us, and I turned to see the men with the hateful stares. They were arguing among themselves.

I let them pull away when the signal changed. There were political stickers and religious symbols on the rear window of the van. I turned off the main road at the first corner.

We rode through back streets for a while, and I worried for the changes I was seeing. Rosanna's faux-bronze panels told a brutal Bombay story, but less brutal than the truth, and less brutal than the politics of faith. The violence of the past was just sand in the swash of a new wave, breaking on the Island City's shores. Political thugs travelled by the truckload, brandishing clubs, and mafia gangs of twenty or thirty men had grown to hundreds of fighters. We are what we fear, and many of us in the city feared reckless days of reckoning.

CHAPTER FOUR

RIDING SLOWLY, WE MADE OUR WAY back to the sweeping curve of Marine Drive, following the necklace of reflections on the gentle waters of the bay. That first glimmer of starry sea started us talking again, and we were still talking when I pulled the bike into the driveway of our apartment building, past the salute of the watchman, and into the covered parking bay.

'You go up,' I said to Lisa. 'I'm gonna wipe down the bike.'

'Now?'

'Now. I'll be right up.'

When I heard Lisa's footsteps on the marble stairs I turned to the watchman, nodded to him, and pointed after her. Understanding that I wanted him to follow her, he set off quickly, taking the stairs two at a time.

I heard her open the apartment door, and say her goodnight to the watchman. I slipped quickly out through a side gate to the footpath. Moving quietly, I made my way along the line of the leafy hedge bordering the apartment building's ground-floor car park.

As I'd turned to enter the parking area of the building, I'd seen a huddled figure draw backwards into the shadows of the tall hedge. Someone was hiding there.

I drew a knife and came up quietly to the spot near the gate where I'd seen the figure. A man stepped out in front of me, his back turned, and began to move toward the car park.

It was Scorpio George.

'Lin!' I heard him whisper. 'Are you still there, Lin?'

'What the hell are you doin', Scorpio?' I asked from behind him, and he jumped.

'Oh, Lin! You scared the *crap* outta me!'

I frowned at him, wanting an explanation.

The peace pact that had held since the last big mafia gang war in South Bombay was failing. Young men who hadn't fought the war, or negotiated the truce, were attacking one another in violation of rules that had been written in better men's blood. There'd been attacks by rival gangs in our area. I was vigilant, on guard all the time, and angry at myself for coming so close to hurting a friend.

'I've told you guys about creepin' up on people,' I said.

'See . . . I'm sorry . . .' he began nervously, looking left and right. 'It's . . . it's . . .'

Distress had a hand on his chest, and he couldn't lift it to speak. I looked for a place to talk with him.

I couldn't step into the car park with Scorpio. He was a street guy, sleeping in a doorway, and his presence in the compound, if observed by a resident of the building, would lead to complaints. I had no fear of those complaints, but I knew that they'd cost the watchman his job.

Taking Scorpio by the arm, I led the tall, thin Canadian across the street to a collapsed wall of crumbled stones, deep in shadow. Sitting with him in the darkness, I lit a joint and passed it to him.

'What's up, Scorp?'

'It's this guy,' he began, puffing deeply on the joint. 'This guy with the dark suit. The CIA guy. It's creeping me out, man! I can't work the street. I can't talk to tourists. It's like I see him everywhere, in my mind, asking questions about me. Did your guy, that Naveen detective guy, did he find out anything?'

I shook my head.

'One of the boys tailed him out to Bandra, but the kid ran out of taxi money, and lost him. I haven't heard anything back from your guy, Naveen. I thought you might've heard something.'

'No. Nothing yet.'

'I'm scared, Lin,' Scorpio George said, shuddering the fear along his spine. 'All the street boys have tested him. Nothin'. He doesn't buy drugs, doesn't drink, not even beer. No girls.'

'We'll work it out, Scorp. Don't worry.'

'It's weird,' Scorpio frowned. 'I'm really going outta my mind, y'know?'

I tugged a fold of hundred-rupee notes from my pocket, and gave it to him. Scorpio took it in a faltering hand, but then slipped it into a pocket concealed inside his shirt.

'Thanks, Lin,' he said, looking up quickly to meet my eyes. 'I was waiting here to ask you to help me, because I haven't been on the street. The watchman told me you were still out. But then I saw you were with Lisa, and I couldn't let her see me. I didn't want to ask for money in front of her. She has a high opinion of me.'

'We all need money sometimes. And Lisa always has a high opinion of you, whether you need money or not.'

He had tears in his eyes. I didn't want to see them.

'Listen, you and Gemini,' I said, leading him across the street again, 'you guys lay up some supplies, buy some shit, and take a room at the Frantic. Stay there for a couple of days. We'll find out who this guy is, and we'll deal with it, okay?'

'Okay,' he said, shaking my hand with the tremble in his. 'You think the Frantic's pretty safe, yeah?'

'The Frantic hotel is the only one that'll take you and your lifestyle, Scorp.'

'Oh . . . yeah . . . '

'This mystery man won't get past the desk there. Not in a suit. Keep your heads down, and you'll be safe at the Frantic until we figure this out.'

'Okay. Okay.'

He walked away, stooping his tall frame beneath the loose fronds of the hedge. I watched him do the street guy's night walk: slowly, nonchalantly in the pools of street light – *Honest Joe, nothing to hide* – then scurrying faster in the shadowed sections of the street.

I slipped a twenty-rupee note to the watchman, standing beside me, and climbed the marble stairs to the apartment. Lisa stood in the bathroom doorway while I showered, and I told her about Scorpio George's white-haired stalker.

'But who *is* this guy?' she asked as I stepped out of the shower. 'What does he want with the Zodiacs?'

'I dunno. Naveen Adair, the guy I told you about before? He smells lawyer. He might be right. He's a smart kid. One way or another, we'll find out who this guy is.'

Dried off again, I flopped down on the bed beside Lisa, my head resting on the satin breeze of her breast. From that position I looked down along the length of her naked body to her feet.

'Rosanna likes you,' she said, shifting the direction of the conversation with an elegant gesture to the left with both feet.

'I doubt it.'

'Why? What happened with her?'

'Nothing . . . *happened*.'

'*Something* happened when you were talking to her outside. What did you say?'

'We just . . . talked about Goa.'

'Oh, no,' she sighed. 'She's nuts about Goa.'

'So I discovered.'

'But she *does* like you. No matter what you said about Goa.'

'I . . . don't think so.'

'Oh, yeah. She certainly *dislikes* you, too, at the same time. But she definitely *likes* you.'

'What are you talking about?'

'She was angry enough to hit you, when I came out.'

'She was? I thought we reached a good place.'

'She was ready to hit you, so she likes you a lot.'

'Ah . . . how does that work?'

'She was angry enough to hit you, and she doesn't even know you, see?'

I didn't, but that wasn't unusual: Lisa had her own way of incommunicating.

'It's all so clear now.'

'Was she doing her body language thing,' she asked, 'when she was talking to you?'

'What body language thing?'

'She fakes a sore back, and starts rolling her hips in a circle. Did she do that?'

'No.'

'That's good.'

'It is?'

'Yeah, because it's pretty sexy, and she did it for me, and not for you.'

'There's a logic rolling its hips in there somewhere, I'm sure, but I'm gonna let it roll past. I *did* manage to read *Anushka's* body language, however.'

'A *bear* could read *her* body language,' Lisa cut in quickly, giving me a slap on the arm.

'Where did you say she's performing?' I laughed.

'I didn't,' she slapped.

A seashell bracelet jangled on her wrist. It was the present I'd brought for her from Goa. She played the music of the shells, twisting her wrist for a while, and then silenced them in the clutch of her free hand.

'Did you have a shitty time tonight? Should I be sorry I made you go, when you just got back from your trip?'

'Not at all. I really did like your friends, and it was about time I met them. I liked Rosanna, too. She has good fire.'

'I'm so glad. She's not just a partner. She's become close. Do you find her attractive?'

'What?'

'It's okay,' she said, playing with the bedcover. 'I find her attractive, too.'

'What?'

'She's clever, dedicated, brave, creative, enthusiastic, and easy to get along with. She's really great.'

I stared along the soft coastline of Lisa's long, slender legs.

'What are we talking about, again?'

'You think she's hot,' she said.

'What?'

'It's okay. I think she's hot, too.'

She took my hand, and moved it between her legs.

'How tired are you?' she asked.

I looked down at her toes, bent backwards in a fan-shaped arch.

'Nobody's ever *that* tired.'

It was good. It was always good. We shared a loving kindness that was a kind of loving. And maybe because we both knew that it would end some day, some way, we let our bodies say things that our hearts couldn't.

I went to the kitchen to fetch a cold drink of water, and brought a glass back for her, putting it on the table on her side of the bed.

For a while I looked at her, beautiful, healthy, strong, curled into herself like a sleeping cat. I tried to imagine what the vision of love she was clinging to might look like, and how different it was from my own.

I lay down beside her and gathered my body into the contours of her dream. Her toes closed reflexively over mine in her sleep. And more honest than my mind, my sleeping body bent at the knees, pressed against the closed door of her curved back, and beat on it with the fist of my heart, begging to be loved.

CHAPTER FIVE

Riding a motorcycle is velocity as poetry. The fine balance between elegant agility and fatal fall is a kind of truth, and like all truth, it carries a heartbeat with it into the sky. Eternal moments in the saddle escape the stuttering flow of time, and space, and purpose. Coursing on those wheels, on that river of air, in that flight of freed spirit there's no attachment, no fear, no joy, no hatred, no love, and no malice: the nearest thing, for some violent men, for this violent man, to a state of grace.

I arrived at the passport factory used by the Sanjay Company in a good mood. I'd taken the slow way to work that morning, and the ride had cleared my mind, leaving me with a placid smile I could feel in my whole body.

The factory was the main centre where we changed and created false passports. As the principal forger and counterfeiter of passports and other identification documents for the Sanjay Company, I spent at least some hours of most days at the factory.

I opened the door, and my motorcycle-smile froze. There was a young stranger in front of me. He put out his hand in greeting.

'Lin!' he said, shaking my hand as if he was pumping water from a village well. 'My name's Farzad. Come on in!'

I took off my sunglasses, accepted his invitation to my office, and found that a second desk had been lodged in a corner of the large room. The desk was piled high with papers and drawings.

'They put me here . . . about two weeks ago,' Farzad said, nodding toward his desk. 'I hope you don't mind.'

'That depends.'

'Depends on what?'

'On who the hell you are, and what the hell you're doin' in my office.'

'Oh,' he laughed, relaxing enough to take a seat at the new desk. 'That's easy. I'm your new assistant. Count on it!'

'I didn't ask for a new assistant. I liked the old assistant.'

'But I thought you didn't have an assistant?'

'Exactly.'

His hands flapped in his lap like fish flung on the shore. I stepped across the room to look through the long windows into the factory below. I noticed that changes had taken place there as well.

'What the hell?'

I walked down the wooden steps leading to the factory floor, and headed toward the new desks and light boxes. Farzad followed me, speaking quickly.

'They decided to expand the false document section to include education stuff. I thought you knew.'

'What education stuff?'

'Diplomas, degrees, certificates of competency and the like. That's why they brought me in.'

He stopped suddenly, watching me as I picked up a document from one of the new desks. It was a Master's Degree in Engineering, purporting to be issued by a prestigious university in Bengal.

It bore the name of a young man I knew: the son of a mafia enforcer from the fishing fleet area, who was as slow-witted as he was avaricious, and who was, by any reckoning, the greediest kid-gangster in Sassoon Dock.

'They ... brought me in ...' Farzad concluded falteringly, 'b-b-because I have an MBA. I mean, a real one. Count on it.'

'There goes the neighbourhood. Doesn't anybody study philosophy any more?'

'My dad does,' he said. 'He's a Steiner-Utilitarian.'

'Please, whoever you are, I haven't had a chai yet.'

Moving to a second table, I picked up another false qualification document. It was a Bachelor of Medicine in Dental Surgery. Reading my features, Farzad spoke again.

'You know, it's okay. None of these fake degrees will ever be used in India. They're all for people who want jobs in foreign countries.'

'Oh,' I said, not smiling, 'that makes it okay, then.'

'Exactly!' He grinned happily. 'Shall I send for tea?'

When the chai arrived, in short, crack-veined glasses, we sipped and talked long enough for me to like him.

Farzad was from the small, brilliant and influential Parsi community. He was twenty-three years old, unmarried, and lived with his parents and extended family in a large house not far from the Bombay slum where I'd once lived.

After two postgraduate years in the United States, he started work at a futures trading firm in Boston. Within the first year, he'd become entangled in a complex Ponzi scheme, run by the head of his firm.

Although he'd played no direct part in his employer's criminal intrigue, Farzad's name appeared in transfers of funds to secret bank accounts. When it seemed that he might be arrested, he'd returned to India, using the fortuitous if unhappy excuse that he had to visit the sick bed of his dying uncle.

I'd known the uncle, Keki, very well. He'd been a wise counsellor to Khaderbhai, the South Bombay don, and had a place on the mafia Council. In his last hours, the Parsi counsellor had asked the new head of the mafia Company, Sanjay Kumar, to protect young Farzad, his nephew, whom he regarded as a son.

Sanjay took Farzad in, telling him that he'd be safe from prosecution in the United States, if he remained in Bombay, and worked for the mafia Company. While I'd been in Goa, Sanjay had put him to work in my false passport factory.

'There's so many people moving out of India now,' Farzad said, sipping his second chai. 'And regulations will lighten up. You'll see. Count on it.'

'Uh-huh.'

'Restrictions and laws, they'll all change, they'll all get looser and easier. People will be leaving India, people will be coming back to India, starting businesses here and in foreign countries, moving money around all over the place. And all of those people, one way or another, they're all going to need or want some paperwork that gives them a better chance in America, or London, or Stockholm, or Sydney, you know?'

'It's a big market, huh?'

'It's a huge market. Huge. We only set this up two weeks ago, and we're already working two full shifts to meet our commitments.'

'Two shifts, huh?'

'Flat out, baba.'

'And . . . when one of our clients, who *buys* his engineering degree instead of *studying* for it, is called upon to build a bridge, say, that won't fall down and kill a couple hundred people?'

'No tension, baba,' he replied. 'In most countries, the fake degree only gets you in the door. After that, you have to do more study to meet the local standards, and get accreditation. And you know our Indian people. If you let them in the door, they'll buy the house, and then the house next door, and then in no time they'll own the street, and start renting houses to the people who used to own them. It's the way we are. Count on it, yaar.'

Farzad was a gentle, open-faced young man. Relaxed with me at last and unafraid, his soft brown eyes stared from a place of unruffled serenity, deep within his sanguine opinion of the world.

His round, full lips parted slightly on the permanent quiver of a smile. His skin was very fair: fairer than my tanned face beneath my short blonde hair. His Western-chic jeans and silk designer shirt gave him the look of a visitor, a tourist, rather than someone whose family had lived in Bombay for three hundred years.

His face was unmarked, his skin showing no scar or scratch or faded bruise. It occurred to me, as I listened to his genial chatter, that it was likely he'd never been in a fight, or even closed his fist in anger.

I envied him. When I allowed myself to look into the half-collapsed tunnel of the past, it seemed that I'd been fighting all my life.

My kid brother and I were the only Catholic boys in our tough, working-class neighbourhood. Some of our tough, working-class neighbours waited patiently for the arrival of our school bus every evening, and fought us all the way home; day after day.

And it never stopped. A trip to the shopping centre was like crossing a Green Line into enemy territory. Local militias, or street gangs, attacked outsiders with the viciousness that the poor only ever visit on the poor. Learning karate and joining the local boxing club were the life-skills classes in my neighbourhood.

Every kid who had the heart to fight learned a martial art, and every week gave him several opportunities to practise what he learned. The accident and emergency department of the local hospital was filled, on Friday and Saturday nights, with young men who were having stitches put into cuts on their mouths and eyes, or having their broken noses repaired for the third time.

I was one of them. My medical file at the local hospital was heavier than a volume of Shakespeare's tragedies. And that was before prison.

Listening to Farzad's happy, dreaming talk of the car he was saving to buy, and the girl he wanted to ask out, I could feel the pressure of the two long knives I always carried at my back. In the secret drawer of a cabinet in my apartment there were two handguns and two hundred rounds of ammunition. If Farzad didn't have a weapon, and the willingness to use it, he was in the wrong business. If he didn't know how to fight, and what it feels like to lose a fight, he was in the wrong business.

'You're lining up with the Sanjay Company,' I said. 'Don't plan too far ahead.'

'Two years,' Farzad said, cupping his hands in front of him as though he was holding the chunk of time and its promises. 'Two years of this work, and then I'll take all the money I've saved, and open a small business of my own. A consultancy, for people trying to get a Green Card in the US, and whatnot. It's the coming thing! Count on it.'

'Just keep your head down,' I advised, hoping that Fate or the Company would give him the years he wanted.

'Oh, sure, I always –'

The phone on my desk rang, cutting him off.

'Aren't you going to answer it?' Farzad asked, after a few rings.

'I don't like telephones.'

The telephone was still ringing.

'Well, why do you have one?'

'I don't. The office does. If it agitates you so much, you answer it.'

He lifted the receiver.

'Good morning, Farzad speaking,' he said, then held the phone away from his ear.

Gurgling sounds, like mud complaining or big dogs eating something, rumbled from the phone. Farzad stared at it in horror.

'It's for me,' I said, and he let the phone fall into my hand.

'*Salaam aleikum*, Nazeer.'

'Linbaba?'

It was a voice I could feel through the floor.

'*Salaam aleikum*, Nazeer.'

'*Wa aleikum salaam.* You come!' Nazeer commanded. 'You come now!'

'Whatever happened to *How are you, Linbaba*?'

'You *come!*' Nazeer insisted.

His voice was a growling thing dragging a body on a gravel driveway. I loved it.

49

'Okay, okay. Keep your scowl on. I'm on my way.'

I put down the phone, collected my wallet and the keys to my bike, and walked to the door.

'We'll talk more, later on,' I said, turning to look at my new assistant. 'But for now, I think this is gonna work out okay, between you and me. Watch the store while I'm gone, *thik?*'

The word, pronounced *teek*, brought a wide smile to the young, unblemished face.

'*Bilkul thik!*' he replied. *Absolutely okay!*

I left the office, forgetting the young MBA making false degrees, and pushed the bike to speed on Marine Drive, sweeping up onto the narrow cutting beside the Metro flyover.

At the Parsi Fire Temple corner I saw my friend Abdullah riding with two others across the intersection in front of me. They were headed for the narrow streets of the commerce district.

Waiting for a break in the almost constant flow of vehicles, and checking to see that the traffic cop on duty was busy accepting a bribe from someone else, I cut the red light and set off in pursuit of my friend.

As a member of the Sanjay Company, I'd pledged my life to defend others in the gang: the band of brothers in arms. Abdullah was more than that. The tall, long-haired Iranian was my first and closest friend in the Company. My commitment to him was beyond the duty of the pledge.

There's a deep connection between gangsters, faith and death. All of the men in the Sanjay Company felt that their souls were in the hands of a personal God, and they were all devout enough to pray before and after a murder. Abdullah, no less than the others, was a man of faith, although he never showed mercy.

For my part, I still searched for something more than the verses, vows and veneration I'd found in the books of believers. And while I doubted everything in myself, Abdullah was always and ever certain: as confident in his invincibility as the strongest eagle, soaring above his head in the hovering Bombay sky.

We were different men, with different ways to love, and different instincts for the fight. But friendship is faith, too, especially for those of us who don't believe in much else. And the simple truth was that my heart always rose, always soared in the little sky inside, whenever I saw him.

I followed him in the flow of traffic, waiting for the chance to pull in beside him. His straight back and relaxed command of the bike were characteristics I'd come to admire. Some men and women ride a horse as if they're born to it, and something of the same instinct applies to riding a motorcycle.

The two men riding with Abdullah, Fardeen and Hussein, were good riders who'd been on bikes since they were infants, riding on the tanks of their fathers' bikes, through the same traffic on the same streets, but they never achieved the same riverine facility as our Iranian friend, and never looked as cool.

Just as I sensed a gap opening beside his bike, and pulled forward to match his pace, he turned his head to look at me. A smile edged serious shadows from his face, and he pulled over to the kerb, followed by Fardeen and Hussein.

I stopped close to him, and we hugged, still sitting on our bikes.

'*Salaam aleikum*,' he greeted me warmly.

'*Wa aleikum salaam wa Rahmatullahi wa Barakatuh.*' *And unto you be Peace, and Allah's mercy, and His blessings.*

Fardeen and Hussein reached out to shake hands.

'You are going to the meeting, I heard,' Abdullah said.

'Yeah. I got the call from Nazeer. I thought you'd be there.'

'I am indeed going there,' he declared.

'Well, you're taking the long way,' I laughed, because he was heading in the wrong direction.

'I have a job to do first. It will not take long. Come with us. It is not far from here, and I believe that you do not know this place, and these people.'

'Okay,' I agreed. 'Where are we going?'

'To see the Cycle Killers,' he said. 'On a matter of Company business.'

I'd never visited the den of the Cycle Killers. I didn't know much about them. But like every street guy in Bombay, I knew the names of their top two killers, and I knew that they outnumbered the four of us by six or seven to one.

Abdullah kicked his bike to life, waiting for us to kick-start our own bikes, and then led the way out into the brawl of traffic, his back straight, and his head high and proud.

CHAPTER SIX

I'D SEEN SOME OF THE CYCLE KILLERS, riding their polished chrome bicycles at suicidal speed through the market streets of the Thieves Bazaar. They were young, and always dressed in the same uniform of brightly coloured, tight-fitting undershirts, known as *banyans*, white stovepipe jeans, and the latest fashion brand of running shoes.

They all slicked their hair back with perfumed oil, wore ostentatious caste-mark tattoos on their faces to protect them against the evil eye, and covered their own eyes with identical mirror-finish aviator sunglasses, as polished as their silver bicycles.

They were, by general agreement among discriminating criminals, the most efficient knife-men money could buy, surpassed in skill by only one man in the city: Hathoda, the knife master for the Sanjay Company.

Deep within the streets and narrower gullies, clogged with commerce and the clamour for cash, we parked our bikes outside a shop that sold Ayurvedic remedies and silk pouches filled with secret herbs, offering protection against love curses. I wanted to buy one, but Abdullah didn't let me.

'A man's protection is in Allah, honour and duty,' he growled, his arm around my shoulder. 'Not in amulets and herbs.'

I made a mental note to go back to the shop, alone, and fell into step with my stern friend.

We entered a shoulder-wide lane, and as the lane darkened, further from the street, Abdullah led us beneath an almost invisible arch bearing the name *Bella Vista Towers*.

Beyond the arch we found a network of covered lanes that seemed, at one point, to pass through the middle of a private home. The owner of the home, an elderly man wearing a tattered *banyan* and sitting in an easy chair, was reading a newspaper through over-large optical sunglasses.

He didn't look up or acknowledge us as we passed through what seemed to be his living room.

We walked on into an even darker lane, turned the last corner in the maze and emerged in a wide, open, sunlit courtyard.

I'd heard of it before: it was called *Das Rasta*, or *Ten Ways*. Residential buildings and the many lanes that serviced them surrounded the roughly circular courtyard, open to the sky. It was a private public square.

Residents leaned from windows, looking down into the action of Das Rasta. Some lowered or pulled up baskets of vegetables, cooked food, and other goods. Many more people entered and left the court-yard through wheel-spoke alleys leading to the wider world beyond.

In the centre of the courtyard, sacks of grain and pulses had been heaped together in a pile twice the height of a man. The sacks formed a small pyramid of thrones, and seated on them at various levels were the Cycle Killers.

In the topmost improvised throne was Ishmeet, the leader. His long hair had never been cut, according to Sikh religious tradition, but his observance of Sikhism stopped there.

His hair wasn't held in a neat turban, but fell freely to his narrow waist. His thin, bare arms were covered in tattoos, depicting his many murders and gang war victories. There were two long, curved knives in decorated scabbards tucked into the belt of his tight jeans.

'*Salaam aleikum*,' he said lazily, greeting Abdullah as we approached his tower of thrones.

'*Wa aleikum salaam*,' Abdullah replied.

'Who's the dog-face you've got with you?' a man sitting close to Ishmeet asked in Hindi, turning his head to spit noisily.

'His name is Lin,' Abdullah replied calmly. 'They also call him Shantaram. He was with Khaderbhai, and he speaks Hindi.'

'I don't care if he speaks Hindi, Punjabi and Malayalam,' the man responded in Hindi, glaring at me. 'I don't care if he can recite poetry, and if he has a dictionary shoved up his arse. I want to know what this dog-face is doing here.'

'I'm guessing you have more experience with dogs than I do,' I said in Hindi. 'But I came here in the company of men, not dogs, who know how to show respect.'

The man flinched and twitched, shaking his head in disbelief. I wasn't sure if it was because of the challenge I'd thrown, or the fact

53

that a white foreigner had spoken it in the kind of Hindi used by street gangsters.

'This man is also my brother,' Abdullah said evenly, staring at Ishmeet. 'And what your man says to him, he says to me.'

'Then why don't I say it to you, Iranian?' the man said.

'Why don't you, by Allah?' Abdullah replied.

There was a moment of exquisite calm. Men working to bring sacks of grain, pots of water, boxes of cold drinks, bags of spices and other goods still moved into and out of the courtyard. People still watched from their windows. Children still laughed and played in the shade.

But in the breathing space between the Cycle Killers and the four of us, a meditation stillness rippled outwards from our beating hearts. It was the deliberate stillness of *not* reaching for our weapons, the shadow before the flash of sunlight and blood.

The Cycle Killers were only a word away from war, but they respected and feared Abdullah. I looked into Ishmeet's smiling eyes, schemed into slits. He was counting the corpses that would lie around his throne of sacks.

There was no doubt that Abdullah would kill at least three of Ishmeet's men, and that the rest of us might account for as many again. And although there were twelve Cycle Killers in the courtyard, and several more in the rooms beyond, and although Ishmeet himself might manage to live, the loss would be too great for his gang to survive a revenge attack by our gang.

Ishmeet's eyes opened a little wider, crimson betel nut staining his smile.

'Any brother of Abdullah,' he said, staring directly at me, 'is a brother of mine. Come. Sit up here, with me. We'll drink *bhang* together.'

I glanced at Abdullah, who nodded to me without taking his eyes off the Cycle Killers. I climbed onto the wide throne of sacks and took a seat a little below Ishmeet, and level with the man who'd insulted me.

'Raja!' Ishmeet said, calling to a man who was polishing the rows of already gleaming bicycles. 'Get some chairs!'

The man moved quickly to provide wooden stools for Abdullah, Fardeen, and Hussein. Others brought the pale green *bhang* in tall glasses, and also a large chillum.

I drank the glass of marijuana milk down in gulps, as did Ishmeet. Belching loudly, he winked at me.

'Buffalo milk,' he said. 'Fresh pulled. Gives a little extra kick. You want to be a king in this world, man, keep your own milking buffalo.'

'O . . . kay.'

He lit the chillum, took two long puffs, and passed it to me, smoke streaming from his nostrils like steam escaping from fissured stone.

I smoked and passed the chillum to the gang lieutenant sitting beside me. The animosity of moments before was gone from his smiling eyes. He smoked, passed the chillum along, and then tapped me on the knee.

'Who's your favourite heroine?'

'From now, or before?'

'From now.'

'Karisma Kapoor.'

'And from before?'

'Smita Patil. What about you?'

'Rekha,' he sighed. 'Before and now and always. She's the queen of everything. Do you have a knife?'

'Of course.'

'Can I see it, please?'

I took one of my knives out of its scabbard, and passed it to him. He opened the flick mechanism expertly, and then flipped the long, heavy, brass-handled weapon around his fingers as if it was a flower on a stem.

'Nice knife,' he said, closing it and handing it back to me. 'Who made it?'

'Vikrant, in Sassoon Dock,' I answered, putting the knife away.

'Ah, Vikrant. Good work. You wanna see my knife?'

'Sure,' I replied, reaching out to take the weapon he offered me.

My long switchblade knife was made for street fighting. The Cycle Killer's knife was designed to leave a deep, wide hole, usually in the back. The blade tapered quickly from the wide hilt to the tip. Gouged into the blade were trenches to facilitate the flow of blood. Backward serrations entered a body on the smooth side but ripped the flesh on the outward pull, preventing the wound from spontaneously closing.

The hilt was a brass semicircle, designed to fit into a closed fist. The knife was used in a punching action, rather than a slash or jab.

'You know,' I said, as I handed back the weapon, 'I hope we never, ever fight each other.'

He grinned widely, putting the knife back into its scabbard.

'Good plan!' he said. 'No problem. You and me, we never fight. Okay?'

He offered me his hand. I hesitated a moment, because gangsters take stuff like that seriously, and I wasn't sure that I could promise not to fight him, if our gangs became enemies.

'What the hell,' I said, slapping my palm into his, and closing my fingers in a firm handshake. 'We never fight. No matter what.'

He grinned at me again.

'I'm ... ' he began in Hindi. 'I'm sorry about ... about that comment before.'

'It's okay.'

'Actually, I *like* dogs,' he said. 'Anyone here will tell you that. I even feed the stray dogs here.'

'It's okay.'

'Ajay! Tell him how much I like dogs!'

'Very much,' Ajay said. 'He loves dogs.'

'If you don't stop talking about dogs right now,' Ishmeet said through the sliver of a smile, 'I'm going to kick you in the neck.'

Ishmeet turned away from his man, displeasure a crown pressed on his forehead.

'Abdullah,' he said. 'You want to talk to me, I think so?'

Abdullah was about to reply when a crew of ten workingmen entered the courtyard, pulling two long, empty handcarts.

'Make way!' they shouted. 'Work is close to God! Workingmen are doing God's work! We are here for the sacks! Old sacks going out! New sacks coming in! Make way! Work is close to God!'

With a disregard that might've cost other men their lives, the workers ignored the status and comfort of the murderous gang and began pulling sacks from the improvised throne. Deadly Cycle Killers tumbled and stumbled from their places on the pile.

As quickly as his dignity would allow, Ishmeet scrambled off his vantage point to stand close to Abdullah while the demolition continued. I climbed down with him to join my friends.

Fardeen, nicknamed the Politician, stood at once and offered his wooden stool to Ishmeet. The leader of the Cycle Killers accepted, sat beside Abdullah, and called importantly for hot chai.

While we waited for the tea, the workers removed the tall hill of sacks, leaving only scattered grains and straws on the bare stones of the courtyard. We sipped adrak chai, spicy ginger tea strong enough to bring tears to the eyes of someone judging judges.

The workers brought fresh sacks into the open ground. Within minutes a new mound began to appear, and men who worked for the Cycle Killers began to shape it into a series of throne-like seats once more.

Perhaps to cover the embarrassment of having his estrade so abruptly dismantled, Ishmeet turned his attention to me.

'You . . . foreigner,' he asked, 'what do you think of Das Rasta?'

'*Ji*,' I said, using the respectful term equivalent to *sir*, 'I was wondering how we were able to come in here without a challenge.'

'We knew you were coming,' Ishmeet replied smugly, 'and we knew you were friends, and how many you were. Dilip Uncle, the old man reading the newspaper, do you remember him?'

'Yeah. We passed right through his house.'

'Exactly. Dilip Uncle, he has a button on the floor under his chair. The button rings a bell here in the courtyard. From the number of times he presses the button, and for how long, we can tell who is coming, friend or stranger, and how many. And there are many uncles like Dilip, who are the eyes and the ears of Das Rasta.'

'Not bad,' I allowed.

'Your frown is another question, I think.'

'I was also wondering why this is called Das Rasta, Ten Ways, when I can count only nine ways in and out.'

'I *like* you, *gora*!' Ishmeet said, using the word that meant *white man*. 'Not many have noticed that fact. There are, in truth, ten ways into and out of this place, which is the reason for the name. But one of them is hidden, and only known to those of us who live here. The only way that you could pass through that exit is to become one of us, or be killed by us.'

Abdullah chose the moment to reveal his purpose.

'I have your money,' he said, leaning in toward Ishmeet's well-oiled smile. 'But there is a matter I must make clear, before I give it to you.'

'What . . . *matter*?'

'A witness,' Abdullah said, speaking in a tone that was loud enough for me to hear. 'You have a reputation for being so fast, in your work, that even the Djinn cannot see your blade strike. But in this assignment we gave to you, someone was allowed to see the deed. Someone who made a clear description of your men to the police.'

57

Ishmeet locked his jaw shut, glanced around quickly at his men, and then looked back at Abdullah. The smile returned slowly, but the teeth were still locked together as if they were holding a knife.

'We will, of course, kill this witness,' he hissed. 'And at no extra charge.'

'No need for that,' Abdullah replied. 'The sergeant who took the statement is one of ours. He thrashed the witness, and convinced him to change his story. But you understand that with a matter such as this, I must speak of it in the name of Sanjay himself. Especially since it is only the second assignment we have given to you.'

'*Jarur*,' Ishmeet hissed again. *Certainly*. 'And I can assure you that you will never have to raise the question of witnesses again, for so long as we do business together.'

Ishmeet took Abdullah's hand in his, held it for a moment, then stood, turned his back, and began to clamber to the top of his new throne of sacks. As he settled himself at the top of the pile once more, he spoke one word.

'Pankaj!' he said, speaking to the Cycle Killer who'd been sitting with me.

Fardeen took a package of money from his backpack. He passed it to Abdullah, who handed it on to Pankaj. As the Cycle Killer turned to climb up the pile of sacks he hesitated, and swung his gaze around to face me.

'You and me, we never fight,' he grinned, offering his hand once more. '*Pukkah?*' *Correct?*

His wide smile and obvious, innocent pleasure in a new friendship would've been derided as naïve by the gangsters and outlaws I'd come to know in the Australian prison. But we were in Bombay, and Pankaj's smile was as sincere as his willingness to fight me had been only minutes before; as sincere as mine.

Until I'd heard Ishmeet use his name, I hadn't realised that the man I'd traded insults with was the second-in-command of the Cycle Killers, and as feared a knife-man as Ishmeet himself.

'You and me,' I said in Hindi, 'we never fight. No matter what.'

His wicked grin widened, and he scampered athletically up the pile of sacks to give the package to Ishmeet. Abdullah raised his hand to his chest in farewell.

We followed Abdullah out through the labyrinth of lanes, through the living room where Dilip Uncle still sat, reading his newspaper, his foot hovering close to the button set into the floor, and then out into the street.

As we kicked the bikes to life, Abdullah caught my eye. When I met his gaze, his face opened in a rare, wide smile of happiness and exhilaration.

'That was close!' he said. '*Shukran Allah.*'

'Since when did you start subcontracting?'

'Two weeks ago, while you were in Goa,' he replied. 'The lawyer we hired, who betrayed our men to the police, and told them everything he had said in private?'

I nodded, recalling the anger we'd felt at the life sentence the Company men had received, based on their own lawyer's treacherous information. An appeal of the conviction was pending in the courts, but our men were still in prison.

'That lawyer has joined the long line of his fellows in hell,' Abdullah said, his golden eyes gleaming. 'And there will be no appeal of his sentence. But let us not disturb our peace with talk of dishonour. Let us enjoy the ride, and be grateful that, today, Allah has spared us the necessity to kill the killers we paid to kill for us. It is a great and wonderful thing to be alive, *Alhamdulillah.*' *By the grace of God.*

But as Fardeen, Hussein and I fell in behind Abdullah for the ride back to the Sanjay Council meeting, it wasn't God's grace that I was thinking about. Other mafia Companies hired the Cycle Killers, from time to time. Even the cops put them on clean-up duty now and then. But Khaderbhai, who'd founded the mafia group, had always refused.

Anywhere humans gather, from boardrooms to bordellos, they seek and agree upon a moral standard for themselves. And one standard, upheld by Khaderbhai, was that if a man had to be killed, he was given the chance to look into the eyes of the men who claimed that right. Hiring assassins, rather than being assassins, was a change too far for some, I was sure. It was a change too far for me.

Order and chaos were dancing on a slender blade, held by the outstretched arm of conscience. Subcontracting the Cycle Killers tilted the blade. At least half the men in the Company were more loyal to the code than to Sanjay, the leader who was changing it.

The first glimpse of the sea on Marine Drive filled my heart, if not my head. I turned away from the red shadow. I stopped thinking of that pyramid of killers, and Sanjay's improvidence. I stopped thinking about my own part in the madness. And I rode, with my friends, into the end of everything.

CHAPTER SEVEN

I F ABDULLAH HADN'T BEEN WITH US, Fardeen, Hussein and I would've raced one another to the Council meeting, cutting between the cars and overtaking all the way to the Nabila mosque. But Abdullah never raced, or cut between the cars. He expected the cars to make way for him, and for the most part, they did. He rode slowly, his back straight, head held high, his long, black hair fluttering at his wide shoulders.

We reached the mansion in some twenty minutes, and parked our bikes in places reserved for us, outside a perfume shop.

The entrance to the mansion was usually open to the street and unguarded. Khaderbhai believed that if an enemy had a death wish strong enough to make him attack the mansion, he would prefer to drink tea with him, before killing him.

But as we approached, we found the high, heavy street door of the mansion closed, and four armed men on duty. I knew one of them, Farukh, who operated a Company gambling outpost in the distant town of Aurangabad. The others were Afghan strangers.

We pushed open the door and found two more men inside, carrying assault rifles.

'Afghans?' I said, when we'd passed them.

'So many things have happened, Lin Brother, since you have been in Goa,' Abdullah replied as we entered the open courtyard at the centre of the mansion complex.

'No kidding.'

I hadn't visited the mansion in months, and I saw with regret how neglected the paved courtyard had become. In Khaderbhai's time there was a constant fountain drenching the huge boulder in the pond at the courtyard's centre. Lush potted palms and flower boxes had once provided splashes of colour in the white and sky-blue space. They'd long since died, and the dry earth that remained was covered with a sprinkling of cigarette butts.

At the door of the Council meeting room there were two more Afghans armed with assault rifles. One of them tapped at the closed door, and then opened it slowly.

Abdullah, Hussein and I entered, while Fardeen waited outside with the guards. When the door closed, there were thirteen of us in the long room.

The meeting room had changed. The floor was still tiled in cream pentagonal tiles, and the walls and vaulted ceiling still bore the mosaic pattern of a blue-white clouded sky. But the low inlaid table and plump brocade floor cushions were gone.

A dark boardroom table ran almost the length of the room, swarmed by fourteen high-backed leather executive chairs. At the far end of the table was a more ornate chairman's seat. The man sitting in that chair, Sanjay Kumar, looked up with a smile as we entered. It wasn't for me.

'Abdullah! Hussein!' he called out. 'We've gone through all the small stuff already. Now you're here, we can finally deal with some real trouble.'

I assumed that Sanjay would want me to wait outside until the meeting was over, and tried to excuse myself.

'Sanjaybhai,' I said. 'I'll wait in the courtyard, until you need me.'

'No, Lin,' he said, waving his hand vaguely. 'Go sit down with Tariq. Come on, the rest of you, let's get started.'

Tariq, Khaderbhai's fourteen-year-old nephew and only male relative, sat in his uncle's emperor chair at the end of the room.

He was growing fast, already almost as tall as any man in the room. But still he seemed small and frail in that winged chair, once a throne for the king of South Bombay crime.

Behind Tariq was Nazeer, his hand resting on the handle of a dagger: the boy's protector, and my close friend.

I moved past the long table to greet Tariq. The boy brightened for a moment when I shook his hand, but quickly assumed the cold impassive stare that had hardened the bronze of his eyes since the death of his uncle.

When I looked at Nazeer, the older man gave me a rare smile. It was a grimace that could tame lions, and one of the favourite smiles of my life.

I took a seat beside Tariq. Abdullah and Hussein took their places, and the meeting recommenced.

For a while, Sanjay directed the discussions through business matters: trouble with striking workers at the Ballard Pier dockside had slowed the supply of drugs into South Bombay; some fishermen at Sassoon Dock, anchorage of the biggest fishing fleet in the Island City, had formed an association and were resisting the payment of protection money; and a friendly city councillor had been caught by a police raid on one of the Company's prostitution dens, requiring a favour from the mafia Council to hush the matter up, and save the man's career.

The mafia Council, which had carefully set up the raid to force the city councillor deeper into its embrace, authorised the sums required to bribe the police, and determined that twice the amount should be charged to the councillor in question, for doing him the favour.

The final matter was something more complicated, and went beyond business. The Sanjay Company, and the Council that ordered its affairs, ran the whole of South Bombay, an area that stretched from Flora Fountain to the Navy Nagar near the very southern promontory of the Island City, and included everything in between, from sea to sea.

The Sanjay Company was the sole black market authority in the area, but wasn't generally despised. In fact, a lot of people took their disputes and grievances to the Company, in those years, rather than the police. The mafia was usually quicker, often more just, and always cheaper than the cops.

When Sanjay took the leadership, he called the group a Company, joining a gangster trend that divided the city along business lines. Khaderbhai, the dead Khan who'd founded it, was strong enough for the mafia clan to have no other name but his own. Echoes of Khaderbhai's name gave the Sanjay Company an authority that Sanjay's name didn't, and still held the peace.

Occasionally, however, someone decided to take matters into his own hands. One such rogue element was an ambitious landlord in the Cuffe Parade area, where tall, expensive apartment buildings stood on land reclaimed from the sea. He'd begun hiring his own thugs. The Sanjay Company didn't like it, because the Company had the reputation of its own thugs to consider.

The private goons had thrown a rent defaulter from the window of a second-storey apartment. The tenant survived the fall, but his body landed on a cigarette and hashish shop owned by the Company, injuring the operator, known as Shining Patel, and a popular customer who was a renowned singer of Sufi songs.

Shining Patel and his black-white-market shop was just business for the Sanjay Company. The injury to a great singer, loved by every hash smoker in the southern peninsula, made the offence personal.

'I told you this would happen, Sanjaybhai,' a man named Faisal said, clenching a fist on the table. 'I've been warning you about this kind of thing for months.'

'You warned me that someone would fall on Shining Patel's shop?' Sanjay sneered. 'I must've missed that meeting.'

'I warned you that respect was slipping,' Faisal said, more quietly. 'I warned you that discipline was slipping. Nobody's afraid of us, and I don't blame them. If we're so scared that we put mercenaries on the door, we're the ones to blame.'

'He's right,' Little Tony added. 'This problem with the Scorpion Company, for example. That's what gives *chutiyas* like this landlord *bahinchudh* the idea that he can go past us, to create his own little army.'

'It's not a *Company*,' Sanjay spat back at them. 'Those Scorpion fucks haven't been recognised, not by any of the other Companies in Bombay. It's a gang. They're just North Bombay guys, trying to squeeze into the south. Call it what it is, man, a cheap little gang.'

'Call it what you will,' Mahmoud Melbaaf said softly, 'it is still a problem. They have attacked our men in the street. Not a kilometre from here, two of our best earners were hacked with choppers, in the middle of the day.'

'That's right,' Faisal added.

'That's why we have our Afghan brothers on duty,' Mahmoud Melbaaf continued. 'The Scorpions have been trying to cut into our areas at Regal and Nariman Point. I kicked them out of there, but there were five of them, and if Abdullah hadn't been with me it would've gone the other way. My name alone, and yours, too, Sanjay, doesn't scare them. And if Little Tony hadn't cut that dealer's face last week, they'd still be selling drugs outside KC College, fifty steps from your door. If that's not a problem, I haven't seen one.'

'I know,' Sanjay replied more gently, glancing quickly at the boy, Tariq.

The cold stare in the boy's eyes never wavered.

'I know what you're saying,' Sanjay said. 'Of *course* I know. What the hell do they *want*? Do they *want* a war? They really think they can *win* that? What do they want, those *fucks*?'

We all knew what the Scorpion Gang wanted: they wanted it all, and they wanted us dead, or gone.

In the silence that followed his rhetorical question I looked at the faces of the Council members, trying to judge their mood, and their willingness to fight yet another turf war.

Sanjay lowered his eyes, cold eyes in a sensitive face, as he considered the options open to him. His prudent instinct, I knew, was to avoid a fight and negotiate a deal, even with predatory enemies like the Scorpions. What mattered to Sanjay was the deal, not how, or where, or who was on the other end.

He was brave and ruthless, but his first impulse always led him to buy his way out. It was Sanjay who'd put the boardroom table in the Council room, and I realised, staring at his puzzlement and indecision, that the table wasn't an expression of pride or self-aggrandisement: it was a visible representation of his true nature to negotiate, and seal the deal.

The seat next to Sanjay, on his right, was always empty in memory of his childhood friend Salman, who'd died in battle during the last big power struggle against a rival gang.

Sanjay had spared a survivor of that defeated group. It was the man he'd spared, Vishnu, who'd built up the Scorpion Gang, and now threatened Sanjay himself.

Sanjay knew that the men on his own Council who'd disagreed with that clemency, and who'd insisted that the man had to be killed and the book closed on the matter, would see the current trouble as a vindication of their views, and a weakness of leadership.

As I watched him, Sanjay's hand slowly drifted to his right across the polished surface of the table, as if searching for the hand and the warrior advice of his dead friend.

To Sanjay's right, beside the empty chair, was Mahmoud Melbaaf, the slim, watchful Iranian whose serene stare and equable temperament never faltered, no matter how fierce the provocation.

But his calm was the child of sadness, and he never laughed, and almost never smiled. Some great loss had struck at his heart and settled there, smoothing out peaks and troughs of emotion, as wind and sand smother mountains in the desert.

Beside Melbaaf was Faisal, the ex-boxer, the almost-champion. A crooked manager, who stole all Faisal's competition earnings, had driven the knife deeper by running off with his girl. Faisal killed him, and the girl left the city, never to be seen again.

Emerging from eight years in prison, with instincts as quick and deadly as his fists, he'd worked as an enforcer for the Sanjay Company for several years. He had a reputation for rapid resolutions of debt problems. Although his skills as a boxer were sometimes exercised, very often his scarred face and fierce stare were enough to provoke debtors into finding the necessary funds.

After the last big turf war, which left a few places on the Council empty, Faisal had been rewarded with a permanent seat.

Next to Faisal, leaning in close to him, was his constant companion, Amir. With his large head, round and blunt as a river stone, scarred face, luxuriant eyebrows and elaborate moustache, Amir had the mysterious allure of a South Indian movie star.

A notoriously good dancer, despite his considerable paunch, he recounted stories in a bellowing basso, played jokes on everyone but Abdullah, was the first to hit the dance floor at any party, and the first into any fight.

Amir and Faisal controlled the drugs in South Bombay, and their street dealers brought in one quarter of all the Company's profits.

Sitting close to Amir was his protégé, Andrew DaSilva, a young street gangster who'd been appointed to the Council as a concession to Amir. He'd taken control of the prostitution and pornography rackets, captured from the defeated gang in the last turf war.

The fair young man, with light brown hair and camel-coloured eyes, had the illusive innocence in his bright smile that cruelty fashions from fear, and cunning. I'd seen the mask fall. I'd seen the snarl of the whip in his eyes. But others didn't seem to see it: his reflexive smile restored the disguise quickly enough to save him from the distrust that his true nature should've provoked in others.

And he knew that I knew. Every time he looked at me, there was a question in his eyes. *Why can you see me?*

We'd come close to violence, DaSilva and I, and we both knew that one day, one night, in one situation or another, there'd be a head count that would leave one of us behind.

Looking at him then, at that Council meeting, I was sure that when it did finally come, Andrew wouldn't be alone: he'd be leaning, hard, on the strong, wide shoulders of his friend Amir.

Next around the table was Farid, known as Farid the Fixer, whose devotion to Khaderbhai had rivalled that of grizzled Nazeer. Farid blamed himself for Khaderbhai's death in Afghanistan, convincing himself, despite our assurances, that if he'd been there with us in the snow, Khaderbhai might've survived.

His guilt and despair drove him to recklessness, but it also pushed him into a deeper friendship with me. I'd always liked Farid. I liked his furiousness, and his willingness to run into the storm: the shadow that fell before rather than behind his every step.

As I looked at him, that day, in the long pause while Sanjay decided what action to take about rogue landlords, unlicensed thugs, and predatory Scorpions, Farid looked up at me with embers of sorrow burning his eyes. For a moment I was back there, on the snow-scattered mountain, staring into the dead, snow-stone face of Khaderbhai: the man Farid and I had both called father, father, father.

The last man at the table before Hussein and Abdullah coughed politely. His name was Rajubhai, and he was the controller of currencies for the Company. A fat man, who carried his sumptuous girth with ingenuous pride, Rajubhai had the look of an elder from a distant village, but he was a born Mumbaikar.

A splendid pink turban covered his head, and he wore the traditional white *dhoti* beneath his knee-length sleeveless serge tunic. Never fully relaxed beyond the serene boundaries of his currency counting room, Rajubhai fidgeted in his place, glancing at his watch whenever Sanjay wasn't looking.

'Okay,' Sanjay said at last. 'This landlord has got big balls, I'll give him that, but it's not acceptable, what he did. It will send out all the wrong signals, and this is a bad time to be sending wrong signals. Abdullah, Hussein, Farid, go pick up one of those thugs he hired, the biggest, toughest one, the leader. Take him to the second floor of that other building, the new apartment tower they're building at Navy Nagar.'

'*Ji*,' Abdullah replied. *Sir.*

'Use that new place, where they paid the Scorpion Gang instead of us last month. Throw the *madachudh* off the second floor of that building. Make sure he hits the site management office, if you can, or something else that will send a message to the construction company and the Scorpion fuckers both. Give the guy some cheerful fucking encouragement, first. Find out everything he knows. If he survives after you throw him out the window, the goon is free to leave.'

'*Jarur.*' Abdullah nodded. *Certainly.*

'After that,' Sanjay added, 'round up the rest of those thugs, and take them to visit the landlord who hired them. Make them beat him up. Make his own hired goons kick the shit out of him. Be sure they give him a solid pasting. Then cut their faces, and send them out of the city.'

'*Jarur.*'

'When he wakes up, tell the landlord his tax has doubled. Then make him pay for all the time and trouble he's caused. And the hospital bills, for Shining Patel and Rafiq. Best qawwali singer I ever heard, that guy. A damn shame.'

'That it was,' Mahmoud Melbaaf agreed.

'A damn shame,' Amir sighed.

'You got all that, Abdullah?' Sanjay asked.

'Got it.'

Sanjay took a deep breath, puffing his cheeks as he let the air out, and looked around at the other members of the Council.

'Are we done?' he asked.

There was a little silence, but then Rajubhai spoke up quickly.

'Time and money wait for no man,' he said, searching for his sandals.

All the others stood. One by one, they nodded toward Tariq, the boy who sat in the emperor chair, before they left the room. When only Sanjay remained, and he, too, began to walk toward the door, I approached him.

'Sanjaybhai?'

'Oh, Lin,' he said, turning quickly. 'How was Goa? Those guns you brought back, that was good work down there.'

'Goa was . . . fine.'

'But?'

'But two things, actually, since I've been away. Cycle Killers, and Afghans. What's going on?'

His face moved into the shadowland of anger, and his lip began to curl. Leaning in close to me, he spoke in a whisper.

'You know, Lin, don't mistake your usefulness for your value. I sent you to Goa to get those guns because all my better men are too well known down there. And I wanted to make sure that none of my better men got busted on that first run, if it didn't go well. Are we clear?'

'You called me here to tell me that?'

'I didn't call you to this meeting, and I didn't permit you to sit through it. I wouldn't do that. And I didn't like it. I didn't like it at all. It was Tariq who called you, and Tariq who insisted that you be allowed to stay.'

Together we turned to look at the boy.

'If you have the time, Lin?' Tariq said, quietly but firmly.

It wasn't a request.

'Well,' Sanjay said, in a louder voice, slapping me on the shoulder, 'I'll be going. Don't know why you came back, Lin. Me, I fucking *love* Goa. If it was me, I'd have disappeared, man, and stayed on the beach forever. I wouldn't have blamed you if you did.'

Sanjay walked from the meeting room. I sat down beside Tariq again. I was angry, and it took me a while to look directly into the boy's expressionless eyes. A full minute passed in slowly breathing silence.

'You're not going to ask me?' Tariq began at last, smiling faintly.

'Ask you what, Tariq?'

'Why I called you to the Council meeting today.'

'I'm assuming you'll get around to it, sooner or later,' I smiled back at him.

Tariq seemed about to laugh, but regained his severe composure.

'You know, Lin, that's one of the qualities that my uncle liked most about you,' he said. 'Deep down, he said to me a few times, you're more *Inshallah*, if you know what I mean, than any of us.'

I didn't respond. I assumed that using the term *Inshallah*, meaning *The will of God*, or *If God wills it*, meant that he considered me to be fatalistic.

It wasn't true. I didn't ask questions about what we did, because I didn't care. I cared about people, some people, but I didn't care about anything else. I didn't care what happened to me in those years after escaping from prison. The future always looked like fire, and the past was still too dark.

'When my uncle died,' Tariq continued, 'we all worked according to the instructions in his will, and divided his many assets.'

'I recall.'

'As you know, I myself received this house, and a considerable sum of money.'

I glanced around to look at Nazeer. The old soldier's scowl remained, fierce and immutable, but one shaggy eyebrow twitched a flicker of interest.

'And you,' Tariq continued. 'You never received anything from Khaderbhai. You were not mentioned.'

I'd loved Khaderbhai. Damaged sons have two fathers: the wounded one they're born with, and the one their wounded hearts choose. I'd chosen Khaderbhai, and I'd loved him.

But I was sure, alone in that room inside where truth is a mirror, that even if he'd cared for me, in some way, he'd also seen me as a pawn in his great game.

'I never expected to be mentioned.'

'You did not expect to be remembered?' he insisted, inclining his head to emphasise his doubt.

It was exactly the same gesture that Khaderbhai had used when he was teasing me in philosophical discussions.

'Even though you were so close to him? Even though he acknowledged you, more than once, as a favourite? Even though you, and Nazeer, were with him in the mission that cost him his life?'

'Your English is getting damn good,' I observed, trying to change the direction of the conversation. 'This new tutor's doing a great job.'

'I like her,' Tariq replied, but then his eyes flickered nervously, and he amended his hasty reply. 'I mean, I *respect* my teacher. She is an excellent tutor. Rather better, I might say, than you were yourself, Lin.'

There was a little pause. I put the palms of my hands on my knees, signalling that I was ready to leave.

'Well —'

'Wait!' he said quickly.

I frowned, looking hard at the boy, but relented when I saw the pleading crouched in his eyes. I sat back once more, and crossed my arms.

'This ... this week,' he began again, 'we discovered some new papers of my uncle. Those papers had been lost in his copy of the Koran. Or not *lost*, but simply not found, until this week. My uncle placed them there, just before he went to Afghanistan.'

The boy paused, and I glanced back at the brawny bodyguard, my friend Nazeer.

'He left you a gift,' Tariq said suddenly. 'It is a sword. His own sword, that had belonged to his great-grandfather, and that twice has been used in battle against the British.'

'There must be some mistake.'

'The papers are quite specific,' Tariq said stiffly. 'In the event of his death, the sword was to go to you. Not as a bequest, but as a gift, from my hands, directly to yours. You will honour me now, by accepting it.'

Nazeer brought the sword. He unwrapped layers of silk cloth protection, and presented the sword to me in his upturned palms.

The long sword was in a wide silver scabbard, chiselled to show a flight of hawks in relief. The apical portion of the scabbard showed an inscription from the Koran. The hilt was made of lapis, inlaid with turquoise to cover the fixing rivets. A hand guard of beaten silver swept in a graceful curve from the pommel to the cross guard.

'It's a mistake,' I repeated, staring at the heirloom weapon. 'It should be yours. It *must* be yours.'

The boy smiled, grateful and wistful in equal measure.

'You are quite right, it should be mine,' he said. 'But the papers, written in Khaderbhai's own hand, are very specific. The sword is yours, Lin. And don't think to refuse it. I know your heart. If you try to give it back to me, I will be offended.'

'There's another consideration,' I said, still staring at the sword. 'You know that I escaped from prison in my country. I could be arrested and sent back there at any time. If that happens, the sword could be lost.'

'You will never have trouble with the police in Bombay,' Tariq insisted. 'You are with us. No harm can come to you here. And if you leave the city for some long time, you can give the sword to Nazeer, who will protect it until you return.'

He nodded to Nazeer, who leaned in closer, urging me to take the weapon from his hands. I looked into his eyes. Nazeer's mouth tightened in a willow-droop smile.

'Take the sword,' he said in Urdu. 'And draw the sword.'

The sword was lighter than I'd expected it to be. I let it rest on my knees for a time.

In that silent minute in the neglected mansion I hesitated, thinking that if I drew the sword from its scabbard, memories would bleed out from the sheath of forgetfulness, where some of the time, enough of the time, they were hidden. But tradition demanded that I draw the sword, as a sign of accepting it.

I drew the blade into the light and stood, holding the naked sword at my side, the point of the blade only a finger's breadth from the marble floor. And it was true. I felt it: the power in a thing to swell a tide of memory.

I sheathed the sword again, and faced Tariq. The boy indicated the chair beside him with a nod of his head. I sat once more, the sword balanced across my knees.

'The text on the sword,' I said. 'I can't read the Arabic.'

'*Inna Lillahi wa inna –*' Tariq began in the poetry of the Koran.

'*– ilayhi raji'un,*' I finished for him.

I knew the quote. *We belong to God, and unto God do we return.* Every Muslim gangster said it on the way into battle. We all said it, even if we weren't Muslim, just in case.

The fact that I couldn't even read the Arabic inscription on the ancestor-sword Khaderbhai had left to me was a bitter pinch on Tariq's face. I sympathised with him: I agreed with him, in fact, that I didn't deserve the sword, and couldn't know the blood significance that the heirloom had for Tariq.

'There was a letter among those papers we found in the Holy Book,' he said, controlling every breath and word. 'It was a letter to you.'

I felt the cobra rising within me. A letter. I didn't want it. I don't like letters. Any dark past is a vampire, feeding on the blood of the living moment, and letters are the bats.

'We began to read it,' Tariq said, 'not knowing that it was addressed to you. It was not until halfway through it that we realised it was his last letter to you. We stopped reading immediately. We did not finish the letter. We do not know how it ends. But we know that it begins with Sri Lanka.'

Sometimes the river of life takes you to the rocks. The letter, the sword, the decisions made at the Council meeting, *Don't mistake your*

71

usefulness for your value, the Cycle Killers, guns from Goa, Sri Lanka: streams of coincidence and consequence. And when you see the rocks coming, you've got two choices: stay in the boat, or jump.

Nazeer handed Tariq the silver envelope. Tariq tapped it against his open palm.

'My uncle's gifts,' he said, even more softly, 'were always given with conditions, and never accepted without –'

'Consequences,' I finished for him.

'I was going to say *submission*. This house was a gift in Khaderbhai's will, but it was given to me on the condition that I never leave it, even for a minute, until I reach the age of eighteen years.'

I didn't hide my shock. I wasn't sensitive to what he was going through, and becoming.

'*What?*'

'It is not so bad,' Tariq said, setting his jaw against my indignation. 'All of my tutors come here, to me. I am learning everything. English, science, Islamic studies, economics, and the fighting arts. And Nazeer is always with me, and all of the household servants.'

'But you're fourteen years old, Tariq. You've got four more years of this? Do you ever meet any other kids?'

'Men in my family fight and lead at fifteen years old,' Tariq declared, glaring at me. 'And even at this age, I am already living my destiny. Can you say the same of *your* life?'

Young determination is the strongest energy we ever have, alone. I didn't want to criticise his commitment: I just wanted to be sure that he was aware of alternatives.

'Tariq,' I sighed. 'I don't have the slightest idea what you're talking about.'

'I will not simply *follow* in the footsteps of my uncle,' he said slowly, as if I was the child, 'I will *become* Khaderbhai, one day, and I will lead all of these men who were here today. Including you, Lin. I will be *your* leader. If you are still with us.'

I looked once more at Nazeer, who gazed back at me, a softly burning diamond of pride in his eyes. I began to walk away.

'The letter!' Tariq said quickly.

Suddenly angry, I spun round to face him again. I was about to speak, but Tariq raised the letter in his hand.

'It begins with a mention of Sri Lanka,' Tariq said, offering me the silver envelope. 'I know that it was his wish. You gave your word to go there, isn't it so?'

'I did,' I said, taking the letter from his slender fingers.

'Our agents in Trincomalee tell us that the time will soon be right for you to fulfil your promise.'

'When?' I asked, holding the twin legacies, letter and sword.

'Soon,' Tariq said, glancing at Nazeer. 'Abdullah will let you know. But be ready, at any time. It will be soon.'

The interview was over. A cold courtesy kept the boy in his seat, but I knew that he was anxious to leave: even more anxious, perhaps, for me to leave him.

I walked toward the door leading to the courtyard. Nazeer accompanied me. At the door, I looked back to see the tall boy still sitting in the emperor chair, his face supported by his hand. His thumb extended downwards against his dimpled cheek, and the fingers fanned out across his forehead. It was exactly the gesture I'd seen when Khaderbhai was lost in thought.

At the street door of the mansion, Nazeer retrieved a calico pouch, complete with a shoulder strap. The sword fitted neatly inside, concealed by the cloth, and could be worn across my back as I rode my bike.

Slipping the pouch over my shoulder, Nazeer adjusted the sword fussily until it hung to just the right aesthetic angle. He hugged me quickly, furtively and fiercely, crunching my ribs in the hoop of his arms.

He walked away without a word or a backward glance. His bowed legs waddled at his fastest pace, hurrying him back to the boy, the young man who was his master and his only love: Khaderbhai, come back to life, so that Nazeer might serve him again.

Watching him leave, I remembered another time when the mansion had been filled with plants and the music of falling water, and tame pigeons had followed Nazeer's every step through the huge house. They loved him, those birds.

But there were no birds in the mansion, and the only sound I heard was a metal-to-metal stutter, like teeth chattering in a freezing wind: cartridges, being inserted into the magazine of a Kalashnikov, one brass burial chamber at a time.

CHAPTER EIGHT

O UTSIDE ON THE STREET EARLY EVENING glowed on every face, as if the whole world was blushing to think what the night would bring. Abdullah was waiting for me, his bike parked beside mine. He gave a few rupees to the kids who'd stood guard over our bikes. They shouted their delight, and ran to the sweet shops on the corner to buy cigarettes.

Abdullah swung out beside me into the traffic. At a red light, I spoke for the first time.

'I'm picking up Lisa, at the Mahesh. Wanna come?'

'I'll ride with you that far,' he replied solemnly, 'but I will not join you. I have some work.'

We rode in silence along the shopping boulevard of Mohammed Ali Road. The allure of the perfume bazaars gave way to the sugared scents of *firni*, *rabri*, and *falooda* sweet shops. The glittering splendour of bangle and bracelet shops surrendered to the gorgeous fractals of Persian carpets, displayed side to side for a city block.

As the long road ended in a thatch-work confusion of handcarts, near the vast Crawford Market complex, we took a short cut, riding the wrong way into streams of traffic, threading through the wide eye of another junction.

Back in the right flow of traffic again, we paused for the long signal at Metro theatre junction. A movie poster covered the first floor of the cinema. Bad Guy and Good Guy faces, drenched in green, yellow and purple, told their story of love and anguish from behind a thorny hedge of guns and swords.

Families jammed into cars and taxis stared up at the movie poster. A young boy in a car near to me waved, pointed at the poster, and made his hand into a gun, to fire at me. He pulled the trigger. I pretended that a bullet had struck my arm, and the boy laughed. His family laughed. People in other cars laughed.

The boy's kindly faced Mother urged the boy to shoot me again. The boy pointed his finger-gun, aimed with a squinting eye, and fired. I did the-Bad-Guy-coming-to-a-bad-end, and sprawled out on the tank of my bike.

When I sat up again everyone in the cars clapped or waved or laughed.

I took a bow, and turned to see Abdullah's ashen mortification.

We are Company men, I heard him thinking. *Respect and fear. One or the other, and nothing else. Respect and fear.*

Only the sea on the coast ride to the Mahesh hotel finally softened his stern expression. He rode slowly, one hand on the throttle, one hand on his hip. I rode up close beside him, resting my left hand on his shoulder.

When we shook hands goodbye, I asked one of the questions that had been on my mind throughout the ride.

'Did you know about the sword?'

'Everyone knows about it, Lin, my brother.'

Our hands parted, but he held my eyes.

'Some of them,' he said carefully, 'they are jealous that Khaderbhai left the sword to you.'

'Andrew.'

'He is one. But he is not the only one.'

I was silent, my lips tight on the curse that was staining the inside of my mouth. Sanjay's words, *Don't mistake your usefulness for your value*, had forked through my heart like summer lightning, and a voice was calling me to go, to run, anywhere else, before it ended in bad blood. And then there was Sri Lanka.

'I'll see you tomorrow, *Inshallah*,' I said, standing to park my bike.

'Tomorrow, *Inshallah*,' he replied, stepping his bike into gear and pulling away from the kerb.

Without looking back, he called out to me. '*Allah hafiz!*' *May Allah be your guardian!*

'*Allah hafiz*,' I replied, to myself.

The Sikh security guards at the door of the Mahesh hotel looked with some interest at the sword-shaped parcel strapped to my back, but let me pass with a nod and a smile. They knew me well.

Passports, abandoned by guests who skipped out of the hotel without paying their bills, found their way to me through the security teams or desk managers at most of the hotels in the city.

It was a steady stream of books, as illegal passports were known, running to fifteen or more a month in the skip season. And they were the best kind of books: the kind that people who lose them don't report.

Every security office in every five-star hotel in the world has a wall of pictures of people who skipped out on a hotel bill, some of them leaving their passports behind. Most people looked at that wall to identify criminals. For me, it was shopping.

In the lobby of the hotel, I scanned the open-plan coffee lounge and saw Lisa, still at a meeting with friends beside the wide, tall windows that looked at the sea.

I decided to wash some of the street dirt off my face and hands before greeting her, and made my way toward the men's room. As I reached the door I heard a voice, speaking from behind me.

'Is that a sword on your back, or are you just furious to see me?'

I turned to see Ranjit, the budding media tycoon, the handsome athlete and political activist: the man that Karla, my Karla, had married. He was smiling.

'I'm always furious to see you, Ranjit. Goodbye.'

He smiled again. It looked like an honest, earnest smile. I didn't look close enough to find out, because the man smiling at me was married to Karla.

'Goodbye, Ranjit.'

'What? No, wait!' he said quickly. 'I'd like to talk to you.'

'We just did. Goodbye, Ranjit.'

'No, really!' he said, dodging in front of me, his smile almost intact. 'I've just finished a meeting, and I was on my way out, but I'm damn glad that I ran into you.'

'Run into someone else, Ranjit.'

'Please. Please. That's . . . that's not a word I use every day.'

'What do you want?'

'There's . . . there's something I've been wanting to talk to you about.'

I glanced around toward Lisa, sitting with her friends. She looked up and caught my eye. I nodded. She understood, and nodded back, before returning her attention back to her friends.

'What's on your mind?' I asked.

A ripple of surprise scudded across the flawless landscape of his fine features.

'If it's a bad time —'

'We don't have a *good* time, Ranjit. Get to the point.'

'Lin . . . I'm sure we could be friends, if we just —'

'Don't make this about you and me, Ranjit. There *is* no you and me. I'd know it, if there was.'

'You speak as if you don't like me,' Ranjit said. 'But you don't know me at all.'

'I don't like you. And that's just already. If I know you better, it's sure to get worse.'

'Why?'

'Why what?'

'Why don't you like me?'

'You know, if you stand in the lobby stopping everyone who doesn't like you, and asking them why, you better get a room, because you'll be here all night.'

'But, wait . . . it's . . . I don't understand.'

'Your ambition is putting Karla at risk,' I said quietly. 'I don't like it. I don't like *you*, for doing it. Is that clear enough?'

'It's Karla that I wanted to talk to you about,' he said, studying my face.

'What about Karla?'

'I want to be sure she's safe, that's all.'

'What do you mean, safe?'

His brow furrowed into a discomfited frown. He fatigue-sighed, allowing his head to fall forward for a moment.

'I don't even know how to start this . . . '

I looked around, and then directed him to a space in the wide foyer, with two empty chairs. Pulling the sword from my shoulders, I sat facing him, the calico-wrapped weapon resting on my knees.

A waiter approached us immediately, but I smiled him away. Ranjit hung his head for a time, staring at the carpet, but then shrugged himself together.

'You know, I've been pretty deep in the political stuff lately. Running some important campaigns. People have been getting at me, in any press that I don't own. I suppose you've heard.'

'I heard you've been buying vote banks,' I said. 'That's making people nervous. Back to Karla.'

'Have you . . . have you talked to Karla?'

'Why do you ask that?'

'Have you?'

'We're done, Ranjit.'

I began to stand, but he pressed me to stay.

'Look, let me get this out. I've been running a strong press campaign against the Spear of Karma.'

'A spear that'll hit Karla, if you don't stop provoking people into throwing it.'

'That's . . . that's just what I wanted to talk to you about. You see . . . I know that you're still in love with her.'

'Goodbye,' I said, standing to leave again, but he grasped at my wrist. I looked at his hand.

'That's not advised.'

He pulled his hand away.

'Please, wait. Please, just sit down, and hear what I've got to say.'

I sat down. My brow was all fault lines, and it was Ranjit's fault.

'I know you're going to think I'm really out of line,' he said quickly, 'but I think you'd want to know, if Karla was in danger.'

'*You're* the threat to her, and you should back off. Soon.'

'Are you threatening me?'

'Yes. So glad we had this talk.'

We stared at one another, across the space that hovers between predator and prey: hot, imminent and driven.

Karla. My first sight of her, on my first day in Bombay, years before, had put my heart like a hunting bird on her wrist.

She'd used me. She'd loved me, until I loved her. She'd recruited me to work for Khaderbhai. When the blood was washed from floors of love, and hate, and vengeance, and the wounds had healed to a braille of scars, she'd married the handsome, smiling millionaire staring into my eyes. Karla.

I glanced around at Lisa, beautiful and bright, in the company of her artist friends. My mouth tasted sour, and my heartbeat was rising. I hadn't spoken to Karla for two years, but I felt like a traitor to Lisa, sitting there while Ranjit talked about Karla. I looked back to Ranjit. I wasn't happy.

'I can see it in you,' he said. 'You still love her.'

'Do you want me to slap you, Ranjit? Because if that's it, you're mostly there.'

'No, of course not. I'm sure you still love her,' he said honestly and earnestly, it seemed, 'because, you know, if I was you, *I'd* still love her, even if she left me to marry another man. There's only one Karla. There's only one crazy way for any man to love her. We both know that.'

The best thing about a business suit is that there's always plenty to hang on to, if need be. I grabbed at his suit, and shirt, and tie.

'Stop talking about Karla,' I said. 'Quit while you're behind.'

He opened his mouth to shout, I think, but thought better of it. He was a powerful man, peering through a political window at more power, and couldn't make a scene.

'Please, please, I'm not trying to upset you,' he pleaded. 'I want you to *help* Karla. If something happens to me, will you promise —'

I let him go, and he pulled away quickly, sitting back in his chair and adjusting his suit.

'What are you talking about?'

'There was an attempt on my life last week,' he said sorrowfully.

'You're an attempt on your own life, Ranjit, every time you open your mouth.'

'There was a bomb in my car.'

'Tell me about the bomb.'

'My driver was away from the car for only a few minutes, buying *paan*. Luckily, he noticed a trailing wire when he returned, and he found the bomb. We called the police, and they took it away. It wasn't a real bomb, but the note said that the next one would be. I managed to keep it from the press. I have a certain amount of influence, as you know.'

'Change your driver.'

He laughed weakly.

'Change your driver,' I said again.

'My driver?'

'He's your weak link. Odds are, he found the bomb there, because he put it there. He was paid. It was done to scare you.'

'I . . . you're joking, of course. He's been with me for three years . . .'

'Good. Give him a nice severance package. But get rid of him.'

'He's such a loyal man . . .'

'Does Karla know about this?'

'No. And I don't want her to know.'

It was my turn to laugh.

'Karla's a big girl. And she's smart. You shouldn't be keeping this from her.'

'Still . . .'

79

'You're wasting your best resource, if you don't tell her. She's smarter than you are. She's smarter than anybody.'

'But —'

'Tell her.'

'Maybe. Maybe you're right. But I just want to try to get a *handle* on this thing, you know? I think it'll be okay. I have good security. But I worry for *her*. That's my only real worry.'

'I told you before, back off,' I said. 'Lay off the politics, for a while. They say the fish starts to stink at the head. I say if it stinks anywhere, you've been there too long.'

'I won't stop, Lin. These guys, these fanatics, that's how they win. They scare everybody into silence.'

'You're gonna teach me politics now?'

He smiled: the first smile of his that I almost liked, because it was sewn at the edges by something kinder than bright victory.

'I . . . I think we're on the edge of a truly big change in the way we think, and act, and maybe even the way we *dream* in this country. If better minds win, if India becomes a truly modern, secular democracy, with rights and freedoms for all, the next century will be the Indian century, and we'll lead the world.'

He looked into my eyes and saw the scepticism. He was right about India's future, everyone in Bombay knew it and felt it in those years, but what he'd given me was a speech, and one he'd delivered before.

'You know,' I said, 'every guy on every side makes the same speech.'

He opened his mouth to protest, but I stopped him with a raised palm.

'I don't do politics, but I know hatred when I see it, and I know that poking hatred with a stick will get you bit.'

'I'm glad you understand,' he sighed, letting his shoulders sag.

'I'm not the one who has to understand.'

His back straightened again.

'I'm not *afraid* of them, you know?'

'It was a bomb, Ranjit. Of course you're afraid. I'm afraid just talking to you. I'll prefer it when you're far away.'

'If I knew you'd be there for her, with your . . . your *friends*, I'd be able to face this situation with a quiet heart.'

I frowned at him, wondering if he understood all the ironies that were packed into his request. I decided to throw one back.

'Couple weeks back, your afternoon newspaper carried a pretty rough article about the Bombay mafia. One of those *friends* of mine was mentioned by name. The article called for him to be arrested, or banned from the city. And he's a man who hasn't been charged with anything. What happened to innocent before guilty? What happened to journalism?'

'I know.'

'And as I recall, some other articles in your newspaper called for the death penalty to be applied, in a case involving another one of my *friends*.'

'Yes –'

'And now you're asking me –'

'For protection for Karla, you're right, from the same men. I know it's hypocritical. The fact is, I've got nowhere else to turn. These fanatics have got people everywhere. The cops, the army, teachers, the unions, government services. The only people in Bombay not contaminated by them are . . . '

'My people.'

'That's right.'

It was pretty funny, in its own way. I stood up, holding the sword in my left hand. He stood with me.

'Tell Karla everything,' I said. 'Anything you've hidden from her about this, tell her. Let her make up her own mind about staying or leaving.'

'I'll . . . yes, of course. And about our arrangement? For Karla?'

'We don't have an arrangement. There's no *our*. There's no you and me, remember?'

He smiled, opened his mouth to speak, but then pulled me into a hug with surprising passion.

'I know I can count on you to do the right thing,' he said. 'No matter what happens.'

My face was close to his neck. There was a powerful perfume: a woman's perfume, that had settled on his shirt not long before. It was a cheap perfume. It wasn't Karla's perfume.

He'd been with a woman in a suite at the hotel, minutes before he asked me to watch over his wife, the woman I still loved.

And there it was: the truth, suspended on a thread of suspicion between our eyes as I shoved him from the hug. I still loved Karla. I still loved her. It had taken that, a different woman's scent on Ranjit's skin, to make me face a truth that had circled my life for two years, like a wolf circling a campfire.

I stared at Ranjit. I was thinking murder, and feeling shamed love for Lisa in equal measure: not a peaceful combination. He shifted his feet awkwardly, trying to read my eyes.

'Well . . . okay,' he said, taking a step away from me. 'I'll . . . I'll get going.'

I watched as he walked to the doors of the hotel. When he climbed into the back seat of his Mercedes sedan, I saw him glance around nervously, a man who made enemies too easily, and too often.

I looked back to see Lisa, sitting at the table near the window, and reaching out to shake hands with a young man who'd stopped to say hello.

I knew she didn't like him. She'd once described him as more slippery than a squid in the pocket of a plastic raincoat on a rainy night. He was the son of a successful diamond trader, and he was buying an upper berth in the movie industry, shredding careers along the way.

He was kissing her hand. She withdrew her hand quickly, but the smile she gave him was radiant.

She once told me that every woman has four smiles.

'Only four?'

'The First Smile,' she'd said, ignoring me, 'is the unconscious one that happens without thinking about it, like smiling at a kid in the street, or smiling back at someone who's smiling at us from a TV screen.'

'I don't smile at the TV.'

'Everybody smiles at the TV. That's why we have them.'

'I don't smile at the TV.'

'The *Second* Smile,' she'd persisted, 'is the polite one, the kind we use to invite friends into a house when they come to the door, or to greet them in a restaurant.'

'Are they paying?' I'd asked.

'You wanna hear this, or not?'

'If I say *not*, will you stop?'

'The *Third* Smile is the one we use against other people.'

'Smiling *against* people, huh?'

'Sure. It's a good one. With some girls, the best smile they've got is the one they use to keep people away.'

'I'm gonna let that pass, and skip to the fourth.'

'Aaah! The *Fourth* Smile is the one we only give to the one we love. It's the one that says *You're the one*. Nobody else ever gets that smile. No matter how happy you are with someone, and no matter how much you like someone, even if you like them so much that you love them really, really a lot, nobody ever gets the Fourth Smile except the one you're truly in love with.'

'What happens if you break up?'

'The Fourth Smile goes with the girl,' she'd said to me that day. 'The Fourth Smile always goes with the girl. For ex-boyfriends it's the Second Smile from then on, unless he's a bad ex-boyfriend. Bad ex-boyfriends only ever get a Third Smile, no matter how charming they are.'

I watched Lisa give the young producer manqué her best Third Smile, and walked to the men's room to wash off the new dirt I'd accumulated talking to Ranjit.

The black and cream tiled restroom was larger, more elegantly lit, better appointed, and more comfortable than eighty per cent of the homes in the city. I rolled up the sleeves of my shirt, ran some water over my short hair, and washed my face, hands and forearms.

The attendant handed me a fresh towel. He smiled at me, wagging his head in greeting.

One of the great mysteries of India, and the greatest of all its joys, is the tender warmth of the lowest paid. The man wasn't angling for a tip: most of the men who used the washroom didn't give one. He was simply a kind man, in a place of essential requirement, giving me a genuinely kind smile, one human being to another.

It's that kindness, from the deepest well of the Indian heart, that's the true flag of the nation, and the connection that brings you back to India again and again, or holds you there forever.

I reached into my pocket to give him a tip, and the silver envelope containing Khaderbhai's letter came out in my hand with the money. Handing the man his tip, I put the envelope down on the wide counter beside the basin, and then supported myself with both arms, staring into my own eyes in the mirror.

I didn't want to read the letter: I didn't want to roll that stone away from the cave where I'd hidden so much of the past. But Tariq said that the letter mentioned Sri Lanka. I had to read it. Locking myself in a stall, I stood the sword against a corner of the door and sat down on the hard seat-cover to read Khaderbhai's letter.

I held in my hand this day a small blue glass ball, of the kind that they call a marble in English, and I thought about Sri Lanka, and those who

83

*will journey to there in my name, as you have promised that you will
do for me. For a long time I stared at that blue glass ball in the palm of
my hand after I found it on the ground and picked it up. In such fragile
things and subtle ways is the pattern of our lives revealed to us. We are
collections of things that we find and experience and value and keep
inside ourselves, sometimes knowingly, sometimes unknowingly, and that
collection of things is what we finally become.*

*I collected you, Shantaram.You are one of the ornaments of my life.
You are my dear son, like all my dear sons.*

My hands began to shake: maybe angry, maybe sad, I couldn't tell. I
hadn't let myself mourn him. I didn't visit the gravestone monument,
in the Marine Lines cemetery. I knew his body wasn't buried there,
because I'd helped to bury him myself.

A fever boiled up through my face, chilling my scalp. *My dear son . . .*

*You will hate me, I think, when you come to know all of the truth about
me. Forgive me, if you can. The night is heavy on me. It may be that all
men would be hated if all of the truth were known about them. But with
the honesty required of a letter such as this, written on the night before
we go to war together, I cannot say that I do not deserve to be hated by
some. And to them in this moment I say go to hell, the lot of you.*

*I was born to leave this legacy. I was born to do it no matter what the
cost. Do I use people? Of course I do. Do I manipulate people? As many
as I need. Do I kill people? I kill anyone who opposes me violently. And I
am protected in this and I endure and I grow stronger, while all around
me fall, because I am following my destiny. In my heart I have done no
wrong, and my prayers are sincere. I think somehow you understand
that.*

*I have always loved you, even from the first night that we met. Do
you remember? When I took you to see the Blind Singers? That is as true
as any bad thing you will come to know of me. The bad things are true
and I freely admit it. But the good things are just as true even though
they are truths of the heart and have no reality outside what we feel
and remember. I chose you because I love you and I love you because I
chose you. That is the whole of the truth, my son.*

*If Allah wills me to Him, and you are reading this after I have gone,
that is no cause for sadness. I have many questions, and Allah, as you*

know, is the answer to all questions. And my spirit has mixed with yours, and with all of your brothers. You will never fear. I will always be near you. When you are lost and outnumbered and abandoned you will feel the touch of my father's hand on your shoulder, and you will know that my heart is there next to you in battle, and all my sons.

Please find a way to let my soul kneel with yours in prayer even though you are not a man of prayer. Try to find a moment for at least a little prayer every day if you can. I will visit you there sometimes when you pray.

And remember this last advice from me. Love the truth that you find in the hearts of others. Always listen to the voice of love in your own heart.

I slid letter and envelope into my wallet. The words *that blue glass* appeared in the fold of letter still visible in the wallet, and my heart ran to the top of the hill.

I saw his hand. I saw afternoon light, glowing on his cinnamon-coloured skin. I saw the fine, long fingers moving as he spoke, as delicate as things born in the sea. I saw him smile. I saw the light of his thoughts, streaming from his amber eyes, reflecting off the blue glass ball, and I mourned him.

For a moment I found us, my adopted father and his abandoned son, in a different somewhere beyond judgement and fault: a place forgiven, a place redeemed.

Love unlived is a sin against life, and mourning is one of the ways we love. I felt it then, and I let it happen, the longing for him to return. The power in his eyes, and the pride when I did something he admired, and the love in his laugh. The longing: the longing for the lost.

A blood-filled drum was beating somewhere. I was hot, suddenly, and breathing too hard. I clutched at the sword. I had to leave. I had to get up and leave.

It was too late: sorrows hidden behind banners of rage for years fell as tears. It was messy, and noisy.

'Sir?' the washroom attendant called out after a while of my blubbering. 'Are you urgently requiring more toilet paper?'

I laughed. Bombay saved me, as she did so many times.

'I'm good,' I called back. 'Thanks for asking.'

I left the stall, put the sword on the towel stand, and washed my face with cold water. Mirror check: *Terrible, but you've looked worse.* I gave the very kind attendant another tip, and made my way back through the lobby toward Lisa's table.

She was alone, staring out at the dark sea streaked with silver. Her reflection stared back at her, taking the chance to admire. Then she saw me approaching her in the glass.

A rough day. Cycle Killers, and the Sanjay Council, and Ranjit, and Karla, and the threat of Sri Lanka, sooner rather than later. A rough day.

She turned, running the eyes of her gentle intuition over the loss and wounded love still prowling on my face.

I started to speak, but she silenced me with a fingertip on my lips, and kissed me. And it was okay again, for a while. It was a crazy love we shared: she wasn't in love with me, and I couldn't be in love with her. But we made the night bright and the sunlight right a lot of the time, and never felt used or unloved.

We looked through the huge picture windows to the waves rolling into the bay. Waiters carrying trays behind us were reflected on the glass, moving back and forth as if they were walking on the waves. A black sky struck the sea, melting horizons.

If the hour comes, and there's no-one to beg or blame but yourself, you learn that what we have in the end is just a handful more than what was born in us. That unique handful, what we add to what we are, is the only story of us that isn't told by someone else.

Khaderbhai collected me, as his letter said. But the collector was dead, and I was still an exhibit in the museum of crime he created and left to the world. Sanjay had used me to test his new gun-running contact, and that made it clear: I had to leave the collection and find my freedom again, as soon as possible.

Lisa took my hand beside me. And we stood for a while, looking out, two pale reflections painted on the endless penance of the sea.

PART TWO

CHAPTER NINE

Stories from the wounds of seven wars and power struggles gushed across the blotter on my desk in the passport-counterfeiting factory.

An Iranian professor, a scholar of pre-Islamic texts who'd escaped the Revolutionary Guard's purges, required a full work-up: false birth certificate, false international motor vehicle licence, bank documents, and a false passport, complete with a travel history covering the last two years, supported by valid visa stamps.

The documents had to be good enough to pass close inspection, and get the customer on a plane. When he got wherever he was going, on my false documents, he planned to ditch them, and appeal for asylum.

The marks of torture on him were severe, but he had to take a chance with a false passport because no legal authority would give him a genuine one, except the legal authority that wanted him back in chains.

A Nigerian, an Ogoni activist who'd campaigned against government collusion with oil powers to exploit Ogoni resources, had become a target. He'd survived an assassination attempt, and had arrived in Bombay, in the cargo hold of a freighter, without papers, but with money from supporters in his community.

He bribed the cops at the port, who followed procedure and sent him to us. He needed a new identity, with a passport that changed his nationality and kept him safe.

A Tibetan nationalist had escaped from a Chinese work camp, and had walked across snow-covered peaks into India. He'd made his way to Bombay, where Tibetan exiles provided the money and the contact to the Sanjay Company for new documents.

And there were others: an Afghan, an Iraqi, a Kurdish activist, a

Somali, and two men from Sri Lanka, all of them trying to avoid, escape, or survive the bloody dehiscence of wars they didn't start, and couldn't fight.

But wars are good for bad business, and we didn't just work for good guys. The Sanjay Company was an equal opportunity exploiter. There were crooked businessmen wanting to hide their profits, and thugs who needed a new reputation to ruin, and runaway generals, and people who faked their own deaths, and they always bought their way to the front of the line.

And to one side, there was another passport. It was a Canadian book, bearing my photograph, and with a new visa stamp for Sri Lanka. It had a Reuters News Agency press card attached.

While I was preparing documents that enabled others to escape from wars and vicious regimes, I was making the document that would carry me into a conflict that had cost tens of thousands of lives.

'Do you actually *read* all this?' my new assistant asked, picking up the pages of biographical notes that had been prepared for us by the Ogoni activist.

'Yeah.'

'All of it?'

'Yeah.'

'Really? I mean . . . it's pretty gruesome stuff, man.'

'That it is, Farzad,' I said, not looking up.

'I mean, stuff like this, it's worse than the newspapers.'

'It's all in the newspapers, if you look past the stock market reports and the sports pages,' I said, still not looking at him.

'I'm not surprised. This is some damn depressing shit, yaar.'

'Uh-huh.'

'I mean, a guy could get himself well and truly into a state of depression with stuff like this, day after day, and really need a break. Count on it.'

'Okay,' I said, pushing away the file I'd been reading. 'What's the problem?'

'Problem?'

'If there's an ocean at the end of this stream of consciousness, you should start flowing into it. Right about now.'

'The ocean?' he asked, mystified.

'The *point*, Farzad. Get to the *point*.'

90

'Oh,' he smiled. 'The point. Yes. There's definitely something quite like a kind of a point, that's for sure. Count on it.'

He stared at me for a few moments, then lowered his eyes and began making circles on the surface of the wooden desk with his fingertip.

'Actually,' he said at last, still avoiding my eyes, 'I was trying to find a way to ask you to . . . to come to my house for . . . for lunch or dinner, and to meet . . . to meet my parents.'

'That's it?'

'Yes.'

'Why didn't you just ask me?'

'Well,' he said, the little circles becoming smaller and smaller, 'you've got a reputation, you know?'

'What kind of a reputation?'

'A reputation for being kind of a grouchy guy, yaar.'

'*Grouchy?*' I snarled. '*Me?*'

'Oh, yes.'

We stared at one another. In the factory below, one of the large printing machines grumbled to life, dropping quickly into a chatter of metal clamps and rollers, advancing and retreating, rumbling and turning on a barrel drum.

'Has anyone ever told you that you're completely crap at this invit-ing-people-to-dinner thing?'

'Well,' he laughed, 'this is really the first time I've ever asked anyone to my parents' house in years. We're kind of . . . *private*, if you know what I mean.'

'I know private,' I sighed. 'Private is what I had, before you.'

'So . . . will you come? My parents are really dying to meet you. My Uncle Keki used to talk about you a lot. He said you were –'

'Grouchy. I know.'

'Well, yes, that, too. But he also said you were big on philosophy. He said you were Khaderbhai's favourite for arguing and talking philoso-phy. My pop is a great one for that. My Mom's even worse. The whole family have these big philosophical discussions. Sometimes there's thirty of us, arguing at the same time.'

'Thirty of you?'

'We have this . . . kind of . . . extended family. I can't really describe it. You have to see it. I mean, see *us*. But you won't be bored, that I can promise you. No way. Count on it.'

91

'If I agree to visit your indescribable family, will you leave me alone and let me get back to work?'

'Is that a *yes*?'

'Yes, one of these days.'

'Really? You'll come?'

'Count on it. Now get outta here, and let me get these books done.'

'Great!' he shouted, dancing a few steps left and right with his hips. 'I'll talk to my pop, and set it up for one day this week. Lunch or dinner! Great!'

He gave me a last smile and a wag of his head, and then closed the door behind him.

I pulled the file back toward me, the Nigerian's file, and began to draw out the basic elements of the man's new documented identity. A much kinder but completely artificial life began to develop on my sketchpad.

At one point I opened a drawer full of photographs of clients who wanted passports: the survivors, the lucky ones who weren't shot, drowned, or imprisoned in the attempt to find a better life.

Those faces from war and torture, brushed and cleaned and smeared with artificial calm for our passport photo studio, held my eyes. Once we wandered a free Earth, carrying a picture of our God or king to ensure safe passage. Now the world is gated, and we carry pictures of ourselves, and nobody's safe.

And the bottom line, for the Sanjay Company, was always black: black money. Every black market in the world is the child of tyranny, war or unpopular laws. We turned over thirty to forty passports per month, and the best of them sold for twenty-five thousand US dollars apiece.

Treat war like business, Sanjay once said to me, villainy bright as a newly minted coin in his eyes, *and business like war*.

When the background work on passports for current clients was done, I collected the files and photographs to take them down to the factory floor. I took my own passport, the new one I'd prepared for the trip to Sri Lanka, and shoved it into the centre drawer of the desk. I knew that sooner or later I'd have to hand it over to my best counter-feiters, Krishna and Villu, who were, as Fate would have it, Sri Lankan refugees. But I wasn't ready to face that journey yet.

I found Krishna and Villu sleeping on two couches I'd installed for them in a quiet corner, away from the printing machines. The challenges of new passport work always excited the Sri Lankan forgers, and quite often they'd work through the night without sleep, to complete an assignment.

I watched them for a while, listening to their snoring drift in and out of chorus, swelling sometimes to a grinding roar, in almost perfect unison and then separating once more into rasp and gasp. Their free arms hung loosely at their sides, hands open, receiving the blessing of sleep.

The two other workers who helped me were running errands, and at that moment the factory was silent. I stood for a few moments in that snoring, peaceful place, envying the sleepers.

They'd come to Bombay as refugees. When I'd met them, they were living as pavement-dwellers under a sheet of plastic with their families. Although their work for the Sanjay Company paid well, allowing them to move to comfortable, clean apartments not far from the factory, and they had flawless identity cards, forged by their own hands, they still lived in fear of deportation.

The loved ones they'd left behind were lost to them, perhaps never to be seen or heard from again. Yet despite everything they'd endured and continued to suffer, they slept like children in a placid, insensible peace.

I never slept as well as they did. I dreamt too often and too hard. I always woke in a thrashing struggle to be free. Lisa had learned that the safest way for her to sleep in the same bed was to hold me close, and sleep inside whatever circle my dreaming mind was trying to break.

I left the pile of documents on Krishna's desk, and climbed the wooden stairs quietly. They had their own keys, so I locked the door behind me.

I'd arranged to meet Lisa, to visit the slum clinic with her and have lunch afterwards. She'd developed a relationship with our local pharmacist, who'd provided a few boxes of medicines. The medicines were packed into the saddlebags of my motorcycle, and she'd asked me to deliver them with her.

I cruised the gradual creep of noon traffic, because sometimes it's enough of everything to be moving slowly on a motorcycle, on a sunny day.

In the rear-view mirror of my bike I saw a cop on a motorcycle quite similar to my own. He was drawing alongside me.

The peaked cap and a revolver in a leather holster at his side said that he was a senior officer. He raised his left hand, and pointed to the kerb with two outstretched fingers.

I pulled my bike into the kerb, behind his. He pushed out the side-stand on his bike, then swung a leg over the seat and turned to face me. With his right hand resting on the holster, he slid two fingers of his left hand across his throat. I killed the engine, and remained on the bike.

I was calm. Cops pulled me over from time to time, wanting to talk or collect a bribe. I always kept a rolled-up fifty-rupee note in my shirt pocket for just that purpose. And I didn't mind. Gangsters understand police graft: cops don't get paid enough to risk their lives, so they tax the community the shortfall.

But something in the officer's eyes, a glimmer reflected off a flaw more jagged than corruption, made me uneasy. He slipped the catch off the holster and slid his hand under the stiff cover, on to the butt of the revolver.

I stood from the bike. My hand began to move slowly toward the knives in the scabbards under the flap of my shirt. Cops didn't just take bribes in Bombay in those years: they shot gangsters, from time to time.

A calm, deep voice spoke from very close behind me.

'I wouldn't be doing that, if I were you.'

I turned to see three men standing with me. A fourth man was at the wheel of a car, parked close behind them.

'You know,' I said, my hand on the knife, underneath my shirt, 'if you were me, you probably *would*.'

The man who'd spoken looked away from me to nod his head at the policeman. The officer saluted, climbed back onto his bike, and rode away.

'Nice trick,' I said, turning back. 'I must remember it, if I ever lose my balls.'

'You can lose your motherfucking balls right here and now, *gora*,' a thin man with a pencil moustache said, showing the blade of a knife he hid in his sleeve.

I looked into his eyes. I read a very short story, told by fear and hatred. I didn't want to read it again. The leader raised an exasperated hand. He was a heavy-set man in his late thirties, and a quiet talker.

'If you don't get in the car,' he said quietly, 'I'll shoot you in the knee.'

'Where will you shoot me if I *do* get in the car?'

'That depends,' he replied, regarding me evenly.

He was magazine dressed: hand-tailored silk shirt, loose-fitting grey serge trousers, a Dunhill belt, and Gucci loafers. There was a gold ring on his middle finger that was a copy of the Rolex on his wrist.

The other men looked around at the flow of traffic and pedestrians in the gutters of the road. It had been a fairly long silence. I decided to break it.

'Depends on *what?*'

'On whether you do as you're told or not.'

'I don't like being told what to do.'

'Nobody does,' he replied calmly. 'That's why there's so much power attached to it.'

'That's pretty good,' I said. 'You should write a book.'

My heart was racing. I was scared. My stomach dropped like a body thrown in a river. They were the enemy, and I was in their hands. I was probably dead, whichever way you looked at it.

'Get in the car,' he said, allowing himself a little smile.

'Get to the point.'

'Get in the car.'

'If we play it out here, you go with me. If I get in the car, I go out alone. Arithmetic says we should do it here.'

'*Fuck* it!' the pencil moustache snapped. 'Let's kill this *chudh*, and get it over with.'

The heavy-set leader thought about it. It took a while. My hand was still on my knife.

'You're a logical man,' he said. 'They say you argued philosophy with Khaderbhai.'

'Nobody argued with Khaderbhai.'

'Even so, you can see that your position is irrational. I lose nothing by killing you. You gain everything by staying alive long enough to find out what I want.'

'Except for the part about you being dead. I'd lose that. And so far, that's the best part.'

'Except for that,' he said, smiling. 'But you've seen how much trouble I went to, just to talk to you. If I wanted you dead, I'd have run over your motorcycle with one of my trucks.'

'Leave my motorcycle out of this.'

'Your bike will be safe, yaar,' he laughed, nodding at the thin man with the moustache. 'Danda will ride it for you. Get in the car.'

He was right. There was no other logical choice. I let my hand fall from my knife. The leader nodded. Danda stepped forward at once, started the bike, and kicked back the stand. He gunned the engine, impatient to leave.

'You hurt that bike —' I shouted at him, but before I could finish the threat he tapped the bike into first gear, and roared off into the stream of traffic, the motor screaming in protest.

'Danda has no sense of humour, I'm afraid,' the leader said as we watched Danda sway and skid through the traffic.

'Good, because if he hurts my bike, he won't find it funny.'

The leader laughed, and looked me hard in the eyes.

'How could you exchange philosophies with a man like Khaderbhai?'

'What do you mean?'

'I mean that Khaderbhai was insane.'

'Sane or not, he was never boring.'

'What *doesn't* bore us, in the long run?' he asked, getting into the car.

'A sense of humour?' I suggested, getting in beside him.

They had me, and it was just like prison, because there was nothing I could do about it. He laughed again, and nodded to the driver, whose eyes filled the soft rectangle of the rear-view mirror.

'Take us to the truth,' he said to the driver in Hindi, watching me closely. 'It's always so refreshing, at this time of day.'

CHAPTER TEN

T HE DRIVER BULLIED HIS WAY THROUGH TIGHT, midday traffic, reaching a warehouse in an industrial area in minutes. The warehouse was freestanding, with a screaming space between it and the nearest buildings. Danda was already there. My bike was parked on the gravel driveway in front.

The driver parked the car. A roller door opened to a little over halfway. We got out, stooped under the door, and a chain clattered noisily as it rolled shut again.

There were two big worries. The first was that they hadn't blindfolded me: they'd allowed me to see the location of the warehouse, and the faces of the eight men inside. The second worry was the supply of power tools, torches and heavy hammers arranged on benches along one wall of the warehouse.

It took an effort not to stare. Instead, I focused on the long low chair standing alone in the open space near the back wall of the small warehouse. It was a piece of pool furniture: a banana lounge, upholstered in strands of acid-green and lemon vinyl. There was a wide stain under the chair.

Danda, the skinny moustache with short-story eyes, gave me a thorough pat-down. He took my two knives and passed them on to the leader, who examined them for a moment, before putting them down carefully on the long bench.

'Sit down,' he said, turning to face me.

When I refused to move, he folded his arms patiently and nodded to a tall, powerfully built man who'd been with us in the car. The man came for me.

Hit first, and hit hard, an old con used to tell me.

As the big man stepped in quickly, swinging out with an open-handed

97

slap to the right side of my head, I rolled with the blow, and hit him with a short, sharp uppercut. It good-luck connected with the point of his chin.

The big man stumbled back a step. Two of the men drew guns. They were old-fashioned revolvers, military issue from a forgotten war.

The leader sighed again, and nodded his head.

Four men rushed forward, pushing me onto the green and yellow lounge chair. They tied my hands to the rear legs of the chair with coconut-fibre ropes. Slipping another length of rope under the front, they tied down my legs.

The leader finally unfolded his arms and approached me.

'Do you know who I am?'

'A critic?' I suggested, trying not to show the scared that I was feeling.

He frowned, looking me up and down.

'It's okay,' I said. 'I know who you are. I know a Scorpion when I see one.'

The leader nodded.

'They call me Vishnu,' he said.

Vishnu, the man Sanjay spared after the war that cost so many, the man who came back with a gang called the Scorpions.

'Why do so many gangsters name themselves after gods?'

'How 'bout I name you *dead*, you *bahinchudh*!' Danda spluttered.

'Come to think of it,' I said thoughtfully, 'Danda's not a god. Correct me if I'm wrong, but Danda's just a demigod. Isn't that right? A minor deity?'

'Shut up!'

'Stay cool, Danda,' Vishnu soothed. 'He's just trying to keep the subject off the subject. Don't let him bait you.'

'A demigod,' I mused. 'Ever asked yourself how often you get the short stick around here, Danda?'

'Shut up!'

'You know what?' Vishnu said, stifling a yawn. 'Fuck him. Go ahead, Danda. Fuck his happiness, if you want.'

Danda rushed at me, swinging punches. As I moved my head quickly, left and right, he only connected with one in every three. Suddenly he stopped. When I held my head still long enough to glance up, I saw the big man, the man I'd hit on the point of the chin, pulling Danda away by the shoulder.

The big man punched at my face. He was wearing a brass ring on his middle finger. I felt it crunch along the curves of my cheek and jaw. The big man knew what he was doing. He didn't break anything, he just made it unwell. Then he changed tactic, and smacked me hard on the sides of the head with open-handed slaps.

If you beat a man with your fists for long enough, your knuckles will shatter, or the man will die, or both. But if you break him up a little with your fists, to make sure that a good, hard slap is filled with pain, you can go on beating him all day long with an open hand.

Torture. It's heavy and flat in that space. There's a density to it, a centripetal pull so strong that there's almost nothing you can take from it; so little you can learn that isn't dark all the way through.

But one thing I came to know is that when the beating starts, you shut your mouth. You don't speak. You keep your mouth shut, until it ends. And you don't scream, if you can help it.

'Okay,' Vishnu said, when the month of two minutes ended.

The big man stepped back, accepted a towel from Danda and wiped his sweat-soaked face. Danda reached up to rub the big man's shoulders.

'Tell me about Pakistan,' Vishnu demanded, holding a cigarette to my lips.

I drew in the smoke with dribbles of blood, and then puffed it out. I had no idea what he was talking about.

'Tell me about Pakistan.'

I stared back at him.

'We know you went to Goa,' Vishnu said slowly. 'We know you picked up some guns. So, I will ask you again. Tell me about Pakistan.'

Guns, Goa, Sanjay: it was all coming home with one turn of the karmic wheel. But there's a voice inside my fear, and sooner or later it says, *Let's get it over with*.

'A lot of people think the capital of Pakistan is Karachi,' I said, through swollen lips. 'But it's not.'

Vishnu laughed, and then stopped laughing.

'Tell me about Pakistan.'

'Great food, nice music,' I said.

Vishnu glanced at the tip of his cigarette, and then raised his eyes to the big man.

And it started again. And I limped through thick mud as each new slap on the side of my head smacked me closer to the fog.

When the big man paused, resting his hands on his thighs, Danda seized the moment to flog me, with a thin bamboo rod. It left me soaking wet with suffered sweat, but woke me up.

'How are your balls *now*, *madachudh?*' Danda screamed at me, kneeling so close that I could smell mustard oil and bad-fear sweat in the armpits of his shirt.

I started laughing, as you do sometimes, when you're being tortured.

Vishnu waved his hand.

The sudden silence that followed the gesture was so complete that it seemed the whole world had stopped for a moment.

Vishnu said something. I couldn't hear him. I realised, slowly, that the silence was a ringing in my ears that only I could hear. He was staring at me, with a quizzical expression, as if he'd just noticed a stray dog, and was wondering whether to play with it or kick it with his Gucci loafers.

Another man wiped the blood from my face with a rag smelling of petrol and rotting mould. I spat out blood and bile.

'How do you feel?' Vishnu asked me, absently.

I knew the survivor's rules. *Don't speak. Don't say a word.* But I couldn't stop anger writing words, and couldn't stop saying them once they were in my head.

'Islamabad. The capital of Pakistan,' I said. 'It's not Karachi.'

He walked toward me, drawing a small semi-automatic pistol from his jacket pocket. The star sapphire in his eyes showed a tiny image of my skull, already crushed.

The entry door of the warehouse opened. A chai wallah, a boy of perhaps twelve, stepped through from the bright light of the street, bringing six glasses of tea in one wire basket, and six glasses of water in another.

'Ah, chai,' Vishnu said, a sudden wide smile smoothing out wrinkles of rage.

He put the pistol away, and returned to his place near the long bench.

The chai boy handed out glasses. His ancient street-kid eyes drifted over me, but showed no reaction. Maybe he'd seen it before: a man tied to an acid-green and lemon-yellow banana lounge, and covered in blood.

The gangster who'd smeared some of the blood from my face untied my legs and hands. He took a glass of chai from the boy, and handed it to me. I struggled to hold it in both numbed hands.

Other gangsters took their glasses of chai, courteously working their way through the ritual of refusing, so that others could drink, and then accepting the compromise of half-shares, spilled into emptied water glasses.

It was a polite and convivial scene. We might've been friends, sitting together at Nariman Point, and admiring the sunset.

The boy hunted around the space for the empty glasses of the last round, filling his wire baskets as he went. He noticed that one of the glasses was missing.

'Glass!' he growled, in a feral percolation of whatever it was that accumulated in his throat.

He held up one of the baskets, showing the offending empty space where the last glass should've rested.

'Glass!'

Gangsters immediately scrambled to find the missing glass, turning over empty cartons and shoving aside heaps of rags and rubbish. Danda found it.

'*Hain! Hain!*' he said, revealing the glass with a flourish. *It's here! It's here!*

He handed it to the boy, who snatched it suspiciously and left the warehouse. Danda looked at Vishnu quickly, his eyes bright with grovelling: *Did you see that, boss? Did you see it was me who found the glass?*

When I was sure that I could move without trembling, I put my glass of chai on the ground beside me. It wasn't all pride and anger: my lips were split and swollen. I knew I'd be drinking blood as well as chai.

'Can you stand?' Vishnu asked, setting his empty glass aside.

I stood. I started to fall.

The big man who'd slapped me around rushed to catch me, his strong arms encircling my shoulders with solicitous care. With help, I stood again.

'You can go,' Vishnu said.

He shifted his eyes toward Danda.

'Give him the keys to his bike, yaar.'

101

Danda fished the keys from his pocket on impulse, but approached Vishnu, rather than me.

'Please,' he begged. 'He knows something. I know it. Just . . . just give me a little more time.'

'It's okay,' Vishnu replied, smiling indulgently. 'I already know what I need to know.'

He took the keys from Danda and threw them to me. I caught them against my chest with both numbed hands. I met his gaze.

'Besides,' Vishnu said, looking at me, 'you don't even know about Pakistan, do you? You don't have any damn idea what we're talking about, isn't it?'

I didn't answer.

'That's it, my friend. *Ja!' Go!*

I held his eyes for a moment, and then held out my hand, palm upwards.

'My knives,' I said.

Vishnu smiled, folding his arms again.

'Let's call that a fine, shall we? Your knives will go to Hanuman, as a fine for that shot you took at him. Take my advice. Go now, and keep this place a secret. Don't tell Sanjay or anyone else about it.'

'A secret?'

'I let you know about this place, because you can use it to contact us. If you leave a message here, it will get back to me, very quickly.'

'Why would I wanna do that?'

'Unless I have misjudged you, and I'm really quite good at judging characters, you may decide, one day, that you have more in common with us than you think now. And you may want to talk to us. If you're smart, you won't tell anyone about this address. You'll save it, for a rainy day. But for now, for today, as the Americans say, *fuck off*!'

I walked with Danda to the side door, stepping through as he opened it for me. He cleared his throat noisily, and spat on the leg of my trousers before slamming the door shut.

On the ground, beside my bike, I found a scrap of paper, and used it to wipe the mess of spit from my jeans. I put the key into the ignition of the bike. I was about to kick-start the engine, when I caught sight of my battered face in the rear-view mirror. My nose wasn't broken, for once, but both eyes were pulpy and swollen.

I kicked the bike alive, but left her in neutral gear, resting on the side-stand with the engine turning over slowly. I twitched a control lever on a panel beneath one long edge of the seat. The panel dropped down, showing my Italian stiletto knife.

I hammered on the door of the warehouse with the butt of the knife. I heard an angry voice inside as someone approached the door, cursing whoever was disturbing the peace. It was Danda. I was glad.

The door opened. Danda was swearing angrily. I grabbed at the front of his shirt, slammed him against the doorjamb, and jabbed the stiletto against his stomach. He tried to break free, but I pushed the point deeper into his stomach until the knife spit red onto his pink shirt.

'Okay! Okay! Okay!' he shouted. '*Fuck! Arey, pagal hai tum?*' Have you gone mad?

Several men began to approach me. I pressed the knife a little harder.

'*No! No!*' Danda shouted. 'Get the hell back, you guys! He's *cutting* me here!'

The men stopped. Without taking my eyes off Danda's face, I spoke to Vishnu.

'My knives,' I mumbled, my lips as numb as the heel of a bricklayer's hand. 'Bring them here. Give them to me.'

Vishnu hesitated. I saw the terror in Danda's sweat. He was more afraid of his employer's disregard than he was of my anger.

At last, Vishnu slouched toward us with the two knives. When he handed them to me, I shoved them into the belt at the back of my trousers, holding the stiletto at Danda's belly.

Vishnu began to tug on Danda's shirt, wanting to pull him away from me, and back into the warehouse. I resisted, pressing the knife just a little harder against Danda's soft stomach. A half-centimetre of the blade was inside his body. One centimetre more would penetrate an organ.

'*Wait! Wait!*' Danda shrieked in panic. 'I'm bleeding! He's gonna *kill* me!'

'What do you want?' Vishnu asked.

'Tell me about Pakistan,' I said.

Vishnu laughed. It was a good laugh, clear and clean. It was the kind of laugh that would've endeared him to me on another day, when he hadn't introduced me to his pool furniture.

I paid the cloth-seller, found an open drain, and washed my face with a cloth soaked in vodka, cleaning off the running wounds with dabs from the clean towel.

A barber serving clients beneath a conversation-tree offered me his mirror. I fixed it to a ribbon on the tree, and dressed the two worst cuts on my face. Finally I took the cloth-seller's black rag, and wound it around my forehead in an Afghan turban.

The clients and friends squatting around the barber's chair in the shade nodded and wagged varying degrees of disapproval or consolation.

I took an empty glass, poured myself a shot of vodka and drank it. Holding bottle and glass in one hand, I ripped open a packet of codeine tablets with my teeth, shook four into the glass, and half-filled it with vodka. The level of approval rose among the shaving club. When I drank the glass down and offered the men the rest of the bottle, a little cheer went up.

I went back to sit on my bike, out of view, and stared through desert-dry leaves of sun-withered trees at the warehouse, where my blood was still wet on the floor.

They came out in a laughing, joking group, shoving and teasing the thin man with the moustache, Danda. They squeezed into two Ambassador cars, and drove out into the flow of traffic heading toward Tardeo.

Giving them half a minute, I followed the cars, careful to stay out of mirror range.

They passed through Tardeo, kept on through Opera House junction and into the main road. It was a long, leafy boulevard, running parallel to one of the city's main train lines.

The cars stopped at the gate of a mansion complex, not far from the main station at Churchgate. The high, metal gates opened quickly, the cars drove inside, and the gates swung shut again.

I rode past, glancing up at the tall windows of the triple-fronted mansion. Wooden storm shutters covered all the windows. Dusty, blood-red geraniums spilled over the rail of the first-floor balcony. They dripped all the way to the rusted iron spears on top of a security wall, concealing the ground floor.

I slammed the bike into the heavy traffic, moving toward Churchgate station and beyond, past the thirsting, ochre playing fields of Azad Maidan.

I took my rage and fear out on the road, cutting between cars, fighting back against the city by challenging and beating every other bike that I passed.

I pulled up near KC College, close to Sanjay's mansion. The school was one of Bombay's finest. Well-dressed, fashion-conscious students crowded the street, their young minds glittering in the compass of their smiles. They were the hope of the city: the hope of the world, in fact, although not many knew it, at the time.

'I swear,' a voice from behind me said. 'Fastest white man in Bombay. I've been trying to catch you for the last five –'

It was Farid the Fixer, the young gangster who blamed himself for not being with Khaderbhai at the end, in the killing snows of Afghanistan. He broke off suddenly as I removed the soft black cloth I'd used as a turban.

'Oh, *shit*, man! What happened to you?'

'Do you know if Sanjay's at home?'

'He is. Sure. Come on, let's get inside.'

When I made my report to Sanjay, sitting at the glass and gilt table in his dining room, his expression was calm and almost dismissive. He asked me to repeat the names I'd heard them use, and the faces I'd seen.

'I've been expecting this,' he said.

'Expecting it?' I said.

'Why didn't you tell Lin?' Farid demanded. 'Or me, so I could ride with him.'

Sanjay ignored us and began to pace the long room.

His handsome face had begun to age beyond his years. The ridge-and-valley depressions below his eyes had deepened to dark, hard-edged troughs. Worry lines flared out from the corners of his bloodshot eyes, fading in the new grey that began at his temples, and streaked the gloss-black hair.

He drank too much, and he did too much of everything else he enjoyed. He was a young man in charge of an empire, burning youth into age.

'What do you think they were really after?' he asked me, after a long pause.

'Why don't you tell me? What's the deal with Pakistan? What else didn't you tell me, when you sent me to Goa?'

'I tell you what you need to know!' Sanjay snapped.

107

'This was something that I needed to know before today,' I said evenly. 'You weren't tied to that lounge chair, Sanjay. I was.'

'Damn right!' Farid said.

Sanjay let his eyes drift to his hands, resting on the glass table. His biggest fear, reasonably enough, was a bloody gang war that took most of the lives and power from one gang, and all the lives and power from another. Anything short of that, in his eyes, was a victory. It was the only thing we agreed on, in all the missions and battles of the last two years.

'There are things in play here that you don't know, and can't understand,' he said. 'I'm running this Company. I tell you both what you need to know, and nothing more. So, fuck you, Lin. And fuck you, Farid.'

'Fuck *me*, Sanjay?' Farid spat at him. 'That's all the respect I get? How about I fuck your happiness right here and now?'

He took a step toward Sanjay but I stopped him, my hands on his chest.

'Take it easy, Farid brother,' I said. 'This is just what they wanted, when they slapped me around today – us, falling out with each other.'

'Fuck *me*?' Farid snarled. 'Say it again, boss. Say it again.'

Sanjay stared at the young fighter for a while, and then his cold eyes drifted to mine.

'Tell me the truth, Lin. What did you tell them?'

It was my turn to anger. Rage drew in a breath. My lips widened, splitting cuts.

'What are you trying to say, boss?'

He frowned, irritated.

'Come on, Lin,' he said. 'This is the real world. People talk. What did you tell them?'

I was angry enough to beat him senseless; angrier at him, in fact, than the men who'd nearly beaten *me* senseless.

'Of *course* he didn't say anything!' Farid said. 'It's not the first time he's been kicked by the other side. Me, too. And you, too, Sanjay. Stop being so disrespectful. What's the matter with you, boss?'

Sanjay flashed a look, exasperated to the point of being vicious, revealing how close he was to the edge. Farid held his gaze for a moment, but then looked away.

Sanjay turned back to me.

'You can go, Lin,' he said. 'And whatever you did or didn't say before, keep your mouth shut about this from now on.'

'About what, Sanjay? About the act they put on today? One minute they're gonna kill me, the next minute they're letting me go. They wanted me to come back here, in this condition, and say the word *Pakistan* to you. It's a message. I'm the message. This Scorpion guy, Vishnu, is big on messages.'

'So am I,' Sanjay smiled. 'And I write messages in blood, like they do. In a time and manner of my own choosing.'

'Whatever you do, don't do it for me.'

'Are you telling me what to do? Who the fuck do you think you are?'

There was a dragon inside me, all fire, but I didn't want some other soldier to sit in a chair, as I'd done, until the ceiling turned red.

'Don't square up for me, boss. When the time comes, I'll handle that myself.'

'You'll do what you're told, and when you're told.'

'I'll square this up myself, Sanjay,' I repeated. 'In a time and manner of my own choosing. Just so we're clear that I told you, in advance.'

'Get out,' Sanjay said, his eyes narrowing. 'Both of you. Don't come near me, Lin, unless I send for you. Get out.'

On the street Farid stopped me, angrier than I was.

'Lin,' he said quietly, his eyes wider than rage. 'I don't give a shit what Sanjay says. He's weak. He's nothing. I have no respect for him any more. We'll find Abdullah. We'll go, just the three of us, without saying a thing. We'll kill this Vishnu, the one in charge, and those other *gandus*, Danda and Hanuman.'

I smiled, bathing my wounded face in the warmth of his brave heart.

'It's okay. Leave it alone. Right place and right time, brother. One way or another, I'll see those guys again, and if I need you, I'll make sure to call you.'

'Night and day, man,' he replied, shaking hands.

He rode away, and I looked back at Sanjay's mansion: another mansion, in a city of slums. The street windows were sealed, red metal shutters rusted into their slides. A withered hedge clung to a wrought-iron fence.

It was a lot like the house the Scorpions returned to, after they'd worked me over. It was too much like that house.

You can respect a man's rights or opinions without knowing the

I rode along beside the fishermen's coves to the Colaba Back Bay, to keep the appointment in the slum.

The land everywhere around me had been reclaimed from the sea, stone by stone. Tall, modern apartment buildings crowded together on the new stone ocean, and showered precious shade on wide, leafy streets.

It was an expensive, desirable area, with the President hotel as a figurehead on the prow of the suburb. The little shops that lined the three main boulevards were freshly painted. Flower boxes decorated many of the windows. The servants who moved back and forth from the residential towers to the shops were dressed in their best saris and bleached white shirts.

As the main road swung left and then right beside the World Trade Centre, the scene changed. The trees became more sparsely planted, and then stopped altogether. The shade began to fade as the last shadow cast by a tower surrendered to the sun.

And the heat from that sun, hovering, obscured by heavy clouds, beat down on the dust-grey ocean of the slum, where the ridges of low rooftops rolled away to the tattered horizon in ragged waves of worry and struggle.

I parked the bike, took the medicines and bandages from the saddle-bags, and tossed a coin to one of the kids who offered to watch the bike for me. There wasn't really a need. No one stole anything in that area.

As I entered the slum, making my way along a wide, sandy, uneven path, the smell of the open latrine that lined the road flattened the breath in my lungs. A fist of nausea twisted my stomach.

The beating in the warehouse came back hard and fast. The sun. The beating. The sun was too hot. I staggered to the side of the path. The surge of nausea erupted and I stooped, my hands on my knees, and threw up anything I still had inside onto the weeds beside the road.

The children of the slum chose that moment to rush out of the lanes to greet me. Crowding around me as I shuddered and shivered, they tugged at the sleeves of my shirt and shouted my name.

'Linbaba! Linbaba! Linbaba!'

Pulling myself together I allowed the children to drag me with them into the slum. We worked our way through the narrow, stumble-foot lanes between huts made from plastic sheets, woven mats and bamboo poles. The huts, covered in dust accumulated through eight months of the dry season, looked like desert dunes.

Gleaming towers of pots and pans, garlanded images of gods, and smooth, highly polished earthen floors glimpsed their way through low doorways, attesting to the neat, ordered lives that persisted within.

The children led me directly to Johnny Cigar's house, not far from the seashore boundary.

Johnny, who was the head man in the slum, was born on the streets of the city. His father, a Navy man on temporary assignment in Bombay, had abandoned Johnny's mother when he learned that she was pregnant. He left the city on a warship, bound for the Port of Aden. She never heard from him again.

Cast out by her family, Johnny's mother had moved into a pavement-dweller settlement made from sheets of plastic strung across a section of footpath near Crawford Market.

Johnny was born in the day-long shout, shove and shuffle heard from one of Asia's largest covered markets. His ears rang from early morning until last light with shrill or braying cadenzas of street sellers and stallholders.

He'd lived the whole of his life in pavement communities and crowded slums, and only ever seemed truly at home in the surge and swirl of the crowd. The few times I'd seen him alone, walking the strip of sea coast beside the slum, or sitting in a lull of afternoon outside a chai shop, he'd seemed diminished by the solitude; withdrawn into a smaller sense of himself. But in any crowd, he was a jewel of his people.

'Oh, my *God*!' he cried, when he saw my face. 'What the hell happened to you, man?'

'It's a long story. How you doin', Johnny?'

'Oh, shit, man. You got a solid pasting!'

I frowned at him. Johnny knew that frown. We'd lived together as neighbours in the slum for eighteen months, and had continued as good friends for years.

'Okay, okay, *thik hai*, baba. Come, sit down. Have some chai. Sunil! Bring chai! *Fatafat!*' Super quickly!

I sat on an empty grain drum, watching Johnny give instructions to a team of young men, who were making final preparations for the coming rain.

When the previous head man of the slum retired to his village, he nominated Johnny Cigar as his successor. A few voices grumbled that Johnny wasn't the ideal choice, but the love and admiration everyone felt for the retiring head man silenced their objections.

It was an honorary position, with no authority beyond that contained within the character of the man who held it. After almost two years in the job, Johnny had proven himself to be wise in the settlement of disputes, and strong enough to inspire that ancient instinct: the urge to follow a positive direction.

For his part, Johnny enjoyed the leadership role, and when all else failed to resolve a dispute, he went with his heart, declared a holiday in the slum, and threw a party.

His system worked, and was popular. There were people who'd moved into that slum because there was a pretty good party every other week to settle a dispute peacefully. People brought disputes from other slums, to have them resolved by Johnny. And little by little, the boy born on the pavement was Solomon to his people.

'Arun! Get down to the mangrove line with Deepak!' he shouted. 'That flood wall collapsed yesterday. Get it up again, fast! Raju! Take the boys to Bapu's house. The old ladies in his lane have no plastic on the roof. Those fucking cats pulled it off. Bapu has the sheets. Help him get them up. The rest of you, keep clearing those drains! *Jaldi!' Fast!*

The tea arrived, and Johnny sat down to drink with me.

'Cats,' he sighed. 'Can you explain to me why there are cat people in this world?'

'In a word? Mice. Cats are handy little devils.'

'I guess so. You just missed Lisa and Vikram. Has she seen your face like this?'

'No.'

'Hell, man, she's gonna have a fit, yaar. You look like somebody ran over you.'

'Thanks, Johnny.'

'Don't mention,' he replied. 'Hey, that Vikram, he doesn't look too good either. He's not sleeping well, I think.'

I knew why Vikram didn't look too good. I didn't want to talk about it.

'When do you think?' I asked, looking at the black, heaving clouds.

The smell of rain that should-but-wouldn't fall was everywhere in my eyes, in my sweat, in my hair: first rain, the perfect child of monsoon.

'I thought it would be today,' he replied, sipping at his tea. 'I was sure.'

I sipped my tea. It was very sweet, laced with ginger to defeat the heat that pressed down on every heart in the last days of the summer.

The ginger soothed the cuts on the inside of my mouth, and I sighed with pleasure.

'Good chai, Johnny,' I said.

'Good chai,' he replied.

'Indian penicillin,' I said.

'There is . . . there is no penicillin in this chai, baba,' Johnny said.

'No, I mean —'

'We never put penicillin in our tea,' he declared.

He seemed offended.

'No, no,' I reassured him, knowing that I was heading down a dead-end street. 'It's a reference to an old joke, a joke about chicken soup, a joke about chicken soup being called Jewish penicillin.'

Johnny sniffed at his tea charily.

'You . . . you smell *chickens* in the tea?'

'No, no, it's a joke. I grew up in the Jewish part of my town, Little Israel. And, you know, it's a joke everybody tells, because Jewish people are supposed to offer you chicken soup, no matter what's wrong with you. You've got an upset stomach, *have a little chicken soup.* You've got a headache, *have a little chicken soup.* You've just been shot, *have a little chicken soup.* And in India, *tea* is like chicken soup for Jewish people, see? No matter what's wrong, a strong glass of chai will fix you up. Geddit?'

His puzzled frown cleared in a half-smile.

'There's a Jewish person not far from here,' he said. 'He stays in the Parsi colony at Cuffe Parade, even though he's not a Parsi. His name is Isaac, I believe. Shall I bring him here?'

'Yes!' I replied excitedly. 'Get the Jewish person, and bring him here!'

Johnny rose from his stool.

'You'll wait for me here?' he asked, preparing to leave.

'No!' I said, exasperated. 'I was joking, Johnny. It was a *joke*! Of *course* I don't want you to bring the Jewish person here.'

'It's really no trouble,' he said.

He stared at me, bewildered, trapped a half-step away, uncertain whether he should fetch Isaac-the-Jewish-person or not.

'So . . .' I said at last, looking at the sky for an escape from the conversational cul-de-sac, 'when do you think?'

He relaxed, and scanned the clouds churning in from the sea.

'I thought it would be today,' he replied. 'I was sure.'

'Well,' I sighed, 'if not today, tomorrow. Okay, can we do this now, Johnny?'

'*Jarur*,' he replied, moving toward the low doorway of his hut.

I joined him inside, closing the flimsy plywood door behind me. The hut, made of thin, tatami-style matting strung to bare bamboo poles, was paved on the bare earth with extravagantly detailed and coloured tiles. They formed a mosaic image of a peacock, with its tail fanned out against a background of trees and flowers.

The cupboards were filled with food. The large, metal, rat-proof wardrobe was an expensive and much-prized item of furniture in the slum. A battery-powered music system occupied a corner of a metal dresser. Pride of place went to a three-dimensional illustration of the flogged and crucified Christ. New floral-print mattresses were rolled up in a corner.

The traces of relative luxury attested to Johnny's status and commercial success. I'd given him the money as a wedding present, to buy a small, legal apartment in the neighbouring Navy Nagar district. The gift was intended to allow him to escape the uncertainty and hardship of life in the illegal slum.

Aided by the enterprising spirit of his wife Sita, the daughter of a prosperous chai shop owner, Johnny used the apartment as collateral for a loan, and then rented it out at a premium. He used the loan to buy three slum huts, rented the three illegal huts at market rates, and was living in exactly the same slum lane where I'd first met him.

Moving a few things aside, Johnny made a place for me to sit. I stopped him.

'Thanks, brother. Thanks. I don't have time. I have to find Lisa. I've been one step behind her all day long.'

'Lin brother, you'll always be one step behind that girl.'

'I think you're right. Here, take this.'

I gave him the bag of medicines that Lisa had given me, and pulled a wad of money bound with tight elastic bands from my pocket. It was enough to pay two months' wages for the two young men who worked as first aid attendants in the free clinic. There was also a surplus to cover the purchase of new bandages and medicines.

'Is there anything special?'

'Well . . . ' he said, reluctantly.

'Tell me.'

'Anjali – Bhagat's daughter – she went for the exams.'

116

'How'd she do?'

'She came top. And not just top of her class, mind you, but top of the whole Maharashtra State.'

'Smart kid.'

I remembered the little girl she was, years ago, when she'd helped me from time to time in the free clinic. The twelve-year-old kept the names of all the patients in the slum in her head, hundreds of names, and became a friend to every one of them. In visits to the clinic in the years since, I'd watched her learn and grow.

'But smart is not enough in this, our India,' Johnny sighed. 'The Registrar of the university, he is demanding a *baksheesh* of twenty thousand rupees.'

He said it flatly, without rancour. It was a fact of life, like the diminishing numbers of fish in fishermen's nets, and the daily increase of cars, trucks and motorcycles on the roads of the once genteel Island City.

'How much have you got?'

'Fifteen thousand,' he replied. 'We collected the money from everyone here, from all castes and religions. I put in five thousand myself.'

It was a significant commitment. I knew Johnny wouldn't see that money repaid in anything less than three years.

I pulled a roll of American dollars from my pocket. In those days of the rabid demand for black market money, I always carried at least five currencies with me at any one time: deutschmarks, pounds sterling, Swiss francs, dollars and riyals. I had about three hundred and fifty dollars in notes. At black market rates it was enough to cover the shortfall in Anjali's education bribe.

'Lin, don't you think . . . ' Johnny said, tapping the money against his palm.

'No.'

'I know, Linbaba, but it's not a good thing that you give money without telling the people. They should know this thing. I understand that if we give without praise, anonymously, it is a ten-fold gift in the eyes of God. But God, if He'll forgive me for speaking my humble mind, can be very slow in passing out praise.'

He was almost exactly my own height and weight, and he carried himself with the slightly pugnacious shoulder and elbow swing of a man who made fools suffer well, and fairly often.

His long face had aged a little faster than his thirty-five years, and the stubble that covered his chin was peppered with grey-white. The sand-coloured eyes were alert, wary, and thoughtful.

He was a reader, who consumed at least one new self-help book every week, and then unhelpfully nagged his friends and neighbours into reading them.

I admired him. He was the kind of man, the kind of friend, who made you feel like a better human being, just for knowing him. Strangely, stupidly, I couldn't bring myself to tell him that. I wanted to do it. I started to do it a few times, but wouldn't let myself speak the words.

My exile heart at that time was all doubt and reluctance and scepticism. I gave my heart to Khaderbhai, and he used me as a pawn. I gave my heart to Karla, the only woman I've ever been in love with, and she used me to serve the same man, the man we both called father, Khaderbhai. Since then I'd been on the streets for two years, and I'd seen the town come to the circus, the rich beg paupers, and the crime fit the punishment. I was older than I should've been, and too far from people who loved me. I let a few, not many, come close, but I never reached out to them as they did to me. I wouldn't commit, as they did, because I knew that sooner or later I'd have to let go.

'Let it go, Johnny,' I said softly.

He sighed again, pocketed the money, and led the way outside the hut.

'Why are Jewish people putting penicillin in their chickens?' he asked me as we gazed at the lowering sky.

'It was a joke, Johnny.'

'No, but those Jewish people are pretty smart, yaar. If they're putting penicillin in their chickens, they must have a damn good –'

'Johnny,' I interrupted, with a raised hand, 'I love you.'

'I love you, too, man,' he grinned.

He wrapped his arms around me in a tight hug that woke every one of the wounds and bruises on my arms and shoulders.

I could still feel the strength of him; still smell the coconut oil in his hair as I walked away through the slum. The smothering clouds threw early evening shadows on the weary faces of fishermen and washer-women, returning home from the busy shoreline. But the whites of their tired eyes glowed with auburn and rose-gold as they smiled at me. And they all smiled, every one of them, as they passed, crowns gleaming on their sweated brows.

CHAPTER THIRTEEN

When I stepped into the laughing broil of Leopold's, I
scanned the tables for Lisa and Vikram. I couldn't see them,
but my eyes met those of my friend Didier. He was sitting with Kavita
Singh and Naveen Adair.

'A jealous husband!' Didier cried, admiring my battered face. 'Lin!
I'm so *proud* of you!'

'Sorry to disappoint you,' I shrugged, reaching out to shake hands
with him and Naveen. 'Slipped in the shower.'

'Looks like the shower fought back,' Naveen said.

'What are you, a plumbing detective now?'

'Whatever the cause, I am delighted to see sin on your face, Lin!'
Didier declared, waving to the waiter. 'This calls for a celebration.'

'I hereby call this meeting of Sinners Anonymous to order!' Kavita
announced.

'Hi, my name's Naveen,' the young detective said, buying in, 'and
I'm a sinner.'

'Hi, Naveen,' we all replied.

'Where to begin . . . ' Naveen laughed.

'Any sin will do,' Didier prompted.

Naveen decided to think about it for a while.

'It suits you, this new look,' Kavita Singh said to me as we sat down.

'I'll bet you say that to all the bruises.'

'Only the ones I put there myself.'

Kavita, a beautiful, intelligent journalist, had a preference for other
girls, and was one of the few women in the city who was unafraid to
declare it.

'Kavita, Naveen will not reveal his sins!' Didier pouted. 'At least tell
me some of yours.'

She laughed, and began reciting a list of her sins.

'Those rocks in your shower,' Naveen remarked quietly, leaning close to me, 'did a professional job.'

I glanced at him quickly. I was ready to like him. I already did like him. But he was still a stranger, and I wasn't sure that I could trust him. How did he know that I'd received a *professional* beating?

Reading my expression, he smiled.

'All the hits, on both sides of your face, are bunched up in a tight pattern, left and right,' he said quietly. 'Your eyes are blacked, but they're still open, and you can see okay. That's not easy to do. Your wrists are marked, too. It's not hard to figure that somebody who knew what he was doing smacked you around pretty good.'

'I'm guessing there's a point in there, somewhere.'

'The point is, I'm hurt.'

'*You're* hurt?'

'You didn't invite me.'

'I wasn't the one sending out cards.'

'Likely to be any more parties?' he smiled.

'I don't know. You feeling lonely?'

'Count me in, if you need a date, next time.'

'I'm good,' I said. 'But thanks for the offer.'

'Please!' Didier insisted as a glowering waiter slammed the drinks down on the table. 'Stop whispering, you two. If it's not an illicit lover or jealous husband to boast about, you'll have to offer another sin to discuss.'

'I'll drink to that,' Kavita encouraged.

'Do you know why sin is banned?' Didier asked her, his blue eyes glittering.

'Because it's fun?' Kavita offered.

'Because it makes fun of people who ban sin,' Didier said, raising his glass.

'I'll make the toast!' Kavita announced, raising her glass to Didier's. 'To tying people up and giving them a good smack!'

'Excellent!' Didier cried.

'I'm in,' Naveen said, raising his glass.

'No,' I said.

It wasn't the day to toast people being tied up; not for me.

'Okay, Lin,' Kavita snapped. 'Why don't *you* make the toast?'

120

'To freedom, in all its forms,' I said.

'I'm in again,' Naveen said.

'Didier is always for freedom,' Didier agreed, raising his glass.

'Alright,' Kavita said, banging her glass against ours. 'To freedom, in all *her* forms.'

We'd just put our glasses back on the table when Concannon and Stuart Vinson joined us.

'Hey, man,' Vinson said, offering a handshake like a good-natured smile. 'What the hell happened to you?'

'Someone kicked his fuckin' arse,' Concannon laughed, his Northern Irish drawl prowling. 'And it looks like they threw in his head, n'all. What ya been up to, boyo?'

'He has shower issues,' Kavita said.

'Shower issues, does he, indeed?' Concannon grinned, leaning close to Kavita. 'And what issues do you have?'

'You first,' Kavita replied.

He grinned again, as if he'd won.

'Me? I take issue with everything that isn't already mine. And since I've let that cat out of the bag, I repeat, what issues do you have?'

'I have loveliness issues. But I'm in treatment.'

'Aversion therapy is said to be very effective,' Naveen said, staring at Concannon.

Concannon looked from one to the other, laughed hard, seized two chairs from a neighbouring table without asking, dragged them to our table and pushed Vinson down into one of them.

He turned his own chair around backwards, and rested his solid forearms on the back of it.

'What are we drinkin'?' he asked.

I realised that Didier hadn't called for drinks, his habit whenever anyone joined him in Leopold's. I turned my head and saw him staring at Concannon. The last time I'd seen Didier look at someone that hard, he'd had a gun in his hand. Thirty seconds later he'd used it.

I raised my hand to call the waiter. When the drinks were ordered I moved the subject across Didier's eye line.

'You look good, Vinson.'

'I'm damn happy,' the young American replied. 'We just made a killing. Fell right into my lap. Well, into *our* laps, Concannon's and mine. So, hey, the drinks are on us.'

The drinks arrived. Vinson paid and we raised our glasses.

'To sweet deals!' Vinson said.

'And to the suckers who sweeten them,' Concannon added quickly.

Our glasses clashed, but Concannon had soured the toast.

'Ten thousand American dollars each!' Concannon said, slamming his glass down hard on the table. 'No better feelin'! Just like comin' in a rich girl's mouth!'

'*Hey*, Concannon!' I said.

'There's no call for talk like that,' Vinson added.

'What?' Concannon asked, his arms wide with wonder. '*What?*'

He turned his head and leaned the side of his chair toward Kavita.

'Come on, darlin',' he said, his smile as wide as if he was asking her to dance, 'you can't be tellin' me you're a stranger to the experience. Not with a face and a figure like yours.'

'Why don't you talk to me about it?' Naveen Adair muttered through clenched teeth.

'Unless you're a fuckin' lesbian!' Concannon continued, laughing so hard that his chair tilted sideways and almost fell.

Naveen began to stand. Kavita put a hand against his chest, holding him back.

'For Chrissakes, Concannon!' Vinson spluttered, surprised and confused. 'Like, what the hell's the matter with you? You brought me a solid-gold customer, we made a bundle of cash, and we're supposed to be, like, happy and celebrating. Stop antagonising everybody already!'

'It's alright,' Kavita said, staring evenly at Concannon. 'I believe in free speech. If you put a hand on me, I'll cut it off. But if you just sit there, talking like an idiot, hey, you can do that all night long for all I care.'

'Oh, so, you *are* a fuckin' cunt-licker,' Concannon grinned back at her.

'As a matter of fact –' she began.

'As a matter of fact,' Didier interrupted her, 'it's none of your business.'

Concannon's grin hardened at the edges. His eyes glittered, sunlight on the back of a cobra's hood. He turned to face Didier. The menace in his expression was clear. The rudeness to Kavita had been a ruse to provoke Didier.

It worked. Didier's eyes were indigo flames.

'You should powder your nose and put on your dress, sweetheart,' Concannon growled. 'All you fuckin' homos should wear dresses. As a warning, like, for the rest of us. If you get fucked like a woman, you should dress like one.'

'You should have the courage, if not the honour,' Didier replied evenly, 'to discuss this privately. Outside.'

'You're a fuckin' unnatural thing,' Concannon hissed, through barely parted lips.

We were all on our feet. Naveen reached out to grab Concannon's shirt. Vinson and I separated the two men, as waiters rushed at us from all corners of the bar.

The waiters at Leopold's had a unique internship in those years: if they put on boxing gloves and lasted two minutes in the back lane with the very big, very tough Sikh head waiter, they got the job. Six of those waiters, directed by the very big, very tough Sikh head waiter, surrounded our table.

Concannon looked around quickly, his hard smile widening to show an uneven set of yellowing teeth. For a few seconds he listened to the voice within, urging him to fight and die. In some men, that's the sweetest voice that ever speaks to them. Then the viciousness softened into cunning, and he began to back away through the circle of waiters.

'You know what?' he said, stepping backwards. '*Fuck* yez! Fuck yez *all!*'

'What the hell was *that* all about?' Vinson gasped as Concannon stomped out into the street, pushing shoppers aside.

'It is obvious, Stuart,' Didier said as we slowly sat down again.

He was the only one of us who hadn't stood, and the only one who seemed calm.

'Not to me, man.'

'I have seen this phenomenon many times, Stuart, in many countries. The man is almost uncontrollably attracted to me.'

Vinson spluttered beer foam across the table. Kavita howled with laughter.

'Are you saying he's *gay*?' Naveen asked.

'Does a man have to be gay,' Didier asked, giving him a look to tan leather, 'to be attracted to Didier?'

'Okay, okay,' Naveen grinned.

'I don't think he's gay,' Vinson said. 'He goes to prostitutes. I think he's just crazy.'

'You got that right,' Kavita said, waving her glass in front of his bewildered frown.

Sweetie, who'd been standing well away from the confrontation, slapped a filthy rag on our table as a sign that he was ready to take our order. He picked his crooked nose with his middle finger, wiped it on his jacket, and let out a sigh.

'*Aur kuch?*' he menaced. *Anything else?*

Didier was about to make an order, but I stopped him.

'Not for me,' I said, standing and collecting my keys.

'But, no!' Didier protested. 'One more, surely?'

'I didn't finish the last one. I'm riding.'

'I'm with you, cowboy,' Kavita said, joining me. 'I told Lisa I'd call around tonight. I'll come home with you, if you don't mind?'

'Happy to have you along.'

'But . . . can a gay man go to prostitutes, like, a lot?' Vinson asked, leaning toward Didier.

Didier lit a cigarette, examined the glow for a moment, and then addressed Vinson, his eyes narrowing.

'Have you not heard them say, Stuart, that a gay man can do everything that a man wants?'

'*What?*' Vinson asked, adrift as an iceberg.

'They also say that ignorance is bliss,' I said, exchanging a smile with Didier. 'And I'm gonna follow my bliss home.'

We left the bar and made our way through the crush of shoppers to the parking area, where I'd left my bike.

As I put the key into the ignition, a very strong hand reached out and seized my forearm. It was Concannon.

'Fuck *him*, eh?' he said, smiling widely.

'What?'

'Fuck him. The French mincer.'

'You're crazier than you know, Concannon.'

'I can't argue with that. And I don't want to argue. I've got that money. Ten grand. Let's go and get drunk.'

'I'm going home,' I said, pulling my arm free to put the key in the ignition.

'Come on, it'll be fun! Let's go out, you and me. Let's go pick a

124

fight. Let's find some really tough bastards, and hurt them. Let's have fun, man!'

'Attractive and all as that —'

'I've got this new Irish music,' he said quickly. 'It's fuckin' grand. The thing about Irish music, you know, is that it's so good to fight to.'

'No.'

'Ah, come on! At least listen to it, and get drunk with me.'

'No.'

'That Frenchman's a fuckin' *faggot*!'

'Concannon —'

'You and me,' he said, softening his voice and forcing a smile almost exactly like a scowl of pain. 'We're the same, you and me. I *know* you. I fuckin' *know* you.'

'You don't know me.'

He snarled, whirling his head around, and spitting on the ground.

'I mean, that faggot, think about it. If the whole world was like him, the human race would die out.'

'And if the whole world was like you, Concannon, we'd deserve to.'

It was hard; too hard. Who was I to throw stones? But I loved Didier, and I'd had all of Concannon I could take for one long day.

His eyes flashed with sudden murderous fury, and I stared back at him, thinking that I'd been tied up and beat up that day, and he could stare all he wanted.

I started the bike, kicked away the side-stand, and helped Kavita to climb up behind me. We rode away without looking back.

'That guy,' she shouted, leaning over my shoulder, her lips touching my ear, 'is out of his bloody mind, yaar.'

'I only met the guy once before,' I shouted back. 'He seemed kind of okay.'

'Well, somebody emptied his *okay* basket,' Kavita said.

'You could say that about most of us,' I replied.

'Speak for yourself,' Kavita laughed. 'My basket is a horn of plenty, baby.'

I wasn't laughing. The look in Concannon's eyes stayed with me. Even as I brushed aside Lisa's pain and concern, apologised to her, kissed her, and sat on a wobbly stool in the bathroom while she cleaned and dressed the cuts on my face, I saw Concannon's eyes: omens in a cave.

'It suits Lin, this look,' Kavita said to Lisa, claiming a comfortable nearby were empty, and the few sleepers I saw were stretched out near a line of handcarts, three hundred metres away.

I smoked a cigarette, waiting and watching the quiet street. When I was sure that no-one was awake on the block, I put my cotton handkerchief under the downpipe of the petrol tank on my bike, pulled the feeder tube free, flooded the handkerchief with petrol, and then reconnected the tube.

At the door of the warehouse where they'd slapped me around that afternoon, I broke the padlock on the chain across the door, and slipped inside.

I used my cigarette lighter to find my way to the piece of pool furniture: that banana lounge in acid-green and yellow vinyl. There was an empty drum nearby. I dragged it toward the banana lounge, and sat down.

In a few minutes, my eyes adjusted to the darkness. I made out certain objects and pieces of furniture quite clearly. Among them was a large coil of coconut-fibre rope. The rope they'd used to tie me to the pool chair had been cut from that roll.

I stood up and uncoiled the rope until it tumbled into a large, loose pile. Packing the pile of rope under the banana lounge, I stuffed the petrol-soaked scarf within the fibre strands.

There were empty cardboard cartons, old telephone books, oily rags and other inflammables in the warehouse. I dragged them into a line leading from the pool chair to a row of cabinets and benches where the power tools were displayed, and doused them with everything I could find.

When I lit the scarf it flared up quickly. The flames fluttered and then rushed into a fierce fire that began to consume the pile of rope.

Thick, musty smoke quickly filled the open space. The vinyl banana lounge was putting up a fight. I waited until the fire had prowled along the line of combustible refuse, and then left the warehouse, dragging a heavy oxy-acetylene kit with me.

I let the gas bottles rest in the gutter, out of reach of the fire, and walked slowly to my bike.

The firelight in the windows of the warehouse rippled and throbbed for a time, as if a silent party was underway inside. Then there was a small explosion.

I guessed that a container of glue or paint thinner had exploded.

Whatever it was, it brought the fire into the rafters of the warehouse, and sent the first flames and pieces of orange ash into the heavy, humid air.

People began emerging from surrounding shops and houses. They ran toward the fire, but there was nothing they could do. There was little water to spare. The warehouse was a stand-alone building. It was lost to the fire, and everyone knew it, but other buildings wouldn't burn with it.

As the crowd swelled, the first chai and *paan* sellers arrived on bicycles to profit from the pool of spectators. Not long behind them were the firemen and the police.

The firemen trained hoses on the sides of the burning building, but the hoses only produced a thin stream of water. The police lashed out with bamboo canes at a few of the spectators, established a command post opposite the fire, and commandeered a chai seller for themselves.

I was getting worried. I wanted to burn down the torture shed. It had seemed like a good idea at the time. Vishnu wanted me to leave a message there, and I was sure that he'd get my message clearly. But I didn't want the fire to spread.

The firemen in their brass Athenian helmets were helpless. It seemed, for a handful of heartbeats, that the fire might jump the open space to the next building.

Thunder boomed the drum of sky. Every window in the street shuddered. Every heart trembled. Thunder smashed the sky again and again, so fearsome that lovers, neighbours and even strangers reached out to one another instinctively.

Lightning lit lanterns of cloud everywhere at once, directly overhead. Dogs cowered and scampered. A cold wind gusted through the humid night, the blade of it piercing my thin shirt. The freezing wind fled, and a warm, plunging wave of air as damp as sea spray moved through the street like a hand rustling a silk curtain.

It rained. Liquid night, heavy as a cashmere cloak: it rained. And it rained.

The crowd shivered and shouted with delight. Forgetting the fire they jumped and whooped and danced together, laughing madly as their feet splashed on the sodden street.

The fire sizzled, defeated in the flood. Firemen joined the dancers. Someone turned on music somewhere. Cops swayed in a line beside their jeeps. The dancers laughed, soaked through, satin-skin clothes reflecting colours in the puddles at their feet.

I danced on a river of wet light. Storms rolled, while the sea came to the earth. Winds leapt at us like a pack of happy dogs. Lakes of lightning splashed the street. Heat sighed from every stone. Faith in life painted our faces. Hands were laughter. Shadows danced, drunk on rain, and I danced with them, the happy fool I was, as that first flood drowned the sins of the sun.

PART THREE

'How often do you think about Karla?' Lisa asked.

Damn, I thought, waking up, *how do women do that?*

'A lot, lately. That's the third time I've heard her name in as many days.'

'Who else talked about her?'

'Naveen, the young private detective, and Ranjit.'

'What did Ranjit say?'

'Lisa, why don't we *not* talk about Karla and Ranjit, okay?'

'Are you jealous of Ranjit?'

'What?'

'Well, you know, I've been spending a lot of time with him lately, late at night.'

'I haven't been here lately, Lisa, so I didn't know. How much time have you been spending with Ranjit?'

'He's been damn helpful with the publicity for the shows. We've had lots more people coming through the doors since he got on board. But there's absolutely nothing going on between us.'

'O . . . kay. What?'

'So, how often do you really think about Karla?'

'Are we doing this *now*?' I asked, turning over to face her.

She raised herself on an elbow, her head tilted to her shoulder.

'I saw her yesterday,' she said, watching me closely, her blue eyes innocent as flowers.

I frowned silence at her.

'I ran into her at my dress shop. The one on Brady's Lane. I thought it was a secret, my secret, and then I turned around and saw Karla, standing right beside me.'

'What did she say?'

'What do you mean?'

'I mean, what did she say to you?'

'That's . . . kinda bizarre,' she said, frowning at me.

'Whaddaya mean, bizarre?'

'You didn't ask how she *looks*, or how she's *feeling* – you asked what she *said*.'

'And?'

'So . . . you haven't seen her for almost two years, and the first thing you ask me about is what she *said*. I don't know what's more freaky, that you *said* that, or that I kinda understand it, because it's about Karla.'

'So . . . you *do* understand.'

'Of course I do.'

'So . . . it's *not* bizarre.'

'The bizarre part is what it tells me about you and her.'

'What are we talking about, again?'

'Karla. Do you want to know what she said, or not?'

'Okay,' I said. 'No.'

'Of course you do. First, let me say she looked great. Really great. And she seems fine. We had a coffee at Madras Café, and I laughed myself silly. She's on a thing about religion at the moment. She said – no, wait, let me get it right – oh yeah, she said *Religion is just a long competition to see who can design the silliest hat*. She's so funny. It must be damn hard.'

'Being funny?'

'No, always being the smartest person in the room.'

'You're smart,' I said, turning onto my back, and putting my hands behind my head. 'You're one of the smartest people I know.'

'*Me?*' she laughed.

'Damn right.'

She kissed my chest, and then nestled in beside me.

'I've offered Karla a place with me in the art studio,' she declared, her feet wriggling in time to the words.

'That's not the best idea I've heard this week.'

'You just said I was smart.'

'I said you were smart,' I teased her. 'I didn't say you were wise.'

She punched me in the side.

'I'm serious,' I laughed. 'I . . . I don't . . . I mean, I'm not sure I want Karla walking back into the apartment of my life. The rooms where she used to live are boarded up now. I'd kinda like to keep it that way, for a while longer.'

'She's a ghost in *my* mansion, too,' she said wistfully.

'Oh, I see. I've got an imaginary apartment, and you've got an imaginary mansion?'

'Of course. Everybody's got a mansion inside. Everyone except people with self-esteem issues, like you.'

'I don't have self-esteem issues. I'm a realist.'

She laughed. She laughed for quite a while: long enough to make me wonder what it was that I'd said.

'Be serious,' she said when she settled down. 'That was the first time I've seen Karla in almost ten months, and I . . . I looked at her . . . and . . . I realised how much I love her. It's a funny thing, don't you think, to remember how much you love somebody?'

'I'm just saying –'

'I know,' she murmured, leaning across to kiss me. 'I know.'

'What do you know?'

'I know it's not forever,' she whispered, her face close, her lips still touching mine, and those blue eyes challenging the morning sky.

'Every time you answer a question, Lisa, I get more confused.'

'I don't even *believe* in forever,' she said, tossing eternity away with a flash of blonde curls. 'I never did.'

'Am I going to like what we're talking about, Leese, when I know what it is?'

'I'm kind of a *now* fanatic, if you know what I mean. Kind of a *now fundamentalist*, you could say.'

She began to kiss me, but she began speaking again, her lips bubbling the words into my mouth.

'You're never gonna tell me about that fight you had, are you?'

'It wasn't much of a fight. It wasn't really a fight at *all*, if you wanna get technical.'

'I *do* wanna get technical. What happened?'

'Happened?' I said, still kissing her.

She pulled herself away from me, and sat up on the bed, her legs crossed.

'You've gotta stop doing this,' she said.

'Okay,' I sighed, sitting up and resting my back against a stack of pillows. 'Let's have it.'

'The Company,' she said flatly. 'The passport factory. The Sanjay Company.'

'Come on, Lisa. We've been through this before.'

'Not for a while.'

'Seems like yesterday to me. Lisa –'

'You don't have to do it. You don't have to be that.'

'Yes, I do, for a little while longer.'

'No, you don't.'

'Sure. And I'll make money, as a fugitive, with a price on my head, working in a bank.'

'We don't live big. We'll be okay on what I'll make. The art market is starting to take off here.'

'I was doing this before we got together –'

'I know, I know –'

'And you accepted it. You –'

'I've got a bad feeling,' she said bluntly.

I smiled, and put the palm of my hand against her face.

'I can't shake it off,' she said quietly. 'I've . . . I've got this really bad feeling.'

I took her hands in mine. Our feet were touching, and her toes closed around mine, grasping with surprising force. Dawn began to burn gaps in the wooden shutters.

'We've been through this before,' I repeated slowly. 'The government of my country put a price on my head. And if they don't kill me, trying to catch me, they'll take me back to the same prison I escaped from, and they'll chain me to the same wall, and go to work on me. I'm not going back, Lisa. I'm safe here, for now. That's something. For me, if not for you.'

'I'm not saying give yourself up. I'm saying don't give up on yourself.'

'What do you want me to do?'

'You could write.'

'I *do* write, every day.'

'I know, but we could really *focus* on it, you know?'

'We?' I laughed.

I wasn't mocking her: it was simply the first time she'd mentioned my writing, and we'd lived together for almost two years.

'Forget it,' she said.

She was silent again. Her eyes drifted slowly downwards, and her toes released their fierce grip on mine. I brushed a stray curl from her eye, and ran my hand through the sea-foam of her blonde hair.

'I owe them a promise,' I said flatly.

'You don't,' she said, but there was no force in her protest, as she lifted her eyes to meet mine. 'You don't owe them anything.'

'Yes, I owe them. Everyone who knows them, owes them. That's how it works. That's why I don't let you meet any of them.'

'You're free, Lin. You climbed the wall, and you don't even know you're free.'

I stared back into her eyes, a sky-reflected lake. The phone rang.

'I'm free enough to let that phone ring,' I said. 'Are you?'

'You never answer the phone,' she snapped. 'That doesn't count.'

She got out of bed. Staring at me, she listened to the voice on the other end of the line. I watched sadness settle like a shawl across her shoulders as she handed me the phone.

It was one of Sanjay's lieutenants, passing on a message.

'I'll get on it,' I said. 'Yeah. What? I told you. I'll get on it. Twenty minutes.'

I hung up the phone, went back to the bed, and knelt beside her.

'One of my men has been arrested. He's at the Colaba lock-up. I gotta bribe him out.'

'He's not one of *your* men,' she said, pushing me away. 'And you're not their man.'

'I'm sorry, Lisa.'

'It doesn't matter what you did, or what you were. It doesn't even matter what you are. It's what you try to be that counts.'

I smiled.

'It's not that easy. We're all what we were.'

'No we're not. We're what we want ourselves to be. Don't you get that yet?'

'I'm *not free*, Lisa.'

She kissed me, but the summer wind had passed, and clouds fell across a grey field of flowers in her eyes.

'I'll start the shower for you,' she said, jumping from the bed and running toward the bathroom.

'Look, this is no big deal, getting this guy outta the lock-up,' I said, passing her on my way into the bathroom.

'I know,' she said flatly.

'You still want to meet up? Later today?'

'Of course.'

I stepped into the bathroom and stood under the cold shower.

'Are you gonna tell me what it's all about?' I called out to her. 'Or is it still a big secret?'

'It's not a secret, it's a *surprise*,' she said softly, standing in the doorway.

'Fair enough,' I laughed. 'Where do you want me for this surprise, and when?'

'Be outside the Mahesh, on Nariman Point, at five thirty. You're always late, so make four thirty the time in your head, and you'll be on time at five thirty.'

'Got it.'

'You'll be there, right?'

'Don't worry. It's all under control.'

'No,' she said, her smile falling like rain from leaves. 'It's not. Nothing is under control.'

She was right, of course. I didn't understand it then, as I walked beneath the high arch of the Colaba police station, but I could still see her sorrowful smile, falling like snow into a river.

I climbed the few steps leading to the wooden veranda that covered the side and rear of the administration building. The cop on duty outside the sergeant's office knew me. He wagged his head, smiling, as he allowed me to pass. He was glad to see me. I was a good payer.

I gave a mock salute to Lightning Dilip, the daytime duty sergeant. His bloated drinker's face was swollen with smothered outrage: he was on a double shift of bad temper. Not a good start.

Lightning Dilip was a sadist. I knew that, because I'd been his prisoner, a few years before. He'd beaten me then, feeding his sad hunger with my helplessness. And he wanted to do it again as he stared at the bruises on my face, his lips tremors of anticipation.

But things had changed in my world, if not in his. I worked for the Sanjay Company, and the group poured a lot of liquid assets into the police station. It was too much money to risk on his defective desires.

Allowing himself the semblance of a smile, he tilted his head in a little upward nod: *What's up?*

'Is the boss in?' I asked.

The smile showed teeth. Dilip knew that if I dealt with his boss, the sub-inspector, the trickle-down of any bribe I'd pay would barely dry his sweaty palm.

'The sub-inspector is a very busy man. Is there something that *I* can do for you?'

'Well . . . ' I replied, glancing around at the cops in the office.

They were doing an unconvincing job of pretending not to listen. To be fair to them, pretending not to listen isn't something we get a lot of practice at in India.

'Santosh! Get us some chai!' Dilip grunted in Marathi. 'Make fresh, yaar! You lot! Go and check the under barrack!'

The under barrack was a ground-floor facility at the rear of the police compound. It was used to house violent prisoners, and prisoners who violently resisted being tortured. The young cops looked at one another, and then one of them spoke.

'But, sir, under barrack is empty, sir.'

'Did I ask you if there was anyone *in* the under barrack?' Dilip demanded.

'N-no, sir.'

'Then do as I say, all of you, and check it out thoroughly! Now!'

'Yes, sir!' the constables shouted, grabbing their soft caps and stumbling from the room.

'You guys should have a code or something,' I suggested, when they'd gone. 'Must get tedious, having to shout them out of here, every hour or so.'

'Very funny,' Dilip replied. 'Get to the point, or get the fuck out. I've got a headache, and I want to give it to someone.'

Straight cops are all alike; every crooked cop is corrupt in his own way. They all take the money, but some accept it reluctantly, others hungrily; some angrily, others genially; some joke and some sweat as if they're running uphill; some make it a contest, while others want to be your new best friend.

Dilip was the kind who took the money resentfully, and tried to make you bleed for giving it to him. Fortunately, like all bullies, he was susceptible to flattery.

'I'm glad you can deal with this personally,' I said. 'Dealing with Patil can take all day. He doesn't have your *finesse* for getting things done decisively and quickly, *fatafat*, like lightning. They don't call you Lightning Dilip for nothing.'

They called him Lightning Dilip, in fact, because his shiny boots, lashing out from the darkness of his rage, always struck a chained man when he least expected it, and never twice in exactly the same place.

'That is very true,' Dilip preened, relaxing in his chair. 'What can I do for you?'

'There's a guy in your lock-up, Farzad Daruwalla by name, I'd like to pay his fine.'

'Fines are imposed by the court, not by the police,' Dilip observed, a sly grin wet on his lips.

'Of course, you're completely right,' I smiled, 'but a man of your vision can see how dealing with this matter in a forceful fashion, right here and now, will save the valuable time of the court, and the public purse.'

'Why do you want this fellow?'

'Oh, I can think of five thousand reasons why,' I replied, pulling a prepared wad of rupee notes from my pocket, and beginning to count them.

'A man of vision could think of many more reasons than that,' Dilip frowned.

It was too late. He was already looking at the money.

'Lightning-*ji*,' I said softly, folding the notes over double and sliding them across the desk beneath the cover of my hand. 'We've been doing this dance for almost two years now, and we both know that five thousand reasons is all I'd have to give the sub-inspector to make a full . . . *explanation* . . . of my interest. I'd be grateful if you'd save me that trouble, and accept the explanation personally.'

Santosh approached with the tea, his footsteps thumping on the floorboards of the wooden veranda. Lightning Dilip flashed his hand out to cover mine. I let my hand slide back across the desk. Dilip's hand slithered the notes to his side of the desk, and into his pocket.

'The college man,' Dilip said to Santosh, as the young constable placed the tea in front of us. 'The one we brought in from the nightclub, late last night. Bring him here.'

'Yes, sir,' Santosh replied, hurrying from the room.

The young cops returned to the office, but Dilip stopped them with an upturned hand.

'What are you doing here?'

'We . . . we checked the under barrack, sir, just as you said. All is in order. And we saw that you ordered chai, so we thought we might . . . '

'Check it again!' Lightning Dilip snapped, turning his attention back to me.

The young cops stared at me, then shrugged and slouched out of the office again.

'Is there anything else I can help you with?' Dilip asked sarcastically.

'Matter of fact, there is. Have you heard anything about a man with

141

'Sanjay's not gonna be happy about this. He spends a lot of money keeping a lid on this ward. You're gonna have to buy him a new hat.'

'I . . . I . . . but, do you know . . . what size is his head?' he asked, desperately worried. 'I've only seen him the one time, and, by my recollection, his head looked, no disrespect, a little on the *big* side.'

'He doesn't wear a hat.'

'But . . . you said –'

'I was kidding. But only about the hat.'

'I . . . I'm so sorry. I really fucked up badly. It . . . it won't happen again. Can you, maybe, put in a good word for me with Sanjay?'

I was still laughing when a taxi pulled up beside us. Naveen Adair got out of the taxi and reached back through the window to pay the driver. Opening the back door, he helped a beautiful young woman out of the cab. He turned and saw me.

'Lin! Damn good to see you, man. What brings you here?'

'Six thousand reasons,' I replied, staring at the girl.

Her face was familiar, but I couldn't place it.

'Oh,' Naveen said, 'this is Divya. Divya Devnani.'

Divya Devnani, daughter of one of Bombay's richest men. Photographs of her short, athletically fit body, draped in expensive designer dresses, claimed eye-line positions in the coverage of every A-list event in the city.

And that's what had thrown me: the unglamorous clothes she wore on that morning. The simple blue T-shirt, lapis bead necklace and jeans weren't from that other world, in which she was born to rule. It was the girl in the woman standing in front of me, not the woman on the page.

'Pleased to meet you,' I said.

'Got any hash?' she demanded.

I flicked a glance at Naveen.

'It's a long story,' he sighed.

'No, it's not,' she contradicted him. 'My dad, Mukesh Devnani – you've heard of Mukesh Devnani, I take it?'

'He's that guy with the crazy daughter who solicits drugs outside police stations, isn't he?'

'Funny,' she said. 'Careful now, I'm going to pee in my pants.'

'You were gonna tell me why it's not a long story,' I prompted.

'I don't want to tell you, now,' she sulked.

144

'Her father hired a lawyer I know —' Naveen began.

'Who then hired *this* guy,' she quickly cut in, 'to be my bodyguard, for a couple of weeks.'

'I'd say you're in very good hands.'

'Thank you,' Naveen said.

'Fuck you,' she said.

'Nice meeting you,' I said. 'So long, Naveen.'

'And all because I get mixed up with this Bollywood wannabe movie star,' Divya continued, ignoring me, 'I mean, not even a *real* movie star, just a *wannabe*, for fuck's sake. And he's such a fucking jerk, he starts to threaten me when I refuse to go out with him. Can you believe that?'

'It's a jungle out there,' I smiled.

'You're telling *me*,' she said. 'Have you got any hash, or not?'

'*I* have!' Farzad said quickly. 'Count on it!'

We turned to stare at him.

He reached down into the front of his pants, fiddled there for a while, and pulled his hand out to reveal a ten-gram block of Kashmiri hashish, wrapped in clear plastic.

'There,' he said, offering it to Divya. 'It's all yours. Please accept it as . . . as a gift, like.'

Divya's lips peeled a lemon of horror.

'Did you just pull that thing . . . out of your underpants?' she asked, gagging a little.

'Er . . . yes . . . but . . . I changed my underpants only yesterday night. Count on it!'

'Who the fuck is this guy?' Divya demanded of Naveen.

'He's with me,' I said.

'I'm sorry!' Farzad said, beginning to put the hash in his pocket. 'I didn't mean to —'

'Stop! What are you doing?'

'But . . . I thought you —'

'Peel the plastic off it,' she commanded. 'And then don't touch it. Just leave it in your hand, on the open plastic. Don't touch it with your fingers. And don't touch me. Don't even think about touching me. Believe me, I'll know it, if you do. A mind like yours, it's a toy to me. It's a toy to any woman. So, don't think about me. And gimme the fuckin' hash already, you *chudh*.'

145

Farzad began to unwrap the block of hashish, his fingers trembling. He glanced at the petite socialite.

'You're thinking!' Divya warned.

'No!' Farzad protested. 'I'm not!'

'You're disgusting.'

Farzad finally succeeded in unwrapping the parcel, leaving the hashish exposed on his palm. Divya picked it up between forefinger and thumb, broke off a little piece, and dropped the rest of it into the silver fish-mouth of her purse.

She took out a cigarette, squeezed some tobacco out of the end of it, and placed the little piece of hash into the blank end. She put the cigarette between her lips, and turned to Naveen for a light. He hesitated.

'You think this is a good idea?'

'I'm not going in there to talk to the cops unless I have a smoke,' she said. 'I don't even talk to the downstairs maid until the upstairs maid has given me a smoke.'

Naveen lit the cigarette. She puffed at it, held the smoke in her lungs for a few moments, and then let out a solid stream of smoke. Naveen turned to me.

'Her father filed a complaint against the wannabe actor, before I came along,' Naveen said. 'The actor acted heavy. I paid the actor a visit. We talked. He agreed to back off, and to stay backed off. Now we need to lift the complaint, but she has to do it in person. I want to get it done early, before any reporters get onto it, and –'

'Let's fucking *go*, already!' Divya snapped, grinding out the cigarette under the sole of her shoe.

Naveen shook my hand. I held it firmly for a moment.

'The guy following the Zodiac Georges,' I said. 'His name's Wilson, registered at –'

'The Mahesh,' Naveen finished for me. 'I know. In all this, I forgot to tell you. I tracked him down last night. How did *you* find out?'

'He came here, looking for information.'

'Did he get any?'

'Dilip, the duty sergeant – do you know him?'

'Yeah. Lightning Dilip. We've got a little history.'

'He says Mr Wilson wouldn't pay, so he threw him out.'

'You believe him?'

'Not usually.'

'You want me to go see this Wilson?'

'Not yet. Not without me. Check him out. Find out what you can about him. Get back to me, okay?'

'*Thik*,' Naveen smiled. 'I'll get on it, and –'

'This is the fucking *longest* I've ever stood up,' Divya interrupted angrily, 'on my *legs*, for God's sake, in the same fucking *place*, for God's sake, in my whole fucking *life*! Do you think we can get *on* with it now?'

Naveen smiled a goodbye, and escorted the poor little rich girl through the arched gate.

'It's *Farzad*!' Farzad called after her. 'My name's *Farzad*!'

When he lost sight of her, the young Parsi turned to me, grinning widely.

'Damn it all to *hell*, yaar! What a beautiful girl! And such a nice nature! Some of those super-mega-rich girls, they can be very stuck-up and all, so I've heard. But she's so natural, and she's –'

'Will you cut it out!'

He opened his mouth to protest, but the words withered when he saw my expression.

'Sorry,' he said bashfully. 'But . . . did you see the colour of her eyes! Oh, my *God*! Like bits of shining stuff, you know, dipped in something . . . really, really full of . . . really lovely stuff, like a bucket of . . . loveliness . . . honey.'

'Please, Farzad. I haven't had my breakfast.'

'Sorry, Lin. Hey, that's it! Have breakfast! Can you come to my place? Can you come home with me, now? You promised to come this week!'

'That's gonna be a *no*, Farzad.'

'Please come! I have to see my Mom and Pop, take my bath and change my clothes before I go to work. Come with me. They'll still be having breakfast at home, some of them, and they'd *love* to meet you. Especially after you saved my life, and all.'

'I didn't save your –'

'Please, baba! Trust me, believe me, they're waiting to meet you, and it's very important that you come, and you'll find it *damn* interesting at my house!'

'Look, I –'

'Please! Please, Lin!'

Four motorcycles pulled up hard beside us. They were Sanjay Company men. The leader of the group was Ravi, a young soldier in Abdullah's enforcement group.

'Hey, Lin,' Ravi said, his eyes behind mercury lens mirrors. 'We heard some Scorpions are having breakfast at one of our places in the Fort. We're all heading there to kick the shit out of them. Wanna come along?'

I glanced at Farzad.

'I've already got a breakfast date,' I said.

'Really?' Farzad said.

'Okay, Lin,' Ravi said, putting his bike in gear. 'I'll bring you back a souvenir.'

'Please don't,' I said, but he was already riding away.

The Fort area was only a thirty-minute walk from where we were standing, and roughly the same distance from Sanjay's mansion. If the Scorpions were really provoking a fight so close to home, the war that Sanjay had tried to deal away was already on his doorstep.

'Do you think they might take me with them, one of these days?' Farzad asked, watching the four motorcycles vanish in the traffic. 'It would be so cool, to kick some ass with them.'

I looked at the young forger, who'd been kicked unconscious the night before but was already thinking of kicking someone else. It wasn't cruelty or callousness: Farzad's violent fantasy of brotherhood and blood was a boy's bravado. He was no gangster. After just a few hours in the cells, he was already breaking down. He was a good kid, in a bad Company.

'If you ever go with them, and I come to hear about it,' I said, 'I'll kick your ass myself.'

He thought about it for a moment.

'Are you still coming to breakfast, please?'

'Count on it,' I said, putting an arm around his shoulder, and leading him to my bike.

CHAPTER FIFTEEN

B OMBAY, EVEN NOW, IS A CITY OF WORDS. Everyone talks, everywhere, and all the time. Drivers ask other drivers for directions,
strangers talk to strangers, cops talk to criminals, Left talks to Right,
and if you want a letter or parcel delivered, you have to include a few
words about a landmark in the address: opposite the Heera Panna, or
nearby to Copper Chimney. And words in Bombay, even little words
like *please, please come*, still have adventures attached, like sails.

Farzad rode pillion with me for the short trip to the Colaba Back
Bay, near Cuffe Parade, pointing out his favourite places. He liked to
talk, that kid, and started three stories inspired by places we passed,
but didn't finish any of them.

When we parked outside his parents' home I looked up at a huge
house, at least three storeys high, with gabled attics. The impressive,
triple-fronted house was one of three between streets on either side,
forming a small inner-city block.

Joined to the similar homes on either side, the Daruwalla mansion
presented a façade that we South Bombay partisans love: the architec-
tural flourishes inherited from the British Raj, cast in local granite and
sandstone by Indian artists.

The windows boasted stained-glass embellishments, decorative
stone arches, and wrought-iron security spirals, sprouting elegant
metal vine leaf traceries. A flowering hedge gave privacy and shaded
the morning sun.

The wide, wooden door, flanked by Rajasthan pillars and adorned
with complex geometric carvings, swung open silently as Farzad used
his key and led me into the vestibule.

The high, marble-walled entry hall was decorated with garlands of
flowers trailing from urns set into scalloped alcoves. Incense filled the

air with the scent of sandalwood. Directly ahead of us, opposite the main door, was a ceiling-high curtain made of red velvet.

'Are you ready?' Farzad asked theatrically, his hand on the partition of the curtains.

'I'm armed,' I smiled. 'If that's what you mean.'

Farzad pulled one half of the curtains aside, holding it back for me to pass. We walked on through a dark passageway and arrived at a set of folding doors. Farzad slid the panels back. I stepped through.

The vast space beyond the corridor was so high that I could only vaguely make out the detail of its sunlit uppermost reaches, and the width clearly encompassed a far greater space than Farzad's home alone.

At ground level, two long tables had been set for breakfast, with perhaps fifteen place settings at each table. Several men, women and children were sitting there.

What appeared to be two fully equipped kitchens, open to view, formed the left and right boundaries of the ground floor. Beyond them, doors at the back and sides of the vast chamber led to other closed rooms.

My eyes roved to the upper floors. Ladders led to head-height walkways. Ladders from those wooden pathways led to still higher boardwalks, supported on bamboo scaffolding. Several men and women chipped or scraped at the walls serenely, here and there on the walkways.

A parting in the monsoon cloud sent sunlight spilling from high turret windows. The whole space was suddenly a topaz-yellow lucency. It was like a cathedral, without the fear.

'Farzad!' a woman screamed, and every head turned.

'Hi, Mom!' Farzad said, his hand on my shoulder.

'Hi, Mom?' she yelled. 'I'll take your *Hi, Mom*, and beat you black and blue with it. Where have you been?'

Others came to join us.

'I've brought Lin,' Farzad said, hoping it might help his cause.

'Oh, Farzad, my son,' she sobbed, pulling him to her in a suffocating embrace.

Just as swiftly she pushed him away and slapped his face.

'Ow! Mom!' Farzad pleaded, rubbing his face.

Farzad's Mother was in her fifties. She was short, with a shapely figure and a neat, gamine haircut that suited her soft features. She wore a floral apron over her striped dress, and a string of well-matched pearls at her neck.

'What are you doing, you wicked boy?' she demanded. 'Are you working for the hospitals now, drumming up trade for those doctors by giving everybody a this-thing?'

'Heart attack,' a grey-haired man I guessed to be her husband helped her.

'Yes, giving everybody a this-thing,' she said.

'Mom, it wasn't my –'

'So, you're Lin!' she said, cutting him off and turning to face me. 'Keki Uncle, may his spirit shine in our eyes, used to talk about you a lot. Did he mention me? Anahita? His niece? Farzad's mom? Arshan's wife? He said you were quite the one for talking philosophy. Tell me, what is your take on the free will versus determination dilemma?'

'Give the boy a chance to relax, Mother,' Farzad's father said as he shook my hand. 'My name is Arshan. I'm very pleased to meet you, Lin.'

He turned to Farzad then, fixing him with a stern but loving frown.

'And as for *you*, young man –'

'I can explain, Pop! I –'

'You can explain my hand across your backside!' Anahita growled. 'You can explain how we worried so much we didn't get a wink's worth of sleep the whole night? You can explain how your poor father was roaming on the road at two o'clock in the morning, looking for you, because maybe a water truck ran over you and left you crunched up like scrambled eggs in a ditch?'

'Mom –'

'Do you know how many ditches there are in this area? This is the peak area for ditches. And your father searched through every one of them, looking for your scrambled eggs corpse. And you have the shamelessness to stand here, in front of us, without a scratch on your miserable hide?'

'You might at least be limping,' a young man said as he approached us to shake hands with Farzad. 'Or slightly disfigured, *na?*'

'This is my friend Ali,' Farzad said, exchanging a penitent smile with the young man, who was his twin in height and weight, and seemed to be roughly the same age.

'*Salaam aleikum,*' I said.

'*Wa aleikum salaam*, Lin,' Ali said, shaking hands. 'Welcome to the dream factory.'

'Lin got me out of jail this morning,' Farzad announced.

'Jail!' Anahita shrieked. 'Better you should have been in one of those ditches, with your poor father.'

'Well, he's home now, Mother,' Arshan said, gently pushing us toward the tables on the left side of the huge room. 'And I'll bet these boys are both very hungry.'

'Starving, Pop!' Farzad said, moving to take a place at the table.

'No you don't!' a woman countered, tugging at Farzad's sleeve.

She was wearing a colourful *salwar kameez* of pale green tapered trousers and a flowing yellow-orange tunic. 'Not with those hands full of jail germs! Who knows what diseases you're infesting us with, even as we speak. Wash your hands!'

'You heard her!' Anahita said. 'Wash your hands! And you, too, Lin. He might have infected you with his jail germs.'

'Yes, ma'am.'

'I have to warn you in advance, though,' she cautioned. 'I lean towards determinism, and I'm ready to roll my sleeves up, if you're a free will man.'

'Yes, ma'am.'

'And I don't pull my punches,' she added. 'Not when it comes to philosophy.'

'Yes, ma'am.'

We washed our hands at a sink in the open kitchen, and then sat down at the long table on the left-hand side of the huge room. The woman in the *salwar kameez* immediately served us with bowls of meat in fragrant gravy.

'Have some mutton now, you young fellows,' she said, seizing the moment to pinch Farzad's cheek between her fingers. 'You're a naughty, naughty boy!'

'You don't even know what I've done!' Farzad protested.

'I don't need to know any such thing,' the woman averred, giving his cheek another mutilating twist. 'You are always a naughty, naughty boy, no matter what you're doing. Even when you're doing good things, you're naughty also, isn't it so?'

'And cheeky,' I added.

'Oh, don't get me started on *cheeky*,' Anahita agreed.

'Thanks, Lin,' Farzad muttered.

'Don't mention it.'

The woman in the *salwar* tunic twisted one more bruise into Farzad's cheek.

'You're a cheeky, cheeky, cheeky boy.'

'This is Zaheera Auntie,' Farzad said, rubbing his face. 'Ali's mom.'

'If you have a taste for pure vegetarian,' another woman, wearing a pale blue sari, suggested brightly, 'you might like to try this daal roti. It's fresh. Made from just now.'

She placed two small bowls of the saffron-coloured daal on the table, and unwrapped a napkin of freshly cooked rotis.

'Eat! Eat!' she commanded. 'Don't be shy.'

'This is Jaya Auntie,' Farzad stage-whispered. 'It's kind of a competition between Zaheera Auntie and Jaya Auntie as to who's the best cook, and my Mom stays out of it. We'd better be diplomatic. I'll start with the mutton, and you start with the daal, okay?'

We pulled the bowls of food closer, and began to eat. It was delicious, and I ate hungrily. The two women exchanged knowing glances, happy with the drawn result, and sat down beside us.

A few adults and children joined us at the long table. Some came from the ground-floor apartments, while others climbed down from the interconnected catwalks to stand near us, or sit further along at the table.

As Farzad took a hungry bite of his mutton in masala gravy, Anahita approached from behind and smacked him on the back of the head, as swiftly and unexpectedly as Lightning Dilip might've done. All the children near us laughed and giggled.

'Ow! Mom! What did you do *that* for?'

'You should be eating stones!' she declared, waving the side of her hand at him. 'Stones from those ditches your poor father was searching, instead of tasty mutton chunkies.'

'The daal is also tasty, isn't it?' Jaya Auntie asked me.

'Oh, yes,' I said quickly.

'Your poor father, out the whole night in those bloody ditches.'

'Enough about the ditches, Mother dear,' Farzad's father said gently. 'Let the boy tell us what happened.'

'I was at the Drum Beat last night,' Farzad began.

'Oh! What music did they play?' a pretty girl of perhaps seventeen asked.

She was sitting a little way along the table, and she leaned in to catch Farzad's eye.

'This is Kareena Cousin, Jaya Auntie's daughter,' Farzad said, without looking at her. 'Kareena, this is Lin.'

'Hi,' she said, smiling shyly.

'Hi,' I answered her.

Having finished the bowl of vegetables, I gently pushed it away. Zaheera Auntie immediately shoved the spare bowl of mutton in front of me, so close that it almost fell into my lap. I grasped the bowl with both hands.

'Thanks.'

'Good mutton,' Zaheera Auntie confided, with a wink. 'Good for all of your angers and such.'

'My angers. Yes, ma'am. Thanks.'

'So, you were at the Drum Beat nightclub,' Arshan said quietly, 'which I warned you against, many a time, son.'

'What warnings?' Anahita asked, slapping Farzad on the back of the head.

'Ow! Mom! Cut it out, yaar!'

'Your warnings are delicious to him! He eats them up like sweeties. Yum, yum, yum! I've told you, operant conditioning is the only thing that works on this boy, but you're such a Steiner fan. I'd say your son got fairly Steinered last night, wouldn't you?'

'I don't think you can blame the Steiner School,' Jaya cut in.

'Indeed,' Zaheera agreed. 'The methodology is pretty sound, *na*? My Suleiman was saying only last night —'

'And, while you were at the nightclub ...' Arshan prompted patiently.

'Well,' Farzad said, casting a wary eye about for his Mother's hand. 'There was this party and all, and we —'

'Were they doing any new dances?' Kareena asked. 'Did they play the music from the new Mithun picture?'

'I can get you that music this afternoon,' Ali answered her casually, taking a piece of Farzad's bread and biting off a chunk. 'Whatever you want. Even stuff from movies that haven't come out yet.'

'Wow!' the girl sighed.

'And while you were at this club,' Arshan persisted resolutely.

'And while you were at this Steiner School nightclub,' Anahita interrupted, raising her hand, 'free as a bird, your father was in the ditches!'

'No,' Arshan said, his patience a sympathetic string. 'I'm pretty sure the ditches came later, sweetheart. So, what happened at the club, that put you in jail?'

'I'm . . . I'm not sure,' Farzad said, frowning. 'I drank too much. That I'll freely admit. And there was this argument, when the cops came to close the place down. Next thing I know, I was lying on the ground. I fell, I think. And then this cop kicked me in the back of the head, right where *you* keep hitting me, Mom, and I passed out. I woke up in the police jeep, and they locked me up, without a phone call or a by your leave. Somebody there called the Company, and they called Lin, and he came and got me out. He saved my hide. Count on it.'

'That's it?' Farzad's Mother asked, contempt drawing down the corners of her mouth. 'That's your big adventure?'

'I didn't *say* it was a *big adventure!*' Farzad protested, but his Mother was already gone, headed for the open kitchen.

'Thank you, Lin, for bringing our boy home to us,' Arshan said, his hand resting on my forearm for a moment.

He turned his attention back to Farzad once more.

'Let me get this straight. A policeman kicked you in the head, while you were on the ground. Kicked you so hard that you lost consciousness?'

'That's right, Pop. I wasn't doing anything. I was too *drunk* to do anything. I was just lying there, where I fell over.'

'Do you know this policeman's name?' Arshan asked thoughtfully.

'Lightning Dilip, they call him. He's a duty sergeant at the Colaba lock-up. Why?'

'My dad's gonna go nuts about this!' Ali said. 'He'll have this Lightning Dilip's badge. He'll bring the entire law faculty with him.'

'And my dad will bring the medical fraternity on board,' Kareena added, her eyes fierce. 'We'll have this cop kicked off the force.'

'Absolutely!' Jaya agreed. 'Let's get started!'

'Can I say something here?'

Everyone turned toward me.

'I know this Lightning Dilip pretty well. He doesn't bear grudges easily. He doesn't even bear bribes easily.'

I paused, feeling the attention in the group.

'Go on,' Arshan said softly.

'You can't badge this cop. You can make his life very unpleasant for a while, and get him moved somewhere for a while, maybe, but you can't badge him. He knows too much about too many people. No-one's saying he doesn't deserve it, but if you make his life unpleasant, sooner or later he'll come back. And when he comes back, he'll disturb your happiness again. Probably forever.'

'Are you saying we shouldn't do anything about this?' Ali asked.

'I'm saying that if you go up against this guy, be prepared for a war. Don't underestimate him.'

'I agree,' Arshan said quietly.

'What?' Ali and Jaya asked together.

'Farzad is lucky. Lin's right. It could've been much worse. And the last thing we need, right now, is a sociopathic policeman on our doorstep.'

'And operant conditioning takes another beating,' Anahita said, returning from the kitchen. 'What is it with you Steiners, and running away?'

'Don't go to that nightclub again, Farzad,' Arshan said, ignoring her. 'Do you hear me? I forbid you.'

'Yes, Pop,' Farzad said, hanging his head.

'Okay,' Arshan said, standing to clear the dishes. 'Are you finished with these?'

He and Anahita took the dishes to the near kitchen, and returned bearing two fresh bowls and two bottles of soft drink.

'Nice custard,' Anahita said, dropping bowls of sweet custard in front of us. 'To fill your blood with sugar.'

'And Rogers Raspberry,' Arshan said, placing the crimson-coloured soft drink bottles beside our bowls. 'There's not many problems in life that a long, cold glass of Rogers Raspberry can't make look much rosier. Drink up!'

'I like what you've done with the place,' I remarked. 'Who's your decorator? Harlan Ellison?'

Farzad turned to face his father.

'He saved my life, Pop. The families voted. I think this is the time. What do you say?'

'It seems that it is,' Arshan murmured, glancing around at the

Escheresque web of ladders, handmade stairs and catwalks scaling upwards around him in the vast, half-bell chamber.

'Is that a *yes?*' Farzad asked.

Arshan swung his leg across the bench seat we were sitting on, and faced me directly.

'What's your guess that we're doing here?' he asked.

'Taking a wild stab in the step-ladder, I'd say you're looking for something.'

'Precisely,' Arshan grinned, showing a row of neat, small, perfectly white teeth. 'I see why Keki Uncle liked you. That's exactly what we're doing. All of this, everything you see here, is one great big treasure hunt, for a very valuable treasure chest.'

'As in . . . a pirate's treasure chest?'

'In a way, yes,' he replied. 'But a merchant's treasure — smaller, and much more valuable.'

'It must be, for all this remodelling.'

'Farzad,' Arshan said. 'Get the list.'

When Farzad left us, his father began to explain.

'My great-grandfather was a very successful man. He amassed a considerable fortune. Even after putting much of his money into charities and public works, in the Parsi tradition, his wealth was still equal to that of any industrialist or merchant of his age.'

Farzad rejoined us, sitting beside me on the long bench seat. He passed a folded parchment document to his father. Arshan's hand rested on the document while he finished his explanation.

'When the British could see the writing on the wall, and they knew their rule here was coming to an end, they began to leave Bombay, some of them in great haste. Many of the most successful British businessmen and their wives feared that after independence there would be a violent backlash against them. There was something of a mad scramble, in the last weeks and days.'

'And your great-grandfather was in the right place, at the right time.'

'It was pretty well known that my great-grandpa had loads of undeclared cash that he didn't keep in bank accounts,' Farzad said.

'Money that was never adequately accounted for,' Arshan added.

'And that missing cash,' I said, 'bought stuff from the departing British.'

'Exactly. Fearing that the Indian authorities might think they'd

157

stolen or looted the jewels they had, and who knows, maybe some of them did, many of the British sold off their jewellery in advance, for cash. My great-grandfather bought a very large quantity of those jewels in the last months before independence, and he hid them –'

'Somewhere in this house,' I concluded for him.

Arshan sighed, and allowed his gaze to roam along the catwalks and conduits that wound their way around the woven basket of the chamber.

'But there was no clue where the treasure was hidden?'

'Not a word,' Arshan sighed, opening the parchment letter, and holding it between us. 'The document we found in an old book is very specific about the number and type of gems, and the fact that they were hidden somewhere, even to describing the chest they were hidden in, but there was no hint about exactly *where*. My great-grandfather owned all three of the houses in this block, and in his time he lived and worked in them all.'

'So you started looking.'

'We searched the rooms, and all the furniture. We turned every-thing over, looking for secret drawers. Then we searched the walls for secret panels, or hidden sliding doors, or suchlike. When we found nothing, we knew we had to start breaking into the walls.'

'We started here, on the joining walls in our own house,' Anahita said, as Kareena placed a bone china cup of chai in front of me. 'But then, when we started on the this-thing –'

'The common wall,' Arshan helped her.

'Yes, when we started breaking into the this-thing, a lot of stuff started falling down inside the house of our neighbours, the Khans.'

'My favourite illuminated clock, for one thing,' Zaheera said rue-fully. 'It had a waterfall, you know, so it looked like water was falling down all the time. Then the whole clock fell down, and it smashed into a million pieces. I haven't found one as good since.'

'And when things started falling down in their house, the Khans came here, asking us what we were doing.'

'Which is where my dad came in,' Farzad's young friend, Ali, said.

'Literally,' Farzad joked.

'Our two families have been close for ever,' Ali said. 'Arshan Uncle and Anahita Auntie decided to tell my dad exactly what they were doing, and to invite him to join in the hunt for the treasure.'

'We thought that my great-grandfather might have hidden the box of jewels inside the common wall,' Arshan added. 'There were a lot of renovations and changes made to these houses, in his time, and there was no way into the walls without involving the Khans.'

'My Suleiman came home that night, after visiting here,' Zaheera Auntie said, 'and sat the whole family down for a meeting. He told us about the treasure, and the invitation to join in the hunt, even if it meant breaking down the wall between our two houses. We were all talking at once, like crazy people!'

'It was damn cool,' Ali added.

'And arguing also,' Zaheera said. 'But after a lot of heart-to-heart, we decided to join in the hunt for the treasure, and we started breaking down the wall the very next day.'

'But the treasure wasn't in there,' the pretty girl, Kareena, said. 'Not that we've found so far. And that brought *my* dad into the *mela*.'

'Arshan and Anahita invited us in for a talk,' Jaya explained, smiling at the recollection. 'When we got here, we found all the Daruwallas and all the Khans, and all the breaking-down inside. Then they invited us to join in with them, because they thought maybe the treasure was inside the wall between *our* two houses, on the other side. And to search through the upper floors, they needed cooperation from us. My husband, Rahul, agreed right there, on the spot. He's mad for adventure.'

'He skis,' Kareena said. 'In the snow.'

People shook their heads in wonder.

'And you're completely sure this treasure is really here?'

'Count on it,' Farzad said. 'When we didn't find the treasure in *that* wall, we started working on the ceilings and floors between us and the roof. It's here, and we'll find it.'

'It's a kind of madhouse, for sane people,' Kareena finished for him. 'With three happy families, one Hindu, one Muslim and one Parsi, all living together in it.'

The people around me, members of three extended families from three faiths, shrugged and smiled.

'There's no first and last here,' Arshan said softly. 'We're in this together. We all agreed to split the treasure three ways, with equal shares to each family.'

'If you find it,' I said.

'*When* we find it,' a few voices corrected me.

'And this has been going on for how long?'

'Nearly five years now,' Farzad answered. 'We started right after we found the parchment. The Khans came in a year after that, and the Malhotras came in about six months later. I went to college and Wall Street and back again, in the time we've been searching.'

'But this isn't our real job, or anything,' Kareena Malhotra said. 'My dad's a doctor. Ali's pop, Suleiman Uncle, teaches law at Bombay University. Arshan Uncle is an architect, which is how we can do all this renovation, without the whole thing falling down. And we're all studying, those of us who don't work full time outside, or with the kids here at home.'

'The treasure hunt is what we do at night and holidays, mostly,' Ali added. 'Or if we get a free day, like this one, where everybody was so worried about Farzad being missing all night. Thanks for the holiday, cuz.'

'Any time,' Farzad smiled.

'And we have two kitchens,' Anahita declared triumphantly. 'Veg and non-veg, so there's no problem.'

'Indeed,' Jaya Auntie said. 'Really, you know, a lot of differences between communities come down to ghobi and gosht, cauliflowers and kebabs. If there are two kitchens, everybody eats the food they like, and everything is hunky and this-thing –'

'Dory,' Anahita said, and the two women exchanged smiles.

'And we're all in this together, make or break,' Ali added, 'so we don't have a reason to argue.'

'Except for philosophy,' Anahita contradicted him.

'As interesting as this mystery is –' I said, but Farzad cut me off.

'I *told* you it would be interesting, didn't I?'

'Ah . . . yeah. But we still didn't get to the part where I know why you're telling me about all this.'

'We have a problem,' Arshan said simply, staring his earnest frown directly into my eyes. 'And we were hoping you would help us with it.'

'Okay. Tell me.'

'An inspector from the City Council came here a few weeks ago,' Ali said, 'and he got a look inside at some of the work.'

'He doesn't know what we're doing, of course,' Farzad added. 'We told him we're renovating the houses to make apartments.'

160

'What brought him here in the first place?' I asked.

'We think it was a neighbour down the street,' Arshan explained. 'He saw us taking delivery of some heavy steel girders a few months ago. We use them to support the arches, when we take out sections of the walls.'

'He tried to buy our house a few years back,' Anahita said. 'The rascally fellow tried every trick in the book to make us sell. When we refused, he was angrier than a scalded cat.'

'It's bad luck to hurt a cat,' Zaheera said, nodding sagely.

'You mean, even in similes?' Anahita asked earnestly.

'I'm just saying, one must be prudent, where cats are concerned. Probably even in similes.'

The whole group nodded.

After a few moments of silence, I spoke again.

'So . . . cats aside, you need what, from me?'

'Planning permits,' Arshan said, coming back to the moment. 'The City Council official agreed, after a lot of negotiation, to accept a bribe to let us get on with the . . . *renovations*. But he insists that we get the proper planning permit certificates, or damn good copies.'

'To cover his arse,' Ali said.

'He can't fake the permits, and he can't steal them,' Farzad added. 'But if we can fake them, he promised that the investigation will end with him.'

'If *you* can fake them for us, Lin,' Arshan corrected him.

'Yeah, if *you* can fake them, the inspector will sign off on them, and leave us alone to search for the treasure, like always. No problem. Count on it.'

'So, that's it,' Arshan sighed, resting his elbows on the long table. 'If you can't help us, we'll have to stop. If you *can* help us, we can go on until we find the treasure.'

'You can make those documents yourself,' I said to Farzad. 'You're pretty good. You don't need me.'

'Thanks for the compliment,' he grinned, 'but there's a couple of problems. First, I don't have any contacts at the City Council. And second, the boys in the factory won't take orders from me on a job like this, and they'll probably tell Sanjay about it. But *you*, on the other hand . . . '

'Why am I always on the other hand?'

161

'You can do it discreetly, or let me do it, because you're the boss at the factory,' Farzad said, pushing on. 'With your help, it could be done without anyone coming to know about it.'

'You might think this is a strange question,' I said, glancing around at the expectant faces staring at me, 'but it's probably a lot stranger *not* to ask it. What makes you think I won't help you out, and then tell Sanjay anyway?'

'It's a fair question,' Arshan allowed, 'and I hope you won't be offended if I tell you it's not the first time it has been raised in this room. The bottom line is that we need your help, and we believe we can trust you. Keki Uncle thought very highly of you. He told us, many times, how you were with Khaderbhai at the end, and that you are a man of honour.'

The use of the word *honour* struck at my chest, especially when they were asking me to conceal something from my boss, Sanjay. But I liked them. I already liked them more than I liked Sanjay. And Sanjay was rich enough. He didn't need a piece of their treasure, if they ever found it.

'I'll have your paperwork this week,' I said. 'I'll tell Sanjay it's a favour to a friend, which it is. I've done off-the-books jobs before. But I want it to end here. I don't want this coming back to me from Sanjay, Farzad. Are we clear?'

The group of people around me burst into applause and cheering. Several of them rushed forward to pat me on the back, hug me, and shake my hand.

'Thank you so much!' Arshan said, smiling happily. 'We've been so worried about this City Council thing. It's the first real challenge to what we've been doing here. We . . . we've come to enjoy this treasure hunting of ours, and we . . . well . . . I think we'd be as lost as the treasure is, if the council shut us down.'

'And we're not expecting you to do this for nothing,' Farzad added. 'Tell him, Pop!'

'If you'll accept it, we want to give you one per cent of the treasure,' Arshan said.

'If you find it,' I smiled.

'*When* we find it,' several voices corrected me.

'*When* you find it,' I agreed.

'Now, how about some more daal roti?' Jaya asked.

'And some chicken pieces,' Zaheera suggested.

'And a nice egg and curry sandwich,' Anahita offered, 'with a long glass of raspberry.'

'No, no, thank you,' I said quickly, stepping up and away from the table. 'I'm still completely full. Maybe next time.'

'*Definitely* next time,' Anahita said.

'Sure, definitely.'

'I'll see you out,' Farzad said, as I made my way to the long curtain closing off the front of the house. The whole group walked with us to the door.

I said my goodbyes, shaking hands and exchanging hugs, and stepped through the vestibule to the street beyond with Farzad.

A monsoon shower had soaked the street, but the heavy clouds had passed, and bright sunshine steamed the moisture from every mirrored surface.

Somehow, that first glimpse of the street seemed strange and unfamiliar, as if the weird megacosm of catwalks and crawlspaces in the gigantic bell-chamber of Farzad's house was the real world, and the gleaming, steaming street beyond was the illusion.

'I . . . ah . . . I hope my mixed-up family didn't freak you out,' Farzad muttered.

'Not at all.'

'You don't think, you know, it's a bit . . . *crazy, na?* What we're doing?'

'Everybody's searching for something. And from what I can see, you're all happy.'

'We are,' he agreed quickly.

'What kind of crazy person doesn't like happy?'

Impulsively, the young Parsi reached out and hugged me stiffly.

'You know, Lin,' he said, as we parted from the hug, 'there is actually something else I wanted to ask you.'

'Something else, yet?'

'Yes. You know, if you ever get the phone number of that girl, that beautiful girl with the loveliness in her eyes, that Divya, the one we met outside the police station this morning, I –'

'No.'

'No?'

'No.'

163

'Really no?'

'No.'

'But —'

'No,' I said gently, smiling at his puzzled frown.

He shook his head, turned, and walked back inside the building, the hive, the home. I faced the sun and stood for a while on the rain-scented street.

Money's a drug too, of course, but I wasn't worried for Farzad's extended family. They weren't hooked. Not yet. They'd torn their homes apart, true enough, but they'd replaced them with a common space of sharing. They'd turned their lives upside down, but it was an adventure: a voyage within themselves. They made sense of the dream they lived. It was still fun, for them, and I liked them very much for it.

I was standing, with my face in the sunlight, looking calm, very calm, and crying, somewhere inside. Sometimes the sight of what you lost, reflected in another love, is too much: too much of what was, and isn't any more.

Family, home: little words that rise like atolls in earthquakes of the heart. Loss, loneliness: little words that flood the valleys of alone.

In the island of the present, Lisa was slipping away, and a spell had been cast by the mention of a name: Karla. Karla.

It's a foolish thing to try to love, when the one you really love, the one you're born to love, is lost somewhere in the same square circle of a city. It's a desperate, foolish thing to try to love someone at all. Love doesn't try: love is immediate, and inescapable. The mention of Karla's name was fire, inside, and my heart wouldn't stop reminding me.

We were castaways, Karla and I, because we were cast out, both of us. Lisa and all the other bright people we loved, or tried to love, were volunteers, sailing to the Island City on dreams. Karla and I crawled onto the sand from ships we'd sunk ourselves.

I was a broken thing. I was a lonely, broken thing. Maybe Karla was, too, in her own way.

I looked at the domed house: separate entrances on the outside, joined lives on the inside. Whether they found the treasure or not, it was already that marvel, that miracle, an answered prayer.

I turned to the storm-faded sunlight again, and rejoined the world of exiles that was my home.

CHAPTER SIXTEEN

I SWUNG THE BIKE AWAY FROM FARZAD'S HOUSE and into the wide, divided boulevard that followed the Island City coast north. Densely packed, sodden rainclouds closed in overhead, darkening the street.

I began to pass a wide, sheltered inlet, and slowed down.

Long wooden fishing boats painted vivid blue, red and green had been dragged onto the shore for maintenance work. The fishermen's simple huts leaned into one another, their plastic sheet coverings secured to the corrugated roofs against storm winds by bricks and pieces of broken concrete.

Nets were strung between wooden poles. Men worked on them, threading spools of nylon through holes and woven loops. Children played on the sand, defying the gathering rainstorm, and chased one another between the boats and webs of netting.

From dawn, the little bay was a small but important part of the local fishing community. After midnight it was a small but important part of the local smuggling community, who used fast boats to bring in cigarettes, whiskey, currencies and drugs.

Every time I passed the sandy beach I scanned it, looking for faces I knew, and signs of illicit trade. I had no personal interest: Farid the Fixer administered the bay, and the profits and opportunities were his. It was professional curiosity that drew my eye.

All of us in the black market knew every place in South Bombay where crime flourished, and all of us sent a discreet, searching eye into them, every time we passed. *We began in caves and dark places*, Didier once said, *and we criminals still miss them terribly*.

I let my eyes glance back to the wide divided road, and saw three motorcycles pass me on the other side. They were Scorpions. The man riding in the centre was Danda. I recognised one other as

165

Hanuman, the big man who'd given me a professional beating in the warehouse.

I stopped my bike, shifted into neutral gear, and adjusted the rear-view mirror until I could see them. They'd stopped at a traffic signal, some way in the distance behind me. As I watched in the mirror, they talked, argued, but then swung their bikes around and came after me. I sighed, and hung my head for a moment.

I didn't want to fight them, but I was in my own area, and I didn't want to lead them into any of the Company operations. And too proud to run, I didn't want to let them chase me into the arms of my Company friends, only a few streets away.

Kicking the bike into gear, I let out the clutch, rapped the throttle, and spun the bike around in a tight circle. Gunning the engine, I accelerated toward the oncoming Scorpions, on the wrong side of the divided road.

I had nothing to lose. There were three of them, and if the charge didn't go well for me, I was in trouble anyway. I'd come off motorcycles before, and preferred to take my chances with an accident than a massacre. And my bike was in everything with me, all the way, as I was with her.

They must've had something to lose, or less loyal motorcycles: at the last moment they turned their bikes aside.

Two of them rattled away into spiralling arcs, as they tried to keep their bikes under control. The third bike spun out, crashing into a slide against a wall at the side of the road.

I braked hard, whirling through a half-turn, one boot sliding on the wet road, and threw my bike onto the side-stand, cutting the engine with the kill-switch.

The fallen rider struggled to his feet. It was Danda, and me with no aftershave. I met him with left and right punches that threw him backwards onto the ground.

The other Scorpions let their bikes fall, and ran at me. I felt bad for their bikes.

Ducking, weaving and throwing punches where I could, I battled the two Scorpions on the side of the road, beside the tumbled scatter of their motorcycles. Cars slowed on the road as they passed, but none stopped.

Recovering from the blows, Danda ran at us. He stumbled past his friends and into me, grasping at my vest to steady himself.

I lost my footing on the wet road and fell backwards. Danda landed on top of me, growling like an animal.

He was burrowing his head in next to mine, trying to bite me. I felt his mouth against my neck, the wetness of his tongue, and the blunt nub of his head, as he strained to get close enough to put his teeth on my throat.

His fingers were locked in a clutch of my vest. I couldn't throw him off. The other two Scorpions kicked at me, trying to land blows in the gaps between Danda's body and mine. They missed, and kicked Danda a couple of times. He didn't seem to notice.

I hadn't been hurt, or even properly hit by anyone. I could feel my two knives pressing against my back on the ground. I had a policy. I never drew the knives unless the other man was armed, or if it became a question of life or death.

I managed to roll over, wrestled away Danda's grip on my vest, and stood up quickly. I should've stayed down. Hanuman was behind me. He wrapped an arm around my throat from behind. His powerful arm began to choke off my air.

Danda rushed at me again, trying to burrow his head in close. He was a biter. I knew one in prison: a man whose anger suddenly became biting, until pieces were missing from anyone he attacked. A victim knocked his teeth out, leaving the rest of us in peace, and I was thinking of doing the same to Danda.

He was pressed up close against me, his head tucked in under Hanuman's arm, his teeth against my arm. I couldn't hit him in any place that might make him let go.

I reached up, closed my fingers around Danda's ear, and ripped at it hard. I felt the whole flap of his ear give way, tearing itself from the side of his head. When he stopped biting, I stopped ripping.

He screamed, hurling himself backwards, clutching at the bloody wound.

Shifting my hand around, I tried to shove it between Hanuman's body and mine. I wanted to reach one of my knives, or one of his balls; either one would do.

The third man rushed at me. In his fury, he began to slap at my head, standing too close. I kicked him in the balls. He fell as if he'd been shot.

I closed my hand around the hilt of my knife, as darkness closed a hand around my throat. The knife was free. I tried to stab the big man in the leg. I missed. The knife slid away to the side.

167

I tried again. I missed. Then the blade found flesh, a small cut on the outer edge of Hanuman's thigh. He flinched.

It was enough to get a bearing. I struck again and rammed the blade into the meat of his thigh. The big man lurched suddenly, and I lost my grip on the knife.

The arm didn't weaken. I'd followed my training, turning my chin into the crook of his elbow to lessen the choking effect. It was no use. I was going under.

A voice, blurred and rumbling, seemed to be calling my name. I twisted my head against the locked muscle and bone of Hanuman's arm. I heard a voice.

'Look away, now, boyo,' it said.

I saw something, a fist, coming at me from the sky. It was huge, that fist, as big as the world. But just when it should've smashed into my face it struck somewhere else, somewhere so close that I felt the shudder of it. And again it struck, and again.

And the arm around my neck released its grip, as Hanuman fell to his knees and flopped forward, his head made of lead.

I rolled and stood, shaping up, my fists close to my face, coughing and breathing hard. I turned to look around me. Concannon was standing near the fallen Hanuman, his arms folded.

He smiled at me, and then nodded his head in a little warning.

I turned quickly. It was Danda, all blood-streaked teeth, blood-streaked eyes, and blood-streaked ear. And me with no aftershave.

He swung a wild punch trying to knock me out. He missed. I snapped a fist at the gash where the ragged flap of his ear was hanging by a tongue-tip of skin. He screamed, and it rained. Sudden rain spilled and splashed on us.

Danda ran, clutching at the side of his head, rain running red into his shirt. I turned to see Concannon swinging a kick at the other departing Scorpion. The man yelped, and joined Danda, stumbling toward a stand of taxis.

Hanuman groaned, wakened by the rain. He crawled to his knees, stood unsteadily, and realised that he was alone. He hesitated for a moment.

I turned to look at Concannon quickly. The Irishman was grinning widely, all clenched teeth.

'Oh, Lord,' he said softly. 'Please make this man too stupid to run away.'

Hanuman lurched away, limping after his friends.

My knife was lying in the rain, still bleeding into the bitumen. Some way down the wide road, the Scorpions tumbled into a taxi as it sped away from the rank. I picked up the knife, cleaned it, closed it and slid it into the scabbard.

'Fuckin' grand fight!' Concannon said, slapping me on the shoulder. 'Let's get stoned.'

I didn't want to, but I owed him that, and more.

'Okay.'

There was a chai shop beneath a very large tree, close to where we stood. I pushed my bike under the shelter of the tree. Accepting a rag from the chai stall owner, I dried the bike off. When the job was done, I began to walk back to the road.

'Where the fuck are you goin'?'

'I'll be back in a minute.'

'We're havin' a civilised cup of fuckin' tea here, you Australian barbarian.'

'I'll be back in a minute.'

The abandoned Scorpion motorcycles were still lying in the rain by the side of the road, leaking petrol and oil. I picked them up, stood them on their stands in the cover of the stone wall, and returned to Concannon as the tea arrived.

'Lucky for you I came along,' he said, sipping at a glass of chai.

'I was doin' okay.'

'The fuck you were,' he laughed.

I looked at him. When a man's right, he's right.

'The fuck I was,' I laughed. 'You really are one mad Irish mother-fucker. What are you doing here, anyway?'

'My favourite hash shop used to be near here,' he said, jerking his thumb over his shoulder in the direction of Cuffe Parade. 'But somebody threw a fella off a building next door, and he landed right on top of the shop. And on top of Shining Patel, the owner.'

'You don't say.'

'The upside is that a notorious singer was also hit, which saved me quite a bit. I used to pay him, regularly. It was the only way I could get him to stop singin'. Where was I?'

'You were telling me what you're doing here.'

'Oh, so ya think I was followin' ya? Is that it?' Concannon asked.

'You must have a mighty high opinion of yourself, boyo. I'm just here buyin' hash.'

'Uh-huh.'

Some time passed. It was a strangely brooding silence between men, brooding in strangely different directions.

'Why did you help me?'

He looked at me with an expression that seemed genuinely hurt.

'And why the fuck would one white man not help another white man, in a fuckin' heathen place like this?'

'There you go again.'

'Alright, alright,' he said quickly, putting a hand on my knee to calm me down. 'I know you've got a soft heart. I know you're a compassionate sort. That's the beauty of ya, and there it is. You've even got compassion for motorcycles, may God have pity on you. But you don't like my plain talk. You don't like it when a man calls a spade a heathen, or a faggot a mincer.'

'I think we're done here, Concannon.'

'Hear me out, man. I know it offends your sensibilities. I understand that. I truly do. I don't *like* that about you, and I don't respect it. I'll be straight up about that. You can't respect kindness. Not really. You know what I'm talkin' about. You've done time behind the wall, on the other side of things, as I have. But you're a compassionate man, even though you're more like me than you think.'

'Concannon –'

'Wait. I'm not finished. Compassion's a very strange thing. It comes from deep inside. People know it when they see it, because you can't fake it. I know. I've tried. I was terrible at it. I got sick, when I tried. I had to go back to being a genuine, uncaring cunt, just to get well again. It's genuine, see, even being an uncaring cunt, and I'm drawn to genuine things, even if I don't like them. Do you see what I mean?'

'You don't know me at all,' I said, meeting his eye.

'Well, that's where you're wrong,' he smiled. 'I've been in Bombay for a while, you know. A few days after I got here, I heard your name in a conversation of unsavoury types at an opium den. Then I heard it again, twice in quick succession. At first, I thought it was *two* foreign fellas they were talkin' about, until I figured out that Lin and Shantaram were one and the same bad-mannered miscreant. You.'

'So you *were* following me.'

'I didn't say that. What I said was that I got intrigued. I started asking about you. I made it my business to get to know people you know, and people you do business with. I even know your girlfriend.'

'What?'

'She didn't tell ya that she met me?'

He grinned. I was beginning not to like that grin.

'I wonder why she didn't tell you? Maybe she likes me.'

'What the fuck are you talking about?'

'It's no big deal,' he said. 'I met her at an art exhibition.'

My raised eyebrow provoked him.

'Oh, *what*? Because I'm a big lump of a Northern Irish potato-muncher, I can't be interested in art? Is *that* it?'

'Get to the point.'

'There *is* no point, boyo. I met Lisa – that's her name, right? – at an exhibition. We talked, that's all.'

'Why?'

'Look, I didn't even know she was your girlfriend, until one of her friends mentioned your name, then I put two-and-you together, so to speak. I swear.'

'Keep away from her, Concannon.'

'Why? She seemed to like me. I think we hit it off, a little bit. I certainly liked her. You'll have to let her go, one of these days, but I'm sure you already know that, don't you?'

'That's it,' I said, standing.

'Wait a minute!' he implored, standing with me and putting a hand gently on my arm. 'Please. I don't want to fight you, man. I didn't . . . I mean . . . I'm not tryin' to upset you. It's just my way. I know it's fucked up. I really do. But I don't know any other way to be. It's like I said before, about you. Even if you don't like it, you have to see that it's genuine. This is what me being genuine looks like. I truly don't mean to hurt your feelings. And I truly would like to talk.'

I resisted, staring back at him and trying to read his eyes. The pupils were tiny: pinpoints vanishing in an ice-blue tide. I looked away.

On the road nearby, a traffic warden's truck pulled up beside the Scorpion gang motorcycles. Leaping from the back, the team of lifters dragged the motorcycles to the side of the truck, then hoisted them onto the back, cramming them up against others that had been seized for parking illegally.

Concannon followed my gaze as I watched the operation.

'If I hadn't come along when I did,' he said softly, 'it might've been your dead body bein' thrown onto the back of a truck.'

He was right. I didn't like him, and I was pretty sure that he was crazy. But he'd stepped in at exactly the right time, and he'd saved me.

I sat down again. Concannon called for two more glasses of chai. Working quickly, his thick fingers made a small joint.

'Will you smoke with me?'

I took it and puffed it alight as he held the match in the lantern of his cupped hands. After a time, I passed the joint back to him.

'Seein' as how you're always gettin' so offended, and jumpin' up, and wantin' to fight with me or run off somewhere, I'll come straight to the point,' he said, exhaling a stream of grey-blue smoke.

'The point of what?'

'I'm startin' a new gang, and I want you to join me.'

It was my turn to laugh.

'What's so funny?'

'How about . . . *why?*'

'Why a gang?' he asked, passing back the joint. 'The usual. So we can buy guns, do a little menace and mayhem, scare people into giving us truc.kloads of money, spend the truckloads of money, and die in the effort.'

'Dying in the effort? That's your sales pitch?'

Just then a man named Jibril, a horse-breeder from the stables in the nearby slum, approached me. I stood to greet him.

He was a gentle man, shy and a little uncomfortable speaking with human beings, but talkative and loving when dealing with his horses.

His eldest daughter had developed a fever a few weeks before that day, and had become desperately ill. Jibril called me, and agreed to have the girl screened via wide-spectrum viral toxicity.

I'd paid for the testing at a private clinic, and the tests had revealed that the girl was suffering from leptospirosis, a sometimes fatal disease carried in the urine of rats. Because it had been detected early, the girl was responding well to treatment.

Holding my hand between his, Jibril assured me that his daughter was feeling much better, and invited me to take tea with him and his family in their home.

I thanked him in return, and invited him to join us for a glass of chai. He declined, apologising for the refusal, and hurried off to an appointment with a grain merchant who supplied feed for his horses.

'You see what I mean?' Concannon said, when I sat down again. 'These people *like* you. They don't like me. And I don't want them to. I don't want to eat their food. I hate their bloody food. I don't want to watch their movies. I don't want to speak their fuckin' language. But *you* do. You understand them. You communicate with them, and they respect you for it. Think about it. We'll be unbeatable. We could take over this part of the city, you and me.'

'Why would we want to do that?' I laughed.

'Because we *can*,' he said, leaning in close to me.

Because We Can: the motto of power, since the idea of power over others was born in our kind.

'That's not a reason, that's an excuse.'

'Look around you! Ninety-nine per cent of people are just doin' what they're told. But you and me, we're in the one per cent. We take what we want, while the rest of them, they take what they're *given*.'

'People rise up.'

'Aye, they do,' he agreed, his pale blue eyes gleaming. 'From time to time. And then the one per cent take all their privilege back from them, and usually their pride and dignity for good measure, and they go back to being the slaves they're born to be.'

'You know,' I sighed, returning his stare. 'It's not just that I disagree with what you're saying, it's that I actually despise it.'

'That's the beauty of it!' he cried, slapping his thighs with both palms.

He read my mystified frown for a moment, and then continued in a softer tone.

'Look . . . me Ma, she died when I was just a baby. Dad tried his best, but he couldn't manage. There was five of us kids, all under ten years old, and he was a sick man. He sent us to these orphanages. We were Protestants. The girls went to Protestant places, but me little brother and me, there was no place for us, and we ended up with the Catholics.'

He paused for a while, allowing his gaze to fall to his feet. The rain squalled again, striking the plastic awning of the chai shop with the sound of drummers at a wedding.

His foot began to scrape away at the earth slowly, his running shoe leaving a pattern of scrolls and whorls in the muddy ground.

'There was this priest, you see.'

He looked up. Fractal patterns in the irises of his ice-blue eyes glittered around the pinpoint pupils. The whites of his eyes were suddenly red, as if burned by the sea.

'I don't talk about this,' he said, lapsing into a leaden silence again.

His eyes filled with tears. He clenched his jaw, swallowing hard, and willing the tears away. But they fell, and he turned his head.

'You're a fuckin' cunt, you are!' Concannon snapped, wiping his eyes with the back of his hand.

'*Me?*'

'Yeah, fuckin' *you*! This is what all your nice reasonableness does to people. You turn 'em into weak cunts. That's the first time I've let a tear fall in many a long year, and it's the first time I've talked about that fuckin' priest in longer still. And that's . . . that's why we'd be so good together, don't you see?'

'Not . . . really.'

'I got out of that orphanage when I was sixteen. By my eighteenth birthday I'd killed six men. One of them was that fuckin' priest. Shoulda seen how he begged for his life, the miserable sick thing.'

He paused again, his mouth pressed into a bitter wrinkle. I was hoping that he'd stop talking. He didn't.

'I forgave him, you know, before I killed him.'

'Concannon, I —'

'Will you not hear me out, man?'

He seemed desperate.

'Alright.'

'I never forgave anyone, after that,' he began, brightening with violent recollection. 'I was a full ranked volunteer with the UVF. And I went on breakin' heads, shootin' Catholics in the knees, sendin' pieces of the IRA cunts we captured to their widows, and a lot more. We worked together with the cops and the army. Unofficial like, of course, but we had a fuckin' green light. Hit squads, killin' and maimin' on demand, no questions asked.'

'Concannon —'

'Then it all fell apart. It got too hot. *I* got too hot. *Too violent*, they said. It was a fuckin' war. How can you be *too violent* for a war? But they sent me out. Scotland first, then London. I fuckin' hated the place. Then I went on the road, and ended up here.'

'Look, Concannon —'

'I know,' he said quickly. 'I know what you're thinkin' and I know what you're gonna say. And it's true. I can't deny it. I like hurtin' people who deserve it. I'm a twisted cunt. Lucky for me, there's a lot of twisted girls out there, so I'm happy bein' twisted. But you're not like that. You have your principles. Don't you get it? You're the *talk softly*, and I'm *the big stick*. You look 'em in the eyes, do business with 'em, and shake their hands. I chop their hands off, if they disobey.'

'Chopping people's hands off. There's a leap forward.'

'I've given it a lotta thought,' he said alarmingly. 'That's why I've been tryin' to pull you away from that French mincer.'

'You just don't know when to quit, do you?'

'No, wait, hear me out. It's . . . it's like . . . if you strip a religion down to its most basic parts, the parts that make it work so well and last for hundreds and hundreds of years, it boils down to this — nice words and the fear of horrible punishments that never end. You and me. You can't beat a combination like that. Popes and heathen mullahs have got fat on it for centuries.'

I let out a long sigh, and put my palms on my knees, preparing to stand. He reached out to put a hand on my wrist. The grip of his hard fingers was fierce, and there was enormous strength in it.

'That's not advised,' I said.

He released his grip on my arm.

'Sorry, I . . . just . . . *think* about it,' he said, the grin leaning in through the doorway of his eyes again. 'I'll talk to you in a few days. We won't be alone in this, if you throw in with me. I'm already talkin' with others, and there's plenty of them that's interested, make no mistake. Think about it. That's not too much to ask for savin' your *talk softly* arse today, is it? I'd like to have you in this with me. I'll need someone to talk to. Someone I trust. Just think about it, that's all I ask.'

I rode away, leaving him standing there under the blue plastic awning. I didn't think about his offer, but I did think about him, that afternoon, as I made the rounds of cafés and bars we used as passport drops.

I talked with my contacts. I listened to gangster street music: gossip, slander, lies and denunciation. Always funny. But in every idle moment my thoughts returned to Concannon, and to those tears he resented so bitterly, but failed to stop.

What dream, what hope, what despair drives us to the things we do, just to desert us when the deed is done? What hollow things are they, motive and reason, born at night to fade so quickly in the sunlight of consequence? What we do in life lives on inside us, long after ambition and fear lie frosted and opaqued on forgotten shores. What we do in life, more than what we think or say, is what we are.

Concannon was running into crime, and I was already running away from it. For too long I'd done things because the fear of capture became a mirror, a face in the water, not really me, and I absolved myself of my own sins. But the waters were stirred, and the face I'd always put on the things that I did was blurred, and vanishing.

CHAPTER SEVENTEEN

I WAITED FOR LISA OUTSIDE THE MAHESH HOTEL, enjoying the city. It had rained intermittently but heavily through the afternoon, yet the early evening air was hot and dry beneath the brooding sky.

Occasional waves struck at the low sea wall, crashing up and over to splash across half the wide street. Children courted the waves, running from spray to spray, while couples skipped away.

Hopeful carriage drivers slowed beside the strollers, trying to entice them into their rickety, high-wheeled carts. Peanut sellers wandered among the walkers, fanning the glowing coals they carried in baskets around their necks. Smoke from the little fires, filled with the flavour of roasted peanuts, drifted among the strollers, temptation turning their heads.

The whole city, washed clean by the heavy rains, was more fragrant than usual. The cloud-soaked sky locked in scents of food cooking on hundreds of small street stalls, *bhel puri*, *pav bhaji*, *pakodas*, and sweet pungencies from *paan* sellers, incense traders, and the frangipani garlands being sold at every traffic signal.

I counted thoughts on perfumed strands, and then I heard her voice.

'A penny,' Lisa said.

I turned.

'They don't make pennies any more,' I said, pulling her close to me and kissing her.

'Are you forgetting this is Bombay?' she asked, not resisting me. 'People get arrested for kissing in public.'

'Maybe they'll put us in the same prison cell,' I suggested, holding her close.

'I . . . don't think so,' she laughed.

'Then I'll escape, and come bust you out.'

177

'And then what?'

'And then I'll bring you back here, on an evening just like this, and kiss you again, just like this.'

'Wait a minute,' she said, studying my face. 'You've been fighting again.'

'Are you kidding?'

'Come off it. You're trying to distract me! That's a dirty trick, buster.'

'What?'

'Jesus, Lin! Fighting again? What the fuck?'

'Lisa, it's cool. I'm fine. And I'm right here, with you.'

I kissed her face.

'We better go,' she said, as she frowned out of the kiss, 'or we'll miss him.'

'Miss who?'

'Miss *whom*, writer,' she said. 'You'll find out, soon enough.'

She led me on the short walk from the seafront to the promenade that surrounded the nearby Air India building. The offices were closed, but the dim night-lights in the ground-floor reception area revealed the desks and doorways within.

When we reached a locked glass door, close to the back of the building, Lisa signalled me to wait. She glanced around nervously at the wedge of street we could see from the rear door, but there was no-one in sight.

'So . . . what are we —'

'We're waiting,' she interrupted me.

'Waiting . . . for?'

'For *him*.'

There was a flicker of light within the building. A security guard carrying a torch approached the door. He opened it with a key on a heavy chain, and held the door open for us. He urged us to enter quickly, and then locked the door again behind us.

'This way,' he said. 'Follow me closely.'

Weaving his way along a series of corridors and between rows of silent desks, he brought us to a service elevator at the rear of the building.

'Emergency lift,' he said, smiling happily. 'After stop at top, walk two floors to roof. My bonus, please.'

Lisa handed him a roll of notes. The guard saluted us, pressed the button to open the doors of the elevator, and waved us inside.

'So, we're gonna rob the Air India company,' I said as we ascended in the lift. 'And ten minutes ago, you were worried about a public kiss.'

'I wasn't worried,' she laughed. 'And we're not here to rob the place. We're here for a private party.'

The doors opened on a storage floor, with walls of filing cabinets and open shelves stacked with dusty folders.

'Ah, the Kafka Room. Can't wait to see the menu.'

'Come on!' Lisa said, rushing to the stairwell. 'We have to hurry.'

Taking the steps two at a time, she led me up the stairs. At the top she hesitated, with her hand on the emergency release bar of the closed door.

'I hope he remembered to leave this door unlocked,' she said breathlessly, and then pushed on the bar.

We stepped through onto the roof of the building. It was a vast area, with several small metal huts on the periphery.

A huge structure towered ten metres over us, braced by heavy steel girders. It was the illuminated logo of the Air India company: a stylised archer, with a drawn bow, circled by a great disc.

The gigantic figure rose from a central support pylon, fixed to a rotating steel table, which was in turn supported by an array of girders and cables.

Like every other Mumbaikar, I'd seen the huge sign rotating above the Air India building hundreds of times, but standing so close to it, so high above the rolling sea, was a different truth.

'*Damn!*'

'We made it in time,' Lisa grinned.

'There's a *bad* time for this? What a view!'

'Wait,' she said, staring up at the archer. 'Wait.'

There was a whirring, grinding sound, as if a generator had started up nearby. The throb of an electric turbine began, building from a soft purr to a persistent whine. Then the click and stutter of a condenser, or several of them, chattered from somewhere very close, at the base of the immense sign.

Suddenly, in one burst of flickering crimson colour, the great circular logo lit up, bathing the whole space in blood-red light. Moments later, the crimson archer began to rotate on its pylon axis.

Lisa was dancing little excited steps, her arms wide.

'Isn't it great?'

She was laughing happily.

'It's brilliant. I love it.'

We watched the huge wheel of scarlet light turn for some time, and then shifted to face the open sea. The clouds had swollen together to fill the whole of heaven with black brooding. Distant lightning strikes forked through the darkness: ribs of cloud, rolling and shifting on the bed of night.

'You like it?' she asked, leaning in beside me as we watched the sky and sea.

'I love it. How'd you come up with it?'

'I was here a couple weeks ago with Rish, from the gallery. He was thinking about making a full-size copy of the Air India archer for a new Bombay exhibition, and he invited me to come take a look. When we got here, he changed his mind. But I liked it so much up here that I cultivated the guard, and bribed him to let us come up here, you and me.'

'You cultivated the guard, huh?'

'I'm a cultivated girl.'

For a time we gazed at the rejoicing sea, far below. It was a dangerous view, irresistible, but my thoughts slithered back to that afternoon, and Concannon.

'Did you meet a tall Irishman named Concannon, a while back?'

She thought for a moment, one of my favourite frowns curling her upper lip.

'Fergus? Is that his name?'

'I only know him as Concannon,' I said. 'But you can't miss this guy. Tall, heavyset, but athletic, kinda rangy, a boxer, with sandy hair and a hard eye. He said he met you, at an exhibition.'

'Yeah, Fergus, that's his name. I only spoke to him for a while. Why?'

'Nothing. I was just wondering why he was at the exhibition. I don't figure him for an art lover.'

'We had lots of men at that show,' she said thoughtfully. 'It was our most successful show so far. The kind of show that brings people who don't normally go to galleries.'

'What kind of a show?'

'It was all about the broken lives that spin out from bad or troubled relationships between fathers and sons. It was called *Sons of the Fathers*.

There was a big piece about it in the paper. Ranjit gave us great coverage. It pulled in a crowd. I told you all about it. Don't you remember?'

'No,' I replied. 'I've been in Goa, Lisa, and you didn't tell me about it.'

'Really? I was sure I did. Funny, huh?'

'Not really.'

Sons of the Fathers. Was it that phrase, those words, *Sons*, *Fathers*, glimpsed on a poster that had drawn Concannon to the exhibition? Or had he followed me, and then followed Lisa to the gallery, using the show as a pretext to meet her and talk to her?

Acid memories had burned his eyes, when he spoke to me. I had memories of my own. I woke too often still chained to a wall of the past, being tortured by the ghosts of men whose faces I'd already begun to forget.

I turned my head to look at Lisa's gentle profile: the deep-set, hooded eyes; the fine, small nose; the sculpted flow of her long, graceful chin; the half-smile that almost always played in the stream of her lips. The wind was picking up, lifting the blonde curls of her hair into a feathered halo.

She was wearing a loose, knee-length black dress with a high, stiff collar, but no sleeves or shoulders. She'd kicked off her sandals, and her feet were bare. The only jewellery she wore was a thin necklace of irregular turquoise beads.

She read my face, frowning a little, as she made her way back into my mind.

'Do you know what today is?' she asked, laughing as my eyes widened with alarm. 'It's our anniversary.'

'But, we got together in —'

'I'm talking about the day I let myself love you,' she said, her smile showing how much she was enjoying my confusion. 'This is exactly the day, two years ago, that you stopped your bike beside me on the causeway, a week after Karla got married, when I was waiting for the rain to stop.'

'I was hoping you forgot that. I was pretty high, that day.'

'You were,' she agreed, the smile filling her eyes. 'You saw me standing with a bunch of people under the shelter of a shop. You pulled up, and asked me if I wanted a ride. But the rain was pouring down like mad —'

'It was the start of a flood, a big one. I was worried that you might not make it home.'

'Pouring in buckets, it was. And there's you, sitting on your bike in the rain, soaked through to your bones, offering me, dry and comfortable, a ride home. I laughed so hard.'

'Okay, okay —'

'Then you got off your bike and started to dance, right there in front of the whole crowd.'

'So stupid.'

'Don't say that! I loved it!'

'So stupid,' I repeated, shaking my head.

'I think you should make a promise to the universe that you'll always dance in the rain, at least once, if you're in Bombay during monsoon.'

'I don't know about the universe, but I'll make a pact with *you*. I hereby promise that I'll always dance in the rain at least once, in every one of my monsoons.'

The storm was coming in fast. Lightning shocked the theatre of the sea. Heartbeats later, the first thunder smashed the clouds.

'That's a big storm coming in.'

'Come here,' she said, taking my hand.

She led me to an open space beneath the slowly turning wheel of the crimson archer. Ducking into an alcove, she fetched a basket and brought it out.

'I paid the watchman to leave it up here for us,' she explained, opening the basket to reveal a large blanket, a bottle of champagne, and a few glasses.

She handed me the bottle.

'Open us up, Lin.'

While I peeled away the foil wrapper and twisted the wire tether, she spread out the blanket, holding it in place against the gathering wind with spare tiles she found on the roof.

'You really thought this out,' I said, popping the cork on the champagne.

'You don't know the half of it,' she laughed. 'But this is a special place. When I came up here with Rish, I took a damn good look around. This is one of the only open spaces in Bombay, maybe *the* only space, where nobody can see you from any window, anywhere.'

She pulled her dress up over her head, and tossed it aside. She was naked. She picked up the glasses and held them out. I filled them. I put the bottle aside, and held my glass close to hers for a toast.

'What shall we drink to?'

'How 'bout getting your goddamn clothes off?'

'Lisa,' I said, as serious as the storm. 'We've gotta talk.'

'Yeah, we do,' she said. '*After* we drink. I'll make the toast.'

'Okay.'

'To fools in love.'

'To fools in love.'

She drank her glass down quickly, and then threw it over her shoulder. It shattered against a stone buttress.

'I've always wanted to do that,' she said happily.

'You know, we should talk about –'

'No,' she said.

She unfastened my clothes and pulled them off. When we were both naked she picked up another glass and refilled it.

'One more toast,' she said, 'then we talk.'

'Okay. To the rain,' I suggested. 'Inside and out.'

'To the rain,' she agreed. 'Inside and out.'

We drank.

'Lisa –'

'No. One more drink.'

'You said –'

'The last one didn't do it.'

'Didn't do what?'

'Didn't wake the Dutchman.'

She filled the glasses again.

'No toast this time,' she said, drinking half her glass. 'Bottoms up.'

We drank. A second glass shattered in the shadows. She pushed me back onto the tethered blanket, but slipped away again, her body on the sky.

'Do you mind if I dance while we talk,' she said, beginning to sway, the wind happy in her hair.

'I'll try not to object,' I said, lying back to watch her, my hands clasped behind my head.

'This is another anniversary, of sorts,' she said dreamily.

'You know, there's a special place in hell for people who never forget birthdays or anniversaries.'

'This is one that starts tonight, two years after the *other* one started.'

'The other one?'

'Us,' she danced, twirling in a circle, her arms woven in the wind. 'The other us, that we used to be.'

'That we *used* to be?'

'That we used to be.'

'And when did we change?'

'Tonight.'

'We did?'

'Yes.'

'In the elevator, or on the stairs?'

She laughed and danced, her head moving to a beat only her arms and hips and legs could hear.

'I'm doing a rain dance,' she said, her hands already swimming through water. 'It has to rain tonight.'

I glanced up at the immense disc of the archer, rotating slowly, chained to the rock of the city with steel cables. Rain. Rain means lightning. The red archer looked like a very tempting lightning rod.

'It has to rain?'

'Oh, yeah,' she said, flopping at my feet and staring at me, her body supported on one arm. 'And it *will* now, soon.'

She picked up the champagne bottle, took a mouthful and kissed me, trickling the wine into my mouth in the bruised blossom of a kiss. Our lips parted.

'I want to have an open relationship,' she said.

'It can't get much more open than this,' I smiled.

'I want to be with other people.'

'Oh, *that* kind of open.'

'I think you should be with other people, too. Not all the time, of course. Not if we stay together. I don't think I'd like to see you in a permanent thing. But definitely sometimes. I could actually hook you up. I've got a friend who's really hot for you. She's so cute that I wouldn't mind doing a threesome.'

'*What?*'

'It would only take a word,' she said, staring into my eyes.

The storm was close. The wind smelled of the sea. I lifted my eyes to the sky. Pride has most of the anger, and humility most of the right.

184

I didn't have the right to tell her what to do, or what not to do. I didn't even have the right to ask her. We didn't have that kind of love.

'I don't have the right —'

'I want to be with you, if you want to love me,' she said, lying beside me, her hand on my chest. 'But I want us to be with other people as well.'

'You know, Lisa, you picked a pretty weird way to tell me this.'

'Is there a way that isn't weird?'

'Still . . .'

'I didn't know how you'd react,' she pouted. 'I still don't know. I thought, if you don't like it, this'll be the last time we make love. And if you do like it, this'll be the first time we make love as the new us, free to be what we want. Either way, it's a memorable anniversary.'

We looked at one another. Our eyes began to smile.

'You knew I'd completely love this stunt, didn't you?'

'Totally.'

'The whole Air India archer thing.'

'Totally.'

I leaned over her, smoothing the wind-strewn hair from her face.

'You're an amazing girl, Lisa. And I'm constantly amazed.'

She kissed me, her fingers vines around my neck.

'You know,' she murmured, 'I did some research.'

'You did?'

'Yeah, on how often this place gets hit by lightning. Do you want to know?'

I didn't care. I knew what was happening to us, but I didn't know where we were going.

The storm was on us. The sky connected. Rain filled our mouths with silver. She pulled me onto her, into her, locked her feet in the small of my back, and held me inside, tight, loose, and tight again, daring me to follow.

A waterfall of wind and rain drummed on my back. I put my forehead to hers, sheltering her face with mine, our eyes only lashes apart. The monsoon, flesh-warm, poured from my head and splashed up from the ground. We pressed our mouths together, breathing into one another, sharing air.

She rolled me over onto my back, holding me inside her, flattening her long fingers across my chest, her arms stiff.

A roar of thunder smashed new rain from sodden clouds. Water poured in rivulets from her hair and her breasts, running into my open mouth. Water began to fill the roof of the building, ebbing around us in a secret sea, high above the Island City.

Her fingers clawed. Her back arched, cat-fierce. She slid her hands from my chest, down along my body. Sitting upright, she locked me inside, and turned her face to the sky, her arms out wide.

A drum began to beat: a heavy footstep in a hall of memory, my heart. We were breaking apart. In that instant it was clear: what we had was all we ever were, or could be.

Lightning painted the water around us on the roof. They turned above my head, Lisa and the storm and the wheel of Fate, and the whole world was red, blood red, even to that sea the sky, that sea the sky.

PART FOUR

CHAPTER EIGHTEEN

Ruling a criminal enterprise requires an instinct for fear, a flair for ruthless caprice, and a talent for herding your men into that lush minion-pasture between awe and envy. Running a criminal enterprise, on the other hand, is all hard work.

I woke early after the night of the red archer, feeling that an arrow had passed through me leaving a red emptiness inside. I was at my desk in the passport factory before nine.

Three hours of detailed work with Krishna and Villu brought my counterfeit passports up to date. After a call to my contact at the Bombay Municipal Corporation, asking him to deliver copies of the permit documents for Farzad's treasure-hunting family, I headed to the Colaba Causeway for a working lunch.

Most of the five-, four- and three-star hotels in South Bombay were within a three-kilometre radius of the Gateway of India monument. Ninety per cent of Bombay's tourists could be found within the same arc of the peninsula, along with ninety-five per cent of the illegal passport trade, and eighty-five per cent of the drug trafficking.

Most businesses in the south paid protection money, called *hafta*, meaning *a week*, to the Sanjay Company. The Company exempted the owners of seven restaurants and bars in the same area. The owners of those bars allowed touts, pimps, tourist guides, pickpockets, drug dealers and black market traders connected with the Sanjay Company to use their premises as convenient drop-off points for goods, documents and information.

My passport forgery and counterfeiting unit had to monitor those seven drop-off centres for usable documents. For the most part, that job fell to me. To keep enemies and potential rivals guessing, I changed the order of the bars and restaurants every day, rotating between them often enough to confuse any sense of routine.

I started, on that day, at the Trafalgar Restaurant, only a good knife's throw from Lightning Dilip's desk in the Colaba police station. At the door of the corner-facing restaurant, below the three steep steps leading inside, I paused to shake hands with a Memory Man named Hrishikesh.

Memory Men were a criminal sub-caste in those years: men who lacked the foolhardiness to risk prison time by actually committing crimes, but whose intelligence and prodigious memories allowed them to make a modest living, serving the fearless fools who did.

Taking up positions in high criminal traffic areas, such as the causeway, they made it their business to know the latest figures for the day's gold prices, the current black and white market exchange rates for six major currencies, the carat price for white diamonds, rubies, emeralds, and sapphires, and half-hour fluctuations in the price of every illicit drug, from cannabis to cocaine.

'What's up, Kesh?' I asked, shaking his hand.

'No problem, baba,' he grinned, raising his eyes to the sky for a moment. '*Ooperwale.*'

The word he'd used was a reference to God, and one of my favourites. More often used in the singular, *Ooperwala*, it could be roughly translated as *The Person Upstairs*. Used in the plural, the term meant *The People Upstairs*.

'*Ooperwale,*' I replied. 'Let's go.'

'Okay,' he said, becoming serious as he launched into his iterations of the latest prices and rates.

I only needed the gold and currency exchange rates, but I let Kesh run through the whole of his repertoire. I liked him, and admired the subtle genius that allowed him to hold hundreds of facts in his current memory, adjusting them as often as three times in a single day, without a decimal point of error.

Most gangsters held fringe dwellers like Kesh in contempt. I never understood it. The small-scale street outlaws were harmless people, surviving through cleverness and adapted skills in a hostile environment that sometimes didn't treat them well. I also had a soft spot for independent outlaws: men and women who refused to join the ranks of law-abiding citizens, no less resolutely than they rejected the violence of hardcore criminals.

When his recitation ended, I paid him twice the going rate for a

Memory Man's mantra, and he gave me a smile like sunlight streaming off the sea.

Inside the restaurant I sat with my back to a wall. I had a clear view of the street. A waiter nudged my shoulder with his belly. I ordered a vegetable sandwich and a coffee.

I didn't have to signal anyone: I only had to wait. I knew that the information network of the street was already at work. One or more of the endlessly drifting street guys roaming the tourist beat would've seen me park my motorcycle, talk with Kesh, and enter the restaurant. Word would already be spreading through neighbouring lanes and dens: *Linbaba is sitting at Trafalgar.*

Before I finished my sandwich, the first contact arrived. It was Billy Bhasu. Hesitating close to my table, he glanced around nervously, and spoke very softly.

'Hello, Mr Lin. My name is Billy Bhasu. I am working with Dennis, the Sleeping Baba. You might be remembering me?'

'Sit down. You're making the boss nervous.'

He glanced at the restaurant boss, leaning on the counter, his hand playing in the trays of change as if they were pebbles in a stream. Billy Bhasu sat down.

A waiter appeared immediately, slapping a grimy vinyl menu booklet in front of Billy. The rules in all the drop-off bars and restaurants were simple: no fighting or disturbances that might upset the civilians, and everyone buys lunch, whether they eat it or not.

I ordered tea and a takeaway sandwich parcel for Billy. When the waiter left us, Billy came to the point quickly.

'I have a chain,' he said, reaching into his pocket. 'Solid gold it is, with a picture locket attached.'

He put the gold locket and chain on the table. I picked it up, running my thumb over the links of the chain, and then prised open the locket. I found two photographs: a young man and a young woman, facing each other and smiling happily across the hinge of their little world: a world that had found its way into my hand.

'I don't take stolen goods, Billy.'

'What *stolen*, baba?' he demanded indignantly. 'This was a trade, a fair trade, the locket for dope. And good quality. Almost fifty per cent pure. All square and fair!'

I looked at the photographs of the young couple again. They were northern Europeans, bright-eyed and healthy; from the kind of social background that put perfect teeth in untroubled smiles. They looked about twenty years old.

'How much do you want?'

'Oh, baba,' he grinned, beginning the Indian bargaining ritual. 'That is for *you* to say, not me.'

'I'll give you five dollars American.'

'But,' he spluttered, 'it's much too *less*, for such a piece!'

'You said it was for *me* to say.'

'Yes, baba, but it is for *you* to say a *fair* price!'

'I'll give you sixty per cent of the gram weight price. Do you agree it's eighteen carat gold?'

'It's . . . it's maybe *twenty-two* carats, baba. No?'

'It's eighteen. Sixty per cent. Or try your luck with the Marwaris, at Zaveri Bazaar.'

'Oh, no, baba!' he said quickly. 'If I deal with the Marwaris, I'll end up owing *them* money. They're too smart. I'd rather deal with you. No offence.'

'None taken. Fifty per cent.'

'Done at sixty.'

I called the waiter, passed him the locket and chain, and told him to ask the manager to weigh it on his jewellery scale. The waiter slouched over to a desk, and handed over the chain.

Using a fine scale that he kept under the counter, the manager weighed the locket and chain, wrote the gram weight on a piece of paper, and handed them back to the waiter.

The waiter passed the paper to me, hefted the chain and locket in the bowl of his hand for a moment as if checking the accuracy of the scale, and then dropped them into my upturned palm.

I glanced at the figure on the paper, and then showed it to Billy Bhasu. He nodded. Using Kesh's figure for the current rate, I rounded the amount to the nearest ten rupees, and wrote the figure on the same sheet of paper, showing it to Billy. He nodded again.

'You know, baba,' he said, as he put away the money, 'I saw that Naveen Adair before, that Anglo detective fellow. He gave me a message, if I see you in any place today.'

'As it happens, I'm in any place right now.'

'Yes,' he replied earnestly. 'So, I can give you his message.'

There was a pause.

'Would you like another sandwich parcel, Billy?'

'Actually, yes, Linbaba. Jamal is waiting outside.'

I waved for another parcel.

'Are we good for the message, now?'

'Oh, yes. Naveen said, let me be exactly sure, *Tell Linbaba, if you see him, that I have nothing new about the man in the suit.*'

'That's it? That's the message?'

'Yes, baba. It's important, no?'

'Critical. Let me ask you something, Billy.'

'Yes, baba?'

'If I didn't buy your chain, were you gonna give me the message?'

'Of course, baba,' he grinned, 'but for more than just two sandwiches.'

The sandwich parcels arrived. Billy Bhasu put his hand on them.

'So . . . so now . . . I'll take my leave?'

'Sure.'

When he left the restaurant, I looked again at the photographs of the smiling young couple. I closed the locket, and dropped it into my shirt pocket.

For the next four hours, I worked my way through the other six drop-off restaurants and bars in my district, spending about forty minutes in each one.

It was an average day. I bought a passport, three pieces of jewellery, seven hundred and fifty US dollars in cash, an assortment of other currencies, and a fine watch.

That last item, in the last trade of the day, in the last of the bars, involved me in an angry dispute with two of the street guys.

The man who brought the watch to me, Deepak, settled the price quickly. It was a price far below the actual value of the watch, but far more than he could expect to receive from the professional buyers in the Fort area.

At the moment of the handover, a second man, Ishtiaq, entered the bar, shouting for a share of the money. Ishtiaq's strategy was simple: make a big enough fuss to force a concession from Deepak, before the latter had the chance to slip away in the crowded street.

In other circumstances I'd have taken my money back, shoved both men out of the bar, and forgotten about them. My long-standing relationship with the bar's owner was more important than any one transaction.

But when I'd put the watch to my ear, I'd heard the reassuring trip-click movement, twitching toward its rundown cycle: the mechanical heart beating its rhythm reward for the daily winding fidelity of its owner. It was, as it happened, my favourite watch.

Ignoring my instincts, I tried to placate Ishtiaq. The momentary weakness ignited impudence, and he shouted all the harder. Diners at other tables began to stare at us, and it wasn't a big place.

Speaking quickly, I soothed Ishtiaq, pulled some money from my pocket and paid him off. He snatched at the notes, snarled at Deepak, and left the bar. Deepak gave me an apologetic shrug, and slipped out onto the street.

I slid the metal bracelet of the watch over my hand, onto my wrist. I snapped the catch shut. It was a perfect fit. Then I looked up to see the manager and his waiters staring at me. The short story written in their eyes was clear: I'd lost face. Men in my position didn't placate street touts like Ishtiaq.

I glanced again at the watch on my wrist. My greed had weakened me. *Greed is human Kryptonite*, Karla once said to me, as she pocketed all of the commission we'd just made together on a deal.

I needed to work out, and swung the bike through traffic, heading for the mafia boxing gym at Ballard Pier.

The manager of the gym, Hussein, was a veteran gangster who'd lost an arm to a machete blow in a battle with another gang. His long, scarred face found its way into a biblical beard that rested on the prodigious mound of his chest. He was brave, kind, funny, tough, and a match for any of the young gangsters who trained at the gym. Every time I looked into his laughing, dangerous eyes I wondered what he and Khaderbhai must've been like: the young fighters who created a gang that became a mafia Company.

Let my enemy see the tiger, they used to say, *before he dies.*

There was no doubt that Hussein and Khaderbhai had shown the tiger many times, as they'd prowled the city, young and fearless, all those years before. And something of that striped menace lingered in the burnt-clay eyes of the gym master.

'*Wah, wah*, Linbaba,' he said, as I entered the gym. '*Salaam aleikum.*'

'*Wa aleikum salaam*, One Hussein.'

Because another Hussein joined Khaderbhai in those early years, and went on to hold a position on the Council, they were sometimes known as One Hussein and Two Hussein, for the number of arms they possessed.

'*Kya hal hain?*' *How are you going?*

'Busier than a one-armed man in a bar fight,' I replied in Hindi.

It was an old joke between us, but he laughed every time.

'How are you, One Husseinbhai?'

'Still swinging the punches, Linbaba. If you keep punching, you stay hard. If you stop the windmill, there's no flour.'

'You got that right.'

'Are you training full session, Lin?'

'No, One Husseinbhai, just loading the guns.'

Loading the guns was gangster slang for a workout that pumped the biceps and triceps in the same session of supersets.

'Damn good!' he laughed. 'Keep the guns loaded, yaar. You know the two rules of combat. Make sure they *know* they've been hit, and –'

'Make sure they *stay* hit,' I finished for him.

'*Jarur!*'

He handed me a towel as I walked past into the main training room. The gym, which at first had been a small, dirty space where large, dirty gangsters learned the arts of street fighting, had proven so popular with the young men of the Sanjay Company that it had been expanded to include the whole of the neighbouring warehouse.

In the foreground there was an assortment of weight-training equipment: benches, lat and rowing machines, incline and decline presses, squat bars, chin-up and dip bars, and stacks of heavy plates and dumbbells. Beyond that area, lined with mirrors, was the blood-stained boxing ring.

Further into the newly created space was a wrestling and judo mat. Lining the far wall were heavy body bags and suspended speedballs. In the corner leading back toward the entrance was a corridor, two men wide, formed with vinyl-padded walls. The corridor was the training space for knife fighting.

It was hot in the gym. Grunts, moans and shouts of pain pierced humid air that was sweating adrenaline and that high, scrape-bone smell of testosterone.

I've spent a large part of my life in the company of men. Ten years of my life in prisons, seven years in gangs, twenty years in gyms, karate schools, boxing clubs, rugby teams, motorcycle groups, and all my growing years in a boys' school: more than half of my life in exclusively male societies. And I've always felt comfortable there. It's a simple world. You only need one key to every locked heart: confidence.

Nodding to the other young men in the weight-training area, I took the long knife-scabbards from their tucks in the back of my jeans, and folded them with my money, keys, the watch and my shirt on a wide wooden stool.

Strapping on a thick leather weight belt, I slapped the towel on an empty bench, and began my alternate sets of reclining tricep extensions and standing bicep curls. After thirty minutes, my arms were at the peak of their pump. I collected my things, and made my way to the knife-training corridor.

In those years before every handbag thief carried a gun, the techniques of knife fighting were a serious business. The masters who taught their knife skills were cult heroes for young gangsters, and treated with as much deference as members of the Sanjay Council themselves.

Hathoda, the man who'd taught me for two years, had also taught Ishmeet, the leader of the Cycle Killers, who'd passed on the skills to his own men. The knife master was just leaving the corridor with a young street fighter named Tricky as I approached.

They both greeted me with smiles and warm handshakes. The young gangster, exhausted but happy, excused himself quickly, and headed for the shower.

'A good kid,' Hathoda said in Hindi, as we watched him leave. 'And a natural with the knife, *may he never use it in shame.*'

The last phrase was a kind of incantation that Hathoda taught his students. I repeated it instinctively, as we all did, in the plural.

'*May we never use it in shame.*'

Hathoda was a Sikh, from the holy city of Amritsar. As a young man, he'd fallen in with a tough crowd. Eventually, he'd abandoned his studies, and spent almost all of his time with the local gang. When a violent robbery led to conflict with community leaders, Hathoda's family disowned him. As part of the price of peace, his gang had been compelled to cast him out as well.

Alone and penniless, he made his way to Bombay, and was recruited by

Khaderbhai. He apprenticed the young Sikh to Ganeshbhai, the last of the master knife fighters, who'd started with Khaderbhai in the early 1960s.

Hathoda never left the master's side, and through years of study became a master himself. He was, in fact, the last knife teacher in South Bombay, but none of us knew that then, in those years before the glamour of the gun.

He was a tall man, something of a disadvantage for a knife fighter, with a thick mane of oiled hair coiled into a permanent topknot. His almond-shaped eyes, the same Punjabi eyes that with a single, smouldering stare, had seduced travellers to India for centuries, glowed with fearlessness and honour.

His name, the one that everyone in South Bombay knew him by, *Hathoda*, meant *Hammer* in Hindi.

'So, Lin, you want to practise with me? I was just leaving, but I'm happy to stay for another session, if your reflexes are up to it?'

'I don't want to put you out, master-*ji*,' I demurred.

'It's no trouble,' he insisted. 'I'll just drink water, and we'll begin.'

'I'll train with him,' a voice from behind me said, speaking in Hindi. 'The *gora* can work out with me.'

It was Andrew DaSilva, the young Goan member of the Sanjay Company Council. His use of the term *gora*, meaning *white man*, though very common in Bombay, was insulting in the context. He knew it, of course, and leered at me, his mouth open and his lower jaw thrust out.

It was also a strange thing to say. Andrew was very fair-skinned, his part-Portuguese ancestry evident in his reddish-brown hair and honey-coloured eyes. Because I spent so much time riding my motorcycle in the sunlight, without a helmet, my face and arms were darker than his.

'That is,' Andrew added, when I didn't respond, 'if the *gora* isn't afraid that I might embarrass him.'

It was the right moment, on the wrong day.

'What level do you want?' I asked, returning his stare.

'Level four,' Andrew said, his leer widening.

'Four it is,' I agreed.

All training in the knife-fighting arts was done with hammer handles: the reason for Hathoda's enduring nickname. The wooden handles, without their hammerheads, approximated the hilt and heft of a knife, and could be used for practice, without causing the grievous injuries of real knives.

Level one used the blunt end of a basic hammer handle. Level four training used handles shaved to points, sharp enough to draw blood.

Training bouts were usually conducted in five one-minute rounds, with a thirty-second recovery period between them. Stripped down to jeans and bare chests, we entered the training corridor. Hathoda, standing in the entrance to referee the session, handed us one sharpened handle each.

The space was tight, with only a few centimetres of movement possible to left or right. The aim was to teach men how to fight in close quarters, surrounded by enemies. The end of the padded corridor was blocked off: the way in, was the only way out.

Andrew held his sharpened handle in the underhand grip, as if he was holding the hilt of a sword. I held mine with the blade downward, and adopted a boxer's stance. Hathoda nodded to check that we were ready, glanced at the stopwatch hanging around his neck, and gave the signal.

'*Begin!*'

Andrew rushed at me, trying for a surprise early strike. It was an easy sidestep. He stumbled past me, and I gave him a shove that sent him into Hathoda at the open end of the corridor.

A young gangster watching from behind the master began to laugh, but the master silenced him.

Andrew spun around, and stepped toward me more cautiously. I closed the gap between us quickly, and we exchanged a flurry of jabs, thrusts and counter-moves.

For a moment we were locked in a tight clinch, heads knocking together. Using some main strength, I shoved Andrew off balance, and he lurched backward into the closed end of the corridor to regain his footing.

Attacking again, Andrew feinted jabs, lunging at me. Each time I arched my back, pulling out of range, and slapped at his face with my free left hand.

Several of the young gangsters training in the gym had gathered near the entrance to the corridor to watch. They laughed with each slap, infuriating Andrew. He was a full member of the Sanjay Company Council, and the position, if not the man, demanded respect.

'Shut the fuck up!' Andrew screamed at the onlookers.

They fell silent at once.

Andrew glared at me, his teeth clenched on the hatred he felt for me. His shoulders arched around the anger pumping outward from his heart. The muscles stiffened in his arms, and he began to shiver with the strain of suppressing his rage.

It hurt him not to win. He thought he was good with a knife, and I was making him realise that he wasn't.

I should've let him win. It would've cost me nothing. And he was my boss, in a sense. But I couldn't do it. There's a corner of contempt we reserve for those who hate us, when we've done them no wrong: those who resent us without cause, and revile us without reason. Andrew was corralled into that corner of my disdain as surely as he was trapped in the dead end of the training corridor. And contempt almost always conquers caution.

He lunged. I swung around, avoiding the blow, and brought my pointed handle down into his back, between the shoulder blades.

'Three points!' Hathoda called.

Andrew lashed out with his handle, swinging round to face me. He was off balance again, and a sweep of my foot brought him down beside me. Landing heavily on top of him, I jabbed the hammer handle into his chest and kidneys.

'Six more points!' Hathoda called out. 'And stop! Time to rest!'

I stepped back from Andrew. Ignoring Hathoda's command, he stood and rushed at me, jabbing with his wooden blade.

'Stop!' Hathoda shouted. 'Rest period!'

Andrew pressed on, slashing at me, trying to draw blood. Against the rules of training, he was trying to stab me in the throat and the face.

I parried and protected myself, stepping further into the dead-end corridor. Countering with my fists and handle, I struck back at him through every opening. Within seconds our hands and forearms were bleeding. Strikes against our chests and shoulders sent thin streams of blood down our bodies.

We bounced off the padded walls and into one another, fists and handles flashing, breathing hard and fast as our feet began to slip on the stone floor, until the wrestling struggle sent us both to the ground.

Luckier in the fall, I closed an arm around Andrew's neck, locking him in a chokehold. His back was to my chest. As he tried to wriggle free I wrapped my legs around his thighs, holding him immobile. He thrashed around, making us slither on the slippery stone, but my grip on his throat was solid, and he couldn't shake me off or twist himself free.

'Do you quit?'

'Fuck you!' he spluttered.

A voice spoke from a place of ancient instinct.

This is a wolf in a trap. If you let it go, sooner or later, it'll come back.

'*Lin!*' a different voice said. 'Lin brother! Let him go!'

It was Abdullah. The strength drained from my arms and legs, and I let Andrew slide away from me, onto his side. He gasped, choking and coughing, as Hathoda and several young gangsters crowded into the corridor to assist him.

Abdullah reached out and pulled me to my feet. Breathing hard, I followed him to the rows of hooks where I'd left my things.

'*Salaam aleikum,*' I greeted him. 'Where the fuck did you come from?'

'*Wa aleikum salaam.* From heaven, it seems, and just in time.'

'Heaven?'

'It would certainly have been hell, if you had finished him, Lin. They would have sent someone like me to kill you for it.'

I gathered my shirt, knives, money and watch. In the entrance to the gym I used a wet towel to wipe down my face, chest and back. Strapping on the knives, I threw the shirt over my shoulders, and nodded to Abdullah.

'Let us ride, my brother,' he said softly, 'and clear our minds.'

Andrew DaSilva approached me, stopping two paces away.

'This isn't over,' he said.

I stepped in close and whispered, so that no-one else could hear.

'You know what, Andy, there's a lane at the back of this gym. Let's get it over with, right now. Just nod your head, and we'll get it done. No witnesses. Just us. Nod your head, big mouth.'

I leaned back to look at his face. He didn't move or speak. I leaned in again.

'I didn't think so. And now we both know. So back the fuck off, and leave me alone.'

I gathered my things, and left the gym with Abdullah, knowing that it was a foolish thing to humiliate Andrew DaSilva, even privately. A wolf had escaped: a wolf that would probably return, when the moon was bad enough.

CHAPTER NINETEEN

W E RODE TOGETHER IN SILENCE TO LEOPOLD'S. Breaking with the discipline that usually kept him out of any place that served alcohol, Abdullah parked his bike next to mine, and walked inside with me.

We found Didier at his usual table near the small northern door, facing the two wide entrance arches, showing the busy causeway.

'Lin!' he cried, as we approached. 'I was so *alone* here! And drinking alone is like making love alone, don't you think so?'

'Don't take me there, Didier,' I said.

'You are an unordained priest of denied pleasures, my friend,' he laughed.

He gave me a hug, shook hands with Abdullah, and called for the waiter.

'Beer! Two glasses! And a pomegranate juice, for our Iranian friend! No ice! Hurry!'

'Oh, yes sir, I'll rush, and give myself a heart attack just to serve you,' Sweetie growled, slouching away.

He was on my list of top five waiters, and I knew some good ones. He ran the black market franchise in goods that moved through one door at Leopold's and went out the other, without the owners knowing. He took franchise fees from every store on the street, hustled a couple of pimps, and ran a small betting ring. And somehow, he drove the whole thing on nothing more than surliness and pessimism.

Didier, Abdullah and I sat side by side with our backs to the wall, watching the wide bar and the crowded street beyond.

'So, how are you, Abdullah?' Didier asked. 'It has been too long since I've seen your fearsome, handsome face.'

'*Alhamdulillah*,' Abdullah replied, using the expression that meant *Thanks and praise to God*. 'And how goes it with you?'

'I never complain,' Didier sighed. 'It is one of my *sterling* qualities, as the English say. Mind you, if I *did* complain, I could be a master of the complaining arts.'

'So . . . ' Abdullah frowned. 'It means . . . you are well?'

'Yes, my friend,' Didier smiled. 'I am well.'

The drinks arrived. Sweetie slammed the beers in front of us, but carefully wiped every trace of moisture from Abdullah's glass of juice, placing it in front of him with a generous portion of paper napkins to the side.

As Sweetie backed away from Abdullah he bowed, slightly, with each backward step, as if he were leaving the tomb of a saint.

Didier's mouth wrinkled with irritation. He caught my eye, and I laughed, spluttering beer foam from the top of my glass.

'Really, Lin, these people are *insupportable*! *I* sit here every day, and every night, year after year. I have urinated rivers in the lavatories here, and subjected myself to food so miserable, for a Frenchman, that you cannot imagine, and all in the cause of a dedicated, and I think it not *too* immodest to say, magnificent, decadence. Me, they treat like a tourist. Abdullah comes only once in a year, and they are dying of love for him. It is infuriating!'

'In the years that you have been here,' Abdullah said, sipping his fresh juice, 'they have come to know the limit of your tolerance. They do not know the limit of what I will do. That is the only difference.'

'And if you stopped coming here, Didier,' I added, 'they'd miss you more than anyone else in the place.'

Didier smiled, mollified, and reached for his glass.

'Well, you are right, of course, Lin. I have been told, more than once, that I have an unforgettable character. Let us make a toast! To those who will weep, when we are gone!'

'May they laugh instead!' I said, clinking glasses with him.

As I sipped my beer, a street tout named Saleh flopped into a chair across from me, knocking Abdullah's glass, and spilling juice on the table.

'What a fucking idiot that foreign guy is,' he said.

'Stand up,' Abdullah said.

'What?'

'Stand up, or I will break your arms.'

Saleh looked at Didier and me. Didier flapped his fingers at him, suggesting that he stand. Saleh looked at Abdullah again, and slowly stood.

'Who are you?' Abdullah demanded.

'Saleh, boss,' Saleh answered nervously. 'My name is Saleh.'

'Are you a Muslim?'

'Yes, boss.'

'Is this how a Muslim greets people?'

'What?'

'If you say *what* again, I will break your arms.'

'Sorry, boss. *Salaam aleikum.* My name is Saleh.'

'*Wa aleikum salaam,*' Abdullah replied. 'What is your business here?'

'I . . . I . . . but . . .'

He wanted to say *what* again, and I hoped he wouldn't.

'Tell him, Saleh,' I said.

'Okay, okay, I've got this camera,' he said, putting an expensive camera on the table.

'I do not understand,' Abdullah frowned. 'We are sitting here to take refreshment. Why do you tell us this?'

'He wants to sell it, Abdullah,' I said. 'Where did you get it, Saleh?'

'From those fucking idiot backpackers behind me,' he said. 'The two skinny blonde guys. I was hoping you'd want to buy it, Lin. I need money quick, you see.'

'I do not see,' Abdullah said.

'He cheated the backpackers out of their camera, and wants to cash in here,' I said.

'They totally fell for my story,' he said. 'Fucking idiots.'

'If you swear again in my company,' Abdullah said. 'I will throw you into the traffic.'

Saleh, like any street guy in the same circumstances, wanted to escape. He reached out to take the camera, but Abdullah raised a forbidding finger.

'Leave it there,' he said, and Saleh withdrew his hand. 'By what right do you disturb the peace of other men with your commerce?'

'R-right?' Saleh stammered, mystified.

'It's okay,' I said. 'People come up to me with business all the time, Abdullah.'

203

'It is unacceptable,' he grumbled. 'How can you do business with men like this, who have no respect, or honour?'

'Honour?' Saleh mumbled.

'See, Saleh, it's like this,' I said. '*You* see backpackers as victims, ripe for victiming, but we don't see them that way. We see them as emissaries of empathy.'

'What?'

Abdullah grabbed his wrist.

'I'm sorry, boss! I didn't mean to say it!'

Abdullah released him.

'What's the furthest you've been from Colaba in your life, Saleh?'

'I went to see Taj Mahal at Agra once,' he said. 'That's far.'

'Who went with you?'

'My wife.'

'Just your wife?'

'No, Linbaba, my wife's sister also, and my parents, and my cousin-brother and his wife, and all the children.'

'See, Saleh, those guys sitting over there, they've got more guts than you have. They put their world on their backs, go into wild places alone, and sleep under the protection of people they only met a few hours before.'

'They're just backpackers, man. Meat on the hoof.'

'The Buddha was a backpacker, travelling around with what he carried. Jesus was a backpacker, lost to the world for years in travelling. We're all backpackers, Saleh. We come in with nothing, carry our stuff for a while, and go out with nothing. And when you kill a backpacker's happiness, you kill mine.'

'I'm . . . I'm a businessman,' he mumbled.

'How much did you pay them, Saleh?'

'I can't tell you *that*,' Saleh demurred, his face dissolving in sly. 'But I can say that it wasn't more than twenty per cent. I'll take twenty-five, if you've got it.'

Abdullah seized him by the wrist again. I knew the grip. It started out bad, and got worse.

'Are you refusing to tell the truth?' Abdullah demanded.

He turned to me.

'Is this how you do your business, Lin brother? With untruthful men? I will give you this man's tongue, in your hand.'

'My *tongue?*' Saleh squeaked.

'I have been told,' Didier recollected, 'that a certain loathsome woman, named Madame Zhou, uses a human tongue as her powder puff.'

Saleh pulled his hand free and ran, leaving the camera. There was a pause, while we hummed the incident in silence.

'Please, Abdullah,' I said after a while, 'don't cut out his tongue.'

'Something more lenient?'

'No. Let it go.'

'I always say,' Didier observed, 'if you can't say something nice about someone, rob him and shoot him.'

'Sage words,' Abdullah mused.

'Sage words?'

'It is self-evident, Lin,' Didier said.

Abdullah nodded agreement.

'Just because you can't find something *nice* to say about someone?'

'Certainly, Lin. I mean, if you cannot find even one nice thing to say about a man, he must be an absolute swine. And all of us, who have experience of life, know that sooner or later, an absolute swine will cause you grief, or regret, or both. It is simply a prudent precaution to beat and rob negative people, before they beat and rob you. Self-defence, it seems to me.'

'If these waiters knew you as we do, Didier,' Abdullah said, 'they would treat you with more respect.'

'That is undoubtedly true,' Didier concurred. 'The more one knows Didier, the more one loves and respects Didier.'

I stood, leaving my glass.

'But, you're not *going?*' Didier protested.

'I just came in to give you something. I've gotta get home, and get changed. We're going out to dinner tonight, with Ranjit and Karla.'

I unsnapped the stainless steel bracelet from my wrist, and slid the watch off over my hand. For a moment I felt the little clench of regret in losing something that I'd wanted too much. I handed the watch to Didier.

He examined it, turning it over to read the text on the back, and then held it to his ear, listening to the click-whirr of the mechanism.

'But . . . it is a fine watch!' Didier gasped. 'A beautiful instrument. Is it . . . is it really for *me?*'

'Sure, it is. Try it on.'

Didier snapped the bracelet shut on his wrist, and turned his hand up and down, left and right, to admire the watch.

'It suits you,' I said, standing to leave. 'You coming, Abdullah?'

'In fact, my brother, there is a beautiful woman, sitting in the corner,' Abdullah said gravely, his eyes fixed to mine. 'She has been staring at me, for the last fifteen minutes.'

'I noticed.'

'I think I will remain here with Didier, for some time.'

'Waiter!' Didier called out quickly. 'Another pomegranate juice! No ice!'

I scooped up the camera and took a step away from the table, but Didier stood as well, and rushed to stop me.

'You will see Karla tonight?' he asked, leaning in close to me.

'That's the plan.'

'This is *your* idea?'

'No.'

'It is *Karla's* idea?'

'No.'

'Then, who would do such a diabolical thing?'

'Lisa set it up. Kind of a short notice thing. I only heard about it an hour ago. I got a note, while I was sitting at Edward's bar. What's the problem?'

'Can you not find some excuse? Some way not to be there?'

'I don't think so. I don't know what she has in mind, but Lisa's note said she wants me to be there.'

'Lin, it has been almost two years since you have seen Karla.'

'I know.'

'But . . . in matters of the heart, of love –'

'I know.'

'– those two years are simply two heartbeats.'

'I –'

'No, please! Let me say it. Lin . . . you are . . . you are in a darker place than you were two years ago. You are a darker man that you were when you first arrived in Bombay. I have never said this to you. I am ashamed to say that a part of me was glad to see it, at first. It was comforting. I was glad of the company, you might say.'

He was almost whispering, and speaking in a fluid rush of syllables so swift that it was more like a prayer, or incantation, than a shared confidence.

'What are you talking about, Didier?'

'I feel for Karla, perhaps as much as you do, in my way. But being away from *her* did this to you. Loving her and losing her sent you into this shadow, and made you a darker man than God intended you to be.'

'God?'

'I worry, Lin. I worry about what will open, inside you, if you see her again. Some bridges, they should remain burned. Some rivers, they should not be crossed.'

'It's okay.'

'Perhaps, if I were to accompany you? I'm more than a match for her wit, as the world knows.'

'It's okay.'

'Then, if you are determined to see her, perhaps I should arrange a rather inconvenient accident for Ranjit? One that prevents him from attending?'

'No accidents.'

'An unfortunate delay, then?'

'How about we let nature take its course, Didier.'

'That is exactly my fear,' he sighed, 'if you see Karla again.'

'It's okay.'

'Well ...' he murmured, lowering his eyes, and glancing at the watch I'd given him. 'Thank you for the watch. I will always treasure it.'

'Look after Abdullah, with that pretty girl in the corner.'

'I know. We tough guys, we fall fast, and we fall hard. Alas, it is the story of my life. I remember the time –'

'So do I, brother,' I laughed, turning to leave. 'So do I.'

I passed by the two thin backpackers, who were eating for four, with four hands. I put the camera on the table.

'It's worth a grand, US, in the stores here,' I said, 'and any street guy in Bombay will get six for it, and an honest one will give you five back.'

'He gave us a hundred, and promised to get more,' one of the men said.

'He'll be hanging around,' I said. 'And he'll want his hundred back. There's a waiter here, named Sweetie. He does a little on the side. He's a surly motherfucker, but you can trust him. You can do the deal, give Saleh his money back, and be in front. Be safe.'

'Thank you,' they both said.

They looked like brothers, and wherever they'd been in India, it had hungered them.

'Will you join us?'

'I'm on my way to dinner,' I smiled. 'Thanks all the same.'

I walked outside to the bike. Abdullah and Didier raised their hands in farewell, Didier holding an imaginary camera, and sarcastically taking my photo, for helping out two strangers.

I turned away, watching the traffic shuffle beside the bullying shoulder of a bus. Didier and Abdullah: men so different, and yet brothers, in so many ways. I thought of the things we three unwise men had done, together and alone, since we'd met as exiles in the Island City. There were things we regretted, and things buried. But there were also things of triumph, and light. When love cut one of us, the others cauterised with sarcasm. When one had to become two, the others brought their guns. When hope faltered in one, the others filled the hollowness with loyalty. And I felt that loyalty like a hand on my chest, as I looked back at them, and I hoped hard for them, and for myself.

Fear is a wolf on a chain, only dangerous when you set it free. Sorrow exhausts itself in the net of forgetting. Anger, for all its fury, can be killed by a smile. Only hope goes on forever, because hope doesn't belong to us: it belongs to our ancestors, the first of our kind, whose brave love for one another gave us most of the good that we are.

And hope, that ancient seed, redeems the heart it feeds. The heartbeat of any conscious now is poised on the same choice that hope gives all of us, between shadows of the past, and the bright, blank page of any new day.

CHAPTER TWENTY

THE PAST IS A NOVEL, WRITTEN BY FATE, weaving the same themes: love and its glory, hate and its prisoners, the soul and its price. Our decisions become narratives: fated choices that unknowably change the course of the living river. In the present, where decisions and connections are made, Fate waits on the riverbank of Story, leaving us to our mistakes and miracles, because it's our will alone that leads us to one or the other.

Pausing beside my bike that day, I marked the faces on the street. One face held my eyes. It was a young woman, blonde, blue-eyed and nervous. She was standing on the footpath outside Leopold's, waiting for someone. She was fearful but determined, somehow: brave and afraid, in equal measure.

I took out the locket that I'd bought from Billy Bhasu. Prising it open, I looked at the photograph. It was the same girl.

There are a hundred good girls on every bad street, waiting for a guy who usually isn't worth it. The girl was waiting for her boyfriend to return with dope. She wasn't a user: she was thin, but still too healthy, and too aware of the world. Her boyfriend was the user, I guessed, and she'd sold her locket to Billy Bhasu, a street tout, so that the boyfriend could buy drugs.

I'd been on the street long enough to know the signs of somebody's desperate habit, even expressed second-hand. I'd been that habit myself, and I'd seen it in the eyes of everyone who loved me.

The fact that the girl in the locket was waiting outside Leopold's, and not inside, meant that she and her boyfriend were past the early tourist phase, with cold drinks and hot food, and sitting in a restaurant all day long. The fact that she was on the street, and not in a hotel room, meant that they were probably behind on the rent.

She was waiting until the boyfriend came back with the drugs he'd bought with their love locket, and some change to spare for the room.

I'd seen girls like the girl in the locket leave the Island City as ashes, spilled from reluctant hands, not long after they arrived. They were beautiful, as every girl is, and there was always a not so beautiful guy who wrote that part of their story for them.

I could've ridden away without a word. I did it every day: rode past sadness, neglect and futility. You can't jump through every hoop that Fate puts in front of you.

But the locket came to life on the street, imitating art, and I walked over to her.

'I think this is yours,' I said, holding the locket in my open palm.

She stared at it, her eyes wide with fear, but didn't move.

'Go ahead. Take it.'

Hesitantly, she reached out and scooped the locket and chain from my palm.

'What . . . what do you –'

'I don't want anything,' I said, cutting her off. 'This came across my desk, so to speak. That's all.'

The girl smiled awkwardly.

'All the best,' I said.

I turned to leave.

'I must have lost it,' she said quickly, defending herself with a lie.

I hesitated.

'When my boyfriend comes back, we'll give you a reward,' she said, trying on a smile she hadn't used in a while.

'You didn't lose it,' I said. 'You sold it.'

'I what?'

'And the fact that you sold it with your pictures still in it, means your boyfriend did it in a hurry. The fact he did it in a hurry means he did it under pressure. The only pressure that works on people like us, in this city, is drugs.'

She flinched, as if I'd threatened her.

'People like us . . . ' she said, a Scandinavian accent bumping the words from her lips with a pleasant little music that didn't match the sadness in her eyes.

I walked away.

I looked back. She was still cringing in that shocked flinch, her shoulders curved inwards.

I went back.

'Look,' I said more softly, glancing around in both directions to check the street. 'Forget it.'

I handed her a roll of notes, the profit I'd made that day, and began to leave, but she stopped me. She held the money in her closed hand.

'What . . . what are you *talking* about?'

'Forget it,' I said again, taking a step backwards. 'Keep the money. Forget I said anything.'

'No!' she pleaded, folding her arms in on herself protectively. 'Tell me what you're talking about.'

I stopped, and sighed again.

'You have to leave this guy behind, whoever he is,' I said at last. 'I know how this plays out. I've seen it a hundred times. I don't care how much you love him, or how nice a guy he is —'

'You don't know anything.'

What I knew was that the next picture she'd sell to someone would be the one in her passport. I knew she still had her passport, because it hadn't come to me yet. But she'd sell it, I was pretty sure, if her boyfriend asked her to. She'd sell everything, and when there was nothing left to sell, she'll sell herself.

And her boyfriend would feel bad, but he'd take the money she made from selling her body, and he'd buy dope with it. I knew that, just like every street tout, shopkeeper and pimp around us knew it. It was the truth of addiction, waiting to happen, and they were the truth of the street, waiting to use her.

'You're right,' I said. 'I don't know anything.'

I walked to the bike, and rode away. Sometimes you buy in, sometimes you don't: sometimes you try, and sometimes you ride past. A gold chain and a photograph connected me to the girl, somehow, but there were too many girls, in too much trouble, waiting somewhere for troubled boyfriends. And anyway, I was a troubled boyfriend myself.

I wished the girl in the locket well, and stopped thinking about her by the time I parked my bike at home.

Lisa was preoccupied and quiet as I shaved, showered and dressed. I was glad. I didn't want to talk. The dinner with Ranjit and Karla hadn't been my idea.

Although we both lived in the narrow peninsula of the Island City, I hadn't seen Karla in person since I'd been living with Lisa. I saw pictures of her and Ranjit from time to time, in Ranjit's newspapers, but Fate never crossed our paths.

Karla haunts the mansion of my life, too, Lisa said. I understood what she meant, but Karla wasn't a ghost. Karla was more dangerous.

'How do I look?' Lisa asked me, standing near the front door of the apartment.

She was wearing a very short, sleeveless blue silk dress. She had a shell necklace, the shell bracelet I'd given her, and her Roman-style sandals laced all the way up to the knees.

Her make-up was more elaborate than usual, but it suited her: sky-blue eyes in a black aurora. Her thick, blonde curls were as loose and free as ever, but she'd cut the fringe of her hair herself with a pair of kitchen scissors. It was irregular, haphazard, and brilliant.

'You look great,' I smiled. 'Love what you did to your hair. Did you put my throwing knife back, when you were finished with it?'

'Let me show you where to put your throwing knife, buster!' she laughed, punching me hard in the chest.

'Are you serious, about seeing other people?' I seriously asked her.

'Yes,' she said quickly. 'I am. And you should, too.'

'Is that what this sudden dinner party is about?'

'In a way. We can talk about it later.'

'I think we should talk about it now. And about other things.'

'First, talk to Karla.'

'What?'

'She'll be there tonight. Talk to her. Find out what *she's* thinking, and then we'll talk about what *you're* thinking.'

'I don't see —'

'Exactly. Let's ride, cowboy, or we'll be late.'

We rode to the Mahesh hotel during a lull in the rain, arriving at the covered entrance just as a new shower began. I parked the bike in an alcove, away from the main entrance. It was strictly forbidden to park there, so it cost me fifty rupees.

At the bank of entry doors Lisa stopped me, her hand in mine.

'Are you ready for this?' she asked.

'Ready for what?'

'Karla,' she said, her lips a bright, brave smile. 'What else?'

We found Ranjit sitting at a table set for ten. Two mutual acquaintances, Cliff De Souza and Chandra Mehta, were with him. The men were partners in a Bollywood film production company. My association with them had begun a few years before, when they'd approached me to help them dump some of their undeclared, untaxed rupees, in exchange for black market dollars, with which they could bribe taxation department officials, because the taxmen only accepted dollars.

Lisa had worked with them for several months when she was running a small talent agency, sourcing foreigners to work as extras in Indian films. When she'd segued from the agency into work at the art gallery, she'd kept up contact with Cliff and Chandra.

Their films had been hits in recent years. The producers had established a banner that attracted some of the biggest stars in the city. It was a measure of their success that Chandra and Cliff, who'd always adorned themselves on public occasions with a young starlet, had four pretty girls with them for the dinner that night.

We greeted one another, met the four girls – Monica, Mallika, Simple, and Sneha – and took our seats at the table. Ranjit sat us on either side of him, Lisa on his right, and me on the left. There was no place set for Karla.

'Isn't Karla coming?' Lisa asked.

'No, I'm sorry,' Ranjit said, pressing his lips together in a rueful smile. 'She's . . . she's not feeling a hundred per cent. She asks you all to excuse her, and she sends her best wishes.'

'It's nothing serious, I hope? Should I call her?'

'No, she's fine, Lisa,' Ranjit said. 'She's just been overdoing it a bit lately. That's all.'

'Please be sure to give her my love.'

'I will, Lisa. I will.'

Lisa glanced at me, but quickly turned away.

'Are you all actresses, Mallika?' Lisa asked, turning to the girl sitting nearest her.

The girls all giggled and nodded.

'Yes, we are,' Mallika said shyly.

'It's a hard crawl to the top,' Cliff De Souza said, slurring his speech a little, beginning drunk. 'We don't know which one of you will make it to the next level, yaar, and which ones will fail, and never be seen again.'

The girls giggled nervously. Chandra Mehta moved in to mitigate.

'You'll all get your shot,' he assured the girls. 'You'll all get face-on-screen. Guaranteed. In the bank. But like Cliff says, there's no way to know which of you will have that special magic with the camera, the It factor that moves you onwards and upwards, so to speak.'

'I'll drink to that!' Cliff shouted, raising his glass. 'Onwards and upwards!'

'Have you been acting long?' Lisa asked Simple, when the glasses hit the table again.

'Oh, yes,' Simple replied.

'We started *months* ago,' Monica added.

'Veterans already,' Cliff slurred. 'Another toast! To the business that makes us rich!'

'To show business!' Chandra agreed.

'To creative accounting!' Cliff corrected him.

'I'll certainly drink to that,' Chandra laughed, clinking glasses.

Baskets of *pakodas* and narrow strips of Kashmiri *parathas* arrived at the table.

'I took the liberty of ordering for us,' Ranjit announced. 'There's some non-veg for Cliff, Lin and Lisa, and a wide selection of veg dishes for everybody else. Please, begin!'

'Chandra,' Ranjit continued, as we began to eat. 'Did you happen to see the article in my paper last week? The one about the young gay dancer, who was murdered near your studio?'

'He doesn't read anything but contracts,' Cliff replied, pouring another glass of red wine. 'But I saw it. Actually, it was my *secretary* who saw it. She was blubbering like a baby, crying her eyes out, and when I asked her what was going on, she read the article out to me. What about it?'

'I was thinking that it might make a good story line for a movie,' Ranjit said, passing a basket of *pakodas* to Lisa. 'My paper would get behind it, if you did it. And I'd put money in it.'

'Damn good idea!' Lisa agreed.

'So that's what this dinner's about,' Chandra said.

'And if it is?' Ranjit asked, smiling charmingly.

'Forget it!' Chandra spluttered, gasping on a mouthful of food. 'You think we're crazy?'

'Hear me out,' Ranjit insisted. 'One of my columnists, he's a pretty fair writer, and he's written a few screenplays already, for your competitors –'

'We don't *have* any competitors,' Cliff cut in. 'We're at the top of the cinema food chain, hurling coconuts at the others far below!'

'Anyway,' Ranjit persisted, 'this young writer is hot for the story. He's already begun to write a screenplay.'

'That dancer fellow was foolish,' Cliff said.

'That dancer fellow had a *name*,' Lisa said quietly.

Her manner was calm, but I knew she was angry.

'Yes, of course he –'

'His name was Avinash. He was a brilliant dancer, before a mob of drunken thugs beat him unconscious, poured kerosene on him, and tossed matches at him.'

'Like I said –' Cliff began, but his production partner silenced him.

'Look, Ranjit,' Chandra said nervously. 'You can play the hero in the pages of your newspapers, writing about that poor young fellow –'

'Avinash,' Lisa said.

'Yes, yes, *Avinash*. You can write about him, and take the risks, and get away with it. But be realistic. If we put that story in a movie, they'd come after us. They'd close down the cinemas.'

'They'd *burn* down the bloody cinemas,' Cliff added. 'And we'd lose buckets of money, for nothing at all.'

'Some stories, it seems to me,' Ranjit said gently, 'are so important that we should take the risks involved in telling them.'

'It's not just the risks to ourselves,' Chandra replied reasonably. 'Think about it. If we did such a picture, there'd be riots. Cinemas could get attacked. As Cliff says, there could even be fires. People could die. Is it worth a risk like that, just to tell a story?'

'Somebody *already* died,' Lisa said through almost clenched teeth. 'A dancer. A wonderfully gifted dancer. Did you ever see him at the NCPA?'

Cliff spluttered a mouthful of wine on the table.

'The National Centre for the Performing Arts?' he scoffed. 'The only performing that Chandra's interested in is what pretty girls do when the lights are low, isn't that right, brother?'

Chandra Mehta wriggled uncomfortably.

'You should slow down on the booze, Cliff. You started too early tonight.'

'Speak for yourself,' his partner said, glaring at him and pouring another glass of wine. 'Are you worried that I'm going to tell Ranjit I think his phoney campaign is more about his political ambitions than it is about Avinash, the dead dancer? Ranjit should be the one to worry, not us. We buy pages of his newspapers every day.'

'Why don't we leave business in the office?' Ranjit said, through a thin smile.

'You're the one who brought it up,' Cliff replied, waving his glass and spilling a little wine on Sneha's coloured bangles.

'Do you have any *personal* opinion on what happened to Avinash?' Lisa asked Cliff. 'Considering that it happened five hundred feet from your movie studio, and Avinash danced in three of your movies?'

'Lin,' Chandra cut in quickly. 'Help me out here. What do *you* think? I'm right, *na*? If we did a movie like this, there'd be blood on the seats. We shouldn't needlessly offend the sensibilities, and the . . . the feelings, you know, of any community, isn't that so?'

'It's your subject, guys, not mine. You two own the movies, Ranjit owns the newspapers, and neither of them have anything to do with me.'

'Oh, come on,' Ranjit said, glancing at Lisa. 'Let's hear what you honestly think about this, Lin.'

'I already gave you an honest answer, Ranjit.'

'Please, Lin,' Lisa urged me.

'Okay. Someone once said that the sophistication of any community of people is inversely proportionate to their capacity to be aroused to violence by what people say in public, or do in private.'

'I have . . . absolutely . . . no idea . . . what the *fuck* that means,' Cliff said, his mouth gaping open.

'It means,' Ranjit said, 'that sophisticated people don't get upset by what people say in public, or do in the privacy of their own homes. It's the unsophisticated that do.'

'But . . . what does that mean for *me*?' Chandra asked me.

'It means that I agree with you, Chandra. You shouldn't do the story.'

'*What?*' Lisa gasped.

'See?' Cliff said, waving his glass. 'I'm right.'

'Why not, Lin?' Ranjit asked, his charming smile fading.

'It's not their fight.'

'I told you!' Cliff sneered.

'But it's important, don't you agree, Lin?' Ranjit asked me, but directing his frown at Lisa.

'Of course it's important. A man was killed, murdered, and not for something he *did*, but for something he *was*. But it's not their fight, Ranjit. They don't believe in it, and Avinash deserves believers.'

'Last week it was Avinash,' Lisa said, glaring at me. 'Next week it could be Muslims or Jews or Christians or women they're beating up, and setting on fire. Or it could be movie producers. That makes it everybody's business.'

'You should only do it, if you believe in it,' I said. 'Cliff and Chandra don't. They don't really care a damn about Avinash, no offence. It's not their fight.'

'Exactly!' Cliff protested. 'I just want to make lots of money, maybe win a few awards now and then, and live a happy life on the red carpet. Is that so bad?'

The first course arrived, it was impossible to talk, and everyone turned their attention to the small swarm of waiters serving a flower-bed of food.

A messenger from the concierge desk approached as the food was being served. He bowed to the guests, and then bent to whisper in my ear.

'There is a Mr Naveen at the reception, sir. He says it is rather urgent that he speak to you.'

I excused myself, and made my way to the lobby. I had no trouble finding Naveen and Divya: anyone within ten metres could hear them fighting.

'I won't!' Divya shouted.

'You're being so –'

'Forget it!' she snapped. 'I'm *not* doing it!'

'Hey, man,' Naveen sighed, as I joined him. 'Sorry to bust into your dinner.'

'No problem,' I replied, shaking hands with him, and nodding to the sulky socialite. 'What's up?'

'We were coming down from a private party on the eighteenth floor –'

'A party that was just getting *good*!' Divya pouted.

'A party that was about to get busted for rioting,' Naveen corrected her, 'which was why we were leaving. And who gets into the lift, on the way down? None other than our mystery man –'

'Mr Wilson.'

'The same.'

'Did you talk to him?'

'I couldn't resist it. I know we agreed to wait until we could talk to him together, but it seemed like a God-given opportunity, so I thought I'd play the hand.'

'What did you say?'

'I told him Scorpio George was a friend of mine, and I knew he was looking for him. I asked what it was all about, and why he was dogging my friend.'

'And?'

'He's a lawyer,' Divya cut in.

'Will you let me tell it, please?' Naveen grumbled, grinding his teeth. 'He says he's a lawyer, and that he has an important message for Scorpio, only he calls him Mr George Bradley. Is that Scorpio's last name?'

'Yeah. Did Wilson say what the message was about?'

'He keeps the lid screwed down pretty tight, this guy. I'd like him for *my* lawyer. But he did say it wasn't anything that could harm Scorpio.'

'It was *me* who got him to tell you that!' Divya hissed.

'Yeah, by threatening to rip your blouse and shout that he attacked you in the lift. A little over the top, if you ask me.'

'That's what the top is *for*, stupid! It's for going *over*. What else would the top be for?'

'He say anything else?' I asked.

'No. He won't say anything more. Professional ethics, he said.'

'If you'd just let me scream,' Divya said, 'you'd know it all by now. But oh, no! Screaming isn't an acceptable tactic, for the great detective!'

'And if you screamed your way into a police cell, would I be doing my job?' Naveen demanded.

'How come you guys are still together?' I asked. 'Didn't you sort out the wannabe Bollywood actor guy already?'

'We did,' Naveen sighed. 'But her father has this big business deal going down –'

'Mukesh Devnani doesn't do *big* deals, *chamcha*,' Divya interrupted. 'My father does huge, *humungous* deals.'

'Her father has this huge, humungous deal going down,' Naveen

218

continued, 'and apparently there's been some bad blood among the parties who *aren't* party to the deal. There've been some threats. Nasty stuff. Her dad's playing safe. He asked me to stay on with this brat for a couple of weeks, until the deal's done.'

'I'm not a brat!' Divya snapped, sticking out her tongue. 'And the end of this arrangement can't come fast enough for me, I'm telling you!'

'Did you just stick your tongue out at me?' Naveen asked, astounded.

'It's a legitimate response,' she pouted.

'Sure, if you're four years old.'

'So . . . ' I cut in. 'What happened with Wilson?'

'I knew you were here,' Naveen said quickly. 'One of the guests at the party upstairs said he saw you, on the way up. He said you were having dinner with Ranjit Choudry. I thought this might be the only chance to bring this thing to a conclusion, so I told Wilson to meet us outside, on the sea wall. He's waiting there now. What do you think?'

'I think we should talk with this guy. If he's what he says he is, we should take him to the Zodiac Georges. Divya, will you stay here with my girlfriend, Lisa?'

'Don't *you* start!' she growled.

'That's what we were fighting about, before,' Naveen explained. 'I told her if you wanted to go with me to see the Georges with this guy Wilson, she should stay here at the hotel, in safety. She won't buy it.'

'Are you kidding?' she snapped. 'The most interesting thing to happen for like, a grillion years, going with this mystery man to see these Zodiac guys, whoever the fuck they are, and you want me to sit it out like a good little girl? No way. I'm a bad girl. I'm coming with.'

I glanced at Naveen. His half-smile and resigned shrug told me how much he'd become accustomed to giving in to the girl, in the days they'd been together.

'Okay. Wait here. I'll tell Lisa.'

I went back to the table, put my hands on the back of her chair, and leaned in close to whisper in her ear. I told her the situation, and then made an apology to the table.

'Ladies and gentlemen, I'm sorry to say that I've been called to an emergency, involving a friend. Please excuse me.'

'We agreed to have dinner with Ranjit,' Lisa said, furious and loud.

'Lisa —'

'And if you haven't noticed, that's what we're in the middle of doing.'

'Yeah, but —'

'It's just *rude*,' she said flatly.

'It's an emergency. It's Scorpio, Lisa.'

'Is that why you're leaving?' she demanded angrily. 'Or is it because Karla isn't here?'

I stared at her, feeling hurt without knowing exactly why. Scorpio and Gemini were our friends, and it was important for them.

She stared back at me evenly, her eyes betraying nothing but anger. Ranjit broke the silence.

'Well, we'll be very sorry to see you leave, Lin. But rest assured, Lisa will be in good hands. And perhaps you'll return from your . . . pressing matter . . . in time for dessert. I dare say we'll be here for a while yet.'

He looked at me, his smile as open and ingenuous as ever. Lisa didn't move.

'Really,' Ranjit said, putting his hand over Lisa's on the table. 'We'll do our best to keep Lisa entertained. Don't worry.'

'Just go!' Lisa said. 'If it's so important, just go.'

I stared at them for a moment; stared at Ranjit, and their hands together on the table. A perverse and completely honest instinct made me want to hit Ranjit hard. Anywhere would do.

I said goodbye, and I walked away. I know now that if I'd followed that instinct, if I'd dragged Ranjit from the hotel, slapped him around and put him back in his box of snakes, all of our lives would've been better, and safer, maybe even his.

But I didn't. I rose above. I did the right thing. I was the better man I sometimes am. And Fate wrote a new chapter for all of us that night, on starred pages, and dark.

CHAPTER TWENTY-ONE

OUTSIDE, FITFUL GUSTS CARESSED A FINE MIST OFF THE BAY, drifting across the wide road in glittering veils of delicate moisture. The monsoon, brooding for another assault on the city, paced its clouds horizon-wide over the sea.

The lawyer, Mr Wilson, was leaning casually against the hip-high sea wall. He wore a dark blue suit, and carried an umbrella and a fedora in his long, pale fingers. A banded tie was strangling his crisp white shirt. Despondent lawyers sometimes hang themselves with their business ties. Looking at Wilson, I wondered at a profession that wears its own noose.

As I approached him I realised that his hair was actually silver-white, beyond the thirty-five or so years of his thin, unlined face. His eyes were a soft blue that seemed to suffuse the white surrounding them: blue everywhere. They glittered with what might've been courage, or just good humour. Either way, I liked the look of him.

'This is Lin, Mr Wilson,' Naveen introduced us. 'They also call him Shantaram.'

'How do you do,' Wilson said, offering me a card.

The card, bearing the name E. C. Wilson, announced that he worked for a partnered law firm, with offices in Ottawa and New York.

'I understand, from Mr Adair, that you can take me to meet Mr Bradley, Mr George Bradley,' Wilson said when I pocketed the card.

'I understand that you can tell me what the hell you want with him,' I replied calmly.

'That's telling him!' Divya laughed.

'Please, shut up!' Naveen hissed.

'If you are indeed friends of Mr Bradley —'

'Are you calling me a liar, Mr Wilson?' Naveen asked.

'It's *Evan*,' Wilson responded calmly. 'Evan Wilson. And I'm certainly not doubting your word. I'm merely saying that you will understand, as friends of Mr Bradley, that whatever business I have with him is his private business.'

'And it'll *stay* private,' I agreed. 'So private that you'll never see him, if you don't give me some idea of what you want with him. Scorpio George has a nervous disposition. We like him that way. We don't disturb him without a reason. You see that, right?'

Wilson stared back at me, unruffled and resolute. A few strollers braving the wind and imminent rain passed us on the wide footpath. Two taxis pulled up near us, hoping for a fare. Other than that, the street was quiet.

'I repeat,' Wilson said at last, equably but firmly, 'This a private —'

'That's it!' Divya snapped. 'Why don't you two just kick the shit out of him? He'll talk soon enough, if you give him a solid pasting.'

Wilson, Naveen and I turned to look at the small, slim socialite.

'*What?*' she demanded. 'Go on! Fuck him up!'

'I should warn you,' Wilson said quickly, 'that I took the precaution of hiring the services of a security officer, from the hotel. He is watching us now, near that parked car.'

Naveen and I turned. There was a black-suited bouncer from the hotel, standing in the shadows, five metres away. I knew the man. His name was Manav.

Mr Evan Wilson had made a mistake, because he didn't know the local rules. When you needed private security, in those years, you hired a professional, which means either a gangster, or an off-duty cop.

Guys like Manav weren't paid enough to take real risks. As working men, on low salaries, they had no protection if things got messy. If they got hurt, they had no insurance, and couldn't sue anyone. If they hurt someone else, and got charged for it, they went to prison.

More to the point, Manav was a big, well-muscled guy, and like a lot of big, well-muscled guys, he knew that a broken bone would put a dent in his training routine: he'd lose half a year of sculptured gains. Setbacks like that make most bodybuilders take a long, hard look in the wall mirror at the gym.

'It's okay, Manav,' I called out to him. 'You can go back to the hotel now. We'll call you, if we need you.'

'Yes, sir, Linbaba!' he said, visibly relieved. 'Goodnight, Mr Wilson, sir.'

The bodyguard trundled back to the hotel, jogging a bow-legged trot. Wilson watched. To his credit, the lawyer smiled and remained calm.

'It would seem, gentlemen,' he said gently, 'that you have suddenly moved rather closer into the circle of Mr George Bradley's confidentiality.'

'You got *that* right, you damn honky!' Divya spat at him.

'Will you *please* shut up!' Naveen spluttered. 'And what does *that* mean? *Honky?* What are you, from Harlem now, or what?'

'I'm from the famous nation of *Fuck You*,' she retorted. 'Would you like to hear our national anthem?'

'You were getting more confidential, Mr Wilson,' I said.

'It's Evan. I can reveal that Mr Bradley is the recipient of a legacy. As the only living relative of Josiah Bradley, recently deceased owner of the Aeneas Trust, registered in Ottawa, he stands to gain a substantial sum, if I can find him and make the appropriate declarations before duly authorised notary officers.'

'How substantial?' Naveen asked.

'If you will permit me, I will leave that to Mr Bradley's discretion. I rather think it is his business to tell you the full amount of his inheritance, or not, as the case may be.'

Wilson needn't have worried about Scorpio George telling us. When we took Wilson in a taxi to the Frantic hotel, enticed the Zodiac Georges to come down to a meeting, and left them alone with him on the street, it was fifteen seconds before Gemini George shouted out the sum.

'Thirty-five million! Holy Croesus-Christ! Thirty-five million! *Dollars*, for Chrissakes!'

'Tell the whole damn street, why don't you?' Scorpio scolded, glancing around nervously.

'What are you scared of, Scorp? We don't *have* the money yet! They won't kill us in our beds for money we don't have.'

'They could kidnap us,' Scorpio insisted, waving for us to join them and Wilson. 'Isn't that right, Lin? There are people who could kidnap us, and demand a ransom. They could cut off an ear, or a finger, and send it in the post.'

'The Bombay post?' Gemini scoffed. 'Good luck.'

'They're probably planning the kidnapping right now,' Scorpio whined.

'Christ, Scorpio!' Gemini protested, dancing a little with delight. 'Five minutes ago you were freakin' out about bein' mind-controlled by the friggin' CIA. Now, you're blubberin' on about bein' kidnapped. Can't you just sit back for once and smell the good karma?'

'I rather think that Mr Bradley has a point, however,' Wilson remarked.

'Mr Bradley?' Gemini scoffed. 'Mr Fuckin' *Bradley*! That's worth a million, right there, just to hear that! Scorpio, give Wilson a million dollars.'

'One thing is certain, Mr Bradley,' Wilson continued. 'You cannot stay in this hotel. Not when such a significant change in your financial circumstances has shifted you into a, shall we say, more *significant* income bracket?'

'He means a more *vulnerable* income bracket,' Scorpio mumbled. 'He's already talking kidnapping, Gemini. D'you hear that?'

'Calm down, Scorpio,' I said.

'He's right, actually,' Divya chipped in.

'You see?' Scorpio hissed.

'My dad, he's an expert in kidnapping security,' Divya said. 'I've been trained in it since I was five years old. All rich people are. Now that you're rich, you'll have to learn counter-kidnapping techniques, and have all your friends carefully vetted by the police. You'll need to stay in a safe place, too, and have an armoured limousine. No doubt about it. Bodyguards and money go together like handbags and shoes.'

'Oh, no,' Scorpio moaned.

'And you're right about the fingers and ears,' Divya added. 'But kidnappers use couriers, not the post.'

'Oh, no.'

'One case I know, they cut all the fingers but one, before the family paid the ransom.'

'Oh . . .'

'Divya, please,' Naveen sighed.

'In another case, they cut off both ears. Tragic. Had to give away his collection of designer sunglasses.'

'Oh . . .'

'Divya.'

'And hats never looked quite the same,' Divya mused, 'but at least they got him back. And he's still rich.'

'*Divya, you're not helping!*' Naveen snapped.

'*Excuse* me?' she retorted. 'Far as I can see, there are only two millionaires involved in this conversation, Mr Bradley and Miss Me. Hello? So, I'm the only one qualified to talk about rich kidnapping victims, *na?*'

'Oh, no,' Scorpio moaned.

'Where's the *party?*' Gemini laughed, still dancing.

'I have taken the liberty of reserving suites at the Mahesh hotel, on my floor,' Wilson announced. 'I was hoping that sooner or later I would be successful in locating you, and that I would be able to extend a measure of hospitality. My firm has also arranged for a line of credit to be opened for you immediately, Mr Bradley, for you to use until the legal matters are all resolved and you can receive your full inheritance.'

'That's . . . that's amazing,' Scorpio stammered uncertainly. 'A line of credit?'

'How much credit?' Gemini asked.

'I lodged a hundred thousand dollars in your discretionary account. You have immediate access to it.'

'I like this guy,' Gemini said softly. 'Give him another million dollars, Scorpio.'

'We are hoping that you will retain our services, Mr Bradley,' Wilson said. 'Just as your departed great-uncle Josiah Bradley did for so many years. We're fully prepared to offer you the best possible professional advice, on the management of your legacy. We are at your complete service.'

'What are we waitin' for?' Gemini George cried. 'Let's go!'

'What about our stuff?' Scorpio George asked, glancing back at the Frantic hotel.

'Trust me,' Divya said, taking Scorpio's arm, and leading him toward the waiting taxis. 'You'll send a servant to do that. From now on, your servants will do everything that isn't fun.'

'Whiskey!' Gemini said, falling into step behind them, and leaning over Divya's shoulder.

'And a long shower,' Divya said.

'And champagne!'

'And a second shower.'

'And cocaine! Hey, I know! Let's mix the cocaine *in* the champagne!'

'I'm beginning to like you,' Divya said.

225

'And I *already* like you,' Gemini said. 'Let's get that party started!'

'You'll join us, of course, Mr Wilson?' Divya asked, taking his arm as well.

'If you'll pardon the indiscretion, Miss . . .?'

'Devnani. Divya Devnani. Call me Diva. Everyone does.'

'If you'll pardon the indiscretion, Miss Devnani,' Wilson said, smiling and making no move to disengage his arm from hers, 'didn't you advise your friends, not half an hour ago, to *kick the shit out of me?*'

'Silly boy,' she chided. 'That was before I knew you were administering thirty-five million dollar estates. And it's *Diva*, remember?'

'Very well, Miss Diva. I'd be delighted to share a glass in celebration.'

After the short ride back to the Mahesh hotel, Wilson collected the room keys and arranged to have the desk manager visit Scorpio George's suite in an hour, to sign in the new guests.

As he was about to leave the reception area, I put a hand on his arm.

'Are you planning to make a complaint?' I asked him quietly.

'A complaint?'

'About Manav.'

'Manav?'

'Your security guard.'

'Oh, him,' he smiled. 'He *was* rather derelict in his duty. But . . . I think that was because he knew I was in safe hands, with you and young Mr Naveen, even if he did expose me to the risk of Miss Diva.'

'Is that a *no?*'

'It is indeed a *no*, sir. I will not make a complaint against him.'

'Thanks,' I said, shaking hands with him.

I liked Evan Wilson. He was calm, discreet and resolute. He'd shown courage when we'd confronted him. He had a sense of humour, was professional but pragmatic, and seemed to be a good judge of flawed characters, in life's tight corners.

'Don't mention it,' he said. 'Shall we join the others?'

'No, I've got somewhere I already had to be,' I replied, looking at the laughing group, Naveen, Divya, and the Zodiac Georges, waiting by the doors to the elevators.

I looked back to the silver-haired Canadian lawyer.

'Good luck, Mr Wilson.'

I watched him walk away, and then made my way back to the

ground-floor restaurant. Ranjit's table was empty, and had been cleared and prepared for a new setting.

I signalled the manager.

'When did they leave?'

'Some time ago, Mr Lin. Miss Lisa left a note for you.'

He fished the note from his vest pocket and handed it to me. It was written in the red ink she preferred.

Gone to a party with Ranjit, the note said. *Don't wait up.*

I gave the manager a tip, and took a few steps, before a thought made me turn and call back.

'Did they have dessert?' I asked.

'Ah . . . no, sir. No. They left immediately after the first course.'

I pushed through the main doors of the hotel. Outside in the warm night air I saw Manav, the hotel bodyguard, standing on duty with another security officer. He noticed me, and searched my eyes expectantly.

He was a good kid, with a nice combination: big, strong and kind. He was worried that Mr Wilson would make a complaint for abandoning a guest of the hotel. It would cost him his job, and end any hope of a better career in the hospitality industry. I signalled him to come over.

'*Kya hal hain, Manav?*' I asked, shaking hands. *How are you doing?*

There was a tip rolled into the palm of my hand, but he closed his huge hands over mine and resisted the offer of money.

'No, no, Linbaba,' he whispered. 'I don't . . . I can't take anything.'

'Sure you can,' I smiled, forcing him to clutch at the money or let it fall to the ground.

'That's just what Mr Wilson would've given you, if you'd finished your shift with him tonight.'

'M-Mr Wilson . . . '

'It's okay. I just spoke to him.'

'Yes, Linbaba. I saw you coming inside, before. I was waiting here, but I didn't have the guts to talk to him.'

'He won't make a complaint.'

'It's sure, Linbaba? Really?'

'It's sure. He told me. It's okay.'

The gleam in Manav's black-brown eyes followed me as I collected my bike and rode along Marine Drive to the peak of Malabar Hill.

I stopped at a vantage point looking down on the windowed jewels of light lining the bay-wide smile of Marine Drive. I rolled myself a hash joint and began to smoke it.

A beggar, who made the long, winding climb to the summit every night for a safe place to sleep, came to sit nearby. I handed him the joint. He grinned and puffed at it happily, using his hand as a chillum to draw the smoke without touching it to his lips.

'*Mast mal!*' he muttered, smoke streaming out through his nostrils. *Great stuff!*

Nodding sagely, he puffed again, and passed the joint back to me.

I took the piece of hash I'd used to make the joint, and gave it to him. The man became suddenly serious, looking from the large piece of hashish in his palm to my eyes, and back again.

'Go home,' he said at last in Hindi. 'Go home.'

I rode back through storming rain, parked my bike in the shelter beneath my building, slipped a damp twenty-rupee note into the shirt pocket of the sleeping watchman, and entered my apartment.

Lisa wasn't there. I stripped off the wet clothes and boots, showered, ate some bread and fruit, drank a mug of coffee, and lay back on the bed.

The electric fan turned overhead just fast enough to send a cooling flourish into the humid air. A new downpour drummed against the metal gable over the bedroom window, sending rivulets as silver as mercury streaming past the half-open window.

I smoked a joint in the dark, and waited. It was after three when Lisa returned, her footsteps tapping the dissonant dance of the drunk on the marble floor tiles of the entry hall.

She tumbled into the room, throwing her handbag against a chair. It missed, and rolled off onto the floor. She kicked one loose, untied sandal off, and hop-stumbled out of the other.

Turning in struggling little circles, she wriggled out of her dress and panties, trailing them from one ankle as she thumped onto the bed.

I couldn't see her pupils, in the darkened room. One look at them would've told me what she'd taken: all drugs live and die in the eyes. I reached out to switch on the bedside lamp, but she stopped me.

'Leave it off! I want to be Cleopatra.'

When she was deep in sleep I took a wet towel and cooled her down. I dried her off, and she rolled onto her side of the bed, and settled into blameless sleep.

228

I lay back in the darkness, beside her. Bats chittered past the open window, seeking shelter from the dawn. The watchman, who'd woken from his nap to do rounds of the building, tapped his bamboo stick against the ground to warn away foraging rats. The sound faded, and the room was still and quiet. Her breathing was waves on a gentle shore.

I was happy for the Zodiac Georges, sudden millionaires, and happy to see that Naveen and Divya were still together, no matter how much they fought. And I was glad that Lisa was home and safe.

But I was sick inside. I didn't know what Lisa wanted, but I was sure it wasn't me. There were times, I think, when I wanted her to want me, and love me, and let me love her in return. There were times when I hoped that it would happen. But wanting more was a sign of how little we had. We were friends who didn't try hard enough to make it more.

My eyes began to close. In a half-dream I saw Ranjit, his face contorted, a fiend, a malignant thing. I started awake, and listened for a while to the soft echo of the sea, Lisa's breath, until my eyes closed again.

And we slept, together and alone, as rains washed the city cleaner than the kneeling stone in a prison confessional.

CHAPTER TWENTY-TWO

THE FILTHY GEORGES, AS MANY HAD CALLED THEM, were filthy rich. The whole of South Bombay babbled, marvelling at the fate that allowed the meekest of the city's meek foreigners to become inheritors of the earth. The once-shunned beggars were suddenly shunted into social acceptability. *How the fallen are mighty*, Didier laughed happily.

For three weeks the door of the Zodiac Georges' suite opened, day and night, to admit a promissory of experts, devoting their talents to squeezing the square-peg street dwellers into the round holes of sudden wealth: tailors, barbers, podiatrists, jewellers, numerologists, watchmakers, yoga instructors, manicurists, stylists, meditation masters, astrologers, accountants, legal representatives, personal servants, and a frenzy of stress counsellors.

Securing the essential services of those professionals, and driving their fees to vulture leavings, was a task that Divya Devnani applied herself to with considerable energy, and no little flair. She took a suite at the hotel for those weeks, and was almost constantly in the company of the fledgling millionaires. Reinventing Scorpio and Gemini was a duty, she told me.

'I was right there when the Georges came into their money,' she said. 'Me, who just happens to be the richest girl in Bombay, and a girl of supernaturally good taste. This is karma. This is kismet. Who am I to snub my nose? It's my duty to help them rise from the ashes.'

The Zodiac Georges, for all their loving friendship, had completely different strategies for coping with the move from ashes to A-listers.

Gemini George suggested that they should give most of the money away. The Georges never lied, never cheated their customers, and never raised a hand to anyone. Life in the slums and back alleys of

Bombay had given them a long list of friends and deserving recipients: people who'd helped them, managers of cheap restaurants and little shops who'd extended them life-saving lines of credit, a shuffle of beggars and street touts whose kindness had kept them afloat, and even a few cops, who'd always looked the other way.

With what remained of the money, Gemini enthused, they could have a long, unforgettable season of parties, and then put a modest amount into an interest-bearing account, paid monthly, and go back to living happily, and more comfortably, on the street.

Scorpio wasn't tempted. Although he was horrified by the responsibilities and moral burdens of his sudden wealth, and he talked about it to everyone not skilled in the art of escaping pessimists, he couldn't bring himself to part with it.

The first weeks of his prosperity were a nightmare, he said. Money is another word for misery, he said. Money is the ruin of peace, he said. But he wouldn't embrace Gemini's plan, and give the burden away.

He fretted, paced, moaned and mumbled. Shaved and trimmed, exfoliated and massaged, manicured and moisturised, the tall Canadian wandered back and forth in the luxurious suite, prosperously uneasy.

'It will end badly, Lin,' he said to me, when I dropped in to visit.

'Everything ends badly, for everyone. That's why we have art.'

'I guess,' he agreed vaguely, not consoled. 'Did you see Gemini, when you came in? Is he still playing cards?'

'I didn't see him. A Sikh guy let me in. He called himself your major-domo.'

'Oh, yeah. That's Singh. He kinda runs the place. Him and Diva together. He's got a schnozz on him, that guy. If your main job is looking down your nose at people, it helps to have a long one, I guess.'

'He also has a short list, to go with that long nose.'

'That's . . . that's because we had to put a limit on who gets in here, Lin. You wouldn't believe how it's been, since people started hearing about how I've got all this money.'

'Uh-huh.'

'They're hittin' on us, day and night. The hotel had to double its security staff on this floor to cope. And people *still* managed to get up here. One of them was banging on the door, asking for money, while I was taking a dump.'

'Uh-huh.'

'I haven't been on the street for three days. People were crawlin' outta the shadows, man, all of them with their hands out for money.'

I recalled that the Zodiac Georges had themselves emerged from a shoal of shadows over the years, and always brandishing the shell of an upturned palm.

'Uh-huh.'

'But don't worry, Lin,' Scorpio added hastily. 'You'll always be on the short list.'

'Uh-huh.'

'No, I mean it, man. You always did right by us. And I'll never forget it. Hey! Speaking of which, do you . . . do you need any —'

'No, I'm good,' I smiled. 'Thanks anyway.'

'Okay. Okay. Let's go find Gemini. I want to tell him about the new security arrangements.'

We found the Londoner in an annex to the suite, designed for use as a guest's temporary business office. Gemini George had covered the large desk with a tablecloth, and had converted the office into a gambling den.

He was playing poker with a selection of off-duty service personnel from the hotel. The litter of several meals, drinks and snacks indicated that the game had been running for a while.

'Hey, Scorp! Hey, Lin!' Gemini smiled happily, as we entered. 'Pull up a chair. The game's just hotting up.'

'Too hot for me, Gemini.'

Gemini George was a skilful cheat, but he never took large sums of money off people, and he sometimes deliberately lost hands that he could've won. For him, the thrill was in not being detected, no matter how he played the hand.

'Come on, Lin, push your luck.'

'I prefer my *luck* to do the pushing. I'll watch a couple of hands.'

'Suit yourself,' he said, winking at me and throwing a chip on the table to raise a bet. 'Scorpio, did you get our guest a drink?'

'I'm sorry, Lin.'

He whirled on the hotel staff, playing cards.

'C'mon, you guys! You're supposed to be *working* in this hotel. Fetch our guest a drink. Get him a . . . what, Lin?'

'I'm good, Scorpio.'

'No, please, have something.'

'Okay. A fresh lime soda, no ice.'

One of the players wearing room service livery threw his cards into the pot, and left the table to get the juice.

There was a shout, coming from the main door of the suite. As we looked up, Didier entered the office, dragging the major-domo by the length of his prominent nose.

'This imbecile insists that my name does not appear on the list of permitted guests,' Didier huffed and puffed.

'What an outrage,' I said. 'Like, say, pulling someone's nose, for no reason.'

'No reason? When I explained that such an oversight is quite impossible, because my name appears on *every* list, from Interpol to the Bombay Cricket Club, even though I abhor the game of cricket, he actually tried to shut the door in my face.'

'Can I suggest, Didier, that you let go of *his* face?'

'Oh, Lin!' Didier protested, squeezing the man's nose harder in his closed fist.

The major-domo squealed.

'He's only doing his job, Didier.'

'It is his job to *welcome* me, Lin, not to exclude me.'

'I quit this job!' the major-domo quacked.

'Another thing,' I tried, 'is that you don't know where that nose you're squeezing has been.'

'You're right,' Didier agreed, his lip curling in distaste as he released the major-domo's nose. 'Where can I wash my hands?'

'Through there,' Scorpio said, nodding through the doorway. 'Second door on the right.'

Didier glowered at the major-domo, and left the room. The major-domo looked at me. I have no idea why people look at me when I have absolutely nothing to do with anything.

'Might be a good idea to put Didier on your short list, Scorpio,' I said, reaching out to pick up a small bundle of notes from the pile of winnings in front of Gemini George.

'But, Lin,' Scorpio whined. 'Didier grabbed my major-domo by the nose.'

'You're lucky it was only your man's nose he got hold of.'

'Damn right about that!' Gemini laughed. 'Singh! Put Mr Didier Levy on the short list, right away.'

'I quit this job,' Singh mumbled again, clutching at his nose.

'That's your right,' I said, handing him the money I'd taken from the table. 'But if you do, you'll get drummed out of the Guild of Major-Domos. If you'll accept our sincere apology, on behalf of our friend, and this money for your trouble, we can put this behind us.'

The man held his nose with one hand, fondled the notes with the other, and then wagged his head, moving back to his position near the door.

'Are you sure it's major-*domos*?' Gemini asked mischievously. 'Isn't it *majors*-domo?'

'Say, Lin,' Scorpio remarked, brightening suddenly. 'D'ya think . . . maybe . . . you could stay on with us here for a while? We got plenty of room. We're thinking of taking the whole floor, and you'd be a real help in getting the hang of this being rich thing.'

'Great idea,' Gemini agreed. 'Stay here, Lin. Ask Lisa to move in, too. Liven up the place.'

'Nice offer, guys.'

'Is that a *no*?' Scorpio asked.

'You've got Divya on the case,' I said. 'From what I can see, she's doing a pretty good job.'

'She scares the crap outta me,' Scorpio complained.

'*Everyone* scares the crap outta you,' Gemini commented. 'That's one of the reasons why we love you. What are you doin' here, anyway, Scorp? You never come in here. You hate poker.'

'I don't hate poker.'

'Okay then, Maverick, what's up?'

'It's serious.'

'It can't be more serious than the next hand, Scorp. Lin just gave away all my winnings to your majors-domo, because Didier pulled his nose.'

'Quite rightly,' Didier added, rejoining us.

'Can't argue there,' Gemini agreed. 'I've wanted to do it myself, occasionally, but I thought Singh would hit me. Now, gentlemen, I intend to win back all me previous winnings, so let's play.'

'I mean it, Gemini,' Scorpio said. 'It's serious stuff.'

'I'm playin' against Didier. He's a shark. He'll gut me, if I so much as wink. How can it be more serious than *that*, Scorpio?'

'I wanted to talk to you about the new security arrangements.'

'The what?'

'The new security arrangements.'

'It's a five-star hotel,' Gemini replied. 'We're safe as 'ouses, Scorp.'

'No, we're totally and completely *unsafe*,' Scorpio said. 'A kidnapper could hide in a food trolley, or even disguise himself as a concierge. Then we're finished. Everybody trusts the concierge. We're vulnerable to attack here, Gemini.'

'Attack? What are you, Scorp, an evil warlord?'

'We're vulnerable. I mean it, Gemini.'

'Well, if it's so important, get it off your chest, then. Go on.'

'But . . . I can't talk about security in front of other people.'

'Why not?'

'It wouldn't be . . . secure.'

'Don't we want our friends to be secure, too?'

'But there are employees of the hotel here.'

'And if our bein' 'ere poses some kind of risk to them,' Gemini said, shuffling the cards, 'wouldn't it be fair to include the 'otel employees in our security arrangements, especially the ones gambling with me, so that they can stay safe, too?'

'What?' Scorpio said, shaking his head.

Didier cut the deck, and Gemini paused, the cards in his hand.

'How about this, Scorpio,' he said, smiling at the friend he loved more than anyone or anything in the world. 'Let's just invite all of our friends and all their families to live 'ere with us. Everybody. We'll rent three floors of the 'otel, bring in everyone, and all their families, to stay for as long as they like, and shower them with generosity and happy fun, and spend lots and lots of money at the 'otel, so they're 'appy, and we'll be safe. See? That's your new security arrangement, right there, innit?'

He turned from his bewildered friend to me, the smile all hearts and diamonds.

'Last chance, Lin,' Gemini said, waiting to deal the cards. 'Are you in?'

'No, I'm gone,' I replied, pressing my hand onto Didier's shoulder to say goodbye.

When I left them, Gemini was dealing the cards expertly, a wicked gleam in his eyes. Didier Levy was the only man I knew who was a better card cheat than Gemini George. I didn't want to stay long enough to see one of them lose.

In the corridor outside the suite, I found Naveen and Divya.

'Hey, Lin,' Naveen greeted me, a happy smile moving across his handsome face. 'Are you leaving just now?'

'Yeah. Hey, Divya.'

'It's *Diva*, sweetheart,' she corrected, smiling and pressing her small hand against my forearm. 'What's the rush?'

'Stuff to do,' I answered, smiling back at them.

We stood there in silence for a moment. We were still smiling.

'What?' Divya asked at last.

'Nothing,' I laughed. 'It's just, you two seem to be getting on better.'

'Well,' Divya sighed, 'he's not such a *chudh*, when you get to know him.'

'Thank you,' Naveen said.

'I mean, *elements* of the *chudh* are still there,' Divya clarified. 'And they'll probably always be. You can't make a silk tie from a pig's ear, after all.'

'That's a silk *purse*,' Naveen corrected.

'What?'

'A silk *purse*, not a silk tie,' Naveen insisted.

'What's this? You're going to start carrying a purse now, or what?'

'No, of course not. The saying is *You can't make a silk purse from a sow's ear*. It doesn't mention silk ties.'

'What are you, the prince of fucking proverbs, all of a sudden?'

'I'm just saying –'

'I need a licence from you to change a proverb? Is that it?'

'So, anyway, bye,' I said, pressing the button for the elevator.

I stepped inside. They were still arguing furiously. The doors closed, and the elevator descended, but it seemed that I could still hear them through several floors.

On the ground floor I discovered that they'd actually stepped into a neighbouring elevator, and had argued all the way down beside me. They spilled out into the lobby, squabbling still.

'Hello, again.'

'Sorry, Lin,' Naveen said, detaching himself from Divya. 'I realised that I forgot to tell you something.'

'Uh-huh?'

'It's about your friend Vikram,' Naveen said quietly. 'He's moved into Dennis's place. He's sleeping there, on the floor, and he's hitting the smack pretty hard. I haven't been there myself, in a while, but I heard from Vinson that he's in a bad way. Vinson doesn't go there any more, and neither do I, much. I thought . . . maybe you didn't know.'

'You're right. I didn't. Thanks.'

I glanced at Divya, who was waiting near the bank of elevators. Until that moment I hadn't really noticed how pretty she was. Her wide-set eyes tapered gently to almond-shaped points, where the long lashes were born. Her fine nose curled at the edges to meet the bow of her smile in lines that descended along a scimitar curve to the corners of her mouth.

I glanced at Naveen, and he was staring adoration at her.

And then, in that strange little moment of staring at Naveen and Divya, I felt a shadow pass through me. I shivered. I shifted my gaze to meet Naveen's eyes, hoping that he'd felt it too.

My heart was beating fast, and the sudden sense of dread was so strong that I could feel it in my throat. I searched Naveen's eyes, but there was nothing. He smiled back at me.

'Listen,' I said, taking half a step away from them. 'Stay together.'

'Ah, well . . . ' Divya grinned, about to make some joke.

'Don't stop arguing,' I said quickly, taking another step away. 'But stay together. Look after each other, okay?'

'Okay,' Naveen laughed. 'But —'

I fled, making my way quickly to my parked bike and wrestling it out onto the main road. A few hundred metres away I stopped the bike suddenly, and glanced back over my shoulder at the windowed tower of the Mahesh hotel. I rode away, fast.

I parked the bike outside the house where Dennis lived. The concertina of folding French doors was open on the long veranda. I stepped up onto the veranda, and tapped on the open doors.

Sandal-slap footsteps approached quickly. A curtain was drawn aside, and I saw Jamal, the One Man Show. He beckoned me inside, motioning for me to be silent.

I entered the room, squinting my eyes to adjust to the gloom. Hashish scented the air, mixed with a powerful drift from a large wad of incense sticks, burning in an empty vase.

Dennis was in his customary pose, stretched out in the centre of the large bed, with his hands folded over one another on his chest. He wore pale blue silk pyjamas, and his feet were bare.

I heard a rattling cough to my right and saw Vikram, stretched out on a piece of carpet. Billy Bhasu was sitting on the floor beside him. He was preparing another chillum.

A voice spoke from a darkened corner of the room. It was Concannon's.

'Look what the grimalkin dragged in,' he said. 'I hope you've come to join my little gang, boyo. I'm not in a mood for disappointing drugs, or disappointing men.'

Ignoring him, I went to Vikram's side. Billy Bhasu crab-walked out of the way, and continued preparing the chillum. I pushed at Vikram to rouse him.

'Vikram! Vik! Wake up, man!'

His eyes opened slowly, and then fell shut.

'Last chance, Shantaram,' Concannon said softly. 'Are you with me, or against me?'

I shook Vikram again.

'Wake up, Vik. We're going, man.'

'Leave him alone,' Concannon chided. 'Can't you see the man's happy?'

'It's not happiness, if you can't feel it.'

I shook Vikram's shoulder again.

'Vikram! Wake up!'

He opened his eyes, looked at me, and smiled a sloppy grin.

'Lin! How are you, man?'

'How are *you*, man?'

'Nothing to worry,' he replied sleepily, his eyes drooping and closing. 'It's all cool, man. It's all . . . cool . . . '

He began to snore. His face was dirty. He was a shrinking form inside the clothes of a healthier man.

'Vik! Wake up, man!'

'Leave him the fuck alone,' Concannon said aggressively.

'Mind your own business, Concannon,' I said, not looking at him.

'Why don't you make me?'

It's childish, and we all know it, but it often works.

'Why don't I?' I replied, facing him for the first time.

I could just make out the cold fire in his ice-blue eyes.

'How about this?' I suggested. 'I'll take my friend home to his parents, and then I'll come back here, and we'll meet outside. Sound okay?'

He stood up and approached me, standing close.

'There's two things that I hold sacred. A man's right to crush his enemies, and a man's right to destroy himself in any way he sees fit. We're all goin' down. All of us. We're all on the same road. Vikram's just a little way further down the road than you and me, that's all. That's his natural born right. And you're not stoppin' him.'

It was an angry speech, and every word became just a little angrier.

'Rights have duties,' I answered him, staring back into the fury. 'A friend has a duty to help a friend.'

'I don't have any friends,' he said evenly. 'Nobody does. There's no such thing. Friendship's a fairy story, like Father fuckin' Christmas. And what kind of a cunt did that fat bastard turn out to be? A fuckin' lie, that's what he is. There are no friends in this world. There's allies and there's enemies in this life, and any one of them can change their coat as soon as look at you. That's the truth of it.'

'I'm gonna take Vikram outta here.'

'The *fuck* you are!'

He watched me for a moment, for five heartbeats, and slid his right foot backwards on the floor, shaping up for a fight. Not wanting to be caught flat-footed, I did the same. His hands slowly rose, stopping opposite his face, left fist forward. I raised my hands in response, my heart beating hard.

Stupid. Men. We were going to fight, for nothing. You can't fight *for* anything, of course: you can only fight against something. If you're fighting, the part of you that was for something has already been for-gotten, replaced by a part that's violently against something. And in that minute, I was violently against Concannon.

'One Man Show!' the One Man Show said suddenly.

'Shut the fuck up,' Concannon growled.

'Guys!' Dennis said from the bed, his eyes still closed. 'My high! You're killing my *high*!'

'Go back to sleep, Dennis lad,' Concannon said, watching my face. 'This won't take but a minute or two.'

'*Please*, guys,' Dennis pleaded, in his soft, sonorous voice. 'Concannon! Come over here, at once, my wild son. Come and smoke a legendary chillum with me. Help me get my high back, man. And Lin, take Vikram with you. He's been here for a week. Unlike the rest of us in this happy little tomb, he actually has a family to go back to. Take him with you.'

Concannon slowly let his fists fall to his sides.

'Whatever you say, Dennis, me old reprobate,' he grinned. 'It's no skin off my nose.'

He went to sit beside Dennis on the huge bed.

'Concannon,' Dennis said, his eyes beginning to close again. 'You're the most alive human being I ever met. I can feel your energy, even when I'm dead. And that's why I love you. But you're killing my high.'

'Settle down, Dennis me darlin',' Concannon said, his hand on Dennis's shoulder. 'There'll be no more trouble.'

I roused Vikram quickly, and forced him to stand. As we reached the doors, Concannon spoke again.

'I won't forget this, Shantaram,' he said, his teeth showing in a furious grin.

I took Vikram home in a taxi. He spoke only once.

'She was a great chick,' he said, as if to himself. 'She really was. If she loved me, as much as I love her, she'd be perfect, you know what I mean?'

I helped his sister put him to bed, drank three cups of tea with his worried parents, and then took a taxi back to my parked bike.

I'd arranged to meet Lisa for lunch at Kayani's, near the Metro Junction, and I rode there slowly, drifting at a walking pace on the long, leafy avenue of extravagantly coloured clothing stalls called Fashion Street. I was thinking about Concannon and Vikram and his parents, and my thoughts were wolves.

Vikram's father was an older man, long retired, whose youngest son had been born into the autumn of his life. The self-defeating disarray of Vikram's addiction bewildered him.

His handsome young son, who'd been something of a dandy, dressing himself in the black silk and silver buckles of his obsession with Sergio Leone's movies, suddenly wore dirty clothes. His hair, which had once been coiffed to a millimetre's perfection by his barber, hung in drifts, pressed flat where he'd slept. He didn't wash himself or shave, sometimes for days at a time. He didn't eat or speak to anyone at home. And the eyes that occasionally rose to meet his worried father's were drained of light and life, as though the soul had already deserted the man, and was waiting for the body to fall.

Filled with the avalanchine power of love for his English rose, Vikram, the rich boy who never worked, had created a business on the edge of the movie industry. He supplied foreign tourists to play non-speaking parts in Bollywood movies.

It was a daring commercial venture. He had no experience in the industry, and was working with borrowed funds. But Vikram's charm and belief in himself made it a success. Lisa, his first business partner, had begun to discover her talents in their work together.

When the English rose left Vikram without warning or explanation, the confidence that had seen him dance on the top of a moving train, to propose to her, drained from his life like blood from a whittled vein.

'And he's begun to take things,' Vikram's father had whispered, while Vikram slept. 'Little things. His mother's pearl brooch, and one of my pens, the good one, presented to me by the company, when I retired. When we asked him about it, he flew into a rage and blamed the servants. But it's him. We know. He is selling the things he is stealing, to feed his habit for this drug.'

I nodded.

'It's a shame,' the elderly man had sighed, his eyes filling with tears. 'It's a damn shame.'

It was sorrow and dread as well, because love had become a stranger in their home. I was that stranger, once. I was addicted to heroin: so addicted that I stole money to feed my habit. I stopped, twenty-five years ago, and I despise the drug more every year. I feel heart-crushing compassion every time I see or hear of someone still addicted: still shooting in a war against themselves. But I was that stranger in my parents' house of love. I know how hard it is to find the line between helping someone out, and helping someone in. I know that all suffer and die inside, again and again, from the addiction of one. And I know that sometimes, if love doesn't harden itself, love doesn't survive at all.

And that day, in that runaway year before I knew what cards Fate would throw at me, I prayed for all of us: for Vikram and his family and all the slaves of oblivion.

CHAPTER TWENTY-THREE

I PARKED THE BIKE OPPOSITE KAYANI'S TO MEET LISA. Watching the signal, I took two deep breaths and surfed my second-favourite pedestrian-killer Bombay traffic. Madness machines rushed at me, turning and weaving unpredictably. If you don't dance in that, you die.

Across the suicide road I used the hanging rope in the doorway of the restaurant to assist me on the steep marble steps, and entered the café. Perhaps the most famous of Bombay's deservedly famous Parsi tea and coffee houses, Kayani's offered hot chilli omelettes, meat and vegetable pasties, toasted sandwiches, and the largest selection of home-baked cakes and biscuits in the area.

Lisa was waiting at the table she preferred, toward the back of the ground-floor space, with a view of the busy kitchen, seven steps away beyond a serving counter.

Several waiters smiled and nodded as I made my way to her table. Kayani's was one of our places: in the two years since we'd been a couple, we'd had lunch or afternoon tea there every couple of weeks.

I kissed her, and sat close to her on a corner of the table, our legs touching.

'Bun musca?' I asked her, not looking at the menu.

It was her favourite snack at Kayani's: a freshly made buttered bun, cut into three slices that can be neatly dunked into a cup of hot, sweet tea. She nodded.

'Do bun musca, do chai,' I said to the waiter. Two buttered buns, and two cups of tea.

The waiter, named Atif, collected the unused menus and shuffled away toward the serving counter, shouting the order.

'Sorry I'm late, Lisa. I got this message about Vikram, so I went to Dennis's place, and took him home.'

'Dennis? Is that the Sleeping Baba?'

'Yeah.'

'I'd like to meet him. I've heard a lot about him. He's getting kind of a cult status. Rish was talking about making an installation, based around his trance.'

'I can take you there, but you don't actually *meet* him, unless you're lucky. You sort of stand there, trying not to kill his high.'

'Not killing his high?'

'That's about it.'

'I *like* this guy,' she laughed.

I knew her sense of humour, and her quick love for unusual people who did unusual things.

'Oh, yeah. Dennis is a very *Lisa* kind of guy.'

'If you're gonna do something, make an art of it,' she replied.

The tea and buttered buns arrived. We took chunks of the bread, dipped them into our tea until the butter began to run, and ate them hungrily.

'So, how was Vikram?'

'He's not good.'

'*That* not good?'

'*That* not good.'

She frowned. We both knew addiction, and its python grip.

'D'you think we should do an intervention?'

'I don't know. Maybe. I told his parents they should pay for him to stay at a private clinic for a while. They're gonna try it.'

'Can they afford it?'

'Can they afford not to?'

'Point,' she agreed.

'Problem is, even if he goes there, he's not ready for help yet. Not even close.'

She thought for a moment.

'We're not good, you and me, are we?'

'Where did *that* come from?'

'You and me,' she repeated softly. 'We're not good, are we?'

'Define good.'

I tried smiling, but it didn't work.

'Good is more,' she said.

'Okay,' I said softly. 'Let's do more.'

'You're nuts, you know that?'

I was lost, and not sure I wanted to know where we were going.

'When I was arrested,' I said, 'I had to undergo a psychiatric evaluation. So, I've actually been certified sane enough to stand trial, which is more than I can say for most of the people I know, including the psychiatrist who certified me. In fact, to get convicted in a court of law, you've gotta be declared sane. Which means that every convict in the world, in a jail cell, is sane, A-Grade and Certified. And with so many people on the outside seeing therapists and counsellors and all, pretty soon the only people who'll be able to *prove* they're sane will be the people behind bars.'

She looked up at me. The searchlight smile in her eyes tried to cut through.

'Pretty heavy conversation,' she said, 'with a buttered bun in your hand.'

'These days, Lisa, even when I try to make you laugh, it's a heavy conversation.'

'Are you saying it's *my* fault?' she demanded fiercely.

'No. I was just —'

'It's not always about *you*,' she snapped.

'Okay. Okay.'

Atif arrived to clear the dishes and take the next order. When we had a lot to discuss, we had two or even three buns with tea, but I told him just to bring the tea.

'No *bun musca*?' Atif asked.

'No *bun musca*. *Sirf chai*.' Only tea.

'Maybe, you'll be having, just *one bun musca*?' Atif tempted, waggling his shaggy eyebrows. '*To be sharing?*'

'No *bun musca*. Just chai.'

'*Thik*,' he mumbled, deeply concerned.

He took a deep breath, and shouted to the staff in the kitchen.

'*Do chai! Do chai lao!* No *bun musca*! *Repeating, no bun musca!*'

'No *bun musca*?' a voice called back from the kitchen.

I looked at Lisa, and then at Atif, then at Vishal the fast-food cook, glowering from the serving window. I raised my hand, one finger extended.

'One *bun musca*!' I shouted.

'Yes!' Atif shouted triumphantly. '*Ek bun musca, do chai!*'

Vishal wagged his head in the serving widow enthusiastically, his wide grin revealing pearl-white teeth.

'*Ek bun musca, do chai!*' he shouted happily, banging his saucepan of boiling chai on its gas-ring fire.

'I'm glad we got that settled,' I said, trying to shake Lisa happy.

It was the kind of silly, lovely thing that Bombay does every day, and normally we would've enjoyed it together.

'You know, it's kinda weird,' Lisa said.

'Not really. Atif is —'

'I was here yesterday,' she said. 'With Karla.'

'You . . . what?'

'And exactly the same thing happened with that waiter.'

'Wait a minute. You were here with Karla, yesterday, and you didn't say anything?'

'Why would I? Do you tell me who you see, and who you fight with?'

'There's a reason for that, and you know it.'

'Anyway, when I was here with Karla, the same thing happened with that waiter —'

'Atif?'

'See? She knew his name, too.'

'He's my favourite waiter here. Not surprised she likes him. He should be running the place.'

'No, you're not getting me.'

'Do we have to talk about Karla?'

'Talk about her,' she said quietly, 'or think about her?'

'Are *you* thinking about her? Because I'm not. I'm thinking about you, and us. What there is of us.'

She flicked a frown at me, and then went back to folding and refolding the napkin.

The *bun musca* and chai arrived at the table. I ignored it for a moment, but Atif lingered near my elbow, watching me, so I picked up a piece of the bread and took a bite. He wagged his head approvingly, and walked away.

'I guess it's just my busted-up life, you know?' Lisa said, creasing lines in the napkin with her fingers.

I did know. I'd heard her story many times. It was always differently the same, and I always wanted her to tell it again.

'I wasn't, you know, *mistreated*, or anything. It wasn't anything like that. My parents are kinda great, you know. They really are. The fault is in me. You know that.'

'There's no fault in you, Lisa.'

'Yes, there is.'

'Even if there was, there's no fault that can't be loved away.'

She paused, sipped at the chai, and found another way into whatever it was she was trying to tell me.

'Did I ever tell you about the parade?'

'Not at Kayani's,' I smiled. 'Tell me again.'

'We used to have this Founders' Day Parade every year, right down the whole of Main Street. Everybody for fifty miles around got involved, or came to watch the show. My high school band marched in the parade, and we had this big barge –'

'A float.'

'Yeah, the school had this big float that the parents' committee made, with a different theme every year. One year, they picked me to be the one sitting high up on a kind of throne, as the central attraction. The theme that year was *The Fruits of Liberty*, and the barge –'

'The float.'

'The float was filled with produce from the local farms. I was the *Liberty Belle*, get it?'

'You must've looked damn cute.'

She smiled.

'I had to sit on the top, while the whole mountain of fruit and potatoes and beets and all rolled along between the crowds. And I had to wave, regally, like this, all the way down Main Street.'

She waved her hand gently, palm upwards, her fingers curved around the majestic memory.

Atif cleared the table again. He looked at me, posing the question with one raised eyebrow. I held my hand over the table palm downwards, and gestured toward the table twice. It was the signal to wait for a time. He wagged his head from side to side, and checked on the neighbouring tables.

'It was really something. Kind of a big honour, if you know what I mean. Everybody said so. Everybody kept on saying so, over and over again. You know how irritating it is, when people keep telling you how honoured you should be?'

246

'I know the *dishonoured* version, but I get your drift.'

'The thing was, I didn't really *feel* honoured, you know? I was kinda glad, of course, when they picked *me* from all the other girls, some of them way prettier than me. And I didn't even *do* anything to get picked. Some of the girls tried every devious trick they could think of. You don't know how many tricks a girl can find up her sleeve, until you see a bunch of them trying to get picked to be on top of the truck in the Founders' Day Parade.'

'What kind of tricks?' I asked hopefully.

'Me, I didn't do anything,' she said. 'And I was as surprised as anyone when the committee picked me. But . . . I didn't really *feel* anything. I waved my hand, as regal as Marie Antoinette, getting a little drunk on the smell of those apples heating up in the sun, but I looked at all the faces smiling at me, and all those hands clapping me, and I didn't feel anything at all.'

Shafts of sunlight pierced the subdued monsoon shade of Kayani's. One ray of light crossed our table, striking her face and dividing it between the sky-blue eyes in shadow and the lips, wet with white light.

'I just didn't feel anything at all,' the light-struck lips said. 'And I never did. I never felt like I belonged there, in that town, or in that school, or even with my own family. I never did. I never have.'

'Lisa –'

'You don't feel like that,' she said flatly. 'You and Karla. You belong where you are. I finally get it, and it took the waiter to show it to me. I finally get it.'

She looked up from the wrinkled napkin to stare into my eyes, her face emptied of expression.

'I never do,' she said flatly. 'I never belong anywhere. Not even with you. I like you, Lin. I've had a thing for you for a long time. But I never felt anything more than that. Did you know that? I never felt anything for you.'

There'd always been a knife in my chest when I tried to love Lisa. The knife was those words, when she spoke them, because she spoke them for both of us.

'People don't belong to one another,' I said softly. 'They can't. That's the first rule of freedom.'

She tried to smile. She didn't make it.

'Why do people fall apart?' she asked, frowning into a truth.

247

'Why do people fall in?'

'What are you, a psychiatrist now, answering a question with a question?'

'Fair enough. Okay. If you really want me to say it, I think people fall apart when they weren't really together in the first place.'

'Well,' she continued, her eyes drifting down to the table, 'what if you're afraid of being together with someone? Or with everyone?'

'What do you mean?'

'Lately I feel like the committee picked me for the parade all over again, and I didn't even try. Do you see?'

'No, Lisa.'

'You don't?'

'Whatever we are, or we're not, all I know is that you beat the curse, and got back on your feet. That's something to be proud of, Lisa. You're doing what you love, working with artists you respect. And I'm your friend, no matter what happens. It's good, Lisa. You're good.'

She looked up again. She wanted to speak. Her mouth opened. Her lips twitched, tricked into movement by flickering thoughts.

'I gotta go,' she said quickly, standing to leave. 'There's a new show. A new artist. He's . . . he's pretty good. We're mounting it in a couple of days.'

'Okay. We'll —'

'No. I'll get a cab.'

'I'm faster than any cab in this city,' I smiled.

'That you are, and cheaper too, cowboy, but I'll get a cab.'

I paid and walked out with her, descending to the sun-streaked street. There were taxis parked opposite, and we made for the first in line. She stooped to enter the cab, but I held her back.

She met my eyes for a moment, and then threw her glance away again.

'Don't wait up for me tonight,' she said. 'This new installation we're setting up, it's pretty complicated. We're gonna work around the clock for a couple days, to —'

'A couple of days?'

'Yeah. I . . . I'll probably sleep there tonight, and tomorrow, just . . . just to bring the show in on time, you know?'

'What's happening here, Lisa?'

'Nothing's happening here,' she said, and got into the cab.

It took off at once. She turned to look at me as the taxi pulled away, staring back at me until I lost her.

The rapture, born in seconds, is a frail thing. And when rapture dies, no power can restore it to a lover's eye. Lisa and I were staring at one another from a deeper place: the place where rapture lands when it falls.

A light had dimmed, and a shadow moved across the garden of what was. I waited on the footpath for half an hour, thinking hard.

I was missing something, a conflict more fundamental than Lisa's objection to my life on the edge of the Sanjay Company, or even her desire to be with others. Something else was happening, and I couldn't see it right or even feel it right, of course, because it was happening to me.

CHAPTER TWENTY-FOUR

THE STREET WAS HAPPILY LARCENOUS as I parked my bike outside Leopold's beside a lounge of street touts, their salamander eyes roving for business. I looked left, slowly, and then right, taking in every threat or opportunity on the street around me. I'd begun to turn my thoughts away from that shadow, Lisa's shadow, moving across the garden of what was, when I heard a voice.

'Lin! This is *great*, man! I've been trying to find you.'

It was Stuart Vinson, and he was agitated. That was good. After the talk with Lisa that I didn't understand, agitation from a man I almost never understood seemed like the right distraction.

'Vinson. What's up?'

'There's this girl. She's . . . I need your help. You've got some pull with the Colaba cops, right?'

'Define *pull*.'

'You can get things done, man. That's right?'

'I know who's first and last in line, if you're handing out money.'

'That's it! That's great! Can you come with me? Right now?'

'I –'

'Please, Lin. There's this girl. She's in a lotta trouble.'

He read my frown.

'What? No! *She* hasn't done anything wrong. Fact is, far as I can figure it, it's just that her boyfriend's dead. He OD'd, like, just last night, and –'

'Wait a minute. Slow down. Who's this girl?'

'I . . . I don't know her name.'

'Uh-huh.'

'I mean, I haven't heard it yet. I haven't seen her passport, either. I don't even know where she comes from. But I know I've got to save her, and maybe I'm the only one who can, you know? She's got these eyes, like, it's too weird, man. I mean, it's like the universe is tellin' me to save her. It's mystical. It's magical. It's fated, or something. But every time I ask the cops about her, they tell me to shut up.'

'Shut up, Vinson, or talk sense.'

'Wait! Let me explain. I was in the police station, paying a fine for my driver, you know, because he got in this fight with another driver, on Kemps Corner, near the Breach Candy turnoff, and he —'

'Vinson. The girl.'

'Yeah, man, I finished up with the cops, and I saw this girl sitting there. You gotta see her, man. Those eyes. Her eyes ... they're ... they're fire and ice at the same time. You've gotta see it to believe it. What *is* it about the eyes that gets you so fucked up, man?'

'Connection. Back to the girl.'

'Like I said, her boyfriend died of an overdose some time, like, last night or early this morning. Best as I can make out, she woke up and found him like that, stiff as a two-by-four, and long gone. She was stayin' at the Frantic.'

'Go on.'

'Those Frantic guys run a tight ship, and they know how to keep their mouths shut. I've done some deals there. But, like, dead bodies? They draw the line, you know?'

'I know the Frantic. They held the girl, called the cops, and handed her over.'

'Yeah, the fuckers.'

'They were just trying to stay outta jail, like you should be, Vinson. It's not safe to play Good Samaritan in a police station, when you're a drug dealer. It's not ever safe in a police station.'

'I ... I know. I know. But this girl, man, it's mystical, I tell ya. I tried to get the cops to open up about her. The only thing they told me was that she did the identification of the body at the morgue, like they wanted. That must've been hell for her, man. And she made a statement, like they asked her. But she didn't do anything, and they won't let her go.'

'It's about money.'

'I figured. But they won't talk to me. That's why I need you.'

'Who's on duty?'

'Dilip. The duty sergeant. He's on top of it all. She's sitting in his office.'

'That's good.'

'I can pay him, to let the girl go?'

'He'd sell his gun and badge, if you offered enough.'

'That's great!'

'But then he'd find you, and beat you up to get them back.'

'That's not great.'

'He likes fear. Fill your eyes with just enough simulated fear to make him smile, then give him money.'

'Is that what you do?'

'Lightning Dilip and I are past simulated fear.'

'If you go in there with me, will he let us pay, and get the girl out of there?'

'Sure. I think so. But . . . '

'But what?'

I exhaled a long, exhausted breath, and frowned my reservations into his worried eyes.

I liked Stuart Vinson. His lean, handsome face, tanned by six years of Asian sunlight, always carried the kind of brave, earnest, determined expression that might've graced a polar explorer, leading others on a noble adventure, even though he was in fact a wily, lucky drug dealer, who lived lavish in a city where hunger was a constituency. I couldn't read his motive.

'Are you sure you wanna get involved? You don't know this girl. You don't even know her name.'

'Please don't, like, say anything bad about this girl,' he said softly, but with surprising force. 'It will make me not like you. If you don't want to help me, that's cool. But me, I already know everything I need to know about her.'

'Jesus.'

'I'm sorry,' he said, hanging his head for an instant.

Just as quickly he raised his pleading eyes again.

'I know it sounds crazy, but I've been there in Dilip's office for the last two hours, trying to help her. She didn't say anything. Not a word. But this one time she looked up at me, and she gave me this, like, little smile. I felt it in my heart, Lin. I can't explain it. And I . . . I smiled back at her. And she felt it, too. I know it. I'm sure of it. Sure as anything I've ever known in my life. I don't know if you know what it's like to love someone for no reason you can understand, but all I'm asking is that you help me.'

I knew what it was like: everybody in love does. We walked across the street to the Colaba police station, and into Lightning Dilip's office.

The duty sergeant looked me up and down, looked at the girl sitting across the desk from him, and then looked back to me.

'A friend of yours?' Lightning asked, nodding at the girl.

I looked at her, and something curled inside me, like ferns closing. It was the girl whose photograph was in the locket, the girl who'd sold the locket, the girl I'd tried to warn, when I returned the locket to her.

Fate, I thought, *get off my back.*

Her greasy hair was tangled and clinging to the sweat on her neck. She wore a royal blue T-shirt, faded from over-washing, and tight enough to reveal her small, frail physique. Her jeans seemed too large for her: a thin belt gathered them in bunches around her narrow waist.

She was wearing the locket. She recognised me.

'Yes,' I replied. 'A friend. Please, Sergeant-*ji*, turn on the fan.'

Lightning Dilip glanced at the unmoving fan over her head, and almost imperceptibly lifted his eyes to the fan over his own head, rotating swiftly to banish the monsoon smother.

He shifted his eyes to me again, the irises set in honey-coloured hatred.

'*Punkah!*' he bellowed at a subordinate.

The constable hastily switched on the fan over the girl's head, and cooling air streamed onto the sweat bathing her slender neck.

'So, she is your friend, Shantaram?' Dilip asked cunningly.

'Yes, Lightning-*ji*.'

'Very well then, what is her name?'

'What name did she give you?'

Dilip laughed. I turned to the girl.

'What's your name?' I asked.

'Rannveig,' she replied flatly, her hand drifting to the locket around her neck, as her eyes met mine. 'Rannveig Larsen.'

'Her name's Rannveig,' I said. 'Rannveig Larsen.'

Dilip laughed again.

'That's not the name I have written in front of me,' he said, still smiling.

'It's Norwegian,' the girl said. 'You write it like *R-a-n-n-v-e-i-g*, but you pronounce it *Runway* – like the thing at the airport.'

'Her name's Rannveig,' I said. 'Like the thing at the airport.'

'What do you want, Shantaram?' Dilip asked.

'I'd like to escort Miss Larsen home. She's had a pretty rough day.'

'Miss Larsen tells me that she *has* no home,' Dilip retorted. 'She was thrown out of the Frantic hotel this morning.'

'She can stay at *my* place,' Vinson said quickly.

Everyone looked at Vinson.

'It's . . . it's a big place, my place,' Vinson stammered, looking from one to another of us. 'There's plenty of room. And I have a live-in servant. She'll take good care of her. That is . . . if . . . if she *wants* to come to my place.'

Lightning Dilip turned to me.

'Who the fuck is this idiot?' he asked in Hindi.

'This is Mr Vinson,' I said.

'I'm Stuart Vinson,' he said. 'I was here, like, ten minutes ago.'

'Shut up,' Lightning said.

'We'd like to escort Miss Larsen home, Lightning-*ji*,' I said. 'That is, if she's free to leave.'

'*Free*,' Dilip repeated, drawing out the word. 'It's such a little word, but with so many *conditions* attached to it.'

'I'd be happy to meet those conditions,' I said, 'depending, of course, on just how many conditions there are, and how firmly they're attached.'

'I can think of at least ten conditions,' Lightning said, a sly grin sliding off the edge of his irritability.

I counted out ten thousand rupees, and put the money on the desk. As I slid it across, he reached out to cover my hand in both of his.

'What interest does the Sanjay Company have in this girl?'

'This isn't Sanjay Company business. This is personal. She's a friend.'

Still holding my hand against the desk, he glanced at the girl, looking her up and down.

'Ah, of course,' he said, his lips twitching around an oily grin.

'Wait a minute –' Vinson began, but I cut him off, pulling my hand free.

'Mister Vinson would like to thank you, Lightning-*ji*, for your kind and compassionate understanding.'

'Always happy to help,' Dilip snarled. 'The girl must be back here in two days, to sign the papers.'

'What papers?' Vinson demanded.

Dilip looked at him. I knew the look: he was thinking about which part of Vinson's body he would start kicking, after he had his men chain him to a gate.

'She'll be here, Sergeant-*ji*,' I said. 'And exactly what papers will she be required to sign?'

'The transfer of the body,' Dilip replied, picking up a file from his desk. 'The body of the unfortunate young man goes back to Norway, in three days. But she must sign the forms in two days. Now get out of here, before I start adding more conditions to her release.'

I held my hand out to the girl. She took it, stood up, and walked a few steps. She was unsteady on her feet. As she neared Vinson she stumbled, and he reached out to put an arm around her shoulder.

Vinson walked her to the street, helped her into the back seat of his car, and climbed in beside her. The driver started the engine, but I leaned against the open window.

'What happened, Rannveig, like the thing at the airport?' I asked her.

'What?'

'Your boyfriend. What happened?'

'You don't have to worry about me,' she said abstractedly. 'I'm okay. I'm okay.'

'Right now, I'm worried about *him*,' I said, nodding toward Vinson. 'And if I'm gonna go back in there and deal with that cop, I need to know what happened.'

'I . . . I wasn't,' she began, staring at the cloth bag cradled in her lap. I guessed that it held everything she owned.

'Tell me.'

'He . . . he couldn't stop. And things got crazier and crazier. Then, just yesterday, just last night, I told him I was leaving him, and going back to Oslo. But he begged me to stay one more night. Just one more night. And . . . and then . . . He did it on purpose. I saw it in his face. He did it on purpose. I can't go back home. I can't see anyone from there.'

The fierce, electric blue of her eyes glazed over, and she slithered into an exhausted silence. I knew the look: staring at the dead. She was staring at the face of her dead boyfriend.

'Have you got anyone in Bombay?' I asked.

She shook her head slowly.

'Do you want your consulate involved?'

She shook her head more quickly.

'Why not?' I asked.

'I told you. I can't face anyone now.'

255

'She's beat,' Vinson said softly. 'I'll take her home. She'll be safe with me, until she decides what she wants to do.'

'Okay. Okay. I'll talk to Lightning Dilip.'

'You have to do *more?*' Vinson asked. 'I thought that was it.'

'He didn't give back her passport. He's holding out for more money, but he didn't want to go into that. Not with you in the office. I'll handle it.'

'Thanks, man,' Vinson nodded. 'I'll make sure she gets back to sign the forms. Hey, let me give you that money!'

'It's only cool to hand over money inside a police station, Vinson, not outside. We'll settle it later. If I get the passport back, I'll leave it with Didier, at Leo's.'

Vinson turned to the girl, speaking to her softly.

'You'll be okay. My maid will look after you. She's tough, but she's all bark and no bite. A hot bath, some fresh, clean clothes, something to eat, and some sleep. You'll be fine. I promise.'

He gave instructions to his driver, and the car moved off. The girl turned quickly, found me on the street, and mouthed something at me. I couldn't understand what she was trying to say. I watched the car until it disappeared, and then went back to talk with Lightning Dilip.

There wasn't a lot to learn. The girl's story was that she'd woken to find her boyfriend dead in the bed beside her. There was a syringe stuck in his arm. She'd called the manager for help, and he'd called the police and an ambulance.

Lightning Dilip was satisfied that it was a simple overdose. The kid had track marks on the veins in his arms, hands and feet, and the hotel manager testified that no-one had entered Rannveig's room but the couple.

It cost me five thousand rupees to buy back the girl's passport, and another ten thousand to have the name *Rannveig Larsen* removed from the account of the boy's death.

In the revised version of the official record, it was the hotel manager who'd found the body, and Rannveig vanished from the narrative.

It was a lot of money in those days, and I planned to recover it from Vinson soon. As I was leaving Lightning Dilip's office, slipping the Norwegian passport into my pocket, the duty sergeant stopped me.

'Tell the Sanjay Company that this case raises the stakes.'

'What are you talking about?'

'DaSilva,' he said, almost spitting the word at me. 'Andrew DaSilva.

It was his heroin that killed this boy. It's the third heroin death this week. The Sanjay Company is selling some very strong, very bad shit on the street. I'm getting trouble for it.'

'How can you be sure of that?'

It wasn't a polite question, and he didn't have a polite answer.

'Fuck you, and fuck dead junkies. I don't give a shit. The two local kids are a minor problem. But when a foreigner dies in my zone, it leaves a big stain on my desk. I like a clean desk. I told DaSilva he would have to pay me double this month, for the two deaths. Now that it's *three* deaths, the price is triple.'

'Tell Sanjay yourself, Lightning. You see him more often than I do.'

I left the station house, moved through the traffic, and walked to the narrow cement-block and metal rail divider that separated the lanes moving south and north along the busy causeway.

Standing in a gap in the steel fence, I felt the traffic swirl around me: densely packed red commuter buses, scooters carrying five-member families, handcarts, motorcycles and bicycles, black-and-yellow taxis, fish-market trucks, private cars and military transports moving to and from the large naval base at the spear-tip of the Island City's peninsula.

Words cut through the jungle of thoughts.

Our dope. Sanjay Company dope. The girl in the locket, Rannveig, like the thing at the airport. Her boyfriend. The girl in the locket. Our dope.

Horns, bicycle bells, music from radios, the cries of stallholders and beggars rose up everywhere, echoing from covered walkways and the elegantly sagging stones of buildings that supported them.

Our dope. Sanjay Company dope. The girl. The locket. Her boyfriend. Our dope.

The smells of the street punished me, making me dizzy: fresh catches of fish and prawns from Sassoon Dock, diesel and petrol fumes, and the heavy wet-linen smell of monsoon mould, creeping across the brow of every building in the city.

Our dope. Our dope.

I stood on the road divider. Traffic rivers ran in front of me, heading north, and behind me, heading south, along the arm of the peninsula.

Khaderbhai had refused to allow anyone in the Company to deal heroin in South Bombay, or to profit from prostitution. Since his death, more than half of the new Sanjay Company's funds came from both sources, and Sanjay sanctioned more dealers and brothels every month.

It was a new world, not braver but much richer than the one I'd discovered, when Khaderbhai saved me from prison and recruited me. And it was no use telling myself that I didn't sell the drugs or the girls: that I worked in counterfeiting and passports. I was up to the thin silver chain around my neck in it.

As a soldier with the Sanjay Company I'd fought other gangs, and could be called to protect Andrew, Amir, Faisal and their operations at any time, and with no explanation for the blood to be spilled, and no right to refuse.

Our dope.

I felt a touch in the centre of my back, and as I began to turn there was another touch, and another. Three of the Cycle Killers raced away into the flow of traffic on their chrome bicycles.

I looked back quickly to greet Pankaj, second in charge of the Cycle Killers, as he skidded his bicycle to a stop beside me. He rested against the metal rail of the road divider. Traffic eddied around him, and he looked mischief at me, his eyes bright.

'That's how easy it is, brother!' he grinned, wagging his head energetically. 'Not counting me, you are three times dead already, if my boys were using their knives, instead of their fingers.'

He jabbed two hard fingers into my chest, directly under my heart.

'So glad we never fight, brother,' I said.

'You take your hand off the knife at your back,' he said, 'and I'll take my hand off mine.'

We laughed, and shook hands.

'Your Company is keeping us busy,' he said, spinning the pedal of his bicycle backwards as he held the concrete and steel road divider. 'I'll be able to retire, if this keeps up.'

'If your work ever brings you south of Flora Fountain, I'd appreciate a heads-up.'

'You will have it, my brother. Goodbye!'

Pankaj wheeled his chrome bicycle back into the road. I watched him thread his way through the traffic expertly.

And before I lost sight of him, in the time it took me to lift my eyes to the sky, I was done. It was over. I was finished with the Sanjay Company, and I knew it.

I was done. I quit. I'd had enough.

Faith. Faith is in everything, in every minute of life, even in sleep. Faith in Mother, sister, brother, or friend: faith that others will stop at the red light, faith in the pilot of the plane and the engineers who signed it into the air, faith in the teachers who guard children for hours every day, faith in cops and firemen and your mechanic, and faith that love will still be waiting for you when you return home.

But faith, unlike hope, can die. And when faith dies, the two friends that always die with it are constancy and commitment.

I'd had enough. I lost the little faith I'd had in Sanjay's leadership, and couldn't respect myself any more for submitting to it.

Leaving wouldn't be easy, I knew. Sanjay didn't like loose ends. But it was done. I was done. I knew that Sanjay would be at home late. I decided to ride to his house before the night was out, and tell him that I quit.

I looked up at the banner of Leopold's, and remembered something Karla once said, when we drank too much and talked too much, too long after the doors were closed. *Living alone as a freelancer in Bombay, like Didier*, she laughed, *is a cold river of truth*.

I'd been staring into a splintered mirror, and it was a while since I'd faced *alone*. I was walking away from a small army, pledged to defend me as a brother in arms. I was losing quasi-immunity from the law, protected by quasi-ethical Company lawyers, just a billable minute away from quasi-ethical judges.

I was leaving behind close friends who'd faced down enemies with me: men who'd known Khaderbhai, and knew his imperfections, and loved him as I did.

It was tough. I was trying to walk away from guilt and shame, and it wasn't easy: guilt and shame had more guns than I did.

But fear lies, hiding self-disgust in self-justification, and sometimes you don't know how afraid you were, until you leave all your fearful friends.

I felt things that I'd justified and rationalised for too long fall like leaves, washed from my body by a waterfall. Alone is a current in truth's river, like togetherness. Alone has its own fidelity. But when you navigate that closer view of the shore, it often seems that the faith you have in yourself is all the faith there is.

I took a deep breath, put my heart in the decision, and made a mental note to clean and load my gun.

CHAPTER TWENTY-FIVE

KAVITA SINGH, THE JOURNALIST WHO WAS earning a reputation for good writing about bad things people did, leaned back with her chair tipped against the wall. Beside her was a young woman I'd never seen before. Naveen and Divya were on Didier's left. Vikram was with Jamal, the One Man Show, and Billy Bhasu, both from Dennis's tomb.

The fact that Vikram was up and around again after two hours of sleep betrayed the depth of his habit. When you first start on the drug, a high can last twelve hours. When your tolerance crawls into addiction, you need to fix, or search for one, every three to four.

They were all laughing about something, when I approached the table.

'Hey, Lin!' Naveen called out. 'We're talking about our favourite crime. We all had to nominate one. What's *your* favourite crime?'

'Mutiny.'

'An anarchist!' Naveen laughed. 'An argument in search of a reason!'

'A reasoned argument,' I countered, 'in search of a future.'

'Bravo!' Didier cried, waving to the waiter for a new round of drinks.

He moved aside to let me sit. I took the seat next to him, and took the opportunity to pass him Rannveig's Norwegian passport.

'Vinson will collect it from you, in the next day or two,' I said quietly.

I turned my attention to Vikram. He avoided my eyes, and played with a smudge of beer on the table in front of him. I motioned for him to lean close to me.

'What are you doing, Vikram?' I whispered.

'What do you mean?'

'You were out cold two hours ago, Vik.'

'I woke up, man,' he said. 'It happens.'

'And these guys, who buy dope, just happen to be with you?'

He drew away, leaning back in his chair, and spoke to the table.

'You know, Lin, I think you're mistaking me for someone who gives a shit. But I don't. And I think I'm not alone. Didier, do you give a shit?'

'Reluctantly,' Didier replied. 'And infrequently.'

'How about you, Kavita?' Vikram asked.

'Actually,' she replied, 'I give more than a shit, about a lot of things. And –'

'You know, Lin,' Vikram said. 'You used to be a pretty cool guy, yaar. Don't become just another foreigner in India.'

I thought about his father's fear, and how they had to hide their precious things from him, but didn't respond.

'We're all foreigners in Bombay, aren't we?' Kavita said. 'I –'

Vikram cut her off again, reaching out to grasp at Didier's arm.

'Can we do it now?'

Didier was shocked. He never did business in Leopold's. But he took a prepared wad of notes from his pocket, and gave it to Vikram. My proud friend snatched at the money and rose quickly, almost toppling his chair. One Man Show steadied the chair and rose with him. Billy Bhasu was a beat behind them.

'Well . . . I'll . . . I'll take my leave,' Vikram said, backing away and avoiding my eye.

Billy Bhasu waved a goodbye, and left with Vikram. One Man Show wagged his head, jangling the assembly of gods hanging around his thin neck.

'One Man Show,' I said.

'One Man Show,' he replied, and followed the others out of the restaurant.

'What is it, my friend?' Didier asked me softly.

'I give Vikram money, too. But I always ask myself if I just gave him the shot that kills him.'

'It could also be the one that saves him,' Didier responded just as quietly. 'Vikram is sick, Lin. But *sick* is just another way of saying *still alive*, and still possible to save. Without help from someone, he might not survive the night. While he's alive, there's always a chance for him. Let it go, and relax with us.'

I glanced around at the others, and shrugged myself into their game.

'So, what about *you*, Kavita?' I asked. 'What's your favourite crime?'

261

'Lust,' she said forcefully.

'Lust is a sin,' I said. 'It isn't a crime.'

'I told her that,' Naveen said.

'It is the way *I* do it,' she retorted.

Divya broke into helpless giggles, setting the table to laughing with her.

'What about you, Didier?'

'Perjury is the most likeable crime, of course,' he said, with finality.

'Can I believe you?' I asked.

'Do you swear?' Naveen added.

'Because,' Didier continued, 'it's only lying that saves the world from being permanently miserable.'

'But isn't honesty just spoken truth?' Naveen goaded.

'No, no! Honesty is a choice about the truth. There is nothing in the world more destructive to truth, or infuriating to the intellect, than a person who insists on being completely and entirely honest about everything.'

'I completely and entirely agree with you,' Divya said, raising her glass in salute. 'When I want honesty, I see my doctor.'

Didier warmed with the encouragement.

'They slink up beside you, and whisper *I thought you should know*. Then they proceed to destroy your confidence, and trust, and even the quality of your life with their disgusting fragment of the truth. Some scrap of repugnant knowledge that they insist on being honest with you about. Something you'd rather not know. Something you could hate them for telling you. Something you actually *do* hate them for telling you. And why do they do it? *Honesty!* Their poisonous honesty makes them do it! No! Give me creative lying, any day, over the ugliness of honesty.'

'Honestly, Didier!' Kavita mocked.

'You, Kavita, of all people, should see the wisdom of what I am saying. Journalists, lawyers and politicians are people whose professions demand that they almost never tell the whole of the truth. If they did, if they were completely honest about every secret thing they know, civilisation would collapse in a month. Day after day, drink after drink, program after program, it is the lie that keeps us going, not the truth.'

'I love you, Didier!' Divya shouted. 'You're my hero!'

'I'd like to believe you, Didier,' Naveen remarked, straight-faced. 'But that perjury thing, it kinda kicks the stool out from under your credibility, you know?'

'Perjury is being honest with your heart,' Didier responded.

'So, honesty's a good thing,' Kavita observed, her finger aimed at Didier's heart.

'Alas, even Didier is not immune,' Didier sighed. 'I am heroic, in the matter of lying. Just ask any policeman in South Bombay. But I am only human, after all, and from time to time I lapse into appalling acts of honesty. I am being honest with you now, and I am ashamed to admit it, by advising you to lie as often as you can, until you can lie with complete honesty, as I do.'

'You love the truth,' Kavita observed. 'It's honesty you hate.'

'You are quite right,' Didier agreed. 'Believe me, if you honestly tell the whole of the truth, about anyone at all, someone will want to harm you for it.'

The group broke up into smaller conversations, Didier agreeing with Kavita, and Naveen arguing with Divya. I spoke to the young woman sitting near me.

'We haven't met. My name's Lin.'

'I know,' she answered shyly. 'I'm Sunita. I'm a friend of Kavita. Well, actually, I'm working with Kavita. I'm a cadet journalist.'

'How do you like it, so far?'

'It's great. I mean, it's a really great opportunity and all. But I'm hoping to be a writer, like you.'

'Like me?' I laughed, bewildered.

'I've read your short stories.'

'My stories?'

'All five of them. I really like them, but I was too shy to tell you.'

'Just how did you get hold of these stories?'

'Well,' she faltered, confused. 'Ranjit gave me – I mean, Mr Ranjit – he gave me your stories to proofread. I searched them for typos, and such.'

I stared, not wanting to take it out on her, but too angry and confused to hide my feelings. Ranjit had my stories? How? Had Lisa given them to him, behind my back, and against my wishes? I couldn't understand it.

'I've got them right here,' Sunita said. 'I was going to have my lunch alone today, and continue proofing, but Miss Kavita asked me to join her.'

'Give them to me, please.'

She fished around in a large cloth bag, and gave me a folder.

It was red. I'd filed all of my stories by coloured theme. Red was the file colour I'd chosen for some short stories about urban holy men.

'I didn't give permission for these stories to be printed,' I said, checking to see that all five stories were included in the file.

'But —'

'It's not your fault,' I said softly, 'and nothing will happen to you. I'll write a note for Ranjit, and you'll give it to him, and everything will be okay.'

'But —'

'Got a pen?'

'I —'

'Just kidding,' I said, pulling a pen from my vest pocket.

The last page, on the last story, had only two lines on it.

Arrogance is pride's calling card, and crowds everything with Self.
Gratitude is humility's calling card, and is the space left inside for love.

It seemed appropriate, as notepaper for Ranjit. I pulled the typed page from the story, wrote the lines again in hand on the new last page, and closed the file.

'Lin!' Didier cantankered. 'You are not drinking! Put down that pen at once.'

'What are you doing?' Kavita asked.

'If it's a will,' Naveen said, 'there's probably a way.'

'If you must know,' I said, glancing at Kavita, 'I'm writing a note, to your boss.'

'A love letter?' Kavita asked, sitting up straight.

'Kinda.'

I wrote the note, folded it, and gave it to Sunita.

'But *no*, Lin!' Didier protested. 'It is insupportable! You simply must read the note out loud.'

'What?'

'There are rules, Lin,' Didier riposted. 'And we must break them at every opportunity.'

'That's crazier than I am, Didier.'

'You must read it to us, Lin.'

'It's a private note, man.'

'Written in a public place,' Kavita said, snatching the note from Sunita.

'Hey,' I said, trying to grab the note back.

Kavita jumped up quickly and stood a table-width away. She had a raspy voice, the kind of voice that's interesting because of how much it keeps inside, as it speaks.

She spoke my note.

Let me be clear, Ranjit. I think your tycoon model of media baron is an insult to the Fourth Estate, and I wouldn't let you publish my death notice.

If you touch any of my work again I'll visit you, and rearrange you.

The girl who's bringing this note has my number. If you take this out on her, if you fire her, or in any way hurt the messenger, she'll call me, and I'll visit you, and rearrange you. Stay away from me.

'I love it!' Kavita laughed. 'I want to be the one who passes it on.'

A shout, then the sound of broken glass shattering on the marble floor made us look with others toward the large entrance arch. Concannon was there, locked in a scuffle with several of the Leopold's waiters.

He wasn't alone. There were Scorpion gang men with him. The big guy, Hanuman, was behind Concannon and a few other faces I remembered from that red hour in the warehouse.

The last to push his way into the doorway was Danda, the torturer with the pencil moustache. There was a leather ear-patch strapped across his left ear.

Concannon was carrying a sap, a lead weight wrapped in a sewn leather pouch, and fastened by a cord around the wrist. He lashed out with it, striking the Sikh chief of Leopold's security on the temple. Gasps and cries of horror rose up from all those who witnessed it.

The tall Sikh waiter crumpled and fell, his legs melting beneath him. Other waiters scrambled to help. Concannon swung at them while they were trying to support their comrade, drawing blood, and felling men.

The Scorpions burst into the restaurant, pushing tables aside and scattering frightened patrons. Bottles, glasses and plates smashed on the floor, shattering in frothy puddles. Tables rocked and tumbled over. Chairs skittered away from the brawling mass of men. Customers scrambled, falling over the chairs, and slipping on the messy floor.

Kavita, Naveen and I stood quickly.

'Gonna get messy,' I said.

'Good,' Kavita said.

I flicked a glance at her, and saw that she had an empty bottle in one hand and a handbag in the other.

The nearest exit was blocked with people. There was a corner behind us. If we pushed the table back, Divya and the young girl, Sunita, could get behind it and be safe. I looked at Naveen, and he spoke my thought.

'Divya, get in the corner,' he said, pointing behind him, his eyes on the fighting.

For once, the socialite didn't fight. She grabbed Sunita with her into the corner. I looked at Kavita.

'In there?' she scoffed. 'Fuck you.'

Whatever their reasons for the wild attack, Concannon and the Scorpions had chosen their moment well. It was the dozy half of the afternoon, long before the evening rush of patrons. Half of the Leopold's waiters were upstairs, catching up on sleep.

Caught by surprise, the working staff put up a valiant resistance, but they were outnumbered. The struggling, fighting mass of men surged through the restaurant toward us. It had to be slowed, before it could be stopped.

'Let's fuck these guys up,' Kavita growled.

We ran at the gangsters in the mob, trying to move the fight back toward the entrance. A few customers joined us, pushing at the thugs.

Naveen thumped out punches, precision quick. I pulled one man off a semi-conscious waiter. He lost his balance and fell backwards. Kavita swung her empty beer bottle, slamming it against the man's head. Other customers kicked at him, as he fell again.

The sleeping waiters of the night shift, awakened by the owner of Leopold's, began streaming down the narrow staircase behind us. The forward momentum of the Scorpion thugs stopped. The tide turned. The Scorpions began to stumble backwards.

Naveen and I were pushed and dragged toward the street with them, caught between enemies and reinforcements. As we neared the door, I found myself face to face with Concannon.

If he knew he was losing the fight, his eyes didn't show it. They gleamed like the scales of a fish in shallow water, aflame with cold light. He was smiling. He was happy.

He raised the lead sap slowly, until it was level with his shoulder, and spoke to me.

'The devil's got a crush on *you*, boy!' he said, and then lashed out with the sap.

I ducked quickly to my right. The sap hit the back of my left shoulder. I felt the bone beneath the muscle shudder under the blow. Coming up fast, I swung out with an over-hand right. It hit him square on the side of the head, making solid contact. It had everything in it. It wasn't enough.

Concannon shook his head and grinned. He raised the sap again and I grabbed at him, shoving him backwards onto the street.

In the movies, men fight for long minutes, taking turns to hit one another. In a real street fight, everything happens much faster. Everyone swings at anything they can, and if you're knocked to the floor, most of the time you stay there.

Sometimes, of course, the floor is the safest place to be.

Bunching my fists against my forehead, waiting for an opportunity, I stared through my knuckles at Concannon. He was trying to hit me with the sap. I ducked, dodging and weaving, but taking blows as I parried.

As I stepped back, keeping my balance, I came up against Naveen. We glanced at one another quickly, and stood back to back.

We were alone, between Leopold's and the row of street stalls. The waiters hesitated in the large doorway arch. They were holding the line. What happened on the street was none of their business. They were making sure that the fight didn't spill back inside the restaurant.

The Scorpions moved in. Naveen faced four men alone, his back to mine. I couldn't help him. I had Concannon.

I saw an opening, and snapped lefts and rights at the tall Irishman, but for every punch I landed, he replied with a hit from the sap. The deadly weight connected with my face, drawing fast blood. And no matter how hard or how well I connected with my punches, I couldn't put him down.

Words came into my mind, shawls of snow in the wind.

So, this is it . . .

As suddenly as it had started, the brawl stopped. The Scorpions pulled away from us, circling around Concannon.

Naveen and I looked backwards for a second. We saw Didier. He had a gun in his hand. I was very glad to see him. He was smiling, just as Concannon had smiled. Standing beside him was Abdullah.

As we stepped away from the muzzle of Didier's automatic pistol, Abdullah reached out with his left hand, placed it over Didier's hand, and slowly lowered it until the handgun was at Didier's side.

There was a moment of silence. The Scorpions stared hard, stranded on the wet-red footprint between fight and flight. Witnesses hiding behind stalls were breathing fast. Even the ceaseless traffic, it seemed, was softened.

Concannon spoke. It was a mistake.

'You fuckin' ugly, long-haired Iranian cunt,' he said, showing all of his yellow teeth, and advancing on Abdullah. 'You and I both know what you are. Why don't you speak?'

Abdullah had a gun. He shot Concannon in the thigh. People screamed, shouted and scrambled out of the way.

The Irishman staggered, still fighting, wanting to hit Abdullah with the sap. Abdullah shot him again, in the same leg. Concannon fell.

Abdullah fired twice more, faster than my eye could follow. When Hanuman and Danda reeled backwards, I realised that the big Scorpion and his thin friend had been shot in the leg too.

The Scorpions who could still run, ran. Concannon, a born survivor, was crawling away, using his elbows to drag himself between the souvenir stalls toward the road.

Abdullah took two steps, and put his foot down hard on the Irishman's back. Didier was at his side.

'You . . . fuckin' . . . coward . . . ' Concannon spluttered. 'Go on! *Do* it! You're nothing!'

There was a lot of blood coming from the two wounds in his leg. Abdullah held the pistol over the back of Concannon's head, and prepared to fire. The few people still close enough to see what was happening screamed.

'Enough, brother!' I shouted. 'Stop!'

It was Didier's turn to put a hand on Abdullah's arm, gently pushing the handgun to Abdullah's side.

'Too many witnesses, my friend.' He said. '*Dommage*. Go now. Go fast.'

Abdullah hesitated. There was an instinct working in him. I knew it. I'd heard the voice of that instinct, behind the wall. In that moment he wanted to kill Concannon more than he wanted to live. I stepped in beside him, as men had stepped in for me in prison, guarding my heart as much as my life.

'The only reason the cops aren't here,' I said, 'is because the Scorpions must've paid them to stay away while they attacked the place. That won't last much longer. We've gotta go.'

He took his foot off Concannon's back. The Irishman immediately began to drag himself toward the road.

Two cars pulled up. Scorpion men loaded Concannon and the wounded gangsters into the back. They sped away, knocking a taxi full of tourists out of the way.

Naveen Adair had his arm around Divya. Sunita, the cadet journalist, was with them.

'Are you okay?' I asked Divya.

'Fucking *men*,' she replied. 'You're all idiots.'

'Are *you* okay?' I asked Sunita.

She was clutching the red folder of my stories, hugging them to her chest. She was trembling.

'I'm fine,' she replied. 'But, I have a request, and I don't want to ask it, while you are bleeding. Your face is bleeding, do you know?'

'O . . . kay. Can we make it quick?'

She handed me back my short stories, and held up the note I'd written to Ranjit.

'*Please* let me deliver your note,' she said.

'Ah . . . '

'Please. You have no idea how much this man has harassed me, sexually, and I'm almost fainting with the pleasure of thinking about giving this note to him. I didn't have lunch, also, so maybe I'm a little hypoglycaemic, but it feels like a really terrific holiday for me, so, sorry for your face, but please let me give him this note.'

Didier and Kavita joined me.

'Didier, will you give Sunita your phone number, and escort her to Ranjit's office?'

'Certainly, but you must leave now, Lin.'

There was the sound of a gunshot, from not far away.

'Listen,' I said to Didier quickly. 'Lisa's staying at the gallery, on Carmichael Road. Can you go there?'

'Of course.'

'Make sure she's alright. Stay with her, or keep her with you for a couple of days.'

'*Bien sûr*,' he replied. 'What will you do?'

'Stay out of sight. I don't know yet. Take these stories, and keep them for me.'

I handed him the folder, and ran back to find Abdullah ready to ride, his bike beside mine.

'Who's doing the shooting?'

269

'Our man,' Abdullah replied, gunning the engine of his bike.

'Where are the cops?' I asked, starting my bike.

'They were coming, but Ravi fired a shot in the air,' he replied. 'They have gone for body armour and machine guns. We must leave now.'

Heading into the afternoon traffic, Abdullah and I threaded our way through creeping vines of cars. From time to time we took short cuts on empty sidewalks, or through petrol station driveways. In minutes we descended the long hill at Pedder Road and were beside the juice centre, in sight of the island monument of Haji Ali's tomb.

'We should report to Sanjay,' I said, when we stopped at the signal.

'Agreed.'

We pulled into the parking bays at the juice centre. Leaving the bikes with the attendants, we called the mafia boss. He sounded sleepy, as if we'd roused him from a siesta.

He woke up fast.

'What the *fuck*? Where are you fucks now?'

'At Haji Ali,' Abdullah replied, holding the phone between us so that I could hear.

'You can't come back. The cops will be here in minutes, for sure, and I don't want them asking questions you can't answer. Stay away, and stay *quiet* for a couple of days for fuck's sake, you motherfuckers. Tell me the truth, were any civilians shot?'

Abdullah bristled at the phrase *Tell me the truth*. Gritting his teeth in disgust, he handed me the phone.

'No civilians, Sanjaybhai,' I replied.

The term *civilians* referred to anyone who wasn't involved in the criminal underworld: anyone other than judges, lawyers, gangsters, prison guards and the police.

'Two Scorpions took it in the leg, and a freelancer named Concannon. He got it twice, in the same leg, but I wouldn't count him out. There were a lot of witnesses. Most of them were street guys, or waiters at Leo's.'

'You made this fucking mess, Lin, and you're telling me how to clean it up? Fuck you, motherfucker.'

'If memory serves me right,' I said calmly, 'you shot someone outside Leo's, once.'

Abdullah held up two fingers, waggling them at me.

'Twice, in fact,' I said. 'And I didn't *start* this mess, Sanjaybhai. The

Scorpions started it, and that was a while ago. They've hit us nine times in the last month. They hit Leo's, because it's a place we all love, and it's in the heart of Company land. The foreigner, Concannon, just wants Sanjay Company and the Scorpions to kill each other, because he's starting his own gang. That's as much as I know. I can't tell you what to do, and I wouldn't try. I can only tell you what I know. That's *for* you, not against you.'

'*Madachudh! Bahinchudh!*' Sanjay shouted, and then calmed himself again. 'This will cost a fortune to cover up. Who do you think set it up with the Colaba cops?'

'Lightning Dilip was on duty. But I think this is too ambitious for him. He likes his enemies alive, and tied up.'

'There's a sub-inspector, Matre by name, who's been on my back for a while,' Sanjay mused. 'Motherfucker! This has got his sweat all over it. *Thik*. I'll handle everything at this end. You two stay out of sight for a couple of days. Check in with me again tomorrow. Put Abdullah back on the phone.'

I handed the phone back to Abdullah. He glared at me for a moment. I shrugged my shoulders. He listened.

'Yes,' he said twice, and hung up.

'What's the deal?'

'Did he ask you if you were injured?' Abdullah asked me.

'He's not the affectionate kind. He's the disaffectionate kind.'

'He did not ask,' Abdullah snarled, frowning hard.

There was a small, brooding silence, and then he came back to the moment.

'Your face. You are bleeding. We should see one of our doctors.'

'I checked it in the mirror. It's not that bad.'

I tied a handkerchief across the places on my forehead and eye socket where Concannon's sap had drawn blood.

'Right now,' I said, 'our problem is that Sanjay's not going to war for us, and we're on our own.'

'I could force him to war.'

'No, Abdullah. Sanjay let me dangle in the wind, and now he's letting you swing with me. He'll never go to war, until the war's over.'

'I repeat, I can *make* him go to war.'

'Why is war even an option, Abdullah? I'm not *complaining* that Sanjay won't go to war. I'm *glad* he won't go to war. I'm glad that nobody else will get involved in this. We can handle payback on our own.'

'And we will, *Inshallah*.'

'But since we *are* alone, as we seem to be, we gotta work out a strategy, and the tactics to achieve it, because you just shot three people. One of them twice. What do you want to do?'

He looked away from me, checking the surrounding junction of major arterial avenues, cars streaming gleaming metal from one current or the other.

He looked at me again and half-opened his mouth, but there were no words for the experience: he was alone, and his comrades weren't riding to his rescue. He was a soldier behind enemy lines, told that the escape route had just closed.

'I think we should put as much distance as we can between us and them, for a while,' I said, filling the dissonant gap. 'Maybe Goa. We can ride there overnight. But don't tell anyone. Every time I tell someone I'm going to Goa, they ask me to collect their dirty laundry.'

I'd tried to raise a smile, in the sierra of his doubt. It didn't work.

Abdullah glanced back in the direction of South Bombay. He was wrestling with the desire to return, and kill every Scorpion that ever crawled out from under a rock. I waited for a few moments.

'So, what's the deal?'

He wrenched himself into the minute, and let out two long breaths, charging his will.

'I came to Leopold's to invite you to come with me to a special place. It is a lucky thing, perhaps, that I came when I did, but let us wait, until we see what the consequences of this day are, for each of us.'

'What special place?'

He looked again to the horizon.

'I was not expecting that we would be going there with such a dark shadow following us to the mountain, but, will you come with me, now?'

'And, again, where might that be?'

'To see the teacher of teachers, the master who taught his wisdom to Khaderbhai. Idriss is his name.'

I tasted the name of the fabled teacher.

'Idriss.'

'He is there,' Abdullah said, pointing to a range of hills on the northern horizon. 'He is in a cave, on that mountain. We will buy water, here, to carry with us. It is a long climb, to the summit of wisdom.'

PART FIVE

CHAPTER TWENTY-SIX

Refreshed and prepared we rode the hot monsoon highway between lumbering trucks loaded with high, lopsided bundles, swaying at us at every curve. I was glad of the ride, and glad that Abdullah was racing for once. I needed the speed. Reaction times between speeding cars from lane to lane were so small that fierce concentration killed the pain. I knew pain would come. Pain can be deferred, but never denied. *After the ride, let it come*, I thought. *Pain is just proof of life.*

In two hours we reached the turnoff that led into the Sanjay Gandhi National Park. We paid the entrance fees and began the long, slow ride through the jungle-thick forest at the foot of the mountain.

The winding road leading to the tallest peak in the reserve was in surprisingly good condition. Recent storms had shaken branches loose from trees close to the road, but local forest dwellers, whose huts and hand-built compounds could be seen here and there through the lush undergrowth, quickly swept them up for firewood.

We passed groups of women dressed in flower-garden saris, walking single file and carrying bundles of sticks on their heads. Small children dragging their own sticks and bunches of twigs trailed behind the women.

The park was wild with rain-soaked life. Weeds rose to shoulder height, vines writhed and squirmed across the treillage of branches. Lichens, mosses and mushrooms flourished in every damp shadow.

Pink, mazarine blue and Van Gogh yellow wildflowers trailed across the leafy waterlogged carpet of the forest. Leaves burned red by rain covered the road like petals in a temple courtyard. Earth's frayed-bark perfume saturated the air, drawn up into every sodden stem, stalk and trunk.

Councils of monkeys, meeting in assembly on the open road, scattered as we approached. They scampered to nearby rocky outcrops and boulders, their mouths pinched in simian outrage at our intrusion.

When one particularly large troop of animals scattered into the trees, making me start with fright, Abdullah caught my eye and allowed himself a rare smile.

He was the bravest and most loyal man I'd ever known. He was hard on others, but much harder on himself. And he had a confidence that all men admired or envied.

The great, square forehead loomed over the ceaselessly questioning arc of his eyebrows. A deep, black beard covered everything but his mouth. The deep-set eyes, the colour of honey in a terracotta dish, were sad: too sad and kind for the wide, proud nose, high cheekbones and lock-firm jaw that gave his face its fearsome set.

He'd grown his hair long again. It descended to his broad, thick shoulders, a mane that became the strength prowling in his long arms and legs.

Men followed his face, form and character into war. But something in him, humble reticence or cautious wisdom, pulled him back from the power that some men in the Sanjay Company urged him to take. They begged him, but he refused to lead. And that, of course, made them urge him all the more.

I rode the jungle road beside him, loving him, fearing for him, fearing for myself if ever I lost him, and not thinking about what had happened to me in that fight, and how it might be working on my body, if not my mind.

As we reached the cleared gravel parking space at the foot of the mountain, and turned off our bikes, I heard Concannon's voice.

The devil's got a crush on you, boy.

'Are you alright, Lin brother?'

'Yeah.'

The drift of my eyes found a phone, on the counter of a small shop.

'Should we call Sanjay again?'

'Yes. I will do it.'

He spoke to Sanjay for twenty minutes, answering the mafia don's many questions.

It was quiet, at the foot of the mountain. A small shop, the only structure in the gravel parking lot, sold soft drinks, crisps and sweets.

The attendant, a bored youth with a dreamy expression, lashed out now and then with a handkerchief tied to a small bamboo stick. The swarm of mites and flies scattered, for a second or two, but always returned to the sugar-stained counter of the shop.

No-one else approached the parking area, or descended from the mountain. I was glad. I was shaking so hard that it took me all of those twenty minutes to get myself together.

Abdullah hung up the phone, and signalled for me to follow him. I couldn't tell him that I felt too weak and beat up to climb a mountain: sometimes, all the guts you have is the guts you pretend, because you love someone too much to lose their respect.

We climbed up some steep but wide and well-made stone steps to the first plateau of the mountain. There was a large cave that featured heavy, squat columns supporting a massive granite plinth. The arched entrance led to a chambered sanctum.

Further along the upward path, we stood before the largest and most spectacular cave. At the high, arched entrance to the main cave, two enormous statues of the Buddha, five times the height of a man, stood guard in alcoves, left and right. There were no fences or railings to protect them, but they were remarkably well preserved.

After climbing for some twenty minutes past dozens of caves, we entered a small plateau where the path widened into several well-trodden tracks. The summit was still some distance above.

Through a glade of tall, slender trees and sea-drift lantanas, we came upon a temple courtyard. Paved in large, white marble squares and covered by a solid dome, the columned space ended in a small, discreet shrine to a sage.

Sombre, and perhaps a little sorrowful, the stony gaze of the bearded saint peered into the surrounding jungle. Abdullah stopped for a moment, looking around him in the centre of the white marble courtyard. His hands were on his hips, and a small smile dimpled his eyes.

'A special place?'

'It is, Lin brother. This is where Khaderbhai received most of his lessons from the sage, Idriss. It was my privilege to be with them, for some of those lessons.'

We stood in silence for a while, remembering the dead Khan, Khaderbhai, each of us pulling a different cloak of recollections over our shoulders.

'Is it far from here?'

'Not far,' he said, leading the way out of the courtyard. 'But it is the hardest part of the climb.'

Clinging to branches, grasses and vines, we dragged ourselves up a steeper path that led to the summit.

It was a climb that might've been easy work in the dry season, with rocks and stones solidly embedded in the earthen cliff face and the narrow track. But in those twilight days of the long monsoon, it was a hard climb.

Halfway to the summit we encountered a young man, who was descending the same path. The incline at that point was so steep that he had to slide down backwards on weeds and vines.

He was carrying a large plastic water can. In the encounter with us on the narrow path, he had to crush against us, slipping shirt to shirt and grasping at us, as we did with him.

'What fun!' he said in Hindi, grinning happily. 'Can I bring you something from down?'

'Chocolate!' Abdullah said, as the young man slipped below us, dis-appearing into the vegetation that crowded the vertical path. 'I forgot to buy it! I'll pay you, when you come up!'

'*Thik!*' the young man called back from somewhere below.

When Abdullah and I reached the summit, I discovered that it was a mesa, flat-topped and expansive, giving onto the last jagged half-peak of the mountain.

Several large caves, cut into that steep fragment of the peak, offered views of the mesa, and the many valleys rolling into one another below, and to the Island City, shrouded in mist and smoke on the horizon.

Still puffing I glanced around, trying to get a feel for the place. It was paved with small white pebbles. I hadn't seen any of them in the valley below, or during the climb. They'd been carried to the summit, one sack at a time. As punishing as the work must've been, the effect was dazzling: serene and unsullied.

There was a kitchen area, open on three sides and covered with a stretched green canvas, faded to a colour that neatly matched the rain-bleached leaves of the surrounding trees.

Another area, completely obscured by canvas shrouds, looked to be a bathroom with several alcoves. A third covered area contained two desks and several canvas deck chairs, stacked in rows.

Beyond them, the open mouths of the four caves revealed a few details of their interiors: a wooden cabinet in the entrance to one, several metal trunks heaped inside another, and a large, blackened fireplace with a smouldering fire visible in a third.

As I was looking at the caves, a young man emerged from the smallest of them.

'You are Mr Shantaram?'

I turned to Abdullah, frowning my surprise.

'Master Idriss asked me to bring you here,' Abdullah said. 'It was Idriss who invited you here, through me.'

'Me?'

He nodded. I turned back to the young man.

'This is for you,' he said, handing me a business card.

I read the short message: *There are no Gurus*

Mystified, I handed the card to Abdullah. He read it, laughed, and handed it back to me.

'Quite a calling card,' I said, reading it again. 'It's like a lawyer, saying there are no fees.'

'Idriss will explain it himself, no doubt.'

'But, perhaps, not tonight,' the young man said, gesturing toward the cave that held a fireplace. 'Master-*ji* is engaged with some philosophers tonight, in a temple below the mountain. So, please come. I have made tea, just now.'

I accepted the invitation gratefully, sat down on a handmade wooden stool some little way into the cave, and sipped at the tea when it arrived.

Lost in my thoughts, as I too often am, I guess, I let my mind worry itself back to the fight with Concannon.

Cooler and clearer after the long ride and the long climb to the summit, I looked back into Concannon's eyes, as I sat there, sipping sweet tea in the cave of the sage, Idriss.

I suddenly realised it wasn't anger that I'd felt after Concannon's mindless and brutal attack: it was disappointment. It was the kind of disappointment that belongs to friends, not enemies.

But by joining the Scorpions, he'd made himself new enemies. Our guys had no choice but to hit back at the Scorpions: if they didn't, the Scorpions would see it as weakness, and hit us again. The trouble had started. I had to get Karla out of the city: she was connected to the Sanjay Company.

And there it was. I didn't think of Lisa, or Didier, or even myself. I thought of Karla. Lisa was at risk. Concannon knew her: he'd met her. I should've thought of Lisa first, but it was Karla; it was Karla.

In that twisted knot of love, staring at the scatter of ember-roses in the soft ashes of the fire, I became aware of a perfumed scent. I thought someone must've been offering frankincense at another fire, nearby. But I knew that perfume. I knew it well.

Then I heard Karla's voice.

'Tell me a joke, Shantaram.'

The skin on my face tightened. I felt the chill of fever. A blood-river rushed upwards through my body and shuddered in my chest until my eyes burned with it.

Snap out of it, I said to myself. *Look at her. Break the spell.*

I turned to look at her. It didn't help.

She stood in the mouth of the cave, smiling at the wind, her profile defying everything, her black hair and silver scarf trailing banners of desire behind her. High, strong forehead, crescent eyes, fine sharp nose, and the gentle jut of a pointed chin protecting the broken promise of her lips: Karla.

'So,' she drawled, 'you got a joke, or don't you?'

'How many Parsis does it take to change a light globe?' I asked.

'Two years, I don't see you,' she said, still not turning to face me, 'and the best you can do is a light-bulb joke?'

'It's twenty-three months and sixteen days. You want a joke, or don't you?'

'Okay, so how many Parsis does it take to change a light globe?'

'Parsis don't change light globes, because they know they'll never get another one as good as the old one.'

She threw her head back and laughed. It was a good laugh, a great laugh, from a great heart, strong and free, a hawk riding dusk: the laugh that broke every chain in my heart.

'Come here,' she said.

I wrapped my arms around her, pressing her against that hollow tree, my life, where I'd hidden the dream that she would love me, forever.

CHAPTER TWENTY-SEVEN

EVERYONE HAS ONE EYE THAT'S SOFTER AND SADDER, and one that's hard and bright. Karla's left eye was softer and sadder than her right, and maybe it was because I could only see that soft light, greener than new leaves, that I had no resistance to her. I couldn't do anything but listen, and smile, and try to be funny now and then.

But it was alright. It was okay. It was a renegade peace, in those moments on the morning after the mountain brought her back to me; the morning of that softer, sadder eye.

We'd spent the night in separate caves. There were three other women on the mountain-top mesa, all of them young Indian students of the wise man, Idriss. The women's cave was smaller, but cleaner and better appointed.

There were rope beds and mattresses, where we'd slept on blankets stretched over the bare ground, and there were several metal cupboards, suspended on blocks of stone to keep out rats and crawling insects. We'd made do with a few rusted hooks to keep our belongings off the dusty floor.

I hadn't slept well. I'd only spoken to Karla for a few minutes after that first hug, that first sight of her for almost two years. And then she was gone, again.

Abdullah, bowing gallantly to Karla, had drawn me away to join the other men, gathered for a meal at the entrance to the men's cave.

I was walking backwards, looking at her, and she was already laughing at me, two minutes after we re-met. Two years, in two minutes.

During the meal, we met six young devotees and students, who exchanged stories of what it was that had brought them to the top of the mountain. Abdullah and I listened, without comment.

By the time we'd finished eating the modest meal of daal and rice, it was late. We cleaned our teeth, washed our faces, and settled down to sleep. But my little sleep drowned in a nightmare that choked me awake before dawn.

I decided to beat the early risers to the simple bathroom. I used the long-drop toilet, then took a small pot of water and a piece of soap, and washed myself with half a bucket of water, standing on the pallet floor of the canvas-screen bathroom.

Dried and dressed and cold awake, I made my way through the dark camp to sit by the guttering fire. I'd just built the embers into a flame with twigs of kindling around a battered coffee pot, when Karla came to stand beside me.

'What are you doing here?' Karla purred.

'If I don't get coffee soon, I'm gonna bite a tree.'

'You know what I mean.'

'Oh, you mean, on the mountain? I could ask you the same thing.'

'I asked you first.'

I laughed gently.

'You're better than *that*, Karla.'

'Maybe I'm not what I used to be.'

'We're *all* what we used to be, even when we're not.'

'That's not telling me what you're doing here,' she said.

'What we tell, is rarely what we do.'

'I'm not doing an aphorism contest,' she said, frowning a smile and sitting down beside me.

'We are the art, that sees us as art.'

'No way,' she said. 'Keep your lines to yourself.'

'Fanaticism means that if you're not against me, you're against me.'

'I could report you for aphorism harassment, do you know that?'

'Honour is the art of being humble,' I replied, deadpan.

We were speaking softly, but our eyes were sharp.

'Okay,' she whispered, 'you're on. My turn?'

'Of course it's your turn. I'm already three up on you.'

'Every goodbye is a dress rehearsal for the last goodbye,' she said.

'Not bad. Hello can lie, sometimes, but goodbye always tells the truth.'

'Fiction is fact, made stranger. The truth about anything is a lie about something else. Come on, step it up, Shantaram.'

'What's the rush? There's plenty more where they came from.'

'You got somethin' or not?'

'Oh, I see, it's to throw me off, and put me off my game. Okay, tough girl, here we go. Inspiration is the grace of peace. Truth is the warden in the prison of the soul. Slavery can't be unchained from the system: slavery *is* the system.'

'Truth is the shovel,' she fired back. 'Your mission is the hole.'

I laughed.

'*Every* fragment is the whole entire,' Karla said, firing at will.

'The whole cannot be divided,' I said, 'without a tyranny of parts.'

'Tyranny is privilege, unrestrained.'

'We're privileged by Fate,' I said, 'because we're damned by Fate.'

'Fate,' she grinned. 'One of my favourites. Fate plays poker, and only wins by bluffing. Fate is the magician, and Time is the trick. Fate is the spider, and Time is the web. Shall I go on?'

'Dark funny,' I said, happier than I'd been in a while. 'Nice. Try this — all men become their fathers, but only when they're not looking.'

She laughed. I don't know where Karla was, but I was with her, at last, in a thing we both loved, and she was my heaven.

'The truth is a bully we all pretend to like.'

'That's on old one!' I protested.

'But a good one, and worth a second run. Whaddaya got?'

'Fear is the friend who warns you,' I offered.

'Loneliness is the friend who tells you to get out more,' she countered. 'Come on, let's move it along here.'

'There's no country too unjust, too corrupt, or too inept to afford itself a stirring national anthem.'

'Big political,' she smiled. 'I like it. Try this on for size — tyranny is fear, in human form.'

I laughed.

'Music is death, made sublime.'

'Grief is ghost empathy,' she hit back quickly.

'Damn!'

'You give up?'

'No way. The way to love, is to love the way.'

'Koans,' she said. 'Grasping at straws, Shantaram. No problem. I'm always ready to give love a kick in the ass. How about this — love is a mountain that kills you, every time you climb it.'

'Courage –'

'Courage defines us. Anyone who doesn't give up, and that's just about everybody, is a man or woman of courage. Stop with the courage, already.'

'Happiness is –'

'Happiness is the hyperactive child of contentment.'

'Justice means –'

'Justice, like love and power, is measured in mercies.'

'War –'

'All wars are culture wars, and all cultures are written on the bodies of women.'

'Life –'

'If you're not living for something, you're dying for nothing!' she parried, her forefinger on my chest.

'Damn.'

'Damn, *what*?'

'Damn . . . you got . . . better, girl.'

'So, you're saying I won?'

'I'm saying . . . you got . . . a lot better.'

'And I *won*, right? Because I can do this all day long, you know.'

She was serious, her eyes filled with tiger-light.

'I love you,' I said.

She looked away. After a time she spoke to the fire.

'You still haven't answered my question. What are you doing here?'

We'd been husky-whispering in the contest, trying not to wake the others. The sky was dark, but a ridge of dawn the colour of faded leaves hovered over the distant, cloudy horizon.

'Oh, wait a minute,' I frowned, realising at last. 'You think I came up here, because *you're* here? You think I set this up?'

'Did you?'

'Would you want me to?'

She turned the half-profile on me, that sadder, softer eye searching my face as if she was reading a map. Red-yellow fire shadows played with her features: firelight writing faith and hope on her face, as fire does on every human face, because we're creatures of fire.

I looked away.

'I had no idea you were here,' I said. 'It was Abdullah's idea.'

284

She laughed softly. Was she disappointed, or relieved? I couldn't tell.

'What about you?' I asked, throwing a few sticks on the fire. 'You didn't suddenly get religion. Say it ain't so.'

'I bring Idriss hash,' she said. 'He's got a taste for Kashmiri.'

It was my turn to laugh.

'How long has this been going on?'

'About . . . a year.'

She was dreaming something, looking out at the dawning forest.

'What's he like?'

She looked at me again.

'He's . . . authentic. You'll meet him later.'

'How did *you* meet him?'

'I didn't come up here to meet him. I came to meet Khaled. He's the one who told me that Idriss was here.'

'Khaled? Which Khaled?'

'Your Khaled,' she said softly. '*Our* Khaled.'

'He's alive?'

'Very much so.'

'*Alhamdulillah*. And he's up here?'

'I'd pay good money to see Khaled up here. No, he's got an ashram, down in the valley.'

The hard-fisted, uncompromising Palestinian had been a member of the Khader Council. He'd been with us on the smuggling run into Afghanistan. He killed a man, a close friend, because the friend endangered us all, and then he walked alone and unarmed into the snow.

I'd been a friend, a close friend, but I'd heard nothing of Khaled's return to the city, or anything about an ashram.

'An ashram?'

'Yeah,' she sighed.

Her face and manner had changed. She seemed to be bored.

'What kind of ashram?'

'The profitable kind,' she said. 'It has a majestic menu. *That*, you've got to give him. Meditation rooms, yoga, massage, aromatherapies and chanting. They chant a lot. It's like they never heard of funk.'

'And it's at the base of *this* mountain?'

'At the start of the valley, on the west side.'

She frowned a yawn at me.

'Abdullah goes there all the time,' she said. 'Didn't he talk to you about it?'

Something staggered inside me. I was glad to know that Khaled was alive and well, but the cherished friendship felt betrayed, and my heart stumbled.

'It can't be true.'

'The truth comes in two kinds,' she laughed gently. 'The one you want to hear, and the one you should.'

'Don't start that again.'

'Sorry,' she said. 'Sucker punch. Couldn't resist it.'

I was suddenly angry. Maybe it was that sense of betrayal. Maybe it was old crying, finally forcing its way past the shield of softness, gleaming in her kinder eye.

'Do you love Ranjit?'

She looked at me, both eyes, soft and hard, staring into mine.

'I thought I *admired* him, once upon a time,' she said, 'not that it's any of your business.'

'And you don't admire me?'

'Why would you ask that?'

'Are you afraid to tell me what you think?'

'Of course not,' she said evenly. 'I'm wondering why you don't already *know* what I think of you.'

'I don't know what that means, so how about you just answer my question?'

'Mine first. Why do you want to know? Is it disappointment in yourself, or jealousy of him?'

'You know, the thing about disappointment, Karla, is that it never lets you down. But it's not about that. I want to know what you think, because it matters to me.'

'Okay, you asked for it. No, I don't admire you. Not today.'

We were silent for a while.

'You know what I'm talking about,' she said at last.

'I don't, actually.'

I frowned again and she laughed: the little laugh that bubbles up from an in-joke.

'Look at your face,' she said. 'What happened to you? Fell off your pride again, right?'

'Happily, the fall's not too far.'

She laughed again, but it quickly became a frown.

'Can you even explain it? Why you've been fighting? Why a fight always finds you?'

Of course I couldn't. Being kidnapped and strapped to a banana lounge by the Scorpion gang: how could I explain that? I didn't understand it myself, not any of it, not even Concannon. Especially not Concannon. I didn't know, then, that I was standing on a tattered corner of a bloody carpet that would soon cover most of the world.

'Who says I *have* to explain it?'

'Can you?' she repeated.

'Can *you* explain the things you did to us back then, Karla?'

She flinched.

'Don't hold back, Karla.'

'Maybe I should chase to the cut, so to speak, and *tell* you the answer.'

'Go ahead.'

'Sure you've got the stomach for it?'

'Sure.'

'Okay then, the –'

'No, wait!'

'Wait what?'

'My conversation sub-routine is crying out for that coffee.'

'You're kidding, right?'

'No, I'm grievously coffee-deprived. That's how you kicked my ass.'

'So I *did* win?'

'You won. Can I have the coffee now?'

I used my sleeve to snatch the pot from the fire and pour some coffee into a chipped mug. I offered it to Karla, but she wrinkled her lip in a proscenium arch of disgust.

'I'm reading a *no*,' I guessed.

'How's that magic act workin' out? Drink the damn coffee, yaar.'

I sipped at the coffee. It was too strong and too sweet and too bitter, all at the same time. Perfect.

'Okay, good,' I croaked, coffee shivering hello. 'I'm good.'

'The –'

'No, wait!'

I found a joint.

'Okay,' I said, puffing it alight. 'I'm good. Lemme have it.'

'Sure you don't need a manicure, or a massage?' Karla growled.

'I'm so good, now. Smack me around all you like, Karla.'

'Okay, here goes. The marks on your face, and all the scars on your body, are like graffiti, scrawled by your own delinquent talent.'

'Not bad.'

'I'm not finished. Your heart's a tenant, in the broken-down tenement of your life.'

'Anything else?'

'The slumlord's coming to collect the rent, Lin,' she said, a little more softly. 'Soon.'

I knew her well enough to know that she'd written and rehearsed those lines. I'd seen her journals, filled with notes for the clever things she said. Rehearsed or not, she was right.

'Karla, look –'

'You're playing Russian roulette with Fate,' she said. 'You know that.'

'And your money's on Fate? Is that what this is about?'

'Fate loads the gun. Fate loads every gun in the world.'

'Anything else?'

'While you do this,' she said, even more softly, 'you're only breaking things.'

It was just true enough to hurt, no matter how softly she said it.

'You know, if you keep coming on to me like this . . . '

'You got funnier,' she said, laughing a little.

'I'm still what I used to be.'

We stared at one another for a few moments.

'Look, Karla, I don't know what it is with Ranjit, and I don't know how it's two whole years since I looked at you and heard your voice. I just know that when I'm with you, it's wild horse right. I love you, and I'll always be there for you.'

Emotions were leaves in a storm on her face. There were too many different feelings for me to read. I hadn't seen her. I hadn't been with her. She looked happy and angry, satisfied and sad, all at the same time. And she didn't speak. Karla, lost for words. It hurt her, in some way, and I had to break the mood.

'*Sure* you don't want to try that coffee?'

She raised a rattlesnake eyebrow, and was about to fang me, but sounds from the caves alerted us to the presence of others, waking with the dawn.

We breakfasted with the happy devotees and were drinking our second mug of chai, when a young student appeared at the ridge of the camp where the steep climb from the forest ended. He accepted a chai gratefully, and announced that the master wouldn't be joining us until after lunch.

'That's it,' Karla muttered, moving to the open kitchen, where she rinsed out her cup and set it on a stand to dry.

'That's what?' I asked, joining her at the sink.

'I've got time to go down, visit Khaled, and be back before Idriss gets here.'

'I'm coming with,' I said quickly.

'Wait a minute. Call off the myrmidons. Why are *you* coming?'

It wasn't an idle question. Karla didn't idle.

'*Why?* Because Khaled's my friend. And I haven't seen him since he walked into the snow, nearly three years ago.'

'A good friend would leave him the hell alone, right now,' she said.

'What's *that* supposed to mean?'

She fixed me with that look: hunger burning in a tiger's eyes, staring at prey. I loved it.

'He's happy,' she said quietly.

'And?'

She glanced at Abdullah, who'd come up to stand beside me.

'Happy's hard to find,' she said at last.

'I've got absolutely no idea what you're talking about.'

'Happiness has a sign on it,' she said. 'It says *Do Not Disturb*, but everybody does.'

'Interfering is what we do,' I insisted, 'if we care about someone. Weren't you interfering, when you ripped some skin off me just now?'

'And were you interfering, between Ranjit and me?'

'How?'

'When you asked me if I love him.'

Abdullah coughed politely.

'Perhaps I should leave you for some time,' he suggested.

'No secrets from you, Abdullah,' Karla said.

'But you keep plenty of your own, brother,' I said. 'Not telling me that Khaled is here?'

'Fire away at Abdullah, Lin,' Karla interjected. 'But answer my question first.'

'When you know where we are in this conversation, come get me.'

'You were answering a question.'

'What question?'

'Why?'

'Why what?'

'Why do you love me?'

'Dammit, Karla! You're the most indiscernible woman who ever spoke a common language.'

'Give me a ten-minute head start,' she laughed. 'No, make it fifteen.'

'What are you planning?'

She laughed again, and pretty hard.

'I want to warn Khaled that you're coming, and give him a chance to escape. You know how important that is, don't you? A chance to escape?'

She walked to the edge of the mesa, then slipped out of sight on the steep path. I waited for the essential fifteen minutes to pass. Abdullah was looking at me. I didn't bite. I didn't want to know.

'Perhaps . . . she is right in this,' he said, at last.

'Not you, too?'

'If Khaled looks at what he has through your eyes, instead of his own eyes, he may believe in himself less than he does now. And I need him to be strong.'

'Is that why you never told me Khaled was here in Bombay?'

'Yes, that was a part of it. To protect his little happiness. He was never a very happy man. You remember that, I am certain.'

He was, in fact, the most dour and stern man I'd ever known. Every member of his family had been killed in the wars and purges that pursued the Palestinian diaspora into Lebanon. He was so callused by hatred and sorrow that the most vicious insult in his Hindi vocabulary was the word *Kshama*, meaning *forgiveness*.

'I still don't get it, Abdullah.'

'You have an influence over our brother Khaled,' he said solemnly.

'What influence?'

'Your opinion matters very much to him. It always did. And your opinion of him will change, when you come to know of his life now.'

'Why don't we cross that bridge, before we blow it up?'

290

'But another part,' Abdullah said, his hand on my arm, 'the biggest part, was to protect him from harm.'

'What do you mean? He was a Council member. That's for life. No-one can touch him.'

'Yes, but Khaled is the only man who has the authority to challenge Sanjay for the leadership of the Council. That can make some resent him, or fear him.'

'Only if he challenged Sanjay.'

'In fact, I have asked him to do just that.'

Abdullah, the most loyal man I knew, was planning a coup. Men would die. Friends would die.

'Why are you doing this?'

'We need Khaled, perhaps more than you know. He has refused, but I will ask him again, and keep on asking him, until he agrees. For now, please keep his presence here a secret, just as I have done.'

It was a long speech for the taciturn Iranian.

'Abdullah, none of this applies to me any more. That's what I've been trying to tell you. I've been trying to find a way to bring this up with you since we got here.'

'Is it too much to ask of you?'

'No, brother,' I replied, moving half a step away from him. 'It's not too much to ask, but it has nothing to do with me any more. I made a decision, and I've been waiting for a chance to tell you. It's such a big thing that I've pushed it away, after Concannon and the Scorpions, and then seeing Karla up here, after so long. I guess . . . now is the right time to face it, and get it out there.'

'What decision? Has anyone talked to you about my plan?'

I let out a heavy sigh. Straightening up, I smiled, and leaned back against a squared-off boulder.

'No, Abdullah, nobody talked about your plan. I never heard about it, until you told me just now. I made the decision to leave after Lightning Dilip told me that three kids cancelled on the dope that DaSilva and his crew are selling.'

'But you do not have anything to do with that, and I do not. It is not our operation. We both disagreed with Sanjay, when he started *garad* and girls in South Bombay. It was not our decision to make.'

'No, it's more than that, man,' I said, looking out at the spirals of storm swirling over the distant city. 'I can give you ten good reasons why I should leave, and why I have to leave, but they're not important, because I can't think of one good reason to stay. Bottom line is, I'm just done, that's all. I'm out.'

The Iranian warrior frowned, his eyes searching left and right through an invisible battlefield for the Lin he knew, while his mind made war on his heart.

'Will you permit me to persuade you?'

'Trying to persuade isn't just permitted, among good friends,' I said, 'it's required. But please, let me spare you the kindness. I don't want to hear you plead a lost cause for me. I know how you feel, because I feel it myself. The truth is, my mind's made up. I'm already gone, Abdullah. I'm long gone.'

'Sanjay won't like it.'

'You're right about that,' I laughed. 'But I don't have any family ties to the Company. I don't have any family, so he doesn't have the mafia card to play against me. And Sanjay knows I'm good with passports. I could always be useful, sometime down the line. He's a cautious guy. He likes options. I'm guessing he won't put fire in my way.'

'That is a dangerous guess,' Abdullah mused.

'Yeah. That it is.'

'If I kill him, your odds will improve.'

'I don't know why I even have to say these words, Abdullah, but here goes, *Please don't kill Sanjay, for me.* Are we clear on that? It would ruin my appetite for a month, man.'

'Granted. When I take his life, I will purge your benefit from my mind.'

'How about not killing Sanjay at all?' I asked. 'For *any* reason. And why are we talking about killing Sanjay? How did you let this happen, Abdullah? No, no, don't tell me. I'm out. I don't want to know.'

Abdullah mulled it over for a while, his jaw locked, and his lips twitching with the tide of reflection.

'What will you do?'

'I think I'll freelance,' I answered him, my eyes following a shadow of thoughts across his wind-shaped face. 'I thought I might string with Didier for a while. He's been asking me to throw in with him for years.'

'Very dangerous,' he mumbled.

'More dangerous than this?' I asked, and when he opened his mouth to speak, I stopped him. 'Don't even try, brother.'

'Have you told anyone else about this?'

'No.'

'Make no mistake, Lin,' he said, suddenly stern. 'I am starting a war, and I must win it. Your belief in Sanjay's leadership has been lost, as has mine, and you are no longer with the Company. Very well. But I hope that your loyalty to me will ensure your silence, concerning my plans.'

'I wish you hadn't told me about it, Abdullah. Conspiracies contaminate, and I'm contaminated now. But you're my brother, man, and if it's a choice between them and you, I'll stand with you every time. Just don't tell me any more about the plan, okay? Didn't anyone ever tell you, there's no curse as cruel as another man's plans?'

'Thank you, Lin,' he said, smiling softly. 'I will do what I can to ensure that the war does not come to your door.'

'I'd prefer it didn't come to my subcontinent. Why war, Abdullah? Walk away, man. I'll stand with you, out here, outside the Company, no matter what they throw at us. A war will kill our friends, as well as our enemies. Is anything worth that?'

He leaned back against the squared stone beside me, his shoulder touching mine. We both looked out over the forest canopy, and then he rested his head on the stone to look into the troubled sky.

I lay back against the stone, lifting my face to fields of cloud, ploughed by the storm.

'I cannot leave, Lin,' he sighed. 'We would be good partners, it is true, but I cannot leave.'

'The boy, Tariq.'

'Yes. He is Khaderbhai's nephew, and my responsibility.'

'Why? You never told me.'

His face softened in the sad smile we reserve for the memory of a bitter failure that brought eventual success.

'Khaderbhai saved my life,' he said at last. 'I was young, an Iranian soldier running away from the war with Iraq. I got into bad trouble, here in Bombay. Khaderbhai intervened. I could not understand why a mighty don would reach out to save me, from a death that my pride and my temper had earned.'

His head was close to mine, but his voice seemed to be coming from somewhere else, somewhere beyond the great stones at our backs.

'When he granted me an audience, and told me the matter was resolved, assuring me that I was safe from harm, I asked him how I could repay him,' Abdullah continued. 'Khaderbhai smiled at me for a long time. You know that smile so well, Lin brother.'

'I do. Still feel it, sometimes.'

'And then he made me spill my blood, with my own knife, and swear on that flowing blood to watch his nephew, Tariq, as a protector, offering my life, if necessary, for as long as I or the boy should live.'

'He was a master of the devil's compact.'

'Ah, yes,' Abdullah said quietly, as we sat up and turned to face one another. 'But that is why I cannot simply walk away from what Sanjay is doing. There are things you do not understand. Things I cannot tell you. But Sanjay is bringing fire on our heads, maybe even on the city itself. Terrible fire. The boy, Tariq, is in danger, and I will do whatever it takes to keep him safe.'

We stared at one another for a while, not smiling but at peace, somehow. At last he stood up, and slapped me on the shoulder.

'You will need more guns,' he said.

'I've got two guns.'

'Exactly. You need more guns. Leave it to me.'

'I have enough guns,' I said, starting to catch up.

'Leave it to me.'

'I don't need new guns.'

'Everybody needs new guns. Even armies need new guns, and armies have many guns. Leave it to me.'

'Tell you what. If you can find a gun that makes people go to sleep for a couple of days without hurting them, get me one, and a lot of ammunition.'

Abdullah stopped, and drew me close to whisper.

'This will be bad, before it is good, Lin. It is not a joke. Please know that I value your silence very highly, the silence of friendship, because I know that you are risking your life, should Sanjay come to know of it. Be prepared for war, the more so if you despise war.'

'Okay, Abdullah, okay.'

'Let us go to Khaled,' he said, walking away.

'Oh, so now it's *okay* to disturb his *little happiness*, huh?' I said, following him.

'You are not family now, Lin brother,' he said quietly, as I drew alongside him at the edge of the mesa. 'Your opinion no longer has influence.'

I stared into his eyes, and it was there: the blur of indifference, the diminishment of love's light and friendship's bright trust, the subtle change in the aura of affections when one still inside the fold looks into the eyes of what lives outside.

I'd found a home, a broken home, in the Sanjay Company, but the gates were closed there forever. I loved Abdullah, but love is a loyalty of one, and he was still in a band of brothers, loyal to all. That's why I'd waited to tell him: why I'd let myself drift inside the other tides of Karla's soft-eyed cleverness and Concannon's martial madness.

I was losing Abdullah. I struck the tree-inside, what we were together in the Company, with the axe of separation. And my friend, his eyes drifting on stranger currents, led us over the mesa on the downward path, as thunder tumbled in that threatening sea, the drowning sky.

CHAPTER TWENTY-EIGHT

A T THE BASE OF THE MOUNTAIN Abdullah led me away behind the valley of the sandstone Buddhas and its well-cleared paths. We followed a jungle track through thick forest for a few minutes, and then entered a tree-lined approach, rising on a gentle slope to meet a concrete and hardwood house, three storeys tall.

Before we reached the steps leading up to the wide ground-floor veranda, Khaled walked out of the vestibule to greet us.

Dressed in a voluminous yellow silk robe, and with garlands of red and yellow flowers around his neck, he stood with his fists locked onto his hips.

'Shantaram!' he shouted. 'Welcome to Shangri-La!'

He'd changed. He'd changed so much in the years since I'd seen him. His hair had thinned to the point that he was almost bald. The fighter's frame had expanded until his hips and belly were wider than his shoulders. The handsome face that had frowned its rage and recrimination at the world was swollen, from temple to vanishing jaw, and his smile all but concealed his golden-brown eyes.

It was Khaled, my friend. I rushed the steps to greet him.

He extended his hands, holding me two steps below. A young man in a yellow kurta took a photograph of us, let the camera fall to a strap around his neck, and pulled a notebook and pen from his shirt pocket.

'Don't mind Tarun,' Khaled said, nodding his head toward the young man. 'He keeps a record of everyone I meet, and everything I do and say. I've told him not to do it, but the naughty lad won't listen. And hey, people always do what their hearts tell them to do, isn't it so?'

'Well –'

'I got fat,' he said.

It wasn't regretful or ironic. It was a flat statement of fact.

'Well –'

'But *you* look very fit. What have you been doing, to get all those bruises? Boxing with Abdullah? Looks like he got the better of you. No surprise, eh? Certainly, you both look fit enough to make that climb up my mountain, to see Idriss.'

'Your mountain?'

'Well . . . *this* part of it is mine, *na*? It's actually *Idriss* who thinks he owns the whole mountain. He's such a *chudh*. Anyway, come here, let me give you a hug, and then we'll take a look around.'

I climbed the last two steps, and fell into a fleshy cloud. Tarun flashed a photograph. When Khaled released me he shook hands with Abdullah, and led the way inside.

'Where's Karla?' I asked, a step behind him.

'She said that she will meet you again on the path,' Khaled replied breezily. 'She is jogging, I think, to clear her mind. I am not sure whether it is you or me that disturbs her peace, but my money is on you, old friend.'

The entrance to the huge old house opened into a wide vestibule, with staircases left and right, and archways leading to the main rooms of the ground floor.

'This was a Britisher's monsoon retreat,' Khaled announced, as we moved beyond the vestibule to a sitting room featuring walls of books, two writing desks, and several comfortable leather chairs. 'It passed to a businessman, but when the national park was established here, he was forced to sell it to the city. A rich friend of mine, one of my students, has rented it from the city for some years, and he gave it to me, to use.'

'Your students?'

'Indeed.'

'Oh, I see. Is this where you learn how *not* to contact your friends, when you come back from the dead?'

'Very funny, Lin,' he replied, in that flat tone he'd used when he'd described himself as fat. 'But I think you'll understand my need for discretion.'

'Fuck discretion. You're not dead, Khaled, and I want to know why I didn't know that.'

'Things are not as simple as you think, Lin. And anyway, what I teach people here has nothing to do with the outside world. I teach love.

297

Specifically, I teach people how to love themselves. I think you're not surprised that for some people, that's not easy.'

We walked through the sitting room, opened the louvred French doors and entered a wide sunroom, running the whole width of the house. There were many wicker armchairs, with glass-topped tables between them.

Softly whirring overhead fans disturbed the slender leaves of potted palms. A wall of glass panels looked out into an English-style garden of rosebushes, and neatly clipped hedges.

Two pretty young Western girls dressed in tunics approached us, bowing to Khaled, their palms pressed together.

'Please, take a seat,' Khaled invited, pointing toward two of the wicker chairs. 'What will you have, hot drinks, or cold?'

'Cold,' Abdullah answered.

'The same.'

Khaled nodded at the girls. They backed up a few steps, before walking away out of sight. Khaled watched them leave.

'Good help is so easy to find these days,' he sighed contentedly, as he lowered himself into a chair.

Tarun made notes.

'What happened?' I asked.

'What . . . *happened*?' Khaled repeated, mystified.

'The last time I saw you there was a dead lunatic on the ground, and you walked into a snow storm, without a gun. Now you're here. What happened?'

'Oh,' he smiled. 'I see. We're back to that.'

'Yeah. We're back to that.'

'You know, Lin, you got harder, since I saw you last.'

'Maybe I did, Khaled. Maybe I just like the truth, when I can get it.'

'The truth,' he mused.

He glanced up at Tarun, who was still making notes. The assistant stopped, caught Khaled's eye, sighed, and put his notebook away.

'Well,' Khaled continued, 'I walked from Afghanistan. And I walked. And I walked. It's surprising, really, how far you can walk, when you don't care if you live, or if you die. To be precise, when you don't *love yourself*.'

'You walked *where*, exactly?'

'I walked to Pakistan.'

298

Tell me about Pakistan, a voice said in my head.

'And after Pakistan?'

'After Pakistan, I walked to India. Then I walked through India, to Varanasi. By the time I got there, word had spread about me. A lot of people were talking about the *Silent Walking Baba*, who never spoke a word to anyone. It took me a while to realise they were talking about me. I didn't speak, because by then I actually *couldn't* speak. Physically, I mean. I was quite sick, from malnutrition. Almost died from it. The hunger, for so many starving months, caused my hair to fall out, and many of my teeth. My mouth was swollen with ulcers. I couldn't say a word, to save my life.'

He laughed softly, chuckling motes in a sunbeam of memory.

'But people took my silence for wisdom, you see? Less really *is* more, sometimes. And in Varanasi, I met an Englishman, Lord Bob, who claimed me as his guru. As it happens, he was very rich. A lot of my students have been rich, in fact, which is funny, when you think about it.'

He paused, staring out into the English garden, a smile of wonderment pulling at the edges of his mouth.

'Lord Bob . . . ' I prompted.

'Oh, yes. Lord Bob. He was such a kind and caring man, but he was in need of something. Desperately in need. He spent his whole life searching in vain for the one thing that would give his life meaning, and then he finally came to me for an answer.'

'What was it?' I asked.

'I have no idea,' Khaled replied. 'I had no idea what he was searching for, frankly. Not a clue. He was stinking rich, after all. What could he possibly want? But I don't think it mattered much to Lord Bob that I couldn't help him, because he left me everything, when he died.'

The girls returned with two trays, and set them down on tables near us. There were drinks in long glasses, and several dishes of dried papaya, pineapple and mango, and three varieties of shelled nuts.

Bowing deeply to Khaled, their hands pressed together reverently, the girls backed away and then turned, gliding across the tiled veranda on bare feet.

I watched the girls out of sight, and turned to see Khaled, staring dreamily at the garden, and Abdullah staring fixedly at Khaled.

'I was there, in Varanasi, for nearly two years,' Khaled reflected. 'And I miss it, sometimes.'

He looked around then, and picked up one of the glasses. He handed it to me, passed another to Abdullah, and took a long sip himself.

'They were good years,' he said. 'I learned a lot from Lord Bob's willingness to subjugate himself, and surrender to me.'

He chuckled. I glanced at Abdullah. *Did he say subjugate? Did he say surrender?* It was a strange moment, in an already strange hour. We sipped our drinks.

'And he wasn't the only one, of course,' Khaled continued. 'There were many others, even elderly sadhus, all of them too happy to kneel and touch my feet, even though I said nothing at all. And that's when I understood the power that comes into us when another man, even if it's only one other, bends his knee in devotion. I understood that men sell the power of that dream to women, every time they propose.'

He laughed. I stared at my drink, at the lines of moisture that zig-zagged through the silver filigree design on the surface of the ruby-red glass. I was becoming increasingly uneasy. The Khaled who spoke so complacently about others kneeling before him wasn't the friend I'd loved.

Khaled turned to Abdullah.

'I think our brother, Lin, is rather surprised that while my English has improved, in the years with Lord Bob, my American sensibility has declined, wouldn't you say?'

'Every man is responsible for his own actions,' Abdullah replied. 'That law applies to you, and to those who choose to kneel before you, as it does to Lin, and to me.'

'Well said, old friend!' Khaled cried.

He placed his glass on the table, and lifted himself with some grunt-ing effort from the chair.

'Come! I want to show you something.'

We followed him back into the house and through to the staircases flanking the entrance vestibule. Khaled paused at the foot of the stairs for a moment, his hand resting on the turned wooden pommel.

'I hope you liked the juice,' he asked earnestly.

'Sure.'

'It's the drop of maple syrup that makes the difference,' he pressed.

There was a pause. I understood, at last, that he wanted a reply.

'The juice was fine, Khaled,' I said.

'Good juice,' Abdullah echoed.

'I'm so glad,' Khaled said flatly. 'You've got no idea how long it took me to train the kitchen staff on the juices. I had to flog one of them with a spatula. And the drama I had with the desserts, don't let me go there.'

'You have my word,' I said.

He took one step, but then turned quickly to speak to Tarun, who'd been following us.

'You can wait here, Tarun,' Khaled said. 'In fact, take a break. Get yourself a biscuit.'

Crushed, Tarun ambled away. Khaled watched him leave, suspicion squinting in his eyes.

The old Khaled could've taken the steps three at a time, and beaten any man in Bombay to the top floor. The new Khaled paused twice on the first flight.

'This floor,' he puffed, as we reached the first floor, 'has all of our main meditation and yoga halls.'

'Do a lot of yoga, then?' I asked, channelling the impish spirit of Gemini George for a moment.

'No, no!' Khaled replied seriously. 'I'm much too fat and unfit for that. I was always a boxing and karate man, anyway. You remember that, Lin.'

I remembered. I remembered when Khaled could fight any man in the city but Abdullah into the ground, and still have energy to spare.

'Uh-huh.'

'But yoga is very popular, with my people. They're at it all the time. They'd do it all night, if I let them. I practically have to hose them down to make them stop.'

Through the nearest door in the corridor, we could see a class of a dozen people, sitting on mats. Flute music came from speakers fixed to the walls.

Regaining his breath, Khaled led us to the second floor.

The corridor at that level showed many closed doors, running the length of the building.

'Dormitories,' Khaled wheezed. 'And single rooms.'

He gently eased open the door to the nearest room. We saw several girls, sleeping on single beds under tent-pole mosquito nets. The girls were naked.

'My most devoted students,' Khaled said, in that same bewilderingly flat tone.

'What the fuck, Khaled?' I snapped, but he put his finger to his lips, silencing me.

'Please, Lin, be quiet! We won't get a minute's peace, if you wake them up.'

'Okay, bye, Khaled,' I said, leaving.

'What are you doing?' Khaled asked, a puzzle stamped on his forehead.

'Well, I'm gonna keep on walking until I'm not here. That's what goodbye means.'

'No, Lin, what's the matter?' he asked, pulling the door closed gently.

'The matter?' I said, stopping at the top of the stairs. 'What's that in there, a harem? Have you gone nuts, Khaled? Who do you think you are?'

'Everyone here is free to leave, Lin,' he said flatly, his frown darkening at the edges. 'Including you.'

'What a coincidence,' I sighed, turning to go. 'I was just leaving.'

'No, no, I'm sorry,' he said, rushing forward and putting a hand on my shoulder to stop me. 'There's something you have to see! Something I must show you! It's a secret. A secret I want to share with you.'

'I've had enough secrets for one day, Khaled. Call me, when you come down off the mountain.'

'But Abdullah hasn't seen the secret yet. You can't deprive *him*, as well, can you? That would be cruel. Abdullah, wouldn't you like to know the secret?'

'I *would*, Khaled,' Abdullah replied, all fascinated innocence.

'Then, tell Lin. Convince him to stay. Whatever the case, I'm going up to see the secret, and you're welcome to come along, if you want, my brothers.'

He released his grip on my shoulder, braced himself with a deep breath for the climb to the third floor, and then trudged up the stairs.

I held Abdullah back.

'What are we doin' here, Abdullah?'

'What do you mean?'

'A room full of naked girls? What's the matter with him? There's plenty of girls. The world's full of girls. Having your own roomful of girls is what gives creepy a bad name. Come on, brother. Let's go.'

302

'But, Lin,' Abdullah whispered. 'What about the secret?'

'Are you kidding?'

'It is a secret. A real secret.'

'I don't like the secret I heard already, Abdullah.'

'How can you *not* want to know?'

'Let's just say I've got psychic asthma, and right now, I need fresh air. It's medicinal. Let's go.'

'Please stay with me, Lin, just until the secret is unveiled.'

I sighed.

'Are you guys coming?' Khaled called out from his resting place, halfway up the flight of stairs. 'These stairs are killing me. I'm getting an elevator installed next week.'

Abdullah gave me his pleading frown.

'Okay, okay,' I called back, heading up the stairs.

Plodding wearily, Khaled followed the elbow turn of the stairs and finally came to a closed door. Fetching a key from the folds of his kaftan, he opened the door, and ushered us inside.

It was dark. The light from the stairwell revealed an attic room, with the folded arms of roof beams above our heads. Khaled closed the door, locked it, and clicked on a suspended light bulb.

It was a hoard of objects in gold and silver: jewelled necklaces and chains, spilling from little wooden chests, scattered across several tables.

There were candlesticks and mirrors, picture frames, hairbrushes, strings of pearls, jewelled bracelets, watches, necklaces, brooches, rings, earrings, nose-rings, toe rings and even several black and gold wedding necklaces.

And there was money. A lot of money.

'No matter how I tried to explain this,' Khaled said, breathing through his open mouth, 'nothing could ever be clearer than seeing it for yourself, *na*? This is the power of the bended knee. Do you see? Do you *see*?'

There was a softly breathing silence. Pigeons brooded in a distant corner of the roofline, their warbled comments echoing in the long, closed room.

Finally, Khaled spoke again.

'Tax free,' he wheezed.

He looked from Abdullah, to me, and back again.

'Well? What do you think?'

'You need more security,' Abdullah observed.

'Ha!' Khaled laughed, clapping the tall Iranian on the back. 'Are you volunteering for the job, my old friend?'

'I *have* a job,' he replied, even more seriously.

'Yes, yes, of course you do, but –'

'Your students gave you all this stuff?' I asked.

'Actually, I *call* them students, but they refer to themselves as devotees,' Khaled said, staring at the hoard. 'There was even more than this.'

'More than *this*?'

'Oh, yes. A lot of other gifts from my devotees in Varanasi. But I had to leave there rather quickly, and I lost everything.'

'Lost it how?'

'To the police, as a bribe,' Khaled replied. 'That's why Lord Bob set me up here, in this house, just before he died.'

'Why did you have to leave Varanasi so quickly?'

'Why do you want to know, Lin, my old friend?'

The jewels from the treasure were glittering in his eyes.

'You brought it up, man.'

He stared at me for a while, hesitating on the glacial edge of cold-hearted truth. He decided to trust me, I guess.

'There was a girl,' he said. 'A devotee, a very sincere devotee, who came from a prominent Brahmin family. She was beautiful, and ultimately devoted to me, body and soul. I didn't know she was below the age.'

'Come on, Khaled.'

'I couldn't know. You live here, Lin, you know how precocious these young Indian girls can be. She looked eighteen, I swear. Her breasts were swollen like ripe mangoes. And the sex was fully mature. But, alas, she was only fourteen.'

'Khaled, you just officially freaked me out.'

'No, Lin, understand me –'

'Understand sex with kids? You want me to see it *your way*? Is that it, Khaled?'

'But it won't happen again.'

'*Again?*'

'It *can't* happen again. I've taken measures.'

'You're making this worse every time you open your mouth, Khaled.'

'Listen to me! I make every one of them show me a birth certificate now, especially the younger ones. I'm protected, now.'

'*You're* protected?'

'Let's stop all this serious talk, yaar. We all have things in the past that we regret, no? We have a saying, in Arabic. *Take counsel from he who makes you weep, not from he who makes you laugh.* I haven't made you laugh today, Lin, but that doesn't mean my counsel is worthless.'

'Khaled —'

'I want you to know that you, and Abdullah, my only remaining brothers, will always be safe, now. This power, this money and my inheritance, it's all ours.'

'What are you talking about, Khaled?'

'Money, to expand the business,' he unexplained.

'What business?'

'This business. The ashram. The time has come to franchise. We can run this together, and spread out through India, and eventually to America. The sky's the limit. Literally, in fact.'

'Khaled —'

'That's why I've waited so long to contact you. I had to accumulate this fund base. I brought you here to show you something that's yours, as much as it is mine.'

'You're right about that,' I said.

'I'm so glad you understand.'

'I mean that this stuff you've got here isn't ours, Khaled, and it isn't yours.'

'What does *that* mean?'

'It was given to something bigger than we are, and you know it.'

'But, you don't understand,' he insisted. 'I want you both in this with me. We can make millions. But the spiritual industry is a vicious business. I'll need you, as we move on.'

'I've already moved on, Khaled.'

'But we can franchise!' Khaled hissed, all teeth. 'We can franchise!'

'Khaled, I must leave the city,' Abdullah said suddenly, urgency rasping his voice.

'What?' Khaled asked, shaken from a tree of plans.

'I want to ask you, one more time, to leave this place, and these people, and come back to Bombay with me.'

'Again, Abdullah?' Khaled said.

'Take your rightful place at the head of the Council that was Khaderbhai's. We are in a time of trouble, and it will become much worse. We need you to lead us. We need you to push Sanjay aside, and lead us. If you come now, Sanjay will live. If you don't, one of us will kill him, and then you will have to lead anyway, for the sake of the Company.'

In that new avatar, Khaled was the opposite of what I considered to be a leader of men. But Abdullah, an Iranian who'd tuned his heart to the music of Bombay's streets, didn't see the man who stood with us in the attic room. Abdullah saw the prestige that attached itself to Khaled's long and intimate friendship with Khaderbhai, and the authority that bled from the many battles and gang wars Khaled had presided over, and won, for the Company.

I was done with the Sanjay Company, my mind was made up, but I knew that New Khaled's taste for subjugation would add fire to Old Khaled's unhesitating use of power.

Crime mixed with anything is fatal, which is why we're fascinated by it. Crime mixed with religion redeems saviours with the sacrifice of sinners. I didn't want Khaled to accept Abdullah's offer.

'Once more, I tell you that I can't accept,' Khaled smiled. 'But with friendship and respect, I want you to consider my offer. It's a golden opportunity to get in on the ground floor, before the spiritual industry really takes off. We can make millions from yoga alone.'

'You must think of the Company, Khaled,' Abdullah pressed. 'You must follow your destiny.'

'It will not happen,' Khaled responded, the little smile still on his lips. 'But I do appreciate your kindness, in considering me again. Now, before you take a final decision, I ask you to think on all my treasures, and join me at lunch. I'm starved, I don't mind telling you.'

'I'm done,' I said.

'You're . . . what?'

'Khaled, I was already done when you showed me the harem. I'm leaving.'

'Does that mean you won't be taking any food?' Khaled asked, locking the door.

306

'It means goodbye, again, Khaled.'

'But, it's bad luck not to eat food that has been prepared for you!' he warned.

'I'll have to risk it.'

'But it's Kashmiri sweets. A Kashmiri sweet chef is one of my devotees. You have no idea how hard they are to get.'

I crossed the entry hall, Khaled bustling behind me. Tarun joined us, trotting at his master's side.

'Oh, well,' he puffed, walking with us onto the front veranda.

He gave me a damp, spongy hug, shook hands with Abdullah, and waved as we walked the gravel path.

'Come back any time!' he called. 'You're always welcome! We show movies, on Wednesday nights! We serve ice-cold *firni*! And we dance, on Thursdays! I'm learning to dance. Can you believe it?'

Beside him, Tarun made new entries in his notebook.

At the first bend in the path we found Karla waiting for us. She was sitting on a fallen tree, and smoking a cigarette.

'So, did you piss on his pilgrimage, Shantaram?'

'You could've given me a little more warning, before I saw him,' I said, feeling beaten by the truth. 'What the hell happened to him?'

'He got happy, more or less,' she answered softly. 'In his case, a little more than less.'

'Are *you* happy to see him like this?'

They both stared at me.

'Oh, come on!'

They continued to stare.

'Okay, okay,' I conceded. 'Maybe ... maybe I just want my friend back. Don't you miss him?'

'Khaled is here, Lin,' Abdullah replied.

'But —'

'Save your breath for the climb,' Karla said, heading back toward the path. 'Do you gangsters ever shut up?'

We approached the ascent to the first caves, and she began to run at a slow jog. When we reached the steep climb she was still ahead of us.

As we struggled upwards, I couldn't help staring at the sand-line curves of her body, contoured by the climb.

Men are dogs, Didier once said to me, *without the manners.*

'Are you staring at my ass?' she asked.

'Afraid so.'

'Forgive him, Karla.' Abdullah said to cover somebody's embarrassment. 'He simply stares, because you are climbing like an ape.'

Karla laughed, clutching at the vines on the path to hold her place. That big, true laugh rang through domes of branches risen with the cliff. She held her free hand out to Abdullah, warning him not to say another word until the laughter rushed away from her.

'Thank you, Abdullah,' she said at last.

'Don't mention.'

And laughing, and joking, we three exiles climbed the mountain that would change everything, for each of us, forever.

CHAPTER TWENTY-NINE

WHEN WE REACHED THE SUMMIT there was just enough time to freshen up. Karla changed into a sky-blue *salwar kameez*, and joined us for the last of the lunch that had been served. As we finished, an announcement was made that Idriss was on the mountain. I looked back toward the steep slope, but everyone else turned to stare at the caves.

'There's another way up this mountain?' I asked Karla.

'There's another way up every mountain,' she purred. 'Everybody knows that.'

'O . . . kay.'

Within seconds an older man I assumed to be Idriss and a younger man, both of them wearing white kurta tops and loose, sky-blue calico pants, appeared on a path that led past the women's cave. The younger man, a foreigner, carried a hunting rifle slung over his shoulder.

'Who's the gun?'

'That's Silvano,' Karla replied.

'What's the rifle for?'

'To frighten tigers away.'

'There are tigers?'

'Of course. On the next mountain.'

I wanted to ask how close the next mountain was, but Idriss spoke.

'Dear friends,' he said, clearing his throat. 'That's quite a climb, even on the easy path. I apologise for being late. A squabble of philosophers set upon me this morning.'

His deep, gentle voice tumbled from his chest and hummed into the air. It seemed to roll around us on the mesa. It was a voice that comforts: a voice that could wake you softly from a nightmare.

'What was their dilemma, master-*ji*?' a student asked.

309

'One of them,' he replied, fishing a handkerchief from the pocket of his kurta and wiping his forehead, 'had produced an argument to prove that happiness was the greatest of all evils. The others couldn't defeat his argument. So, naturally, they became desperately unhappy. They wanted me to relieve them of their distress by refuting the argument.'

'Did you do it, Idriss?' another student asked.

'Of course. But it took forever. Would anyone but philosophers fight so hard against the proposition that happiness is a good thing? And then, when their minds were convinced that happiness was a good thing, the sudden surge of all their pent-up happiness was too much for them. They lost control. Has anyone here seen hysterical philosophers?'

The students looked around at one another.

'No?' Idriss prodded. 'Just as well. And there's a lesson. The more slender your grip on reality, the more dangerous the world becomes. On the other hand, the more rational the world you find yourself in, the more carefully it must be questioned. But enough of that, let's get started. Gather around, and get comfortable.'

The devotees and students brought stools and chairs, ranging them in a semicircle around Idriss, who lowered himself gently into an easy chair. The young man with the rifle, Silvano, sat a little behind Idriss and to his right. He sat on a hard wooden stool, his back rigid and his eyes passing back and forth among us. Very often his eyes stopped on me.

Abdullah leaned in to speak to me.

'The Italian with the rifle, Silvano, is watching you,' he whispered, with a little flick of his head.

'Thanks.'

'Don't mention,' he replied gravely.

'I see that we have a new visitor to our little study group,' Idriss said, looking at me.

I turned to see if he wasn't staring at someone behind me.

'It's a pleasure to have you with us, Lin. Khaderbhai spoke of you quite often, and I'm very glad you could come.'

Everyone turned to look at me. They smiled and nodded, welcoming me. I looked back at the holy man, resisting the temptation to say that Khaderbhai, for all the many conversations on philosophy we'd shared, had never once mentioned Idriss to me.

'Tell us, Lin,' he asked, smiling widely, 'are you looking for enlightenment?'

'I didn't know anyone lost it,' I replied.

It wasn't exactly rude, but it wasn't as respectful of the famous teacher's dignity as it should've been. Silvano bristled, clutching reflexively at the barrel of the rifle.

'Please, Master,' he said, his deep voice riffling spiky malice. 'Allow me to enlighten him.'

'Put the rifle down, Romeo,' I replied, 'and we'll find out who sees the light first.'

Silvano had a lightly muscled, athletic frame and moved it gracefully. Square-jawed and square-shouldered, with soft brown eyes and an expressive mouth, he looked more like an Italian fashion model or movie star than a holy man's acolyte, or so it seemed to me then.

I didn't know why he didn't like me. Maybe the cuts and bruises on my face made him think he had to prove something. I didn't care: I was so angry at Khaled and Fate that any fight would do.

Silvano stood. I stood. Idriss waved his right hand gently. Silvano sat, and I slowly sat down again.

'Please forgive Silvano,' Idriss said gently. 'Loyalty is his way of loving. I think the same might be said of you, isn't it so?'

Loyalty. Lisa and I couldn't find a way to be in love with each other. I was in love with Karla, a woman who was married to someone else. I'd resigned my heart from the brotherhood of the Sanjay Company, and had a conversation about murdering Sanjay in the same day. Loyalty is something you need for things you don't love enough. When you love enough, loyalty isn't even a question.

Everyone was staring at me.

'Sorry, Silvano, rough decade,' I said.

'Good. Very good,' Idriss said. 'Now, I want, no, I *need* you two boys to be friends. So, I will ask you to come here, both of you, in front of me, and shake hands with one another. Bad vibrations will not help us move toward enlightenment, will they, boys?'

Silvano's square jaw clenched on his reluctance, but he stood up quickly and took a step to stand before Idriss. His left hand held the rifle. His right hand was free.

A foolish impulse to resist being told what to do held me in place. The students began to murmur, their hushed voices buzzing between them. Idriss looked at me. He seemed to be suppressing a smile. His brown eyes glittered, more brilliant than the jewels in Khaled's attic.

Silvano squirmed, anger and humiliation pressing his lips together hard. White ridges formed around his mouth.

I didn't care, in that empty instant. The Italian had started it, by asking for permission to enlighten me. I was happy to show him some lights of my own. And I was happy to leave the mountain, the sage, Abdullah and Karla, that minute.

Karla slammed an elbow into my ribs. I stood, and shook hands with Silvano. He made a contest of it.

'Thank you,' Idriss said at last, and we released our knuckle-crushing grip. 'That was . . . enlightening. Now, take your places, and let's get started.'

I returned to my chair. Abdullah was shaking his head slowly. Karla hissed a single word at me.

'*Idiot!*'

I tried to frown, but couldn't, because she was right.

'Okay,' Idriss said, his eyes glittering. 'For the benefit of our visitor, what is Rule Number One?'

'Rule Number One – there are no gurus!' the entire group responded, quickly and firmly.

'And Rule Number Two?'

'Rule Number Two – you are your own guru!'

'And Rule Number Three?'

'Rule Number Three – never surrender the freedom of your mind.'

'And Rule Number Four?'

'Rule Number Four – inform your mind with everything, without prejudice!'

'Okay, okay,' Idriss laughed. 'That's enough. Personally, I don't like rules. They're like the *map* of a place, rather than the place itself. But I know some people do like rules, and need them, so there you are. Four more damn rules. Maybe Rule Number Five, if you get there, should be *There are no rules.*'

The group laughed with him, settling more comfortably on their stools and chairs.

Idriss was something more than seventy years old. Although he walked with the help of a long staff, his thin but healthy frame was flexible. From time to time he crossed his legs effortlessly on the easy chair, without the assistance of his hands.

His curly, grey hair was cut close to the scalp, throwing all of the attention to his eloquent brown eyes, the magnificent swoop of his hooked nose, and the swollen crest and quiver of his dark, full lips.

'If I recall correctly, Karla,' he began softly, 'our last discussion was on the subject of obedience. Is that right?'

'It is, master-*ji*.'

'Please, Karla, and all of you. We are one searching mind here, and one heart in friendship. Call me Idriss, as I also call you by your names. Now, tell us your opinion on the subject, Karla, finally.'

Karla looked back at the teacher, her eyes a forest on fire.

'You really wanna know, Idriss?'

'Of course.'

'Really?'

'Yes.'

'Okay. Adore me. Worship me. Obey me. *Me, Me, Me*, that's all God ever says.'

The students gasped, but Idriss laughed with open delight.

'Ha! And now you see, my young seekers after wisdom, why I so highly prize Karla's opinion!'

The students murmured among themselves.

Karla stood, walked to the edge of the mesa, and lit a cigarette. She stared out at the surrounding hills and valleys. I knew why she'd left. She was uncomfortable with being told that she was right; she'd rather be considered clever or funny, even if she was wrong.

'Adoration is submission,' Idriss said. 'All religions, like all kingdoms, require you to submit, and obey. Of all the tens of thousands of faiths that have existed since the beginning of human time, only those that could enforce obedience have survived. And when obedience decays, the devotion that depended on it becomes as remote as the once great religion of Zeus, Apollo, and Venus, which for so long ruled all the world it knew.'

'But, Idriss, are you saying we should be proud, and not obedient?' a young man asked.

'No, I'm not. Of course not,' Idriss replied softly. 'And you're quite right to raise the point, Arjun. What I'm saying has nothing to do with pride. There is much to be gained by lowering your head and falling to

313

your knees once in every while. None of us should ever be so proud that we cannot fall on our knees and admit that we do not know everything, and that we are not the centre of the universe, and that there are things for which we should be justly ashamed, and also happily grateful. Do you agree?'

'Yes, Idriss,' several students replied.

'And pride, the good pride that we need to survive in a brutal world, what is it? Good pride does not say *I am better than someone else*, which is what bad pride says. Good pride says *For all my faults, I have a born right to exist, and I have a will, which is the instrument I can use to improve myself*. In fact, it is quite impossible to change and improve yourself without a measure of good pride. Do you agree?'

'Yes, Idriss.'

'Good. What I'm telling you is this: kneel in humility, kneel in the knowledge that we are all connected, every one of us, and every living thing, kneel in the knowledge that we are all together in this struggle to understand and belong, but don't blindly obey anyone, ever. Do you young people have anything to offer on this point?'

There was a pause, as the students looked at one another.

'Lin. Our new visitor,' Idriss asked me quickly. 'What do *you* say?'

I was already there, thinking of prison guards who'd beaten men in prison.

'Enough obedience will let people do just about anything to other people,' I said.

'I *like* that answer,' Idriss said.

Praise from the wise is the sweetest wine. I felt the warmth of it inside.

'Obedience is the assassin of conscience,' Idriss said softly, 'and that is why every lasting institution demands it.'

'But surely we must obey *something*?' the Parsi student asked.

'Obey the laws of the land, Zubin,' Idriss replied, 'except where they would cause you to act in a manner that is not honourable. Obey the Golden Rules. Do unto others, as you would have them do unto you, and do not do to others, what you would not have them do to you. Obey your instinct to create and love and learn. Obey the universal law of consciousness, that everything you think or say or do has an effect greater than zero, even if it's only an effect on yourself, which is why you must try to minimise the negative in what you think and say and do, and maximise the positive. Obey the instinct to forgive, and to share with others. Obey your faith. And obey your heart. Your heart will never lie to you.'

He paused, looking around at the students, many of them writing notes on what he'd said. He smiled, then shook his head, and began to cry.

I looked at Abdullah. *Is he crying?* Abdullah nodded, and then flicked his head at the students. Several of them were crying, too. After a while, Idriss spoke though his tears.

'It took so long, fourteen billion years, for this part of the universe to bring into being a consciousness, right here, capable of knowing and actually calculating that it took fourteen thousand million years to make the calculation. We don't have the right to throw those fourteen billion years away. We don't have the moral right to waste or damage or kill this consciousness. And we don't have the right to surrender its will, the most precious and beautiful thing in the universe. We have a duty to study, to learn, to question, to be fair and honest and positive citizens. And above all, we have a duty to unite our consciousness, freely, with any free consciousness, in the common cause of love.'

I came to hear that speech many times from Idriss, and in modified forms from some of his students, and I liked it, in all its forms. I liked Idriss the mind: but what he said immediately after that speech made me like Idriss the man.

'Let's tell jokes,' he said. 'I'll go first. I've been wanting to tell this all day. Why did the Zen Buddhist keep an empty bottle of milk in his refrigerator? Anyone? No? Give up? It was for guests who drink black tea!'

Idriss and the students laughed. Abdullah was laughing out loud, happily and freely, something I'd never seen in all the years that I knew him. I painted that laugh on a wall of my heart. And in a small, simple way I loved Idriss for releasing that happiness in my stern friend.

'Okay, okay, my turn!' Arjun said excitedly, standing to tell his joke.

One by one the other students stood to tell their jokes. I left, threading my way through the rows of students to find Karla, at the edge of the mesa.

She was writing notes from the lecture Idriss had given, but she wasn't using a notepad. She was writing the notes on her left hand.

Long sentences looped their way back and forth across her hand, up along the length of each finger to the nail, and down again to the knuckle, and then in between the fingers, across the webbing and up again, between two more fingers.

The words continued on the palm-side of her hand, until the whole span of skin, hand and fingers, was covered with a tattooed web of words, like henna decorations on the hands of a Bombay bride.

It was the sexiest thing I'd ever seen in my life: I'm a writer. I found the strength at last to move my eyes and stare out at the forest, already smothered by the heavy swell of cloud.

'So that's why you asked me to tell you a joke,' I said.

'It's one of his things,' she replied, raising her eyes to stare ahead. 'He says that the one sure sign of a fanatic is that he has no sense of humour. So, he gets us to laugh, at least once every day.'

'Are you buying it?'

'He's not selling anything, Lin. That's why I like him.'

'Okay, what do you think of him?'

'Does it matter, what I think?'

'Everything about you matters, Karla.'

We faced one another. I couldn't tell what she was thinking. I wanted to kiss her.

'You've been talking to Ranjit,' she said, a frown searching my eyes.

I stopped thinking about kissing her.

'He's a talkative guy, your husband.'

'What did he talk about?'

'What *would* he talk to me about?'

'Don't play games with me!'

She was speaking softly, but it was still like a trapped animal's cry. She calmed down.

'What, exactly, did he tell you?'

'Lemme guess,' I murmured. 'You and Ranjit do this to people for kicks, right?'

She smiled.

'Ranjit and I do have an understanding, but not about everything.'

I smiled.

'You know what,' I said. 'To hell with Ranjit.'

'I'd agree with you,' she said, 'if I didn't think I might have to join him there one day.'

She looked away at the clouds, churning over the distant city, and the first rain showers simmering and frothing at the edges of the forest.

I was confused, but I was mostly confused when I talked to Karla. I didn't know if she was telling me something intimate about her and Ranjit, or talking about us. If she was talking about Ranjit, I didn't want to know.

'Big storm,' I said.

She looked back at me quickly.

'It was because of me, wasn't it?'

'What was because of you?'

She shook her head, and then stared at me again, her green eyes the only bright things left in the grey-sky world.

'What Ranjit talked to you about,' she said, suddenly determined and clear. 'He's worried about me, I know. But the fact is, *he's* the one who needs help, not me. He's the one in danger.'

She stared into my eyes, trying to read my thoughts. I was reading what looked like pure and honest concern for her husband. It hurt more, somehow, than Concannon's club.

'What do you want, Karla?'

She frowned, let her eyes fall from mine, and then raised them to stare at me again.

'I want you to help him,' she said, almost as if it were an admission of guilt. 'I'd like him to stay alive, for a few more months, and that's not a sure thing.'

'A few *months*?'

'Years would be acceptable, but a few months are essential.'

'Essential for what?'

She looked at me, trying out emotional responses, before relaxing in a smile.

'My peace of mind,' she said, not telling me anything.

'He's a big boy, Karla, with a big bank account.'

'I'm serious.'

I stared back at her for a moment, and then smiled my way into a soft laugh.

'You're something, Karla. You're really something.'

'What do you mean?'

'All that stuff, this morning, asking me if I came up here because of you, just to throw me off the track, because *you* came up here to ask me to help Ranjit.'

'Do you think I'm lying to you?'

317

'Talking about keeping Ranjit *alive* for a few months, is the same as talking about him being *dead* in a few months. It's pretty cute, Karla.'

'You think I'm *manipulating* you?'

'It wouldn't be the first time.'

'That's not —'

'It doesn't matter,' I said, not smiling. 'It never did. I love you.'

She tried to speak, but I put my fingers across her lips.

'I'll ask around, about Ranjit.'

Thunder silenced her reply: thunder rumbling into blasts, shaking the forest trees.

'I gotta go,' I said, 'if I'm gonna beat that storm back to the city. I have to make sure that Lisa's okay.'

I turned to leave, but she held my wrist. It was the tattooed hand: the hand covered with a tracery of words.

'Let me ride with you,' she said.

I hesitated. Instinct flinched.

'Just that,' she said. 'Let me ride back to town with you.'

'Okay. Okay.'

We collected our things and made the rounds of the students, saying our goodbyes.

The students liked Karla. Everyone liked Karla, even when they didn't want to understand her.

At the edge of the mesa, Idriss and Silvano came to say goodbye. Silvano still had the rifle slung over his shoulder.

'No hard feelings, Silvano,' I said, offering my hand.

He spat on the ground.

Nice, I thought. *Okay, rise above.*

'Your name, Silvano, means forest.'

'And what if it does?' he demanded, his jaw jutting on the words.

'I know it,' I smiled, 'because an Italian friend of mine changed his name from Silvano, to Forest. Forest Marconi. And I remember thinking that it's a beautiful name, in both languages.'

'What?' Silvano frowned.

'I'm just saying, I have a friend, whose name is Silvano, and I like him very much. I'm sorry we got off on the wrong foot. I hope you'll accept my apology.'

'Well, yes, of course,' Silvano agreed quickly, reaching out to accept my hand.

There was no contest in it, and the young Italian smiled at me for the first time.

'You speak Italian?' he asked.

'I can swear, if it's required.'

Idriss laughed.

'You *must* come back, Lin!' he demanded. 'You must hear my little talk on the animal nature, and the human nature. You'll get a kick out of it. Maybe *two* kicks!'

Lightning forked a cobra-strike through the black clouds. The teacher's face and body were illuminated for an instant with blue-silver light.

'I'd like that,' I replied, when the flashes of lightning had passed. 'I'll make sure to bring my animal nature along.'

'You're always most welcome.'

Abdullah, Karla and I made our way down the slopes, clinging to one another from time to time on slippery paths.

At the gravel parking area, Abdullah used the phone. Waiting for him, I looked around at the brooding sky.

'We might not make it before the storm. It might hit us on the highway.'

'With any luck,' she grinned. 'Say, that was a pretty fast turnaround back there with Silvano.'

'He's okay. It was my fault. I've got a lot on my mind.'

'Fuck you, Lin. Why do you do that?'

'What?'

'Allude to things on your mind, but then never tell anyone what they are.'

'That's a glass house you're throwing stones at,' I replied, but she was right, again, and I knew it.

I wanted to tell her. It was all upside down. Lisa and I were lost. Ranjit was attracting bombers. I was leaving the Sanjay Company. Wars had started between gangs and within them, and the only safe place in the city was somewhere else.

'You should leave town for a while, Karla. I should, too.'

'Not a chance of that yet, Shantaram,' she laughed, and walked over to the small shop to talk with the attendant.

Abdullah returned and spoke softly, his head close to mine.

'Sanjay has paid everyone,' he said. 'There will be no trouble. But it is as I expected. I must go north to the brothers in Delhi for at least a week. I must go tonight.'

'A week?'

'Not a day less, out of the city.'

'I'm coming with you. You've got enemies in Delhi.'

'I have enemies everywhere,' he said softly, lowering his eyes. 'As I have friends. You cannot come with me. You will leave for Sri Lanka, and complete your mission there, while this matter of the shooting at Leopold's is resolved.'

'Slow down, brother. I'm quitting the Sanjay Company, remember?'

'I told that to Sanjay, and —'

'You what?'

'I told Sanjay that you want to leave.'

'It should've been me who told him,' I said, quietly angry.

'I know, I know,' he replied. 'But I have to leave for Delhi, tonight. I will not be there, when you tell Sanjay, and that would be too dangerous without me. I decided to do it now, to see if his reaction presents any danger to you.'

'Did it?'

'Yes, and no. He was surprised, and very angry, but then he calmed down enough to say that if you complete this last mission for the Company, he will allow you to leave. What do you think, Lin?'

'That's all he said?'

'He also said that if you had any family here, they would already be dead.'

'And?'

'And that he will throw you to the dogs, very happily, when your mission is completed.'

'Is that it?'

'All but the cursing. He is a foul-mouthed man, and he will die cursing, *Inshallah*.'

'When do they want me to leave?'

'Tomorrow morning,' he sighed. 'You take the train to Madras. Then you will leave by cargo ship, for Trincomalee. Company men will be waiting at VT station tomorrow morning, at seven. They will have all of your tickets and instructions.'

Sri Lanka, cargo ship, instructions: I took a deep breath, and let it out slowly.

'Sri Lanka?'

'You gave your word, that you would do it.'

'I did, and I regret it.'

'After this mission, you will be free. It is a clean way out. I think it is wise for you to agree. I will not be able to remove Sanjay for some time, and this way, you will be safe.'

'Okay. Okay. Okay, *Inshallah*. Let's ride.'

'Wait,' he said, leaning in close. 'In the next weeks of your life, my brother, you must walk and talk very carefully.'

'You know me,' I smiled.

'I do know you,' he said solemnly. 'And I know the demon inside you.'

'Uh-huh?'

'There are demons in all of us. Some of them do not mean us any harm. They just want to live inside us. Some of them want more. They want to eat the souls that hold them.'

'You know, Abdullah, I'm not really same-page with you on the demon thing.'

He looked at me for a while, wind-worried leaves drifting in his amber eyes.

'Hey, it's okay –' I began, but he cut me off.

'I have heard you say that there are no bad or good men. That the deeds we do are good and bad, not the people who do them.'

'It was Khaderbhai who said that,' I replied, looking away.

'Because he heard it from Idriss,' Abdullah said quickly, and I looked back at him. 'Every wise thing Khaderbhai said, was first said by Idriss. But in this, I do not agree with Idriss or Khaderbhai or you. There are bad men in this world, Shantaram brother. And in the end, there is only one way to deal with them.'

He started his bike and rode away slowly, knowing I'd catch him.

Karla joined me, and I kicked the bike to life. She got up behind me. That perfume: cinnamon, and pure *oud*. For a satin second her hair was against my neck.

The engine rumbled, warming. She leaned close, one arm over my right shoulder, and one under my left. Her word-tattoo hand was on my chest.

I heard the music, inside. Home. Home is the heart you're born to love.

We rode gentle curves and slopes, as the shadow of the mountain that brought us together vanished in the praying hands of trees. I had to brake hard on the dark road to avoid a fallen branch. She fell into me softly and held me. I didn't know where her body ended, and I began. I didn't want to know.

I pulled away at speed to make the steep climb over the next hill. She braced herself, her hands hard on me. At exactly the right moment her palms and fingers slid across my ribs to find my heart, and held me as we crested the last dome of trees.

When we reached the main road I swung shakily, love-clumsy, into fast clever traffic. A prodigal wind kissed her hair around my neck. And she clove to me, her starfish hand on my chest, as we rode through splashes of light streamed from desire, dying on billboards along the stingray tail highway home.

CHAPTER THIRTY

'That was a long goodbye,' Karla said, watching Abdullah ride away from the wide space in front of the Mahesh hotel.

'It was a long ride,' I said.

'Yeah, but, Abdullah, emotional. That's not something you see every day.'

'What can I tell you, Karla?'

'What you can tell me is what you're not telling me.'

Khaled's money will buy many guns, Abdullah had whispered to me in goodbye. It wasn't especially emotional.

'It's complicated,' I said.

'Still not telling me.'

She was still sitting behind me on the bike. In one hand she held the bag that Abdullah had carried for her on his bike. The other hand was on my hip. For once, I was glad to be on the other hand.

'You know,' I said happily, 'I like this.'

'Still not telling me.'

'But I really *do like* this.'

'What?'

'Sitting here, on the bike, and having a conversation with you like this.'

'We're not having a conversation.'

'Technically, I think we are.'

'*Not* telling me something doesn't qualify as any kind of conversation, technically or otherwise.'

'Maybe it's a reverse conversation.'

'There's a forward step.'

There was a little pause. The space around us was clear and free. The storm had passed, and fresh monsoon winds cooled the coast behind us.

'You know, it really is damn nice, talking to you like this, I gotta say.'

'Since you gotta say it, does the bike have to be a part of the conversation?'

I turned the bike off.

'So, what is it about this you like so much?' she asked. 'That we're sitting so close, or that I can't see your face?'

'It's because I can't see *your* face. And . . . because we're sitting so close.'

'I thought so. Hey, wait a minute. *My* face is the problem?'

'Your eyes, actually,' I said, watching people, cars and horse-drawn carriages passing back and forth in front of the hotel.

'My eyes, huh?'

I felt her voice everywhere that her body touched mine.

'If I can't see your eyes, it's like we're playing chess, and you just lost your queen.'

'Is that so?'

'Oh yeah.'

'And I'm powerless and defenceless?'

'Not defenceless. But there's definitely some lessness here.'

'Lessness?'

'The opposite of moreness.'

'And that turns you on?'

'Kinda.'

'Because you like *lessness* in a woman?'

'Of course not. It's because *looking* at you is like we're playing chess, and I've got *one* queen, and you've got four queens, eight queens, sixteen queens –'

'I've got sixteen queens in the game?'

'Oh yeah. All green. Sixteen green queens. And I can't see any of them right now, in this bike-talk. And I love it. It's liberating.'

There was a pause. It didn't last long.

'*This* is the quality of your motorcycle conversation?'

'It's just a fact. A recently discovered fact, in fact. For now, sitting here like this, all your queens are locked in a box, Karla, and I'm loving it.'

'You're messed up, you know that?'

'Oh yeah.'

'My eyes are nothing,' she said after a while, some puzzle in her voice.

'Well, your eyes, and the heart behind them, are everything to me.'

She thought about it, maybe.

'No, my will is everything.'

She repeated the last word, as if pushing it from her body.

'Everything.'

'I'm with you and Idriss on will, but it's the direction it takes that interests me.'

She rested her forearms on my back.

'When you were in prison,' she asked slowly, 'did you ever lose your will?'

'Does getting chained to a wall and kicked unconscious count?'

'Maybe. But when it happened, did you ever lose your will? Did they ever take your will from you?'

I thought about it for a while. Once again, I wasn't sure where she was leading the conversation, or whether I'd like it when we got there. But her big question had a small answer.

'Yeah. You could say that. For a while.'

'I had my will taken from me, too,' she said. 'I'd rather kill, than let that happen again. I killed the man who did it to stop it from happening to some other me, somewhere else. I'll never let anyone take my will again.'

The rebel yell: you'll never take me alive.

'I love you, Karla.'

She was silent, even her breathing soundless.

'Did that freak you out?' I asked after a while, staring ahead at the moving street.

'Of course not. Honesty is my only addiction.'

She moved away from me, resting on her hands, and was silent again.

'This bike-talk is fun,' I said after a while. 'You gotta admit.'

'Then try holding up your end of the conversation. It's tumbleweeds back here, Shantaram.'

'Okay. Here goes. You talked about Ranjit, on the mountain. I didn't say much then, but now that we're bike-talking, I have a question. Why doesn't Ranjit, who must keep living for a few months, just sell up and take you a long way from anywhere?'

'He told you about the bomb, didn't he?'

'What did he tell *you*?'

'He said you told him to fire the chauffeur. You were right, by the way. The guy was crooked.'

'Ranjit went to a lot of trouble, asking me not to tell you, and then he went home and told you all about it.'

'He's a politician. Politics isn't lying. It's the art of knowing who's lying.'

'That still doesn't answer the question. Why doesn't he take the money and run? He's a rich man.'

She laughed, surprising me, because I couldn't read her face, and because I didn't think any part of it was funny.

'You can't run away from the game, Lin,' she said.

'I like this conversation. What are we talking about?'

'Wherever you find it,' she said, leaning in close, her breath on my neck. 'Whatever it looks like, when you find the game that hooks you, there's nowhere else you can be. Am I right?'

'Are we talking about Ranjit, or Karla?'

'We're both players.'

'I don't like games. You know that.'

'Some games might be worth the play.'

'Like being king of Bombay, for instance?'

I felt the tension move through her as she pushed away again.

'How do you know that?'

'He's ambitious,' I said. 'It shows. He has enemies.'

She was silent for a while, and I had no clue to her thoughts. Bike-talking had its drawbacks.

'Ranjit's an imitation good guy,' she said, 'in a cast of genuine bad guys.'

'An imitation good guy? They're usually the ones who give genuine bad guys a bad name.'

'Bad guys do a pretty good job of that on their own,' she replied, laughing a little.

'Why play games, Karla? Get out of this, now.'

'I *game*, because I'm good at it. I game good.'

'Walk away. If Ranjit's so determined to be political, you've gotta be the one to walk away.'

'Is this about Ranjit and me, or about you and me?'

'This is about you. If we weren't doing bike-talk, I probably wouldn't be able to say it at all. Not to your eyes. I don't like what's going on. I don't think Ranjit has any right to put you at risk. No ambition's worth that.'

'I'll buy a bike,' she said, leaning close again, and smiling on my back. 'You'll teach me to ride.'

'I mean it, Karla. He's rattling the unfriendly cage. Sooner or later, whatever's inside the cage is gonna get out.'

'Why are we talking about this?'

'It's like this. Ranjit can do politics, and I'll ask friends to watch out for him, but you don't have to be Ranjit's wife *here*. You can be Ranjit's wife a long way away from here. In London, for example.'

'London?'

'A lot of Indian wives escape to London.'

'But I'm a Bombay girl, yaar. What would I do in London?'

'You're also American, and Swiss, and a lot of other nice places. You could set up a house in London for Ranjit, with Ranjit's money, and hope he rarely visits it. Make it cool. Bombay cool. But make it so you can walk away, and never look back.'

'And I'm still asking, what would I do there?'

'You'd keep a low profile. And you'd use any extra money to make money for yourself, until you don't need anyone else's extra money any more.'

'Uh-huh?'

'Yeah. The real reason why so many people want to be rich is because they want to be free. Freedom means that you don't need anyone else's money.'

'How does that work again?' she asked, laughing.

'Maybe you shave your lifestyle, save some money, and put a down payment on a house for yourself. You're smart. In no time, you'll turn one house into five.'

'My lifestyle?'

'What do I know? But whatever you do in London or anywhere would be safer than what you're doing here, with Ranjit. Someone's gonna hit him, and hit him hard, because he won't shut up, and his political ambitions are making people nervous. Hell, I want to hit him, and I hardly even know him.'

'His mouth is what put him in the game. That's his table stake. If he wins this fight, his face will be on the political poster of his choice. He'll get elected, too. I'm sure of it. And anyway, why the hell should he shut up, when he's right?'

'It's not safe for you, that's why.'

'Let me tell you a little something about safety,' she murmured, her face against the pillow of my back. 'Safety is a cave, a nice warm cave, but the light is where the adventure is.'

'Karla,' I said, careful not to move, 'you've got no idea how cool this is, listening to you, but not seeing you.'

'You're such an ass,' she said, not moving.

'No, really, it's just great. And I was listening. I heard every word. Look, in my view, but who am I, the right woman is a big enough dream. If a guy wants a whole city, there's something wrong with him.'

'*Less* wrong than you, or *more* wrong than you, on a scale of *you?*' she laughed.

'You can't go back home,' I said firmly, my hands tight on the handlebars, 'because you don't know what's waiting for you. And you can't stay here, because you *do* know what's waiting for you.'

I was glad she couldn't see my face, and glad she didn't pull away.

'Look, you're probably on a most-wanted list, Karla. And I'm definitely most-wanted. We're who we are, and who we are has no place in lives of public ambition. It's bad for them, and it's a lot worse for us if it falls down, and they're looking for someone to blame for it.'

'I'm okay,' she murmured. 'I know exactly what I'm doing.'

'I don't want to think of something happening to you, Karla. Ranjit's *making* me think of it. A lot. I don't like him for it. One way or another, this guy puts himself on everybody's hurt list. Have mercy. Send me a postcard from London, and give me some peace of mind.'

'Mercy,' she said softly. 'My favourite inessential virtue. I think you've done this motorcycle talk before.'

'I was right about this, wasn't I? It's damn cool.'

'It's okay,' she murmured. 'Is it my turn now?'

'Your turn?'

'Yeah.'

'For motorcycle talk?'

'Yeah.'

'Sure, talk away,' I said confidently, not careful what I wished for.

She nestled in tighter, her lips close.

'Are you ready?'

'Ready for what?'

'You don't need coffee, or a joint?'

'I'm good. I'm so good.'

'Okay,' she said. 'Gimme a dramatic pause.'

'But –'

'Shut up! You're dramatic pausing.'

There was a dramatic pause.

'That . . . truly . . . fucking . . . transcendent ride home,' she said at last, murmuring the words onto my skin, 'was a rip through space and time, baby. When you crashed down two gears and gunned it, passing between the passenger bus and the water tanker, my soul left my body. When we slid the closing gap and roared through, a voice in my head said Oh yeah . . . Oh yeah . . . Oh God . . . Oh God . . . all the way home.'

She stopped, and stopped my heart.

'How am I doin' here, Shantaram, without all of my queens?'

Fine. She was doing fine. I turned in the saddle until I could see a corner of her face.

'I thought you didn't believe in God, Karla,' I smiled.

'Who are *we* to believe in God?' she said, her lips only lashes from my face. 'It should be enough for anyone that God believes in us.'

We could've kissed. We should've kissed.

'I'm thinking that I have to talk to Lisa,' I said, words cutting my own throat. 'Are you thinking that you have to talk to Ranjit?'

She drew away slowly, until shadows took her face. I turned to the front again. She didn't say anything, so I spoke.

'I have to talk to her.'

'Well, you can do that here,' she said quietly.

'What do you mean?'

'Lisa's here, at the hotel. Gemini and Scorpio are throwing a party, in the penthouse suite. They've taken the whole floor, in fact. Tonight's the official housewarming. Everyone in town is up there. That's why the limos are prowling. That's why I asked you to drop me here.'

'But . . . why didn't you mention this before?'

'Why didn't you know?'

It was a good question. I couldn't answer it.

'Are you going?' I asked her, still staring ahead.

'I was going to ask you to be my door date.'

'Ranjit isn't here?'

'Ranjit is otherwise detained, this evening. A monthly meeting with the City Council. Didier agreed days ago to walk me out, and have a drink with me at home. But I'd like *you* to walk me in. Are you up for it?'

I wanted to see Lisa, and know that she was safe. I wanted to see Didier for a report about the fallout from the shooting at Leopold's. Good reasons to go. But I was afraid of spending more time with Karla. I hadn't seen her for two years, but she'd been as close to me on the ride home to the Island City as wings on my back. And it was Karla, so there wasn't an easy way to anything. She wanted to keep her husband alive for at least a few months more: it was cold-blooded, but I didn't care. She'd been hurt, and she hurt back, but I knew there was nothing bad in her, just as I knew that she wouldn't harm Ranjit or anyone else without reason. She was too strong for the world she knew, and I loved that about her, and I thought that if I looked at her again, I wouldn't have the courage to leave her side.

'I'd be honoured to escort you to the party, Karla,' I said, staring straight ahead.

'I'd be honoured to accompany you, Shantaram. Let's get moving. I wanna see if you dance like you ride, or ride like you dance.'

CHAPTER THIRTY-ONE

I PARKED THE BIKE UNDER THE SHELTER at the entrance to the hotel, and when I turned to look at her all sixteen queens stared back at me. I froze.

'Are you okay?'

'Sure, why?'

'You look like somebody stood on your foot,' she said.

'No, I'm fine.'

'Sure?'

'Yeah,' I said, glancing away from checkmate. 'I'm good.'

'Okay, let's go to the party. There'll be plenty of people to stand on our feet there.'

We crossed the lobby, found a lucky elevator, and pressed for the penthouse.

'Every time an elevator door closes on me,' she said, as the elevator doors closed, 'I want a drink.'

The doors opened on a drinking party, already bumpy happy. Guests had spilled from crowded suites into the corridor, where they sat in groups or stumbled back and forth, laughing and shouting.

We made our way inside and found Gemini George, dancing with Didier to music just loud enough to ruin a shout. Didier had a table cover over his head and was holding the edge in his teeth, as a woman might with her shawl.

'Lin! Karla! Rescue me! I am watching an Englishman dance. I am in pain.'

'French git,' Gemini called back, laughing happily.

He was having, quite literally, the time of his life.

'Come, Lin! Karla! Dance with me!' Didier shouted.

'I'm looking for Lisa!' I called back. 'Have you seen her?'

'Not . . . recently,' Didier replied, frowning questions of his own at me, then at Karla, then at me again. 'That is to say . . . not . . . recently.'

Karla leaned in close to kiss him on the cheek. I kissed him on the other cheek.

'Hey! I'm havin' some of that!' Gemini shouted, offering his cheek to Karla, who obliged with a kiss.

'I'm so glad to see you both!' Didier shouted.

'Likewise! Got a minute, Didier?'

'Certainly.'

I left Karla with Gemini, and followed Didier back into the hallway. We crossed the corridor stream on patches of bare carpet, stepping over flowing groups of people smoking, drinking, and laughing out their other selves.

Didier opened the door to one of the adjoining suites with a key and led me inside.

'Some of these party people know no boundaries,' he said, locking the door behind him.

The main room was well appointed, but untouched. There was a tray on the writing desk: brandy and two glasses. Didier gestured with the brandy bottle.

'No, thanks. But I'll smoke a joint with you, if you've got one.'

'Lin!' he gasped. 'When have you ever known Didier *not* to have one?'

He poured himself a thumb of brandy, selected a slender joint from a polished brass cigarette case, lit it, and passed it to me. As I smoked, he raised his glass in a toast.

'To battles lived,' he said, drinking a sip.

'How's Lisa?'

'She is very well. She is happy, I think.'

'Where is she now?'

'She stayed with me, until just a few hours ago,' he replied, drinking the measure of brandy. 'She said she was returning to your apartment.'

'How bad was it, after Abdullah and I left?'

'Well, I wouldn't go back to Leopold's for a while, even with my influence.'

My thoughts went back to the fight at Leopold's, Concannon cracking the lead sap into the fallen Sikh head waiter.

'Dhirendra took a beating. He's a good man. How is he?'

'He recuperates. Leopold's is not the same without him, but we must go on.'

'Anyone else get hurt?'

'A few,' he sighed.

'What about the cops?'

'Lightning Dilip rounded up all the witnesses who had any money, myself included, and fined us all.'

'What about the street?'

'From what I know, nobody's talking about this. It died, in the newspapers, after the first day. I think . . . Karla used her influence with Ranjit to kill the story, as they say. And those who are not scared of the Sanjay Company are scared of the Scorpions. It is quiet now, but it cost Sanjay a lot of money, I am sure. A lot of people had to piss on this fire.'

'I'm sorry you got dragged into this, Didier. And in Leopold's, of all places. It's sacred ground.'

'Didier is never *dragged*,' he sniffed, 'even when he is unconscious. He freely marches, or he is transported.'

'Still . . . '

'An American friend of mine has a saying, for occasions like this. *It's a mess, but we didn't make it.* Yes, it's a mess, but Concannon made it happen. The question is, what are we going to do about it?'

'Got any ideas?'

'My first impulse is that we should kill him.'

'I love you, Didier.'

'I love you, too, Lin. So we will kill him, yes?'

'No, that was a no. I'm travelling tomorrow. I'll be away for a week, maybe a day or two more, and we'll work this out somehow, when I get back. We'll have to find a way without killing anybody, Didier.'

'As solutions go,' he mused, 'killing is a winning hand. Anything less, at this point, is only bluff.'

'Concannon's a man. There must be a way to reach him.'

'Through his chest,' Didier observed. 'With an axe. But I suppose you're right. We should be aiming higher. The head, perhaps?'

'I've spoken to him, I've listened to him. I met a dozen Concannons with a dozen different faces in prison. I'm not saying I like him. I'm saying that if he was born into a different life, Concannon could be an amazing man. In his own way, he already is an amazing man. There must be a way to reach him, and stop all of this.'

'Men like Concannon don't change, Lin,' he said, letting out a gust of sighs. 'And the proof is very simple. Did you change, when you went to prison? Did you change, when you joined the Company? In your true self, deep inside yourself, did you change? Are you not the man you always were?'

'Didier —'

'You are. You did not change. You could not change, and neither do the Concannons of this world. They are born to harm and destroy, Lin, until time or temper stops them. And now that this one wants to harm and destroy us, the kindest thing we can do is to kill him, take the karmic burden on ourselves, and hope that the good we cause, by saving the world all the future harm this man will do, if he lives, is enough to save our souls for a better incarnation. Although I cannot think of a better incarnation than the one you see before you, so I would only ask that Didier may come back as Didier is, and do it all again.'

'Just don't do anything until I get back, okay? We'll talk first, then we'll do whatever else we have to do, okay? In the meantime, watch Lisa for me, while I'm away. When I see her, I'll try to talk her into going to Goa for a while, but we both know Lisa.'

'Not a chance,' he shrugged.

'I know —'

'She's a clever fox, my friend,' he said. 'And she knows what she wants, and how to get it.'

'Look after her for me, until I get back. Ask Naveen to give you whatever time he can spare from Divya, if you need extra eyes. I'll speak to him, if I can find him.'

'I need no help, of course, but I have come to like Naveen,' Didier said thoughtfully.

'I like him, too. You make a good team, the two of you. Speaking of teams, I'd like to join you, Didier, when I get back, if you still want me.'

'Lin . . . you mean . . . to work together?'

'We'll talk about it when I get back.'

'But, you're leaving the Sanjay Company?'

'I am. I did.'

'You did? Sanjay let you go?'

'After this job, I have Sanjay's blessing. Actually, I think he's glad to see me leave.'

'You are not afraid to disagree with him. There are only two kinds of leaders, those who welcome the truth, and those who despise it. Sanjay is a despiser, I am afraid.'

'That he is,' I smiled.

'I am very happy to hear you are leaving him. Are you happy?'

'I am. Just keep an eye on Lisa.'

'I will, I will, and with pleasure.'

'Shall we head back to the others?'

'Yes! This is wonderful news, Lin, and it calls for celebration. But . . .'

'But what?'

'You and Karla.'

'What, me and Karla? There's no me and Karla.'

'Lin, this is Didier. No fleeting suspicion of love is hidden from Didier. I saw you together. I know everything.'

'Forget Karla.'

'I can, if you can,' he said, a half-worried smile confusing his face. 'Whatever you do, I am with you.'

'Thanks, brother,' I said, sharing a hug that pressed his curly hair into my face.

We made our way back to Karla and Gemini. Karla looked from Didier to me, and then back again, smiling just enough condescension to put a bite in her affection.

Two young foreign girls, carrying drinks in each hand, danced their way up to Didier and Gemini, who took the drinks, still dancing.

'Are you with someone?' one of the girls asked Gemini.

'I'm with myself,' Gemini replied. 'I don't know if that qualifies. I'm Gemini. What's your name then?'

'Hey!' the girl shouted back. 'I'm a Gemini, too.'

'That's great, you'll get this — what did one Gemini say to the other?'

'What?'

'Nothing. The other Gemini already left.'

They laughed, spilling wine and bumping together.

Karla and I made our way through party-sway to shout at friends as we were shouted unto, until we found the deserted bar.

'Nice bar,' Karla said, greeting the bartender. 'Free, well-stocked and empty.'

'Welcome,' the barman said.

'I'd shoot three men for a glass of champagne,' Karla said, waving an elegant wrist.

'Certainly, ma'am,' the bartender replied. 'And for sir?'

'Plain soda, no ice,' I said. 'How's it been, tonight?'

'At the end of the road, there are only two questions,' the bartender said, inscrutably, preparing the drinks. '*What did I do?* and *What did I miss?*'

'Unless,' I offered, 'the last question is, *Who the hell turned off my life support?*'

'Life is short,' the tall young bartender said, easing the cork from the bottle with a fist. 'But made of long nights.'

'That's why it's so lonely at the top,' Karla put in.

'It's lonely at the top,' he replied quickly, filling Karla's glass, 'because it's so crowded at the bottom.'

'What's your name?' Karla asked, laughing.

'Randall, ma'am.'

'Randall,' she said, accepting the glass, 'This is Lin, I'm Karla, and I couldn't agree with you more. Where's your family place?'

'My parents are from Goa,' he said, handing me the soda. 'But I'm from here.'

'We're from here too, for as long as here lasts,' I said. 'What's with the one-liners, Randall?'

'It's not that interesting a story,' he replied.

'Why don't you let us judge that, Randall?' Karla suggested.

'Well, at first, I used to talk,' he said, washing a glass. 'I used to ask questions. *Are you here on a business trip? Do you have any kids? Why do you think your wife doesn't understand you?* But, after a while, I started breaking my part of the conversation down into little pieces of the truth. Barmen never get more than a line or two. It's a narrative rule, I'm afraid. Am I boring you folks?'

'No,' we said together.

'So, I don't converse any more. I'm making this exception, tonight, because my shift has ended, and because I like you. I liked both of you, from the moment you walked in. And when I like something, I'm never wrong about it.'

'Nice talent to have up your sleeve,' Karla smiled. 'Go on, about the one-liners.'

'Most of the time, I prune the conversation tree. It's all bonsai. It's all punchlines now. And it's better that way, in little pieces of the truth. It's like a code, the truth. When people hear it, the doors unlock.'

'Randall,' Karla said, her eyes gleaming coloured glass, 'if you stop conversing, I'll never darken this joint again. A refill, if you please.'

He poured two fresh glasses of champagne, and another long soda.

'My replacement hasn't arrived, but my shift was officially over half an hour ago, so I'd like to join you folks in a toast,' he said, offering Karla the champagne and the soda to me. 'May words never fail you.'

'Can't drink to that, because words never fail,' she said quickly. 'This is the first toast that Shantaram and I have shared in two years, Randall, and I think this is a fated meeting. Let's make this toast to the three of *us*.'

I moved to clink glasses with them, but she swerved away from me.

'No! It's bad luck to toast with water,' she said.

'Oh, come on.'

'I'm serious.'

'You're kidding, right?'

'Just because you don't believe it, that's no reason to mess with it, Lin. Do you need any more bad luck?'

'You've got me there.'

'I always get you there.'

A newcomer to the bar bumped Karla into me, and our glasses clashed together anyway.

'Looks like we've done that toast after all,' I said.

She stared at me from a hard frown for a moment, but then she smiled again.

'Okay,' she said. 'Make another toast, without drinking water yourself. That should keep us safe.'

'To green eyes – may they always be protected.'

'I'll certainly drink to that,' Randall said, sipping champagne.

'To green queens,' she said, smiling light at me.

She raised her glass, took a small sip, and stared back at me. It was the moment to break through, and we both knew it. It was perfect.

'Lin!' Vinson said, bouncing against me and slapping his long, strong fingers onto my back, Rannveig at his side. 'Good to see you, man!'

I was still looking at Karla. She was looking at me.

'Vinson,' I said, the voice in my ears sounding like something hard,

337

breaking. 'I don't think you've met. This is Karla. Karla, this is Stuart Vinson. And this is Rannveig, like the thing at the airport.'

'Say, *Karla!*' Vinson shouted. 'I'm damn glad to finally meet you.'

'It won't do any good,' Karla replied, playing it straight.

'It . . . it won't?' Vinson smiled, already confused.

'No. Anything you heard is out of date.'

'Out of . . . what?'

'I reinvented myself.'

Vinson laughed.

'Oh. Wow. Like, when did this happen?'

'It's happening now,' Karla said, holding his gaze. 'Try to keep up.'

My heart stumbled like a drunk dancing. God, I loved her. There was no-one like her.

Then she turned to the girl, Rannveig, and asked her if she was okay. I looked at the girl. She wasn't okay.

'She's fine!' Vinson said, clapping an arm around her.

Rannveig's face was drawn and pale.

'I told her,' Vinson continued, 'I said, hey, you've been through a lot. Time to get out and see people, have a few laughs, you know? The best medicine, they say.'

He hugged her to him, shaking her. Her arms flapped at her sides.

'How you doing, kid?' I asked.

She looked up quickly, ice-chips glittering in her blue eyes.

'I'm not a kid!' she snapped.

'O . . . kay.'

'Don't take it personally,' Karla said. 'He's a writer. He thinks he's older than his grandfather.'

'That's pretty funny,' Vinson laughed.

'And as for *you*,' Karla said. 'Let that girl out of your armpit, right now.'

Surprised, Vinson allowed Karla to peel Rannveig away from him.

'Randall,' Karla said, 'I know you're off duty, but this in an emergency. I want your cleanest glasses and your dirtiest jokes, and make it snappy.'

'Your command is my wish, ma'am,' Randall said, glasses like eels swimming in his hands.

'How 'bout that?' Vinson mumbled. 'She stole my girl.'

'She's *your girl* now?'

338

'Oh, man,' he said, turning a big, open-mouthed smile on me. 'I told you, didn't I, back there at the station house? I told you she was the one. I'm crazy about her. She's really something, isn't she? My heart beats faster every time I look at her.'

'She's been in a plane crash,' I said.

'A plane? But . . . what?'

'You know what I mean. She woke up a few days ago with a dead boyfriend in the bed. That's a big fire to put out. Go easy, man.'

'Oh, sure, sure. I mean, like – hey, wait a minute! You don't think I'm taking advantage of her *situation*, do you? I'm . . . I'm not that kinda guy.'

'I know.'

'I haven't put a hand on her.'

'I know.'

'I wouldn't do that.'

'I know.'

'I'm not that kinda guy,' he said again gruffly.

I was suddenly tired: the kind of angry-tired that's irritated by everything that isn't flat, and white, and has a pillow at one end.

'If I thought you were that kinda guy, I wouldn't have let you get near her, or any girl I know.'

He bristled, young manhood straightening his spine.

'Any time you think you're good enough, sport.'

'I really haven't got time for this shit, Vinson. I met Rannveig before you did. And I got her out of jail, remember? That gives me the right to tell you not to push her too hard. If you don't like it, and you want to get slappy, I'll be downstairs by my bike, in about five minutes.'

We stared at one another, his pride riding out to meet my irritation. Men. I liked Vinson, and he liked me, and we were ready to fight.

'When did you meet her?' he asked, after a long stare.

'Before that day at the police station.'

'Why didn't you tell me?'

'Why didn't she? Maybe because it's none of your business. Look, I met her once, on the street, outside Leo's. She was waiting for her boyfriend to score. Ask her about it.'

'Okay, okay. But I care about her. Don't you see that?'

'Of course I do. I'm glad she's with you. That's what I was trying to tell you before, maybe in the wrong way. You're a nice guy. She'll be safe with you. I know that. Just ease up a little. She had a boyfriend. He's dead. What she needs is a friend. The boy-part can wait, while the friend-part does the work. You see that, right?'

He relaxed, letting out a gush of air.

'Wow! You really had me going there, Lin. *Jesus!* I thought –'

'Listen, the best thing you can do for that girl, right now, is to tell her that her boyfriend didn't commit suicide. She feels guilty, but she had nothing to do with it. The dope was too strong. Three kids died in the same week. Check on it. Make sure she understands that, and clear her mind.'

'Thanks,' he said. 'Hey, I'm sorry we got off on the wrong –'

'It's my fault. Got a lot on my mind. Have you seen Lisa anywhere?'

'She was with that artist, last time I saw her. The tall guy, with the slicked-back hair.'

'Thanks. He's one of the partners in her gallery. If I can't find her, I'm gonna go home. If you see her or the artist, please tell her that. You take care.'

'Wait!' Vinson said, reaching out to offer his hand. 'Thanks. Thanks. I mean . . . I'll take care of Rannveig. I mean –'

'It's good,' I said, shaking hands with him, smiling at him, liking him, wishing happiness for him and the girl, and not really caring, so long as they were happy, if I ever saw either one of them again. 'It's good.'

Little tornadoes of laughing-drinking people whirled in every room. I went from whirl to whirl, searching for Lisa. Nobody had seen her for a while at the party. I finally made my way to the door.

Karla was dancing with Rannveig. For a minute, I watched: her hips the sea, her eyes the flute, her hands the cobra. Karla.

CHAPTER THIRTY-TWO

W HEN THE ELEVATOR DOORS OPENED, Scorpio George, Naveen
Adair and Divya Devnani stepped out.

'Lin!' Naveen cried. 'Where are you going, man? The party's just getting started!'

'I'm beat,' I said, stepping into the elevator and holding the button to keep the doors open. 'But can you give me a minute?'

'Oh, please come with us!' Scorpio pleaded. 'I want you to tell me about that shooting incident at Leopold's. Nobody's talking, and I'm dying to know what happened.'

'Another time, Scorp.'

'Okay, then we'll ride back down with you,' Naveen said, pulling the others into the elevator with him.

The doors closed, leaving us with our reflected selves in the mirrored walls.

'There was a very pretty American girl, all blonde hair and brown eyes, waiting upstairs,' Divya said. 'Did you meet her?'

'There's a very pretty girl waiting for me at home,' I said.

'But this girl –'

'Forget it, Divya!' I snapped, too harshly.

'You should take a little time off from that Charm School, mother-fucker,' Divya said matter-of-factly. 'You sweep a girl off her feet.'

'I'm sorry, it's been a rough –'

'*I'll* meet the American girl with brown eyes,' Scorpio said brightly.

We turned to look at him.

'I mean . . . if Lin's, you know, not going to be there at the party, and . . .'

'You spruced up some, Scorpio,' I remarked.

His longish hair was pulled into a ponytail. He wore a yellow shirt, new jeans, a silver-buckled belt and cowboy boots. A ring on his middle finger featured a Greek helmet, in gold, gleaming from the centre of an onyx square.

'Is it too much?' he asked, checking himself quickly in the wall mirror. 'It was Diva's idea. She said –'

'It's good,' I said. 'You look like a million dollars. Kudos, Divya.'

'*Thirty-five* million dollars, actually,' Divya replied. 'And it's *Diva*, remember? I swear, if you call me Divya again, I'll punch you straight in the balls. And I'm short enough and mean enough to do it.'

'That's not hyperbole,' Naveen averred.

'Okay. You're Diva, from now on.'

I looked down at her proud, pretty face. She was a short girl, who wore high-heeled shoes so often that it gave her a slightly forward-leaning stance, on the balls of her feet: a leopard-footed posture that made her look as if she was stalking prey. I liked it, and liked her, but just wanted to go home.

The doors opened on the lobby, and I stepped out quickly.

'Sure we can't tempt you?' Naveen asked.

'Not tonight.'

I pulled him close enough to whisper.

'That thing at Leopold's,' I said quietly. 'I'm glad you were there, Naveen.'

'When there's a reckoning,' he said, just as quietly, 'count me in.'

'I will. Listen, if Didier asks you for any help, do me a good. He's watching Lisa, while I'm away.'

'Away?'

'A week or so. I'll check in with you, when I get back.'

'*Thik.*'

'And, hey, Scorpio,' I said, in a louder voice, as Naveen rejoined Diva. 'Be careful with the girl.'

'The blonde, with brown eyes?'

'*Any* girl,' I said.

The doors closed, and the lift carried them back to the penthouse party.

I made my way to the bike, paid a tip to the security guards, and rode out into the coursing rain.

Soothing cleansing showers, cold so close to the sea, rolled with me

342

as I rode the length of Marine Drive twice, before turning again and making my way home.

I didn't know it then, but that fall of purging rain, drops as big as flowers, was the last heavy fall of the Bombay season. The torrents that had swamped the streets of the Island City, and left every patch of dusty earth lush with weeds, was drifting south toward Madras, before riding the sea lane up-drift to Sri Lanka, and the great oceans that had birthed them.

I took the steps two at a time, and rushed into the apartment, spilling water onto the silver-flecked marble of the hallway floor. Lisa wasn't there.

I stripped off my sodden boots and clothes, scrubbed the cuts on my face clean with disinfectant, and stood in the shower, letting the cold water run on my back, the suburban penitent's scourge.

I dressed, and was just about to make a pot of coffee, when Lisa walked in.

'Lin! Where the hell have you *been*? Are you okay? Oh, God, let me look at your face.'

'I'm fine. How are *you*? Has everything been quiet here?'

'Are you proud of yourself?'

'What?'

She shoved me, two hands on my chest, then picked up a metal vase, and threw it at me. I ducked, and it crashed into a wall unit, sending things clattering to the floor.

'Coming home, all beat up like that!'

'I –'

'Gang wars in the street! Grow *up*, for God's sake!'

'It wasn't –'

'Shooting people at Leopold's! Are you a *complete* asshole?'

'I didn't shoot any –'

'Running off to the mountain with Karla.'

'Okay, okay, so *that's* what this is about.'

'Of *course* it is!' she shouted, throwing an ashtray at the wall unit.

She suddenly cried, then suddenly stopped crying and sat down on the couch, her hands folded in her lap.

'I'm calm now,' she said.

'Okay . . .'

'I am.'

343

'Okay.'

'It's not about you,' she said.

'Fair enough.'

'No, really.'

'Lisa, I didn't even know she was there. But since you mention Karla, there's something —'

'Oh, Lin!' she cried, pointing at the things that had fallen from the wall unit. 'Look what happened to the sword! I'm so sorry. I didn't mean that to happen.'

One of the things that had fallen from the cabinet was Khaderbhai's sword: the sword that should've been willed to Tariq, the boy king, Khaderbhai's nephew and heir. The sword was broken. The hilt had snapped completely free from the shaft of the sword. It lay in two pieces beside the scabbard.

I picked them up, wondering at the strange frailty of a weapon that had survived battles in the Afghan wars against the British.

'Can you get it fixed?' she asked anxiously.

'I'll do it when I get back,' I said flatly, putting the pieces of the sword into the cabinet. 'I'm going to Sri Lanka tomorrow, Lisa.'

'Lin . . . no.'

I went to the bathroom, and showered again to cool down. Lisa showered, and joined me as I was drying off. I leaned into the mirror, and put a plaster on the ugly cut that Concannon's lead sap had left on my cheek.

She talked, warning me about the dangers of going to Sri Lanka, telling me what she'd read in the newspaper, Ranjit's newspaper, explaining to me that I had no obligation to go, and that I owed the Sanjay Council nothing, nothing, nothing.

When she finished, I pleaded with her to leave Bombay for a while, told her everything I knew about the Leopold's incident, and warned her that things wouldn't get better, until I reached some kind of an understanding with Concannon.

'Enough horrible stuff,' she said at last. 'Is it my turn, now?'

I lay back against a stack of pillows on the bed. She was leaning against the doorjamb, her arms folded across her waist.

'Okay, Lisa, your turn.'

'If I can't stop you leaving, it's time to talk about other things.'

'As a matter of fact —'

'Women want to know,' she said quickly. 'You're a writer. You're supposed to know that.'

'Women want to know . . . what?'

She joined me on the bed.

'Everything,' she said, a hand resting on my thigh. 'All the stuff you never tell me, for example. The stuff you don't tell any woman.'

I frowned.

'Look, they say that women are emotional, and men are rational. Bullshit. If you saw the stuff you guys do, saw it from our point of view, the last thing you'd call it was rational.'

'Okay.'

'And women are actually pretty rational. They want clarity. They want an answer. Are you in this, or are you out? Women want to know. Anything less has no guts, and women like guts. That's rational, in our book, if you'll forgive the literary metaphor.'

'Forgiven. What are you talking about?'

'Karla, of course.'

'I've been trying to talk to you about —'

'You and Karla,' she said. 'Karla and you. On the mountain, and off it. I get it. And I'm cool with it.'

And suddenly it was done: we were two minds, two ways of being, two paradigms whirling apart, leaving phantom limbs where once they'd touched.

'I can't shake it, Lisa,' I said. 'It's not Karla, it's me, and I —'

'Karla and I have an understanding about you,' she said impatiently.

'An . . . understanding?'

'That's what the lunch with her at Kayani's was all about. Weren't you paying attention?'

Feynman once said that if you understand quantum theory, you don't. I had no idea what Lisa was talking about.

'What are you talking about?'

'It's not about her, and it's not about you. It's about me.'

'That's what *I* was trying to talk about.'

'No, you weren't. You were talking about you and Karla. Fine. I get that. But this isn't about that. This is about me.'

'This . . . what?'

'This conversation.'

'Didn't I start this conversation?'

'No, *I* did,' she frowned.

'Was I there, when you did?'

'Here it is. You can't love two people, Lin. Not in the right way. Nobody can. She can't do it, and neither can you. I get that. I really do. But sad and romantic and fucked up and thrilling and wonderful as all that is, it's irrelevant. This isn't about her, and it's not about you. It's my turn. It's about me. It's my shot at the mike, Lin.'

'It's *what* about you?'

'It's *all* about me.'

'You think you could start this conversation again?'

She looked directly into my eyes, challenging me to stay with her.

'See, women need to know, it's that simple.'

'I got that bit.'

'And once they know, they can deal with anything.'

'Deal with . . . what?'

'Stop beating yourself up, Lin. You're good at beating yourself up. You could get a prize, if they gave prizes for beating yourself up, and I kinda love that about you, but it's not needed here. I'm breaking up with you, tonight, and I wanted to talk about it, because I thought you should know why.'

'I . . . sure . . . of course. *What?*'

'I really think you should know.'

'Can I *pretend* to know?'

'Stop kidding around, Lin.'

'I'm not kidding, I'm just lost.'

'Okay. It's like this – I don't want to explain you any more.'

'Explain me to your friends, or my enemies?'

'I don't give a shit what anybody says about you,' she said, burning blue into my eyes. 'And I wouldn't listen to it. You know that. What I don't like about what you do is that *you* like it.'

'Lisa –'

'You like having two guns and six false passports and six currencies in the drawer. And you can't say you do it to survive. You're smarter than that. I'm smarter than that. The fact is, you like it. You like it a lot. And I don't want to explain that to myself any more. I don't like that you. I can't like that you. I won't like that you. I'm sorry.'

A man's a prison. I should've told her that I'd quit the Sanjay Company, and the Sri Lanka run was my ticket home. I'd taken a step away from the me that she didn't like. It wouldn't have changed her mind, but it was something she had a right to hear. A man's a prison. I didn't speak.

'Karla *likes* that you,' she said casually. 'I think she likes *that* you even more than *you* do.'

'Where did you go, Lisa?'

She laughed, and pretty hard.

'You really want to know?'

'Enough with the wanting to know, Lisa.'

She sat up on the bed, her legs crossed. Her blonde hair was tied into a swallowtail, dipping and shaking as she spoke.

'You know Rish, my partner in the gallery?'

'How many partners have you got now?'

'Six. Well –'

'Six?'

'So, anyway –'

'Six?'

'So, anyway, Rish has been doing a lot of meditation –'

'Oh, no.'

'And a lot of yoga studies –'

'Okay, Lisa, stop. If you tell me there's a guru behind all this, I'll be obliged to slap him.'

'He's not *my* guru, he's Rish's guru, and that's not the point. It wasn't said by a guru, and Rish didn't say it. A woman said it, I think. I don't know who she is, actually. But Johnny Cigar gave me a self-help book, and Rish gave me exactly the same book, on the same day. And the quote was in that book – the thing she said.'

'What thing?'

'The thing that Rish heard from somewhere, and said to me.'

'What thing?'

'*Resentment is unmet need or desire*,' she said. 'That's what I've been trying to tell you.'

I thought about it. A writer's worst instinct, and too often the first, is to look for the flaw in any written or spoken thing that looks good. I didn't find it.

'That's pretty good,' I conceded.

'Pretty *good*! She should get the Nobel Prize for Saying Cool Shit.'

'Okay,' I smiled.

'It ripped my mind apart, Lin, I gotta tell ya. It made so much sense. I suddenly understood exactly why I was feeling so *resentful*, these last months. I was really out of it on resentment, you know? Like, when you get to the stage where you get irritated by things that used to be cute, only now they're not cute any more?'

'How much not cute are we talking about?'

'A lot not cute.'

'A lot?'

'I was muttering,' she confessed.

'You were muttering?'

'I was.'

'Muttering?'

'I thought you must've heard me, a couple times.'

'About irritating things I did?'

'Yes.'

'Like what?'

'Well, for starters –'

'No, don't tell me. I don't wanna know.'

'It might be helpful to your process,' she suggested.

'No, I'm good. I've already been processed. Go on. You were muttering.'

'See,' she said, smoothing out the bedcover in front of her folded legs, her feet asleep against her calves. 'When I heard those words, *resentment is unmet need or desire*, I knew how to *think* about what I was *feeling*. Do you get that?'

'Think-feeling. I . . . think I get it.'

'I had a frame, you know, for the painting of me. I knew what my unmet need was. I knew what my unmet desire was. And when I knew that, I knew it all.'

'Can you divulge the unmet need?'

'I need to be free of you,' she said flatly, her hands pressed into stars on the bed.

'The new you gave up sugar.'

'I don't need it. Not any more,' she said, tracing a circle on the bedcover with her finger. 'I don't have to sugar anything, especially not what I tell myself.'

'And the unmet desire?'

'I want to be one hundred per cent inside my own *now*. I want to *be* the moment, instead of just watching the moment pass. You know what I'm talking about, right? You get me?'

'Maybe.'

'Now. *This* now. *My* now. *All* my nows. That's what I want. Do you get that?'

'You're in the now. I get it. I swear, Leese, if there's a guru involved in this —'

'This is all me. This is all mine.'

'And it's what you want?'

'It's the beginning of what I want, and I'm completely sure of it.'

She was tough. She was superb.

'Then, if it's really what you want, I love it, Lisa.'

'You do?'

'Of course. You can do anything you put your heart into.'

'You really think so?'

'It's great, Lisa.'

'I knew you'd get it,' she said, her eyes blue pools of relief. 'It's just that I want a special now, one that's *mine*, instead of a constant now, that I constantly share with someone else's now.'

A constant now, that you constantly share with someone else's now. It was a pretty good definition of prison.

'I hear you.'

'I want to know what it's like to be me, when it's just me.'

'Go get 'em, Lisa.'

She smiled, and let out a weary sigh.

'It sounds so selfish, but it wasn't. It was generous, you know, not just to me, but to you and Karla, too. It let me see us all clearly, for the first time. It let me see how much you're alike, you and her, and how different you both are than me. Do you understand that?'

In a damning way, in a kind and loving way, she was telling me that Karla and I were made for each other: Karla's edges fitting my scars. True or not, strangely hurtful or not, it didn't matter, because those minutes weren't Karla's or mine: they were hers.

The fall and summit within, what we do, and what we choose to become, are ours alone, as they should be, and must be. Lisa was deep in that serene, uncontradictable stillness born in resolution, and she was gloriously alone with it. She was clear, determined, brave and hopeful.

349

'The new you is really something,' I said quietly.

'Thank you,' she said softly. 'And the new me, broken up with old you, and not sleeping in the same bed as the new you, needs to rent the guest bedroom to sleep in.'

'Well,' I laughed, 'if your *now* isn't too compromised by it, no problem.'

'Oh, no,' she said seriously, snuggling in beside me, her head on my chest. 'But I do think, now that we're separated under the same roof, we should have a few rules.'

'Uh-huh.'

'Like with sleepovers. We should have a sleepover rule.'

'Sleepovers? Your *now* is getting more crowded by the minute.'

'We could hang a sign on the front door.'

'A *sign*?'

'I mean, a sign that only we understand. Like a garden gnome, for example. If the garden gnome is on the left side of the door, one of us has a sleepover guest. If it's on the right side of the door, no sleepovers.'

'We don't have a garden gnome. We don't have a garden.'

'We could use that cat statue you don't like.'

'I didn't say I didn't like it. I like it plenty. I said it didn't seem to like me.'

'And you'll have to forgive the rent, for at least six months.'

'Just to be clear on the sleepover cat signal,' I asked. 'Was it the left side of the door, or the right?'

'The left. And you'll have to forgive the rent.'

'The rent's already paid for a year, Lisa.'

'No, I mean *my* rent, for the guest room. I'll pay the market rate. I insist. But I put everything I have into the next show, and I'm skinned alive. I won't be able to pay you for at least six months.'

'Forget about it.'

'No, really, I insist on paying,' she said, punching me in the ribs.

'Forget about it.'

She hit me again.

'I give up. I'll let you pay me back.'

'And . . . I'll need an advance,' she added.

'An advance?'

'Yeah.'

'You don't work for me, Lisa.'

'Yes, but I hate the word *loan*. It sounds like the noise a dog makes, when it's in pain. I've decided, from now on, that when I need a loan I'll ask for an advance. It's a much more inspiring word.'

'Advanced thinking.'

'But I won't be able to pay for food, electricity, phone or laundry bills for a while. Every penny of my advance will be tied up.'

'Covered.'

'I insist on paying it, when I have enough to spare from my next advance.'

'Right.'

'And I'll need a car, but we can talk about that when you get back.'

'Sure. Is that it, with the house rules?'

'There is one other thing.'

'Let's have it.'

'I don't know. I mean —'

'Let's have it.'

'I'm not cooking any more,' she said, pressing her lips together until the bottom lip pouted free.

She'd cooked three times, in two years, and it wasn't pleasant eating.

'Okay.'

'To be brutally honest, I absolutely hate cooking. I can't stand it. I only did it to please you. It was a living hell for me every time, from beginning to end. I'm not doing it any more. I'm sorry, but that's just how it is, even as a roommate.'

'Okay.'

'I don't want to hurt you, but I don't want you to get any expectations, either. I'm big into expectations at the moment, as part of my process, and I hose them down before they become —'

'Resentments?'

'Exactly! Oh, God, I feel so much better. Do you?'

'I feel okay,' I said.

'You do? Really? It's important to me. I don't want to drag any guilt or shame into my *now* with me. It's important to me that you care enough to let me do this, and that you feel good about it.'

Good is only half the truth, and truth is only half the story. A small part of me was aggrieved that she was demanding so much and taking so much from the little that we had left. But the bigger part of me had always supposed or expected, however silently and reluctantly, that we'd part from one another one day, and probably with little more than

351

we could hold in our hands. And then there was Karla, always Karla. I had no right to shade a minute of Lisa's happiness. Good is only half the truth, and truth is only half the story.

'I'm good, Lisa. I just want you to be happy.'

'I'm so glad,' she said, smiling through her lashes. 'I was dreading this, you know.'

'Why? When have I ever *not* listened to you, or *not* supported you?'

'It's not that. It's more complicated than that.'

'How?'

'There are other things and other people to consider.'

'What things, Lisa? What people?'

'I don't want to go into it, now.'

Women want to know? I thought. *Men want to know, too.*

'Come on, Lisa —'

'Look, you're leaving tomorrow, and I want us to keep feeling happy about how far we've come tonight, okay?'

'If that's the way you want it.'

'I do. I'm happy, Lin, and don't want to spoil it.'

'I'll be back soon, a week or so, and we'll talk again. Whatever help you need, it's yours. If you want a new place, I'll set it up, and clear the rent for a year. Whatever you want. Don't worry.'

'You've really evolved, you know,' she said wistfully.

'From what?'

'From what I met,' she said.

She looked up at me with an expression I couldn't recognise, at first, and then I did. It was endearment; the kind of endearment we reserve for very dear friends.

'Do you remember our first kiss?' she asked.

'Afghan Church. They chased us out. We almost got arrested.'

'Let's find out,' she said, moving to sit across me, 'how we'll remember our last kiss.'

She kissed me, but the kiss dissolved in whispers and we talked, lying side by side in the dark, until the storm softened and died. When she slept, I rose and packed a bag for the morning's train ride.

I put my guns, ammunition, long knives, some passports and a few bundles of money in a compartment I'd had made in the back of a heavy chest of drawers. I left extra money for Lisa in the top drawer of the dresser, where she'd find it.

When everything was set, I went to the window and sat in the wicker chair I'd bought for her, high enough to give a view of the street below.

The last lonely chai seller walked past our window, gently ringing the bell on his bicycle to attract the attention of dozing nightwatchmen. Little by little the *thring-thring* of the bell faded, until the street was silent.

All life orbits that sun, Fate's heart. Ranjit, Vikram, Dennis the Sleeping Baba, Naveen Adair, Abdullah, Sanjay, Diva Devnani, Didier, Johnny Cigar, Concannon, Vinson, Rannveig, Scorpio, Gemini, Sri Lanka, Lisa: my thoughts, a voyager, sailed from sea to sea, with one star in the black-ink sky, Karla.

Lisa was still asleep when I left, at dawn. I walked, contrition-brisk, to a taxi stand on the causeway. My shadow played like a laughing dog in the yellow morning. A sleepy taxi driver reluctantly accepted double the fare. The empty streets we drove were bright, cleaned by light.

The station, Bombay's pagan cathedral, urged porters, passengers and burdens into passageways of crucial consequence, every seat precious; every seat important; every seat essential to someone's destiny.

And when the Madras Express pulled out, at last, my window woke the streets for me, all the way through rain-stained suburbs to the tree line of green mountains and valleys, beyond the city's grey hunger.

Again-and-again, again-and-again, the train's rhythm chanted. I felt good: bad and good at the same time. My heart was a question; my head was a command.

Sri Lanka was risky. Lisa was right about that. But Abdullah had spoken to Sanjay, wresting my freedom from him in exchange for the mission I'd promised to do. And one job, like fifty others I'd done, was a small price to pay for a clean exit from the Company.

I was happy for Lisa, happy that she was free of me, if that was what she wanted. I was still feeling the same worried affection for her, but I had to start getting used to the fact that she was already gone: she was gone, and I was on a war train.

Lisa found her truth, and I found mine. I was still in love with Karla, and I couldn't love anyone else.

It didn't matter what intrigues Karla was plotting, with Ranjit or against him. It didn't matter that she'd married someone else, or that I'd tried to love someone else. It didn't matter if we couldn't be more than friends. I loved her, and I always would.

I felt good, and bad: one bad mission away from good.

Again-and-again, the train wheels sang, again-and-again, again-and-again, as farms and fields and towns of dreams streamed past my window, and a shawl of sky misted distant mountains with the last of that year's rain.

PART SIX

CHAPTER THIRTY-THREE

THERE WAS NO MOON. CLOUDS HID, AFRAID OF THE DARK. Stars
were so bright that whenever I shut my eyes they burned sparks
on the dark inside. The wind was everywhere, playful, happy to see
us out there on the surface of nowhere, and the ship plunged and
rose gently, as if swimming through the waves, rather than floating
on them.

I'd waited three days in Madras for just such a night, as had the seventy-seven others with me. Those waiting days had shrunk to minutes:
minutes before midnight, minutes before leaving the danger of the ship
for the greater danger of small boats, on the open ocean.

Waves licked at the prow, streaming in salted mists all the way to the
stern where I stood, dressed in dark blue fatigues and jacket, one more
camouflaged bundle on the camouflaged deck.

I looked at the stars, as the ship sighed through the waves, drifting
between dark night and darker sea.

Most ocean-going cargo ships are painted white, cream or pale
yellow above the waterline. In the event of an emergency at sea, such
as dead engines or a ruptured hull, they can be seen from far by search
and rescue vessels, or aircraft.

The *Mitratta*, a Panamanian coastal freighter of fifty thousand tons,
was painted dark blue, everywhere, and dark blue tarpaulins covered
the cargo and rig on the deck.

The captain ran the bridge on instrument lights. The ship was so
dark that the forward running lights seemed like tiny creatures, diving
into and out of the waves.

Figures huddled together like bundles of cargo, which, of course,
we were. Smuggled people smuggle their dreams with them, and they
whispered to one another often, but no word could be heard. Their

whispers were always just softer than the lush of the waves. Victims of war become masters of silence.

I suddenly needed company. I made my rolling way along the deck to the first of several groups. I smiled at them, teeth in the darkness. They smiled back at me, teeth in the darkness.

I sat down beside them. They began whispering again.

They were speaking in Tamil. I couldn't understand a word, but I didn't mind. I was in the bubble-murmur of their voices, the gentle music of it dripping shadows around us on the painted steel deck.

A figure approached, and squatted down beside me. It was Mehmood, nicknamed Mehmu, my contact on the ship.

'It's a young war,' he said softly, looking at the faces of the Tamils near us on the deck. 'The Tamil homeland in Sri Lanka is an old idea, but the young are dying for it. Can you come with me now?'

'Sure.'

I followed him until we reached the afterdeck.

'They don't trust you,' he said, lighting two cigarettes, and passing me one. 'It's nothing personal. They don't know who you are, or why you're in the group. When you're in a situation that only ever gets worse, like theirs, everyone's a threat, even a friend.'

'You stay on this ship for every tour?'

'I do. We unload the legit cargo, and I go back with the ship to Madras.'

'I wouldn't want to do this every month. Those patrol boats we saw weren't far away, and they've got big guns.'

He laughed quietly.

'You know anything about the Tamil Muslims in Sri Lanka?'

'Not much.'

'Pogroms,' he said. 'Look it up.'

He laughed, but it was just sadness, finding a different way to his face. He straightened up.

'The gold and passports you're bringing will help,' he said. 'We have to buy people out of prison, and then we have to get them out of Sri Lanka to tell the world about our situation. For the others, it's a new civil war. For us, this is a war we never start, but always have to fight. For us, this isn't a matter of nationality, it's a matter of faith.'

Faith, again. There wasn't any pure or noble cause in what I was doing. There was no cause but my own. I was ashamed to think it, standing next to a man who risked his life for what he believed.

The hundred-gram gold ingots I was smuggling had been melted down from jewellery that the Sanjay Company had stolen or extorted. There was blood on it already, and I was carrying it: nothing noble, and nothing pure.

But there was still a stained-glass shard of faith somewhere inside. Mehmu's sacred mission was a job, for me, it was true, but the same dark vessel carried both of us to the same dark war. And it was a war of one, for me: one man's freedom from a gang that was once a band of brothers.

Faith is belief without fear, and freedom is one of faith's perfections. Standing there on that smothered deck, listening to prayers in Arabic, Hindi, English, Sinhalese and Tamil, the stars so bright those tiny suns burned my eyes, I put my faith in freedom, and asked Mehmu for my gun.

He lifted his sweater to show me the handgun, stuffed into the belt of his trousers. It was a Browning HP, standard issue to Indian Army officers. The penalties for trading in them were severe, which was why the officers who sold them to us charged a premium.

I liked Mehmu, and wished that he could come with me to Sri Lanka. He was a fit, knowledgeable thirty-year-old, fluent in six languages, and had a confident eye. I didn't like Mehmu's gun.

'What's with the cannon?'

'It's a bit ... conspicuous, I'll give you that,' he replied, looking around as he handed me the weapon and a magazine.

'Conspicuous? This thing is a zebra in a line-up.'

I checked the gun, and flipped the safety on.

'If you're gonna get caught with a gun in this war,' he said, 'it's gotta be this one. Any other gun, they'll go to work on you for a long time, before they drop you from a helicopter into the sea, right about here, actually.'

'But *this* gun?'

'This gun gives you a chance. The Indian Army has the island nailed down, but there's so many freelancers everywhere now. Americans, Israelis, South Africans, and all of them are working with the Research and Analysis Wing. If the Indian Army catches you with this gun, you can try to pass yourself off as a RAW agent. It's a long shot, but you wouldn't be the first that got away with it. It's the Wild East out there.'

'So, I carry a big gun, and when they see it, because it's so big, I talk them into believing I'm working for them, and then actually start working for them, if they let me live?'

'It happens,' he shrugged. 'A lot, actually.'

'Gimme a *little* gun, Mehmu. I don't wanna kill wildebeest. I just wanna make enough noise to give me time to run away. If they catch me, I'll ditch the gun and deny it. I'd rather do that than start working for them.'

'But a little gun,' he mused. 'I always say, if you have to shoot someone in the eye to kill him, your gun's too small.'

I looked at him for a while.

'A small gun?' He sniffed. 'It's right in the eye, man, or it's like gravel rash, with a little gun.'

'You don't say.'

'I do say. It happens. A lot, actually.'

'You got a little gun, or not?'

'I do,' he mused. 'If you'd be prepared to exchange?'

'Show me.'

He took a small box of cartridges and a .22-calibre automatic from his jacket pockets. It was the kind of weapon designed to fit snugly next to lipstick, perfume and a credit card in a purse: a girl's gun.

'I'll take it.'

We swapped guns. I checked the weapon and put it in my jacket pocket.

'I'd wrap that lot in plastic,' he said, tucking the Browning into his trousers again. 'And lock it up with surgical tape.'

'In case I end up in the water?'

'It happens.'

'Uh-huh?'

'A lot, actually. What is this, your first smuggling run or what?'

I'd smuggled passports and gold to nine countries, but always by plane, and always on Czechoslovakian Airways. The communist airline was the only one in Bombay that accepted payment for tickets in rupees, and checked for weapons, but nothing else. Whatever else you had on you in transit flights, from gold bars to bundles of money, was your problem. And because nobody but Czechoslovakians actually went all the way to communist Czechoslovakia on Czechoslovakian Airways, it wasn't their problem either.

'I fly. Back and forth, in seventy-two hours. I don't do ships.'

'You don't like ships?'

'I don't like power, on land or sea.'

'Power?'

'Power. Absolute power. The law of the sea.'

'You mean the captain?'

'Any captain. I think the *Bounty* was the last free ship.'

Voices whispered hoarsely near the piles of cargo secured to the deck. People began to stand. We saw figures moving back and forth between clusters of shadows.

'What are they doing?'

'They're passing out cyanide capsules, to those who want them.'

'People do that?'

'A lot, actually.'

'You know, Mehmu, the whole morale thing. You're shit at it.'

'You want a suicide capsule, while they're still handing them out?'

'See what I mean?'

'You want one, or not?'

'I'm more your kicking and screaming all the way type, but thanks all the same.'

The commotion on the deck increased. The ship's first officer strode to the port side with several members of the Filipino crew. They uncovered bundles of rope-and-plank ladders, and began to roll them over the side.

'Better get below, and get your stuff,' Mehmu said. 'I'll wait for you at the ladders.'

I worked my way around the comparatively empty starboard side of the vessel to my crewman's berth.

Wrapping the small automatic and the box of ammunition in plastic bags, I sealed them with tape and shoved them into my backpack. I pulled off my jacket and sweater, put on the heavy vest I'd hidden, and dressed again.

The vest contained twenty kilos of gold and twenty-eight blank passports. With an effort, I zipped up my jacket, and paced up and down in the cabin to adjust my step to the extra weight.

There was an open journal on the bed. I'd been trying to write a new short story. I was challenging myself with a difficult subject. It was about happy, loving people in a happy, loving place, doing happy, loving things. It wasn't going well.

I scooped the journal, the pen and everything else on the bed into the backpack, and turned to leave. I reached out to turn off the light and caught sight of my face in a mirror, set into the door panel.

The reckless truth of travel into countries and cultures far from your own is that sometimes, you're just rolling with the dice. Fate, the tour guide, can lead any traveller, at any moment of the journey, into a labyrinth of learning and love, or the long tunnel of a dangerous adventure. And every traveller knows those moments in the mirror: the last, long look at yourself before *Okay, let's do this.*

I switched off the light, and made my way back on deck.

Lines of people were assembled at the ladders. The first officer gave the whispered command, and the smuggled people began to disembark.

I shuffled forward, last in line. A crewman was handing out life-preserver vests, and helping people to fit them.

Mehmu was standing beside him.

'Take mine, as well,' he said, when the crewman fitted me with a vest.

Our eyes met. He knew that if I ended up in the sea, one vest might not hold me afloat, with twenty kilos of gold on my body.

The crewman handed me a second vest, and then gave me a small metal object, and urged me forward.

'What's this?' I asked, when Mehmu and I paused, away from the crowded rail.

'It's a clicker,' he said.

It was a child's toy, made from two pieces of tin that made a *click-clack* sound, when it was pressed. I pressed it.

Click-clack.

'If you're in the water,' Mehmu said, 'stay where you are. Keep together with the others in the water.'

'The *others?*'

'A boat will come back to the ship,' he continued, 'and the ship will circle you from a klick or so away, until we get the all clear.'

'A klick or so away?'

'When you see or hear anything, use the clicker to let them know where you are. Most people keep it in their teeth, like this, so they don't lose it.'

He reached out, took the clicker, and held the edge of it in his teeth.

My clicker was shaped like a pink dragonfly. He was looking at me with a pink dragonfly in his mouth, and he was sending me into the sea.

'It's from a movie,' he said, handing back the clicker. '*The Longest War*, I think it's called.'

'*The Longest Day*.'

'Yeah, that's the one. Have you seen it?'

'Yeah. Have you?'

'No. Why?'

'I think you should take a peek. Thanks for everything, Mehmu. It was nice sailing with you, even if I don't like sailing.'

'Me, too. If you run into a chunky girl, thirty years old, about five-five high, wearing a sky-blue hijab, don't show her the little gun.'

'You stole it off a girl?'

'Kind of.'

'An enemy, or a friend?'

'Does it make a difference?'

'Hell, yeah.'

'It was a bit of both. She's my wife.'

'Your wife?'

'Yeah.'

'And you love her?'

'I'm mad about her.'

'And . . . if I show her the gun . . . she might –'

'Shoot you,' he said. 'It happens. A lot, actually. She shot me once. She's a fighter, my wife.'

'Okay, let me get this straight. Chunky, thirty, five-five, blue hijab. Right?'

'Right. That's her name, in fact. Her comrade name.'

'What?'

'Blue Hijab. That's her name.'

'Her name is Blue Hijab?'

'Yeah.'

'O . . . kay. Thanks for the heads-up.'

'No sweat,' he smiled. 'I warn everyone about her. She's so danger-ous, I love her to death.'

'I hear you.'

'And remember, there's only one rule on the way to shore. Anyone tries to take your place on the boat, push him overboard.'

'It happens?'

'A lot, actually.'

'You!' the first officer grunted, jabbing a finger at me.

I walked to the rail, swung over, and started descending the rope-and-wood ladder.

It was much more difficult than I'd thought. The ladder swirled and swung out over the sea, forcing me to hug ropes and bits of wood like family. Then the ladder slammed back into the unyielding steel of the hull, scraping skin from unprepared fingers.

I came to the last few steps of the ladder. The three boats seemed tiny: pilot fish, hovering against the shark-hide of the freighter.

They were fishing boats, flat and open, like oversized versions of the lifeboats on the deck of the ship, but with a motor. We were still in open sea. The boat I was dropping into was already crowded. It didn't look safe. I took the last steps, and the smell of fish, oiled into the ribs of the ship, reassured me.

Fishermen, I thought. *Fishermen know the sea.*

Friendly hands guided me aft, stepping over feet and small bundles. Friendly hands guided others forward. The crew was distributing the weight.

I counted twenty-three people. The crew of the freighter waved all clear, and drew up the ladders. Our tillerman shoved us away from the ship, and moved into open sea under power.

The motor was quiet, muffled by a soundproofed cabinet.

Click-clack.

A boat nearby in the darkness signalled to us. *Click-clack.* We all turned to see it. *Click-clack*, somebody signalled back. *Click-clack.*

'You know what the difference is, between war and peace?' the man sitting next to me whispered, a smile in his voice.

'I'm guessing you'll tell me,' I whispered back.

'In peace time, you sacrifice twenty to save one. In war time, you sacrifice one to save twenty.'

'Nice try,' I smiled.

'You don't agree?'

'We don't sacrifice for numbers. We sacrifice for love, and land.'

'The numbers in *this* war, are high enough to make a difference.'

'You were talking about war *and* peace.'

'And?'

'War has the blood on the outside. Peace has the blood on the inside, where it belongs. That's pretty much the difference, so far as I've seen. War knocks the buildings down, and peace builds them up again.'

He laughed quietly, his lips closed.

'I'm your contact,' he said.

'Uh-huh?'

'I came with the boat. I'm here to make sure you get where you're going.'

He was a little younger than I was, short and lean, with a cheeky grin that must've won him lips, and cost him slaps.

'Glad to know you. How long before we make shore?'

'Not long.'

He handed me a plastic jug and started bailing out the water that lapped into the boat with occasional waves. I joined in. People all along the shallow boat were bailing out. The tillerman laughed softly.

Click-clack.

The sea, that restless sleeper, rolled shoulders of current beneath us. Water splashed into the boat, soaking us in salt. *Click-clack.*

When the boats reached the shore we jumped out into waist-deep water and struggled for the beach. The boats began to pull away.

We ran for the trees. At the tree line, I looked back at the sea. Some of the slower men and women were still running, scuffing sand as they kicked and ruffled across the beach: a thing of fun, a foot race, maybe, on a sunny day, but a thing of fear that night.

There was no sign of the ship: no light but the stars.

My contact waved to me from another stand of trees. I joined him, and we moved deeper into the jungle. After a while he paused, listening.

'What's your name?' I whispered, when we were sure no-one was following us.

'No names here, man,' he said. 'The less you know, the better. Truth's a sweet thing, unless someone's cutting it out of you, and then it's a very bitter thing. Ready to move?'

'I'm good.'

'There's a truck heading south on the main road. It'll wait for us, but it won't wait long. The boats were a little off course. We've got a lot of country to pass, and not much time.'

We headed into the surrounding bushes, and in a few minutes we were moving through a swathe of jungle that ran parallel to the coast.

Every now and then we glimpsed dark waves through a tree break, but after a while the sea was too far away to hear, and even the scent faded in the stronger fragrances of jungle damp.

My contact led us again and again into a smothering mass of leaves as big as elephants' ears, to emerge on a narrow path that was invisible until he plunged us into it.

He wasn't navigating by the stars: we couldn't see them. His mental map of the jungle was so precise that he never hesitated in his rapid walk.

I lost him, twice. Each time I froze, listening for his step. Each time I heard nothing until he tapped me on the shoulder, and we headed off through the jungle again.

With my backpack and the smuggling vest, I was carrying thirty-five kilos. But the weight wasn't the problem. To stop the vest from shifting, and accidentally dislodging the tablets, I'd strapped it tightly to my chest and waist. Every breath was a struggle.

We pushed through a verge of leaves and bushes onto a main road.

'Gotta save time,' my companion said, glancing at his watch. 'We'll risk a side road, for a while. Much faster. If you see any light at all, hit the trees and hide. I'll draw it off. You stay put. You got that?'

'Yeah,' I puffed.

'You want me to carry the vest, for a while?'

'I'm good.'

'Let me at least take the backpack,' he whispered.

I slipped the backpack off my shoulder gratefully, and he strapped it on.

'Okay, let's jog.'

We ran along the rough side road in a silence so complete that the occasional animal or bird cry was shocking. Every breath strained against the constricting vest.

In truth, a Nigerian gunrunner once said to me, *the smuggler only really smuggles himself. All the other stuff that he carries, it's just an excuse, you know?* By the time we reached the pickup point, my excuse was threatening to stop my heart.

'We're here,' my contact said.

'Hallelujah,' I puffed. 'You guys ever heard of motorcycles?'

'Sorry, man,' my contact smiled, handing me my backpack. 'But I think we're in time.'

'You *think*?' I gasped, resting my arms on my knees.

'Have you got a gun?' he asked.

'Of course.'

'Get it handy. Now.'

I unwrapped my pistol, as he checked and reloaded his ten-shot automatic. He glanced around and saw the small .22-calibre purse pistol.

'If you run into a chunky woman, wearing a sky-blue hijab —'

'I know. Don't show her the gun.'

'Fuck, man,' he grinned. 'You like living dangerously.'

'Something tells me that this Blue Hijab leaves a lasting impression.'

'She's fine. A great comrade,' he laughed. 'Just don't show her the gun.'

He glanced at his watch again, and stared into the darkness that ate the road where starlight failed.

'If this goes south, so do you,' he said, glancing at his watch again. 'Head due south. This road goes to Trincomalee. Stay in the jungle, as much as you can. If you make it, report at the Castlereagh hotel. You're booked in for two weeks. You'll be contacted there.'

'This is where you get off?'

'Yeah. You won't see me again.'

He began muttering indistinctly.

'What?'

'A diamond, for a pearl,' he said.

I waited.

'We shouldn't be here, us Tamils. We left a diamond, Mother India, for a pearl. And no matter what we do, no matter how many of us die, it'll never be worth it, because we gave up a diamond, for a pearl.'

'Why do you still fight?'

'You don't know much about us Tamils, do you? Wait! Did you hear that?'

We listened for a while to the darkness. A small animal moved through the jungle nearby, swiftness hissing through the leaves. The jungle was silent again.

'I'm fighting the army that trained me,' he said softly, staring north along the road.

'The Indian Army?'

At that time, the major military presence in Sri Lanka was the IPKF, the Indian Peace Keeping Force.

'RAW,' he replied. 'They trained all of us. Bombs, weapons, tactical coordination, the whole lot.'

The Research and Analysis Wing was India's counter-intelligence unit. It held a fearsome reputation throughout the region. RAW operatives were highly trained and motivated, and their *By Any Means Necessary* status gave them a licence that left a lot of questions where their commando boots landed, and not many answers.

Indian intelligence agents collected information from many sources, including the gangs. Every mafia Company in Bombay knew someone from RAW, openly or undercover, and every mafia Company knew better than to fight them.

'And now they're at war with us,' my contact sighed, ruefully. 'A diamond, crushing a pearl.'

We heard a noise, maybe the distant grating of gears, and hunkered down in the bushes, staring at the tunnel of the road. Then we heard the unmistakeable grunt and cough of a truck engine, labouring uphill.

The tall, tottering cargo truck rolled into view, and began coasting downhill toward us.

'Is it ours?'

'It's ours,' he grinned, pulling me up with him.

We walked to the edge of the road, where he waved a small blue-light torch. The truck squealed and creaked to a stop, the engine racing on idle.

As we approached, I noticed that a jeep had been driving behind the truck, lights out, and had stopped in its shadow.

My contact led me to the jeep. I glanced into the back of the truck and saw fifteen or more people sitting on bales of cotton.

'You're in the jeep,' my contact said. 'You're a journalist, remember? Can't have you travelling with the common folk.'

My cover name was James Davis, Canadian, a stringer for Reuters news agency. My passport and accreditation were impeccable: I'd made them myself.

We shook hands, knowing that we'd probably never see one another again, and that one or both of us would probably be dead within the year.

He leaned in close to me.

'Remember, check in at the Castlereagh, keep a low profile, you'll be contacted within forty-eight hours. Good luck. May Maa Durga be your guardian.'

'And yours.'

He broke away to clamber up the tailgate of the truck and onto a cotton bale. He waved, and smiled at me.

For an instant, it looked exactly like the throne of sacks in the courtyard of the Cycle Killers, but with ghosts of war, instead of hired assassins.

I took the passenger seat of the jeep, shaking hands with the driver and the two young men sitting in the back.

The truck pulled away and the jeep followed. My contact's face hovered in the swaying shadow, carrying him south. His eyes held mine.

People who abhor crime, as I do, often ask why men who commit crimes, as I did, do such things.

One of the big answers is that the low road is always easier, until it crumbles away beneath desire. One of the small answers is that when life and freedom are at stake, the men you meet are often exceptional. In other lives, they'd be captains of industry, or captains of armies.

In the jungle, on the run, they're friends, because a friend is anyone prepared to die beside you. And men who'll die beside you without even knowing you are hard to find, unless you know a lot of cops, soldiers or outlaws.

The truck turned onto a side road. Shadows closed over my contact's face. I never saw him or heard about him again.

We rode on for twenty minutes, and then the driver stopped the jeep in a clearing, beside the road.

'Get your passport and papers ready. We're going through a few checkpoints. Sometimes they're manned, sometimes, not. Things have been quiet here, for a while. Put this on.'

He handed me a dark blue flak vest with the word PRESS on the chest. The driver and the two men in the back donned flak vests, and the driver stuck a white square bearing the same word on the windshield.

We rode on past scattered cabins and shacks, and then the first large houses. What seemed to be the light of a forest fire on the horizon was the bright city, only ten kilometres away.

We passed through three unmanned checkpoints, slowing to a crawl each time, and then speeding up quickly. Skirting the city, we reached the coastal vantage point of Orr's Hill, and the Castlereagh hotel, in just under an hour.

369

'Damn lucky,' the driver said, as he stopped the jeep in the drive-way. 'There's a Bollywood actress doing a show tonight for the Indian troops. Guess they couldn't tear themselves away.'

'Thanks for your help.'

'Don't mention,' he smiled. 'May Jesus be with you, comrade.'

'And with you.'

The jeep backed out of the driveway and sped away. The local contacts had been a Muslim, a Hindu, and a Christian, and they'd all used the word *comrade*. My contacts were always black market hustlers: men you knew how far to trust. The comrades were a new touch. I wondered what other surprises Sanjay had in store for me. I shouldered my backpack, and looked up at the gabled prow of the Castlereagh hotel.

It was in the white colonial style that colonial white men built for themselves, wherever they could steal gold. The gold in the vest, strapped to my chest, was coming back home to one of those colonies, and I couldn't get rid of it fast enough.

I paused, and did a name check. A smuggler has to live in a new fake name and accent for a while, before using it. As a fugitive with a price on my head, I collected accents and practised them whenever I could.

I'm James Davis. James. My name is James Davis. Maybe not. I'm Jim Davis. Was I Jimmy, as a kid? Jim Davis, pleased to meet you. No, please, call me Jim.

When I found the fake name I could trust, I found my way into the new life I had to live for a while. The problem was simplified by war for my companion, my contact, who'd ridden away as a shadow in the back of a truck. When he wasn't with those he loved or trusted, he had no name at all.

I climbed the granite and tile steps, crossed the wooden veranda and tapped on the filigreed glass of the main door. In a few moments, the night porter opened the door a crack.

'Davis,' I said, flipping easily into a Canadian accent. 'Jim Davis. I have a reservation.'

He waved me inside, locking the door securely, and led me to the reservations desk, where he copied my passport details into a ledger that was half the size of a pool table. It took a while.

'The kitchen is closed, sir,' the attendant said at last, closing the book a page at a time as if he was making a bed. 'There are very few guests at the moment. The season proper begins in three months. But

370

there are cold snacks, and I can mix you a very nice drink, if you like. The house special.'

He walked across the large hotel reception area and switched on a lamp beside a comfortable, linen-covered couch. Moving nimbly, he crossed the room again, and opened a door leading to the bathrooms.

He switched on another light, and plucked a towel from the rail.

'If you'd like to freshen up, sir?' he said.

I was hungry and thirsty. I didn't want to spend half an hour or longer creating a safe hiding-place in the hotel room for my golden vest. So long as I was wearing it, the vest was safe.

I accepted the towel, washed my face and hands, and then sat down on the couch, where a place had already been set for me.

'I took the liberty of preparing a drink, sir,' he said, placing a tall glass in front of me. 'With coconut, fresh lime, a bite of ginger, a dash of bitter chocolate flakes, and a few secret ingredients of my own. If it's not to your liking, I'll prepare another of your choosing.'

'So far, I'm happy to let you do the choosing, Mr – may I know your name?'

'Ankit, sir,' he replied. 'My name is Ankit.'

'A nice name. *The Complete*. I'm Jim.'

'You know Indian names, sir?'

'I know Indian names, Ankit. Where are you from?'

'I'm from Bombay,' he said, placing a tray of sandwiches in front of me. 'Like you.'

He was either my contact at the hotel, or he was an enemy. I was hoping for the contact. The sandwiches looked good.

'Wanna sit down?'

'I can't,' he said, speaking softly. 'It wouldn't look right, if someone came in. But thank you, anyway. Are you okay?'

He meant, *Did you bring any trouble with you?* It was a fair question.

'I'm good,' I said, dropping the Canadian accent. 'We passed through empty checkpoints. We were lucky. There's a movie star in town, entertaining the troops.'

He relaxed, allowing himself to lean on the back of an armchair.

He was a little taller than I was, thin, perhaps forty-five years old, and had thick, grey hair. His eyes were sharp, and he was fit. I guessed that his confident, graceful movements had been learned in boxing, or some other martial art.

371

'I made veg, and non-veg options,' he said, gesturing toward the tray of sandwiches.

'Right now I'm hungry enough to eat the napkin option. Mind if I go ahead?'

'Eat! Eat!' he said in Hindi. 'I'll fill you in, while you fill yourself in, so to speak.'

I ate everything. The cocktail was good, too. My contact, Ankit, a Hindu from Bombay in the middle of a war involving Buddhists, Muslims and other Hindus, was a good host and a valuable resource. While I ate, he listed the requirements for my two- or three-day role of journalist.

'And most importantly, you have to report to the checkpoint every day before noon, to get stamped,' he said in conclusion. 'That's a must. If you're here for a few days, and they see a single day missing, you'll be detained. Have you ever had the feeling that you're not wanted?'

'Not recently.'

'Well, if you miss a day, and they catch you, you're going to feel like the *Universe* doesn't want you any more.'

'Thanks, Ankit. Doesn't anyone in this war have a sense of humour? *The Universe doesn't want me any more?* That's such a depressing thought that I insist on one more of your special cocktails, immediately.'

'Just don't miss that checkpoint,' he laughed, returning to the small bar in the lounge area.

He went back to the bar several times, I guess. I lost count after the third time, because everything after that was the same thing, somehow, like watching the same leaf float past on a stream, again and again.

I wasn't doped. Ankit was a damn good bartender: the kind who knows exactly how drunk you don't need to be. His voice was soft, kind and patient, although I had no idea what he was saying, after a while. I forgot about the mission, and the Sanjay Company.

Flowers so big I couldn't put my arms around them tried to press my eyes closed. I was tumbling, slowly, drifting, almost weightless, in feathered petals.

Ankit was talking.

I closed my eyes.

The white flowers became a river. It carried me to a place of peace, among the trees, where a dog ran toward me, frantic with happiness, and pawed at my chest happily.

CHAPTER THIRTY-FOUR

'D AVIS!'
The dog scratched and pawed at the edge of the dream, trying to claw me back to that place, that sacred space.

'Davis!'

I opened my eyes. There was a blanket over me. I was still sitting where I'd slept, but Ankit had put a pillow behind my head, and a blanket over my chest. My hand was in my jacket pocket, holding the small automatic. A deep breath told me that the golden vest was still in place.

Okay.

There was a stranger stooping over me.

Not okay.

'Back off, friend.'

'Sure, sure,' the man said, straightening up and offering his hand. 'I'm Horst.'

'Do you often wake people up to meet them, Horst?'

He laughed. It was loud. Too loud.

'Okay, Horst, do me a favour. Don't laugh like that again, until I've had two coffees.'

He laughed again. A lot.

'You're kind of a slow learner, aren't you?'

He laughed again. Then he offered me a cup of hot coffee.

It was excellent. You can't dislike someone who brings you good, strong coffee, when you've been thirty-minute drunk only four hours before.

I looked up at him.

His eyes were sun-bleached blue. His head seemed unnaturally large, to me. I thought that Ankit's coconut lime drinks were to blame until I stood, and saw that he had an unnaturally large head.

'That's a big head you've got on you,' I said, as I shook hands with him. 'Ever played rugby?'

'No,' he laughed. 'You can't imagine how hard it is to find a hat that fits.'

'No,' I agreed. 'I can't. Thanks for the coffee.'

I started to walk away. It was still in the half-light. I wanted to beat the dawn to my bedroom, and sleep a little more.

'But you have to report, at the checkpoint,' he said. 'And believe me, it's much safer for us just after dawn, than at any other time, *ja*.'

I was still wearing the flak vest marked PRESS. He was inviting me, as a fellow journalist. If I had to do it, it was better in company. Sleep no more.

'Who are you with?' I asked.

'*Der Spiegel*,' he replied. 'Well, I'm freelancing for them. And you?'

'How long have you been here?'

'Long enough to know the safest time to report to the checkpoint.'

'Do I have time to wash up?'

'Make it quick.'

I ran upstairs to my room, stripped off, had a cold shower, and was dried and re-vested in six minutes.

I came down the stairs in a jog, but found the lounge area empty. The windows of dawn light were at exactly the same intensity as the lights in the room: a light without shadows.

A soft, scraping sound stirred the stillness. Gardeners were working already.

I walked through to the long, wide veranda, directly above the open wound of lawns surrounding the hotel: a wound that the jungle ceaselessly sought to heal.

Seven servants were hard at work, hacking, chopping and spraying herbicide on the perimeter: the urban front line in the war with nature.

I watched them for a while, waiting for Horst. I could hear the jungle, speaking the wind.

Give us twenty-five years. Leave this place. Come back, after twenty-five years. You'll see. We'll heal it of all this pain.

'I'd like to have a few of those fellows working for me,' Horst said, as he came to stand beside me. 'My girlfriend has a place in Normandy. It's lovely, and all that, but it's a lot of work. A couple of these guys would fix it up in no time.'

'They're Tamils,' I said, watching them drift across lawns lit by hovering dew. 'Tamils are like the Irish. They're everywhere. You'll find hard-working Tamils in Normandy, if you look hard enough.'

'How do you know they're Tamils?' Horst asked suspiciously.

I turned to face him. I wanted another coffee.

'They're doing the dirty work,' I said.

'Oh, yeah, yeah,' he laughed.

It wasn't funny. I wasn't laughing. He pinched his laugh to a frown.

'Which agency did you say you're with?'

'I didn't say.'

'You're a real secretive guy, aren't you?'

'The shooting is wallpaper. The real war is always between us, the journalists.'

'What are you talking about?' Horst asked nervously. 'I just asked you who you're with, that's all.'

'See, if I make friends with you, and I break a story, and then I find out you stole it from me, I'd have to hunt you down and beat you up. And that's not good.'

He squinted at me. His eyes flared.

'*Reuters!*' he said. 'Only you Reuters pricks are so stingy with a story.'

I wanted another coffee. Ankit appeared at my elbow. He was carrying a small glass of something.

'I thought that a fortification might be required, sir, if you will forgive the impertinence,' Ankit said. 'The road you walk this morning is not kind.'

I drank the glass, discovering that it was sherry, and damn good.

'Ankit,' I said, 'we just got related.'

'Very good, sir,' Ankit replied equably.

'You there,' Horst said to Ankit. 'Can you find out, please, if any of these fellows have work permits for outside of Sri Lanka?'

I held Ankit's response with a raised hand.

'Are we gonna get going, Horst, before the bears wake up?'

'Bears?' he said, making it sound like *beers*. 'There are no bears. It's tigers, not bears. The Tamil Tigers. They're absolutely crazy, those fucks. They all carry suicide capsules, in case they're caught.'

'You don't say.'

'They don't seem to realise that when they do that, commit suicide like that, they make the other side even more determined to throw them out of the country.'

'Are we gonna do this?'

'Yeah, yeah, sure. Don't set fire to your pants.'

'What?'

'Don't set fire to your pants,' he repeated crossly, crossing the lawn.

'Already with the rules,' I said, following him out onto the main road.

Fighting in Trincomalee had ceased, and a slender ceasefire had prevailed for weeks. The German staff of *Der Spiegel* had returned to their home offices for other assignments. Horst, an Austrian stringer, had stayed on.

He was holding out for a new story: one that he could break without competition. He was hoping, in fact, that the Tamil Tigers would launch an offensive in the area, and that his faded-blue eyes would be the first eyes on a new war.

He was a tall, healthy, well-educated young man, in love with a girl, probably a nice girl, who lived on a farm in Normandy, and he was hoping for more war in Sri Lanka. *Journalism*, Didier once said to Ranjit, the media baron, *the cure that becomes its own disease.*

'You haven't got a camera?' Horst asked, after we'd walked and talked about Horst for about fifteen minutes.

'In my experience, checkpoints are allergic to any cameras but their own.'

'True,' he agreed, 'but there was a severed head on the road, yesterday. The first one for a month.'

'Uh-huh.'

'And . . . if we see another one today . . . I'm not going to share the pictures.'

'Okay.'

'It's not my fault that you left your camera.'

'Got it.'

'Just, you know, so we're straight on that, okay?'

'I don't want your pictures of severed heads, Horst. I don't even want to think about them. If there's another severed head on this road, he's all yours.'

There was another severed head on that road, only fifty metres further along.

At first, I thought it was a trick: a pumpkin, or a squash, shoved onto a pole as a macabre joke. In a few steps, I saw that he was a dead kid, maybe sixteen or seventeen.

His head was propped on a bamboo pole, driven into the ground so that the boy's dead face was face to face with any living face that passed, on the main road.

The eyes were shut. The mouth was wide open.

Horst was adjusting his camera.

'I told you so,' he said. 'I told you so.'

I started to walk along the road. He called out to me.

'Where are you going?'

'Catch me up.'

'No, no! It's not safe, alone on this road. That's why I wanted to walk together. You should stay with me. I mean, for *your* safety.'

I kept walking.

'Two, in two days!' Horst said, as distance lost him. 'Something's up. I can feel it. I *knew* I was right to stay.'

He was clicking his camera.

Click-clack. Click-clack.

Killing the kid was a crime, but spiking his head was a sin, and sin always demands expiation. My heart wanted to find a way to return the kid's head to his parents, help them find the rest of him, somehow, and lay him to rest.

But I couldn't listen to my heart. I couldn't even lay his dead young head on the earth, which every instinct inside me cried to do. I had a vest full of gold and passports, and my own passport was as false as my journalist accreditation. I was a smuggler, on a mission, and I had to walk away.

Alone on the road I grieved for that kid, whoever he was, whatever he'd done. I walked on, finding my hard face again, trying to lose all thought of it in the jungle, bright in a brief halo of sunlight between storms.

Trees were plentiful, growing tall and strong in nurseries of shrubs and plants, some waist-high, some reaching to my shoulders.

The leaves shivered drops of the last rain onto the thick roots of the trees: devotees pouring scented oil on the feet of tree-saints, whose raised-arm branches, and million-hand leaves had prayed the storm from the sea. *Without trees to pray for it, there's no rain*, Lisa once said to me, as we'd rushed out to enjoy a warm, monsoon rainstorm.

Winds from the sea pacified storm-shaken trees. Branches dipped and swayed, foaming leaves waving with the sound of surf on the shore of the sky. Birds hovered and swooped, vanishing in walls of green, and darting out again, their shadows glittering on the wet road.

Nature was healing me, as Nature does, when we let it. I stopped grieving for the lost kid beside the road, and the lost kid inside me, and I stopped saying the words *severed head*.

A car approached me from the north. It was a battered white sedan, with the headlights covered in stars of black tape. The driver was a woman. She was chunky. She was short. She was thirty. She was wearing a sky-blue hijab.

She stopped beside me and leaned over to roll down the window.

'What the fuck do you think you're doing?' she demanded.

'I –'

'Don't tell me.'

'But, you just asked –'

'Get in the car.'

'Who are you, again?'

'Get in the car.'

I got in the car.

'You're compromised,' she said, a pinched frown of contempt looking me up and down.

'*Salaam aleikum*,' I said.

'You're compromised,' she repeated.

'*Salaam aleikum*,' I said.

'*Wa aleikum salaam*,' she replied, squinting at me angrily. 'We've got to get out of here.'

She drove off but in a few seconds we saw Horst, still standing beside the kid's head, still trying to get that perfect shot. She wanted to drive on but I stopped her, some ten metres past the journalist.

'He'll ask questions, if I disappear from the road. Let me handle this.'

I got out of the car, and jogged back to Horst.

'What's going on? Who's that with you?'

'I've just heard,' I said breathlessly. 'Fighting has started again. I'm getting the hell out of here. You want a ride back to the hotel?'

His eyes narrowed, as he looked north on the deserted road.

'No, see, I think I'll hang around. You go. It's okay.'

'I don't like to leave you like this, when it's getting dangerous.'

'No, no, I'm fine. I'll go see what's happening at the checkpoint. You go on.'

He fumbled with the camera, and offered his hand. I shook it.

'Good luck,' I said.

'Same to you. And do me a favour? Since you're going, keep this to yourself for as long as you can, okay?'

'Not a problem. Bye, Horst.'

He was already walking away, preparing his camera.

Click-clack.

When I got back in the car, I saw that Blue Hijab had a pistol in her hand. She was pointing it at me.

'All good,' I said.

She drove off at speed, one handed. She was changing gears with the hand that held the pistol, and making me nervous enough to flinch as she nudged the lever violently with the heel of her hand.

'What are you two, sweethearts?' she demanded. 'Blah, blah, blah. What did you tell him?'

'What he wanted to hear. Are you going to shoot me?'

She seemed to consider it.

'I don't know,' she said. 'What did you tell that man? Whose side are you on?'

'Your side, I hope. And if you shoot me, you'll put a hole in one of the passports.'

She swung the car into a clearing that became a parking bay amid the trees. She turned off the engine, and put both hands on the gun.

'You think this is funny? I'm dragged from a cover that I've worked on for two years, to pick you up at the hotel, collect the stuff, and drive you to the airport.'

'A cover? What are you, a spy?'

'Shut up.'

'Aaah . . . okay, who are you again?'

'I find you on the road, alone,' she said, staring enigmas at me. 'Then you stop to talk to a stranger. Convince me this isn't a mistake, or by Allah I'll put a bullet in your head, and strip the gold off your body.'

'If you know your Holy Koran,' I said, 'it should be enough for me to give you the number of a verse.'

'What the hell?'

'Two, two hundred and twenty-four,' I said.

'The Cow,' she sneered, giving the name of the verse from the Koran. 'Are you trying to make a point about me? Are you saying I'm fat?'

'Of course, not. You're . . . curvy.'

'Cut it out.'

'You started it.'

'Back to the verse, smart guy.'

'If you're *not* a Muslim, and you're gonna learn a few verses from the Koran, verse two, two hundred and twenty-four, is a nice place to start. *And make not Allah's name an excuse in your oaths against doing good and acting piously —*'

'*— and making peace among mankind*,' she finished for me, smiling for the first time.

'Shall we do this?' I asked, beginning to wrestle out of my jacket.

She put the gun in a pocket of her skirt, opened the back door of the car, and began to pull the back seat upright.

There was a hiding place underneath, behind a false cover. When I handed her the vest, she did a thorough check of every pocket and each passport.

Satisfied, she put the vest into the hiding place, and concealed it with the snap-fit cover. The seat clicked back into place, and we got back in the car.

'We'll stop at the hotel,' she said, driving off. 'You have to check out. We need you to be a ghost from here.'

'A ghost?'

'Shut up. We're here. Go inside, get your stuff and check out. I'll put petrol in the car, and meet you here in fifteen minutes. Not a second more.'

'Do you —'

'Get out!'

I got out. I ran the steps, entered the reception area and heard my name.

'Mr Davis!'

It was Ankit, the night-and-day porter, standing in a bay window. He had a tray in his hand.

'I saw Blue Hijab,' he said, as I approached him, 'and thought you might be needing this.'

I took a long sip of the long drink.

'They don't call you *The Complete* for nothing, Ankit.'

'One strives to please, sir. Your things are with me at the desk. You need only sign the register, when you're ready.'

'Let's do it now.'

'You've got a six-hour drive ahead. I'm here, if you want to take a minute to freshen up.'

When I returned, Ankit had refilled the drink, and there was a packet of sandwiches, some water, and two bottles of soft drink beside my backpack on the counter.

I gave him a small roll of money. It was about five hundred American.

'No, I can't take this,' he said. 'It's too much.'

'We may never see each other again, Ankit. Let's not part fighting.'

He smiled, and put the money away.

'The snacks will keep you going, and this might help, if things get . . . a little tense . . . with Blue Hijab.'

It was a dime of hashish, and a packet of cigarettes.

'I should smoke hash, if things get tense with an armed, angry woman?' I asked, accepting the gift.

'No,' he said. '*She* should.'

'Blue Hijab smokes hash?'

'Loves the stuff,' Ankit said, packing the drinks and food into my backpack. 'It's like catnip. But save it, for as long as you can. She gets mean when it runs out.'

A car stopped hard outside. The horn sounded three times.

'You should imagine that she's Durga, the warrior goddess, mounted on a tiger, and behave accordingly.'

'How's that, exactly?'

'Be respectful, devoted and afraid,' Ankit said, wagging his head wickedly.

'It's been a pleasure, new-old friend. Goodbye.'

I turned at the door to see him smiling and waving. I looked back at the car to see Blue Hijab, jabbing a finger at me, the engine of the car revving.

We roared out of the driveway and onto the main road, heading south toward Colombo. She leaned forward in her seat, her arms taut and her knuckles white.

After ten minutes of listening to her teeth grinding the pepper of her temper, I decided to make conversation.

'I met your husband, Mehmu.'

'*This* is how you break a serene silence? With mention of my bloody husband?'

'Serene? I've seen more serenity under interrogation.'

'To hell with you,' she said, but she relaxed against the seat, drained of rage. 'I've been . . . tense. And I don't want to get any tenser.'

I wanted to say something funny, but she had a gun.

She drove well. I studied her style for a while as she passed trucks, slowed for temporary barriers, and hit sharp corners. I love being driven by a driver I trust. It's a rollercoaster, with fatal risk.

The windscreen was a bubble, moving through space and time. Tree shadows arched over the car as we passed, trying to comfort us as the forests ended and fenced houses became beads and baubles on another chain of civilisation.

'I shot a man, yesterday,' she said, after a while.

'A friend or an enemy?'

'Does it make a difference?'

'Hell, yeah.'

'He was an enemy.'

We drove in silence, for a while.

'Did you kill him?' I asked.

'No.'

'Could you have killed him?'

'Yes.'

'The mercy outweighs the shame,' I said.

'Fuck you,' she said.

'All that cursing isn't exactly in line with Islam, is it?'

'It's in English, it doesn't count, and I'm a Muslim communist,' she said.

'O . . . kay.'

She pulled the car into a roadside stop amid fields of flowers, sprung from sodden earth. She looked around, and turned the engine off.

'Did Mehmu look well?'

'He did.'

'Really?'

'Yeah, I like him. A lot, actually.'

She sobbed, suddenly, tears falling as freely as the raindrops that began to spatter the windows.

Just as quickly she recovered, dried her eyes, and began to open the bag of sandwiches.

She cried again, and couldn't stop: something inside her was all of it, everything at once. I didn't know what it was: I didn't know her.

382

I saw the new-moon chips of nail polish near her cuticles, the bruise on her face, about the size of a man's ring, the cuts on her own knuckles, the fragrance of fresh soap in her clothes, hand-washed in a hotel basin, the bag on the back seat, carrying essentials for a quick escape, and the quick escape she made every time her eyes detected that I might be looking into her, and not just at her.

But observation only took me to a tough, brave, devout girl on the run, who's meticulous in her hygiene, but won't clean the last coloured fragment of the girl she was from her fingernails. The *why* of her was still a mystery, because the why of anyone only comes with connection.

I felt helpless to console her. There were tissues in the bag. I handed them to her, one at a time, until the tears dried and the sobbing stopped, as the rain all around us stopped.

We got out and stood by the car. I tipped a stream of water from a bottle into her cupped hands, so that she could wash her face.

She stood there for a while, breathing air scented by white flowers, clinging to vines all around us.

We got back in the car, and I mixed a cigarette joint. She wouldn't pass it back to me, so I mixed another. She wouldn't give that back either, so I made a couple more cigarettes.

Minds floated free across fields of green velvet to memory's greener pastures: that place, inside, where the soul is always a tourist. And I don't know what memories danced for Blue Hijab, in those minutes, but for me it was Karla, turning and twirling, as she danced at the party. Karla.

'I'm starving,' Blue Hijab said. 'And by the way —'

'I know. If I speak a word of this to anyone, you'll shoot me.'

'I was going to say, thank you. But damn right. Pass me a sandwich.'

She started the car, and eased it out of the parking bay.

'You don't want me to take over for a while?'

'I drive,' she said, heading out onto the highway again, at speed. 'I always drive. Give me a sandwich.'

'What kind do you want?'

'Give me one of those I-don't-give-a-fuck sandwiches. You got one of those?'

'A whole sack, as it turns out.'

She never spoke again on the trip. Sometimes she muttered *zikr*, phrases spoken in remembrance of God. Once, she broke into a chorus from a song, only to fade again in a few bars.

And when we stopped, before the road swerved into the entrance of the airport in Colombo, she simply turned the engine off and stared at me, in a continuation of that long silence, as strange as it was surprisingly sad.

'*I-muh'sinina*,' I said.

'*The doers of good?*' she translated.

'You were saying it, while you were driving.'

'Do you have a second passport?'

'Of course.'

'Get the first flight out that you can. Get home, as fast as you can. Do you hear me?'

'Get home, as fast as I can. Okay, Mummy.'

'Be serious. Do you need anything?'

'You never told me how the mission was compromised.'

'And I won't,' she said evenly.

'You're tighter with a story than a Reuters correspondent. Anyone ever tell you that, Blue Hijab?'

She laughed, and I was glad to see it.

'Go. Now.'

'Wait,' I said. 'I have something to give you. But if I do, you have to promise me something.'

'What . . . something?'

'Promise me not to shoot Mehmu . . . again. At least, not for something connected to me. I like the guy.'

'I *married* the guy,' she snarled. 'But okay, okay, I won't shoot him. I've already shot him twice, and he never stops whining about it.'

I took the small automatic from my pocket, took the spare shells from the other pocket, and handed them to her.

'I think he wanted me to give you this,' I said.

She cradled the small gun in her palms.

'Mehmu, *mehboob*,' she muttered, then tucked the gun away into another of the pockets in the pleated curtain of her black skirt. 'Thank you.'

I stood from the car, stooping to say goodbye.

'He's a very lucky man,' I said. '*Allah hafiz*.'

'Much luckier, now that I pledged not to shoot him again. *Allah hafiz*.'

She drove away, and I made my way on foot up the entrance ramp to the airport.

In forty-five minutes I'd checked in. I was lucky, or Blue Hijab's timing had been perfect. I only had an hour to wait.

I found a place where I could watch the people walking past, look at the faces, study the walk, see tension or empathy, lethargy or urgency, listen to the tenor of a laugh or a shout, feel a baby's cry ripple through the hearts of almost all who hear it: a still moment in a public space, watching and waiting for the expression or cadence that writes itself.

A man came to sit beside me. He was tall and thin, with a bushy moustache and slicked-back hair. He was wearing a yellow shirt and white trousers.

'Hello,' he said out loud, and then changed to a whisper. 'We should greet one another as friends, and go to the bar. I'm your contact here. It will look less suspicious if we're having a drink.'

He offered his hand. I took it, drawing him in closer.

'I think you've made a mistake, Jack,' I said, holding his hand fast in mine.

'It's okay,' he said. 'Blue Hijab called, and gave me your description.'

I released his hand and we stood together, pretend friends.

'Her description was perfect,' he said. 'She really studied you.'

'Somehow, that doesn't fill me with reassurance,' I said, as we walked to the airport bar.

'Hell, no,' he replied, throwing an arm around my shoulder. 'With Blue Hijab, it's better to keep it to fuzzy recollections.'

'What is it, with the communist connection?'

'When you're looking for fighters, the enemy of your enemy is a good place to start.'

'What does that mean?'

'I can't say any more than that.'

We talked the waiting minutes. He told me stories that might've been true, and I listened with what might've been belief, and then I cut him off before he started a new story.

'What's this all about?'

'What do you mean?'

'Nobody has an exit contact at the airport,' I said. 'And Blue Hijab said I was compromised. What's going on?'

He looked me over for a while, and seemed to conclude that my patience was drifting toward a storm. It was a good call.

'I can't say anything,' he said, looking away.

'You can. And you should. What the fuck is going on?'

'Going on?'

'Is there a threat to me in this airport, or not? Am I in danger? Am I gonna get busted? Spit it out, or spit your teeth out.'

'*You* are not in danger,' he said quickly. 'But you *are* the danger. I was sent to watch you, that you didn't do anything crazy.'

'Crazy?'

'Crazy.'

'Crazy, like, what?'

'They didn't say.'

'And you didn't ask?'

'Nobody asks. You know that.'

We looked at one another.

'What were you going to do, if I did something crazy?'

'Smooth it over with the authorities, and get you out of the country and back to Bombay as quick as possible.'

'That's it?'

'I swear. And I don't know any more.'

'Okay. Okay. I'm sorry for that crack, about spitting your teeth out. I felt like I was walking into a trap for a minute or two there.'

'*You* are not in danger,' he said comfortingly. 'But do not go directly to your house when you return.'

'What do you mean?'

'Just report to the Company as soon as you return.'

'Does this have something to do with how the mission was compromised?'

'I don't know. Sanjay was very specific about reporting to him. Very specific. But he didn't explain.'

My flight was called. We shook hands again, and he slipped away through the crowds.

I took my seat on the plane, and had two drinks before take-off. I'd done the job. It was over. It was my last mission for the Sanjay Company. I was free, and my heart, the fool in that castle in the sky, sang all the way to thirty thousand feet.

CHAPTER THIRTY-FIVE

I ARRIVED IN BOMBAY LATE, BUT LEOPOLD'S WAS STILL OPEN, and I knew Didier would probably be there. I wanted a report. The tall, thin airport contact had told me to go directly to the Company, which was unusual. I had a standing appointment with Sanjay, twenty-four hours after I returned from any mission. It was a mandatory cooling-off period, in case I was being followed, and Sanjay never varied that routine. But nothing about the job was usual policy, and none of it made sense. Before I went to my apartment, or Sanjay, I wanted Didier to tell me everything that had happened while I'd been away, and where Lisa was staying.

And Didier gave me a report, but not there.

We took a taxi in solemn silence. Didier answered every question with a raised hand. We stopped at a quiet place, with a view of the shrine at Haji Ali.

'Lisa is dead,' he told me, beside the windy sea, 'from an overdose of drugs.'

'What? What are you saying?'

'She is gone, Lin.'

'From drugs? What drugs?'

'Rohypnol,' Didier replied sadly.

'No. No.'

'Yes. Yes.'

'It's not possible.'

How could she be dead, I thought, *and me not feel it, not know it somehow, not sense it?*

'It is a fact, my friend. She is no more.'

Splinters of lost time stabbed at me. All the things I should've said and should've done with Lisa, all the minutes I didn't use to cherish her, everything stabbed me in the chest. I wasn't there, with her, at the end.

'It can't be true.'

'Sadly, it is true, Lin.'

I felt my knees wanting to run, or give way. A world without Lisa. Didier put an arm around me. We rested against the promenade wall.

A force of life drained away from me into the air. Atoms of love separated from the Source, because the world was turning too fast to hold them. The sky was hiding behind black cloaks of cloud, and the city-light on the water was the ocean crying. Something inside me was dying, and something else, a ghost, was trying to free itself.

I choked a breath, slowing my frantic heart, and faced my friend.

'Her family?'

'They were here,' he said. 'Very nice people.'

'Did you talk to them?'

'I did, and they talked to me, until they found out that I was *your* friend, as well as Lisa's. I am sorry to tell you, Lin, but they blame *you*, in part, for Lisa's death.'

'Me?'

'I spoke to them about you, for you, and for you and Lisa together, but they did not believe me. They do not know you, so it is easier for them to blame a stranger than to know the truth. They left the city yesterday, with the body of our sad, sweet Lisa.'

'She's gone? They took her home?'

'She's gone, Lin. I am so sorry. I am desolate.'

Cars passed us in swarms between traffic signals, leaving the wide boulevard open and then empty again. All along the sea wall people sat alone, in couples or in families, most of them gazing at the Haji Ali shrine, floating on the sea and lit for the soul.

'What happened? Tell me everything you know.'

'You are sure that you are ready, my friend? Could we get drunk first?'

'Let me have it.'

'Could *I* get drunk first?'

'Didier, come on.'

'I loved her, too, you know,' he said, taking a sip from his flask. 'And I've been through quite an ordeal, these last few days, without you.'

He put the flask away, took his brass cigarette case from his pocket, and selected a joint. Smoking peacefully for a few moments, he offered it to me.

'I'm good.'

'You're good?' he doubted, offering the joint again.

'I'm not good, but I'm okay. I'm . . . not-good-okay. Tell me what happened.'

'It was the night after you left. I —'

'*The night after?* That's five days ago.'

'I tried everything to find you, Lin. The Sanjay Company would not say a word, and I could not find Abdullah. I think that wherever he is, he still does not know, as you did not.'

Abdullah, my heart said. *Where are you?*

'He'll be hurt,' I said. 'He liked Lisa, and she always liked him.'

'Very much so. She was his Rakhi sister.'

'His Rakhi sister? She never told me that. And neither did he.'

A Rakhi is a simple bracelet that a girl can tie on a boy's wrist, indicating that from that day onwards he must behave as her brother, and defend her staunchly. The bracelet is a symbol of the new brother's victory, whenever he fights for her honour.

'I was her Rakhi brother too, Lin.'

'When did that happen?'

I had no idea that Lisa even participated in the Rakhi ceremony, let alone that she'd chosen Abdullah and Didier as Rakhi brothers.

'And it is my fault that she died,' he said quietly. 'I failed, in my duty to protect her, while you were away.'

He smoked for a while, refusing tears. He looked at me once, and started to speak, but when our eyes met he turned away. We both knew it was true: I'd left her in his care, and he'd promised to watch over her.

A street sweeper scraped his broom against the kerb. He looked up at me, and nodded amiably. I watched him swish and step, swish and step: a bayside boulevard, measured in sweeps of a broom.

'She pulled a prank on me,' Didier said. 'And it was not fair of her to do such a thing, because I trusted her.'

'Go on.'

'We . . . we were watching a selection of excellent French films, which I had chosen for her personally, when she suddenly developed a headache. She retired early to bed, and sent me out to buy a certain medicine. When I returned, I discovered that I had been tricked. I found a note, saying that she was attending a party, and would return at dawn.'

He sighed, shaking his head, as tears fell.

'Where did she go?'

'I learned that she was at a party for Bollywood movie stars, somewhere in Bandra. You know how many parties there are in Juhu and Bandra every night, and how late those parties run. I did not expect her to return before dawn, so I decided to remain awake, during the night, with Gemini, who never sleeps, and wait for her to call me. I left messages everywhere, including with your watchman.'

'You're saying what, Didier? You were supposed to keep her safe, and she's dead, and I don't get it, so far.'

'You are right, Lin, to condemn me.'

Who am I, to condemn anyone? I thought. And Lisa had played a lot of tricks on me, too. A few times she'd left me wondering for a long time where she was, and what she was doing.

'Okay, okay, Didier. I get it. Lisa knows . . . Lisa knew . . . how to escape. She was good at it. It's not your fault. Tell me the rest of it.'

'I left messages for her, as I said, and I went to play poker with Gemini George, at the Mahesh. I was playing cards when our Lisa died. One of the street boys sent a note to me that Lisa had just been found, dead. I was desolate.'

'And.'

'When the autopsy was performed –'

No. No. Lisa, cut open, organs removed. *Don't think of it. Don't picture it, in your mind.*

'An autopsy?'

'It was . . . it was not pleasant,' Didier said. 'The police report confirmed that she died from an overdose of tranquillisers. She was alone, when she was found.'

'Rohypnol?'

'Rohypnol,' Didier frowned. 'Did you ever know her to use it, recreationally?'

'Never. It doesn't make sense. She didn't do tranqs. She hated them, as much as I do. She didn't even like it when other people did them.'

'The police called it suicide, at first. They think she took a fatal dose of the drug intentionally.'

'Suicide? No way. She's a fighter.'

390

'She *was* a fighter, Lin. She is no more.'

Is hadn't become *was*, yet. Lisa was still too strong: I could hear her teasing laugh, every time I let my mind go to her.

'Derelict as I was in my duty, when she was alive,' Didier said, 'I ensured that the word *suicide* was removed from the record of her death. Her death is ruled as accidental, involving an accidentally fatal dose of the tranquilliser, Rohypnol. Lightning Dilip made me pay a tidy sum for it. That police station should establish itself as a bank. I would buy shares, if they did.'

'Who found her? The nightwatchman?'

'No, Lin, it was Karla who found her.'

'Karla?'

'She said that she had a late rendezvous with Lisa, at your apartment. When she arrived, she found the door open, walked inside, and found Lisa. She alerted the watchman, and he called an ambulance, and the police.'

'Karla?'

The ground was trembling, as if the waves were sweeping over the wall and through the road in murmured secrets.

'Yes. It was a terrible shock for her, but she was a tower of strength, as the English say.'

'What . . . what was that?'

'The police questioned Karla . . . quite physically, in fact. I advised her to leave the city, for some time, but she refused. It was Karla who helped Lisa's parents through the whole of the thing.'

'When was the last time you spoke to her?'

'The last time? Yesterday. There was a small service for Lisa at the Afghan Church, and she was there.'

'A service, for Lisa? Even though Lisa was gone?'

'Yes. Karla organised it.'

It was too much, too many hits in a single round: too long to the bell and a safe corner.

'Karla did it?'

'She did it alone, in fact. When she mentioned the idea to me, I offered to help, but she took charge of it herself.'

'Who else was there?'

'Her friends from the art gallery, a few of us from Leopold's, Kavita, Vikram, Johnny Cigar and his wife, Naveen Adair and Diva Devnani, the Zodiac Georges, and Stuart Vinson and his Norwegian girlfriend. Lisa's parents had already left the city, with her body, so it was a quiet affair.'

'Who spoke for Lisa?'

'No-one spoke. We just sat, silently, and then one by one we all left the church.'

Yesterday, when I should've been there, with others who loved Lisa. But yesterday I was staring at a severed head, on the side of the road. Yesterday, I was being warned by my tall, thin contact at the airport not to go home.

You are not in danger, he'd said. I hadn't been paying attention. I hadn't realised that what he'd said was specific to me. He'd hesitated, after the first word, for just an eyelid flicker: *You, are not in danger*.

He was telling me that *I* wasn't in danger, but that someone else was. Did he know? Did he already know that Lisa was dead, when he met me at the airport?

And then I remembered Blue Hijab's tears, the sadness in them, the long, silent stare, when she dropped me at the airport. Did she know about Lisa?

It happened days ago. The Sanjay Company knew, for sure: they knew everything that happened in their ward. I guessed that Sanjay was worried I might find out about Lisa somehow, at the airport, and lose control. He sent the thin man, in case I found out about Lisa, and compromised his mission.

'I have done some research, with Naveen Adair,' Didier said, examining me closely.

The ground was moving or my knees were moving as if I was back on the deck of the *Mitratta*. I couldn't focus on what Didier was saying. There was ocean-sound in most of my mind. *Lisa. Lisa. Lisa.*

'Lin?'

'Sorry, what?'

'I have been checking some facts, with Naveen.'

'What facts?'

'It is not possible to determine how the Rohypnol came to be in Lisa's hands, but we did find out who supplied it.'

'You did? How?'

'We examined the pills from the evidence locker, and they have very distinctive markings.'

'You stole police evidence?'

'No, of course not. I *bought* police evidence.'

'Well done. Whose dope was it?'

He hesitated, squinting at me, a net of concern covering his face.

'If I tell you, will you promise, truly, that you will not kill him without me?'

'Who is it?'

'Concannon,' he sighed.

That slippery slide shivered through the street again. I held the wall tighter, to stop falling. I couldn't tell if I was dizzy, or the world was unbalanced. Everything was out of sync.

I looked around me, trying to get my head straight. The night was new-moon clear. The stars were paled city light. Behind us cars passed in shoals, as fish passed in shoals before us, in the bay.

'She was not raped,' Didier said.

'What . . . did you say?'

'When this drug is involved, there is always a suspicion of rape,' he said softly. 'The police report said that there was no sign of rape. I . . . thought you should know that.'

I looked down at the waves, lapping and splashing on boulders at the base of the sea wall: waves cleaning shells and driftwood twigs from stony teeth, and soothing granite shoulders with patience, softened in the sea.

The waves laughed. The waves cried. That glorious living second, ending as wind, and sea, and earth: the waves laughed, and cried, calling me. I was falling, hard. I had to get a grip. I had to pull myself together. I needed my motorcycle.

'I have to go home,' I said.

'Of course. I will come with you.'

'Didier –'

'Why do you always fight affection, Lin? It is truly your great, personal flaw.'

'Didier –'

'No. When a friend wants to do a loving thing, you must allow him. What is love, but this?'

What is love, but this?

The words chanted themselves to me in the taxi, and only stopped when we reached the apartment, and sat down with the nightwatchman to ask about Lisa.

He cried for her, and for what we were for him: always happy, kind and generous, on every festival and name day.

When he calmed down, he told me that Lisa had returned around an hour after midnight, with two men in a black limousine.

One of the men returned to the car, after fifteen minutes or so, and drove away. The other man left about an hour later. Karla arrived a few minutes after, and called the watchman.

'Did you know the men?'

'No, sir.'

'What did they look like?'

'One was a foreigner. He was the first one to leave. He had a loud voice. He was walking with two sticks, and he was shouting in pain, like maybe he had a broken leg.'

'Or maybe two fresh bullet wounds in the leg,' Didier observed.

'Concannon. And the other man?'

'I never saw his face. He looked away from me, and he covered his mouth with a handkerchief, coming and going.'

'Did he have a car?'

'No, sir. He walked away, very fast, in the direction of Navy Club.'

'Did you get the number of the car?'

'Yes, sir.'

He went through his logbook, and gave me the number.

'I'm so sorry, sir. I should have —'

'Your job is to guard the gate, not the apartments. It's not your fault. She liked you. Very much. And I know you would've saved her, if you could, just like I would've done. It's okay.'

I gave him a chunk of money, asked him to keep his eyes open for the cops, and climbed the steps to my apartment.

I opened the door, walked through the living room and stepped into the bedroom. That place of quarrel and love, for us, had become a tomb for Lisa, alone.

The mattress she'd bought because she liked the seahorse pattern on the cover was stripped bare, but for two pillows at the head, and a pair of Lisa's well-worn, well-loved hemp sandals at the base.

After a minute, I stopped staring at the place where Lisa's breath had faded, and ceased, and stopped, and died, and I moved my eyes away.

The room was clean, and empty. Everything of hers was gone. I looked at the few things of mine that remained.

The red movie poster, Antonioni's *Blow Up*, art and abandon becoming death and desire, and the wooden horse head on the window sill, my belts, strung on a suit stand in the corner, the sword, in two pieces in the wall unit, and a few books.

And it was all: all there was of me in the apartment. Without Lisa's flowers and paintings and coloured sarongs, the place we'd called home was cold, and alone. *What is civilisation?* Idriss once remarked. *It's a woman, free to live as she wants.*

'There is a picture of her, in death, on that bed,' Didier said, standing in the doorway. 'It is in the police report. Do you want to see it?'

'No. No. Thanks.'

'I thought it might console you,' he said. 'She looked very, very peaceful. As if she simply went to sleep, forever.'

We listened to the silence, echoing off the walls in our hearts. Just the thought of that picture, of her dead sleep, made my stomach churn with dread.

'You are not safe, I am afraid, Lin,' Didier said. 'The police are very hot for you. If they come to know that you have returned to Bombay, they will come here, looking for you.'

He was right: right enough to shake me awake.

'Give me a hand,' I said, beginning to wrestle the heavy chest of drawers away from the wall.

We pushed the chest wide enough to expose the false back panel. It looked untouched. I released the cover.

'Have you got a man you can trust to hold my guns, a lot of money, some passports and half a key of the best Kashmiri that ever rolled down the Himalayas?'

'Yes, for ten per cent.'

'Of the money only?'

'Of the money.'

'Done. Call him here.'

'I must insist that he brings something to drink with him, Lin. Do you know how many hours it has been, since I last made contact with alcohol?'

'You drank from your flask three minutes ago.'

'The flask,' he sighed, genius to child, 'does not count. Shall I tell him to bring food, as well?'

'I don't want any food.'

'Good. Food is for people who don't have the courage to take drugs. And food kills half of the alcohol effect. There was a test done on a drunken mouse, once, or perhaps it was a drunken rat —'

'Just call him, Didier.'

I stuffed a few bundles of rupees in one inside pocket of my denim vest, and a bundle of US dollars in the other. I cut a piece off the Kashmiri key, and put the rest back in the compartment. I strapped on my knives in their scabbards.

After snapping the cover in place, I shoved the chest against the wall again, in case someone other than Didier's man entered the apartment.

Didier was in the open kitchen, searching through the cupboards.

'Not even cooking sherry,' he muttered, and then he saw me and smiled. 'My man, Tito, will be here in half an hour. How are you, my friend?'

'Not-good-okay,' I said absently.

I was looking at the refrigerator. The photographs that Lisa had taped to the door, photographs of her that she'd asked me to take, were gone. Strips of clear tape remained, framing empty spaces.

She'd insisted on tape, instead of magnets. *I hate magnets*, she said. *They're such treacherous things*.

'Her parents,' Didier said, 'gathered everything that was hers, and took it with them. There were many tears.'

I went to the bathroom and washed my face with cold water. It didn't work. I fell forward on my knees at the toilet, and emptied every dark, acid thing that was inside me.

Didier found me, and did the right guy thing. He backed away, and left me in pieces.

I washed up again, and looked into the mirror.

A photo that Lisa had pushed in the top of the mirror frame had been torn away. Lisa's face had been ripped from the picture, and only my foolish, smiling face remained. I took it down, tore it up and threw it in the bin.

Sitting in the living room, Didier and I drank strong, black coffee, and smoked strong, black Kashmiri. It was Lisa's stash: her perfect, heavenly high, only for the most special occasions, which was why I'd had to hide it with my things.

And when the brandy and the food arrived, with Tito, we drank a toast, with Lisa, to the loved.

Tito helped me shove the heavy chest away from the wall again.

'Nice,' he said, when he saw the guns, passports and money. 'Ten per cent.'

'Done.'

He began to stuff the bundles into a sack.

It was my safety net in the Island City, the stake I was bringing to the table as a partner with Didier: everything I owned that wasn't in my pockets, or my pack.

Tito was about to tie the sack closed, but I stopped him.

'Wait a minute.'

There was a place I hadn't looked, and that the police might've overlooked. There was a gas-fired hot water heater in a closet. Lisa had made a shelf on top of the heater to dry out some tripping mushrooms, which a friend had brought from Germany.

I opened the door and searched on top of the panel. There was a shoebox in the back. I saw the words REASONS WHY written on the end panel.

I pulled it toward me, feeling around inside, and my hand shivered through keepsakes and pictures as if through reeds in a pond.

They were simple things: a thin, silver scarf she'd worn, the first time we met, a wind-up child's toy, a brass Zippo lighter that Didier had given to us as a housewarming present, and that she couldn't bear to let me use, for fear that I might lose it, which I would've done, a dog whistle that she used whenever we walked on Marine Drive, so she could get the attention of every dog she passed, a paperweight I'd made for her from silver rings, and a scatter of stones, shells, pictures, amulets and coins.

It was a box of nothings, bits of stuff that had no value or meaning for anyone else in the world. *And isn't that love, Lisa*, I thought, looking at the box of charms. When it means nothing to anybody else, and it means everything to us, isn't that love? *Didn't we love, Lisa? Didn't we love?*

I put the box in Tito's sack along with the pieces of Khaderbhai's sword and the pair of Lisa's hemp sandals. He tied it tightly, and slung it over his shoulder.

'What's your family name?' I asked him.

I was studying his face. It was an important face. He had all my worldly goods in his hands, and we'd known each other fourteen minutes. I wanted to recognise that face, no matter how it changed.

'Deshpande,' he said.

'Take care of our percentages, Mr Deshpande.'

'No tension,' he laughed.

We shook hands. He nodded to Didier, and trotted down the stairs.

'So, how do we kill him?' Didier asked, pouring a measure of brandy, after Tito left.

'Kill who?'

'Concannon, of course.'

'I don't want to kill Concannon. I want to find him, and make him tell me who bought that dope off him, and gave it to Lisa.'

'I would recommend that we do both,' he mused.

'I need to talk to Naveen,' I said. 'Can you call him, and set it up? I have to report to Sanjay, early in the afternoon. Tell Naveen I'll meet him at five, at Afghan Church, if he can make it.'

'Certainly. Do you know when Abdullah returns?'

'No.'

'You need him now, inside the Company.'

'I know.'

I looked around the room, and into the bedroom beyond.

'I'm gonna sleep here, tonight.'

'Surely not?' Didier protested. 'It is not secure. I know a place, near Metro. The manager has a splendid collection of manias and obsessions. You will love him. Let me take you there, now.'

'I'm gonna sleep here.'

'You, my friend, are –' he began, but then laughed. 'Well, if there is no persuading you, then Didier will sleep in this place of such sadness and sorrow with you.'

'You don't have to –'

'Didier insists! But on the couch, of course. And thank my foresight, in asking Tito to bring two bottles.'

I slept on the floor, beside Lisa's bed, with the pillow that was hers. Didier slept like a child, his arms and legs flung wide, on the couch.

Morning stumbled into a cold breakfast of the food I couldn't eat the night before, and brandy with a dash of coffee in it.

We cleaned the kitchen, and Didier joined me at the door of the apartment that he'd visited so often: that place where love had laughed for the last time.

'I'm ashamed,' he said softly. 'I'm so ashamed, Lin.'

'Shame is the past. If it isn't now, it soon will be.'

He thought for a moment.

'That's one of Karla's, isn't it?'

'Of course.'

We both thought, for a while.

'When you see her —'

'Didier.'

'No, I was going to say, when you see Karla, be gentle with her.'

'I'll talk nice to Karla. I always talk nice to Karla. I want to ask her how come she was the one who found Lisa's body. You just get all those eyes and ears of yours on Concannon, Didier. And set it up for me with Naveen. Are we good?'

I was trying to move, trying to escape from the cage of sorrow, and Didier knew it. We stood in silence for a while, staring at the empty rooms, before he spoke.

'I am not-good-okay, my friend. Shall we ... I mean, if you will permit it, I would like to say some words, for Lisa, here at this door that we will never open again.'

'Nice idea. Go ahead.'

'Lisa, we loved you, and you knew that, in your heart. We loved your smile, and your free mind, and your habit of dancing for no reason, and your cheating at charades, and the way you loved us all, every time you saw us. But most of all, we loved your sincerity. You never faked it, Lisa, as you Americans say. You were always the real person. If there is any essence of your spirit lingering here, come into our hearts, now, and stay with us, when we leave this place where you left us, so that we can carry you inside us, and always love you.'

'Didier,' I said, after a while. 'Thank you. That was really nicely put.'

'Of course,' he replied, pulling me through the door, and closing it for the last time. 'If you could only hear the words that I have prepared for you, my dear friend.'

'You already wrote lines for when I'm dead?' I asked, taking the stairs.

'Didier should not be caught on the hop, as they say. Especially if it concerns a beloved friend.'

'I ... guess not. Have you composed farewells for all your beloved friends?'

'No, Lin,' he said, as we reached the courtyard of the building. 'Only you. I have only written such words for you. What I said just now for Lisa, it was from my heart. And you, my still-living friend, are attracting interest from bookmakers, ready to give odds on your survival outside the Sanjay Company.'

I looked back at the apartment building. Without her body to see dead, and believe dead, the apartment we'd shared was all I had of her, and what we were. It had been a light, happy place for both of us, most of the time. But I knew that for me alone, every time I saw it would be a conversation with the ghost of God.

CHAPTER THIRTY-SIX

IT WAS HARDER TO GET INTO RANJIT's media headquarters than it was to break out of prison. After three levels of security, each one checking my VISITOR tag and none checking my metal, I finally reached his private secretary.

'The name is Shantaram,' I said, for the fourth time. 'It's a private, and personal, matter.'

She picked up a phone, spoke the mantra, and then opened the door.

Ranjit rose from his leather chair, extending his hand over the desk. The secretary left, closing the door.

'Sit down,' I said.

'What do you —'

'All that security, and no-one thought to ask me if I was carrying a gun.'

'A gun?' he gasped.

'Sit down.'

He sat down, his hands floating on the glass-topped desk.

'Where's Karla?'

'Karla? You're here about Karla?'

'Where's Karla?'

'Why?'

'Pick up the phone.'

'What?'

'Pick up the phone, and call Karla.'

'Why don't . . . why don't *you* call her?'

'I don't like phones. And I don't need one, because I can make you call her for me. You see that, right?'

'See . . . what?'

'Call Karla.'

'I –'

'Call Karla.'

'You call me,' Karla's voice said from behind me, 'and I come.'

She was sitting in an armchair in a corner of the large office. Potted palms beside her chair had hidden her from sight.

She seemed angry, and very glad to see me. I'd walked into a fight they'd been having.

'Hello, Karla. In the corner for bad behaviour?'

'Ranjit and I have a new agreement,' she said, lighting a cigarette, shafts of light and dark on her face through the palm leaves. 'If we find ourselves in the same room, we sit as far apart as we can.'

'Are you done here?' I asked, staring into queens.

Ranjit laughed. I faced him. The laugh stopped so quickly that he almost choked on it.

'What are you laughing at?'

'I . . . well . . . I . . . really have no idea.'

He was terrified. It didn't make sense. Sure, I'd mentioned a gun, but I wasn't carrying one, and Karla was there, and she was. He was safe, but he was sweating hard.

'You know that expression, where you tell someone they look like they've seen a ghost?'

'I . . . I suppose,' he replied.

'Well, you look like the ghost.'

'The . . . ghost? *Whose* ghost?'

'What's wrong with you?'

'You . . . said you had a gun.'

He was shaking.

'I said that no-one thought to *ask* me if I was carrying a gun. I didn't say I had one.'

'Well, yes . . . I mean, no.'

'Is there anything you want to tell me, Ranjit?'

'No!' he said quickly. 'Nothing at all.'

'What do you know about Lisa's death?'

'Nothing. Nothing. The poor girl. A tragic accident. That is, I mean . . . nothing at all.'

'Goodbye, Ranjit, and please don't wait up,' Karla said, standing, and walking to the door.

I opened the door for her and we left the office. Ranjit was still sitting in his chair, his hands splayed on the desk as if he was trying to stop it floating away.

When the elevator doors closed, she took out a flask, drank a sip, closed it and turned to me, all queens.

'Do you think I had something to do with her death?'

'*What?*'

'The cops did. Worked me over pretty good. Only left bruises where I won't show.'

I felt my stomach drop. Anger filled the empty inside.

'Lightning Dilip?'

'He sends his regards,' she said.

The doors opened on a small crowd in the lobby. She stopped me in the doorway, blocking the people. Our faces were inches apart.

'I didn't have anything to do with it,' she said. 'I would never hurt Lisa. Or let anyone else hurt her.'

'Of course not,' I replied, but she was already gone.

I made my way to the desk, hurled the visitor tag across the counter, and bounced through people until I found Karla, unruffled, a little way from the front entrance.

We rode to the Bandra sea-face. She clung to my back, her face pressed into me, a ready-to-die passenger.

I could've gone to a dozen places closer, but I needed to ride. When we stopped, near the sea, I was as calm as the waves on the bay.

We walked that little smile of the coast in the midday heat, but we were comfortable: two foreigners who'd learned to love a sun-blessed city.

'We had a date,' she said, as we walked.

'We had a date?'

'No.'

I thought about it.

'You and Lisa had a date?'

'Yeah.'

We walked on for a while, and then I got it.

'You mean, you and Lisa had a *date*-date?'

'Kind of.'

'Kind of?'

'Kind of.'

'There's no kind-of *date*-date.'

'There was always this . . . *thing* between us, you know —'

'A thing, huh?'

'On her side, sure.'

'And this thing took you there that night?'

'She said she wanted to have a little booze, and a lotta fun, or a lotta booze, and a little fun.'

'I'm not understanding this.'

'It was her plan.'

'What plan?'

'I said I'd go three or four drinks with her, and see what happened after that. She said you were cool with it.'

'Really?'

'Yeah,' she frowned.

We walked on a few more steps in silence, our shadows clinging to us, hiding from the heat.

'And with you, and the *date*-date? Was that serious?'

'Not for me,' she smiled, and then frowned her gaze at our feet. 'Lisa was a flirt. She couldn't help herself. I played along, because she liked it when I did.'

'I'm sorry, Karla. I'm sorry I wasn't here to stop this, and to stop you being the one to find her. If I could take that from you, I would.'

'The only beauty the past has is that it can't be changed. There was nothing you could've done, and there's nothing you can do now.'

'It . . . must've been . . . so hard, finding her.'

'The door was open,' she said, staring at her feet. 'She was on the bed. I thought she was asleep. Then I saw how still she was, and the bag of pills. I shook her, but she was gone. Cold. I got the watchman to call the ambulance and the cops, but she was gone, Lin. She was long gone, poor baby.'

I put my arm around her, and she settled into me, as softly as married.

'Who was with her?' I asked. 'Who gave her the stuff?'

'I don't know, yet. I've been trying to find out, but I haven't mixed in those circles for a while.'

'When the cops . . . worked you over, did they let anything slip?'

'Only that they want *your* ass pretty bad,' she said. 'That came in clear as a boot on the spine. And I could see their point. Let's face it, you vanish from the city, and your girlfriend dies. Or was it the other way around?'

'Wait a minute,' I asked, pulling my arm away from her to look into her eyes. 'You can't think I'd hurt Lisa? You can't think that.'

She laughed. It was the first time she'd laughed since I'd seen her in Ranjit's office, sitting behind the plants.

'It's good to see you laugh, Karla.'

'It's the first time since I found her. I've been uncomfortably numb for a while, and hazing purple most of the time. Of course you wouldn't hurt her. I wouldn't love you, if you could.'

She turned to the sea, the wind clearing her face for the sun. The breeze made lines of sea-foam music and frothy notes on parallel waves in the mouth of the bay.

'Karla, what the hell happened? What do *you* think happened?'

'I told you, I don't know yet. Where the fuck were *you*, anyway?'

Where was I?

Click-clack. Severed head. Blue Hijab.

'I had a job. Have you heard anything from Abdullah?'

'No, but he has my number, and he always calls me when he gets back to town.'

'Abdullah has your number?'

'Of course.'

'I don't have your number.'

'You don't use phones, Shantaram.'

'That's not the point.'

'And the point is?'

'Well —'

'I'm not going back to Ranjit,' she said quickly, not smiling.

'What? I mean, good, but what?'

'I'm already checked in at the Taj.'

'The Taj?'

'My things will arrive by evening.'

'You're not going home, to Ranjit?'

'Let me tell you, if you're gonna make a move, Shantaram, this is your time.'

The worst part of being in love with a woman who's smarter than you are, is that you can't stop coming back for more, which, as it happens, is also the best part.

'What?'

'What did you tell me, once,' she asked, not wanting an answer, 'about *before*, and *after*?'

'I . . . ah . . .'

405

'*After* just started, Lin. After started today. You can't go home. I won't go home. The only question is, are you in it with me, or in it without me?'

I felt stupid not understanding what she was telling me, and looking back now, I guess I was. But I didn't know what decisions she'd made, or why she was telling me then.

Seconds fell, pollen in the wind. It was everything. It was nothing.

'We just lost Lisa,' I said. 'We just lost Lisa.'

'Lisa would —'

She cut herself off, laughed again, and gave me about eight unhappy queens.

'*Jesus!*' she said. 'Am I . . . actually . . . trying to talk *you* . . . into coming with *me*?'

'Well, I —'

'Fuck you,' she said.

'Fuck . . . me?'

She stood quickly, and hailed a taxi.

'Wait a minute, Karla.'

She got in the cab, and drove away.

I sprinted to the bike, and rode too fast and too loose until I found her cab. I followed her all the way back to the Taj hotel, riding around her cab and trying to catch her eye. She never turned to look.

I parked the bike, and watched her climb the wide steps and walk into the hotel. I went to the reservations desk, and left a note for her.

I rode away from the proud galleon of the Taj hotel through rivers of traffic, and questioned every man or woman I could still trust about Concannon. I checked gambling dens, opium parlours, country liquor bars, hash hangouts and numbers-racket corners. I didn't learn much, but street voices confirmed that Concannon was running a heroin franchise for the Scorpion Company.

Everyone called them the Scorpion Company, rather than the Scorpion Gang: everyone recognised their status as a full mafia Company.

I had to report to Sanjay. I had a standing appointment for two in the afternoon on the day after my return from Sri Lanka, whatever the date.

No doubt, Sanjay had expected me to report sooner. He wouldn't be in a good mood. But that was okay. Since the death of his friend Salman, Sanjay didn't have a good mood.

I parked the bike in a row of motorcycles outside KC College. I gave the parking attendant a hundred-rupee note, and asked him to keep his eyes open for dangerous types.

'They're college kids,' he said in Hindi. 'They're *all* dangerous. Who knows what they'll do next?'

'More dangerous than the kids are.'

'Oh, okay. You got it,' he winked.

I walked the half-block to Sanjay's mansion, and rang the bell. An armed Afghan guard opened the door, recognised me and ushered me inside.

I found Sanjay in the breakfast room, at the end of the house. A row of windows looked out on a distressed garden, bound by high walls. Sanjay was in his pyjamas and a dark blue dressing-gown with a monogrammed pocket.

A breakfast big enough for three big henchmen covered the table, but Sanjay was drinking tea, and smoking a cigarette.

There was only one chair in the room, and Sanjay didn't rise from it.

'Good work,' he said, looking me up and down. 'But then, you always did good work, didn't you? Your money, for this job, will be delivered to you. All your things from the passport factory have been removed. They're in that red case, near the front door. That leaves only goodbye. So, goodbye.'

'How was the mission compromised? Why did I come home early?'

He stubbed out the cigarette, took a sip of tea, placed the cup very delicately on the saucer and leaned back in the chair.

'You know why I'm glad to see you go, Lin?' he asked.

'Because you think I'm made for better things?'

He laughed. I'd known him for years, but I'd never heard that laugh before. It must've been one he saved for the right goodbye. Then he stopped laughing.

'Because, you're not a team player,' he said grimly, 'and you never will be. You're a black sheep. Look around you. Everyone belongs to something or someone. You're the odd man out. You don't belong anywhere. You don't belong to anyone. And now, you don't belong here.'

'Was it because Lisa died? Is that why you had a man at the airport?'

'Like I said, you're not a team player. There was no way to know how you'd react. You were in Madras, when it happened.'

'When did you know?'

'Five minutes after the cops, of course. But you had already started, and the job was too important to stop.'

'Five minutes?'

'You never use the phone, so I knew there was a good chance you wouldn't come to know about it. It was my decision to keep it quiet until the job was complete, and it was my decision to have contacts for you, every step of the way.'

'Your decision.'

'Yes. If you don't like it, well, you know, there's always the fuck-you option.'

'You didn't tell me that my girlfriend died.'

'*You're* the one who wanted to keep her out of the family. It was *your* choice that we never met her, when we know the Mothers, sisters and wives of every brother in the Company.'

I looked at him, angry enough to fight him. My heart was thumping tribal music. I wondered how many times leaders lived through murderous seconds like those, without ever knowing that Death, Himself, had been lured into the room on a false alarm.

'You still have a faint shadow of my protection,' Sanjay said. 'It covers you, because it would not look well for *me*, if a former employee was killed in the first two weeks that he left my service. But the clock is ticking. Don't make me brush that shadow from your back sooner. Now, get the fuck out of here, and let me finish my breakfast in peace.'

I opened the door and was about to leave, but he spoke again. They always speak again: they always want the last word, even when they already had it.

'I'm sorry about your girl,' he said. 'It's a sad business. Must be hell for her family. But don't let your feelings push you into hasty action. The Company will let you burn, the next time you fuck up.'

I left the mansion and rode to the food stands for office workers at Nariman Point. I was still angry, and hungry. Standing with dozens of others, I ate hot bread rolls, filled with eggs, fried potatoes and spiced vegetables, and drank a pint of milk.

I'd been skipping meals, and ducking sleep. I had to work out. I had to stay sharp. Every street guy in the south would know within hours that I was officially out of the Company. There were a few, with grudges, who'd only held back because I was a Company man. They could come out snapping, when they knew I was a lone wolf.

408

Half an hour's ride away on that cold river of truth was a gym, in Worli. Some abandoned mill complexes had been transformed into beauty parlours and health centres. A retired gangster from the Sanjay Company, named Comanche, had set up a gym there as his home and place of business.

He was a friend, a stand-up gangster, and we'd fought with knives against rival gangs together, twice, and been cut both times. That's stuff you don't forget.

Comanche was a true independent, allowing members of any mafia Company to exercise in his gym, and cops as well, so long as no-one said a word against the Sanjay Company.

I stripped to jeans and boots, and pushed weight for an hour. Half an hour of shadow boxing gave me a cool-down.

The kids in the gym, all local and poor, were shy at first, although doing the young manhood thing of making sure I clearly understood they weren't afraid. When they saw that I was okay, they joined in the shadow boxing with me, training hard.

Showered, dressed and refreshed, I looked in the spotted mirror.

My eyes were bright, and clear. Calm settled on me like flakes of autumn. *When all else fails*, the sign above the mirror said, *steel it out*.

'You need a lat machine,' I said to Comanche, passing him enough money to buy a new lat machine.

Comanche looked at the money.

'That was an expensive training session,' he said, frowning.

'Loved every minute of it. But put a little window in there, yaar. If someone ever forces me to imagine what a snake's asshole smells like, I now know where to start.'

'Fuck you,' he laughed. 'Seriously, what's the money for?'

'I'm hoping you'll consider it a membership fee.'

'But Company men are free. You know that.'

'I'm not with the Company any more, Comanche. I'm freelance, now.'

I hadn't said it to anyone but a close friend, and after so long in the brotherhood it sounded strange, even in my own ears.

'What?'

'I'm out, Comanche.'

'But, Lin, it's —'

'It's okay. Sanjay's good with it. Happy, in fact.'

'Sanjay's . . . Sanjay's . . . *good* with it?'

'I just came from there, man. He's good with it.'

'He is?'

'My word.'

'Okay.'

'But, I'll need a new place to train, now that I can't use the Company gym. So, how about it? Will you have me as a member?'

He was confused and afraid, but he was a friend, and he trusted me. His face gradually softened, and he extended his hand.

'*Jarur*,' he said, shaking hands. 'You're welcome here. But I have to say, you'd be wiser to leave Bombay, man, under the circumstances.'

'Maybe, brother,' I said, walking away. 'But would She let me go?'

CHAPTER THIRTY-SEVEN

Karla will be pleased
to accept the company of Shantaram
at 8 pm, in her suite.

It was written in her hand: the precise, fluent script I liked more than any other calligraphic style I'd ever seen. I wanted to keep it, but I was trading punches with a dirty world: if an enemy put his fingers on the note, I'd want to beat him for it.

I sat on the bike, burned the note, and then rode slowly toward Afghan Church to meet with Naveen.

I parked the bike behind a nearby bus stand. When I was with the Sanjay Company, I parked on any footpath in town. As a freelancer, I parked my bike out of sight.

The commemoration nave in the church featured dusty flags and pennants, with stone inscriptions to soldiers lost in two Afghan wars.

It was a military church and a battle chapel, erected as a monument to the fallen. There were still grooves in the pews for unforgotten soldiers to rest their rifles when they prayed, before and after obeying the order to kill Afghans, a people whose language they couldn't speak, and whose culture they couldn't understand.

The mournful church was almost empty. An elderly lady was sitting in a rear pew, reading a novel. A man and a boy knelt on the approach to the altar. The circle of stained glass above the altar seemed to float above their heads.

Naveen Adair was examining the brass eagle supporting the Bible stand. He was young, but confident. His hands were behind his back, respectfully, but his step was strong as he paced back and forth: a young man, fully inhabiting the space of his life.

He saw me watching him, and followed me to the deserted garden behind the church.

We sat beneath a tree, on a support made of stone and cement.

It was quiet. The fading light of evening became the stained-glass light of the altar window above our heads, lighting the dark garden below with church-light.

'I'm so sorry about Lisa, man,' he said.

'Me, too. Naveen, gimme a minute, will you?'

I had to be quiet, for a minute.

I had to think, for a minute.

I hadn't stopped, to think. And now that I'd stopped to think, I was thinking.

Lisa. Lisa.

'What did you say, Naveen?'

'. . . and the police report, that's what we know, so far,' Naveen said.

I hadn't heard any of it but the last words.

'Sorry, Naveen. I'm not really with it. You'll have to run that by me again.'

He smiled at me, a good friend, feeling bad.

'Okay. But, listen, stand up first.'

'Come again?'

'Stand up, man.'

'What for?'

'Stand up, for fuck's sake.'

He stood up, pulling me up with him.

'Give me a hug,' he said.

'No, I'm good.'

'All the more reason. Come on, give me a hug.'

'I'm really, really good.'

'Fuck it, man, your girlfriend died a week ago. Give me a hug, yaar.'

'Naveen —'

'Either you hug the Indian in me, or you fight the Irishman in me,' he said. 'There's no other way, in a situation like this.'

He was holding his arms out. There was no other way.

He hugged me like a brother, like my brother in Australia, and it was bad.

'Let it go,' he said, as my tears fell on his shoulder. 'Let it go.'

Tears, in a garden of stained light: tears on the shoulder of a volunteer brother.

'Fuck you, Naveen.'

'Let it go.'

I let it go, and then I let him go.

'You feel better?' Naveen asked.

'Fuck you, Naveen. And yeah, I do.'

We sat down again, and he told me the little that he knew. It didn't add much.

'Where's Concannon running the dope gig?'

'I don't know,' he said, smiling for the first time. 'Do you want him?'

'I want to talk to him.'

'Talk?'

'Talk, then listen, while he tells me who went with him to Lisa's that night.'

'You don't think it was Concannon who gave Lisa the drugs?'

'He left, according to the watchman, after fifteen minutes. The second man was there for almost an hour. I want to know who the second man was.'

'Okay. I'll get on it.'

'The watchman gave me the number of the black car they came in that night,' I said, handing him the number I'd jotted down. 'If you could detective out the owner for me, it would help.'

'I'll have the owner for you tomorrow, but it might not help. Lots of people have cars registered under other people's names.'

'Didier set up a place for me at the Amritsar hotel, on Metro. You can leave a message there, or I'll be at Kayani's, tomorrow, between one and two. Okay?'

'You left your place?'

'I did. And I'm not going back.'

'Where are you going now?'

'I have to meet Karla, at eight. I'm gonna buy a shirt, and check in at the Amritsar. What are you doing?'

'I have to pick up Diva, at seven thirty. I'm free till then. Mind if I come along?'

'I'd be glad of the company.'

We rolled the bike out from behind the bus stop, I kicked the engine happy, and he climbed on behind me.

'I've been learning how to ride,' he said.

'Uh-huh.'

'I've got my eye on this tricked-out vintage 350. It's damn cool, and really fast.'

'Uh-huh.'

'And the racer boys have been teaching me how to stunt ride.'

'The racer boys, huh?'

'Yeah. Rich kids on imported Japanese bikes. They're Diva's friends. And good riders.'

'Uh-huh.'

'Would you like me to show you what I can do on your bike?'

'Naveen, don't ever talk about my motorcycle that way again.'

'Got it,' he laughed. 'But just wait till you see mine!'

We rode along Fashion Street, where a stallholder in a drive-by-shirt-shop brought a new shirt and a couple of T-shirts to the bike, and then we rolled on to the Metro Junction.

I parked the bike in an alleyway behind the hotel's façade, which passed beneath an arch, connecting the second to fourth floors of the whole block.

The Amritsar was in a curved building that faced the junction like a cliff-face, rising from pelagian traffic swirling around the vast intersection.

At ground level, there were sporting goods shops, office supply outlets, a music store, and Kayani's restaurant, served by the alley behind the hotel's façade.

At the second floor and up, the whole building was connected by a network of corridors and hidden stairways, leading from shuttered street balconies to the last private apartment, at the end of a city block. If you knew your way, you could be in another postal code, in the same building, while the cops or other bad guys were still banging on the door.

It was rumoured that the Amritsar had twenty-one exits. I was happy with three. The first thing that a man on the run does in any new place is find the exits. Before I went to the desk, I explored the building with Naveen. I found three suitable hasty exits, leading to three different places on surrounding streets. Nice.

When Naveen and I reached the reception desk we found Didier, rolling dice with the hotel manager. He rose to hug me.

'Lin,' he whispered in the hug. 'I am about to win a discount on your rent, before you are even a registered guest.'

'Let's pay the rent *first*,' I whispered back, 'and you can win the discount later.'

'Shrewd,' he said, pulling apart again.

I checked in with one of my false passports, and took a look at my new rooms.

There was a large living room, with a bedroom and bathroom leading from it through high, wooden doors. A kitchenette filled one corner alcove.

At the far end of the room there was an archway of French doors, leading to a shadowed balcony. I walked through, opened the shutters, and looked out at the busy junction below.

The view was superb: a giant child's toy, wound up and whirling through its cycle of light, sound and movement. Beyond were the trees of the Bombay Gymkhana, their leafy shadows making a tunnel of the road.

I looked around me and saw that there were only short, flimsy partitions between my balcony and the two sets of rooms beside it. The rooms looked deserted.

The hotel manager was standing beside me.

'Anyone in the next rooms?' I asked.

'Not at the moment, but we've got two parties coming tomorrow.'

'Tomorrow never comes,' I said in Hindi. 'We're here now, and we'd like to take all three of these front-facing suites for a year, cash in advance.'

'*Suites?*' the manager and Didier said, at the same time.

'Suites,' I said. 'All three. From tonight. A year in advance. Are we good?'

'Hold on a minute,' the manager said. 'I just have to check with my greed.'

He paused, for a bit, with a thinking face, and then made up his mind.

'What do you know,' he said, 'we're suddenly unbooked.'

You've got to like a man who anthropomorphises his own greed: at the very least, it's a conversation.

'What's your name, sir?'

'Jaswant,' he said. 'Jaswant Singh. And how shall I call *you*, sir?'

'Just call me baba. Is that okay?'

'Sure, sure, baba. No problem. A year, you said? In advance?'

I paid the money, and he left us alone to go through the rooms.

We took down the temporary barriers between balconies, and walked all the way around, from hotel room to hotel room.

'Why do you need three of these *rooms*, Lin? I refuse to call them *suites*.'

'The walls at the ends of these balconies are sealed, Didier. If I have all three suites to myself, nobody can sneak up that way.'

'I see,' he said.

'But I only need two of them. The other one is for you, Naveen, if you want it.'

'For me?' Naveen asked.

'You haven't got an office yet, have you?'

'No. I work from my apartment.'

'Well, now you have an office, detective, if you want it.'

He looked at Didier, who shrugged a smile.

'This just occurred to you now?' Naveen asked.

'Yeah.'

'Because you have an extra room?'

'Yeah.'

'I love it. You're on,' Naveen said, shaking my hand. 'Nice to have you at the other end of the balcony.'

Didier joined us, placing his hands on ours.

'This is the beginning of something very –'

'Shit!' Naveen said, breaking away. 'She'll kill me!'

'Who will kill a detective?' Didier demanded.

'Diva. If I don't pick the spoilt brat up on time, she'll give me hell for two days. I have to run. I'll grab a key on the way out, Lin. The room on the right, okay with you?'

It was exactly the room that I wanted him to take.

'You got it, Naveen.'

'You're going to meet Karla?' Didier asked me, as we watched him leave.

'At eight.'

'I have some things to do, my friend, so I will leave now. But I will be available for you later, and I will wait in the Taj for some time, if I discover any news.'

'Thanks, Didier.'

'It is nothing.'

'No, I mean it. The owner of this building is your friend, and this is one of your areas, because the local don is your friend, and that's why I'm safe here. Thanks, for everything.'

'I love you, Lin. Please, do not suffer that I say it. We French have no chains on the heart. I love you. We will solve the mystery of sad, sweet Lisa, and then we will march on.'

He left, and I stood in each of the strange, new rooms I'd just rented for a year, on instinct. It was my first home, after the home I'd made with Lisa. I was trying to live again: trying to plant a new tree, in a new place.

I walked back to the balcony, folded my arms on the rail and watched the wheel of lights, red-yellow-white, making slow fireworks where five avenues met and dispersed.

A crow landed on my balcony for a moment, inspected me, ruffled its feathers and flew away. A group of teenagers crossed with the signal, laughing and happy, on their way to the budget shops on Fashion Street.

A distant temple bell sounded, followed by chanting. Then the Azaan rang out from somewhere nearby, clear and beautifully sung.

Is this the place? I asked myself. I wanted a place. Any place. I wanted a home.

Is this where I find it? I wanted connection. I wanted to give every-thing I had to one love, and be loved in return.

Is it here? I stared at the crossroad, hoping for an answer, as white, red and yellow lights made dragons from weaving lines of cars.

CHAPTER THIRTY-EIGHT

I WAS EARLY, AND SO WERE THE STARS arriving at the Taj in limousines for a gala to promote a new movie. I parked the bike beneath a palm tree, across from the hotel, waiting for snail minutes to make the long creep to eight and my appointment with Karla.

Through the wide doors of the lobby I saw the sponsor wall, with special guests posing for photographs in front of brand names that had paid them by the second. Flash, flash, turn this way, turn that way: the mug shots of the privileged, caught in the act.

The limousines stopped, the photographers hurried to other headlines, and the sponsor wall was dismantled. The spacious, gracious lobby, where great thinkers had discussed great ideas on rainy Bombay afternoons, for rainy decades, was barren and businesslike again.

To hell with early. I walked around the hotel to a back door, guarded by a man I knew, and climbed the promenade stairs to Karla's door. I knocked, and she opened it.

Her feet were bare. She wore a black silk lounging suit. It was trousers and top all in one, sleeveless, with zip pockets, and a zip front.

Her hair was tied up in a knot behind her head. There was a thin, silver letter opener, in the shape of a Damascan sword keeping the knot together. Karla.

'You're early,' she said, smiling but not inviting me in.

'I'm always early, or late.'

'That's a talent, for a man in your line of not-working. You wanna come in?'

'Sure.'

'Rish!' she called, over her shoulder. 'Our interview is over.'

She pushed the door wide, and I saw Rish, one of Lisa's partners at the gallery. He rushed forward.

'I'm so sorry, Lin,' he said, holding my hand in both of his. 'It's a terrible shock. Dear Lisa. A terrible loss. I'm . . . I'm just beside myself with grief.'

He squeezed past Karla, sidestepped me and scuttled away down the corridor. It was a long corridor.

'A man who's beside himself,' Karla said, as Rish scuttled, 'usually has a fool for company. Come in, Shantaram. It's been a long day.'

She walked back into the suite and sat on the window-seat couch.

'Make me a drink, please,' she said, when I'd closed and locked the door. 'I love it when I don't make the drink.'

'What'll it be?'

'I'll have a Happy Mary.'

'A *Happy* Mary?'

'It's a Bloody Mary, without the red corpuscles. And rocks. Lots of rocks.'

I made the drinks and brought them to sit with her.

'Shall we toast?' she asked.

'To running away angry?' I suggested.

She laughed.

'How about to old times, Shantaram?'

'To fallen friends,' I countered.

'To fallen friends,' she agreed, clashing glasses with me.

'You've gotta snap out of it,' she said, taking a long sip of her drink, before putting it down.

'I'm okay.'

'Bullshit. I just gave you four leads — fool, happy, blood, and rock — and you didn't go for any of them. That's not you. That's not you and me.'

'You and me?'

She saw my mind working, and smiled.

'Why are you so determined to find out who gave Lisa the dope?'

'Aren't you?'

She picked up her glass again, studied it for a while, drank off a coalminer's finger, and turned all the queens on me.

'If I find out who did it, or if you do, I'll probably want to kill who-ever it is. It's the kind of true that makes people kill people. You really wanna go there?'

'I just want to find out what happened to Lisa, that's all. I owe her that, Karla.'

419

She put her palms on her thighs, let out a gasp of air, and quickly stood up.

She crossed the room to the escritoire, opened her handbag, and took out a brass cigarette case exactly like Didier's.

With her back to me she lit a joint, and smoked it doggedly.

'I didn't think I'd need this, tonight,' she muttered, between deep breaths.

My eyes moved down her body, bowing to her. Her silhouette, wrapped in black: love was shouting inside me.

'It was either this,' Karla said, her back still turned to me, 'or breaking a bottle over your head.'

'Right . . . what was that?'

She stubbed out the joint, took two more joints from the case, snapped it shut, dropped it into her handbag and returned to the couch.

'Here,' she said, shoving the two joints at me. 'Catch up.'

'I'm kinda high already.'

'Fuck you, Shantaram. Smoke the fucking joints.'

'O . . . kay.'

I smoked. Every time I made to say something, she pushed the joint at me again gently.

'You know,' I said, when she let me, 'that's twice you've said *Fuck you* to me, in the same day.'

'If it'll make you feel any better,' she drawled, 'say *Fuck you* to *me*, right now.'

'No, I –'

'Come on, get it off your chest. You'll feel better. Say *Fuck you, Karla*. Say *Stop fucking with me, Karla*. Go on. Try it. *Fuck . . . you . . . Karla.*'

I looked at her.

'I can't,' I said.

'I bet you can, if you try.'

'Can I say *Fuck you* to a sunset? Can I say *Fuck you* to a galaxy?'

She smiled at me again, but her eyes were fierce. I had no idea what she was thinking.

'Look,' I said, 'let's get something straight. I just want to know what happened to Lisa. I want some kind of resolution, for Lisa, and for us. Don't you see that?'

'It's a steep slide from resolution to retribution,' she said. 'And a lotta people rush off that cliff.'

'I'm not the cliff-rusher type.'

She laughed. 'I know everything about you, Lin.'

'Everything?'

'Pretty much.'

'You do, huh?'

'Test me,' she purred.

I laughed, and then realised that she wasn't kidding.

'Really?'

'Smoke the fucking joint,' she said.

I smoked.

'Favourite colour,' she began, 'blue, with green: leaves against the sky.'

'Damn. Okay, favourite season?'

'Monsoon.'

'Favourite —'

'Hollywood movie, *Casablanca*, favourite Bollywood movie, *Prem Qaidi*, favourite food, gelato, favourite Hindi song, "Yeh Duniya Yeh Mehfil", favourite motorcycle . . . your current motorcycle, blessings be upon her, your favourite perfume —'

'Yours,' I said, holding up my hands in surrender. 'My favourite perfume is yours. You're damn good.'

'Of course I am. I'm born for you, and you're born for me. We both know that.'

A breeze from the sea ruffled through the room, announcing itself with a flourish of sheer, silk curtains. It suddenly occurred to me that I'd been in the neighbouring suite, years before, visiting Lisa.

Am I mad? Or was it just stupid not to say the words, not to tell Karla the truth: that I didn't understand her relationship with Ranjit, that I hadn't found the way to open the fist my life had closed over memories of Lisa living, and thoughts of her dead? I didn't want to be with Karla wreathed in grief. I wanted to be free, to be hers alone. And that wasn't going to be soon.

'Lisa was —' I began.

'Shut up,' she said.

I shut up. She lit the second joint, and passed it to me. She padded over to the small bar, grabbed a chunk of cubes from the bucket, and three-quarters filled a new glass.

'You're supposed to put the ice in first,' she said, pouring vodka slowly over the cubes, 'and add the Happy Mary with attention.'

She took a sip.

'Ah,' she sighed. 'That's better.'

She thought about things for a while.

'It's been a damn long day,' she said to the ceiling.

'What happened with Ranjit, Karla?'

She flashed a look from the angry part of the feminine divine. My heart got colder in my chest. She was magnificent.

'What did I say?'

She grit her teeth, as if putting them on display.

'You *finally* peer through your shawl of sorrows to ask about *me*, and what *I'm* going through? It's moments like these, Lin, that give *Fuck you* such long legs.'

'Wait a minute. I didn't ask you about Ranjit before, and about why you left him, because I thought it was obvious. He's a prick. I just wanted to know if there was anything specific. Did he threaten you?'

She laughed, pretty hard, and put the glass down. She came to stand in front of me.

'Stand up, Shantaram,' she said.

I stood up. She put her fingers into the front of my jeans, and curled them around my belt. She pulled me toward her.

'Sometimes,' she said, not smiling, 'I just don't know what to do with you.'

I had a few suggestions, but I didn't get to make them. She shoved me back on the window seat, and sat down beside me.

'It's a *week*, for us, since Lisa died,' she said, 'but it's only yesterday, for you. I get that. We all get that. And it's freaking you out that we don't seem to be getting how important this is to you.'

'Exactly.'

'Shut up. Kiss me.'

'What?'

'Kiss me.'

She put her hand behind my neck and drew our lips into a soft, brief kiss, then pushed me away again.

'Look, this isn't about Ranjit, and it isn't about Lisa. I know your heart can't let go of this, because I know you, and I love you. That's —'

'You love me?'

'Didn't I just say it, before? I'm born for you, and you're born for me. I knew it the first second I saw you again, on the mountain.'

'I . . .'

'But I also know all your weaknesses. We've got a couple of them in common, which is always a good start to any relationship. But I –'

'Relationship?'

'What are we talking about here, Shantaram, if it isn't us?'

'I –'

'Back to your weaknesses. We've gotta –'

'You're my only weakness, Karla.'

'I'm your strength. More than half of it at the moment, it seems to me. Your weaknesses are that you whip yourself with guilt and smear yourself with shame. I've been waiting for you to evolve, grow up, and grow out of it.'

'Well –'

'You've made progress,' she said, stopping me with a raised hand. 'No doubt about that. But you're not there yet. You've got self-esteem issues –'

'Well deserved.'

'Funny. But it's okay. Self-esteem issues? Lightweight stuff. Nothing we can't fix. I'm homicidal. Nobody's perfect. But Lisa's gone, and no amount of self-flagellation will bring her back. If it would, I'd save you the trouble, and flog you myself. I might anyway, if you don't snap out of it.'

'Okay, so I lost the thread, there.'

'Let Lisa go. At least around me. I just told you that I love you. I've never said that to any other man. If you weren't so numb with guilt, you'd react.'

I kissed her with everything I had, everything I was, and everything I wanted.

'That's better,' she said, pushing me away again gently. 'Right now, I can wait for my lover, but I need my friend while I wait. There's too much happening. I need you to catch up, Shantaram, and get with the faith. I need you to trust me, because I can't tell you anything. Not until it's over.'

'Why not?'

'That's why,' she smiled. 'Because you're curious, and you're loyal. And some of the things you hear about me, until I get this done, might sound crazy, or worse, so I need your faith.'

She meant it. She was completely sincere: no games or tricks. It was compelling, beautiful and scary. I loved it. *Imagine this*, I thought, *all the time*.

She grabbed my shirt, and pulled my face close to hers.

'Look me in the queens, and tell me you've got all this,' she commanded. 'Because, you know what, I love you, but I've got too much happening, at the moment, to put up with drama from the guy I love. So, you know, tell me you got this.'

'I got this,' I said, diving into that pool, that green lagoon so close, so deep.

'Good,' she said. 'Now get out.'

'You say that like you mean it,' I said, standing there, kind of floppy.

'No, I'm just saying it while I can.'

'But, I . . .'

We walked to the door and she shoved me through, no kiss, hug or handshake. The door closed, and I walked the marble halls of the hotel alone.

What was happening? It was wrong. It was all wrong.

I sprinted back to her door and rang the bell. She answered immediately, startling me.

'Look,' I said, trying to get the words out quickly. 'It's you. It's always been you, since the first time I –'

'– saw you on the street,' she interrupted me, leaning against the doorframe. 'Smiling, and about to walk in front of a bus. I remember you were smiling at a kid on the pavement. And there was a leaping dog at your feet. Do you know anything about the Tarot?'

'It's that Chinese mafia gang, isn't it?'

She laughed happily. I heard a temple bell inside.

'I knew it, the minute I yanked you back from in front of the bus,' she said. 'When I looked into your eyes, all the lights went on. And time –'

'– slowed down,' I continued. 'For really long seconds. And the effect –'

'– lasted for days,' she said, straightening up to face me. 'Lin, I just want you to be in this with me, by believing in me, but I can't involve you in it. Do you see?'

'Favourite colour,' I said, ticking an imaginary list in my hand, 'corpuscle red.'

She relaxed against the doorway again, the too-smart smile beginning.

'Favourite season, winter. In Basel, to be exact. Favourite movie, *Key Largo*, favourite food, barbecued steak, favourite song, "The Internationale", favourite car, because you're not into motorcycles yet, the Chevy Camaro, 1967, matt black with blood-red interior —'

She kissed me. I closed my eyes. A light hovered in my mind. The light faded in waves, falling beneath the world. Love like water, searching for the sea. Love like Time, searching for meaning. Love like all that was, and ever will be.

'Stop it!' she said, pushing me away.

She put the back of her hand to her lips, and wiped away the sea. I opened my mouth to speak, but she slapped me, pretty hard.

'Don't get killed,' she said. 'I want to do that again.'

'The kiss, or the slap?'

'Both, but maybe in a different order.'

She slammed the door in my face.

Love. Love like a marble echo in an empty hotel corridor.

Didier was waiting for me in the lobby.

'I was rather hoping you would stay the night with Karla,' he said as we left the hotel.

I stopped, and stared at him.

'I only mean,' he said, 'that I have dangerous news. I know, now, where Concannon is making his dope business.'

The night was looking up. And I was in just the right mood.

'How reliable is your information?'

'He was seen there today, at three in the afternoon.'

'Where is he?'

'In a house owned by the Scorpions.'

'On Marine Lines road?'

'Yes. How do you know?'

'I followed Vishnu and his guys there, after they slapped me around. It's one of their hangouts.'

'What are you going to do?'

'I'm gonna walk up to the door, and ring the bell.'

'With a hand grenade?' Didier asked, pondering.

'No. You're going to call Vishnu, and tell him that I'll visit him, at ten tonight.'

'What makes you think I have this Vishnu's telephone number?'

'Didier,' I sighed.

'Oh, very well, Didier has every number, of course, or can find it. But do you think it wise, to walk into the den of lions?'

'I think he'll want to talk. He's a talkative guy.'

'What makes you think he wants to talk to you, no offence?'

'None taken. I quit the Sanjay Company, and I'm still alive. He'll want to talk to me.'

'Very well,' he said. 'I will make the call.'

I watched him walk back into the hotel, and signalled one of the Sikh doormen. The man walked across the courtyard to join me at the bike.

'Yes, baba?' he asked, offering his hand.

I passed him some money in the handshake, as I'd done many times before.

'For the boys, when the shift is over.'

'Thank you, baba. There were several big functions tonight, with many distinguished guests, so not many tips. Anything I can do for you?'

'Keep an eye on Miss Karla. If you hear anything I should know, I'm staying at the Amritsar, on Metro.'

'*Thik*,' he said, rushing to rejoin his colleagues. 'No problem!'

Didier returned, his expression thoughtful, a fisherman studying the rain.

'It is established,' he said. 'Vishnu is expecting you. We do not have much time. We need more guns, and more cartridges.'

He began to look around for a taxi.

'I'm not taking a gun. And you're not coming, Didier.'

'Lin!' he said, stamping his foot. 'If you deny me this adventure, I will spit on your grave. And when Didier says such a thing, it is written on stone.'

'My grave? Why am I always dying before you do?'

'And dance on it, like Nureyev.'

'You'd dance on my grave?'

'Like Nureyev.'

'Okay. You're coming.'

'Should we not get some others with us?'

'Who would go?' I asked, starting the bike.

'Good point,' he conceded, still looking for a taxi.

'Get on.'

'Pardon me?'

'Get on the bike, Didier. I don't want to rely on a taxi, if we have to leave that place in a hurry. Get on.'

'But, Lin, you know about my motorcycle hysteria.'

'Get on the bike, Didier.'

'If cars fell over, when we got out of them, I wouldn't ride in cars, either. It is hysteria and physics combined, you see.'

'You don't have motorcycle hysteria, Didier. You're motophobic.'

'I am?' he asked, intrigued.

'No doubt.'

'Motophobic. Are you sure?'

'It's nothing to be ashamed of. A lot of my friends are motophobic. But it's okay. There's a treatment for it.'

'There is?'

'Get on the bike, Didier.'

CHAPTER THIRTY-NINE

I PARKED THE BIKE A BLOCK AWAY FROM THE MANSION, and waited in the quiet side street. Moonlight wrote tree poems on the road. A thin, black cat ran through the streaks of light and shadow in front of us, sprinting to safety.

'Thank you, Fate,' Didier said. 'A black cat. Of course.'

We approached the gate. I paused, looking up and down the long street. Cars passed, but it was quiet.

'You sure you want to do this, Didier?'

'How *dare* you!' Didier said.

'*Okay. Okay.* Sorry.'

I pushed open the gate, and walked to the front door. I was about to press the buzzer but Didier stopped me. He smiled, paused, and then pressed the buzzer himself.

A man approached the door. There were pieces of stained glass and frosted scroll panels on the door. I saw through the glass that he was a big man: a big man, walking slowly, with a cane. Hanuman.

He opened the door, saw me, and sneered.

'You again,' he said.

'Tell me about Pakistan,' I said.

He grabbed my shoulder as if it was a grapefruit, and shoved me along the corridor. Fit, crazy-eyed henchmen appeared from rooms at the end of the hall. Goons appeared on the stairs. Hanuman shoved me toward a door near the end of the hall.

'*Madachudh! Bahinchudh! Gandu! Saala!*' they shouted back at me, itching to rush me.

Every gun in the world is a death wish, and they were all armed, and wishing us harm. I was scared, because I hadn't expected guns, and because outlaws, by definition, don't go by the rules.

428

There was a heavy, hairy guy in a white undershirt standing closest to me in the hallway. He slowly raised a crowd pleaser, a sawn-off twelve-gauge shotgun, and pointed it at me. Hanuman frisked me. Satisfied that I wasn't carrying a gun, he lifted my shirt to show the two knives at my back, and let the shirt fall again, stifling a yawn. The gangsters laughed, pretty hard. He turned to Didier, who stopped him with a raised palm. He took his automatic pistol from his pocket and handed it to Hanuman.

A door opened, a little way along the hallway in front of me. Vishnu walked out into the hall, standing with his men.

'You don't just wear out the welcome mat,' he said calmly. 'You cremate it. Come in, before you cause a riot.'

He walked back into the room, Hanuman shoved me forward, and we joined Vishnu in his study.

There was a mahogany desk, two plush visitor chairs and a row of wooden chairs behind them. Political and religious posters competed for space on the walls, but there were no books. A screen on the desk gave different views around the mansion, one image of security after another.

Vishnu paused at the entrance to speak with Hanuman. The tall man stooped to listen, wagging his head.

When Vishnu rejoined us he was alone. It was very confident, or very foolish. He poured three bourbons on the rocks and passed them to us, taking his place behind the desk in a high-backed office chair.

'Mr Levy, isn't it?' Vishnu asked as we took our seats in front of his desk. 'We haven't met, but I've heard reports of you.'

'*Enchanté, monsieur*,' Didier replied.

'My wife is ill,' Vishnu said, turning to me. 'She is being attended by our doctor, and two nurses. That's why I keep her close to me. That's why my men wanted to kill you, just now. Because my wife is in this house. That's why *I'm* thinking about killing you. Are you quite mad, to come here?'

'I'm sorry that your wife is ill, and that I disturbed her peace,' I said, standing to leave. 'I'll find another way.'

'You give up so easily?' Vishnu sneered.

'Look, Vishnu, I thought this was your gambling den, your club, I didn't know it was your home. I'll find another way.'

'Sit down,' Vishnu said. 'Tell me what this is all about.'

'I know how you would feel if anything happened to your wife,' I began, sitting again, 'because something happened to my girlfriend. She died. The man who provided the pills that killed her is under your protection. I came into your clubhouse to ask you to let me talk to him, out on the street.'

'Why don't you just wait for him, outside?'

'I don't lie in wait for people. I'm a front door guy. That's why I asked to see you. The man's working for you, so I'm asking.'

'What do you want to know?'

'I want to know what he knows. The name of the man who was with him, the one who gave my girlfriend the pills.'

'And what could you give me in return?'

'Whatever you ask of me, that we both think is fair.'

'A favour?'

He laughed a grin at me.

'It's not a small thing,' I said. 'If you let me have time with this man, I'll do anything you ask that we both think is fair. You have my word.'

'Cigar?' he asked.

'No thanks.'

'Very gracious,' Didier said, reaching for one, and inhaling its fragrance. 'You know, Vishnudada, if you plan to kill us, this is almost exactly how I would choose to go.'

Vishnu laughed.

'I did something like this myself, once, when I was seventeen,' he said, staring an unsatisfactory smile at me. 'I carried a tray of chai glasses, all the way to the local don's living room, put down the tray, and put my knife to the don's throat.'

'What happened?' Didier asked, engrossed.

'I told him that if his *goondas* didn't stop molesting my sister, I'd come back, just as silently, and cut his throat.'

'Did he punish you?' Didier asked.

'Yes, he did. He recruited me,' Vishnu replied, taking a sip of his drink. 'But even though it reminds me of my youthful self, I cannot approve of what you have done, in coming to my home. Who is this man, under my protection?'

'The Irishman. Concannon.'

'Ah, then you are too late. He is gone.'

'He was here today, monsieur,' Didier said quietly.

'Yes, Mr Levy. But here today, gone tonight, that is the nature of our business, isn't it? The Irishman left three hours ago. Where he went, or if I ever see him again, I don't really care.'

'Then, I'll take my leave, and I apologise again, if I disturbed your wife.'

'Is it true,' he asked, waving me back into my seat, 'that you're no longer with the Sanjay Company?'

'It is,' I said.

'If you will permit me, Vishnudada,' Didier said, trying to change the subject, 'you did not know this girl, who died. But I had the honour to know her. She was a jewel, a very rare human flower. Her loss is simply insupportable.'

'And this intrusion is insupportable, Mr Levy. Order must be maintained. Rules must be obeyed.'

'Regrettably so,' Didier replied. 'But love is a poor master, and a poorer slave.'

'Shall I tell you something about the poor,' Vishnu said, rising to top up our glasses, but keeping an eye on me.

'With pleasure,' Didier said, puffing the cigar.

'If you build a nice house,' Vishnu said, sitting again, 'they break the floor, so they can sit in the dirt. If you build it up stronger, they bring dirt in from outside, so they can sit in the dirt again. I run a construction business. I know. What do you think, Shantaram?'

What did I think? *You're a megalomaniac, and you'll die violently.*

'I think it sounds like you're a man who hates the poor.'

'Oh, come on,' he protested. '*Everyone* hates the poor. Even the *poor* hate the poor. My point is that some are born to lead, and most are born to follow. You have taken a big step in the right direction.'

'What step?'

'Leaving the Sanjay Company. There is only one small step, now, between you and me. If you were to join me, and tell me everything you know about the Sanjay Company, you would be a leader, and not a follower. And I would make you richer than you can imagine.'

I stood up.

'I apologise again for busting in on you. If I'd known you had family here, I wouldn't have come. Will your men let us leave, without waking everyone upstairs?'

'*My* men?' Vishnu laughed.

'Your men.'

'My men won't lay a finger on you,' he said. 'You have my word.'

I turned to leave, but he stopped me.

'The Irishman isn't the only one who knows,' he said.

I faced him again. Didier was standing beside me.

'There was a driver,' he said. 'My driver. The black car was one of mine.'

'Yours?'

'The Irishman borrowed it that night. He'd been shot the day before, I understand, but still insisted on going out. I let him have my driver.'

'Where do I find this driver?'

'He will not tell you anything,' Vishnu said.

'He might,' I said through clenched teeth.

'He's dead. But, he did tell me everything he knew, before he died.'

'What do you want, Vishnu?'

'You know what I want. I want to stop the Sanjay Company from pumping weapons and bomb-makers from Pakistan into Bombay's streets.'

'That's a little exaggerated –' I began, but he cut me off, standing behind his desk with his fists on his hips.

'You can't deny it, because it's happening everywhere,' he said, raising his voice to a shout as he warmed to his theme. 'Money from the Arabs, training in Pakistan, an army already on the move across the world. They're about to take their first country, Afghanistan. It won't be the last country the Islamic army takes, before this is over. If you can't see what that means, you're an idiot.'

'Now *you're* the one who's disturbing your wife. I don't want a political debate with you, Vishnu. I want the Irishman.'

'Forget my wife, motherfucker, and forget the Irishman. Tell me what you think about all this. You've both been here long enough to feel the love of Mother India. Where do you stand?'

I looked at Didier. He shrugged.

'The real fight,' I replied, 'is between Sunni and Shia Islam. Muslims are killing a hundred or more Muslims for every non-Muslim, one mosque and marketplace at a time. We don't have a dog in that fight. We should stay out of it. And we definitely shouldn't bomb or invade their countries, while they're fighting that family feud. Or at any other time, for that matter.'

432

'We Indians do have a dog in the fight,' he said more seriously, his hands working. 'Kashmir. That's why they are hitting us, again and again. They want Kashmir as an independent Islamic State. Where do you stand on Kashmir?'

'Kashmir is a war no-one can win. There should be blue United Nations helmets everywhere in Kashmir, protecting the people until it gets worked out.'

'And would you feel the same way, if it was a state from your country?'

'He has a point,' Didier observed, gesturing with his cigar.

I looked at him, then back to Vishnu.

'I don't have a country. And I don't have a girlfriend any more. Do you know anything that can help me find the man who killed her?'

He laughed, and his eyes flickered to the clock on the wall. It occurred to me, too late, that he was stalling.

The door opened behind us, and Lightning Dilip walked through. Six cops crowded into the room. Two cops grabbed me. Two cops grabbed Didier.

Lightning Dilip came to stand close to me, his belly bursting through his shirt.

'I've been searching for you, Shantaram,' he said. 'I've got some unhappy questions to ask you.'

I looked at Vishnu. He was smiling. Lightning Dilip began to shove us toward the door.

'Wait!' Vishnu commanded, pointing at Didier. 'I need Mr Levy. We have matters to discuss.'

'Jarur!' Lightning responded.

The cops released Didier. He looked at me, asking me with his eyes if we should fight and die, there and then. I shook my head, and he gave me a broken half-smile, sending courage into the prairie in my heart where fear was already running. It was okay. We'd both been in Lightning Dilip's custodial care, and we both knew what to expect: the boot and the baton and exhaustion as the only mercy.

CHAPTER FORTY

The cops dragged and shoved me out of the house. Scorpion gangsters jeered and mocked me from the stairwell. Danda kicked at me, as he slammed the door.

Eight hands and a few boots pushed me face down in the back of a jeep. They drove too fast to the Colaba police station, threw me out of the jeep, stomped on me a few times, and then dragged me into the stony courtyard.

They passed the row of offices where normal interrogations were held, and dragged me toward the under barrack, where abnormal interrogations were held.

I got up, and resisted arrest. I got in a couple of good shots, too. They didn't like it. They slapped me around, and shoved me into one of the wide, dark cells.

There were four scared men in the cell, and I was one of them. The other three scared men, chained together in the far corner, were sitting on their haunches. Their faces were dirty, and their shirts were torn. They looked like they'd been there a while.

The cops chained me to the entry gate, low, forcing me to curl up in a ball on my knees.

Boom. A kick came out of nowhere. Hello, Lightning. Kick, punch, baton, punch, kick, kick, baton, kick, punch, punch, baton.

You beat Karla like this, you coward, I thought, finding an image I could use to lock my mind. *Your karma's waiting for you. Your karma's waiting for you.*

Then it stopped, like the last thunder, and I could hear the thudding storm rolling away.

When I thought it was safe, I risked a look and caught a glimpse of Lightning Dilip. He was staring at the three men huddled in the corner. He was breathing hard. His face was all the wrong happiness.

I got it. I was the warm-up act. The guys in the corner were the main event.

The guys in the corner got it too, and started to beg. I had time to breathe and move and check to see the damage.

I was lucky. No bones broken, nothing ruptured, arms and legs still working. It could've been worse, and had been before.

When Lightning Dilip went to work on the chained men, two cops uncuffed me from the gate, and took me back to the duty sergeant's office, to decide how much of my money to keep. They took it all, of course: it cost me all I had to buy back my clothes, personal effects and knives. They threw my stuff into the road, and threw me after it, dressed in my shorts.

I stood in the deserted, late-night street beside a traffic island, picking up my clothes, one by one, until I was dressed. For a while I stayed there, staring at the police station, as you do, sometimes, out of that stubbornness born of injustice.

I was bleeding, beat up, in the middle of the fluorescent street. I could hear the screams of Lightning Dilip's new victims. The flashing light on the corner bathed me in red with a slow heartbeat. I stared at the place where the screaming came from.

A black Ambassador car pulled to a stop beside me. The windows were down. I saw Farid in the front seat, beside a Company driver, named Shah. Faisal, Amir and Andrew DaSilva were in the back seat.

DaSilva had his elbow on the window. He reached under the dashboard of the car, and I instinctively pulled one of the knives. The gangsters laughed.

'Here's your money,' DaSilva said, passing a package through the window. 'Thirty grand. Severance pay, for the Sri Lanka run.'

I reached out to take the package, but he wouldn't release it.

'Two weeks, you've got, of Sanjay's protection,' he said, grinning into my eyes. 'After that, why don't you try to kill me, huh? And we'll see what happens.'

'I don't want to kill you, Andy,' I said, grabbing the package from his hand. 'I have too much fun making you look bad, in front of your friends.'

'Good one!' Amir laughed. 'I'm going to miss you, Lin. *Challo!* Let's go!'

The black Ambassador drove away, leaving blue smoke swirling in the fluorescent haze. I put the money inside my shirt, and heard the screaming, beginning again.

A headache said hello behind my right eye. There were bruises making themselves acquainted all along my back and shoulders.

I walked back under the wide arch at the entrance, climbed the steps to the long porch and stepped into Lightning Dilip's office.

'Call him,' I said to the sleepy constable watching the desk.

'Fuck you, Shantaram,' he said, lounging in his chair. 'You better not let him see you in here.'

I reached inside my shirt, pulled out a few hundred-dollar bills, and threw them on the desk.

'Call him.'

The constable snatched the notes off the desk, and ran out of the office.

Lightning Dilip was back in seconds. He didn't know whether I wanted to make trouble, or make up with a bribe, and he didn't know which one he wanted more. He was oily with sadism, his bulging shirt stained with sweat.

'This must be my lucky day,' he said, the riding crop in his hand twirling.

'I want to bail out three prisoners.'

'What?'

'I want to bail out three prisoners, with cash money.'

'Which three?' Lightning asked, suspicion pinching his face.

'The three you're kicking the shit out of.'

He laughed. Why do people laugh, when you're not trying to be funny? Oh, yeah: when you're the joke.

'I'm happy to do it,' he grinned. 'For the right price. But will it make a difference to you, to know that one of those men has raped several little girls, and I don't know which one of them it is yet, until I get a confession? Of course, the choice is yours.'

You try to do something right. My ears were ringing, and pain was waking my face. It was the kind of angry-pain that shivers in you, and won't stop shivering until something very good or very bad happens. The bells wouldn't stop ringing. A child molester? Fate is Solomon, forever.

'I'd like,' I croaked, and then cleared my throat. 'I'd like to pay you to stop beating the three prisoners. Have we got a deal?'

'We would have a deal for five hundred American,' he said, 'whenever you find it.'

He knew he'd cleaned me out. And the constable had wisely kept the hundred-dollar notes I'd given him to himself. Dilip gasped when I pulled the notes from my shirt and threw them on the table.

'I have eighty more prisoners upstairs,' he said. 'Would you like to pay me not to beat them?'

At that moment, beat up and crazy, thinking that Lisa's body had been at that police station, and that every cop in the place had seen her dead, and knowing that Lightning Dilip had beaten Karla, probably on the same gate he chained me to, I didn't care. I just wanted the screaming to stop for a while.

I threw some more money on the desk.

'Tonight, everybody,' I said.

He laughed again, scooping the money from the desk. The cops in the doorway laughed.

'This has been a profitable night,' he said. 'I should beat you more often.'

I walked out of the office, and along the white porch to the steps.

I passed under the archway, leading to the street, knowing that all I'd bought was silence for one night, but that they'd be beaten the following night, and others would be beaten after them, every night.

I hadn't stopped anything, because all the money in the world can't buy peace, and all the cruelty won't stop until kindness is the only king.

A black limousine pulled up in front of me, and Karla got out with Didier and Naveen. My happiness was a cheetah, running free in a savannah of solace. And pain ran away, afraid of love.

They hugged me, and settled me in the car.

'Are you okay?' Karla asked, her hand cool on my face.

'I'm okay. How did you know I was out?'

'We've been waiting. Didier called us, and we've been waiting across the road, outside Leo's. We saw you get thrown out of the station house, and we gave you a minute.'

'That was Karla's idea,' Naveen added. 'She said *Let him get his pants on in peace*. Then we were just coming toward you, when the black Ambassador stopped.'

'And then, after it left, you went back inside,' Didier said.

'Which seemed a little brazen,' Naveen smiled, 'so we waited again, getting ready to bust you out, and then you came outside.'

'We have news,' Didier said.

'What news.'

'Vishnu talked to me, after you left,' Didier said. 'He told me who it was, that went with Concannon to see Lisa.'

'Who?'

'It was Ranjit,' Karla said flatly, taking the cigarette back from Didier.

'*Your* Ranjit?'

'Matrimonially speaking,' she said. 'But it looks like I could be a widow, before a divorcee.'

Ranjit? I remembered how scared he'd been, when I'd gone to his office looking for Karla. He thought I knew. *That's why he was so afraid.*

'Where is he?'

'He skipped town,' Karla said. 'I've called all his friends. I drove them nuts, but nobody's seen him since yesterday evening. His secretary booked a flight for him, to Delhi. He disappeared completely after he landed there. He could be anywhere.'

'We'll find him,' Naveen said. 'He's too successful to remain discreet for long.'

Karla laughed.

'You got that right. He'll come up for bad air, sooner or later.'

'You can relax now, Lin,' Didier added, 'for the mystery is solved.'

'Thanks, Didier,' I said, passing Karla her flask. 'It's not solved, but at least we know who can solve it.'

'Exactly,' Karla concluded. 'And until we track Ranjit down, let's focus on matters at hand. You look a little beat up, Shantaram.'

'Sorry to intrude,' the uniformed driver asked. 'But may I offer you the first aid kit, sir?'

'Is that you, Randall?'

'It is indeed I, Mr Lin, sir. May I offer the kit, and perhaps a refreshing towel?'

'You may, Randall,' I said. 'And how do you come to be steering this big, black bar around Bombay?'

'Miss Karla offered me the opportunity to serve,' Randall said, passing the first aid kit across the seat.

'Knock it off, Randall,' Karla laughed. 'No-one serves anything but drinks and first aid in this car.'

I looked at Karla. She shrugged her shoulders, opened her hip flask, poured some vodka onto a swab of gauze, and passed the flask to me.

'Drink up, Shantaram.'

'Any opportunity to serve, Miss Karla,' I said, smiling at her acquisition of the barman from the Mahesh hotel.

She cleaned up the few cuts on my face, head and wrists expertly, because she'd done it before, to a lot of soldiers. One of Karla's best friends from the Khaderbhai Company days was a corner man, who kept fighters fighting. He'd taught her everything he knew, and she was a good corner man herself.

'Where to, Miss Karla?' Randall asked. 'Although the destination is the journey, of course.'

'Where do you want to go?' Karla laughed, asking me.

Where did I want to go? I wanted to say goodbye to Lisa with my friends, and let a branch of grieving fall. Knowing that it was Ranjit who gave the pills to Lisa gave me the little peace that I needed for goodbye.

'There's something I'd like to do. And I'd like you all to do it with me, if you're up for it.'

'Sure, okay, certainly,' they all said, none of them asking what it was.

'Didier, do you think we can wake up your friend, Tito?'

'Tito doesn't sleep, as far as I know,' Didier replied. 'At least, no-one has ever actually *seen* him sleeping.'

'Good. Let's go.'

Didier gave Randall directions to the fishermen's colony behind Colaba market. We parked beside a row of tilted handcarts and wound through dark lanes and alleys to find Tito, who was reading Durrell by kerosene lantern. He was lonely, he said, so he taxed us time: ten per cent of two hours. We smoked a joint with him, talked books, and then collected my kit.

'What is our new destination, sir?' Randall asked, when we were all in the car.

'The Air India building,' I said. 'And a funeral in the sky.'

CHAPTER FORTY-ONE

THE NIGHTWATCHMAN REMEMBERED ME, accepted some money, and sent us up to the roof of the deserted Air India building.

The red archer was turning slowly. The night was clear, the star-horizon wider than the sea. The waves below seemed fragile, their crests of foam like strips of floating seaweed, seen from our perch in the sky.

While they were admiring the archer and the view, I set about making a small fireplace. Naveen helped me gather bricks and broken tiles from the wide concrete roof. We made a base of tiles and built a small hearth around them with bricks and stones.

I'd taken a newspaper from the nightwatchman, and began screwing the pages up into small, tight balls. When it was ready, I uncovered Lisa's box of things from the bag that Tito had kept safe.

The metal wind-up toy was a bluebird, attached to a device with finger holes like a pair of scissors. I pressed the scissors together, and the bird moved its head and sang. It was Lisa's. She'd had it since she was a child. I gave it to Karla.

There was a yellow tube with brass fittings at the end, which held all of my old silver rings. I'd made it as a paperweight for Lisa. I gave it to Naveen. The stones, acorns, shells, amulets and coins fit inside a blue velvet jewel box. I gave it to Didier.

I tore the photographs into fragments and fed them into the fireplace, along with anything that would burn, including the hemp sandals and the box itself, marked REASONS WHY, ripped into small pieces. Her thin, silver scarf was last into the pile, curled and coiled like a snake.

I lit the lowest of the paper balls around the fire, and it caught. Didier helped it along with a swish from his flask. Karla did the same. Naveen fanned the flames with a chunk of tile.

Karla took my hand, and led me to the edge of the building where we could look at the sea.

'Ranjit,' I said softly.

'Ranjit,' she repeated softly.

'Ranjit,' I growled.

'Ranjit,' she growled back.

'How are you holding up?'

'I'm okay. I've got other things on my mind. Are you okay?'

'Ranjit,' I said, my teeth clenched.

'He always liked her,' Karla said. 'I was so busy projecting him into the limelight that I didn't see how close they got.'

'You're saying Ranjit had a thing for Lisa?'

'I don't know. Maybe. I never asked him anything about his sex life, and he never told me anything. Maybe it was just because *we* liked her so much. He's a competitive man. But like all competitive men, his balls fell off when the going got hard.'

'What does that mean?'

'I'll tell you, one day, after we find him. My problem with Ranjit isn't important now, and it had nothing to do with Lisa. His problem was a fear of success. Surprising, how common that is. There should be a name for it.'

'Ambition fatigue?' I suggested.

'I like it,' she laughed softly. 'What do you think Ranjit was doing with Lisa, that night?'

'Rohypnol is a rape drug, but sometimes people take it together because they like it. So, either Ranjit is a rapist, and it went wrong, or they had a thing, and that went wrong. Thing is, I didn't think they were that close, except that she liked his politics.'

'His politics?' Karla laughed, to herself.

'How is that funny?'

'I'll explain it one day. How was it tonight, Shantaram, in the cage with Lightning Dilip?'

'The usual. Short back and sides.'

'Bad cops are bad priests,' she said. 'All confession, and no absolution.'

'How are *you* comin' along, Slim?'

'I'm okay. I've got bruises like Rorschach tests. One of them looks like two dolphins, making love. But, you know, maybe that's just me.'

441

I wanted to see the bruise. I wanted to kiss it. I wanted to beat the man who put it there.

'The car and Randall,' I said, 'and staying at the Taj. It costs. I've got some money put away, a hundred and fifty thousand dollars. I can set you up in a safe place somewhere, with the car and Randall and whatever else you need. While Ranjit's on the loose, you should play it safe.'

'Listen,' she said. 'I told you that I've been working with the economists and analysts at Ranjit's paper. I made some money, and put a little aside.'

'Yeah, but –'

I spent two years on it, with the best advice the boss's money could buy, and quite a bit of the boss's money.'

I remembered the bike-talk, me telling her to save money and put a down payment on a house. And she was working with professional economists and stock market analysts all the time, and didn't say a thing. She was even sweet to me.

'You've been playing the market?'

'Not . . . exactly.'

'Then *what* . . . exactly?'

'I've been manipulating it.'

'*Manipulating* it?'

'A bit.'

'How much of a bit?'

'I used a proxy vote to leverage the theoretical worth of all of Ranjit's shares in communications, energy, insurance and transportation, and I built a secret buying block, for sixteen minutes, and then I closed it down.'

'A buying block?'

'And I bought my brains out, with six guys on six phones, for sixteen minutes.'

'Then what?'

'I moved the stock prices in selected arm's-length companies, where I'd already bought preferential stock.'

'What?'

'I rigged the market a couple of times. No big deal. I made my cut, and got the hell out.'

'How much did you make?'

'Three million.'

'Rupees?'

'Dollars.'

'You made three million dollars on the market?'

'I skimmed it *off* the market, to be precise. It's actually not that hard, if you're stinking rich to begin with, which I was, with Ranjit's proxy shares. So, there's no problem for money. I have it in four different accounts. I don't need Ranjit's money, or yours, Lin. I need your help.'

'Three million? And I was talking to you about –'

'Being a London Bombay wife,' she ended for me. 'I loved it. Really. And –'

'Wait. You said you need my help?'

'An old enemy of mine is back in town,' she said. 'Madame Zhou.'

'I detest that woman, and I've only met her once.'

'Detest is the doormat,' Karla said. 'What I feel for that woman is a whole mansion of malice.'

Madame Zhou was an influence peddler who'd sweated secrets from influential patrons of her brothel, the Palace of Happy, for more than a decade. When she drew Lisa into her maze of stained sheets, Karla got Lisa out, poured gasoline on the Palace of Happy, and burned it to the ground.

'She put it around that she's looking for me. And this time, it's not just the twins.'

I knew the twins, Madame Zhou's bodyguards and constant companions. The last time I'd seen them, they were bleeding, because I was losing a very untidy fight with them, and because Didier shot them.

'I detest those twins, and I've only met them once, as a pair.'

'This time,' Karla said, looking out at the night, 'she's got personal cosmeticians with her. Two acid throwers.'

One of the retribution services offered in those years was acid-throwing. Although usually limited to so-called honour burnings, acid throwers hired themselves out for other matters, when the price was right.

'When did she get back to Bombay?'

'Two days ago. She found out about Lisa's death, somehow. She knows I burned down her palace for Lisa. She wants to look me in the eyes, and laugh, before she burns me.'

Stars wandered their dark pastures. Early dawn pressed all the shadows flat. Faint light began to wake waves in brilliant peaks: seals of candescence, playing.

443

I turned my head slowly, so that I could look at Karla's profile as her heart talked to the sea.

She'd been afraid, for days. She'd discovered our sweet, dead friend, and she'd been beaten by the cops, and she'd broken up with Ranjit, permanently, for whatever reason, and she had Madame Zhou's acid throwers looking for her, and then she'd discovered that Ranjit was the one who was with Lisa, at the end.

She was the bravest girl I ever met, and I'd been so much in my own guilt and loss that I hadn't been beside her, where I belonged, when she needed me.

'Karla, I –'

'Shall we do this now?' Didier asked, from beside the small fire. 'We are ready.'

Didier and Naveen had tended the fire well. The residue of fine ashes, cooled by fanning them out on the ground, was enough for each of us to have a handful.

We went to a corner facing the open sea, and scattered those little ashes we had of her, in the place she would've chosen to scatter mine.

'Goodbye, and hello, beautiful soul,' Karla said, as the ashes drifted from our fingers. 'May you return, in a longer and happier life.'

We followed the wind and ashes with thoughts of her. I was so angry at Fate that I couldn't cry.

'Well, we'd better get out of here,' Naveen said, cleaning up the impromptu fireplace. 'The cleaning staff will arrive soon.'

'Wait, guys,' I said. 'Madame Zhou's back in town, with acid throwers, and she's asking around about Karla.'

'Acid throwers,' Didier said, spitting the words in a shiver of dread.

'Who's Madame Zhou?' Naveen asked.

'A loathsome woman,' Didier said, drinking the last sip from his flask. 'Imagine a spider, the size of a small woman, and you will be very close.'

'We'll keep a watch on Karla round the clock,' I suggested, 'until we throw Madame Zhou and her acid throwers in the sea. We –'

'I thank you, and accept your help, Didier and Naveen,' Karla cut me off. 'Much appreciated. But *you* can't, Lin.'

'I can't?'

'No.'

'Why not?'

'Because you won't be here. You're going away.'

'I am?'

'Yes.'

'When?'

'This morning.'

'Goodbye, Lin,' Didier said, rushing to hug me. 'I never wake before the afternoon, so I fear that I will miss your departure.'

'My departure?'

'To the mountain,' Karla said. 'To stay with Idriss, for two weeks.'

'Goodbye, Lin,' Naveen said, hugging me. 'See you when you get back.'

'Wait a minute.'

They were already walking to the door. We joined them, and as the elevator doors closed, Karla sighed.

'Every time an elevator door closes on me –' she began.

Didier handed her a flask.

'I thought you were out,' she said, taking a swig.

'It is my *reserve*.'

'Will you marry me, Didier, if I can divorce Ranjit, or kill him?'

'I'm already married to my vices, Karla dear,' Didier replied, 'and they're very jealous lovers, all of them.'

'Just my luck,' Karla said. 'All my guys are vices, or married to them.'

'Which one am I?' Naveen asked. 'Now that I'm one of the guys.'

'Maybe both,' Karla said. 'Which is why I have such high hopes for you.'

We reached Karla's car, and Randall opened the doors. I told them that I wanted to walk back to my bike, still parked near the Scorpion house. Karla walked me to the sea wall to say goodbye.

'Stick it out,' she said, her palm on my chest.

Her fingers were truth, touching me.

Imagine this, every day.

'As it happens,' I smiled, 'I'm a stick-it-out guy.'

She laughed. Temple bell.

'I'd like to be beside you, when Madame Zhou pops out of the shadows.'

'You can help me by staying two weeks up there, Lin. Let everything cool down. Let me set this in motion. Let me do what I have to do, and keep you out of it while I do it. Stay longer up there with Idriss, if you need.'

'Longer?'

'If you need.'

'What about us?'

She smiled. She kissed me.

'I'll come and see you.'

'When?'

'When you least expect it,' she said, walking back to the car.

'What about Madame Zhou?'

'We'll be merciful,' she said out the window as Randall drove away, 'until we find her.'

I watched the car out of sight, and began to walk the sea wall promenade. Early walkers brisked elbows and ankle socks at me, too serious to look at anything but the pavement.

Morning rose behind eastern buildings, shadow-veils lifting slowly from their faces. Dogs, impatient for action, barked here and there. Flocks of pigeons tested their skills, swooping the flourish of a dancer's dress over the path, and soaring invisible again.

I was a funeral procession of one. I could still feel the ashes on my fingers as I walked. Tiny fragments of Lisa's life were floating across the sea, and along the promenade.

Everything leaves a mark. Every blow echoes in the forest inside. Every injustice cuts a branch, and every loss is a fallen tree. The beautiful courage of us, the hope that defines our kind, is that we go on, no matter how much life wounds us. We walk. We face the sea and the wind and the salted truth of death, and we go on.

And every step we take, every breath we spend, every wish fulfilled is a duty to those lives and loves no longer graced, as we still are, with the spark and rhythm of the Source: the soul we loved, in their eyes.

PART SEVEN

CHAPTER FORTY-TWO

'LET ME BEGIN OUR LESSONS BY TELLING YOU where Khaderbhai was wrong in his instruction of you,' Idriss said, when I'd been with him on the mountain for three restless, sleep-sluggish nights, and three days filled with chores.

'But —'

'I know, I know, you want the Big Answers, to the Big Questions. Where did we come from? What are we now? Where are we going? Is there a purpose to life? Are we free, or are we determined by a Divine plan? And we'll get to them, irritating as they are.'

'Irritating, Idriss, or irresolvable?'

'The Big Questions only have small answers, and the Big Answers can only be found through small questions. But first, we need a little R and R.'

'Rest and Recuperation?'

'No, Repair and Rectification.'

'Rectification?' I asked, an eyebrow dissenting.

'Rectification,' he repeated. 'It is the duty of every human being to help others toward rectification, whenever the discourse between them is private, and of a spiritual nature. You will help me in this, and I will help you.'

'I'm not a spiritual person,' I said.

'You're a spiritual person. The very fact that we're having this conversation is the proof, although you don't have the eyes to see it.'

'Okay. But if the club lets me in, you should look at the membership criteria.'

We were sitting in a corner of the white-stone mesa with a view directly into the tallest trees in the valley. The kitchen was to our left. The main areas were behind us.

It was late afternoon. Small birds chittered from branch to branch, fussing and fidgeting among the leaves.

'You seek escape in humour,' he observed.

'Actually, I just try to stay on my game. You know Karla, Idriss, and you know she likes to raise the bar.'

'No, you are escaping, all the time, except for this woman. You are escaping everything, even me, except her. If she were not here, you would escape Bombay, as well. You are running, even when you are standing still. What are you afraid of?'

What was I afraid of? Take your pick. Let's start with dying in prison. I told him, but he wasn't buying it.

'That's not what you're afraid of,' he said, pointing the chillum at me. 'If something happened to Karla, would you be afraid?'

'Oh, yeah. Of course.'

'That's what I mean. The other things are things you already know, and things you can survive, if you have to. But Karla, and your family, that's where your real fear lives, isn't it?'

'What are you saying?'

He settled back again, smiling contentedly.

'It means that you are carrying fear within you, Lin. Fear should be outside us. It should only jump into us, when it is required. The rest of the time, we are designed by nature, and culture, to flourish in peace, because it's very difficult to maintain a connection to the Divine, when you're living in fear.'

'Which means?'

'You need to be rectified.'

'What if I *like* being unrectified? What if I think the unrectified part is the best part? What if I'm beyond rectification? Are there rules to this procedure?'

He laughed.

'You might be right,' he smiled. 'It might be the best part of you. But you can't know, unless you submit yourself to rectification.'

'*Submit?*'

'Submit.'

'See, when the language strays into cult territory, Idriss, the unrectified part of me yanks me outta there.'

'Let me put it this way,' Idriss said, leaning back in his chair. 'Suppose you know someone, know him fairly well, and suppose there

450

are some likeable things about him, but suppose this person is just a taker, and never a giver. Are you with me, so far?'

'Yes.'

'Very well. Suppose this person is ruthless with those not close to him, and never hesitates to ride on the success, talent, or money of others, but never works himself, and never puts anything back into the loop. Are you with me so far?'

'I met this guy,' I said, smiling. 'Go on.'

'Well, in that case it's your duty, as a more rectified person, to speak to him, and attempt to moderate his damaging behaviour. But that can only work, if the other man submits himself to your counsel. If he is too proud, or too unrectified, you cannot perform your duty with him, and you must perform it with a more receptive person instead.'

'Okay. I get it. But, Idriss, I wouldn't call that submission. I'd call that meeting me halfway.'

'And you're right, it's both of those things. It's also common ground, and agreement, and a free discourse, but none of those things are possible without a measure of submission from everyone involved. Civilisation is submission, in a good cause. Humility is the doorway to submission, and submission is the doorway to rectification. Are we clear?'

'I'm . . . with you, so far, Idriss.'

'Thank the Divine,' he sighed, relaxing and letting his hands fall into his lap. 'You have no idea how many people make me go through that, again and again, with example after example, just to shove their fucking pride or prejudice out of the way for a fucking minute.'

It was the first time I'd heard him swear. He saw the glimmer in my eye.

'I have to swear, and talk crazy, and shout, now and then,' he said, 'or I'd go out of my fucking mind.'

'I see . . .'

'I don't know how the Tantrics do it. All that physical penance, sacrifice and performing strenuous rituals, every day, for the whole of their lives. We teachers have it easy, compared to that. But we still go nuts, once in a while, under the sheer weight of being so fucking nice to everybody. Light the damn chillum, please. Where were we?'

'Khaderbhai's errors,' I said, lighting the chillum for him.

He puffed for a while, found the stream, and floated his eyes into mine.

'Tell me what you know about the movement toward complexity,' he said, staring fixedly at me.

'Khaderbhai said that if you take a snapshot picture of the universe, every billion years, all the way back to the Big Bang, we can see that the universe is always getting more complex. And that phenomenon, the continuous movement toward complexity, from the Big Bang to now, is the irreducibly defining characteristic of the universe as a whole. So, if this movement toward complexity defines the entire history of the universe –'

'– then it's a pretty good candidate as a reference point, for a definition of Good and Evil that is objective, and also universally acceptable,' Idriss finished for me. 'Anything that tends toward complexity is Good. Anything that tends against complexity is Evil.'

'And the quick moral test,' I added, 'is to ask yourself the question: *If everybody in the world did this thing I'm doing, or thinking of doing, would it help us get to more complexity, or hold us back?*'

'Excellent,' Idriss said, smiling and blowing smoke through his teeth. 'You're a good student. Let me ask a question. What is complexity?'

'Excuse me, sir.'

'Idriss. My name is Idriss.'

'Idriss, can I ask a question?'

'Of course.'

'Is the concept of Good and Evil really necessary?'

'Of course.'

'Okay. Well, what do you say to people who argue that Good and Evil are culturally defined, arbitrary constructs?'

'I have a simple answer,' he said, puffing contentedly. 'I tell them to fuck off.'

'That's your answer?'

'Certainly. I ask you, would you appoint someone who doesn't believe there's any such thing as Good and Evil as a babysitter to your child, or your aged grandfather?'

'With all due respect, Idriss,' I laughed, 'that's an appeal to cultural bias, and not an answer. Are Good and Evil arbitrary, or not?'

He leaned in closer to me.

'Because we have a destiny, which is undeniable, our journey is a moral journey. Understanding what is Good, and what is Evil, and the differences between them, is a required step for us to assume our role

452

as guardians of our own destiny. We are a young species, and assuming our destiny is a big step. We only became self-aware yesterday.'

'I'm not completely getting it,' I said, looking up from my notes. 'Thinking of things in terms of Good and Evil is required, at this stage in our spiritual evolution, is that it?'

'If there were no Good or Evil in the world,' he said, leaning back again, 'why would we have laws? And what are laws, but our fumbling, and constantly evolving attempt to establish what is Evil, if not what is Good?'

'I'm still not understanding it,' I said. 'I hope you'll be patient with me, but from what you've said, we could just as easily substitute some other words, like *right and wrong*, or *positive and negative*, for Good and Evil. And we might be better off, if we did.'

'Oh, I see,' he said, leaning in closer. 'You mean the *semantics* of it. I thought you were talking about the cultural architecture of Good and Evil.'

'Ah . . . no.'

'Very well, on that level, the terms Good and Evil are required, because they are connected to the Divine.'

'And what if people don't believe in the Divine?'

'I tell them to fuck off. I can't waste my time with atheists. They don't have an intellectual elbow to lean on.'

'They don't?'

'Of course, not. The fact that light has both physical and metaphysical characteristics means that it is nonsense to refuse the metaphysical. And an absence of doubt is an intellectual flaw. Ask any scientist, or holy man. Doubt is the agnostics' parachute. That's why agnostics have a softer landing than atheists, when the Divine speaks to them.'

'The Divine speaks?'

'Every day, to everyone, through the soul.'

'O . . . kay,' I said, more confused than when I'd asked the question. 'Maybe I'll put that one in the later file. I'm sorry for the intrusion.'

'Stop apologising. I asked you to define complexity.'

'Well, Khaderbhai never let me pin him down on that. I asked him, a few times, but he always slipped away.'

'What are your thoughts?'

My thoughts? I wanted to be with Karla. I wanted to know that she was safe. And if I had to be on the mountain, I wanted to listen to the

453

teacher, rather than talk. But I'd learned, after three days of discussion, that there was no escape from the fortress of his mind.

I took a sip of water, put the glass back on the table beside us carefully, and threw my hat in the psychic ring.

'At first, I started thinking of complexity as being about complicated things. The more complicated things are, the more complexity. A brain is more complex than a tree, and a tree is more complex than a stone, and a stone is more complex than space. Like that. But . . . '

'But?'

'But the more I think about complexity, the longer I stay with two things. Life, and will.'

'How did you get there?'

'I thought about a much more evolved and advanced alien species, travelling through space. I asked myself what they might be looking for. Wherever there's life, I think they'd be very interested. Wherever there's fully evolved will, I think they'd be fascinated.'

'That's pretty good,' Idriss said. 'I'm going to enjoy telling you more about this. Make me another chillum. Hey, Silvano!'

The holy man's constant companion, Silvano, crossed the white-stone space to join us.

'*Ji?*'

'Keep everyone away, for a while, please. And eat some food. You skipped lunch, again. What's that, man? Next, you'll be shaving your head. Don't be holier than the fucking holy man, okay?'

'*Ji,*' Silvano laughed, backing away, and catching my eye.

Since I'd returned to the mountain, Silvano had been an almost constant companion. He was always ready to help, and always good-humoured.

The fierce scowl was only and ever the fruit of his protective love for Idriss. In every other hour of morning or evening he was a kind, happy soul, in a place that was home.

'Complexity,' Idriss began again, when Silvano left, 'is the measure of sophistication in the expression of the set of positive characteristics.'

'Can you run that by me again, please?'

'A thing is complex, to the degree that it expresses the set of positive characteristics,' he replied.

'The *positive* characteristics?'

454

'The set of positive characteristics includes Life, Consciousness, Freedom, Affinity, Creativity, Fairness and many others.'

'Where does this set of positive characteristics come from? Who made the list?'

'They are universally recognised, and would be recognised by your more evolved and advanced alien species, I am sure. If you look at their opposites, you'll see why they are *positive* characteristics – Death, Unconsciousness, Slavery, Enmity, Destruction, and Iniquity. You do see what I am saying, don't you? These positive characteristics are universal.'

'Okay, if we accept the set of positive characteristics, how do we measure it? Who gets to measure it? How do we decide what's *more* positive, and *less* positive, Idriss?'

A black cat came to stand near us, arching its back.

Hello, Midnight. How did you get here?

The cat jumped into my lap, tested or punished my patience with claws, and sat down to sleep.

'There are two ways of looking at us,' Idriss said, glancing out at the trees, throbbing with birds. 'One says that we are just a cosmic accident, a fluke, and the lucky survivors of the real masters of the earth, the dinosaurs, after the fall of the Jurassic. That view says we're all alone, because a fluke like this is unlikely anywhere else. And that we live in a universe that has us, and billions of planets with nothing more than microbes, meek little methanogens, archaea and bacteria, inheriting alkaline seas.'

A dragonfly buzzed around him for a while. He coaxed it with an extended hand, muttering to himself. He pointed his finger at the forest, and the dragonfly flew away.

'The other view,' Idriss said, turning to me again, 'says that we're everywhere, in every galaxy, and here in this galaxy, in our solar system, about two-thirds of the way out from all the action at the Milky Way's hub, we're the lucky ones, where evolution happened to achieve it locally. Which explanation is more plausible, do you think?'

What did I think? I dragged myself back to the bridge of ideas.

'My money's on the latter. If it happened here, it's likely to be some-where else, as well.'

'Precisely. It's likely that we're not alone. And if the universe produces us, and creatures like us, when the soup is cooked just right, then the set of positive characteristics becomes tremendously significant.'

'For us?'

'For us, and in themselves.'

'Are we talking about essential and contingent distinctions?'

He laughed.

'Where did you study?' he asked, looking me over, as if for the first time.

'Here, at the moment.'

'Good,' he smiled. 'Good. There is no distinction between the two. Everything is contingent, and essential, at the same time.'

'I don't follow you, I'm sorry.'

'Let's take a short cut,' he said, leaning in close again, 'because I'm dispensing with the Socratic-Freudian-question-with-a-question-bullshit. Khaderbhai loved that, may he be at peace, but I prefer to get it off my chest, and argue it out afterwards. Is that okay with you?'

'Ah . . . yes. Sure. Please, go ahead.'

'Very well, here it is. I believe that every atom in existence has a set of characteristics, given to it by light at the instant of the Big Bang. Among those characteristics is the set of positive characteristics. Everything that exists, in the form of atoms, has the set of positive characteristics.'

'Everything?'

'Why do you say such a doubtful thing?'

'Doubtful, or doubting, Idriss?'

He leaned forward in his chair, and reached for the chillum.

'Do you doubt *yourself*, as well?'

Did I? Of course, I did. I'd fallen: I was one of the fallen.

'Yes.'

'Why?'

'At the moment, because I'm not paying for something I did.'

'And that troubles you?'

'Very much. I only made a down payment so far. I'll have to pay the rest sooner or later, one way or another, and probably with interest.'

'Maybe you're already paying for it now, and you don't know it.'

He was smiling, and sending gentle calm toward me.

'Maybe I am,' I said. 'But not enough, I think.'

'Fascinating,' he said, holding out the chillum for me to light. 'How do you get on with your father?'

'I love my stepfather. He's kind, and brilliant. He's one of the finest human beings I've ever known. I've betrayed him, with my life. I've betrayed his integrity with what I've become.'

I didn't know why I'd said it, or how the words had spilled from an urn of shame. I'd closed a steel door on the hurt I'd caused that fine man. Some things we do to others kneel so long in our hearts that bone becomes stone: a scarecrow in a chapel.

'Sorry, Idriss. I got emotional.'

'Excellent,' Idriss said softly. 'Have a smoke.'

He passed me the chillum. I smoked, and settled down.

'Okay,' Idriss said, leaning back and tucking his feet under his calves, 'let's wrap this up before some nice, sweet fellow comes along, with some girlfriend problem that I have to listen to. What's the matter with these young people? Don't they know it's *supposed* to be problematic? Are you ready?'

'Please,' I said, not ready at all, 'go ahead.'

'The set of positive characteristics is in every particle of matter in existence, expressed at its own level of complexity, and the more complex the arrangement of the matter, the more complex the manifestation of the set of positive characteristics. Are you with me so far?'

'Yes, I am.'

'Very well. At our human level of complexity, two remarkable things happen. First, we have non-evolutionary knowledge. Second, we have the capacity to override our animal nature, and behave like the unique human-animals that we are. Do you see?'

'Master!' Silvano said, rushing into the space. 'Can I take Lin with me, for a minute? Please!'

Idriss laughed happily.

'Of course, Silvano, of course. Go with him, Lin. We'll have more talks, later.'

'As you say, Idriss. I'll go through my notes, and be prepared when we talk again.'

Silvano rushed through the mesa, and onto the gentler path leading from the mountain.

'Hurry!' he called, sprinting ahead.

He branched off onto a side path, climbing very steeply to a break in the trees. There was a knoll, with a view toward the setting sun. Breathless, puffing hard, we stood side by side and stared at the view.

'Look!' Silvano said, pointing at a place near the centre of the horizon.

There was a building: a church, it seemed, with a spire.

'We have not missed it.'

As the red shimmer of the sun began to set, rays of light struck the ornament at the top of the church spire.

From our vantage, I couldn't see what the ornament was, a cross, or a cross within a circle, but the light radiating from the spire for a few moments was a field of coloured light, bathing all the homes and buildings in the valley.

It vanished in evening's haze, as the sun slept.

'Brilliant,' I said. 'When did you find this?'

'Yesterday,' he grinned, heading back to the camp, and his protected sage. 'I was dying to show it to you. I don't know how long it will last. Maybe another day or two, before the glory is gone.'

CHAPTER FORTY-THREE

WHEN WE REJOINED THE GROUP ON THE MESA I saw Stuart Vinson, with Rannveig, talking to Idriss in the same chairs where I'd been sitting. What was it Idriss had said? *Some nice, sweet fellow comes along, with some girlfriend problem that I have to listen to.*

I left them alone with him, and did some chores in the kitchen. I was washing dishes when Vinson and Rannveig joined me. Rannveig picked up a tea towel, and began drying the dishes. Candles in mounds like wax models of the mountain lit the space with yellow light. Vinson watched us from the doorway. Rannveig turned ice-blue eyes on him. He jumped forward, and began putting the dry dishes away.

'You know,' I said to the girl, 'there's an alternative to *Rannveig, like the runway at the airport*, in English. You can also be *Rannveig, as in catwalk runway.*'

'I prefer airports,' she said sternly. 'But thank you for your thought. I have seen Karla.'

'Uh-huh?'

'I would like to tell you about it, but in private. Is there somewhere we can go?'

'I guess. Sure.'

'Stuart,' she said, giving him the tea towel. 'I'm talking with Lin, for a while. Come and get me, in twenty minutes.'

I dried my hands and led her from the open kitchen to a fallen tree that many used as a place to read or converse. We sat down alone. I looked at Vinson, in the open kitchen, washing dishes contentedly.

'I lied,' Rannveig said.

'About what?'

'Karla didn't say or do anything that I would have to tell you privately. Karla only told me to tell you that she'll see you soon, and that she was keeping the faith, and changing the faith every day, just to be sure.'

'Nice,' I said, smiling. 'What *do* you want to talk about, Rannveig?'

'Your girlfriend, Lisa,' she said intently.

She was searching my eyes, unsure whether she'd crossed a line or not.

'Because your boyfriend died from an overdose, too?'

'Yes,' she said, lowering her eyes, then raising them quickly to look at Vinson.

'It's okay,' I said.

She turned to face me.

'When I heard about it,' she said, 'I was shocked. I only met her once, but it punched me in the stomach, you know?'

'Me, too. How are *you* coping?'

'How do I look?'

She'd filled out a little, and there was a healthy pink blush in her cheeks. Her startling eyes, blue light through blue ice, were clear. Her hands, which had fidgeted and curled into themselves whenever I'd seen her before, were as calm as sleeping kittens in her lap.

She wore a sky-blue T-shirt, a man's suit vest, and faded jeans. Her feet were bare. She wore no jewellery or make-up. Her oval-shaped face was driven by a strong nose, and full lips.

'You look very pretty,' I said.

She frowned at me. Maybe she thought I was coming on to her.

'I'm not coming on to you,' I laughed. 'I'm taken, for this and many lifetimes, past and to come.'

'You are? You found someone again, after –'

'Before. And after. Yeah.'

'And you're connected to someone? Like before?'

'Oh, yeah. But not like before.'

'Better?'

'Better. And it'll get better for you.'

She looked at Vinson, drying dishes.

'My family, in Norway, they're very strict Catholics. My boyfriend was everything they hated, so, you know, to show my independence I followed him to India.'

'What was he doing in India?'

'We were supposed to be going to an ashram, but when we got to Bombay, we never moved.'

'He'd been here before?'

'A few times, yes. Now, I know it was for drugs, each time.'

'But it hurt, when he died. And it still hurts, right?'

'I wasn't in love with him, but I liked him a lot, and I really tried to care for him.'

'And what about Vinson?'

'I think I'm falling in love with Stuart. It's the first time I've ever felt like this about anyone. But I'm not letting myself go to him. I can't. I know he wants it, and I want it too, but I can't.'

'Well . . .'

'How are you coping with it?' she demanded, her mouth wide with pleading. 'How did you get connected again?'

How did I get connected again? It was a good question, for a man who was a mountain away from the woman he loves.

'Stuart will be generous, I think,' I said. 'He'll give you time. There's no rush. From what I can see, he's much happier than when I first met him.'

'He could be happier,' she sighed. 'And so could I. Do you get stuck, sometimes, in memories?'

'Sure.'

'You do?'

'Sure. It's a natural thing. We're emotional minds. And it's okay, so long as it's a ride, and not a way of life. Are you flashing back?'

'Yeah. I see him in my mind, when I stop thinking. It's like he's still with me.'

'You know, the guy you were talking to, the sage, Idriss, he told someone yesterday that they can release a departed spirit by offering food, on a plate, by a river, and leaving it there for the crows and the mice to eat.'

'How . . . how does that work?'

'I'm no expert, but apparently the appeased spirits are released, to the next part of the journey.'

'I'd try anything, at the moment. Whenever I relax and stop thinking, he's right beside me.'

I'd started the conversation about appeasing departed spirits as a distraction, to raise her own spirits, but the words opened a door in her eyes, showing how afraid she was inside. She was shaking. She hugged herself.

461

'Listen, Rannveig, you know, there's a river you have to cross, on the way back to the main road. I'll prepare a plate for you, and you can leave it by the river, if you like. Did your boyfriend have a sweet tooth?'

'He did.'

'Good. There's plenty of sweets prepared for tonight. Maybe your boyfriend will be so happy he'll move on, and leave you alone.'

'Thank you. I'll definitely try it.'

'It's gonna be okay,' I said. 'It gets easier.'

'Do you meditate?'

'Only when I'm writing. Why?'

'I've been thinking I should start meditating or something,' she said absently, then quickly found my eyes again. 'What do you think of him?'

'Vinson?'

'Yes, Stuart. I don't have a brother or father here to ask about him. What do you think of him?'

I looked at Vinson, stacking the last of the pots and dishes on the shelves, and wiping down the long stainless steel sinks.

'I like him,' I said. 'And I'm absolutely sure he's nuts about you. If you're not his soul mate, Rannveig, you should break it to him. Soon. This is it, for him.'

'Do you ever get depressed? Stuart told me some things about you. About your life. Do you ever get days when you think of suicide?'

'Never in captivity, and one way or another, most of my life has been spent in captivity.'

'Seriously. Do you ever have days when you simply want it to end? All of it, at once?'

'Look, suicide and I are nodding acquaintances. But I'm more your till-the-last-dying-breath kind of guy.'

'But life can be so shit, sometimes,' she said, looking at me again.

'It's all good, even the bad stuff. It's all blood, flowing through the heart, and wonderful minutes, of wonderful things. I'm a writer. I have to believe in the power of love. Suicide isn't an option.'

'Not for you.'

'And not for you. If you're thinking about it, you can also put some thought into the fact that you don't have the right to take your own life. Nobody does.'

'Why not?' Rannveig like the runway asked, her eyes wide, innocent of the cruel, broken question she'd just asked.

'Think of it this way, Rannveig, does a deranged person have the right to kill a stranger?'

'No.'

'No. And when suicide is in your head, *you're* the deranged person, and you're also the stranger, in danger of the harm you might do to yourself. No matter how bad things get, you don't have the right to kill the stranger that you might become, for a while, in your own life. The rest of your life would tell you, at that point, it's not an option.'

'But you don't get the blues, ever?' she asked.

She was so earnest that I wanted to put my arm around her.

'Of course. Everybody does. But you're young, and your life is so rich. It's a hoard of minutes. We don't have the right to destroy them, or even waste them, as I'm doing. We only have the right to experience them. So, get that crap out of your head. Not an option, okay? And don't stress. It'll pass. Vinson's a good guy. He'll wait as long as it takes for you to make up your mind, and get your feelings right, whichever way they fall. Everything will pass. Get up and fight.'

'You're right, I know, but sometimes the cloud takes a long time to clear the sun.'

'You're a very nice, very serious girl, who went through the same burning door that I did. It knocked you around, like it did me. You're doing fine. You're doing great. Look at me. I was running around town getting kicked by the cops. You're so much healthier than when I saw you last time. Talk to Idriss before you leave. He's pretty cool.'

'You are a criminal,' she said flatly.

It was a statement.

'Ah . . . sure.'

'Can a woman who is *not* a criminal, love a criminal? Have you seen this?'

I had, but not often.

'Ah . . . sure.'

She looked doubtful, but I didn't want to convince her.

'You're gonna have to talk to Vinson, about crime and punishment,' I said. 'It's none of my business, how another man makes his money on the street.'

'Do you know that Stuart killed someone?'

463

'You know,' I said, looking up at the small groups of people talking and doing chores on the mesa, 'if we're gonna talk about Vinson, we should invite Vinson.'

'Not now,' she said softly. 'Not yet.'

I stood, and she stood with me.

'Do you wish,' she said falteringly, 'do you constantly wish that you had done something else?'

'It's just regret,' I said.

'Regret,' she repeated absently.

'You know how they have *proof of life*, in a kidnapping?'

'Not really.'

'When someone's kidnapped, the negotiator wants proof that the kidnapped person is still alive. A phone call, or film. Proof of life.'

'Okay.'

'Regret is just proof of soul, Rannveig. If you didn't feel it, you wouldn't be the nice person you are, and Vinson wouldn't be deranged about you. It's a good thing. And it's a better thing when it fades, which it will, soon enough.'

We walked back toward the centre of the mesa. Vinson joined us, a smile like an empty beach on his face.

'I'm going to talk to Idriss now, Stuart,' Rannveig said, walking past him. 'Please collect me after twenty minutes.'

'Okay, babe,' he said, grinning after her, his eyes following her like puppies.

'What brings you to the mountain, Vinson?'

'It was Rannveig's idea. She was talking to Karla. That Karla's something, isn't she? I don't understand half of what she says.'

'You're doin' okay with half. She's the quickest draw I ever saw.'

'How did you meet her?'

'She saved my life,' I said. 'Listen, they've just started the main fire. We can sit there, while Rannveig talks to Idriss. Sound like a plan?'

'You bet.'

Most of the students on the mountain were involved in cooking, or preparing devotional idols for prayers. I asked one of them to prepare the plate of sweets for Rannveig's persevering ghost, and to leave it with Silvano.

There was no-one sitting by the fire. Vinson and I sat on box crates, looking through the flames at the flame of Vinson's heart, twenty metres away with Idriss, and beyond sound.

'You know, Lin,' he said, turning to me, 'I wanted to come, anyway. I wanted to tell you how sorry I am for your loss. Lisa was a fine girl.'

'Thanks, Vinson. You were at the service Karla organised. This is the first chance I've had to tell you, I appreciate it.'

'It was nothing. We were honoured to attend, man.'

'How's Rannveig doing?'

'Well,' he said, scratching at his short beard, and stretching his mouth into a struggle with words.

He sighed, and let his hands fall to his thighs.

'She's hurt. She's really hurt. I think, sometimes, that maybe I should get some professional help, a grief counsellor, but then, like, I always come back to the fact that nobody will ever care about her as much as I do.'

'Except for Rannveig herself.'

'Yeah, of course, kinda, when she's better.'

'Now, actually.'

'But, like, she's not a hundred per cent yet, man.'

'She has to be her own principal caregiver, Vinson, just like you are for Vinson, see? Cut her as much slack as she needs. Let her explore.'

'Explore?'

'Whatever she wants to do, or try, support her in it. Just give her time, and space. If she's yours, sooner or later she'll come to know it.'

Advice, from a man who wasn't with the only woman he ever loved, because he couldn't reach out from a shadow of the lost. Who the hell was I to give advice?

'Who the hell am I to give advice, man?' I said. 'Do your best, Vinson. We mess up. We all mess up. We'll probably never *stop* messing up. But if we just keep doing our best, sooner or later it's gotta be good enough for somebody. Am I right?'

'Amen to that, brother!' he said, slapping hands with me. 'You know, I saw Concannon the other day. I was in Null Bazaar, visiting one of my dealers. He came in with a few guys. He was walking with a stick. It's black, with a silver skull for a knob. Pretty cool, although I wouldn't mind betting he's got a sword in it.'

'No doubt. Did he say where he was staying?'

'No. But I heard a rumour he's got a place way out, in Khar. But it's only a rumour. There's a lotta rumours floating around about that guy. He asked about you.'

'What did he say?'

'*Where's the Australian convict?*'

'What did you tell him?'

'I said, *Is that a trick question?* Lucky for me, he's got a sense of humour. I got outta there pronto, man. That guy was okay, when I met him, kinda, but now, like, a whole city isn't far enough away.'

'Don't stress about Concannon. There's a line ahead of you there.'

Idriss and Rannveig stood up. We walked around the fire to join them. Silvano was a step behind, the rifle on his shoulder.

'You're sure you won't stay the night?' Idriss asked her, holding her hands in his.

'Thank you, sir, no. Stuart's maid has a bad cough, and I want to be sure she is okay. She has been so kind to me, and there is no-one at home with her until we return.'

'Very well, please give her our blessings. And come again, whenever you wish.'

She knelt to touch the earth before the teacher's feet. Vinson shook hands amiably.

'Thank you for your hospitality, sir,' he said.

'You are most welcome,' Idriss said.

Silvano drew two young men to his side.

'These two men are walking down now by the safer path,' he said. 'They will guide you, one torch in front, and one torch behind.'

'They've got the plate of food for the sweet tooth spirit,' I told her. 'It's wrapped in red cloth. They'll give it to you at the base, and tell your driver where to stop. You'll find the riverbank by torchlight.'

'Thank you,' she said dreamily. 'Thank you for everything.'

They said their farewells, and walked into the darkness beyond the fire.

And I dreamed of them, that night, and a few times in the week that followed. And Didier visited my dreams, reminding me of the priorities. And Abdullah, the shadow-rider, visited dreams that raced over rooftops. And Lisa, calling to me in echoes of sorrow and remorse, hers and mine.

The world below the mountain was changing, of course, as everything does, but I couldn't connect to it, except in those dreams. I wasn't just physically separated from the life I'd made my own, and the people who'd become my society of friends: the mountain was my heart's retreat from that world, and it faded in that cleaner, clearer air, only forcing its way back through visitors and dreams.

They were hard dreams. They woke me, most nights and mornings, before the sun and songbirds could ease me from sleep. And the dream-words that woke me that night were Rannveig's, asking me about regret.

I sat up, listening to night sounds in the forest. A figure dressed in a robe as white as the stones beneath his feet walked across the courtyard of the mesa.

It was Idriss, carrying his long staff. He stopped at the edge of the clearing, where a break in the tree line gave a view of the city's lights on the horizon.

He stood there for a while, appeasing spirits of his own, perhaps, or walking his own tightrope between attrition and contrition. Then he walked back to his cave slowly, his face drawn in sadness, and his steps quiet on the shifting stones.

Regret is a ghost of love. Regret is a nicer self that we send into the past from time to time, even though we know it's too late to change what we said, or did. We do it because it's human: a thing of our kind. We do it because we care, drawn by threads of shame that only fray and wither in the sea of regret.

Along the way regret, even more than love, teaches us that harm creates harm, and compassion creates compassion. And having done its work, regret fades to the nothing that all things become.

I lay back, wondering if Rannveig had placed the food beside the river on her way home from the mountain, and if the spirit she was resurrecting with remorse was free to leave her, in peace.

CHAPTER FORTY-FOUR

I SAW MANY VISITORS SWEAT THEIR WAY into the mountain camp, and glow like stones in clear water when they strolled out again. The teacher was always gentle and serene. Nothing dislodged his benign smile. Nothing interrupted his trance of patient empathy. Until, that is, he was with Silvano and me, playing cards behind the shower screen.

His equanimity capsized in the cardroom-washroom, and he swore oaths against stupidity and cursed the *malignantly uninformed*.

The devotees beyond the curtain could hear his tirades and cursing, but the thin sheet was enough to preserve the dignity that never failed when Idriss was in public, and the heir to their eyes.

It was a peaceful enough place: an open prison. There was no authority, and no walls but those you had to climb inside. Yet the chains that bound the devotees who lived with Idriss were no less severe.

They loved him, and couldn't leave him without weeping distress. Mind you, he was an easy man to love.

'Non-evolutionary knowledge,' he said, in one of our rare, undisturbed hours, two weeks after I'd arrived on the mountain. 'Summarise.'

'Again, Idriss?'

'Again, impudent intellect,' he said, leaning close so that I could relight his joint. 'Knowledge isn't knowledge, until the truth of it is self-evident in the sharing. Again.'

'Okay, in a world where apples fall from trees, it's sufficient *evolutionary* knowledge to step out of the way from falling apples, or to catch one, or pick one up off the ground and eat it. All the other stuff we know, like the rate at which it falls, and the calculations that allow us to land a craft on Mars, is non-evolutionary. Not required, for evolutionary purposes. So, why do we have it? And what's it for? Is that a fair summary?'

'C-plus. You left out that if you extrapolate all the branches of non-evolutionary knowledge, all the sciences, arts and philosophy to their logical extremes, you get knowledge about how everything does everything.'

'And?'

'Well, in itself, nothing at all. At the moment, for example, based on our record here on Earth, the sciences and philosophies are giving us the means to annihilate ourselves, and most of the other species with us. So, in itself, all our knowledge means nothing. But, combined with our capacity to override our animal nature, and to express our uniquely human nature, which is a very nice nature, as it happens, it is everything.'

'I'm not seeing it.'

'You're looking right at it, but you're not seeing it. All animals have an animal nature. We have an animal nature that's pretty close to that of bonobos, I'm glad to say, but just like bonobos do, we act like chimps when we're under extreme stress.'

'And that's our animal nature?'

'Pretty much. But unlike chimps and bonobos, we don't always *have* to do that. We have the capacity to modify the way we behave. A chimp, is a chimp, is a chimp. But a human being can be anything that he or she wants to be.'

'How, exactly?'

'When we express our truly human nature, we create humane-human things that don't exist in the animal world. Things like democracy, and justice. There's no Democratic Front of Chimpanzees. There's no Court of Justice for lions and zebras.'

'I guess not, but —'

'We humans, uniquely, can shape our behaviour with ideas, and feelings, and devotion and art. Things that come from nowhere else but our humanity. We make ourselves, don't you understand?'

'There's plenty of animal nature on display, Idriss,' I said. 'I've put some of it on display myself.'

'Of course, our animal nature expresses itself very frequently, and not always pleasantly. Most of the bad news, anywhere, caused by man, is our animal nature, expressing itself without constraint. But the stuff in the arts pages and the science pages of the same newspaper, has more to do with our humane-human nature.'

'I don't see a lot of good, where I work.'

'We can be anything we want to be, including angels. The best that we can do, when we're determined to do well by one another, is unmatched in the natural world. And when our humane-human selves release our minds from vanity, and greed, we will not only achieve miracles, we'll *be* the miracles that we're destined to be.'

It was a long speech, and as with many of his longer speeches, he ended it with a question.

'What is your understanding of the difference between Fate and Destiny?'

Fate, Karla once said, *and Destiny, his Twin Sister.*

'I just can't live with the notion that we're not in control of our own destiny, and that Fate can play with us, like so many toy soldiers.'

'Fate doesn't play with us,' Idriss said, finishing a joint. 'Fate responds to us.'

'How?'

He laughed.

It was a day so bright, immaculate heaven so blue, that we were both wearing sunglasses. He couldn't see my eyes, and I couldn't see his. It helped, because very often, when I stared into his leaf-brown eyes long enough, I fell like a kid into a creek, and had to think fast to catch up, when a question shook me from the stream.

The students and devotees talked and laughed in the shade, all the chores done for the day. The sky seemed to hover much higher than it usually did, as if there was more space and light.

'You want to know how Fate works, because you want to fight with Fate, isn't it?' Idriss asked. 'Your instinct is to fight, if you feel yourself under threat. You think that Fate is fighting with you, and you want to gain an advantage in the struggle. Am I right?'

'I'd like to win in a fair fight, but I get the feeling that Fate cheats.'

'And how does Fate cheat?'

'I think Fate and Time have a thing going on. They're partners in crime.'

'Definitely,' he laughed. 'Fate is another name for Karma, which is another name for Time, which is another name for Love. All of them are names for a tendency field, which permeates the universe. In fact, it's not too much to say that it *is* the universe.'

'A tendency field, Idriss?'

'A tendency field.'

'What's it made of, this *tendency field*?'

'Dark energy, probably, but it's not what it's made of that counts. It's what it *is* that matters, just as all the atoms that your body is made of are not what you *are*.'

'Okay, a dark energy tendency field,' I said, trying to follow. 'And what does it do?'

'The tendency field is what drives the movement toward complexity, and it has done so since the singularity. In that sense, it *is* the universe. When conscious self-awareness occurs, emerging from sufficient complexity, a link is established between the tendency field and each individual consciousness that engages with it.'

'What kind of a link?'

'The tendency field is what responds to our instinct for the Divine. We can't know the Divine, directly. We can't directly know the Source of this universe, and its tendency field, and all the other infinite universes like this one, infinitely expanding like flowers and shrivelling again to nothing, and blooming again, in a garden of eternal creation, somewhere in the mind of God. We can't know that. We don't even know all there is to know about our *own* universe, let alone the infinite multiverse, or the Divine that created it. But we *can* know the tendency field very directly, any time we want.'

'How?'

Idriss laughed again, and lit another joint.

'Isn't it your turn to talk?'

He mocked me gently at least once in every talk: to keep me on my game, perhaps, or to provoke me into a revelation. Every guru, even those who tell you there are no gurus, is an excellent psychologist, skilled in the provocation of truth.

'I do interrupt a lot, Idriss, and I'm sorry, but only when I don't understand. Right now, I got it. Please, go ahead.'

'Very well,' he said, relaxing again with his feet tucked up beneath him in the canvas chair. 'Let's do this thing. At the Big Bang, some characteristics were imparted to the born universe. Space, for example, and time, and matter, and gravitation, all examples of characteristics imparted to the universe by the Big Bang. And the tendency field, which drives the tendency toward complexity, was another of the characteristics imparted at the Big Bang. I also want to say that the set of positive characteristics was imparted to every particle of matter, as well. You're with me so far?'

'Space, time, matter, gravitation, classical physics, particle physics, tendency field, positive characteristics, all imparted in the Birth-Bang.'

'Yes,' he chuckled. 'Concisely put. The tendency field operates on a very simple semi-Boolean program – *If This, Then That* – which runs everything, everywhere. The basic algorithm, *if this happens, then that happens*, runs everything, including entropy. If it happens that a fully self-aware consciousness arises, then the connection to the tendency field happens.'

'Doesn't entropy run counter to complexity?'

'No. Entropy runs counter to order. And anyway, infinite entropy only applies in a closed system. And with black holes in our universe, leading who knows where, this isn't a closed system.'

'Sorry to go back. You mean, no matter what you do in life, good or bad, you can always connect to this tendency field?'

'If you get in tune with the tendency field, through expanding and exploring the set of positive characteristics within yourself, the tendency field responds with constant energy, and affirmations. If you work against the tendency field, by being negative, unfair, unloving, and unconscious of the truth, you weaken your connection to the tendency field, and you experience existential dread, no matter how rich or famous or powerful you are.'

'Existential calm, instead of dread? Is that what you're saying?'

'If you remain connected to the tendency field, you have serenity. Life is connection, the world is connection, and both are always impoverished by disconnection.'

'Just about everyone I know, outside of my close friends, has some kind of existential dread. Isn't it a part of the human condition?'

'Nothing is a part of the human condition, but our common humanity. A few hundred of us we were, when we began. A few hundred, with no claws or savage teeth but those we cut from the predators that tried to prey upon us. We learned, through cooperation and love, to fear no creature, and no place on land or sea. We are magnificent, and we are malignant. But we can be anything we want ourselves to be, from killers of neighbours, to saviours of distant neighbours in our galaxy. We can shape our destiny. We have the tools. We can –'

A commotion among the students drew the holy man's attention. We turned to see that Naveen and Diva had arrived on the mountain. They were talking with the small crowd.

'What a pretty girl,' Idriss said quietly. 'Do you know her?'

'Her name's Divya Devnani, but I suggest that you call her Diva.'

'Is her father Mukesh Devnani, the industrialist?'

'The same.'

'Then she must be in trouble. Introduce me, please.'

'Yes, sir.'

I made the introductions. When Idriss took Diva by the hand and led her to the comfortable deckchair I'd vacated, I walked Naveen to sit with me on the log where Rannveig sat with me, weeks before, talking crime and punishment.

Naveen opened the discussion with crime, and punishment.

'Concannon's moving his dope gig around,' he said when we sat down. 'It's a moveable beast, and hard to pin down, but I'm starting to get a line on him. And there's a contract out on Ranjit.'

'You don't say. How much is it?'

Naveen looked at me, all straight-arrow detective.

'Why do you want to know?'

'Just curious,' I said, smiling. 'If there's a pot, I've got some friends who'd like to throw a few bucks in.'

'Matter of fact, there is,' he smiled. 'Legend has it, a local contractor and a local politician were trying to outbid each other to have him killed, but then joined forces, to double the pot.'

'That should keep him out of Bombay for a while. Check with anyone who knows Goa, if you can. I've got some friends from the Company in Delhi. I'll ask around, and see if he's hiding there.'

'Hell, yeah. On another front, there were two fights between Sanjay Company and Scorpion guys in Colaba last week. Shots fired. Two shops wrecked. That little war the Scorpions started at Leo's got hotter. One of their houses on Marine Lines was burned down. In retaliation, the newspapers say. A female nurse died in the fire. There's a helluva racket in the press. Sanjay was detained, but they let him go. Lack of evidence.'

I'd been in that house. I knew that Vishnu's wife was ill. That's why a nurse was in the mansion; a nurse, who died. I knew that Vishnu wouldn't stop until the fire was burning in front of Sanjay's eyes.

'Oh, and your friend Abdullah is back,' Naveen added. 'He said that he'll meet you, when you get off the mountain. But he said to stay here, at least another week.'

'Another week?'

'That's what he said.'

'Damn, that was a news report. Thanks for coming up here, to tell me.'

'Actually,' he said, smiling, 'we came up here with a friend of yours.'

I searched his eyes. He nodded.

'Where is she?'

'In that second cave, over there. She asked me to give her a few minutes before telling you, and nobody says no to Karla!'

CHAPTER FORTY-FIVE

I RAN ACROSS THE SLIPPERY WHITE STONES, stopping before the entrance to the cave. I glimpsed inside. She was sitting on a wooden stool, examining a silver figurine of the Goddess Lakshmi resting in her palm.

I stood in the entrance to the cave, facing the wind as she'd done, the first time I'd seen her on the mountain.

'Tell me a joke, Karla.'

She turned slowly to look at me. From the corner of my eye, I could see that she was smiling.

'So,' I asked, 'you got a joke, or don't you?'

'Okay. Why do cops call informers two-slappers?'

'Three weeks I haven't seen you, and you give me cop jokes?'

'It's sixteen days and eight hours. You want a joke, or don't you?'

'Okay. Why do cops call informers two-slappers?'

'Because you gotta hit them once, to start them talking, and hit them again, to shut them up.'

'Come here,' I said.

She kissed me, arms around my neck, legs stretched to toes, her body pressed to mine like two trees grown as one.

'I'm so glad to see you,' I said. 'What's with the ten minutes Naveen had to stall me?'

'I was a little hot from the climb, and I wanted to look cool. For you.'

'Let's go someplace.'

I took Karla to Silvano's Point, where we sat on stony grass with a wide view of the trees below. A breeze hit the cliff in waves, rolling up from the valley in gusts of warm air. Trees on the cliff-edge swayed, sprinkling feathered shade.

'Tell me everything,' she said.

'That's funny. I was just going to ask you the same thing.'

'No, you go first.'

'There's not much to report. It's generally pretty quiet. It's kind of like a theme park, up here, for people who like housework. They're big on chores.'

'How's that working out?'

'Okay. I prefer chores to rules.'

'Thanks for staying, Shantaram. I love you for it. I know it's not where you wanted to be.'

She hadn't explained why she wanted me out of the city, and I didn't ask her. I was just glad that she was with me.

'It's never boring, though. A lot of people come up to see Idriss, and only stay for an hour or two.'

'What kind of people?'

She relaxed, leaning on her palms, and smiling happily in the sunlight.

'There was a politician up here a couple of days ago. He had an O.K. Corral of guns and bodyguards. He wanted advice. Idriss told him to give up his bodyguards, and armoured cars, and walk among the people in a simple shirt, trousers and sandals.'

'What did the politician say?'

'The politician said that if he did that, he'd be murdered. *There's your problem*, Idriss said. *Go and solve it.*'

'I love that guy,' she said. 'He should do stand-up.'

'And half a dozen Shiva sadhus came and stayed. They preferred their oxygen smoked, argued with Idriss day and night, and started waving their Shiva tridents over their heads, threatening to kill everybody. In the end, Silvano and I had to handle it.'

'With Silvano's rifle?'

'Of course not. You can't shoot holy men. We paid them to leave.'

'Smart move. How's it been, with Silvano?'

'Great. He's a good guy.'

'I knew you'd like him, because he's a lot like you.'

'Like me?'

'Oh, yeah.'

I thought about it, but not for long.

'I like him. I'd like him on our team.'

'Our team? We've got a team?'

'I've been giving it some thought. I've been thinking we could –'

'Let's talk about that later,' she said. 'How's it going with Idriss?'

I wanted to talk about us, and what we were going to do together in the Island City, or away from it. I wanted to talk about us, and I wanted to kiss her.

'I'd rather talk about us,' I smiled.

'How's it going with Idriss?' she repeated.

'Idriss . . . is pretty cool, I gotta admit.'

'Has he opened any doors for you?'

A big question, and a funny one at that: I spent most of my life closing doors, and doing everything I could to keep them closed. There was too much of the past that I didn't want to remember.

'Doors in the mind, certainly,' I said. 'But if you mean, am I a transformed man? No, it's still me.'

She looked out at the view: the valley and the spired village, shimmering in the distance.

'Did you find Madame Zhou?' I asked.

'She's gone to ground,' Karla replied, looking at the point where earth strains to kiss the sky.

'Nothing at all?'

'No-one's seen her or heard from her since Didier and Naveen started asking around. She's probably still here. She's cunning. If she doesn't want to be found, she's invisible.'

'Nobody's invisible. If she's still around, we'll find her. Naveen gave me a message from Abdullah. He –'

'Told you to wait here at least another week. Abdullah called, and told me. That's why I pulled Naveen up here with me.'

'And Diva?'

'That's something else. I wanted her to meet Idriss. I have plans for Diva, and something tells me that Idriss is a cosmic connection.'

'Speaking of cosmic connections,' I said, pulling her on top of me to kiss her.

Earth-smell through her hair. The sun touching us with warm light breaking through leaves, and winds rushing trees on the cliff with hot breath. Karla.

'Can we sleep here tonight, Shantaram?'

'We can sleep here now.'

'Good. Then let's go back to the kids, and play nice.'

'Well . . . I . . . '

We played nice with Naveen and the students. Idriss kept Diva in conversation for two hours, and then insisted that the poor little rich girl stay the night, in a poor little poor girl cave, with the other girls on the mountain.

Diva surprised me by agreeing immediately, and then unsurprised me by sending Naveen back to the car to fetch her essential supplies.

When we'd eaten dinner, and cleaned the dishes, some students left for the night, and others retired to the caves, to study or sleep. The night owls, my friends, sat around the fire, and sipped too-sweet black tea, laced with rum.

I stood to say goodnight to Idriss and Silvano, sitting with me, on the other side of the fire.

Naveen, Diva, and Karla talked and laughed together, firelight painting mysterious beauty.

'That Diva is a remarkable young woman,' Idriss said softly, as she laughed at something Karla said.

In her private conversation with Idriss, Diva had made the sage laugh so hard that he got the giggles, and couldn't stop. Watching her laughing by the fire, the holy man chuckled again.

'Don't you think she's remarkable?'

I looked at her, sitting next to Karla. I couldn't see it.

'I see a very spoilt girl,' I said. 'Smart, pretty, and spoilt.'

'You might be right, now,' Idriss laughed. 'But think of what she will become, and what she could achieve.'

He retired for the night, Silvano at his side.

As I joined the others, Diva dragged Karla by the elbow, and they walked off together to sit in the canvas chairs that faced the eastern forest.

I could just see their profiles, dipping past the edges of the chairs as they talked. I sat down with Naveen.

'Good to see you smiling, man,' he observed.

'Was I smiling?'

'You were smiling. Well, before Karla left you were.'

He prodded at the fire with a stick, throwing up brittle sparks.

'What's on your mind, kid?'

'It can wait till morning,' he said, pestering the fire.

478

'No time like the present. What's up?'

'I'm worried about her,' he said, glancing up at the girls sitting in the canvas chairs, just out of hearing, except for their laughter.

'Karla?'

'No,' he frowned. 'Diva.'

'What's the problem?'

'Her father got mixed up with some very bad guys. I'm talking *supremely* bad guys. It's long money, and they've got short tempers.'

'Wait a minute. Mukesh Devnani is one of the richest guys in Bombay.'

'He took in a lot of black investment money from somewhere. He wanted to move from building convention centres to building whole towns and cities, straight off the plan. The only people with the real money to make that dream come true –'

'– were the short-tempered guys. And now they want their money back, with interest.'

'Right. It's a weird thing that Ranjit is mixed up in this.'

'Ranjit? How?'

'He was running a campaign in his newspapers against one of the big new cities that Mukesh was set to build. The scare stories forced the government to change course, and cancel Mukesh's permits. The whole thing started falling apart. It's gotten so bad that when the cops come to his mansion, we never know if it's to protect him or arrest him.'

'He has to pay up, Naveen, even if it bankrupts him.'

'That's what *I* say. That's what I told him, respectfully. But there's some hitch. I don't know what it is. I don't get up to the mansion in Juhu very often now. I put this together in the few chances I got to rummage around in his office. I think Diva . . . I think she's a kidnap, waiting to happen. Her Mother died six years ago. She's his only child. His only heir. It's a way for his enemies to hurt him. It's just logic, in a twisted way. I'm worried, man.'

'You really think it's that bad?'

'I do. I'm . . . a little freaked out. This is over my head, and I really care about this girl, even if I think her father is a prick.'

'Take her out of the city.'

'I've tried. She knows that something's up with her dad. She won't leave.'

'You could hide her, for a while.'

'How? Where? She's famous, man. I spend more time dodging the press than I do dodging bad guys. And she loves it. I had to ban the phone. She was calling the paparazzi and telling them where she'd be. She knows them on a first name basis. She buys them rounds of drinks. She's a godmother to one of their kids.'

I laughed, but then saw that he was still too serious for laughter.

'She thinks discretion is anything that doesn't involve skywriting, which she's done, for her eighteenth birthday party. She told me. It'll be the same wherever she goes.'

'You could hide her in the slum,' I suggested. 'If she's game for it. I hid there myself once, for eighteen months, and it's one of the safest places I've ever been in my life.'

'Would they take her in?'

'The head man's a friend. And he loves a party. He's gonna love Diva. But it's not for everybody, and Diva certainly isn't everybody.'

'Are you serious, about the slum?'

'Unless you can think of a better place to hide a Bombay Diva from the madding crowd? But no promises. I have to run it by my friend, first.'

He looked again at the girls. Karla and Diva were honking with laughter, covering their mouths and noses to smother the noise.

They were drinking something. It looked good.

'Listen, Naveen, if you still think it's a good idea when I come down from the mountain, I'll ask Johnny Cigar about it. Okay?'

'I'm not sure how I'd to sell it to Diva, but okay. Yeah. Please do it, Lin. I want every choice I've got, if things go bad with her father's friends.'

'You got it, Naveen. Let's find out what the girls are drinking.'

We talked together for a while, four friends bound in fear as much as in faith; in comradeship as much as companionship.

At the first break in laughing-talk, Karla and I said goodnight, gathered a batch of blankets, some water and a lunch box, and walked by torchlight to Silvano's Point.

I set up a bower for us, using two blankets as lean-shelters, and padding the ground with the rest. We settled on hips and elbows. I opened the lunch box to show cold fried *pakodas*, pineapple, cashew and lentil cakes, a few handfuls of nuts, and Bengali custard in small clay pots.

She closed it again, and emptied her purse, throwing two hip flasks, a cigarette case and a gold cigarette lighter with a small watch set into it onto the blanket. The hands on the watch were set at twenty-three minutes past midnight.

'The watch on your lighter has stopped,' I said, reaching for it.

'Don't wind it,' she said quickly. 'I like it that way.'

'Karla, I'll be back in a week, and I've been —'

'Let me go first,' she said.

'Okay.'

'I'm putting some money into a business venture with Didier and Naveen. They're going to expand the detective business, and I think they're on to something.'

'Okay, but I was actually thinking of a black market money franchise. I've got the contacts, and I can buy their cash, if not their loyalty. I can make a good living for us.'

'I've got money.'

'And you should keep it.'

'We don't know how long we'll be here in Bombay,' she said, taking a sip from a flask and passing it to me. 'Let's enjoy this ride as much as we can, and as safely as we can.'

'The detective business isn't on the top ten list of safe occupations. I'm pretty sure it's not on the top hundred.'

'It's still way above crime and punishment, Shantaram.'

Crime, and punishment. How many times had I heard or thought that phrase, that echo of Fate's laugh, in the last few days? How many times does it take?

'I don't see a place for me in that set-up, Karla.'

'You're a silent partner,' she said. 'Like me.'

'I am?'

'The silenter the better.'

'*Silenter?*'

'You talk to people that Didier and Naveen can't reach. If we have to talk to those guys, who's gonna do that but you, or me? Why not you and me together?'

'Karla,' I smiled, wanting to take her clothes off, and my clothes off, and stop talking. 'I can't move from committing crimes to solving them. My skill-set is on the villain side.'

'We're specialising,' Karla said, taking another sip from the flask, 'in missing persons.'

'Karla,' I laughed. 'You and me, we *are* missing persons.'

She laughed again.

'Cases that the cops have given up on,' she said.

'If the cops gave up, there's probably a good reason.'

She selected a joint from the brass case, and lit it.

'Not necessarily. Sometimes they just want the case to go away, and a case that *could* get solved goes unsolved. And sometimes they're paid to look the other way. Runaway husbands, missing brides, prodigal sons, we're the office of last resort, for lost loves.'

'I don't see any money in it, Karla. I'd be living on your dollar, it seems to me.'

'There probably won't be any dollars. Not yet. It'll cost more than it makes. But private security and private detection will boom, in this country. It's a good bet. And fortunately, I've got enough chips to play the game, for a while. If it bugs you, keep a tab, and pay me back when the business takes off.'

'Speaking of missing persons, any word of Ranjit?'

'Not yet. There was a rumour he was seen on a yacht, in the Maldives. I'm trying to check it out. For the time being, his proxy vote makes me a serious player. Good thing he was a lousy boss, and I wasn't. His entire news service is helping me track him down. Ironic, ain't it?'

'Are you still at the Taj?'

'Yeah. It's okay, for now. They've got good security downstairs, and I've got better security upstairs.'

'Have you seen Didier?'

'He's been hanging with me. He's pretty spooked about the acid throwers. You know how vain he is.'

'He doesn't call it vanity. He calls it good taste, and I think we both agree.'

'One way or another,' she said, 'I'm gonna remove that woman from my harm's way.'

She shoved all the things aside and lay back on the blankets, one hand behind her head.

'So, Shantaram, now that you know my plans, are you in?'

Fate leads you to what you desire, and Time makes sure that it's the wrong moment. Was I with her, in her lost love detective agency plan? No. I couldn't work with the cops, and I couldn't turn anyone in to the cops, which made me a lousy detective.

She knew it. She saw it in my eyes, and in my breathing: the heavy breath of worry that we weren't on the same path away from the mountain.

'Stop thinking,' she said. 'Tomorrow is just like you. It's never on time.'

The wind in moonlight, painting leaf-shadow lace on her skin. Love in all the past lives, every time we'd loved each other and lost each other: starlight on her sleeping face. There was no star in my sky that night: no light to guide me on that sea of what we were, and what we weren't. But I didn't care. She was asleep, in my arms, and I was already sailing home.

PART EIGHT

CHAPTER FORTY-SIX

I DIDN'T THROW IN WITH KARLA, NAVEEN AND DIDIER in the Lost
Love Bureau. Call me stubborn. Naveen did. Call me crazy. Didier
did. Call me a free spirit. Karla didn't. She didn't speak to me at all.
She didn't even respond to my messages, but sent a message of her
own, through Naveen, to stay away until she cooled off. I got hotter,
instead, and bought Didier's black market crime portfolio. He'd
become a legitimate businessman, a partner in the Lost Love Bureau,
two doors down from my own, and decided to turn his back on black
business. I let his drug and callgirl rackets slide, and focused on his
money changing operations. It took me a while to sort out the details.
I was buying white money that had become black money, making it
white again through a black bank, and figuring small weekly margins
on a high daily turnover: make or break. It was like the stock market,
without the lies and corruption.

When Karla finally responded, late in the second afternoon after
coming down from the mountain, I raced to meet her at the sea wall
in Juhu where we'd talked of Lisa, our own lost love, weeks before.

And as evening strollers passed us, smiling happily, and the sun
began to fall, Karla wept and told me she wasn't angry with me: she
was troubled by Ranjit and Lisa.

'What was Ranjit doing there with Lisa that night? What was she doing
with him? Since I came back to Bombay, I can't stop thinking about it.'

She cried into my chest, and then stopped crying, as I held her.

'Why don't I understand it, Shantaram?'

Karla was two beats ahead of every mind she met. The mystery tor-
mented her, where it was just a slow burn in me; sand in the wind, for
her, and sand in an hourglass with Ranjit's name on it for me. I had to
tell her to let it go, just as she'd once told me.

'We'll find him,' I said. 'And when we do, we'll find out what happened. Until then we'll have to stop thinking about it, or we'll both go nuts. I mean, more nuts than we already are.'

She smiled.

'There's something not right,' she said. 'Something I should know, but don't know. Something right there in front of me. But you're right – if I don't let it go, it'll drive me crazy.'

Vermilion sunset, the last grace of the sun, washed flaws and faults from every face and form on the promenade: an ocean of evening light showing only the beautiful things we are inside.

Gentle breezes chased one another along the sea wall, playing through skirts and shirts of walkers on the way. The first few car headlights began to pass.

Pale shadows of palm leaves drifted across her face, tracing the exact curve of her neck to her lips, every time a car passed. Karla.

'Is it your pride that won't let you join Didier and Naveen and me?' she asked, a harder eye turned toward me.

'No.'

'Pride is the only sin we can't see in ourselves, you know.'

'I'm not proud.'

'The hell you're not. But that's okay. I like pride in a man. I like it in a woman, too. But don't let it stop you now. We can make this work.'

'How, Karla?'

'We might be here a week, okay, but we might still be here three years from now. This can start to build in three months. Security is the big thing in India in the next fifty years. I'm telling you. I've had two years to study this, with Ranjit's best advisors.'

'You're serious, aren't you?'

'I'm always serious, when it comes to love.'

'Love?' I grinned, like an idiot.

'Pay attention,' she jabbed at me. 'I'm talking business.'

'Okay, I'm attentive.'

'Money isn't gonna flow from the rich to the poor. It's gonna flow from the poor to the rich, faster than ever, and it's gonna stay there. That's so outrageously unfair that personal security can't lose as an investment. See?'

'In a strange way. And the detective agency?'

'We're a bureau, not an agency. We only take on one kind of case.

Lost loves. We don't snoop or peep or shadow. We investigate missing loved ones. That's our way into the wider security business. We're gonna grow, and fast.'

'How?'

'If we want to grow, we need to know all the main players as friends. If we find missing loved ones for them along the way, they can't roll on us later. Plus, we get to know where all the skeletons dance.'

'You really thought this through.'

'Will you stop stating the obvious?'

'Look, I follow your logic, and I see the point —'

'Do you? This is something clean, and right. I don't see the right on your side of the playpen.'

'Right? We're talking about what's *right*, now?'

'You know, whatever else happens on the ride, interesting stuff like success and failure and fun, the bottom line for me, now, is that it's gotta be right, and it's gotta make a difference, or I'm an hour yesterday.'

'Finding lost loves?'

'Would you prefer losing *found* loves?'

She snapped the words at me, because she thought I hadn't taken her seriously, but I was stung.

'Is that at me? At us?'

'I'm not the one who's walking away from this, Shantaram.'

'Karla, I'm yours. But you know I can't work with the cops.'

'You can stay out of that part.'

'The handing people over to the police part, or the giving evidence in court part? I can stay out of that?'

'Didier will handle police liaison. He said he's looking forward to an interview with the cops where he isn't on the floor.'

'It's not just that. I've got too much at stake, Karla. I'm wanted everywhere but here, and that's because I know who to pay. I stay on my side of the line. The cops leave me alone because I don't sell drugs or girls, I don't cheat anyone, I don't beat anyone who hasn't got it coming, I keep my mouth shut when they give me a kicking, and I pay them regularly, and well.'

'Paradise,' Karla said, an eyebrow perched like a mockingbird on a branch.

'They tolerate me. But that could change, and then I'd have to run,

489

and fast. You know that. I can't get into anything serious, and you shouldn't, either. I thought we understood that.'

'I told you, I'm a silent partner,' she said, the queens flashing at me for an instant. 'But I can always find my voice, if you're not in this with me.'

There was a little silence. She was daring me to say the wrong thing, I guess, and maybe I did.

'Have you heard anything new about Ranjit?'

She looked away. I thought I'd hurt her, and I tried to change the subject.

'How about this?' I suggested. 'You check out of the Taj, and move into the rooms next to mine.'

'Next to you?'

'I mean it, Karla. There are three rooms, with a balcony that looks out on a good street, and you said you like security.'

She thought about it, offering me two queens from the corner of her eye.

'Are you talking sleepovers?' she asked, knowing I'm no good at that game.

'I'm gonna leave the sleepovers to another conversation. But I bought new locks for your doors, and installed them.'

'*My* doors?'

'Ah . . . yeah. If you take the rooms.'

'You must've been pretty sure I was gonna say yes.'

'Ah . . . '

'How many locks did you put on?'

'You mean, on the *front* door?'

'How many doors are we talking about?'

'All of them. Bathroom, bedroom, balcony, all of them.'

'O . . . kay,' she smiled. 'Any other surprises?'

'I put a first aid box with a surgical suture kit in the bathroom. You can sew up a sizeable wound, if you have to.'

'And they say romance is dead,' she laughed.

'And I got some other stuff.'

'Other stuff, huh?'

'Yeah, the neighbourhood has some great shops. I had the manager put a small refrigerator in your room, and stocked it with vodka, soda, lemons and the nastiest cheese I could find.'

'Nice.'

'And I taped a knife under the desk drawer. If you open it right, someone standing in the room wouldn't see you slip it out.'

'Won't see me slipping it out, huh?'

'And your bed has painted iron tubes.'

'My bed has tubes,' she laughed.

'Yeah. I checked the end caps. They came unscrewed on the head-end of the bed. I put a roll of money in one, and a skinny knife in the other. Just in case.'

'Handy.'

'And I bought you a sitar.'

'A sitar. What's that for?'

'I'm not sure. It was in the music shop downstairs, and I couldn't resist it.'

'You know —'

'There's no room service,' I said, cutting her off. 'But there's a sitar store downstairs, and the manager upstairs is crazier than I am, and all in all I think it's a good idea for you to move in with us, Karla. Are you game?'

'Honey, for the rest of your life, I *am* the game.'

'Do you mean it?'

'I mean it.'

'Good, let's get you settled, neighbour.'

She rode back with me. We followed Randall, as he returned to the hotel. I resisted the impulse to swing the bike out and pass. It wasn't hard. She had her left arm over my shoulder, her right arm in my lap, and her head resting on my back. I wanted to keep on riding until the bike said enough.

'You know,' I said, as I walked with her to a quiet corner on the steps of the Taj hotel. 'We could just keep on riding until we're far enough away, or the bike says enough.'

'I have things that I have to do, Shantaram,' she smiled. 'And anyway, lost love is the trump card, at least for now. Our first official bureau case is Ranjit, and we're gonna find that rodent, wherever he is.'

'Official case?'

'I registered us with the police, as a bureau. I fast-tracked it, using Ranjit's man. He's a corporator, and he was glad to see me. Since Ranjit's disappearance, the juice has stopped flowing. When I went to see him I had all the right American fruit. He's a nice guy, except that sometimes his face is greedier than his mind.'

It was my turn to laugh.

'Let's talk about it later,' she said, pulling me to her and holding me close, shell-within-a-shell perfect.

'Get a good night's sleep,' she said, beginning to pull away from me. 'Okay . . . what?'

'You're gonna need all the sleep you can get,' she said. 'If you're turning me down at the bureau, and going out as a freelancer.'

'Wait a minute. I can't come back and see you, later tonight?'

'Certainly not,' she said, pushing free and walking the last steps to the door. 'And anyway, it'll still be there, in the morning.'

'What'll still be there in the morning?'

'Lust,' she said, pausing at the door. 'You remember Lust, don't you, Shantaram? Pretty girl, lotta fun, no scruples?'

The door closed. I was confused again. Then I smiled again. *Dammit, Karla.*

I rode back to the Amritsar hotel in a predicament, and found the manager in a quandary: his face was in a large box, labelled *Quandary Inc.*

'What's the dilemma, Jaswant?'

'There's supposed to be a phaser pistol in this box,' he said, looking up at me absently, his hands still searching through foam packaging. 'Ah, here it is!'

He pulled the toy pistol from the box, but his triumph faded quickly.

'This is all wrong! The photon emitter is in the wrong place. And the deflector shield is missing. You can't trust anyone, these days.'

'It's a toy, Jaswant,' I said.

'A replica,' he corrected. 'And not an accurate one.'

'It's a replica of a toy, Jaswant.'

'You don't understand. I've got a Parsi friend who said he could make a *real* one for me, if I have a perfect replica of the original. He won't work with this crap. He's a Parsi.'

He stared at me, sorrow burning him, as sorrow always does, even when it shouldn't.

'Please, Jaswant,' I said sincerely. 'Don't make a laser pistol.'

'A phaser pistol,' he corrected. 'And you could use one. People walk in and out of your rooms all day and night, like it's Buckingham Station.'

'Only people with a key.'

'Well, there are two key holders in there now.'

I found Naveen in the chair, near a desk I'd bought from the trophy store downstairs. He was playing my guitar, and better than I played it, but that put him on a list of anybody.

I looked into my bedroom and saw Didier on the bed, his elegant, Italian shoes on the floor, laces inside. He waved hello.

'Nice playing, Naveen,' I said, throwing myself into a chair.

'Nice guitar,' Naveen replied, playing a popular Goan ballad.

'I found her loitering with intent, in a music store downstairs.'

'No place for a guitar like her,' he said, switching to Pink Floyd's 'Comfortably Numb'. 'She's a high-maintenance crazy love guitar, like Diva.'

'What's the Diva situation?' I asked.

'Not good,' he said, still playing. 'That's why I'm doing guitar therapy.'

'I cleared it with Johnny Cigar, this morning. A Bihari clan moved out, leaving six empty houses. There are two huts reserved, a few steps from Johnny's house. One for her, and one for you.'

'Can't come a minute too soon for me,' Naveen said, putting the guitar aside.

'I think you're right. I asked around today in the Fort area. Her dad's in big trouble. The bookies have him at fifty-to-one. People are talking about him like he's already dead. And people are talking about Diva, and what she might know about her dad's bad deals, or where the money is.'

'Indeed,' Didier agreed, springing off the bed with surprising agility and tiptoeing to the small, chest-high refrigerator.

He'd bought the refrigerator as a housewarming present, stocked it with beer, and put a bottle of brandy on my night table for himself. He threw a beer to me, and one to Naveen, and settled himself again comfortably on my bed.

'I have made some enquiries of my own,' he said. 'There are at least two dangerous and merciless groups after Diva's father, and both of them have deep ties to the police.'

'You're right,' Naveen said.

'One of them, in fact, *is* the police,' Didier continued. 'Something about the police pension fund, I think. This business mogul has amassed

493

a Mongol horde of enemies. He should evaporate from Bombay, and relocate to an anonymous island. Certainly, he can afford to buy one.'

'He's the most stubborn man I've ever met,' Naveen growled. 'He wants to ride it out. He thinks his security is rock solid. And, okay, it's true enough that he's surrounded by guns, day and night, but . . .'

'But what?'

'But there are two separate security outfits working in that mansion, cops and private. Neither of them, far as I can tell, is willing to take a bullet for the richest and crookedest man in Bombay. Some of those guys live in slums, hoping that they can move their family into a one-room apartment the size of his toilet. If the cops are ordered away, I think the private army will run away. I've tried to warn him, but he won't listen.'

'He did listen to you,' Didier said. 'He left his daughter in your care.'

'He called me *son*, yesterday,' Naveen said. 'It was the weirdest thing. I hardly know him.'

He walked to the shuttered windows. When he opened a shutter, the neon lights of the Metro theatre blushed his face.

'He said, *Keep my daughter close to your heart, and safe with you, away from me, my son.*'

'That is a significant responsibility,' Didier mused.

'And a significant job,' I added. 'Diva's a handful. She should leave the city, man.'

'I agree,' Didier said. 'And soon.'

'She won't go. And I know her. If I try to take her to the airport, she'll scream the place down.'

'If you can't get her to leave Bombay,' I said, 'and if the people who want to kill her father might kidnap her, then you'll have to hide her until it blows over. And the slum is the only place I can think of, where no-one will look for the richest girl in town. But I hope you have a better idea.'

'I don't.'

'Neither do I,' Didier said.

'Where is she now?' I asked.

'At her weekly meeting. She gets together with some friends every week at the President.'

'Oh, yes?' Didier asked.

'It's called the Diva Girl Gossip Club,' Naveen explained.

'Fascinating!' Didier said.

'Once a week they swarm like piranhas, and rip to pieces any girl they know who isn't in their clique.'

'Will you get me an invitation?' Didier pleaded, joining us. 'I would love to go.'

'She should be finished by ten,' Naveen said. 'You guys wanna go with me, and pick her up?'

'I will certainly come,' Didier said, slipping on his shoes and tying them.

'I'm going to need both of you,' Naveen said, 'if I'm going to convince Diva to dump her suite at the Mahesh, and come live in a slum for a week. I might need the two of you to restrain her while I just *explain* the idea.'

'You sure you wanna do this now?' I asked.

'No present like the time,' the young detective smiled, but his eyes were serious. 'It's late enough to get her to the slum and settle her in before too many people know about it. What do you think?'

'Didier is ready. To the gossip club, at once!'

CHAPTER FORTY-SEVEN

W E FOUND DIVA IN A SHRIEK OF DIVAS, in the lobby of the President hotel. The three of them stopped, staring at us with well-practised aghast.

Didier was in a rumpled, white linen jacket and faded blue corduroys. I was in boots, black jeans, T-shirt and sleeveless vest. Naveen was in grey fatigues and a thin, brown-suede shirt. He carried a heavy backpack.

The pretty girls made it clear that we didn't present a pretty picture.

'Is *that* him?' one of the Diva girls asked, pointing an accusing false nail at Naveen.

'In the flesh,' Diva sneered, making no introductions.

'Motorcycle maniac,' the other Diva girl said, crossing me off the list.

'Debauched womaniser,' the first said, crossing Didier off.

'Pardon me, mademoiselle,' Didier said. 'But, I am a *man*iser.'

'Debauched maniser,' the girl said.

'And the horse,' Diva said, crossing Naveen off, 'without Prince Charming.'

The Diva girls giggled.

'What's with the backpack?' Diva demanded. 'Setting off for the Himalayas, I hope?'

'I'm not a climber,' Naveen said, staring at her.

'Ooooooh!' the Diva girls said. 'The tomcat has claws.'

'We have to go, Diva,' Naveen said.

'How about you climb a tree,' Diva said defiantly. 'And don't come down.'

The girls giggled.

Naveen was angry, because he was genuinely afraid. Given the threat to her, he thought they were foolishly exposed in the well-lit lobby. He expected a carload of thugs to burst in at any moment and kidnap her.

And strong, confident young Naveen knew he'd be powerless to stop it. I knew him well enough to know that he was unaccustomed to the feeling, and that he didn't like it.

Didier stepped into the awkward silence, bowing elegantly to the girls.

'Allow me to introduce myself, dear ladies,' he said, handing out business cards. 'My name is Didier Levy. I am a native of France, but a guest in your great city for some years. With my associate, the well-known detective Mr Naveen Adair, we are the Lost Love Bureau, and we are at your service, if there is a mystery to be solved.'

'Wow!' one of the girls said, reading the card he'd given her.

'No matter is too trivial,' Didier pitched, 'and no piece of gossip too insignificant for the Lost Love Bureau.'

'We've gotta go,' Naveen repeated, gesturing toward the door.

Diva cheeked goodbye to her friends, and went with us to the doors. We walked out past the entry portico to the beginning of the main street.

Naveen stopped, and looked at me. I glanced around, and realised that Didier wasn't with us. I trotted back into the hotel to snatch him from the girls.

'See you next Tuesday!' he called out, as I dragged him away. 'I assure you, I have gossip about well-known people that you will enjoy more than orgasm!'

The Diva girls shrieked.

We rejoined Naveen and Diva.

'Business cards?' I said.

'I . . . thought it best to be prepared,' Didier replied.

'Show me one.'

'I'd like to see one of those, too,' Naveen said.

'Me, too,' Diva agreed. 'Hand 'em over, Frenchy.'

Reluctantly, he passed out the business cards, and we studied them by the light of a streetlamp.

LOST LOVE BUREAU
Didier Levy, Master of Love
Naveen Adair, Master of the Lost

The back of the card showed a picture of what I assumed to be a listening ear, with the words:

LOOSE LIPS MAKE THE WORLD GO ROUND
Suite 7, The Amritsar Hotel, Metro, Bombay

'Do you think it too . . . subdued?' Didier asked earnestly.

'*Master of the Lost?*' Naveen said. 'It's a bit Tolkien, man.'

'And what's with the ear?' I asked innocently, and should've kept my mouth shut.

'But, Lin! You only object, because you ripped a man's ear off a few months ago,' Didier protested.

'Not *all* the way off,' I protested back. 'And anyway, Didier, so now it's *Suite* 7, and not *Room* 7?'

'Wait a minute,' Diva said, planting a hand like a tiny garden fork on my chest. 'You ripped some guy's ear off?'

'Naveen,' I said, 'you can take over any time now.'

'Diva —' Naveen began.

'Nothing doing from either of you,' Diva said. 'Not until I sit down. Where's the limo?'

We stared at her.

'You don't have a limo,' Naveen said. 'Not any more. I sent the car and driver back to be reassigned at the estate.'

She laughed, but we weren't laughing, so she grabbed Naveen's shirt, yanking it up and down in her fists until she tore it.

'You . . . fucking . . . did . . . *what?*'

'Diva, will you please trust me on this,' Naveen said, tucking strands of his shirt into his pants.

'*Trust* you? I *did* trust you, and you lost my fucking car! Do you know how far a girl can walk or run in these shoes? That's what limousines were *designed* for, idiot, the fucking *shoes*! Where's my four-wheeled shoebox, Naveen?'

'Can we have this conversation off the main street? There's a corner just ahead, with a laneway.'

'You must be —'

'Please, Miss Diva,' Didier said. 'You can surely understand that we three men would not be here, appealing to you in this way, if we did not care about you, and if we did not judge it prudent.'

498

She looked from face to face and then stormed off. She turned into the lane and stopped halfway, her back against the wall.

One foot was raised behind her, resting on the wall. She was wearing an elegant yellow skirt, a white high-necked blouse and ankle-strap heels. Her skirt was split at the side, and her short, fine legs were revealed by the pose. She was a girl who knew how to pose: she'd posed for every magazine in the country.

I glanced at Naveen. He was studying her with the eyes of love: desire, stripped of hunger. *We tough guys fall fast, and we fall hard*, Didier had said. And there was no doubt that Naveen Adair, the Indian-Irishman, was a tough guy falling somewhere.

Naveen let her have it. She was stubborn, and proud. He knew that he had to be brutally honest to have a chance of convincing her of the dangers she faced.

Every twisted deal that untangled itself at the feet of a gangster, a crooked politician or a cop, gunning for him, spooled out in front of her. Her foot slid down the wall, and she straightened up, bracing herself.

'The threat is very real, Miss Diva,' Didier said gently. 'We have all examined this matter, and we have all concluded that your safety is in peril.'

'They're bad guys,' Naveen said. 'And your dad's surrounded by good guys he doesn't trust. I think that's why he gave me the job of making sure you're safe, and told me not to bring you back to the mansion.'

'Mummy,' she moaned very softly, calling out to a ghost.

'I recommend leaving, Miss Diva,' Didier advised. 'Fast, and far away. I would be honoured to arrange it. Lin can provide the false papers. There is sufficient money. You would be safe, until this matter is resolved.'

'I won't leave while my dad's still here,' she pouted. 'What if he goes to jail? He'll need me. No matter what else I have to do, I won't leave Bombay while he's here.'

'The alternative is hiding here, in the slum nearby,' Naveen said. 'That's what I've been trying to tell you.'

'The slum? First, you tell me that my dad is a crook, and that other crooks are trying to kill him, so they might kidnap me or kill me, which I've been dealing with all my life, and now —'

'It's . . . it's really bad,' Naveen said. 'I mean, I told you, Diva. I'm scared myself. Please, listen to us.'

'I lived there, Diva,' I said. 'You'll be safe in the slum, and it shouldn't be for long.'

'The slum?' she repeated, trying again, but there wasn't much fight left in her.

'Do you have someone close enough to you, to trust with your life?' Didier asked.

The slim socialite flinched as if he'd shocked her: more than her father's misdeeds, or the threat to her own safety. She backed away half a step, and then regained her composure.

'I've got a lot of distant relatives, but no-one close. My Mother was an only child, like me, and my father's brother passed away two years ago. Since my Mother died, there's only my dad and me. I'm not going anywhere.'

'Hiding in this place, Miss Diva, will not be pleasant,' Didier advised. 'The people are civilised, but the circumstances are primitive. Do you not wish to reconsider?'

'I'm not leaving.'

'I told you so,' Naveen said, adjusting the backpack.

I left them talking, and went to check the end of the laneway.

The street at the end of the alley led to the white arches and port-hole windows of the World Trade Centre, and then to the slum beyond.

It was quiet. The pavement dwellers had settled down for the night on footpaths. Frisky dogs, hungry for their own hour of power, jerked, jumped and barked. An almost empty bus swept around the corner in front of me. Movie posters adorned the sides like heralds, draped over a war elephant.

Streetlamps showed the entrance to the slum, near the end of the street. I knew how hard the life was in that slum. I knew how rich the rewards were. The slum was a jellyfish, an empathic dome of common cause: filaments of love and common suffering touched every life.

Diva walked toward me slowly, with Naveen and Didier. Naveen put his arm around her. She didn't push it away.

Maybe he'd told her that the backpack she'd been teasing him about was filled with her things, which he'd hastily gathered for her from the suite at the Mahesh. Maybe, as other loves closed for her, she was finally opening to him.

She came into the light, and I saw that she was afraid.

'It's gonna be okay, kid,' I said, making her look me in the eye. 'You've got a pretty cool ride ahead of you, with pretty cool neighbours.'

'I heard the neighbourhood improved a lot when you moved out,' she said, but there was only a candle-fire in it. 'So, tell me, slum dweller, is there anything I should know?'

'The more you go with it,' I said, as we neared the wide path beside the open latrine, leading to the slum, 'the better it gets.'

'That's what my therapist said,' she muttered, 'before I sued him for harassment.'

'You won't be harassed by anything but love in the slum,' I said. 'But that takes some getting used to, as well.'

'Bring it on,' the brave, scared socialite said. 'Tonight, I'll take all the love I can get.'

CHAPTER FORTY-EIGHT

THE PATH WAS ROUGH: DUSTY EARTH AND STONES. To the right, a long wire fence cordoned off the gleaming windows of showcased goods in the World Trade Centre. To the left was a wide field where women and children found a place to relieve themselves among the weeds, and shrubs, and piles of other people's relief.

A woman was squatting in the darkness, obscured by scrubby plants. Some kids were squatting in the stony grass beside the path. As Diva passed, the kids smiled, and said, *Hello! What is your name?*

When the path began to descend toward the sea we caught our first glimpse of the slum: a tattered cloak, thrown over a fragment of coast beside the gleaming towers of the rich, across the little bay.

'Holy fuck,' Diva said.

The slum, at night, was its own dark age. The light in the houses came from kerosene wick-lamps. There was no electricity, and no running water. Rats swept through the lanes in black waves every night, devouring piles of garbage left like dark offerings.

That smell of kerosene, and mustard oil almost-burnt, and incense, and salt-wind from the sea close by, and the soap of desperate cleanliness, and honest sweat, and the scent of horses, goats, dogs, cats, monkeys and snakes: all those aromas assaulted Diva as we wound our way by torchlight to Johnny Cigar's house.

Her eyes were wide, but her lips were pressed into a determined frown. She held Naveen's arm, but her high-heeled shoes staked out a sure path on the uneven ground.

Johnny Cigar was waiting for us, dressed in his temple best.

'Welcome, Aanu,' he said, pressing his palms together, and bowing to Diva. 'My name is Johnny Cigar. I hope you don't mind it, that I'm calling you Aanu. I have told everyone that you are my cousin Aanu, visiting from London.'

'Okay,' Diva said uncertainly.

'To help you settle in peacefully here,' Johnny added, 'I told them that you are a little bit mad. That should explain your angry temperament.'

'My angry temperament?'

'Well, Shantaram said . . . '

'Shantaram, huh?'

'I have also told everyone that some people are searching for you, because you stole something from them, so we must keep your stay with us a secret.'

'Okay . . . I guess.'

'Oh, yes. This is the safest place for thieves outside the parliament building.'

'That's reassuring,' Diva replied, smiling. 'I think.'

'You may be surprised how many famous people hide in the slum with us. We had a cricket player hiding here, once. I can't tell you his name, but when we played together, he told me —'

'Shut up, Johnny!'

Johnny's wife, Sita, emerged from the house, her red and gold sari whirling sails around her slim figure.

'You don't even know what I was talking about,' Johnny said, his feelings hurt.

'Shut up anyway,' Sita snapped. 'And leave the poor girl alone.'

Two other women joined her, and they led Diva to the hut reserved for her, a few paces away. Naveen and Didier followed. I looked at Johnny.

'Coming along, Johnny?'

'I'm . . . I'm going to give Sita a minute,' he said.

'Trouble in paradise?' I asked, opening my big mouth.

'You don't know the half of it,' he said, wiping a hand through his thick, brown hair. 'Sita is driving me nuts.'

'Listen, I'm gonna roll some joints. For Diva. I think she'll need them more than blankets, if she sleeps here tonight. Why don't we sit inside, and I'll get to work, while you talk.'

He talked. I learned more about Sita, in half an hour, than any man should know about another man's wife. I tried to take her side, once, in fairness, but he cried, so I had to stop.

It was all Johnny, after that. His suffering was measured in Stations of the Cross Wife, each one with a scolding image. In the end, it came down to one thing.

'Contraception,' I said, rolling joints for Diva's slum orientation.

'What are you saying?'

'She wants another kid, and you don't. Contraception.'

'I'm *practising* contraception, at the moment,' he pleaded, shifting uncomfortably on his seat. 'We haven't had sex in six months.'

'That's not contraception, Johnny, that's disconception. No wonder she's cranky.'

'Sita believes that sex is for making children. I think sex is for making children, and for making love, sometimes. She won't accept any birth control. When I tried to talk to her about condoms, she called me a pervert.'

'That's a little harsh.'

'What am I going to do? You see how beautiful she is, *na?*'

Sita was named after a kindly, self-sacrificing Goddess, and for the most part she lived up to the name. But she also had a temper, and a tongue that whipped it into shape. We thought about it, for a while, as Diva's joints accumulated.

'You could do the girl thing,' I suggested, 'and talk it out.'

'Not . . . safe,' he said. 'Or?'

'Or you could do the guy thing.'

'The guy thing?' he asked, his eyes squinting suspiciously.

'The guy thing is to ignore it, and hope she gives in before you do.'

'I'm going with the guy thing,' Johnny said, punching his palm. 'It's so much safer than the truth.'

'Don't be too sure,' I said, gathering up the rolled joints. 'Women have a psychic witchy spooky talking-to-the-dead way of knowing everything you think. So, sooner or later, you've gotta do it their way anyway.'

'Of course,' he hissed. 'That's how women get back at men.'

'How's that?'

'By making men become women, for a while. It's cruel, what they do, making us talk to them, Lin. It's scary, and men have difficulty with scary. It makes them want to fight.'

'Speaking of scary, let's go find out how Diva's doing.'

Diva was surrounded by young girls up past their bedtimes, asking her about everything she wore, and everything that spilled from Naveen's pack.

Johnny and Sita had covered the earthen floor with a blue plastic sheet, and they'd covered that with patchwork quilts. There was a clay *matka* water pot in the corner, with an aluminium plate on top, and an upturned glass.

That pot was all of Diva's water for a day: all she had for drinking, cooking and doing the dishes. There was a kerosene pressure cooker in a corner, with two burners. A metal cabinet on high legs held two metal saucepans, some foodstuffs and a carton of milk. Another metal cabinet with three shelves was for her clothes.

A kerosene lantern rested on that cabinet. The low light seemed to hover on faces and in corners. Apart from a decorative swirl of artificial flowers, hanging from one of the bamboo support poles, there was nothing else in the hut.

The walls were made from woven reed matting, the gaps and chinks stuffed with sheets of newspaper. The roof was a bare plastic sheet, draped over the bamboo framework of the hut.

The black plastic roof was so low that I had to stoop a little. I'd spent a lot of time in the humid swelter of a hut just like hers. I knew that an unpleasantly hot day on the city's streets became an inferno in a small hut, each breath a struggle, and sweat dripping like rain from drooping leaves.

I looked at her, the Bombay Diva, sitting on the patchwork blankets and talking with the girls.

I hadn't lied: it did get better, when I lived in the slum, but only after it got so bad that I thought I couldn't stand another minute of teeming crowds, constant noise, lack of water, roaming cohorts of rats, and the constant background hum of hunger and fatally wounded hope.

I couldn't tell her that the better days only ever began after the worst day. And I couldn't know that the worst day, for Diva, was only twenty-four hours away.

'I brought you some supplies,' I said, leaning over to hand her the little pile of rolled joints, and a quarter-bottle of local rum.

'A man of taste and distinction,' she smiled, accepting the gifts. 'Sit down, Shantaram, and join us. The girls were just about to explain whose ass you have to kiss, just to take a shit around here.'

'I'll take a raincheck, Diva,' I smiled, 'but I'm gonna stick around for a bit with Naveen and Didier, until you sleep, so I won't be far. Is there anything else I can get you?'

'No, man,' she said. 'Not unless you can bring my dad here.'

'That would be kinda defeating the purpose,' I smiled again. 'But as soon as this situation with your dad settles down, I'm sure Naveen will put you together again.'

'I hope so,' she said. 'When I first looked at these skinny girls, I thought they could sell their slimming diet for millions, to my friends alone. But then I realised that they're hungry. What the hell is going on here?'

'Welcome to the other side.'

'Well, if I stay here for a week, that's more than enough time to change all that,' Diva said.

One of the girls translated her English words into Hindi, as she spoke. The girls all applauded and cheered. Diva was triumphant.

'You see? The revolution has already started.'

The impish rebel fire was still in her eyes, but her face couldn't hide the fear that crouched in her heart.

She was an intelligent girl. She knew that Naveen, Didier and I wouldn't insist on something as drastic as a week in the slum, if we didn't fear something more drastic on the open street.

I was sure she missed the cosseting luxury of the family mansion, the only home she'd ever known. Naveen said it was always well stocked with friends, food, drink, entertainment and servants. And maybe, in part, she felt that her father had deserted her, by banishing her to Naveen's care.

I watched her smiling that stiff, unflinching smile, and talking with the girls. She was afraid for her father, that much was clear: perhaps more than for herself. And she was alone, and in a different world: a foreign tourist in the city where she was born.

I went to the hut next door, and settled down on a well-worn blue carpet beside Didier and Naveen. They were playing poker.

'Will you play a hand, Lin?' Didier asked.

'I don't think so, Didier. I'm kind of scattered tonight. Can't think straight enough to play in your class.'

'Very well,' Didier smiled good-naturedly. 'Then I shall continue the lesson. I am teaching Naveen how to cheat with honour.'

'Honourable cheating?'

506

'Cheating honourably,' Didier corrected.

'How to *spot* a cheat, as well,' Naveen added. 'Did you know there's exactly one hundred and four ways to cheat? Two for every card in the deck. It's fascinating stuff. Didier could teach a university course in this.'

'Cheating at cards is simply magic,' Didier said modestly. 'And magic is simply cheating at cards.'

I let them play, sitting beside them and sipping one of Didier's emergency flasks. It was a difficult night for me, too, although not the mind-shock that it was for Diva.

I felt the dome of the slum community beginning to close over me with sounds, smells and a swirl of defiant memories. I was back in the womb of mankind. I heard a cough nearby, a man crying out in sleep, a child waking, and a husband talking softly to his wife about their debts in Marathi. I could smell incense, burning in a dozen houses around us.

My heartbeat was trying to find its synchrony with twenty-five thousand others, fireflies, uneven until they learn to flash and fade in the same waves of light. But I couldn't connect. Something in my life or my heart had changed. The part of me that had settled so willingly in the lake of consciousness that was the slum, years before, was missing.

When I escaped from prison I searched for a home, wandering from country to city, hoping that I'd recognise it when I found it. When I met Karla, I found love, instead. I didn't know then that the search for one always leads to the other.

I said goodnight to Didier and Naveen, checked on Diva, already asleep in the arms of new Diva girls, and walked those lanes feeling sadder than I could understand.

A small pariah dog joined me, skipping ahead and then running back to collide with my legs. When I left the slum and started my bike, she joined a pack of street dogs, howling provocatively.

I headed to the Amritsar hotel to do some writing. As I cruised along the empty causeway I noticed Arshan, Farzad's father, the nominal head of the three families that were looking for treasure.

Arshan wasn't treasure hunting: he was staring fixedly at the Colaba police station, across the road from where he stood. I wheeled the bike around in a circle, and pulled up beside him.

'Hi, Arshan. How's it going?'

'Oh, fine, fine,' he said absently.

'It's kinda late,' I observed. 'And this is a rough neighbourhood. There's a bank, a police station and a fashion brand store, all within twenty metres.'

He smiled softly, but his eyes never wavered from the police station.

'I'm . . . I'm waiting for someone,' he said vaguely.

'Maybe he isn't coming. Can I offer you a lift home?'

'I'm fine,' he said again. 'I'm fine, Lin. You go on.'

He was so distracted that his hands were twitching, reflexes driven by violent thoughts, and his expression had unconsciously settled into a grimace of pain.

'I'm gonna have to insist, Arshan,' I said. 'You don't look good, man.'

He gradually brought himself back to the moment, shook his head, blinked the stare from his eyes, and accepted the ride.

He didn't say a word on the way home, and only muttered thanks and farewell abstractedly, as he walked toward the door of his home.

Farzad opened for us, gasping in concern for his dad.

'What is it, Pop? Are you okay?'

'I'm fine, boy,' he replied, resting on his son's shoulder.

'Lin, will you come in?' Farzad asked.

It was a brave offer, because the kid was still in the Company, and we both knew Sanjay wouldn't approve of him hosting me.

'I'm good, Farzad,' I said. 'Let's catch up, one of these days.'

At the Amritsar I threw everything off and took a long shower. Diva, who must've enjoyed baths foaming with scented oils in her father's mansion, would have to wash in a small dish of water in the slum, and like the other girls, she'd have to wash fully clothed.

Poor kid, I thought, as I dressed again, but reminded myself that Naveen was never more than a call for help away. And I wondered how long it would take the Indian-Irish detective to admit that he was in love with her.

I made a no-bread sandwich of tuna fish, tomato and onion between slices of Parmesan cheese, drank two beers, and looked over Didier's black market scams for a while.

He'd made pages of notes, with profiles on the key players, profit margins per month, salaries, and bribery payoffs. When I'd read them, I shoved the papers to the end of the bed, and picked up my journal.

There was that new short story I'd been trying to write, about happy, loving people doing happy, loving things. A love story. A fable.

508

I tried to put a few more lines into the stream of words I'd already composed. I reread the first paragraph.

When it comes to the truth, there are two kinds of lovers: those who find truth in love, and those who find love in truth. Cleon Winters never sought the truth in anything, or anyone, because he didn't believe in truth. But then, when he fell in love with Shanassa, truth found him, and all the lies he'd told himself became locusts, feeding on fields of doubt. When Shanassa kissed him, he fell into a coma, and was unconscious for six months, submerged in a lake of pure truth.

I persisted with the story for a while, but the characters began to change, following their own morphology, and became people I knew: Karla, Concannon, Diva.

The faces blurred, my eyes drooped, and every return to a line was another wave of will. I began to float on the sea of them, real faces and imagined.

The journal fell beside the bed. Loose pages from the notebook swirled free. The overhead fan scattered pages of my happy, loving story into Didier's crime synopses. His pages settled on mine and mine joined his, and the wind wrote crime as love, and love as crime, as I slept.

CHAPTER FORTY-NINE

THERE WILL BE CONSTANT AFFIRMATIONS, Idriss had said, again and
again. If they were there, I didn't see them, even in dreams. Idriss
talked of spiritual things, but the only thing that came to mind for me,
in the word spiritual, was nature. I hadn't found my connection to his
tendency field, and out there on that fringe of the world, I didn't feel
that I belonged to anything but Karla.

I'd searched the faiths I could find. I learned prayers in languages I
couldn't speak, and prayed with believers whenever they invited me
to join them. But I always connected to the people and the purity of
their faith, rather than the religious code they followed. I often had
everything in common with them, in fact, but their God.

Idriss spoke of the Divine in the language of science, and spoke of
science in the language of faith. It made a strange kind of sense to me,
where Khaderbhai's lectures on cosmology only ever left me with
good questions. Idriss was a journey, like every teacher, and I wanted
to learn on the way, but the spiritual path I could see always led to
forests, where talking stopped long enough for birds to find trees, and
to oceans and rivers and deserts. And each woken beautiful day, each
lived and written night, carried inside it a small, ineffaceable emptiness
of questions.

I showered, drank coffee, tidied my rooms and went down to my
bike, parked in the alleyway under the building. I had a breakfast
meeting with Abdullah. I wanted to see him, and I was afraid to see
him: afraid that friendship had faded in his eyes. So I rode and thought
of Diva Devnani, the rich girl in a very poor slum, whose father was
watching the sand run through his fingers. I made a note to buy her
some Kerala grass and a bottle of coconut rum for when I checked on
her.

When I parked my bike beside Abdullah's, across the street from the Saurabh restaurant, I looked up slowly and reluctantly, but the eyes that met mine were as true as they'd always been. He hugged me, and we squeezed onto a small bench behind a table that gave us both a view of the door.

'You are the subject of discussion,' he said, as we worked our way through *masala dosas* and dumplings in mango sauce. 'DaSilva made a bet that you would not live to see the end of the month.'

'Anyone take the bet?'

'Of course not,' Abdullah said, between mouthfuls. 'I beat DaSilva with a bamboo rod. He withdrew the wager.'

'Solid.'

'The talk from Sanjay is what counts, for now, and Sanjay wants you to live.'

'In the way a cat wants a mouse to live?'

'More like a tiger and a mouse,' he replied. 'He thinks the Scorpions are cats, and that they hate you more than DaSilva does.'

'So, am I a target or a useful distraction, for Sanjay?'

'The last. He does not expect that you will survive outside the Company for a long time. But you are useful, in a unique way.'

'Uh-huh?'

'While you live, you are irritating.'

'Thanks.'

'Don't mention. In fact, I think you will probably be irritating, even after you are dead. It is a rare quality.'

'Thanks again.'

'Don't mention.'

'Where do I stand with business?'

'He does not think you will survive long enough, to establish a business.'

'I got that. But if I do survive, say, until the day after tomorrow, when I'd like to get started, how do I stand?'

'Sanjay assured me that he would license you, like everyone else, but at a higher percentage.'

'And they say mafia dons have no heart. Can I do my own passports?'

'He does not think you will –'

'– survive long enough. But if I do?'

'Sanjay has said that you are banned from the passport factory. Your

511

young man there, Farzad, came to see Sanjay personally, asking that he be permitted to learn from you privately. Sanjay said that he did not think –'

'– I'd survive long enough, right, but he didn't rule it out?'

'No. He ordered Farzad not to contact you, or speak to you.'

'And if I bought my own kit, and started modifying books?'

'He does not think –'

'Abdullah,' I sighed, 'I don't care if Sanjay thinks I won't last the winter. The only opinion I respect on that subject is my own. Just tell Sanjay, when you get a minute, that one of these days he might need a good passport from me himself. If he's cool with it, I'd like to start making books. I'm good at it, and it's an anarchist crime. See if you can get him to agree, okay?'

'*Jarur*, brother.'

It was good to hear him call me brother, but I didn't know if he was accepting my defection from the Company, or if his disaffection was driving him closer to my renegade side of the line.

'You will be taking over all of Didier's enterprises?' he asked.

'Not all of them. I'm letting the drugs go. The Company can pick it up, if they want. Amir can have it. And the escorts, too. They can have all of Didier's escort strings in South Bombay. I wrote off the debts, and let everyone run free. They're out there, doing their own things. But the Company can probably negotiate them back again, I guess.'

'It will be done before nightfall,' he intoned, his deep voice rumbling the syllables. 'So, without the girls and the drugs, you will have what, exactly?'

'All Didier's currency touts are with me. I've got enough to float about fifteen of the black money traders from Flora Fountain to Colaba Market, for a month. If it ticks over, I'll do okay. On the side, I'm specialising in watches and technology. Every street guy on the strip will bring stuff to me first, before any other buyer. I think I can make that work.'

'Watches?' he asked, frowning sternly.

'There's a lot of money in collector watches.'

'But *watches*, Lin?' he said, suddenly almost angry. 'You were a soldier, with Khaderbhai.'

'I'm not a soldier, Abdullah. I'm a gangster, and so are you.'

'You were one of his sons. How can you sit here, and talk to me of watches?'

'Okay,' I said, trying to make it light. 'How about we ride our bikes to Nariman Point, and I'll sit *there*, and talk of watches?'

He rose from the table, left the restaurant, and strode to his motor-cycle. He didn't pay a bill in any restaurant in South Bombay. No gangster ever did. I paid, left a tip for the waiters, and caught up to him.

'A ride is necessary,' he said.

I followed him to Bombay University, where we parked the bikes, walked through the colonnades and leafy laneways, and entered the open playing fields called Azad Maidan, behind the campus and other buildings.

There was a fence of iron spears between the vast expanse of the playing fields and the street outside, with only one other entry point, served by a long path across the lawns to the university. The sun's invisible lake of light reflected gold off every surface and feature.

Abdullah and I walked the fence line, side by side, just away from the shaggy weeds that gathered at the base.

It was almost exactly like the walks I'd made with other men every day, in prison, walking and talking, walking and talking in circles of years.

'How bad has it been?' I asked him. 'I heard some stuff on the mountain. What's the deal with the fire, at the Scorpion house?'

He pursed his lips. He'd anticipated that I'd ask him about the fighting in Colaba, and the fire that killed a nurse in Vishnu's house. I knew why that nurse was in the house. I wondered if Abdullah or anyone in the Company knew that civilians were in the house. I hadn't known, when I rang the bell, and I hadn't told Abdullah or anyone else about it.

He let a deep breath escape through his nose, his lips pressed firmly in a rumpled frown.

'Lin, I am going to trust you, as if you are still in the family. It is not what I should do, but it is what I must do.'

'Abdullah, I'm a broad strokes guy, you know that. I don't want intimate details about anything except intimacy, if I can help it. And don't go breaking your oath for me, although I love you for it, man. Just let me know the big picture details, so I know who's shooting at who.'

'It was Farid,' Abdullah said. 'I counselled against it. Fire is indiscriminate. I wanted to discriminate, and kill them personally. All of them, once and for all. Sanjay decided to use fire. Farid set it, and the Scorpions escaped, but a nurse, who was not supposed to be there, she died in the flames.'

'Where's Farid now?'

'He is still here, at Sanjay's side. He refuses to leave the city, when it would be far wiser if he did.'

'There's a lot of that going around at the moment.'

'What is going around?'

'Nothing. Just a stray thought in the wind. The Scorpions will hit back hard, Abdullah. I've met this guy, Vishnu. He's no lightweight. He's smart, and he's got a political agenda. That gives him allies in unlikely places. Don't underestimate his revenge.'

'What does he want?'

'He wants what you want, up to a point. He wants Sanjay dead. But he wants the whole Company dead with him. And he's got a thing about Pakistan.'

'Pakistan?'

'Pakistan,' I repeated. 'Neighbour country, kind people, nice language, great music, secret police. Pakistan.'

'That is not a good thing,' Abdullah frowned. 'Sanjay has made many friends in Pakistan. It was those friends who sent the Afghan guards to protect him.'

We were approaching a curve in the fence. A young couple sat on a blanket in the warm, plush grass. They had several books open in front of them. A message of crows was hopping around them, basking in the morning sun and searching for worms.

Abdullah began to turn away to avoid the couple.

'Wait a minute,' I said. 'I know those guys.'

Vinson and Rannveig looked up, smiling, as we approached. I introduced Abdullah, and stooped to pick up one of the books. It was Joseph Campbell's *The Hero with a Thousand Faces*.

'How did you get into Campbell?'

'We studied him at university,' Rannveig said. 'I'm teaching a crash course to Stuart.'

'It's over my head,' Vinson grinned, waving a hand over the blonde waves of his hair.

'Carlos Castaneda,' I said, reading the covers of other books. 'Robert Pirsig, Emmett Grogan, Eldridge Cleaver, and the Buddha.

514

Nice bunch. You could throw Socrates and Howard Zinn onto that list. I didn't know you're a student here.'

'I'm not,' Rannveig said quickly.

'Technically, I'm the student,' Vinson said. 'I enrolled here nearly two years ago, but I've bunked all my classes. Still have the library card, though.'

'Well, happy reading, guys,' I said, turning away.

'It worked,' Rannveig said. 'That thing, with the plate of food.'

I turned back.

'It did?'

'Yes,' she said. 'Sweet Tooth was happy, I guess. He's gone. Thank you.'

'What are you guys talking about?' Vinson asked, his face as perplexed as a ten-year-old kid's.

One of the things I liked most about Vinson was that his face was so wide open that it gave nowhere for his feelings to hide. Whatever he thought or felt started in his face. He was his own straight man.

'Tell you later,' Rannveig said, waving goodbye.

'Do those people also buy and sell watches?' Abdullah asked, as we continued the loop of the playing fields back toward the campus entrance.

'Are we back to that again?'

Abdullah harrumphed. There actually are people who harrumph. I know quite a few, as it turns out. My theory is that harrumphers have a tiny pinch of extra bear DNA than the rest of us, in their setup.

'I have your guns for you,' he said grudgingly. 'Tell me where you want me to deliver them.'

'I know a guy who'll keep them safe, for ten per cent. I'll give you the details. Thanks, Abdullah. Let me know what I owe you.'

'The weapons are a gift,' he said, stung.

'I'm sorry, brother, of course. Damn nice. And speaking of weapons, I've got a meeting with Vikrant, my knife guy, in Sassoon Dock. Is there anything I can do for you?'

We approached the archway leading back through the campus to the street, but he stopped me before I could join the mill of students passing through the arch.

'There is something,' Abdullah began, but he closed his mouth firmly again, breathing hard through his nose. 'Sanjay has forbidden us from befriending you, or contacting you, for any reason other than Company business.'

'I see.'

'You understand what this means?'

'I . . . guess so.'

'It means that the next time we meet openly, Sanjay will be dead.'

'What?'

'Be confident and unafraid,' he said, hugging me fiercely, and then holding me in his outstretched arms, as solid as a doorjamb. 'You have eyes watching you.'

'You got that right.'

'No. I mean that I have paid some eyes to watch you, for some time,' he said patiently.

'You have? Who?'

'The Cycle Killers.'

'You paid homicidal maniacs to watch out for me?'

'I did.'

'That's very thoughtful. And expensive. Maniacs don't come cheap.'

'You are right. I took some money from Khaled's treasure, to pay for it.'

'How did Khaled feel about that?'

'He agreed. My feeling is that the only way I can lure him back to Bombay, and his true destiny, is to bring his treasure from the mountain to the city, one piece at a time.'

'You're kidding, right?'

He looked me up and down, profoundly offended.

'I never make jokes.'

'You do, too,' I laughed. 'You just don't *know* you do. You're a funny guy, Abdullah.'

'I am?' he asked, grimacing.

'You hired homicidal maniacs to protect me. You're a funny guy, Abdullah. Lisa always laughed when she was with you, remember?'

Lisa.

He looked across the fields, the muscles in his jaw rippling, although his eyes were perfectly still. University students were playing cricket, kicking footballs, sitting in groups, doing cartwheels, and dancing for no reason.

Lisa.

'You were her Rakhi brother,' I said. 'She never told me.'

'Big changes are coming,' Abdullah said, finding my eyes. 'The next time you see me, perhaps it will be at my funeral. Kiss me as a brother, and pray that Allah forgives my sins.'

He kissed my cheek, whispered goodbye, and slipped gracefully into the stream of students flowing through the arch.

The fields, surrounded by the long, speared fence, seemed like a vast green net, cast by the sun to catch brilliant young minds. My eyes searched for Vinson and Rannveig, in the far corner of the park, but I couldn't find them.

Abdullah was already gone when I reached my bike. It was high noon, and he didn't want to explain being seen with me. I wondered when, and how, I'd ever see him again.

I rode back to the Sassoon Dock area, and Vikrant's metal shop. I presented the renowned knife-maker with the two halves of the sword willed to me by Khaderbhai.

Vikrant's bargaining system was to begin with the cheapest solution, sell you on it, and then expose the fatal flaw in the cheapest option. That, of course, led to the next cheapest option, the next hard sell, the next fatal flaw, and the next option, and the next fatal flaw.

I'd tried over the years to get Vikrant to cut straight to the very-expensive-option-with-zero-fatal-flaws, but unfortunately that wasn't an option.

'Do we have to do the option thing again, Vikrant? Can't you just gimme the deluxe deal now? I really don't give a shit how much it costs. And it's really irritating, man.'

'As in everything else in life,' the knife-maker said, 'there's a right way, and a wrong way, to be irritating.'

'Uh-huh?'

'Indeed. Me, for example, I'm *professionally* irritating. *My* irritating goes with the territory. But you, you're irritating without any reason at all.'

'No, I'm not.'

'You're irritating me now, even as we speak.'

'Fuck you, Vikrant. Are you gonna fix the sword, or not?'

He studied the weapon for some time, trying not to smile.

'I'll do it,' he said. 'But only if I can fix it my own way. The hilt has a fatal flaw. A third-rate option.'

'Great. Go ahead.'

'No,' he said, holding the sword in his upturned palms. 'You must understand. If I fix it my way, it will never break, and it will be a partner with Time, but it will not be the same sword that Khaderbhai's ancestors carried into battle. It will look different, and it will feel different. The soul of it will *be* different.'

'I see.'

'Do you want to preserve history,' the knife-maker asked, allowing himself a smile, 'or do you want history to preserve you?'

'Funny guy, Vikrant. I want the sword to last. It's like a trust, and I can't be sure that the next guy will have it repaired if it breaks again. Do the deluxe, Vikrant. Make her last forever, and give her a makeover, but keep her under wraps until you're finished, okay? It makes me sad.'

'The sword, or the trust?'

'Both.'

'*Thik*, Shantaram.'

'Okay. And thanks for the message you sent through Didier, about Lisa. Meant a lot.'

'She was a nice girl,' he sighed, waving goodbye. 'Gone to a better place, man.'

'A better place,' I smiled, thinking it strange that we can think of any life as better than the life we're living.

I avoided better places, and spent the long day and evening doing the rounds of currency dealers and touts, from the Fountain to the Point to the mangroves in Colaba Back Bay.

I listened to Chinese-whispered gangster gossip up and down the strip, made notes on all the money changers' tallies and estimates, checked them against Didier's notes, found out who the principal predators were, which restaurants favoured us and which banned us, how often the cops demanded money, which men could be trusted, which girls couldn't be trusted, which shops were fronts for other businesses, and how much each square foot of black market footpath in Colaba cost.

Crime does pay, of course, otherwise nobody would do it. Crime usually pays faster, if not better, than Wall Street. But Wall Street has the cops. And the cops were my last stop before visiting the slum, to check on Diva and Naveen.

Lightning Dilip gestured toward a chair, when I walked into his office.

'Don't sit in the fucking chair,' he said. 'What the fuck do you want?'

He was looking me over, remembering the last beating he'd given me, hoping for a limp.

'Lightning-*ji*,' I began politely. 'I just want to know if I can still bribe you, now that I'm freelancing, or if I have to go to Sub-Inspector Patil. I'm hoping for you, because the sub-inspector can be a real pain in the ass. But if you tell him that, I'll deny it.'

The constables laughed. Lightning Dilip glared at them.

'Throw this motherfucker in the under barrack,' he said to the cops, lounging in the doorway. 'And kick his head sideways.'

They stopped laughing, and moved toward me.

'Just kidding,' Lightning laughed, holding up a hand to stop his men. 'Just kidding.'

The cops laughed. I laughed, too. It was pretty funny, in its own way.

'Five per cent,' I said.

'Seven and a half,' Lightning shot back. 'And I'll give you a chair to sit in, next time you visit the under barrack.'

The cops laughed. I laughed, too, because I would've given him ten per cent.

'Done. You drive a hard bargain, Lightning-*ji*. You didn't marry a Marwari wife for nothing.'

The Marwaris are trading people from Rajasthan, in northern India. They have a reputation for shrewd business, and sharp deal making. Lightning Dilip's Marwari wife had a reputation for spending money faster than Lightning could beat it from his victims.

He looked at me, tasting the mention of his wife without pleasure. His lip curled. Every sadist has a sadist in the shadows. When you know who it is, just the mention of the name is enough.

'Get out of here!'

'Thank you, Sergeant-*ji*,' I said.

I walked past the cops who'd chained and kicked me, weeks before. They smiled, and nodded good-naturedly. That was pretty funny too, in its own way.

CHAPTER FIFTY

I PARKED OUTSIDE THE SLUM AND MADE MY WAY to Johnny's house. He wasn't there, so I went to the adjoining huts being used by Naveen and Diva. I heard them, as usual, before I saw them.

'Do you know what a woman has to *do* to take a *shit* around here?' Diva demanded, as I walked into the little clear space in front of their huts.

'Wow, that was a long conversation,' I said. 'Weren't you on that last time?'

'Do *you* know, Mr *Kharab Dhandha* Shantaram?' she demanded, using the term for *dirty business*.

'I do. I used to live here. And it ain't right.'

'Damn right, it's not right,' Diva said, turning from me to poke Naveen in the chest. 'A woman can't shit in the daytime, for example.'

There were several people in the group. Naveen and Didier were standing in front of Naveen's hut. Diva was with Johnny's wife, Sita, and three girls from surrounding houses.

'I –' Naveen tried.

'Imagine if someone told you that you can't take a shit, all day, because you're a man, and somebody might see you taking a shit. You'd totally freak out, right?'

'I –'

'Well, that's what *we* get told, because we're women. And when we *are* allowed to take a shit, when the sun goes down, we have to clamber around the rocks, and do it in some miserable fucking place in the total dark, because if we carry a torch, someone might *see* that we're taking a *shit*!'

'I –'

'And women get molested, out there in the dark. There's crazy guys hanging around. Guys who don't mind that the place is full of shit. Guys who actually prefer it that way. I'm not kidding, and I'm not putting up with it. I waited till dark to take a shit, and I'm not doing that again. I'm the fuck out of here, and that means tonight! I'm leaving.'

Naveen was considering whether to say *I* again. He looked at Didier. Didier looked at me. I looked at the fascinating knot on the edge of a bamboo support pole.

There was a commotion, and Johnny rushed in from one of the narrower lanes we used for short cuts.

He saw us, and stopped. His mouth was open. His hands were out in front of him, as if he was holding a branch.

'What is it, Johnny?' Sita asked, in Marathi.

'I . . . I can't . . . '

'Johnny, what's up?' I asked.

He was stiff, as if he was ready to run somewhere. His face struggled. Sita went to him, and led him away. After a minute she returned, and called Naveen and me to her.

Didier and the girls remained with Diva.

'What the fuck is going on?' Diva said. 'I'm leaving! *Hello?* Did everybody *forget* that part?'

Johnny was sitting in a plastic armchair, drinking from a bottle of chilled water.

'They are all dead,' he said.

'Who's dead?' Naveen asked.

'Aanu's father, I mean Diva's father, and everyone at his house. Everyone. Even the gardeners. Even the pets. It was a horrible massacre.'

'When?'

'Just now,' Johnny said breathlessly. 'Lin, how can we tell that girl? I can't do it. I can't.'

'Did you check the story?'

'Yes, Naveen, of course I did. The police and press are going mad. It will be on the news, very soon, and then she will know anyway. Should we just wait? What are we going to do?'

'Turn on the radio, Johnny,' I said.

Sita clicked on the local news channel.

Bad words like slaughter and massacre poured from the mouth

of the radio. Mukesh Devnani and seven of his household had been killed. The household pets had been killed. Nothing, and no-one, was spared.

Divya Devnani, the words said, again and again, the sole heir to the Devnani fortune, might also have been killed in the slaughter, the massacre, the slaughter.

'We can't let her find out by hearing that,' I said. 'She's gotta be told.'

'*I'll* tell her,' Naveen said, soft light in his eyes.

'Good,' I said. 'It's tough on you, but it should be you. But not here. Let's go down to the rocks, and the sea. There's a quiet place I know.'

She didn't protest, when we walked through the slum, but as we stepped among the black stones on the shoreline, she tried to walk back into the slum. I think she sensed that bad news had found a place to drown itself.

Naveen held her in his arms, and told her. She broke the hug, walked a few uncertain steps on the rocky shore, and began to stagger away.

Naveen followed her closely, catching her a few times when her bare feet slipped between the rocks.

She stumbled on in a daze, her eyes blind, her legs moving in an instinct to flee suffering and fear.

I'd seen it before, during a prison riot: a man so scared that he walked into a stone wall, again and again, always hoping for a door. Her mind was somewhere else, searching for the vanished world.

Without her realising it, Naveen led her in a wide arc, and back to me. She sat placidly, then, on a boulder, and very slowly came back to herself. When she did, she started crying uncontrollably.

I left her with Naveen, who loved her, and returned to the huts to bring Sita and the girls to help. Sita was gone, but I found Karla and the Zodiac Georges instead.

I looked at Didier. Diva's hiding place in the slum was a secret.

'I thought it wise, that she have some support,' Didier said. 'Especially since we shall all be spending the night here to support her, in this . . . community facility, is it not so?'

Karla kissed me hello.

'How is she?'

'It hit her like an axe handle,' I said, 'but she came around okay. She's a tough girl. Good that you're here. She's with Naveen, down by the sea. I'd give them a while yet. She's pretty cut up, and Naveen knew her father.'

'Didier is too much of a gentleman to keep a secret,' Didier said, 'and leave Diva without friends, on a night of such terrible disaster as this.'

'And Didier is too scared of ghosts,' Karla added, 'to stay here alone.'

'Ghosts?'

'Clearly,' Didier said, 'the place is haunted. I am sensing presences.'

'Whatever the reason, I'm glad you're here.'

'It's been a while,' she said, looking around at the slum huts. 'Any special attractions this time? Cholera, typhoid?'

There'd been a cholera outbreak years before, while I was living in the slum. Karla had come to help me fight it. She'd accepted the local rats, nursed helpless people, and cleaned diarrhoea from earthen floors on her hands and knees.

'It sounds crazy, I guess, but that time with you, back then, it's one of my happiest memories.'

'Mine, too,' she said, glancing around. 'And you're right. It's crazy. What are the girls doing to Diva's place?'

'They're sprucing it up. Hoping to raise her spirits, I think.'

'There are spirits being raised from the dead in this wild city tonight,' she said. 'That's for sure.'

'Terrible business,' Scorpio added, joining us.

'Poor little thing,' Gemini said. 'We've kept her suite open, at the Mahesh. It's always there, if she wants it.'

'Just keep this place to yourselves,' I said. 'Johnny and the others are taking a risk. Don't let anyone know about Diva. Are we good?'

'Good as gold, mate,' Gemini replied.

'Yes . . . ' Scorpio hedged. 'Unless . . . '

'Unless?'

'Unless someone is forcing me to tell.'

'What's that supposed to mean?'

'Well, suppose somebody started hitting me, to get me to tell, then I would tell. So, I can only promise confidentiality up to the point of physical harm.'

I looked at Gemini.

'It's one of Scorpio's rules,' he shrugged.

'And a good one,' Scorpio added. 'If everyone in the world spilled

523

their guts at the first sign of violence, there'd be no torture any more.'

'SnitchWorld,' Karla said. 'I think you're on to something, Scorp.'

A man came through the lanes toward us, wheeling a bicycle laden with parcels.

'Ah!' Didier cried. 'The relief supplies!'

The man unloaded a sponge mattress, a suitcase, a folding card table, four folding canvas stools and two sacks of booze from the bicycle. I looked at the booze.

'It is for Diva,' Didier said, catching my eye as he was counting the bottles. 'The girl will need to get very drunk tonight, if on no other night in her life.'

'Alcohol isn't the answer to everything, Didier.'

Diva came out of the shadows suddenly.

'I need to get very drunk,' she said.

Didier stared his *Told you so* at me.

'Will you . . . ' Diva said, 'my strange new friends, because none of you are my actual friends, and my actual friends aren't here, and I may never see them again, like my father, will you help me to get very drunk, and clean me up when I get sick, and put me to bed safely, when I don't know what's going on any more?'

There was a pause.

'Of course!' Didier said. 'Come here, sweet injured child. Come here to Didier, and we shall cry into everybody's beer together, and spit into the eyes of Fate.'

She did cry, of course. She ranted, waved her arms, shouted, paced the little hut, tripped on the patchwork blankets, and called the girls in to dance with her.

When the ululating voices and handclap music reached a peak, she began to fall. Naveen caught her quickly and carried her to the bed of blankets, her arms falling at her sides like broken wings. She slowly curled her knees into her heart, and slept.

Sitting vigil in the next hut, Didier played poker with Naveen and the Zodiac Georges. It wasn't a pretty game to watch: Scorpio never saw a crooked card, Didier and Gemini never played him a straight one, and Naveen couldn't take his mind from the sleeping girl in the hut next door.

I looked in on Diva. Several of the neighbour girls were sleeping in the hut to keep Diva company. One girl of eighteen, named Anju, was cuddling the socialite's shoulders in sleep. Another girl had her arm over Diva's belly. Three girls snuggled in close to them. Somebody's little brother was sleeping against their feet.

I trimmed the wick on the kerosene lantern to keep it alight, and lit a mosquito coil and a sandalwood incense stick from the flame. I set the coil and incense on a stand on top of the metal cabinet, and pulled the light plywood door shut on its rope hinges.

Through narrow lanes of sleeping trust I walked back to the rocks and the sea, as black as the sky. I stood watching and listening. In that spot Diva had heard, and realised, that she'd lost everything.

When I stood on the front wall of a prison, between the gun towers, I felt calm. All the terror drained from me, because I knew that if the guards shot me, I'd fall on the right side of the wall.

When I slid down my electric-cord rope to freedom and started running, the calm left me, and the realisation of what I'd lost hit me so hard that I couldn't stop my hands from shaking for weeks.

But I'd chosen my exile, and Diva had hers forced on her. And it was too cruel: her father killed, and everyone else. It was the kind of too-cruel that makes a survivor fall. I hoped that the young socialite, hiding in the real world, had friends who wouldn't let that happen, when she returned to the unreal world.

I heard a sound and turned to see Karla, standing on a rocky outcrop at the edge of the slum. She'd come to find me.

She waved to me, and a stray wave broke high against the rocks nearby. White rivulets of water streamed over black boulders to the shore. A second wave garlanded the rocks with surf as I climbed back toward the light, and love, one wet black stone at a time.

I paused with her at the top, and for a while we watched the sea spilling on the shore of Diva's grief.

We walked back past huts humming and murmuring sleep: fathers sleeping outside to leave more room for the family inside, the silver moon bathing them in soft light.

And we talked softly with Didier, the Georges and Naveen in the hut beside Diva's, all of us wanting to be close, in case she woke.

Diva's Bombay would never be the same again: some of the people she'd known before the tragedy would become true friends, and some would become strangers in press paradise. Either way, when she returned to her destiny, everything would be changed. Naveen was a Bombay boy, and maybe he understood that in ways we couldn't. But in our exile hearts, the Island City was home for all of us. And we waited together, that vigilant night, until the scarlet dawn helped a new exile wake, and struggle to the shore.

PART NINE

CHAPTER FIFTY-ONE

THE LULL THAT FOLLOWED THE STORM of Lisa's death and the massacre at the Devnani estate lasted for long, busy, peaceful weeks. I liked it. I'd seen enough storms for one year.

Diva settled into her role as a slum girl, and the slum settled into its role as host to a Diva. Neither of them had much choice: the girls in the slum were star-struck over Diva, so they formed a permanent honour guard; and the killers of Diva's father hadn't been identified, so Diva stayed in the safest place in the city.

The newspapers still carried the story of the massacre, and the missing heiress. A court-appointed CEO administered the group of companies owned by Diva's father, working with the various boards of directors until the heiress could be found.

There were twenty-five thousand people in the slum, and most of them knew who Diva was. Nobody called a reporter, or tried to claim the reward. She was under the protection of the slum, and in that avalanche of huts and shoulder-width lanes she was Aanu, one of their own. She was safe from thugs with guns or magazine deadlines.

The Georges ran a semi-permanent party and fully permanent poker game from the top floor of the Mahesh hotel. Celebrities who'd closed their windows at traffic signals, when they were poor fixtures of the city, spent more time in the penthouse parties than they did with their therapists.

When the deputy mayor broke the bank, he declared the game a municipal recreation, exempting it from prosecution under gambling laws. When the ward tax collector won a similar pot, the poker game was registered as a charity. And when the prettiest starlet in Bollywood won six hands in a row, cleaning out everyone except the bank, she made the game so hot that one Bollywood actor after another tried, and failed, to restore male pride by beating her record.

For his part, Didier applied himself to the Lost Love Bureau with surprising diligence. He rose early, something so shocking that I jumped with fright the first time I saw him bright and active at eight in the morning. Didier had always said that an hour of sunlight a day is enough for anyone, and the hour before sunset was the only sunlight worth having.

The morning version of the night person I knew was strange, at first. He was punctual. He worked. He even told jokes.

'You know,' Naveen said, a few weeks after the bureau had opened for business, 'I'm so glad that you put Didier and me together. He's a hard-working stiff, if you'll pardon the expression.'

'Maybe. I don't know.'

'You're just nostalgic.'

'It isn't nostalgia, if the first version is better. I don't want Didier to get corporate on me.'

The new Didier did get corporate, and detectived seriously, and business at the bureau was brisk. He put an advertisement for the Lost Love Bureau in the biggest daily newspaper, one of Ranjit's newspapers, offering a reward for information on the whereabouts of Ranjit, the missing owner of Ranjit Media, a Lost Love.

The notice didn't bring any new leads, but it got everyone in town talking about the Lost Love Bureau, and it brought more than a dozen clients, each one clutching a file of photographs and police reports on missing loved ones. And when two of the missing loves were found in as many weeks, due to Didier's street connections and Naveen's deductive skills, the bureau attracted more clients, all of them willing to pay cash in advance.

Karla was right, of course: a market is a need, serving itself. Lost loves, forgotten or abandoned by overstretched police departments, are a constant ache in the heart, no less for the cops themselves, and a need that demands to be served. The bureau did well: lost loves were found, and reunited with the hearts that couldn't stop searching for them.

Vinson and Rannveig dropped in at Gemini George's parties from time to time. Vinson was happy, but never left Rannveig's side unless she sent him away, or told him to wait somewhere.

The girl with the ice-in-a-blue-glass eyes seemed to have accepted the death of her boyfriend. She never mentioned him to me again. But while that ghost might've slipped away on a river of acceptance, some shadow remained in the young face. It was as if every changing expression or movement of a hand was clouded by irresolution.

Nevertheless, she looked healthy and well. And she'd taken to dressing as Karla did, in a thin sheath of *salwar kameez* and tight cotton leggings. It suited her, with her hair pulled back into a high ponytail. And when she smiled happily and openly, as she did from time to time, leaves of doubt parted, and a bright sky of what she could become shone through.

In the mysterious absence of Ranjit, the proprietor, Kavita Singh was promoted from banner journalist to deputy editor of the flagship newspaper. The fact that Karla had a deciding proxy vote in Ranjit Media was influential. The fact that Kavita's columns were the most popular in the city was decisive.

Within two weeks under Kavita's creative hand, the newspaper took a new turn, not left or right, but straight up into something else. The mood was upbeat. Bombay was a great, exciting place to live. *Enough of this comparing ourselves to other places shit*, she wrote in her first editorial. *Open your eyes, and see how wonderful this gigantic social experiment you're living in is, and see how much real love keeps it going.*

People loved it. Sometimes, people born in a place need to have someone wake its beauty for them, and Kavita's editorial started a fire in every Mumbaikar's heart; a fire of pride that none of them knew they'd prepared inside themselves, until Kavita lit it. The newspaper's circulation increased by nine per cent. Kavita was a hit.

Karla laughed, long and happily, when the civic pride campaign became a trend that tumbled into a cascade of social activities across the city. I didn't ask her why, and she didn't tell me.

She moved into the rooms next to mine and transformed them, during a week of deletions and deliveries. Her three rooms, a living room, a bedroom and a wardrobe corridor like mine, became a Bedouin tent.

Waves of sky-blue and white muslin, fixed from the light fittings in the centre of each room, hid the ceilings. The lights were stripped away and replaced by old railway lanterns.

She took all the furniture out of the rooms, except for the bed, and a writing table in the living room. She bought the table from the music store downstairs and had the legs sawn off, so that she could sit at it cross-legged in the middle of the floor.

She covered every linoleum inch of that floor, even the bathroom, with Turkish and Iranian carpets. They were lying on top of one another as if they'd exhausted themselves, wrestling for a place of prominence at her feet.

The balcony that looked out on Metro Junction, and connected with mine, was draped in red silk saris, softening the white heat of day to cooling troughs and stripes of crimson.

There weren't any sleepovers, but it was okay. It was heaven, in fact: the happiest days I'd known since I'd thrown my life in a gutter of shame, nine years before.

Freedom and happiness and justice and even love are all parts of the same whole: peace, within. The first time I put fear into someone to get money for drugs, I crossed a line I'd drawn in the earth of my own life. But the shovel fell from my hand when Karla moved into the Amritsar hotel, and for a while I stopped digging graves of guilt. We ate breakfast, lunch and dinner together almost every day. We did the work we had to do separately, but got together every minute we could.

When we were free, we rode all the way around the Island City. When she felt like it, Karla drove her car, with Randall helping himself to a soda in the back. We saw a couple of movies, visited friends, and went to a few parties.

But any night together, every night together, she went back to the Bedouin tent alone, locking all those locks I'd put on her door.

She was driving me crazy, of course, but in the best possible way. People differ in things like this, I know, but for me it isn't how long you wait for something that counts, it's the quality of the wait. And hours alone with Karla every day was a quality wait.

Sometimes, in all that quality waiting, very occasionally, I found myself thinking about punching a new air vent in the wall of my room. And sometimes, being only a metre away from her behind a connecting wall every night, twisted the guitar string pretty tight. Mind you, there was always the black market, to wind the string tighter.

Crime is a demon, Didier once said, *and adrenaline is his drug of choice.* Every crime, even a little crime like black market money changing, comes with a measure of adrenaline. The people you're doing business with are at least a little dangerous, the cops are more than a little dangerous, and every crime has its own species of predator and prey.

Black market money changing was all but legal in South Bombay in those years, operating openly in every second Colaba cigarette shop. South Bombay had two hundred and ten cigarette shops, all of them licensed by the Municipal Authority and the Sanjay Company. I ran fourteen of them, bought from Didier, and sanctioned by Sanjay. It was usually a safe trade, but criminals, by definition, are violently unpredictable.

I never took Karla on my rounds. I did one round between breakfast and lunch, another after lunch, and a late-night scout of the shops before sleep. It was important for the boss to be seen.

Running a crime franchise requires a sophisticated degree of cooperation, usually bought, and clearly defined roles and rules. I provided the finesse money. The Sanjay Company defined the roles, and enforced the rules.

But every trader changing black money at the street level has his own measure of pride. Rebellion, from frustration or fear, is a constant possibility. The defection of even one of my money changers would bring swift punishment from Sanjay, but it would also cost me the franchise. Making such uprisings impossible, by keeping the shopkeepers between fear and friendship, was my job.

Crime is feudal, and when you understand that, you actually understand quite a lot of it. The Sanjay Company was the castle on the hill, with a moat full of crocodile gangsters, and Sanjay was the feudal lord. If he wanted a girl, he took her. If he wanted a man dead, he killed him.

Because I'd purchased a franchise in the bazaar, that made me a kind of robber baron, and the shopkeepers were the serfs. They had no rights but those granted by the Company.

Crime is a medieval metropolis running parallel to the shining city, complete with absolute monarchy and public executions. And as a robber baron, riding from serf to serf on my steel pony, I had the right to assert my authority.

The first skill in running a crime franchise is projecting an air of unchallengeable entitlement. If you don't believe it yourself, no-one else on the street will. They're too smart. You have to own it, and own it in a way that stops people thinking about challenging you.

In Bombay that involves a lot of yelling and the occasional slap, usually over trivial things, until the air is clear and your voice is the last and the loudest.

After that, it's a matter of observation. This one chews *paan*, this one hates *paan*, this one listens to holy songs from a speaker in the shape of King Kong. This guy likes boys, this guy likes girls, this guy likes girls too much, this guy is confident when he's alone, and this one cowers until his confederates arrive, this one drinks, thinks, smokes, chokes, peeps, talks, walks, and this one is the only one who'll still be standing toe to toe with you, till the last thrust of the knife.

'You hear what happened to Abhijeet?' Francis, my Regal Circle money changer asked, when I pulled up beside him.

'Yeah.'

Abhijeet was a street kid, hustling tourists on the strip. He'd tried to run a police roadblock too fast on a stolen scooter. He crashed into a stone bridge support, and the bridge didn't give way.

'Bloody little prick,' Francis said, handing me the pick-up money. 'He's annoying my mind more, now that he's dead, than he did when he was alive. And when he was alive, he was the most annoying prick in the world.'

'He's annoying you so much that you're light, Francis,' I said, checking the money he gave me.

'What *light*, baba?' he said, raising his voice loud enough for the other traders near him to hear.

I looked around at the faces on the street.

'Don't do this, Francis.'

'I'm not doing anything, baba,' he shouted. 'You are accusing me, and —'

I grabbed him by the collar and dragged him toward an alley, a few steps away.

'My shop!'

'Fuck the shop.'

I shoved him into the alley.

'Let's do it,' I said.

'Let's do what?'

'You're cheating me, in front of your friends. Now we can be honest, alone. Where's the money?'

'Baba, you —'

I slapped him.

'I didn't —'

I slapped him harder.

'In my shirt,' he said. 'Your money is inside my shirt.'

There was a lot of money inside his shirt. I took the money he'd skimmed, and left the rest.

'I don't care where you get your money, Francis, so long as you don't skim it from me. And you'll never make a show in front of your friends again. You see that, right?'

It's an ugly thing, raw power: ugly enough to scare away scavengers. And it's an ugly job, sometimes, keeping street criminals in line. They need to know that reaction will always be fast and violent, and they need to fear it. If they don't, they all turn on you, and then things get bloody.

I did the rounds until I had enough foreign money to knock on the door of the black market bank in Ballard Pier.

Black bankers aren't criminals: they're civilians who commit crimes. By staying on the safe side of the line, they don't risk real prison time. They keep a low profile, when their wealth would bring them into the A-list, because the money's more important. And they're scrupulously apolitical: they hold black money for any party, whether in power or not.

The Sanjay Company used the black bank at Ballard Pier, and so did the Scorpions. But a lot of cops kept their loot there, and some heavy hitters in the armed services, and the politicians, of course. There was construction money, sugar baron money, oil money and slush fund money. In one way or another it was the best protected bank in town.

The bank cared for its customers in return. Whenever one of them messed up, the bank made the mess subside, for a fee. Each scandal was tagged and bagged and locked in the vault. There was more dirt in the black bank at Ballard Pier, it was said, than undeclared gold.

Everyone in town had something to gain from the bank's invisible hand, and everyone had something to lose if the hand became a fist. The bank was so swollen with secrets and secret money that it was too crooked to fail.

For small hustlers like me, given access to a small sub-branch window, the black bank was a convenient way to hand in my US dollars and other currencies, take the equivalent in black rupees, and let the bank forward the foreign cash to the South Bombay buyers' syndicate.

Nobody but partners with too much to lose knew who the buyers were. Some said that a wild bunch of movie producers and actors had set up the syndicate. One rumour insisted that it was a Bombay chapter of the Masonic Lodge.

Whoever they were, they were smart. They controlled eighty per cent of the black dollars in the south, made more profit than anyone in the chain, and never risked an hour behind bars.

After costs, in my small operation, I cleared twenty thousand rupees a month from the money changer operation. If I'd still been living in the slum, it would've made me a king. On the street, it was pin money.

Once crime starts to pay, you soon learn that the key to survival isn't making money, it's keeping it. Every black rupee you make has a hundred hands reaching out to take it away. And you can't call the cops, because the cops are often the ones taking it away.

And when the cash you make comes in bundles, and you don't have any burning desire to spend it, because you're a rainy day kind of a guy, few decisions are more important than where you decide to keep it.

The first rule is not to put it all in one place. If things get bad, and you've gotta give something up, a plump reserve is a good idea. I kept some at home as escape money. I left some with Tito, Didier's man. He gave me friend rates of two per cent. He still called it ten per cent, but only charged me two.

'Forgive me,' he said, when he muttered *ten per cent* again, out of habit. 'My mind is angry with me.'

'Listen, Tito, if someone comes calling, telling you that I'm tied up in a cellar somewhere, and being tortured, and uses the code *300 Spartans*, just give him the money, okay?'

'Done,' he said. 'For ten per cent.'

CHAPTER FIFTY-TWO

EVERY WOMAN OF A CERTAIN AGE is automatically an auntie, in India. Half-Moon Auntie, who ran a black bank in the fish market, was maybe fifty years old, and so voluptuous in her seductive powers that no man could stay more than ten minutes in her company, it was said, without proposing to her. And Half-Moon Auntie, a widow not in mourning, did everything in her considerable range of talents to make the minutes of any transaction roll into double digits.

So far, I'd always been a nine-minute guy with Half-Moon Auntie: deal done, and outta there.

'Hi, Half-Moon Auntie,' I said, handing a paper-wrapped bundle of rupees to her assistant clerk, sitting behind a fish counter. 'How are you?'

She kicked a plastic chair at me. It slid to a stop at my feet. She'd done it before. She did it every time, in fact.

Decades of fish oil, soaked into the concrete, made the surface almost frictionless. It was hard to walk around. It was hard to keep standing up, in fact. It was as if the dead fish, soaked into the stone around Half-Moon Auntie's rope bed, wanted to make us fall down. And people did, every day.

I took the chair, knowing that there was no such thing as a fast getaway from Half-Moon Auntie's black bank.

I was sitting at the end of a very long stainless steel cutting table. It was one of several in the fish market, an area the size of a football field under waves of slanted tin and clotted skylight crests.

Work had stopped for the day, and the shouting had shrunk into a silence that was, perhaps, like the gasps of fish, drowning in our air, just as we drown in theirs.

I could hear Half-Moon Auntie swallowing. I could hear the clock on the wall ticking. I could hear Auntie's assistant, counting the money slowly, carefully.

It was dark, but the shade was hotter than the sunny street outside. The smell had been strong enough to close my mouth, at first, but it began to settle into a low hum of fish not in the sea.

Someone started to run a hose at the far end of the market. Blood and pieces of dead things floated past in a gutter chiselled into the concrete floor.

Beside the gutter was Half-Moon Auntie, standing in her slippers, her rope bed covered by a hand-sewn quilt as silver as the fins of a mirror fish.

'So, Shantaram,' she said. 'They say that a woman has your heart.'

'That's true, Half-Moon Auntie,' I replied. 'How are you doing?'

She put her arms out to her sides. Very, very slowly she lowered herself onto the rope bed, her arms extended at her sides. Then she dripped her feet out of the slippers, and her legs went into action.

I didn't know if it was yoga or contortionism, but Half-Moon Auntie's legs were pythons, searching for something to constrict. They moved left and right, north and south, twirling above her head and extending wide enough to ford a stream, before settling underneath her on the silver quilt, the prehensile feet tucked up against Olympian thighs.

It took about thirty seconds. If it had been a show, I would've applauded. But it wasn't a show, and I wasn't a customer.

She began to roll her shoulders.

'So, how's business, Half-Moon Auntie?' I tried.

Too late. She leaned toward me slowly, arching her back to feline fluidity. Her breasts fell into view, half a moon tattooed on each globe, and she didn't stop until the moon was full.

Her exceptionally long hair fell to the bed around her folded knees, closing a curtain on the moon, and spilling almost to the blood-stained floor.

She raised her eyes, threatening me with mysteries and things we shouldn't know, then curled her arms backwards around her until her hands clasped her own neck, the fingers wriggling like anemones, spawning in the light of that inverted moon.

No-one can say she didn't have her charm. But I liked her, more than I liked her famous routine.

Half-Moon Auntie was always armed, which is invariably interesting, no matter which way you look at it. She had a small automatic pistol, presented to her by the Chief Commissioner. I wanted to know why. I wanted to know the story. I knew that she'd fired it twice, both times to save someone being bullied by thugs from other areas of the city.

She read fortunes in people's hands, and made more money as a sorceress than she did as a fisherwoman and black banker combined.

And she won the girls' wrestling championship in the fishermen's slum, three years in a row. It was a girls-only event, strictly cordoned off by faces of husbands and brothers and fathers, their backs to the girls who wrestled alone. No-one ever got to see it but the girls who fought until they found a champion.

I wanted to know about the event. I wanted to know the story of how the Commissioner gave her the gun. What I didn't want was a game, with a ten-minute deadline.

'A woman always finds a way,' she said, straightening up, and glancing at the clock. 'At least once, when you are with this woman who has taken your heart, you will be thinking of me, while you make love to her.'

'See, Half-Moon Auntie, you're wrong. That's not gonna happen.'

'Are you so sure?' she asked, holding my stare.

'Completely. With all due respect, Half-Moon Auntie, my girlfriend kicks your ass. You're a lovely woman, and all that, but my girlfriend is a goddess. And if it comes to an actual fight, she'd kick your ass there, too. She'd beat both of us together, with change, and have us thanking her for it, after she did it. I'm crazy about her, Auntie.'

She held my stare for a couple of seconds, testing me, maybe, then slapped her thighs and laughed. I liked it so much that I laughed with her.

'All correct,' her assistant called out, putting my bundle of rupees in a metal bin, locking it, and logging the amount in his ledger.

'You're not the first to say such words,' Half-Moon Auntie said. 'But not many do. A few. Most of them beg for their free show, and create lies, as reasons to consult with me.'

'To be fair to them, you put on a great show, Auntie.'

She laughed.

'Thank you, Shantaram. That's how the legend of my palm-reading skills began. An adulterous husband invented it, so that he could hold

539

my hand, and watch the phases of the moon. Some of them sweat with how much they need it. Even people you know. Your friend Didier sits with me every week.'

'I'll bet he does,' I laughed. 'Why do you do it, Half-Moon Auntie?'

I suddenly realised that the question might hurt her.

'I'm sorry,' I said quickly. 'It was a writer's question, so, you know, probably unforgivably rude.'

She laughed again.

'Shantaram, you can only ask that question, when you have the power to do it. So, when you have the power to do it, ask yourself.'

'My girlfriend is gonna love that line.'

'Bring her with you, next time,' she threatened.

'What if she crosses ten minutes, and proposes to you?'

'Of course she will propose to me, and so will you, one day.'

'I thought we covered that,' I frowned, not understanding.

'You write stories, Shantaram,' she smiled. 'One day you will write about me, and that will be a declaration of love. And this woman who has your heart will propose to me, out of happy love, nothing more.'

'Isn't every love happy love?'

'No,' she laughed. 'There is your kind of love. You, and the few like you, who have become my dearest friends.'

'I don't want unhappiness in love,' I said, frowning. 'I don't want unhappiness at all.'

'I'm talking about the real thing,' she replied. 'The real thing is always more painful and more rewarding than anything less.'

'That's . . . very confusing,' I said. 'But I'm so glad we had this talk, Half-Moon Auntie. If I've been unwittingly rude, and you're not gonna shoot me, please give me about two minutes' head start. It'll take me that long to get to the door, on this surface.'

'Go, now, Shantaram,' she laughed. 'You are a VIP customer, from this day. May the Goddess keep your weapons sharp, and your enemies afraid.'

I slowly skated away from her, sliding and slipping my way across slaughter's floor until I reached the golden arch of sunlight leading to the open market beyond.

While I scraped my boots dry, I looked back at her, doing yoga exercises on the bed.

One foot was raised high and enclosed in her palm, like a flame resting in the space above her head. Half-Moon Auntie: business-woman, gangster and Mistress of Minutes. She was right, I thought. Karla probably would propose to her.

My third bank, my Didier reserve, was the floating poker game that Gemini George ran from their penthouse apartment.

Games that turn over a lot of money need a bank to fund the house. The house takes a percentage of the game, win or lose, but the house also plays, because the margin you win, if you play well, is always bigger than the vig paid for running the game.

The best way to keep a house bankable is to have a good dealer who knows when to fold, and another player in the game, who appears independent but is actually giving his winnings to the house.

Even with improved odds like that, it's always possible for some golden child to walk in and break the bank. It happens. Sometimes, it happens three nights in a row.

But a golden child event is rare enough to make a well-run game pay off, five nights from seven, and Gemini George knew how to run a game.

I put money into the bank, with Didier and Gemini, and the three of us primed the pump for the poker games. My winnings, on a weekly basis, were about equal to the interest I would've earned on my money in a well-run fund.

Gemini had given up cheating. It was a mandatory requirement, mandated by Didier and me. We had to run a straight game, or there was no point.

And Gemini did it. He played every game for the house as straight as the bridge between fear and anger. His honesty and skill won him a lot of new friends, and won a lot of money for us.

Gemini needed the game, because his millionaire friend, as it turned out, was stingy with a dollar. Scorpio paid all the bills for the pent-house floor at the Mahesh, because it was the only place in Bombay that he felt safe, and he didn't feel safe enough to leave the city and go somewhere else, where millionaires live in safety.

But he scanned every receipt and invoice for minute economies, and frequently found them, scraping pennies from accounts measured in thousands.

He refused to fund Gemini's parties. Gemini told everyone to bring their own stimulants, and the parties rolled on. They were cheaper, and gaudier, and much more popular. The hotel became a place where famous people met infamous people, and every bar and restaurant was crowded.

Scorpio restricted Gemini to a limited expense account at the hotel, for food, drink, and services. He also gave him two hundred dollars in cash every week.

Gemini made two hundred dollars in cash every hour with us, in the game, and played in a trance of elegant dexterity. He was confident. He lost with a joke or a line from a song, and won without pride.

'I thought of settin' up a support group, a sort of AA, for people like me, who can't stop cheatin', Card Cheats Anonymous, you know, but the trouble is, you wouldn't be able to trust no-one. Not when it actually came down to cards. Know what I mean?'

'Come on, Gemini. A cynic is someone angry at his own soul, and you're no cynic.'

He squinted on the thought.

'I love you, mate,' he said, smiling to himself.

'Love you too, brother. And anyway, you did it, man. You cold-turkeyed cheating at cards, and you're playing straight, and better than ever.'

'Took some doin', I tell ya,' he shuddered. 'I turned to books, at first. I hit Keats pretty hard and got very sad-trippy, then I got totally Kerouaced, as out of it as a drunken chimp and sayin' the first thing that came into me addled mind. I stumbled into Fitzgerald, staggered out of Hemingway, got totally Deronda with George Eliot, stoned with Virginia Woolf, batty with Djuna Barnes and deranged with Durrell, but then I switched back to movies, and three days of Humphrey Bogart had me right as rain.'

'Quite a support group, Gemini.'

'Yeah. Nothin' like writers and actors for company, is there, when you're at the end of your rope.'

'You got that right. I'm glad it worked out for you.'

He looked at me, lifting aside a curtain of reticence.

'It's a nice view, from the other side of the line, Lin. I never thought I'd say this, but it almost feels *good* not to cheat.'

'That's the spirit.'

'You think so? It feels dodgy, sometimes, being straight. Know what I mean?'

'Sure,' I laughed. 'Keep it up. You look great. An abundance of chance and a scarcity of sunlight wear very well on you, card champion. How's it going, with Scorpio?'

'I . . .'

'That bad, huh?'

'He keeps to himself way too much, Lin. He's all alone in the presidential suite, most of the time. I'm not allowed in.'

'Not allowed in?'

'Nobody is, except the staff. He eats most of his meals in there. I mean, if he had some lovely piece of womanhood in there with him, I'd be guardin' the door. But he doesn't, mate, and the two of us, Scorpio and me, we were never alone.'

'Maybe, he just needs a time-out.'

'We split everything, shared every mouthful of food, down to countin' out the peanuts in a packet and sharin' every one of 'em, even and fair. We argued about everything, all the time, but we never ate a thing without the other one there. We haven't broke bread, so to speak, for three days. I'm worried about him, Lin.'

'Gemini, has he thought about leaving Bombay?'

'If he has, he doesn't talk to me about it. Why?'

'He's nervous, being rich. He needs to move on, and he probably won't move on, unless you move him on.'

'Move him where?'

'Anywhere that millionaires live. They tend to stick together, and they know how to look after themselves. He'll be safe there, and you'll get some peace of mind.'

'I'm having enough trouble living with *one* millionaire. I couldn't handle a whole suburb of them.'

'Then take him to New Zealand. Buy a farm, near a forest.'

'New Zealand?'

'Beautiful country, beautiful people. Great place to vanish in.'

'I'm so worried, Lin. You know, I actually lost a game that I should've won, yesterday.'

'You played about three hundred games, yesterday.'

'Yeah, but I'm afraid of losin' my grip, you know? I feel so helpless to help *him*, and I love him, mate.'

I should've shut up. I couldn't know what my suggestion would bring to the Zodiac Georges. If I had three wishes, one of them would be to know when to shut up.

'Maybe, I don't know, you should just get him outside. Take him for a walk around the hotel. It'd be just like old times, except with body-guards. It might shake him awake.'

'That's not a bad idea,' Gemini said thoughtfully. 'I could trick him into it.'

'Or invite him into it.'

'No, I'll have to trick him into it,' he said. 'I'd have to trick him into drinking water in the desert, because he'd think the CIA put it there. But I've got a plan.'

'Please don't tell me,' I said, leaving my bundle of cash for the poker game bank, and heading for the door. 'I'm allergic to plans.'

I should've worried, for my friends. I know that now. Like so many people in the city, I thought that Scorpio's money solved all their problems. I was wrong. The money was a menace, as it often is, that threatened their friendship, and their lives.

CHAPTER FIFTY-THREE

I LEFT THE HOTEL AND RODE TO THE STARLIGHT RESTAURANT, on Chowpatty Beach. The restaurant was an illegal pop-up on a small, appropriated stretch of beach near the beginning of the sea wall.

It had been running for three months. A movie star and a local entrepreneur had the idea to create a restaurant, as a gift to the city, on a derelict section of public beach, so they created a Goan fragment, complete with palm trees, thatched table umbrellas and sand for open toes.

The food was excellent, and the service was efficient and friendly. But the fact that it was completely illegal, and likely to close any time, added a zest so special to the flavour that the city officials charged with closing down the illegal structure waited days, for a table.

The local entrepreneur, whose eccentric, ephemeral gift to the city cost him a lot of money that he knew he'd never recover, was a friend of mine. Karla was waiting at a table he'd reserved for me.

She stood up. Light from a candle on the table lifted her face, as a gentle hand might've done. She kissed me, and hugged me.

She was dressed in a red cheongsam, split to the hip on one side. Her hair was pulled up in a shell of curves and waves, held in place by a poison dart from a blowgun, which she'd modified with a red jewel at the end. She was wearing red gloves. She was beautiful, and it was a beautiful night, until she said the name Concannon.

'Come again?'

'Concannon wrote me a letter,' she repeated, four green queens on me.

'And you tell me this *now*?'

'The other stuff we talked about was more important.'

'I want to read it,' I said.

It was the wrong approach, but I was angry. Concannon got me that way.

'No.'

'*No?*'

'No.'

'Why not?'

'I burned it,' she said. 'Can we go somewhere where I can't blow cigarette smoke on anybody but you?'

We rode to the top of Malabar Hill and a view of the restaurant we'd left, on the strip of coast below. Lights in the curve of Marine Drive garlanded the belly of the great ocean, the Mother of all.

She blew cigarette smoke on me, for a while, and then went easy on me with two green queens.

'What's going on?'

'What *isn't* going on, Karla?'

We were sitting on a stone monument, high enough for a view through trees to the sea. Another couple sat in the shadows a few metres away, murmuring quietly.

Cars and motorcycles passed slowly, preparing themselves for the long, curving road skirting the city zoo, and leading steeply to Kemps Corner junction. The smell of lions in cages followed that road, and the sound of their grieving roars.

Cops passed every thirty minutes or so. Some very rich people lived nearby. A limousine slowed to a creep as it passed us. The windows were blacked out.

I moved gently against Karla, feeling her body, her weight, ready to push her aside and reach for a knife. The car passed, continuing on down Lion-Sorrow Hill.

'Why did you burn the letter?'

'If your body gets infected, and it's more than your immune system can cope with, you fight it off with antibiotics. It was toxic, so I burned it in an antibiotic fire. Now it's gone.'

'But it's not. It's still inside your memory. Everything is still inside your memory. You don't forget anything. What did the letter say?'

'It's already in *two* memories, his and mine,' she said. 'Why should it be in three?'

She drew in a quick breath. I knew that quick breath. It wasn't oxygen, it was ammunition. She was getting angry, and ready to let me have it.

'It concerns both of us,' I said, holding up my hands. 'I get it, that a letter's a private thing. But this is about an enemy. You've gotta see that.'

'He wrote it, hoping that I'd show it to you. It's a trick. He's taunting and tormenting you, not me.'

'Exactly why I want to know what he wrote to you.'

'Exactly why you shouldn't. It's enough that I tell you it wasn't nice, and that you need to know what he's doing. I'd never hide it from you, because you need to know, but I don't want you to read it. You've gotta see *that*.'

I didn't see it, and I didn't like it. For all we knew, Concannon had a hand in Lisa's death. He'd tried to crack my skull. I didn't feel betrayed. I just felt left out. She'd left me out of one too many of her games and schemes.

We rode home, and kissed goodnight. It wasn't good. I couldn't fake it. I was unhappy and disappointed. I almost made it into my room, before she stopped me.

'Spit the long face out,' she said. 'What's the matter?'

She was standing in the entrance to the Bedouin tent. I was standing in the entrance to my monk's cell: the room of an ex-convict, ready to leave in a motorcycle kick.

'Concannon's letter,' I said. 'I think you should've shown it to me. Like this, it feels like a weird secret that I don't want you to keep.'

'A . . . *secret*?' she said, looking me up and down, and tilting her head. 'You know, I've got a pretty busy schedule tomorrow.'

'Uh-huh?'

'And . . . the day after tomorrow.'

'And –'

'Then, too.'

'Wait a minute,' I said. 'Isn't it me, who's supposed to be angry?'

'You're *never* the one who's supposed to be angry.'

'Not even when I'm right?'

'Especially not when you're right. But you're not right about this. And now we're both pissed.'

'You don't have the right to be mad at me, Karla. Concannon's involved with Ranjit and Lisa. Nothing about him should be secret.'

'Why don't we leave it at that,' she said. 'Before we say something we'll regret. I'll stay in touch. I'll slip a note under your door, if I'm feeling low.'

She shut the door, and locked the locks.

I went to my room, but Abdullah knocked on my door a minute later, disturbing my angry pacing. He told me to get ready, and meet him on the street.

He was parked near my bike with Comanche and three others from the Company, all of them on motorcycles. I kicked my bike to life and followed Abdullah and the others south toward Flora Fountain, where we stopped to allow a water tanker to pass through an intersection, elephant-slow.

'You don't want to know where we are going?' Abdullah asked me.

'No. I'm just happy to be riding with you, man.'

He smiled, and led us through Colaba to Sassoon Dock, near the entrance to the Navy base. We parked in front of a wide, shaded entrance gate, closed for the night.

Abdullah sent a kid to buy chai. The men settled on their bikes, each with a different view of the street.

'Fardeen was killed,' Abdullah said.

'*Inna lillahi wa inna ilayhi raji'oon*,' I said, speaking calm words, *We come from God, and to God we return*, but feeling shocked and hurt.

'*Subhanahu Wa Ta'aala*,' Abdullah replied. *May Allah forgive the bad deeds of the returning soul, and accept the good ones.*

'*Ameen*,' I answered.

Fardeen was so polite and considerate, and such a fair arbiter of others' disputes that we knew him as the Politician. He was a brave fighter, and a loyal friend. Everyone but Fardeen had at least one enemy within the brotherhood of the Sanjay Company. Fardeen was the only man we all loved.

If the Scorpion Company had killed Fardeen as a payback for the burning of their house, they'd picked the one man in Sanjay's group whose death punctured every heart with a poisoned sting.

'Was it the Scorpions?' I asked.

The other men with Abdullah, Comanche, Shah, Ravi and Tall Tony, laughed a gasp, and it was a bitter thing.

'They took him between Flora Fountain and Chor Bazaar,' Shah said, rubbing an angry tear away with the heel of his hand. 'He was on his way there, but never arrived. We found his bike in Byculla, parked on the side of the road.'

'They took him somewhere,' Tall Tony continued, 'tied him up, tortured him, tattooed the outline of a fuckin' scorpion on his chest, and stabbed him through it. Pretty safe to conclude it was them.'

Tall Tony, distinguished by his height from the other Anthony in the Company, Little Tony, spat a curse on the ground at his feet. The tattoo was a cruel twist of the knife. Fardeen was a Muslim, and he followed a tradition among some Muslims, forbidding tattoos. Marking Fardeen's body lowered the bar: the conflict wasn't between rival gangs, but between rival religions.

'Holy shit,' I said. 'How can I help?'

They laughed again, but it was the real thing.

'We are here to help *you*, Lin brother,' Abdullah said.

'Help me?'

They laughed again.

'What's up, Abdullah?'

'There is a price on your head, Lin.'

'It's a *limited offer*,' Comanche said. 'One night only, twenty-four hours.'

'Starting when?'

'Midnight tonight to midnight tomorrow night,' Shah said.

'How much?'

'One lakh,' Ravi said. 'A hundred thousand rupees, dude. That makes you the only man here who actually knows his market value.'

It was about six thousand dollars, in those days: enough to buy a pickup truck, in America, and enough to pick up every sneak-killer in the southern zone, in Bombay.

I thought of several men I knew, a couple of friends, in fact, who'd happily kill me for nothing, if it occurred to them, just because they liked killing people.

'Thanks, guys,' I said.

'What do you want to do?' Abdullah asked me.

'I've gotta stay away from Karla,' I said. 'Don't want any crossfire.'

'Wise. Do you need anything from your home?'

Do I need anything, for being hunted to death?

I worked the street. I was always ready. I had good boots, good jeans, clean T-shirt, lucky sleeveless vest with inner pockets, American money, Indian money, two knives at my back, and a motorcycle that never let me down.

I didn't have a gun, but I knew where to find one.

'No, I'm good, until the clock runs down. It's gonna be an interesting night. Thanks for the warning. I'll see you in twenty-four hours. *Allah hafiz.*'

I straightened my bike from the side-stand, and prepared to kick-start.

'Whoa, whoa!' Tall Tony said.

'Where the fuck you goin'?' Ravi asked.

'I know a place,' I said.

'A place?' Abdullah frowned.

'A place,' I said. '*Allah hafiz.*'

'Whoa, whoa!' Tall Tony said.

'What place?' Ravi asked.

'There's a place I know with a way in, that everybody knows, and a way out that only I know.'

'What the fuck?' Comanche asked.

'I'll get my gun,' I said, 'some fruit, and a couple of beers, and retire there for twenty-four. I'll see you guys later. I'm good.'

'Not gonna happen,' Ravi said, shaking his head.

'We are forbidden by Sanjay from helping you,' Abdullah said. 'But in a time of crisis like this, with a Council member like Fardeen killed, many young men from outside the Company are riding the streets with Company men, patrolling the whole boundary of the south with us. Comanche has joined us, and he is retired from the Company.'

'Damn right,' Ravi said.

'There is nothing to stop you riding with us,' Abdullah continued, 'while we make patrols. And nothing to stop you resting with us, for the next twenty-four hours, as a gesture of your support for the Sanjay Company.'

'And if you choose to do that –' Tall Tony said.

'– we can't stop you,' Ravi finished.

'So, come, Lin, and ride the boundary of South Bombay with us for the next twenty-four hours,' Abdullah said, clapping me on the shoulder. 'And offer us your protection, in this time of attacks on the Company.'

It was a nice offer, one you remember, but I didn't feel right accepting it.

'And suppose one of you takes a bullet for me?' I asked. 'How am I gonna feel about that?'

'Suppose you take a bullet saving one of us?' Abdullah replied, starting his bike. 'How will you feel about that?'

The others started their bikes and we rode off together, settling into a slow speed after the bikes were warm, and cruising the streets and boulevards, two in front, three behind.

Men block things out. Men are driven by duty, and block out anything that stands in the way of their duty.

There was a new price on my head, and I had no idea who put it there, but I blocked it out, thinking only of survival. Maybe the fact that I already had a bounty on my head, offered by my own government, made it easier to block, and give myself to the boundary ride with Abdullah and the others, patrolling for surprise attacks by Scorpion Company killers.

It wasn't the first time I'd ridden a patrol in South Bombay. Other gangs had tried to take territory in the tourist-rich peninsula. We'd ridden patrols through the night in anticipation of attacks, which sometimes came: attacks that would've been worse, if we hadn't been able to respond with mobile patrols in less than thirty seconds, anywhere in the south.

Two teams of four men patrolled a four-hour shift, which was the polite limit for the motorcycles.

The dragon's mouth of the Island City is roughly the same size as Manhattan. We cruised dozens of circuits in those hours. Fortunately, South Bombay is ravined with tiny walkways, wide enough for motorcycles. They provided a network of short cuts that shaved minutes of traffic, and offered endlessly surprising entries and exits to major arterial routes.

The times that we stopped patrolling and talked to people were as important as the time in the saddle. Every helpful whisper is a way to strike the enemy. Home ground advantage is the ace of spades, in turf wars. Attention to detail is the ace of hearts. A supportive community that likes and trusts you at least as much as they like and trust the police is the royal flush.

In fact, the cops joined in with the Sanjay Company, after Fardeen's murder, allowing a limited amnesty for Company men to carry weapons.

The Scorpions, Didier's sources assured him, were trying to force their way into the south with a combination of violence and religious nationalism. They felt that the cops should support their control of South Bombay, because they saw themselves as patriots, and the Sanjay Company as traitors.

The cops were under strict orders to react swiftly in matters of religious sentiment, which was a convenient excuse for Lightning Dilip. He joined with Sanjay Company men, who paid him with more than patriotic fervour, and sent his jeep patrols to hunt down Scorpions for disturbing communal harmony.

It was a tense business, during the truce, being immune from police aggression. Most of us preferred the aggression. You know where you stand, when everyone's playing by the same rules. When the cops are the good guys, it's time to think about another game.

It was eerie, stopping at a traffic signal and having a police jeep draw up alongside; having the cops try to smile, and even make small talk, when you've been beaten in the back of the same jeep, by the same cops.

At the end of our patrol, when no-one had heard or seen anything unusual, we stopped near Haji Ali's tomb, where Tardeo met Pedder Road.

Everything south of that point was Sanjay Company territory, from sea to sea. The tomb of the saint was on neutral ground, and gangsters from all over Bombay came to the shrine peacefully, even gangs that were at war.

Abdullah left the bikes with a contact at the nearby service station, and led us on the long walk across the land bridge footpath to the small island tomb of the saint.

We'd all performed the gangster ritual before: a late-night walk to the saint's tomb, before battle.

Haji Ali, then simply a wealthy Uzbek merchant named Ali, gave up all he had to the poor, and went on a pilgrimage to Mecca.

He travelled all of the world that a traveller could reach. It was a difficult thing to do, because it was the fifteenth century, but he went everywhere, carrying his belongings on his back, and learning everything that could be known.

A man of good taste, he settled in Bombay, and was renowned in the city and beyond for his piety. He died while on the annual Haj. The coffin carrying his body was lost at sea, but washed up, miraculously, on the shores of Bombay, where his tomb was built.

Once a day, in high season, the sea washed the path to Haji Ali's tomb away, leaving it invisible below the menacing water. It was as if the saint sometimes said, *Please, enough*, and was released from the world of our sins and sorrows by a drowned path, letting him sleep in peace to restore his power as one of the great protectors of the city.

On that night, the path across the sea was dry and almost deserted. The wind was sharp, and came in ruffling bursts. We walked alone, six gangsters, toward the island tomb, moonlight throwing long shadows on a mirror of shallow tide.

The rounded rocks beneath us on either side of the wide path were exposed: black wet things clinging to the path for shelter, their backs bent to the sea.

Incense, burning in bunches as thick as a camel's hoof, filled the air with fragrances of devotion.

I didn't follow the ritual on the path across the sea to the island shrine. Gangsters going to war walked toward the shrine thinking of the harm they'd done in the past, prayed for forgiveness at the tomb, and walked away from the shrine ready for hell. I didn't do it, that time.

I thought of Karla, and how angry we'd been when we'd said good-night.

I didn't think about who'd taken the contract out on me. The list of suspects was long, and I couldn't shorten it by thinking about it. As it turned out, Abdullah shortened it for me, as we walked back across the sea, on the strip of stone that joined the shore.

'You did not ask me who took out this contract on you.'

'I thought I'd survive the twenty-four, and then find out,' I replied.

'Why do you not want to know now?'

'Because, when I know, I'll want to do something to him. And it would be better to do something to him after everybody stops trying to kill me.'

'It was the Irishman.'

'Concannon?'

'Yes.'

It was my turn to laugh, and about time.

'Good to see you keeping those spirits up,' Ravi said, walking a pace behind us with Shah, Comanche and Tall Tony.

'No,' I laughed, 'it's not funny at all, but it's really, really funny at the same time. I know this guy. I know Concannon. It's his version of a practical joke. It's a gangster joke, to see if I can make it through. That's why the contract expires in twenty-four hours. He's fucking with me.'

I couldn't explain it more, because I was laughing too much, and then the guys understood, all but Abdullah, and they laughed. Every time they tried to straighten up, they reminded themselves how much they wished they'd thought of it first. Then they started exchanging the names of paranoid friends they'd love to do it to, and fell helpless again.

'I love this guy,' Ravi said. 'I've gotta meet him. I mean, we'll kill him, of course, but I've gotta meet him, before we do.'

'Me, too,' Tall Tony said. 'Is this the guy Abdullah shot in the leg?'

'The same.'

'Twice,' Abdullah corrected, 'in the same leg. And now, you can see that mercy is a virtue best reserved for the virtuous, and not for a demon, like this man.'

The guys laughed harder. It was a good sign, in a way. One of our men had been murdered, a man we all loved, and I'd been threatened with murder, but we weren't so afraid that we couldn't laugh. The young street soldiers composed themselves under Abdullah's stern eye, and we completed the walk to the shore.

The walk to Haji Ali's tomb before war was an insult to the saint whose coffin rode miracle-waves back to the Island City, blessing it forever, and we knew it.

But we also knew, or willed ourselves to believe, that saints forgive what the world shuns. And we were sure in those moments of the walk, despite our sacrilege, that he knew we loved him: the eternally patient saint, who listened to our gangster prayer as he slept on the sea.

CHAPTER FIFTY-FOUR

CONCANNON'S PRACTICAL JOKE WAS A BLESSING, after I survived it, because it flushed assassin-minded snakes out of the long grass of Colaba's unconformable jungle. Abdullah and Didier visited every thug who'd asked about the reward for my life, and slapped him around in case the reward was offered again.

I hunted Concannon across the city, following every slender lead. Some of the searches took me to distant suburbs, on rough roads. I spent a lot of time in the saddle, most of it thinking about him. But the Irishman was always a ghost, a rumour, an echo of a taunting laugh, and I finally had to be satisfied, for a while, that if he couldn't be found, he wasn't a threat.

Karla was still mad. She froze me out, and was invisible for days. I tried to stay mad at her, but couldn't pull it off. I thought it was wrong of her to withhold the letter, especially after the writer had paid to have me killed. I felt aggrieved, but I missed her too much. Those days we spent together, connected and happy, were most of the good I knew.

You wanna know a sure sign that you're with your soul mate? a Nigerian smuggler once told me. *You just can't stay mad at her. Am I right?*

He was right, and he was wrong: soul mates can stay mad, for a while, and Karla was still mad. But at least the glacial distance meant that I didn't have to talk about Concannon's joke. I knew she'd heard about it. I knew she'd find it funny, and find a dozen clever ways to tease me about it.

Madame Zhou was still at large. No-one had seen or heard from her in weeks. The word *acid* was burning my mind, every time I thought of it. I didn't want to pester Karla, and I didn't care who she wanted to see. But I wanted to know that she was safe, until she decided to have breakfast with me again, so I kept a discreet watch over her, whenever time allowed.

She spent a lot of her time with Kavita Singh at the newspaper office, and at Lisa's art gallery. I knew where she was at any time of the day or night, but I couldn't talk to her. It was driving me crazy, and I got a little short-tempered.

My money changers were throwing bundles of money at me, instead of passing them to me. People started suggesting anger management remedies, after my third argument in as many days. They ranged from prostitutes, to drugs, to gang fighting, and ended with explosions.

'Blowing shit up is the surest way to get a woman out of your mind,' a friend confided. 'I've blown up lots of stuff. People think it's terrorists, but it's just me, getting a woman out of my mind.'

I didn't want to explode things, but I was still tetchy, and love-confused, so I consulted a professional.

'You ever blow anything up for love?' I asked my barber, Ahmed.

'Recently?' Ahmed replied.

Ahmed's House of Style barber shop was one of the last to resist modernisation into a hairdressing salon. It had three red leather and chromium chairs. They were man-chairs, endowed with hypnotic powers, and no guy I knew could resist them for long.

The mirrors you faced, when you sat in those chairs, were covered with mug shots of previous victims, none of them happy. They were customers who'd agreed to have their photograph posted, in exchange for a free haircut. They were up there as a warning not to ask for, or accept, a free haircut at the House of Style.

Ahmed had a dark sense of humour, which is something you don't search hard for in a barber, but Ahmed was a blood-in-the-bone democrat, and we rated him for that. He tolerated every opinion, and absolute freedom of speech was guaranteed in his barber shop. It was the only place I knew, in the whole city, where Muslims could call Hindus fanatics, and Hindus could call Muslims fanatics, and get all that stuff out of their systems without riots.

It was addictive. It was a bigotry bazaar, and customers seized it by the biased lapels. It was as though everyone in Ahmed's House of Style was on truth serum. And all of it was forgiven and forgotten by everyone, as soon as a customer walked out into the street.

Ahmed shaved me with a razor as sharp as a Cycle Killer's

moustache. When you live on the wrong side of the legal tracks, the number of people you trust to shave you with a straight razor dwindles to not many. Ahmed was trustworthy, because he was so true to his craft that he couldn't possibly kill me with a straight razor. It was against the barbers' code.

If he wanted to kill me, he'd have to use one of his guns, like the gun he'd sold me a few months before, which was in Tito's vault. Safe in the laws of his guild, I opened my throat to his honour and relaxed in absolute trust, and got myself shaved.

He wrapped my freshly skinned face in towels hot enough to force confessions. Satisfied that the punishment fit the crime, he whipped off the towels, and removed the shroud with a bullfighter's flourish.

He brushed me off skilfully, powdered my neck where he'd shaved it, then offered me the entire range of his only aftershave, *Ambrosia de Ahmed*.

I was calm. I was cosseted by Ahmed's professionalism. I was healed, and feeling serene. And I was just rubbing my face down with Ahmed's ambrosia, when Danda walked in the door, calling me a motherfucker.

Danda: and me with aftershave.

I didn't let him finish his tirade. I didn't care what he called me, or why he called me it. I didn't care what he wanted, or why he wanted it. I grabbed his shirt and slapped a cologne-wet palm at his red ear, and kept on slapping it until he broke free and ran away, taking a fair portion of my testiness with him.

I opened the door of the barber shop, and waved goodbye.

'*Allah hafiz*, Ahmedbhai.'

'Wait!' Ahmed said, coming to join me at the door.

He turned up the collar of my sleeveless denim vest, and curled it into place.

'That's better.'

I walked outside and met Gemini George, on the step. He grabbed me by my carefully arranged vest.

'Thank God, mate,' Gemini said, coughing, panting and falling into a hug. 'I've been looking everywhere for you.'

'How'd you find me?'

Gemini George knew it was a professional question.

'A pimp, in First Pasta Lane. He's been following you around. They say you're acting testy. He's been betting you won't last another two days, without visiting a girl.'

'I'm fine,' I said. 'I just got cured.'

'Good,' he said nervously.

'What's the problem?'

'It's Scorpio,' he replied quickly. 'He's gone crazy. You've gotta help me.'

'Slow down. Scorpio can't go crazy. Scorpio's already crazy.'

'Way, way crazier than Scorpio crazy. Twilight Zone crazy. He's freaked out, man.'

'Maybe we should talk about this somewhere.'

We sat in the Madras Café. We had *idli sambar*, followed by two rounds of strong, sweet tea. Gemini was a street guy, even though his friend was a millionaire: he ate first, and talked later.

When he sipped at his tea, washing down the last flavour of chilli and coconut, he told me the story. It began, as so many stories in India do, with a parade of saints.

The previous day there'd been a procession through the streets to venerate the memory of a local saint, who happened to be a lover of hashish. The streets were filled with devout holy men. It was the only day in the year when the cops couldn't bust anyone for smoking, because most of the people smoking were holy men.

It was a festival designed for the Zodiac Georges, and Gemini had used it to lure Scorpio from his eagle's nest at the Mahesh, and get out in the fresh air. It went well, at first, Gemini said. Scorpio found his street-shuffle walk again, remembering the rhythm of the road as Gemini walked beside him. He even got talkative. He began to tell his four bodyguards, hired from the hotel by the hour, about the doorways and alleyways they passed, and the adventures that he and Gemini had experienced in each one of them.

Then they turned a corner and found a sadhu, a holy man, barring their path. His hands were raised, one holding a knotted staff, and the other stained sacred red.

'What happened?' I asked him.

'I said, *Namaste, ji. Like to swap dope? I've got some Manali.*'

'Did he smoke with you?'

'He didn't get a chance. Before he could reply, Scorpio tried to step away, but the sadhu stopped him.'

'What did he want?'

'He said, *Give me a thousand dollars.*'

'How much?'

'A thousand dollars.'

'What did Scorpio say?'

'He said, *Are you crazy?*'

'Did he have a thousand dollars in his pocket?'

'That's exactly what the sadhu asked him,' Gemini said. '*Do you have a thousand dollars in your pocket?*'

'Did he?'

'He had twenty-five thousand on him, Lin. He showed it to me, to explain why we had to have four security guards from the hotel with us.'

'What did Scorpio say?'

'Scorpio, you know, he was getting angry, and he said, *Nobody gives a thousand dollars to a complete stranger. I'll give you a hundred dollars, but just so you leave me alone.*'

'Not very polite,' I said. 'How did the guru take it?'

'He was calm and cool, you know, guru-like, and he said, *If you gave me a thousand dollars, would you even notice its absence from your fortune?*'

'What did Scorpio say?'

'He said, *That isn't the point.*'

'And the sadhu?'

'He said, *Your weakness is greed. And that awakening, itself, is worth a thousand dollars.* I'll remember those words, Lin, until the day I die.'

'He had a point,' I said.

'That he did,' Gemini replied, glancing at the doorway, needing a cigarette. 'And he smiled, as he said it. I'll never forget that smile. It was a spiritual poker face, like. And it might've been that smile, you know, what set Scorpio off. Just that smile.'

'What happened?'

'He tried to push past the holy man, and they kind of struggled. The bodyguards shouted for him to stop. Next thing, the holy man falls down, and bangs his head on the corner of a wall. It was a bad cut. There was a flap of skin missing from his forehead, above the eyebrow. The bodyguards ran to help him. I offered him my handkerchief, and told him we had to call the hotel doctor.'

Gemini stopped. He looked at the street. He wanted to be back out there, in the tide of trick and talent that had carried him so safely, for so long.

'We'll have a cigarette after the story, Gemini,' I said. 'I know you on the street, man. You walk out that door now, you'll be gone in sixty seconds. So chase to the cut, and tell me what happened.'

'Don't you mean *cut to the chase*?'

'Gemini.'

'The holy man cursed him,' Gemini said, shivering.

He was suddenly scared, and I didn't like it, because I liked him.

'And?'

'That's it.'

There's no patience as pure as the patience we spend on loved ones, who make things harder than they need to be. I gave him a patient smile.

'What, exactly, happened?'

'The holy man cursed him. He said that his greed would become his murder weapon. He said that from the day his blood was spilled, Scorpio's money was cursed, and would only bring him sorrow and regret.'

'What happened then?'

'The bodyguards bailed out, right there on the spot.'

'And Scorpio?'

'He ran away. I found him at the hotel, later.'

'And the holy man?'

'I waited with him. I tried to get him to come into the hotel with me. But then some more holy men came, and he told me to run, because they'd be so angry they'd kill me. So, I ran. You know how dangerous holy men are.'

'And Scorpio thinks he's cursed?'

'He kind of *is* cursed,' Gemini moaned. 'I mean, the hotel staff have left our floor. They all think he's cursed, and they won't service his room.'

'How are you getting on, at the hotel?'

'Scorpio talked to the hotel, and hired new people, today. They come from Lithuania, I think. Nice people. Can't understand a word they say. His new bodyguards are Russian. Can't understand them either, and they're speakin' English, and all. He's locked up in the penthouse suite again, but I mean *really* locked up, this time.'

'Drop the poker game for a while,' I said. 'I'll square it with Didier. Let's find the sadhu, and have the curse lifted.'

I was thinking that the sadhu probably wasn't a rich man. I was thinking that we could find him, ask him to forgive the fool who'd touched him without respect, and accept a substantial payment to lift the curse.

The sadhus I knew, and I knew quite a few, would accept the offer without hesitation. It would've worked. I was sure. I couldn't know then that for Gemini, my innocent, loving friend, it would lead to rivers long forbidden, for good reason.

'Fantastic! Lin, you're a genius. This curse thing is rippin' Scorpio to bits. I don't mind tellin' you, I'm not comfortable with it, meself. In my book, you should stand as clear of a holy man's curse as you do from a hand grenade. I was in the spiritual radiation zone, so to speak, and I'd like this cleared up, as much as Scorp.'

'You could ask Naveen Adair for help,' I suggested, opening my suggesting mouth. 'He's running the Lost Love Bureau from the Amritsar, in the rooms next to me.'

'Great idea! I'll ask around, at first, and hand it to Naveen if I can't find him. We'll have Scorpio right as rain in no time.'

'Good,' I said. 'Can I offer you a ride?'

He looked out through the open doorway to my bike, parked illegally at the kerb.

'No, thanks all the same,' he smiled. 'Never was much of a one for motorbikes. I'll scoot back to the hotel in a taxi. Thanks, Lin. I knew I'd feel better, if I talked to you.'

I rode through the southern boulevards, doing my rounds, being seen, and thinking of the Zodiac Georges and how happy they'd been, before an elegant emissary of Fate in a dark suit made one of them rich.

Like Scorpio, I didn't have to stay in Bombay. I knew some parts of Africa pretty well, from my passport smuggling missions. I had contacts in Lagos and Kinshasa. They always had room in their operations for a good passport forger.

I had friends in Singapore. They'd invited me to be the white face for an Indo-Chinese currency ring. It was good money, in a safe city, where everyone left you alone if you respected the local rules, and didn't hurt anybody.

I thought about it, often. But sooner or later, I looked away from every option. And I couldn't decide if it was the city or the woman who wouldn't let me go.

Solemn in the saddle, I rode to the Amritsar hotel, hoping that Karla was there. My touts had tipped me off that she'd left the art gallery an hour before. I had a peacemaker present for her.

Some friends who played in a jazz band had told me they were bringing their acoustic instruments for a jam, by the sea, on the Colaba Back Bay. It was a unique experience: her favourite gift.

'You just missed her,' Didier said, looking up from his cluttered desk. 'She was here for a few minutes, only. She was not alone. She was with Taj.'

'Who the fuck is Taj?'

'A tall artist, rather good looking, with long black hair. He sculpted the Enkidu that stands in the entrance to Jehangir, this month. He's very talented.'

'Artists,' I said, remembering the sculptor.

'Indeed,' Didier agreed. 'Why do we flock to musicians and painters?'

'It's sexy,' I said. 'Painters make them take their clothes off, and musicians make them come.'

'Artist pricks,' Didier hissed.

'Indeed. Did she say when she'd be back?'

'Well . . . '

'What?'

'Well . . . '

'Why don't I want to know this, Didier?'

'She said . . . that she will return . . . in two days, Lin. And I think she meant it. She took her gun. And the tall artist, Taj.'

I was quiet for a while, but I must've been grinding my teeth, or my knuckles, because Didier stood up and gave me a hug.

'No matter what happens, Lin, there is always alcohol,' he said, holding my shoulders in his straight arms. 'Let us get majestically drunk. Do you have a preferred place of abandon?'

'You know, Didier, you're right. We should go anyway.'

'Go?'

'To see Aum Azaan, Raghav's jazz band. They're playing tonight. It's an unofficial concert, on the Back Bay. I was hoping Karla would come. But let's go anyway, and have some fun.'

'You are singing my song, Lin,' Didier answered gleefully. 'But I will take a taxi, if you don't mind.'

CHAPTER FIFTY-FIVE

I RODE ALONE TO MEET HIM AT THE JAM, but as I cruised past the Colaba police station on my way to Cuffe Parade, I saw Arshan, standing in the middle of the road. He had a long, serrated kitchen knife in his hand. He was shouting.

I pulled the bike to a stop, and walked up to stand beside him. A crowd had begun to gather, but they were at a safe distance. So far, the cops hadn't seen him, or they'd chosen not to respond.

'How are you, Uncle?' I asked, my hand close to his.

'This coward!' Arshan shouted. 'He kicked my boy, and now Farzad's in the hospital, with blood on his brain! Come out and fight me! Do you hear me, Lightning Dilip!'

'Whoa, Arshan, take it easy, and keep your voice down.'

Nobody wins, fighting the cops head on. If you've got enough fire or firepower to drive some cops off, they always come back with more cops. And if you beat them, too, they come back with more cops, until you're all dead, or very long gone. That's what it means, to have a police force: you've accepted a group of people who can't afford not to win.

That's part of the unspoken deal they make with any city that hires them: cops put their lives on the line every day, like outlaws, and they can't tolerate a direct attack on themselves. Cops and outlaws bite back, if anything bites them. It's a rule. And cops always bite last.

Softly, I turned Arshan away from the centre of the road, and back onto the footpath across the street. I slipped the kitchen knife from his hand, and passed it to one of the street boys.

There was a taxi stand around the corner. I tumbled Arshan into a cab, and told the driver to wait. When I'd parked my bike in a safe spot, I called out to another street boy to watch over her until I returned. Arshan was sobbing when I returned to the cab.

563

I sat next to the driver, directing him to the triple-fronted mansion near Cuffe Parade. Arshan was stretched out on the back seat, his arm flung over his face. As the taxi pulled away I turned to see Lightning Dilip standing under the arch of the police station entrance, his fists on his hips.

Arshan stopped the taxi before we reached his house, saying that he had to talk to me in private. The chai shop where I sat with Concannon after the fight with the Scorpions was nearby. We sat in a sheltered spot beneath a blue plastic awning tied between trees.

Arshan drank a few breathy gulps of his tea.

'Tell me about Farzad.'

'He was having these headaches. I was so angry I came up here once before, to challenge Dilip, but you brought me home. The headaches got worse. Finally, we convinced him to have it checked, and they discovered a massive blood clot. It happened, they say, when he was kicked in the head.'

'That's tough. I'm sorry, Arshan.'

'While they were testing him, he collapsed. They took him upstairs to the intensive care, right away. He's been there ever since. Seventy-two hours, now, unresponsive.'

'Unresponsive?'

'He's in a coma, Lin.'

'Where is he?'

'Bhatia hospital.'

'It's a good hospital,' I said. 'He'll be okay.'

'He'll die,' Arshan said.

'He won't. You won't let him. But he'll have nothing to live for when he gets well, if Lightning kills you. Promise me you won't do anything like that again.'

'I . . . I can't.'

'You can. And you must. People are depending on you.'

'You don't understand,' he said. 'I found it.'

'You found what?'

'I found the treasure.'

Bells rang somewhere: people were praying at a local temple, and ringing small, hand-held bells.

'*The* treasure?'

'Yes.'

'When?'

He was staring at his own feet in a daze, the empty chai glass slipping through his fingers. I caught it as it fell, and set it on the ground.

'Two weeks ago.'

'The families must be thrilled, even at a sad time like this.'

'I haven't told them.'

'What? You've gotta tell them.'

'At first,' he said quietly, talking to himself, 'I didn't tell anyone because I didn't want to lose what we had. The search was . . . so much fun, you see. We were all so happy. I know the treasure will change us. It has to. We won't be able to stop it. So, I kept it a secret.'

He fell silent, dancing backwards through memories of a treasure unfound.

'And now?'

'When Farzad got sick and he was lying in that bed, not responding to a kiss, I knew that I'd kept the secret because I was greedy. In my heart of hearts, the secret was too wonderful to share, and it gave me pleasure, for a while, to know that it was mine, alone.'

'It's human,' I said. 'And now you can make up for it, like a mensch.'

'Don't you see? I didn't make any protest, when that policeman kicked Farzad, because I didn't want anything to jeopardise the search. I sacrificed my own son, for the treasure.'

'You didn't kick your son in the head, Arshan. And Lightning Dilip has kicked me in the head a few times, without a blood clot. It was bad luck, and bad timing, and that's not your fault.'

'I was . . . so selfish.'

'Well, now you can be generous, and you can afford to bring the best doctors and specialists from the whole world to Farzad's bed. You can make him well with the treasure, Arshan.'

'Do you really think so?'

'I don't know. I don't know anything. But I think you should try. Whatever you do, you've gotta tell the others that you found the treasure. Every day you wait breaks a strand in their trust. You gotta do it now, Arshan, tonight.'

'You're right,' he said, straightening up. 'You're right.'

'Let's get one thing straight, before you do. I don't want any part of the treasure. I don't want to hear about it, ever again, if that's okay with you.'

'What are you saying?'

'I'm saying that I don't need it, and don't want it, and don't want to hear about it, ever again. You see that, right?'

'You're a strange man, Lin,' he said. 'But I like you.'

I walked him to the door of his house. We could hear Anahita, on the other side of it. She'd worked up a good pestering, and let him have it before she opened the door.

'Seven loaves I baked for Farzad's prayers,' the closed door shouted at us, 'and you couldn't get home on time!'

When she opened mid-pester and saw his face, she cried out and pulled him into a cuddle.

'What is it?' she gasped. 'What's the matter, my darling love?'

'I have something to tell you, sweetheart,' Arshan said, leaning on her, as he walked through the red curtains leading to the excavated dome. 'Call everyone together.'

'Of course, my darling,' she said, supporting him on her shoulder as they walked.

'I'm sorry about the loaves, dearest,' Arshan said absently.

'Never you mind about that, my darling.'

I let myself out. Nobody noticed. I was glad.

As I stood outside, waving down a taxi to retrieve my bike, I heard shouts and screams and happy ululations, ringing from the three-family home.

I got my bike, and paid the kid who'd watched it for me. He gave the money back, and change, which wasn't a good thing.

He'd been using my bike as a prop, while I was away. He was a Zone-Drifter. His bing was to sit on other people's motorcycles and in other people's cars to do business. He'd just done a drug deal, sitting on my bike, and he was sharing the take with me. When I was with the Sanjay Company, it wouldn't have occurred to him to use my bike for business. It was insubordinate, and he knew it. He was wondering if I knew it or not.

I grabbed the collar of his shirt, and pushed the money into his pocket.

'What the fuck do you think you're doing, Sid, using my bike?'

'Things are bad on the street, just now, Linbaba! Afghans in Mohammed Ali Road, and Scorpions under the bed. A man doesn't know where to deal his dope any more.'

'Apologise.'

'I'm so sorry, Linbaba.'

'Not to me, to the motorcycle. You were supposed to look after her. Apologise.'

He leaned in toward the bike, both hands pressed together, while I held his shirt. He was a slippery one, and we both knew I'd have to ride him down rather than run him down, if he escaped.

He put his pressed palms to his forehead.

'I'm so sorry, motorcycle-*ji*, for my bad manners,' he said fervently. 'I promise to respect you, in future.'

He reached out to stroke her, but I wouldn't let him.

'That's enough. Don't do it again.'

'No, sir.'

'And tell all the other Zone-Drifters to stay away from her.'

'Yes, sir.'

I rode to the jam on the Back Bay using a route that didn't pass Arshan's home. I didn't want to think about the treasure, or young Farzad, coma-roaming at the hospital. I was blue: blue enough to need jazz.

I parked beside Naveen's bike, near the crowd of fifty or sixty university students sitting on the shore. Jazz was raising people to the same exalted high. I stood on the edge of the group, my hands in my jacket pockets. I was surfing the sounds with thoughts of Karla, knowing how much she would've loved it.

'Musician pricks,' Naveen muttered, joining me.

He was looking at Diva, who was sitting in adoration at the feet of a very talented, good-looking guitar player named Raghav. He was a nice kid, and a friend of mine, but Naveen had a point.

'Indeed.'

Diva was unrecognisable to anyone but her friends, the rich Diva girls, who were with Didier, sitting apart from the main group on the lawns of the Back Bay.

She wore no make-up. The bindi on her forehead was a glass diamond, her earrings were brass, and her bracelets were plastic. Her clothes and sandals came from a slum shop, reflecting the latest fashion for slum girls.

It suited her, as it did all the girls in the slum. But the presence of the Diva girls, from the richer life, worried me.

567

'The girls came along?' I asked.

'I couldn't keep them away,' Naveen sighed. 'Diva says they're sworn to secrecy. I had to let her do this. She's been a prisoner in the slum for nearly two weeks, Lin. She needs this.'

'I guess you're right. And the students might not recognise her. She's got the slum-girl thing down pretty good.'

'You should hear her swear,' Naveen said. 'I wandered into a session the other day. The girls were teaching her what to say when a guy hits on you. It was very instructive. You want to hear some of it?'

'I lived there,' I said. 'I know it starts with *lauda lasoon*, and ends with *saala lukka*. Please, God, don't let Diva unload what she's learned on me.'

'Amen.'

'Have the Diva girls been in the slum?'

He laughed, and I frowned, because I was asking about the security of Johnny Cigar and his family, and it wasn't funny to me.

'That's funny?'

'Yeah,' he laughed again.

'Why?'

'Because if Diva's Divas ever visit the slum, I've got this running bet with Didier.'

'Once again, young detective, I *why* you. Why?'

He sighed, letting out some embarrassment.

'Didier was trying to get the girls to the slum, and have a ghost story night. They were really up for it, but more scared of the slum than the ghosts. I said to Didier, the day they go to the slum, I'll race Benicia around the loop.'

It was a significant boast. Naveen had been practising a few stunts and tricks with Colaba biker boys, and he was becoming a good rider, but racing Benicia was another matter.

She was a Spanish girl who'd lived in Bombay for a couple of years. She bought Rajasthani jewellery, and sold it to buyers from Barcelona. She was a single girl who kept to herself, and was a significant mystery because of it. But everyone knew that when she rode her vintage 350cc bike around Bombay, nobody beat Benicia.

'You know Benicia?'

'Not . . . yet.'

'And you're serious about the bet?'

'Sure,' he laughed, but then smartened up. 'You're not thinking of bribing the Diva girls into the slum, are you?'

'No-one should go there,' I said. 'Diva's there as a guest of Johnny and his family. Until the people who killed her father are caught, no-one should go to see her, in case they expose those people to harm.'

'You're . . . you're right, of course,' he said stiffly. 'I wasn't thinking of that. I'll try to stop the Diva girls, but Didier might've already persuaded them. I'm sorry.'

'It's alright, Naveen. And if the Divas do visit the slum, and you get Benicia to race you, I'll put a thousand dollars on you, kid, here and now.'

'You mean it?'

I fished the money from my pocket, and handed it across.

'Done,' Naveen said, offering his hand.

'Done,' I said, shaking it.

'How's it going with Karla?' Naveen asked.

'Okay,' I said, maybe convincingly. 'How's it going with Diva?'

'I'm going nuts,' he replied, very convincingly.

'Does she know?'

'Does she know I'm going nuts?' he asked, professional concern darkening his face.

'That you love her,' I said, looking for the reaction.

The kid was good. He locked love in the cage of a clenched jaw, betraying nothing, and looked at the slum-girl Diva, clapping her hands in time to the music.

Some of the students wandered from group to group, laughing and talking. Others sat in whispered intimacy. There was some handholding, a little cuddling, and the occasional kiss. In Bombay, in those years, it was as wild as kids could get. It was also more innocent than you can reasonably expect sexually excited twenty-year-olds to be.

It was a sweet thing, the gentle love those kids shared, as their enervated minds recovered from the task of inheriting the city, while the music played, echoing softly from the tall apartment buildings nearby, where many of them lived.

They were sons and daughters of the future. They wore hip clothes, passed joints and bottles of cheap rum around, and played music near the sea. But they also got good grades, and didn't give a damn that the group included every faith, and every caste.

They were already something that had never existed on the foreshore of the Island City, and when their turn came to run the companies and councils, they'd be navigating by different stars.

Diva's two friends were leaning in toward Didier, clutching at him in helpless giggling. They weren't listening to the music. Every sentence Didier whispered made them shriek into his shirt front, trying to stifle the sound.

He saw me, and excused himself from their pout.

'What kept you?' he asked, shaking my hand.

What kept me?

Arshan's suicide attack on the Colaba police station, and a fabled treasure.

'Tell you later. How you doing?'

Didier didn't hear me. He was making a scandalous gesture to the girls.

'How you doing, Didier?'

'I have two very charming ladies over here, who would like to know you better than they should.'

He waved his hand as if presenting a magic trick. We looked at the girls, sitting a few metres away. They were doing something with their faces. It might've been smiling. I couldn't be sure.

Whatever he'd told them about me sent them from fear to fascination, it seemed. They raised their hands, and moved them. It might've been waving, or they might've been warding me off.

They were scary-smiling again, and I couldn't figure it out. Guys never understand what pretty girls do with their faces. They got up, quite athletically for sit-around girls, and began to slow-walk toward us, their bare toes prowling through the grass in step. They weren't sit-around girls at all.

The Divas were dancers: dancers who danced together, and practised. They were good. That part, I understood. Guys always understand what pretty girls do with their hips.

'If they ask you about the man you killed,' Didier said, as the Diva girls slow-stepped across the moonlit grass, 'I'll take it from there.'

'I haven't killed anyone, Didier.'

'You haven't?' he asked, dubious. 'Why do I always think you have?'

'Hi,' one of the girls said.

'Hi,' the second girl said.

'I'm so glad you girls are here,' I said. 'You've gotta hang around, until my wife gets back from church.'

'Your wife?' one girl said.

'Church?' the other peeped.

'Yeah. She's got the kids. Four under four. So glad you're good babysitters. Those kids are demons, and we need a break.'

'Eeeuw!'

'Aren't you the babysitters?' I asked innocently. 'Didier said you'd do Mondays, Wednesdays and Fridays, for twenty rupees an hour.'

'Eeeuw!' they said as they skipped away in step to sit with two pretty, well-dressed boys playing *tabla* drums with the band.

'Now, look what you've done!' Didier protested.

'*The man I killed?*' I countered. '*You'll take it from there?*'

'Well, Lin,' he grumbled, 'Didier is an artist of spin, everyone acknowledges that, but let's face it, you don't give me much to work with. I used a little poetic licence. If I tell people the truth, only Naveen and I will find you interesting, and I am not completely sure of Naveen.'

'What is this? Shit on Shantaram Week? Back up, Didier. I've been crowded all I can take for one day.'

He couldn't reply, because there was a sudden shout.

'It is a fire, I believe!'

We turned to see flames, rising from a place on the coast, not far away.

'It's the fishermen's colony,' Naveen said.

'The boats are on fire,' I agreed.

'Stay with Diva!' Naveen shouted to Didier, as I ran for my bike.

'The girls are safe with me,' he shouted back, his arms around Diva's Divas. 'But please, do not get yourselves killed!'

CHAPTER FIFTY-SIX

NAVEEN AND I RODE PAST CROWDS streaming from the big slum to the fire in the next cove. We stopped the bikes in the middle of the road, next to the concrete divider. From the road, we could see the long boats burning.

It was dark, on the beach, where the fishermen lived in their shamble of huts, but the cove faced a main road with an intersecting street, and the lights made cold pictures of the burning, only twenty metres away.

The boats were already blackened, shrivelled versions of the sturdy craft they'd been. Red-rimmed mouths of glowing coals still burned on their sides.

The boats were lost, but the fire hadn't destroyed the houses, and people were working desperately to save them.

Naveen and I tied handkerchiefs around our faces, ran across the street, and joined the bucket brigades. I filled a space between two women, taking a bucket from one, and passing it to the other. They were fast, and it wasn't easy to keep up with them.

We could hear women and children screaming from the beach, cut off by the fire. They'd saved themselves and the children in shallow waves.

Firemen ran through the flames and smoke to help them. Firemen ran into the burning huts to save children. Firemen caught fire, their sleeves and trousers bursting into quick flames from oil and kerosene spills among the crammed huts.

One rescuer emerged from the swirling smoke close to me with a child in his arms. His own hair was burning, but he ignored it. He passed beside me, but I couldn't break the bucket-chain, and couldn't help him.

The smell of burnt skin went into my mind while I was passing buckets of water and stayed there, like a dead horse found in a prairie of memory.

Is there a limit to the number of horrible things you can see, and experience, in any one life? Of course, there is: the limit is one, and none.

The buckets stopped. Everyone was kneeling, or looking at the sky. It was raining. I hadn't noticed.

I was still smelling the burnt skin, and for some reason, I was remembering the severed head, on the side of the road, in Sri Lanka. I was still in yesterday's prairie.

It poured. The fires sizzled. Firemen broke down the most dangerous structures, and contained the fire. People danced. If I'd been in a better mood, or if Karla had been there, I'd have danced with them.

I walked back along the beach and looked up, beyond the burnt boats, to the wall of trees at the far end of the beach. Grey figures began to walk out of the smoke and the shadows.

Grey figures, ghosts or demons, were coming toward us slowly.

The insides of the boats were saturated with a hundred years of fish oil, and the smoke all around us was blue-black as they burned and smouldered.

The men who stumbled through that black fog and rain toward us were stained with it, because they'd lit the fires. They were grey with ash and smoke and dust from the trees where they'd been hiding.

Rainwater striped their faces, making them grey tigers, moving slowly through a jungle of smoke. It took me a few seconds to realise that they were Scorpions.

Hanuman, as identifiable as a flagpole, and walking with a limp, was the last man out of the shadows.

Time really does slow down, sometimes, when love and fear combine with history, even if it's only the history of a little place like the fishermen's cove in Colaba. Heartbeats become hammers, and you can see everything at once. You're somewhere else, already: somewhere dead, already. And you're never sharper, never more aware of every swirl of smoke.

I saw the Scorpions coming toward us. I saw the people, still dancing behind me. I saw kids, dogs, and elderly people sitting on the sand. I saw firemen, standing amid the huts, steam coming off their burnt uniforms.

The Scorpions were still about sixty metres away. They were carrying knives and hatchets. They'd started the fire as Act One, and were coming to close the play.

I pulled my knives from their scabbards and started jogging toward them. I didn't know what I was doing. The most important thing, it seemed to me at that moment, was to give the people behind me time to react, and run. I was shouting. I was screaming, I guess.

By the third or fourth step I stopped thinking, and something happened to the sound. I couldn't hear anything. Wishes, wings without birds, passed through me like spears of light.

I had a knife in each hand and I was running through a tunnel, numbed of noise. I couldn't even hear my own breathing. It seemed to take forever, but I knew that when I was close, it would be too fast.

There was somebody jogging with me. It was Naveen, but he wasn't running with me, he was grabbing at my vest, he was pulling me to the ground. I hit the sand so hard that the world returned, and all the shouting and screaming and sirens came on at once. Naveen was half on top of me, where we fell.

He was pointing at something. I looked along his extended arm and saw cops, a lot of cops, running hard, and firing at will. Scorpions fell, or surrendered. Lightning Dilip was already kicking one of them.

Naveen and I were still lying on the ground. He was smiling and crying and laughing, all at the same time. He had his hand on my shoulder, the grip fierce.

He loved me after that night, that Indian-Irishman, and he never let me doubt it. Sometimes, the bravest thing we ever do is the thing we never get to do. And sometimes the spark that ignites a brother's love, in men not born brothers, is nothing more than a pure intention.

We rode circles around the area of the cove until Abdullah, Ahmed and Tall Tony arrived. I gave Abdullah what I knew, and then we headed back to the jazz jam, on the Back Bay.

The band had left, and there were only a few kids still there. They told us that Didier, a favourite with the smokers, had left the message that he'd gone back to visit someone named Johnny Cigar.

Diva sat up quickly when we made our way through the slum to her hut.

'What are you doing, you idiot?' she demanded.

'I'm fine,' I said.

'Not you!' she snapped. 'The other idiot. What do you think you're doing, fighting bloody fires? Are you out of your tiny mind?'

'You were safe, with Didier,' Naveen protested. 'I was only gone an hour.'

'And who was keeping *you* safe?' she asked, advancing to poke him in the chest.

Naveen grinned happily.

'What are you so chirpy about?'

'You care what happens to me,' Naveen said, wagging his finger at her defiant nose. 'You care about me.'

'Of course I care about you. Some fucking detective, you are.'

'Wow,' Naveen said.

'That's all you've got to say?'

'Wow.'

'If you say that again, I'll smack you with a pot,' Diva said. 'Shut your mouth, and kiss me with it.'

They almost did, but there was a fierce clatter of pots and pans, and a loud clamour of voices. Somebody was coming through the slum, and making a lot of noise about it.

Naveen put Diva in Sita's hands, ready to make an escape through the back lanes on the sea coast. Johnny Cigar, Didier, Naveen and I faced the only path leading from the main part of the slum.

We heard a voice raised above all the others, shouting in English. It was Kavita Singh. When she came into the open space in front of Diva's hut, we saw that she was smiling, and an honour guard of women was cheering her. Diva returned with Sita to greet her.

'Just for you,' Kavita said, handing Diva a newspaper. 'Today's front page. It'll be on the stands in a few hours, but I thought you should be the first to see it.'

Diva read the lead article, looked at the photographs of her father, handed the paper to me, and fell into Naveen's arms.

The gang responsible for the massacre at the Devnani mansion had been captured. They'd confessed to the crime, and were in prison. It was an African–Chinese crime syndicate, handling most of the pharmaceutical pleasures flowing illegally through Bombay to Lagos.

Smashing the gang and solving the murders was a triumph, the cops said, involving officers from several countries. The temporary CEO of

Devnani Industries, Rajesh Jain, appealed once again for the missing heiress to come forward, and claim her inheritance.

For Diva, the threat was gone and she was free to leave the kerosene lamps, and live in the electric world again.

'Lin,' Didier said. 'Can I offer you a flask?'

He'd been talking and joking with Kavita. Her expression said that I'd interrupted her, and it tested her patience.

'How did you know Diva was here, Kavita?'

'You and Karla are psychically connected,' she snarled, taking a swig from Didier's flask. 'You tell me.'

'What's that supposed to mean?'

'Why don't you just go home, Lin,' she said. 'You do *have* a home, don't you?'

I didn't know what she was so angry about, and I didn't care.

'Bye, Kavita.'

I walked out to the street, and had just started my bike when a motorcycle pulled up beside me, and someone called my name. It was Ravi, the Company street soldier who'd ridden with me on the night of the contract.

'Abdullah sent me to find you,' he said, remaining on his bike, his hands on the high handlebars. 'The Scorpions killed Amir. And Farid is dead.'

'Peace be upon them,' I said. 'What happened?'

'The Scorpions dragged Amir out of his house, and killed him in the street.'

'Oh, shit.'

'Farid went crazy. He shot his way into the police cells.'

'What happened?'

'The cops ran, and Farid killed three Scorpions who were in the cells for the fire. That big guy, Hanuman, he saved Vishnu. He took six bullets, but he's gone for good, the big man. The moustache guy, Danda, he's also gone.'

'What happened to Farid?'

'The cops came back with a lot of guns, and killed Farid. Shot him sixty times, they say.'

'*Y'Allah.*'

'Get the fuck off the street, man. It's cowboys and Indians out there, and I'm too Indian for this shit.'

He rode away quickly, a lone despatch courier in a militarised zone. He was scared, and angry: always a bad combination in a man.

I'd never seen Ravi scared. He was one of the calm ones, and every gang has them. But the loss of blunt-headed Amir, the first to dance when any music played, the first to start punching when the action started, and Farid the Fixer, the champion boxer, both full Sanjay Council members, scared the young gangster.

Scorpions had already died. Company men had died. More would join them in the dark red fall. Ravi was living his life one night at a time. It was war. It was the failure of everything.

I rode back to the Amritsar. I needed to sleep, and then find out what hadn't gone crazy on the street. I needed to know how much of my business was still running, and how much was running away.

I parked the bike in the alleyway that split the hotel. I'd parked there too often, I guess, because I wasn't paying enough attention when I wiped the bike down for the night.

I stood up, and Madame Zhou was there, very close to me. The twins were also there, one on either side of her.

There were two other men: short and thin men, with the kind of hungry in their eyes that nothing can feed. They had their hands in the pockets of the jackets. They were her acid throwers.

'Madame,' I said. 'No offence, but if your acid throwers start to take their hands out of their pockets, I'm gonna go crazy. And when it's all over, I won't be the only one dead or burned.'

She laughed. To be sure that I knew she was laughing, perhaps, she switched on a light beneath her veil. It was a battery-powered party tube-light, curved around her neck like a necklace, inside her black lace veil.

The veil was suspended from a rigid mantilla, high over her head, made from something black and shiny: dead spiders, was my guess. The lace veil met a black taffeta dress that brushed the ground, hiding her feet.

She must've been in very high platform shoes, because the tiny woman was almost eye to veil with me. The light shone through the lace, illuminating her face from below.

I think it was intended to be a devastating revelation of her famous beauty. It wasn't. She was still laughing.

'You know, I'm tired, Madame,' I said.

577

'Your friend, Vikram, died tonight,' she replied quickly, turning off the light.

I got it. The light wasn't for turning on: it was for turning off. In the sudden darkness her face was a shadow, breathing.

'Vikram?'

'The cowboy,' she said. 'He's dead.'

I stared at her black-space face, angry, and thinking about her acid throwers, and Karla.

'I don't believe you.'

'It is true,' she said.

She cocked her head to the side a little, watching me with invisible eyes.

I was watching the acid throwers. I'd seen their victims. I knew some of them: people with faces smeared of feature, a stretched mask of skin, with holes cut for the vanished nose and mouth to breathe, and no eyes at all.

They begged along the strip, communicating through touch. Thinking about them made me angrier, which was good, because I was scared.

'How do you know that?'

'It is a matter of record, now,' she replied. 'It is a police case. He committed suicide.'

'It can't be.'

'It can,' she whispered, 'and it is. He took a week's supply of heroin, and he injected himself with it. There was a suicide note. I have a copy. Would you like to see it?'

'You know, Madame, I've only met you twice, and I already wish I hadn't met you the first time.'

'I gave him the drugs,' Madame Zhou said.

Oh, no, my mind pleaded. *Please, no.*

'Cheapest murder I ever committed,' she said. 'I wish all the people I hate were junkies. It would make life so much easier.'

She laughed. I was breathing hard. It was a tough job keeping a close watch on four of them: five, if you counted the spider about the size of a small woman, named Madame Zhou.

The arched alleyway was dark, and empty. There was no-one on the streets.

'He cheated me,' she hissed, 'and about jewellery. No-one cheats

578

me. Especially not about jewellery. This is a warning, Shantaram. Stay away from her.'

'Why don't you come back, and talk to Karla about it in person? I'd like to watch.'

'Not Karla, you fool, Kavita Singh. Stay away from Kavita.'

I drew my knives, slowly. The twins slipped clubs from their sleeves. The acid throwers shifted on the balls of their feet, ready to throw.

Madame Zhou was only a lunge away. With the right momentum, I could pick her up and throw her at the acid throwers. It was a plan. It was a plan that was a heartbeat away from happening.

'Let's do this,' I said. 'Let's get this over with.'

'Not tonight, Shantaram,' she said, stepping away. 'But I'm sure that's not the first time you've heard those words.'

She backed off slowly, tottering on her platforms, her dress dragging across the ground, a taffeta shadow scaring rats back into their hollows.

The acid throwers scampered away. The twins backed off in step with Madame Zhou, scowling at me.

She'd threatened Karla, and her attention had shifted to Kavita. She was gone a long time before I stopped wanting to follow them, and finish it. But enough dead: enough dead, for one night.

I went back to my rooms, drank something, smoked the last tiny piece of Lisa's heavenly dope, danced to music for a while, and then opened my journal to write.

Farid and Amir, gone. Hanuman and Danda, gone. Boats and huts on the beach burned. And Vikram, gone. Vikram, the love-train rider: Vikram, gone.

Change is the blood of time. The world was changing, out of time, and moving beneath me like a whale, soaring for air. The chess pieces were moving themselves. Nothing was the same, and I knew that nothing would be better, for a while.

The newly dead are ancestors, too. We respect the chain of life and love when we celebrate the life, not mourn the death. We all know that, and we all say it, when loved ones leave.

But even though we know that death is the truth, and we sing stories to ourselves, the pain of loss is something we can't deny, except by wounding tenderness.

It's a good thing, the crying. It isn't rational, and it can't be. It's a

579

purity beyond reason. It's the essence of what we are, and the mirror of what we'll become. Love.

I cried for Vikram. I knew that he wasn't murdered, but released: a soul-prisoner, on the run forever. But still I filled the empty well with dancing, and tears.

And I ranted, and I raved, and I wrote strange things that should be true in my journal. My hand ran back and forth across the pages like an animal in a cage. When my eyes blurred, and the black words I'd written seemed like the black lace of Madame Zhou's veil, I slept in a web of bad dreams: caught, and waiting for death to creep toward me.

PART TEN

CHAPTER FIFTY-SEVEN

S IN IS DISCONNECTION, and nothing disconnects us from one another more completely than the great sin, war. The struggle for control of southern crime caused friends to turn on one another, enemies to strike without warning and the cops to plead for peace, because the feud was ruining business for everyone.

The Scorpions regrouped under Vishnu's leadership, bringing twenty more men to Bombay from the northern state of Uttar Pradesh. They were experienced street fighters, with a patriotic grudge, and within a week of their arrival they took Flora Fountain and the Fort area from the Sanjay Company.

The Sanjay Company, seeing their empire annexed piece by piece, reacted swiftly to the northern invasion: they killed their leader, not a hundred metres from his mansion.

Two-Hussein, the first soldier to fight for Khaderbhai decades before, stepped out in front of Sanjay's car as the crime boss left his mansion. He fired his guns into the windows until Sanjay and his two Afghan guards were dead.

He renamed the Company after himself, as regicides often do, and raised the boy-king, Tariq, to a full place on the Council of the new Hussein Company. Tariq's first act as a Council member was to call for death. *Kill them all*, the boy was widely reported to have said. *Kill them all, and take everything they have.*

It became the new motto of the Hussein Company – *Take Everything They Have* – where once it had been *Truth and Courage*.

Sin piled upon sin until the grave burden tore the last garment of tolerance, and frayed threads of honour and faith floated away on winter winds, leaving hatred naked, for all to see.

Karla started talking to me again, but she was much busier than before: too busy to share more than one meal with me, every other day. Vikram's suicide struck her physically for a while, it seemed to me, but maybe she was just showing me what I wouldn't face myself.

She stopped laughing and smiling. For a time, she was the Karla I'd first met: the Karla who didn't smile. And there were no sleepovers.

It was an endurance test designed for released convicts, or musicians. I was walking through webs of testosterone and adrenaline and pheromones, disconnected from the woman I loved and couldn't make love to, but spoke to, every other day.

And I was still testy. But testiness was the new normal in South Bombay, and nobody noticed.

The measure of a man is the distance between his human self, minute to minute, and his devoted self. I was devoted to Karla, but the distance between us left the devoted self all alone, guarding a candle in the wind, while the human self was outside, roaming the street.

As it happened, every street in town at that time was a carnival for roamers.

Fear is a poverty of Truth, and Greed is a poverty of Faith, Idriss said to me once. Fear and greed took turns to prowl the streets and slums of South Bombay for weeks: six long weeks of tension, pillage, profiteering, and blood in alleyways.

Hashish, marijuana, uppers, downers and flat-liners were all five times the usual price. The sharpest civil servants duly raised the price of bribery, setting off a cascade of corruption that made small fortunes for them, and doubled the ten-rupee bribe that traffic cops demanded at speed traps. Avarice made pay while the moon shone, and fear was the only constant friend on the streets.

I met a kid who'd just been recruited by the Hussein Company, and liked him, and heard that he'd been killed, an hour later. And it happened again, to another young Hussein Company fighter, a few days after that, with just a few hours between a handshake and a handful of dirt.

It hurt, both times, even though it had nothing to do with me. It made me uneasy every time I met a new street soldier, excited by war.

The Cycle Killers accepted contracts from the Hussein Company, and duly executed Scorpion Company men. Scorpions knocked Hussein men from their motorcycles. Hussein men fire-bombed a Scorpion bar.

584

The Scorpions robbed a bank in South Bombay and got away with it. The Hussein Company knocked over a money transport van in Scorpion territory, in revenge, and got away with it. Both gangs used the money they'd stolen in the robberies to bribe or threaten the bank officials and security guards. Without witnesses, the cases were dropped.

Every man with a gun to sell wanted three times the going price. Men who needed a gun sold their wives' wedding jewellery to buy one. The age of hatchets and knives, which was eye to eye, passed away within a season of the winter sun, replaced by eye-for-an-eye shootings.

In a street war, any dark corner can kill you, and dark corners killed people at the rate of four a week until the violence stopped. I paid two of Comanche's best young fighters to shadow Karla from a distance, and keep her safe during those weeks. I wanted to do it myself, but she wouldn't let me.

As suddenly as it had started, the war for South Bombay ended in a day, with a truce between the Hussein Company and the Scorpion Company, and a sit-down between Hussein and Vishnu. Whatever they said to one another in private, the declaration they made when they left the room wasn't just of peace, but of brotherhood and integration.

The two Companies agreed to unite as one. The name of the newly formed Company was an issue, because some Khaderbhai-Sanjay-Hussein men said that they'd shoot themselves before they'd call themselves Scorpions.

The new, combined mafia gang was named the Vishnu Company. Although he had more men, Vishnu had much less territory than Hussein, and it was decided that having the Company named after him would quell rebellion on the streets, and discourage foraging in South Bombay's unrest by outside gangs.

Both leaders presided at Council meetings, and both acknowledged the power of the other. Places on the Council were appointed evenly between members of former gangs, and the spoils of peace were distributed fairly.

It was a complicated balance between limited trust and unlimited hatred, and to help the cooperation along, nephews and nieces from either side were sent to live with the enemy, and consolidated the truce with the pulse in their throats.

And when those hostages went to families whose task it was to care for them as if they were their own, and kill them if the truce failed, six weeks of war ended in a day, and the streets were safely unlawful again.

When peace was reimposed, I paid off the young fighters from Comanche's gym, who'd been guarding Karla. They took the money, but told me they couldn't work for me in the future.

'Why not?'

'Because Karla hired us to work for her, as field agents for the Lost Love Bureau.'

'Field agents?'

'Yes, Linbaba. Pretty cool, *na*? I'm a field agent, investigating missing persons. It's chained and brained, yaar. I was throwing drunks out of Manny's bar, a few weeks ago.'

'I *like* Manny's bar,' I protested.

'I'm keeping a diary,' his friend said. 'I'm going to write a Bollywood movie. Cases we investigate, and stuff. Miss Karla, she's reef, man. She's totally reef. See you round, Lin. Thanks for the bonus!'

'See you round.'

I rode the boundary of my shopkeeper money changers, being friendly and supportive when I could, and slap-nasty when required.

The truce seemed to be holding. I saw Scorpion guys driving around with Hussein guys, and men from both gangs were running the lottery, prostitution and drug rackets side by side, brothers in harm.

I took a break to sit on my motorcycle and watch the sun set on Marine Drive. A call of drummers was rehearsing on the wide footpath. It was the last week of the festival season, and drummers all over Bombay were perfecting their techniques for the processions and weddings that had hired them.

Kids ran from their parents' hands to dance and jiggle next to the drummers. Parents stood behind them, clapping their hands and wagging their heads in time to the infallible rhythm. The children jumped like crickets, their thin arms and legs jerking and leaping. With an audience, the drummers pushed themselves to near-hysterical intensity, sending their heartbeat across the sea to the setting sun. I watched them as evening became night, spilling ink on the waves.

What are we doing, Karla? I thought. *What are you doing?*

I swung the bike around and headed back to Leopold's. I was hoping to catch up with Kavita Singh, and tell her about Madame Zhou. In the weeks since Madame Zhou rose from her wave of shadows beneath the Amritsar hotel, I'd tried several times to contact Kavita, but without success. When the cold stares of reception staff at the newspaper office became a wall of unavailability, I realised that she was avoiding me. I didn't know why Kavita would feel that way, or what I'd done to offend her, and decided to give Fate time to bring us together again. But Madame Zhou's mention of her name worried me, and I couldn't shake off the sense of duty to tell her about it. It was finally one of my street contacts who mentioned that Kavita had been hanging out with Didier, between three and four every afternoon at Leopold's.

Didier had become something of a lost love at Leopold's himself, and his frequent absences wounded the staff. They expressed their disapproval by being scrupulously polite whenever they served him, because nothing irritated him more.

He tried insulting them, to jolt them out of their insupportable civility. He gave it his best shot, calling up a few insults he'd always kept in reserve for emergencies. But they wouldn't relent, and their cruel courtesy pushed a small thorn into his chest with every putrid *please*, and unforgivable *thank you*.

'Lin,' he said, sitting with Kavita Singh at his customary table. 'What is your favourite crime?'

'That again?' I said.

I bent to kiss Kavita on the cheek but she raised her glass to her lips, so I waved hello instead. I shook Didier's hand as I took a place beside him.

'Yes, *that* again,' Kavita said, drinking half her glass.

'I already told you – mutiny.'

'No, this is the *second* round,' Didier said, smiling a secret. 'Kavita and I have decided to play a game. We will ask everyone to nominate a *second* favourite crime, and then test our theories about them against both of their answers.'

'You guys have *theories* about people?'

'Come on, Lin,' Kavita smiled. 'You can't tell me you don't have a theory about me.'

'Actually, I don't. What's your theory of me?'

'Ah,' Didier grinned. 'That would spoil the game. First, you have to nominate a second favourite crime, and then we can confirm our theories.'

587

'Okay, my second favourite crime? *Resisting arrest.* What's your second favourite, Kavita?'

'Heresy,' she said.

'Heresy isn't a crime, in India,' I objected, smiling for help from Didier. 'Is that allowed in the rules of your game?'

'I am afraid so, Lin. Whatever answer that people give to the question, is the answer they give.'

'And you, Didier? Perjury was your first favourite, am I right?'

'Indeed you are,' he replied happily. 'You should be playing this game with us.'

'Thanks, and no thanks, but I'd like to know your second choice.'

'Adultery,' he said.

'Why?'

'Well, because it involves love and sex, of course,' he replied. 'But, also, because it is the only crime that every adult human being fully understands. More than that, because we are not permitted to marry, it is one of the few crimes that a gay man cannot commit.'

'That's because adultery's a sin, not a crime.'

'You're not going all religious on us are you, Lin, talking about sin?' Kavita sneered.

'No. I'm using the word in a less specific and more widely human sense.'

'Can we know any sins, but our own?' Kavita asked, her jaw set in a muscular challenge.

'Heavy!' Didier said. 'I love it. Waiter! Another round!'

'If people don't think there's any collective understanding, in anything at all, I wish them well. If you accept a common language, you can talk about sin in a meaningful, non-religious way. That's all I mean.'

'Then what is it?' she demanded. 'What is sin?'

'Sin is anything that wounds love.'

'Oh!' Didier cried. 'I love it, Lin! Come on, Kavita, let the panther prowl. Riposte, girl!'

Kavita sat back in her chair. She was dressed in a black skirt and a sleeveless black top, unzipped to new moon. Her short black hair, city-chic anywhere in the world, fell in a feathered fringe over a face bare of make-up, thirty-one years old, and pretty enough to sell anything.

'And what if your whole life is a sin?' She sneered. 'What if every breath you draw wounds love?'

'The grace of love,' I said, 'is that it washes away sins.'

'Quoting Karla, are you?' Kavita spat at me. 'How fitting!'

She was angry, and I couldn't understand it.

'I am,' I said. 'She's quotable.'

'I'll bet she is,' she said bitterly.

There was an aggressive edge to her voice and her tone. I didn't see it, then, for what it was.

I'd come to Leopold's to warn her about Madame Zhou's new obsession with her. I hadn't given any thought to the game that she and Didier were playing, because I was just waiting for a break in the conversation to tell her what I knew. If I'd paid closer attention, I might've been prepared for her next remark.

'Sin? Love? How can you even *say* those words, without being struck down?'

'Whoa, Kavita, wait a minute. What do you mean?'

'I mean that Karla was never out of your mind, not even for a minute, when you were in bed with Lisa.'

'Where the hell is that coming from?'

Didier hustled to avert the storm.

'Naveen's second favourite crime was *Harbouring a fugitive*. It completes his profile. Would you like to hear it?'

'Shut up, Didier!' Kavita snapped.

'Kavita,' I said, 'if you've got something to say, spit it out.'

'I'd like to spit it into your face,' she said, putting down her glass.

'Go ahead.'

'Lisa was leaving you for me, Lin,' Kavita said. 'She'd been with Rosanna, at the art gallery, for a while before me, trying things out, but we'd been lovers for months. And if she'd left you sooner, to be with me, she'd be alive today.'

Okay, I thought, *so now we know*. The irony of accusing me of thinking about Karla while I was with Lisa, when she was with Lisa while Lisa was with me, was obviously lost on her. Jealousy has no mirror, and resentment has a tin ear for the truth.

'Okay, Kavita,' I said, standing to leave. 'I came here to tell you that I ran into an unlicensed maniac the other night, named Madame Zhou, and she warned me to stay away from you. I can see that won't be a problem.'

I walked out of the bar.

'Lin, please!' Didier called.

I started the bike and rode from my money changers to the black bank, and back again. I rode to my private stashes of funds. Hours passed, and I talked to a dozen people, but my thoughts couldn't leave Lisa. Lovely Lisa.

Love is always a lotus, no matter where you find it. If Lisa found love or even fun with Kavita Singh, a girl I'd always liked, I'd have been happy for her.

Were we so far apart, she couldn't tell me that she was involved with Kavita?

Lisa was always surprising, and always at least a little confusing. But I'd rolled with the kisses, and I'd always supported her, no matter which direction her Aquarian mind led her. It hurt to think that we hadn't been close enough. It hurt more to think that Kavita might be right, and that Lisa might still be alive and happy, if she'd left me sooner and made a life with Kavita: if I'd been more honest, maybe, and she'd been more willing to tell the truth.

It hurt so much, in fact, that I was glad when I received a message from the Taureg. It obliged me to ride for good hours in bad traffic to visit one of the city's most dangerous minds.

CHAPTER FIFTY-EIGHT

THE TAUREG WAS A RETIRED SPECIALIST, who'd worked for years in the Khaderbhai Company. He was a full Council member, with a vote, but was never present at Council meetings, because he was the Company torturer.

His job was to ensure compliance, and extract information. It was a job that a lot of people in the Company wanted done, and nobody but the Taureg wanted to do. But the Taureg wasn't a torturer by sadistic inclination: he'd simply discovered that he had a talent for it.

He'd been a psychiatrist, of the Freudian persuasion, in northern Africa. Nobody knew exactly where. He arrived in Bombay, and went to work for the Khaderbhai Company. He used his skills as a psychiatrist to discover his subjects' deepest fears, and then magnified those fears until the subjects complied. His success rate, he quietly boasted, was better than Freudian psychoanalysis alone.

I hadn't seen him for years; not since he'd retired from torture, and moved to Khar. I'd heard that he was operating a lottery-racket franchise from a children's toy store.

The note asking me to visit him might've troubled me, on any other day: the Taureg was a troubling man. On that day, I was glad to have something disturbing, to clear my mind.

I headed north to what was then the relatively remote suburb of Khar. Bombay was growing so fast that South Bombay, which had been the creative heart of the city, was itself becoming a remote pulse of the action and activity beating in the bigger heart, the northern suburbs.

Vacant land was already cluttered with new housing and commercial developments. New fashion factories were starting up, designing fame on the debris of construction. Brash brand stores on main roads competed with brash brand-thieves in knock-off street stalls, reflected in the bright windows of the brand stores they copied.

I rode past houses and shopping complexes that were half-built and already sold, as if hope itself had finally found a price. And long lines of crawling traffic stitched those patches of aspiration to acres of ambition: streets of cars that ran like scars on the face and forehead of the thing we made of the Earth.

The Taureg's house was large and modern: a Moroccan palazzo. The dark man dressed in black, who opened the front door, looked like a bearded professor: a scholar, searching absent-mindedly for the spectacles propped on his head.

'*Salaam aleikum*, Taureg.'

'*Wa aleikum salaam*, Shantaram,' he replied, pulling at my sleeveless vest. 'Did you *have* to come on your motorcycle? Come inside. You're scaring my neighbours.'

He led me through his house, constructed with archways everywhere, as if the home was a hive, and we were the bees.

'I hope you understand – I have to run you past my wife, first, to see if she approves of you being here.'

'I . . . see.'

We walked through several archways to a space where the second floor of the house vanished in a high ceiling.

There was a woman in the centre of that room, standing on a platform three steps high. She was dressed in a glittering black burkha, studded with black jewels. There was a net of lace covering her face: her eyes could examine mine, but I couldn't examine hers.

I didn't know if I was supposed to say anything. The Taureg had sent a message, and I'd responded. I had no idea what to expect, facing the woman covered in black stars.

From the tilt of her head I saw that she was looking me up and down a couple of times. I don't think she liked what she saw. Her head cocked to the other side, considering the matter.

'One hour,' she said, her head still on the side as she twirled away through an archway, that led to an archway, that led to an archway.

The Taureg led me through archways to a *majlis* room, with heavy carpets on the floor and soft cushions against the walls. Young men from his family served us with coconut juice and bitter lime hummus dip with asparagus spines, as we sat together on the floor.

By the time we'd eaten the snacks, the young men were ready with hot tea, served from a long-necked samovar. We washed our hands in spouts of warm, tangerine-scented water, poured by nephews and cousins, and then sipped at the tea through sugar cubes.

'I'm honoured by your hospitality, Taureg,' I said, when we were alone, and sharing a hookah pipe of Turkish tobacco, Kerala grass and Himalayan hashish.

'I am honoured,' he said, 'that you responded to my call.'

I knew what he meant: my quick response to his call wasn't something he could expect from anyone else in the Company, or formerly in the Company. While he was a secret member of the Council, he was distantly respected: when he retired, he was shunned.

I didn't understand it. They'd all benefited from his work, and could've pulled out at any time, but they didn't. I worked in passports for the Company, and the Taureg's services were never required. But it was the same Company that protected me for years, in Bombay, so who was I to judge anyone else?

Did I like what he did? No. But what a man does isn't always what a man is, and I'd learned that the hard way.

'Do you know,' he remarked, puffing contentedly, 'you are one of only four men who shook my hand, in all the years that I worked with the Company. Do you want to know the other three?'

'Khaderbhai, Mahmoud Melbaaf, and Abdullah Taheri,' I suggested.

He laughed.

'Correct. My father used to say, put a Viking in front as you go into battle, and a Persian behind you. If the Viking doesn't win, you'll never die alone, because the Persian won't let you die without him.'

'I think we've *all* got enough fight in us when we need it, Taureg.'

'Are you getting philosophical with me, Shantaram?'

Actually, I was getting pretty high. The bowl of the hookah pipe was as big as a sunflower, and I had a long ride home. I had to straighten up. From the few times I'd spoken to him, I'd learned that the Taureg was always in character.

'I mean, when something we love is at stake, we fight. It doesn't matter who we are, or where we come from. Nobody has a franchise on that.'

He laughed again.

'I wish we'd had more talks like this,' he said, 'and that it were possible to have them again. After this day, you will not return to my house unless your life or my own depends upon it. This is a special occasion, with special reasons. But I value my privacy very highly. Are we clear?'

The second hit of the hookah pipe was kicking in: Time yawned, and took a nap. The Taureg's face blurred, suddenly fierce, suddenly kind, but he wasn't moving at all.

It's okay, I calmed myself. *It's not the torturer you've gotta worry about, it's the psychiatrist.*

'I see that,' I said, hoping that my voice didn't sound as squeaky in the room as it did in my head.

'Good,' he said, puffing the hookah alight once more. 'The Irishman. You want him, and I know where he is.'

Concannon. For a second, the irony of finding my personal torturer through a professional torturer was too much. I was pretty high, and I laughed.

'I'm sorry, Taureg,' I said, regaining control. 'I'm glad to hear that you know where he is, and I'd also like to know. I'm not laughing at anything you said. It's just that this Irishman has a way of making you laugh, no matter how much you want to hurt him.'

'Like my cousin, Gulab,' the Taureg said. 'It was not until three of us in the family wounded him that he mended his ways.'

'How's he mending now?'

'Very well. He's a living saint now.'

'A saint, huh?'

'Indeed. It was a miracle that he survived *my* shooting alone, let alone the other corrections. People believe he's blessed. And he certainly is blessed with a new career, dispensing blessings, in fact, near a mosque in Dadar. My advice to you regarding the Irishman is to kill him, before you can't.'

'Look, Taureg, I –'

'Seriously,' he said, leaning toward me seriously. 'You have no idea about this man, do you?'

'I'm always happy to learn more,' I said, trying as hard to get straight as I've ever tried to get high.

'He's the truth.'

'I'm not following you.'

'He's a truth-finder, like me.'

'You mean he makes people tell him things, like you did.'

'It's not the truth that's dangerous,' he said, 'it's someone who always knows how to find it. This Irishman is such a man. I've seen files on him. He was very good at what he did. He's a younger version of me, perhaps.'

He laughed again, and puffed on his hookah pipe.

'You have no idea how much fear you can find inside yourself,' he said after a while, 'until someone helps you find it.'

It was a game, a psychological game, and I don't play games. I didn't answer. He'd called me to his house, and sooner or later I knew he'd get to the point. He gestured with his hookah pipe, urging me to smoke. I smoked.

'In my time with Khaderbhai,' he continued, 'there was no-one more powerful in the Company than I was, although I never appeared at meetings. Khaderbhai knew that I could make the truth spring from any desert, like sacred waters, even from his own lips. When he knew how good I was at my job, he had only two choices – to kill me, or to use me. There is a lesson for you in that.'

He looked at me intently for a moment.

'No advice about killing, please,' I said quickly.

He laughed again, and gestured with the hose of the hookah.

'Smoke!' he commanded.

I puffed until the coals in the lotus bowl glowed like a tiny sun, drew in a deep breath, closed off the pipe again, and blew out a stream of smoke that settled in curling waves on the wall of the arched room.

'Excellent!' he said. 'Never trust a man who can't hold his hashish.'

'Too sane?' I offered.

'Because hashish talks,' he laughed. 'So let us continue talking.'

'Okay. Go ahead.'

'This Irishman, his hatred is not for you. It never was. His hatred is for Abdullah. He attacks you, because he knows how much it hurts Abdullah.'

'What do you know about it?'

'I know that is why the Irishman went to see your girlfriend, on the night that she died.'

I couldn't hide the shock.

'Yes, I know about the last night of your girlfriend's life.'

'How do you know this?'

'Smoke again first,' he said, gesturing at the bowl of the hookah pipe. 'You do understand that some revelations require a trance state, to fully comprehend their import?'

Okay, I thought. *Now I get it.*

'I understand, Taureg, that you're performing psychological experiments on me. I wish you'd include me, so we can get it over with.'

He liked to laugh, the psychoanalytic punitory, and he had a peculiar laugh, high and jagged, but it never varied in pitch or tone. No one thing was ever funnier than another, and the laugh never swelled or chuckled or changed.

The laugh, and the walk, tell you everything, Didier once said to me.

'I do so wish that we could have at least one more interview,' the Taureg said. 'You're quite right. It was another little experiment. Forgive me.'

'Stop with the tests, Taureg.'

'I will, I will,' he laughed. 'I have few visitors, you see, and I never leave this home, nowadays. I miss ... the field experiments. Shall I continue, about the Irishman?'

'Please do.'

'He murdered a man, with Abdullah.'

'He ... what?'

'More than one life was lost, in fact,' the Taureg said.

It couldn't be. I didn't want to believe it.

'How do you know this, Taureg?'

He frowned, hesitating on the shore of puzzlement, ready to laugh again.

'People tell me things,' he said.

'Okay, you know what, Taureg, don't tell me any more. Abdullah will tell me the rest.'

'Wait! Don't be so impatient. This information was *told* to me, not *elicited*, and you need to know this about Abdullah.'

'I won't talk about Abdullah, if he's not in the room. Sorry.'

'Wonderful,' he said softly. 'It was just one more little test. I hope you will forgive me. I am deprived of subjects.'

'What is this, Taureg? You invite me into your home, and now I need a *safe word* just to talk to you?'

'No, no, let me go on. There was a businessman who owed the Company protection money, and wouldn't pay. He was making a case for extortion, in the court, and a lot of noise for Sanjay. Abdullah was with the Irishman, when they fixed the problem. It is for him to tell you what transpired there. What I can tell you, is that it was a very bad affair.'

'What has this got to do with the girl?'

Lisa. Lisa. I couldn't bring myself to speak her name, in the Taureg's hive.

'That is something only one other knows.'

'Something you don't know?'

'Something I don't know . . . yet.'

He looked at me. I think he liked my company. I'm still not sure what that said about me.

'You know what a secret is, Shantaram?' he asked, the wriggle of his smile twitching his long grey beard.

'Something you don't tell me?' I replied, hopefully.

'A secret is a truth untold,' he said. 'And Abdullah has been keeping this a secret from you, and I know that, because I asked him, just yesterday.'

'Why did you ask him?'

'Nice question,' he said. 'What made you ask it?'

'Stop it, Taureg, please. Why did you ask him about me? Was it because this is connected to my girlfriend?'

'This Irishman, Concannon, knows that Abdullah loves you. He thinks that Abdullah told you about the murder they committed together. That gives him two reasons to kill you. The twenty-four-hour contract on your life was not a joke. It was a serious attempt on your life. He meant to kill you, to make Abdullah suffer, and he means to kill Abdullah.'

'I understand, Taureg. And thanks. Where can I find him?'

He laughed again. I was hoping he'd explain the joke. I was sitting in an archway, among an infinite array of archways, and I was so levitationally stoned on the hookah pipe that my legs were jellyfish.

'There are only two kinds of people in this world,' he said, smiling easily for the first time, 'those who use, and those who are used.'

I was thinking that there were probably lots of different kinds of people, and certainly more than two, but I figured that he was actually talking about something else: the reason why he'd called me to his house.

'I'm guessing that this information is gonna cost me something,' I said.

'I want a favour in return, it is true,' he said. 'But it is one that you will be willing to grant, I believe.'

'How willing?'

'I want everything you know, and come to learn, about Ranjit Choudhry.'

'Why?'

'I want to take him into my custody, before anyone else does.'

'Your custody?'

'Yes, at a facility, not far away from here.'

Sometimes, Fate gives you a handful of sand, and promises that if you squeeze it hard enough, it'll turn to gold.

'You know, Taureg,' I said, preparing my jellyfish legs to stand, 'thanks for the offer, but I'll find the Irishman, and Ranjit, on my own.'

'Wait,' the Taureg said. 'I'm sorry. It was my last little test. I promise. I'm finished. Would you like to know the results of my study on you today?'

'I told you. I didn't come here as a subject.'

'Of course,' he laughed, pulling me down beside him again. 'Please, stay, and have another cup of hot tea, before you leave.'

Cousins and nephews cleared the dishes, and brought a new samovar of hot tea.

'You must forgive me,' the Taureg said. 'If you don't, it will have me in analysis for a year.'

I laughed.

'No, seriously,' he said, looking at me earnestly. 'You must forgive me.'

'You're forgiven,' I said.

'I don't feel forgiven,' he said. 'Are you really forgiving me?'

'Come on, Taureg, who the hell am I to forgive anyone?'

'Close enough,' he said. 'And thank you. In a strictly commercial sense, no tests involved, I'm in a position to pay you a considerable sum for a . . . private interview with Ranjit Choudhry.'

'Attractive and all as that sounds . . . ' I began, but he cut me off.

'There are two families, of aggrieved daughters, who will pay us handsomely if Ranjit is in my hands.'

'No.'

'I understand,' he said softly. 'And that's a test I didn't even consider. Thank you. I have enjoyed this very much. Here is the address of the Irishman.'

He slipped a small sheet of paper from his cuff, and passed it to me.

'Tonight, the Irishman will be in the company of only one or two men. He will be vulnerable. Tonight, at midnight, is the time to strike.'

'Thank you,' I said. 'But I'm not handing Ranjit over to you, Taureg, if I find him.'

'That's clear. Do you need help, to kidnap the Irishman?'

'I don't want to kidnap him. I want to make him reconsider his options.'

'Oh, I see. Then, may Allah be with you, and let us smoke one last bowl.'

'You know, I really should be going.'

'Oh, please! Stay, for one more pipe.'

Cousins and nephews replaced the old hookah pipe with a new one, filled with pure Himalayan water, they told me, and then filled the pipe with pure Himalayan herb.

'I taught the mind,' he said, lying back on silk cushions, the tray of tea and dates between us, 'and I've tortured the mind. And you know what? There is no difference. It's funny, isn't it?'

'Not for the patients.'

He laughed that mechanical laugh.

'You know what the elephant in the room is, when it comes to psychiatry?' he asked.

'The success rate?' I suggested.

'No,' he said. 'The success rate only reveals those who *can* be helped by this, and those who *can't*. The elephant in the room is that we can *shape* behaviour more fluently than we can *understand* it. When you know how to make anyone do anything, it makes you start to wonder what we really are.'

'You can't make anyone do anything, Taureg. Not even you. Fact is, some of us are impossible to predict, and impossible to control, and I like it that way.'

'You've been there,' he said, sitting up again. 'You know what it is.'

'Been where?'

'Torture,' he said, his eyes gleaming.

'So that's what this last bowl is about, huh?'

599

'You've been there,' he said. 'Tell me what you learned. Please, confide in me.'

'I know that men you might think are weak, turn out to be strong, and vice versa.'

'Yes,' he said. 'Are you willing to let me . . . *question* you, about it?'

'Actually . . . no,' I said, struggling jellyfish into action.

'Would you like me to make a revelation?' he asked. 'It will bond us, on this day.'

'Actually . . . no,' I said, finding the stuff to stand.

'I took the children's toy shop, because that's what I want to do,' he said. 'I only accepted the Company lottery franchise to make sure they know I'm still a loyal Company man. It's the toy shop, actually, that I wanted, and the crime is just a front.'

'Okay . . .'

'And my name is Mustapha,' he said. 'It was Khaderbhai who gave me the name Taureg. He said that it means *Abandoned by God*, and was a name for the Blue People, because they would not be subdued. But my name is Mustapha.'

'I . . .'

'There, I have confessed two things to you, and we are brothers.'

'Okay . . .'

'And based on the profile I compiled in our meeting today, I will know exactly what to do to you, if you ever speak to anyone of my home.'

He glanced at the clock.

'Oh,' he said. 'I see our time is up.'

CHAPTER FIFTY-NINE

There's a thing that happens when you ride stoned, which no sane person would do, where time vanishes. I arrived in Colaba, from distant Khar, and I had no recollection of the trip. If the destination is the journey, I never arrived.

Whatever happened on the way, I felt freed of worry, and emptied of need when I cruised back into the Island City peninsula. Or maybe it was just because I had Concannon's address, and all I had to do was wait for midnight, to visit it.

I tried to find Karla. She hadn't been avoiding me, but she hadn't been colliding with me. I knew she sometimes had a drink with Didier at Leopold's, late in the night.

I parked the bike outside and walked in, hoping my disappointment didn't show when I saw Didier sitting alone. He gave me a golden smile, and I smiled back, walking toward him. I was glad, on second thoughts, that Karla wasn't there: not if I wanted to reckon with Concannon that night.

Didier rose to greet me, shaking hands strenuously.

'I am *so* glad to see you, Lin,' he said. 'I was wondering where you were. I felt so bad when you left earlier, after that talk with Kavita. It wounded me. Did you not think of *my* feelings?'

'Did you know about Lisa and Kavita?' I asked.

'Of course,' he puffed. 'Didier knows everything. What is the point of Didier, if he does not know every scandalous thing?'

'I'm not sure I understand the question. Why don't we stay with mine.'

'I . . . I knew, Lin. My first thought, when Lisa tricked me, was that she was with Kavita. I checked, but Kavita was at a different party that night, close to here.'

'Why didn't you tell me? Why didn't *she* tell me?'

'Waiter!' Didier called out.

'You're ducking the question, Didier.'

'There were *two* questions, Lin. Waiter!'

'Still ducking, Didier.'

'Certainly not,' he replied. 'I'm simply electing to answer your question *after* I have had two strong drinks. That is not the same thing. Waiter!'

'How can I be of service, sir?' Sweetie asked sweetly.

'Stop with the politeness, Sweetie!' Didier snapped. 'And bring us two cold beers.'

'I am here to serve,' Sweetie said, backing away obsequiously.

It was infuriatingly polite, and Didier was infuriated.

'Get out of my sight!' he shouted. 'Bring my bloody drinks, man!'

Sweetie smiled, too sweetly, backing away.

'Do you know that you get very English, when you get angry?' I remarked.

'These swine!' Didier protested. 'They are only being nice to me, because it hurts me. It is like a strike, but in reverse. It is the most despicable use of courtesy, and courtesy defines us, is it not so?'

'Love defines us, Didier.'

'Of course, it does!' he said, stamping his foot under the table. 'That is exactly why reverse-politeness is so painful. Please, Lin, while you are here, make them more surly and impolite. I beg you.'

'I'll see what I can do, Didier. But, hey, you're a hard act to sell. I might have to *embellish* you, like you did for me, when you sold me to the Divas. Which one of your shootings should I use?'

'Lin, you abuse my sensitivities.'

'Everything abuses your sensitivities, Didier. It's one of the reasons why we love you. What abuses my sensitivities is that you didn't tell me about Lisa.'

'But, Lin, it is such a delicate matter. It is a difficult thing to just say it out loud, like that. Your girlfriend is bisexual, and has a lesbian lover. Was I supposed to make a joke, perhaps? Hey, Lin, the tongue got your cat, so to say?'

'I'm not talking about sex. Lisa told me she was bisexual the first time we got together. I'm talking about relationships. The way it looks to me is that you and Lisa and Kavita all knew something that I should've known, but didn't.'

'I . . . I'm sorry, Lin. Sometimes, a secret is too precious to tell. Do you forgive me?'

'No more secrets, Didier. You're my brother. If it affects you, or me, we have to be straight with each other.'

He couldn't help it. He started giggling.

'Straight with each other?'

His pale blue eyes glittered, lighthouses calling the wanderer home. Worry hid again in laugh lines.

Habits too diligently indulged made caves of his cheeks, but his skin was still taut, his mouth still determined, and his nose imperial. He'd cut his curly hair short, and wore it parted on the side. Diva's influence, I guessed.

The cut made Didier look like Dirk Bogarde at the same age, and it suited him. I knew it would sprinkle new suitors on him at parties.

'Am I forgiven?'

'You're always forgiven, Didier, before you sin.'

'I am so delighted that you came to visit tonight, Lin,' he said, slapping his thighs. 'I feel big things coming in the air. Can you stay, or will you rush off again, as always?'

'I'm sitting here until midnight. You've got me for the duration.'

'Wonderful!'

Sweetie slammed a cold beer in front of me on the table.

'*Aur kuch?*' Sweetie grunted at me. *Anything else?*

'Go away,' Didier snapped.

'Oh, certainly, Mr Didier-*sahib*,' Sweetie said. 'Anything to serve you, Mr Didier-*sahib*.'

'I see what you mean,' I said to Didier. 'This is serious. You're gonna have to do something pretty spectacular, to win back their disrespect.'

'I know,' he pleaded. 'But what?'

A man approached our table. He was tall, and broad, with close-clipped blonde hair and a very short nose that flattened his face, making it seem two-dimensional.

When he got looming-close, I saw that his nose had been squashed flat: broken so many times that the gristle had collapsed. He was either a very bad fighter, or he'd had so many bad fights that the law of averages put a thumbprint where his nose had been.

Either way, it wasn't a pretty sight, looming over our table. Looming over me, in fact.

'How can you sit next to this filthy gay?' he asked me.

'It's called gravity,' I said. 'Look it up, when you have an afternoon to spare.'

He turned to Didier.

'You make me sick!' the big man hissed.

'Not yet,' Didier replied. 'But it happens.'

'How about something happens to your face?' the tall man said, his jaw like a shovel.

'Careful,' I warned. 'My boyfriend has a temper.'

'Fuck you,' the big man said.

There was a second man, standing some distance away. I left him in the periphery, and focused on the flattened moon above our table.

'You know what we do with your kind in Leningrad?' the tall man asked Didier.

'The same thing you do with my kind, everywhere,' Didier said calmly, his hand in his jacket pocket as he leaned back in his chair. 'Until we stop you.'

Leningrad. Russians. I risked a clear look at the second man, standing a few steps behind. He wore a thin black shirt, like his friend. His short brown hair was a little messed, his pale green eyes were bright, and his expressive mouth lifted easily in a smile. His thumbs were hooked in the loops of his faded jeans.

He was leaner and faster than his friend, and much calmer. That made him the most dangerous man in the room, excluding Didier, because everyone else in the room, including me, was nervous. He looked at me, made eye contact, and smiled genially.

I looked back at the man who was blocking out several overhead lights with his face.

'Show me what you've got,' the tall Russian shouted, slapping at his chest. 'Fight me!'

Patrons hastily vacated neighbouring tables. The tall Russian shoved empty tables and chairs aside, and stood in an open space, challenging Didier.

'Come here, little man,' he teased.

Didier lit a cigarette.

'Double abomination!' the tall Russian shouted. 'A gay, and a Jew. A *Jew* gay. The worst kind of gay.'

Waiters established a wide perimeter. They were ready to pounce if the shouting turned to fighting, but no-one wanted to be the first pouncer, punched away by the big, angry Russian.

'Come on, little man. Come here.'

'Certainly,' Didier replied equably. 'When I have finished my cigarette.'

Oh, shit, I thought, and knew that I wasn't the only one in Leopold's thinking it. Didier puffed contentedly, gently easing an urn of ash into his glass ashtray.

In the silence, the Russian companion moved quickly to stand beside me. He held his hands open in front of him, gesturing toward the chair next to mine.

It was a good idea. When he'd moved, I'd leaned back in my chair, put my right arm behind me and closed my hand around one of my knives.

'Is this seat taken?' he asked sociably. 'It might take your friend a minute to finish his cigarette, and I'd rather sit, if it's okay with you.'

'It's a free country, Oleg,' I said. 'That's why I live here.'

'Thanks,' he said, sitting next to me comfortably. 'Hey, don't take it personally, but isn't it a bit of a stereotype? I'm Russian, so my name has to be Oleg?'

He was right. And when a man's right, he's right, even if you're thinking about stabbing him in the thigh.

'My name's Lin,' I said. 'I'm not sure if I'm pleased to meet you.'

'Likewise,' he said. 'Oleg.'

'Are you fucking with me?'

I still had my hand on the knife.

'No,' he laughed. 'It really is my name. Oleg. And your gay Jewish friend is about to get his ass kicked.'

We both looked at Didier, who was examining his cigarette forensically.

'My money's on the Jew,' I said.

'It is?'

'My money's always on the Jew.'

'How much money?' he asked, a wide smile lighting his eyes with mischief.

'Everything I've got.'

'How much is everything?'

'Everything will buy you three thousand,' I said.

'American?'

'I don't deal in roubles, Oleg. The cigarette is running out. Are you in?'

605

'Done,' he said, offering his hand.

I let go the knife, shook his hand, and put my hand back on the knife again. Oleg waved to a waiter. Didier was almost finished his cigarette. The waiter looked past Oleg to me, mystified.

He was worried. The big man was still waiting for Didier in the open space between vacated tables. Service had ceased. The waiter, named Sayed, didn't know what was going on. I nodded my head and he came running, his eyes on the big Russian.

'I would like a chilled beer, please,' Oleg said. 'And a plate of your home-made fries.'

Sayed blinked a few times, and looked at me.

'It's okay, Sayed,' I said. 'I have no idea what's going on, either.'

'Oh,' Sayed said, relieved. 'I'll get the beer and fries, right away.'

He trotted away, wagging his hands and his head.

'It's okay,' he said in Hindi. 'Nobody knows what's going on.'

The waiters relaxed, watching the last seconds of Didier's cigarette.

'I hope your friend wins, by the way,' Oleg said. 'Although I doubt it, unfortunately.'

Didier stubbed his cigarette out.

'You hope my guy wins?'

'*Chert, da,*' Oleg said.

'What does that mean?'

'It means *Hell, yeah*, in Russian.'

'Uh-huh.'

'*Chert, da.* I'd have paid three thousand bucks to have this idiot's bigoted ass beaten senseless, if I was that kind of guy.'

'But you're not that kind of guy.'

'Look, you just met him. I've been working with this asshole for weeks. But I can't bring myself to have someone beaten. Not even him. I've been on the other end a few times, and I didn't like it.'

'Uh-huh.'

'This way, if your guy wins, it's like I paid for it, but I'm free of the karmic debt.'

Didier stood slowly, and stepped away from his table.

'After you pay up,' I said, 'we should talk, Oleg.'

Didier brushed flakes of ash from his rumpled black velvet jacket, and turned up the collar. With his hands pressed deep in the pockets of his jacket, he walked toward the big Russian.

The big Russian was waving his fists in front of him, fists as big as the skulls they frequently hit, and he was weaving back and forth, slowly.

My hand was on my knife. If Oleg got involved, I was sure I could tag him before he left the table. But Oleg put his hands behind his head, leaned back in his chair, and watched the show.

Didier walked to one and a half steps from the big man, and then leapt into a high, balletic pirouette, his arms tucked into his pockets. He flung his arms wide at the peak of the leap, and descended in an arc that put his knees on the Russian's chest, and his pistol on the top of the big man's head.

Didier danced free, his hands back in his jacket pockets, standing away from the big man. The Russian fell from the knees first, as the brain temporarily disengaged, but his arms still flailed until he hit the floor with his face, nose first.

'Pay up, Oleg,' I said, as Didier went to the main counter to make things right with the management.

'Wow,' he said. 'That big guy's a bare-knuckle, no-rules fighter in Russia.'

'Your bare-knuckle fighter just got his ass kicked by ballet and a well-made gun. Pay up.'

'No problem,' he said, grinning in wonder. 'I'm Russian. We invented the well-made gun.'

Oleg pulled a roll from his pocket, peeled a few outer layers from the lettuce, and shoved the head back into his pocket.

'You're a man of mystery, Oleg.'

'Actually, I'm a man unemployed.'

The fact that Scorpio George had hired Russian security guards, and Leopold's was invaded by Russians, couldn't be coincidence.

'Lemme guess,' I said. 'You were working security for the penthouse floor at the Mahesh?'

'That's right. He fired us today, motherfucker.'

'He happens to be a friend of mine, even if he is a motherfucker.'

'Sorry,' he said. 'If you know him, you know how tight he is with a dollar. He counted every minute we'd worked for him, and gave us a two-hundred-dollar kiss goodbye, after guarding his life. Funny, isn't it?'

'That's a bigger roll than two hundred bucks.'

'There was a poker game, at the hotel, run by this guy called Gemini.'

'Uh-huh.'

'Yeah, I had a run of luck, and broke the bank.'

Oleg, a golden-child gambler, broke the bank. Of all the poker games, in all the world, he'd walked into mine.

Sayed brought drinks and food, smiling happily.

'Mr Didier was terrific,' Sayed muttered to me. 'We have not seen such good dancing from him in years! He knocked out that big fellow with just one smack.'

'Where are you dancing the big fellow to now, Sayed?' I asked.

'To the street,' he said, wiping moisture from the table, and offering condiments to Oleg.

Oleg gestured at me with a potato chip dipped in tomato sauce.

'Can I dig in?' he asked politely. 'I love homemade fries.'

'Your friend is being dragged out into the street, Oleg.'

'Is that a *Yes*, or a *No*?'

'I'll be right back,' I sighed, as he dug in.

I knew how it worked. The big Russian's body would be dragged outside Leopold's, twelve inches from the legal obligation line. That would place him in the pavement commercial zone.

The pavement shopkeepers would eventually shove him from their zone to the gutter, twelve inches from their footpath shops.

That would place him in the taxi driver commercial zone, and eventually his body would be dragged to the open road, where an ambulance would collect him, if a bus didn't take him out first.

I'd been that man, that unconscious meat at the mercy of the world. I called a street trader I knew, and paid him to put the big Russian into a taxi, bound for the hospital.

Didier was still accepting praise, and paying handsomely for the interruption to Leopold's business. I walked back to the table, looking for a third Russian. I know it sounds kind of paranoid that I was looking for a third Russian, but they were crazy years, and in my experience, it's always prudent to consider a third Russian.

'Is there a third Russian?' I asked, as I sat down beside Oleg.

He brushed his mouth with a napkin and turned to face me, his pale green eyes looking into mine honestly.

'If there was a third Russian,' he said, 'I'd be gone. Everyone's scared of the Russians. Even Russians are scared of the Russians. I'm Russian. You can trust me on that.'

'Why did Scorpio fire you?'

'Look, he's your friend . . . '

'He's also crazy. Tell me.'

'Well, he's gone kind of nuts, about a curse that was put on him by some holy man. Me, I'd kill the man who put a curse on me, or force him to take it back. But I'm Russian, and we see things differently.'

'So what happened?'

'My ex-boss, your friend, employed food tasters.'

'Food tasters?'

'Have you ever actually met a food taster?'

'No, Oleg, but you did, right?'

'Indian kids. Nice kids. Eating his food, first, to be sure that it wasn't poisoned.'

I knew things weren't good at Scorpio's eagle nest. Gemini had reached out to me. But I hadn't taken Scorpio's obsession with the curse seriously. If what Oleg told me was true, Scorpio was in trouble. He was a good man in a bad situation, which is when friends intervene.

But I had Concannon's address in my pocket, and I was just killing time at Leopold's, waiting for midnight, and I let my friend's distress go.

'Did you quit, or were you fired?'

'I told him I wouldn't let the kids test his food,' he said. 'I offered to do it myself. I'm always hungry. But he didn't take the criticism well. He fired both of us.'

'Who paid you guys to come in here and start trouble tonight?'

'Not me, *him*,' he said. 'He asked me to have one last drink with him. I said okay, hoping it would be the last time I'd ever see him. Then, on the way here, he tells me he's got this private job, roughing up some gay Frenchman, in a bar.'

'And you thought you'd tag along?'

'I thought, if I don't watch this crazy guy he'll kill someone, and that will fuck with my visa.'

'You're a humanitarian,' I said.

'Who the fuck are you, to judge me?'

He was smiling, as friendly as a puppy. And he had a point, again, and when a man has a point there's not much you can do.

'Fuck you,' I said. 'I'm the guy you have to get past, if you came here to hurt my friend.'

'I so *get* you!' Oleg said, disconcerting my concert.

'What?'

'I completely get you,' Oleg shouted. 'Give me a hug.'

He dragged me to my feet, stronger than I'd guessed, and hugged me.

Fate never fights fair. Fate sneaks up on you. The world splashed through lakes of time, and each lake I fell through took me closer to a hug, wild and tender, from my lost brother, in Australia.

I shrugged free, and sat down again. He raised his hand to call for more beer, but I stopped him.

'You're unemployed?' I asked.

'I am. What are you offering?'

'Three or four hours' work.'

'Starting when?'

'Fairly close to now,' I said.

'What do I have to do?'

'Fight your way in, maybe, and fight your way out, maybe. With me.'

'Fight my way into what?' he asked. 'I don't do banks.'

'A house,' I said.

'Why do we have to fight our way in?'

'Because the people inside don't like me.'

'Why?'

'Do you give a shit?'

'That's beside the point.'

'What point?'

'All that money I lost tonight, in the bet,' he said. 'Double.'

'Oh, *that* point. Fine. Are you in?'

'Are we going to get killed?'

'Do you give a shit?'

'Of *course* I give a shit. I give a shit about *you*, and I only just met you.'

'I don't think so.'

'I'm Russian. We bond quickly.'

'I mean, I don't think we'll get killed.'

'Okay, so how many guys are we going up against?'

'Three,' I said. 'But one of them, an Irishman named Concannon, is worth two.'

'What nationality are the other two?'

'What the fuck do you care?'

'Nationality figures in the price, man,' he said. 'Everybody knows that.'

610

'I didn't do a census, but I heard a while back that he's working with an Afghan, and an Indian guy. They might be there.'

'So, there are three guys?'

'Two guys, maybe, and an Irishman worth two.'

'An Irishman, an Afghan, and an Indian?'

'Could be.'

'Against a Russian and an Australian,' he mused.

'If you want to see it that way.'

'Double again.'

'*Double again?*'

'*Chert, da.*'

'Why?'

'An Afghan and a Russian in the same room, right now, is worth extra.'

'Twelve grand to fight with me tonight? Forget it.'

Didier began to walk back toward our table. There was a spatter of applause, and he bowed to dinner patrons a few times before he sat.

'Tell you what,' Oleg said, leaning close, 'I'll come along, and if I don't deliver, don't pay me anything at all, but if I do, pay me my price.'

'Didier, meet Oleg,' I said. 'You're gonna love this guy.'

'*Enchanté, monsieur,*' Didier preened.

'You don't mind that I'm sitting here, monsieur?' Oleg asked politely. 'Considering that I came into your bar with a lunatic?'

'Who has *not* walked into Leopold's with a lunatic?' Didier demurred. 'And Didier can spot a man of character from fifty metres, and shoot him through the heart from the same distance.'

'I can see that we're going to get along very well,' Oleg said, resting his arms on the table comfortably.

'Waiter!' Didier cried. 'Another round!'

I raised my hand to stop the waiters.

'We're leaving, man,' I said. 'Are you okay?'

'But, Lin!' He pouted. 'How can I share my triumph? Who will drink with me now?'

'The next lunatic that walks through the door, brother,' I said, giving him a hug.

CHAPTER SIXTY

WE RODE TO PAREL, AND THE ABANDONED MILLS DISTRICT. The information from the Taureg put Concannon's drug operation in a vacated factory complex, rented out in small private spaces.

The place was a ghost town at night, meaning that many people reported seeing ghosts in the vast network of factory huts after dark. Men and women had lived, worked and died in those acres for two generations, before the mills closed. *You know what ghosts are?* Johnny Cigar once said to me. *Poor people, who die.*

'It looks deserted,' Oleg said, as we parked the bike and walked toward the rows of grey, silent factories.

'It mostly is, at night,' I said. 'He's working from the fourth building. Factory 4A. Keep your voice down.'

We were keeping to a chain-link fence line, shadowed by billboards advertising get-broke-quick schemes for property and the stock market.

'At the very least,' Oleg whispered, 'it's damn good material for my writing.'

I stopped, and stopped Oleg with a palm on his chest.

'Writing?' I whispered.

'Yeah.'

'Are you a journalist, Oleg?'

'*Chert, net,*' he whispered.

'What does that mean?'

'It means *Hell, no*, in Russian. It's like the opposite of *chert, da.*'

'You're teaching me Russian, now?' I whispered. 'Are you a fucking journalist or not, Oleg?'

'No, I'm a writer.'

'A writer?'

'Yes.'

'A Russian writer? You're kidding, right?'

'Well, I'm a writer,' he whispered. 'And I'm Russian. So, I guess that makes me a Russian writer, if you want to think about it that way. Are we still going to the fight?'

I had my hands on my knees, leaning forward into a decision. I was trying to decide if I'd rather face the two-plus-two in factory 4A on my own, or with a Russian writer. It wasn't an easy decision, but maybe that was just a writer thing.

'A Russian writer,' I whispered.

'You've got something against Russian writers?'

'Who hasn't got something against Russian writers?'

'Really? What about Aksyonov? Everybody likes Aksyonov.'

'Fuck you,' I whispered.

'What about Turgenev? Turgenev is funny.'

'Yeah. As funny as Gogol.'

'Gogol wasn't strictly Russian,' Oleg clarified, whispering hoarsely. 'He was a Ukrainian Cossack. One of the great Cossack writers.'

'Enough.'

'Wait a minute,' Oleg whispered, his hand on my arm. 'Are you a writer? That's it, isn't it? Ha! How funny, two writers, engaging on a quest together.'

'Oh, shit. '

'By the way,' he asked. 'What *is* our quest?'

With the Russian, it might be possible to surprise the three men, let me have it out with Concannon, and get out again without anyone getting hurt but Concannon, and me. Without Oleg, I'd have to cut Concannon's men, which was why I wanted Oleg with me. But he was a writer. A Russian writer.

'Then there's Lev Luntz,' Oleg whispered hopefully. 'I love him.'

'Shut the fuck up,' I whispered back.

I straightened up, and looked around. The long, wide street had nature frontage on one side with a railway line behind. The Nissen hut factories on our side were silent, stretching away from us like so many burial mounds.

There was no-one in sight, and even the wandering pariah dogs were scouting other ranges. It was peaceful, in the way that dangerous places are if you're not scared of them. I was channelling that peace, because I was scared, and I wanted to stop Concannon without more blood, but I didn't think it would be that easy.

'By the way, why me?' Oleg whispered. 'Why not your friend Didier, or someone else?'

'You really wanna know?'

'Of course,' he said, searching my eyes. 'It could be good material.'

'Because I've got friends who'd go with me, but they might get hurt, and I'd feel bad about that, but I won't feel bad if *you* get hurt. You see that, right?'

'I see that,' he whispered, grinning happily. 'And it's a very good reason. If I was in the same spot, I'd buy *your* life, too.'

'I'm not buying your life, Dostoevsky. I'm buying your *time*, in a fight. Are we clear?'

'Clear,' he said cheerfully. 'I'm glad we had this talk.'

'Well, here's another talk. If you go near my girlfriend, I'll cut you.'

'You've got a girlfriend?' he whispered, incredulously.

'What's that supposed to mean?'

'Well . . . '

'If you make a Russian-writer move on her, I'll cut you.'

'I got the cutting part the first time,' he whispered. 'It's not something you forget.'

He was grinning at me, and I couldn't read it. He was either a pretty happy guy, wherever he was, or there was something he knew that I didn't know.

'What?' I frowned.

'You've really got a girlfriend?' he asked.

'Keep your Russian epic away from her.'

'I got it, I got it,' he grinned.

'What are you grinning about?'

'It's just so much fun, to do some shit worth writing about with another writer. We should work on a short story together, after this. I've got some great ideas.'

'Will you cut it out. We could get seriously fucked up here. This Irish guy's crazy, and tungsten hard. Stay sharp.'

'Okay, okay, take it easy. I've got twelve thousand bucks invested in this. Let's fuck up the Irishman and his friends, and get drunk.'

He started sprinting toward factory 4A, alone. Russians.

I sprinted after him and caught him outside the entrance. We slipped around the side of the huge, curved hut to sneak a glimpse in a raised window.

Concannon was there with two men, playing cards on the bonnet of an immaculate red Pontiac Laurentian, partially obscured by a silver dust cover.

'Are you good?' I whispered.

'Good for what?' Oleg whispered back. 'What's the plan?'

'We walk in through the door and I challenge the Irishman.'

'Don't you think we should *sneak* in?'

'If I was a sneak-in guy, I would've brought a gun.'

'You didn't bring a *gun*?'

I opened the door and walked into the empty factory. Oleg was a step behind me as we crossed the floor. We stopped a few steps from Concannon and his friends.

The Afghan's hands were in his lap. The Indian's hands were in his lap. I didn't know if they had guns or not.

I knew where Concannon's hands were. They were applauding.

'You're more fun than a drunk nun,' he applauded. 'I heard you were dead. I see it was just a vicious rumour.'

'Let's do this,' I said. 'Just you and me, alone.'

'Is it a *fight* you want, boyo?'

He was still grinning. I'd learned how much you can come to dislike a happy grin.

'I want you to stop all your shit, and stay away from me, and my friends. If you agree to that, I'll sit down, and beat your ass at poker.'

'And if I don't?'

Cold stars filtered through wet light glittered in his eyes.

'Then it's you and me, right here, right now, and we'll settle this, once and for all.'

He leaned back in his plastic chair, and smiled.

'Put your gun on him, Govinda,' he said quietly.

It was the Indian guy who had the gun. The Afghan stood up, his cards still in his hand.

'Yes, boss,' Govinda said.

'Get up, Govinda, and stand beside his friend.'

'Yes, boss.'

Govinda stood up, and moved away from the car.

'Keep your gun on the Australian convict as you walk, lad,'

Concannon warned. 'He's a naughty one. If he moves an inch, shoot him.'

'Yes, boss,' Govinda said, smiling at me.

His eyes shone like opals in the half-light of the factory. When he reached Oleg, he shoved the gun into his stomach. Oleg was still smiling. It looked like I was the only guy in the place who wasn't smiling.

'I come in here, man to man, and you pull a gun?' I said.

He was stung, because we both knew I was right. The fight was rising in him, fast.

'Just a little insurance,' he said, controlling his rage.

'You do this the wrong way, Concannon, we won't be the only ones who die.'

I said it for the benefit of the paid hands, the Afghan and Indian henchmen.

'Govinda will certainly die,' I said. 'And the Afghan, too.'

I turned to the Afghan.

'*Salaam aleikum,*' I said.

He wouldn't reply.

'*Salaam aleikum,*' I said, insisting on one of the kindest Islamic teachings, that a genuine greeting of peace should always be met with an equal or better greeting.

'*Wa aleikum salaam,*' he said, at last.

'What's your name?'

He opened his mouth to speak, but Concannon cut him off.

'Don't tell him that, you heathen half-wit. He's just fuckin' with your mind, don't you see? He's gone native, so he knows native talk. But it's all just to fuck with your fragile heathen minds. Watch a master, while I fuck with *his* mind.'

He stood up and walked around the front of the car to stand close to me.

'If he does anything at all,' he said to Govinda, 'shoot his friend. I'll help you cut the body up meself, later on.'

'Yes, boss.'

He stood opposite me, swaying from side to side slowly, his lips pressed into the shell of a smile.

'I know what you want to know,' he said, standing close to me.

'I want you to stop. That's all.'

616

'Ha! No, you don't. You want the answer to a very important question.'

'What the fuck are you talking about?'

'A question,' he sang at me. 'A question, a question.'

'Spit it out.'

'Mind my words, Govinda!' he commanded, looking at me. 'If he makes a move on me, kill his friend. I'll take care of this cunt.'

'Yes, boss.'

'You only really want to know one thing,' he said, leaning in close. 'Did I fuck her, that sweet little American girlfriend of yours, before I left Ranjit with her that night, or didn't I?'

Veins worked their clotted way upward from my clenched jaw through my eyes and into my forehead. I was sweating with the rage to hurt him. It was something else, something different, something I hadn't brought through the door with me. When he put Lisa in the room, I was fighting for her.

'You know, Concannon,' I said, biting back to make him fight back. 'If the Great Famine didn't starve the English out of you, it's because you're really just an Englishman, with an Irish accent.'

He rushed at my throat, but I dodged away and backed off toward the car.

'Why don't we just do this?' I said, loosening up. 'My guess is, you're all talk. Let's find out, and get this over with. If you kick my ass, and you're prepared to shake and be friends, I'll be happy to admit you're the better man. If I win, you stay the fuck away from me and mine. Sound fair to you, Govinda?'

'Yes, boss,' he answered automatically.

'Shut up, you fool,' Concannon snapped.

'I think your gunman has his conscience on safety,' I said. 'Let's do this without a gun, Concannon. Sound fair to you, Govinda?'

'Shut up!' Concannon shouted. 'Shut up everybody!'

He looked me up and down for a while.

Am I right? Am I right, now, when I look back to that smile on my enemy's face, and see reluctance, in a man who loved to fight?

'Okay, if it's a fight you want, Convict, then you've come to the right place. You don't mind if I play a little music, do ya? I always play music, when I'm beatin' a man black and blue. I've been thinking of bringin' out an album, of my favourite hits, like.'

617

He snapped on a disc player, connected to speakers in the car. Irish music kicked from the red Pontiac. Concannon shaped up, his hands in front, on guard.

'Let's have at you, then,' he said.

I ran at him, falling to the ground, and punching at his thigh, exactly where Abdullah had shot him. I got in two hard shots as I passed. He yelped in pain, and dropped his knee.

I scrambled up, and shoved in under his guard, reaching up for one of his eyes. I let him swing at the back of my head. I felt the blows hit, but didn't feel any pain. I closed my fingers, digging into his eye socket.

He jerked away quickly. I scratched one socket enough to make him close it, blinking blood.

One eye closed, one knee bent, he swung at me in a combination from habit, just as Naveen had warned me. I dodged, ducked, and came in close enough to put my fingers in his collarbone. I pulled it down, putting all my bodyweight in a dead fall to the floor. The bone came loose and he screeched, his arm swaying in the pain.

Prison fighting isn't about fighting. Prison fighting is about winning, and dead.

'So, it's like *that*, is it?' he asked, trying to dance away from me, and rubbing at his eye.

'Yeah. It's like that.'

He danced back again, but I dropped to the floor and grabbed at his balls, twisting as I fell. I didn't let go. He fell awkwardly, trying to protect his legacy.

I scrambled to my knees, and hit him as hard as I could. It wasn't enough, so I hit him again.

He swayed in place, sitting on the floor. He was laughing, and still holding his balls with his good hand. He laughed, rocking back and forth like a baby on a blanket.

'You cheated, as this man is my witness,' he said, pointing at Oleg.

'And that piece of lead you hit me with last time? What was that, Marquess of Londonderry rules? The twenty-four-hour contract you put on my life? That was fair and square? This is your chance to shut up and listen for a change. Leave me alone, Concannon.'

'You cheated, son,' he said, trying to laugh. 'You'll have to confess that sin, you know.'

'If you don't stop coming after me, I'll have a bigger sin to confess.'

618

'You know, boyo, I liked you a lot more when you were dead,' he laughed, one eye closed and bloody. 'Govinda, shoot this fucking convict. Shoot the cunt in the head.'

It happened fast. Govinda moved his hand. Oleg pulled a knife, slashed him across the face, and pulled the gun from his hand before shock hit the floor.

Govinda screamed in pain, knowing that his movie-hero face had been recast. Oleg hit him with his own gun, and he was quiet.

The Afghan still had his cards in his hand, like a tiny fan. I had my knife in my hand. Oleg had the gun.

'If I were you, friend, I'd run,' Oleg smiled, the gun at his side. 'No matter how good your hand is.'

The Afghan dropped his cards and ran.

'You've dislocated me collarbone, ya cunt,' Concannon said, his head lolling to the side. 'I can't even raise me arm. If I could, I could knock you out with a single blow, we both know that.'

'Leave . . . me . . . alone.'

'Lovely, lovely, lovely Lisa,' he said.

I hit him again. He went backwards until the floor stopped him, his arms at his sides, but he wasn't out.

What do I do? I thought. *Can I kill him? Not unless he's trying to kill me.* Concannon was lying on the floor with one eye closed and a busted collarbone. He hadn't even tried to get up. He was still talking, though, and chuckling, as if it was a joke he couldn't stop telling himself.

Oleg didn't like it. He wanted to gag him, but I pointed out that the karmic burden would be his, if Concannon choked to death on the gag.

Oleg hit him, instead, and he was good at it. Concannon slumbered, and we left him in the care of the injured Govinda. I warned him that he'd lose more than a cheek, if I ever saw him in the south again.

'I'm taking your gun,' Oleg told him. 'If you want it back, I'll kill you with it.'

We jogged back to the bike in silence. I stopped him, when we reached it, to thank him.

'The six thousand from tonight,' I said, handing him the money. 'I'll have the rest, and a bonus, tomorrow. I'll be at Leo's at five. What you did back there, I owe you.'

'I would hate to see that Irishman drunk,' he said, glancing over his shoulder.

'I hope I never see him again in any condition. You did really good, Oleg.'

'Thank you,' he said, smiling.

'You smile a lot, don't you?'

'I'm happy, most of the time. It's my cross, but I try to bear it with good humour. I have my sadness, but it doesn't stop me from being happy. You want to work on a short story with me?'

'Are you really a writer?'

'Of course.'

'Those were some pretty snappy lines, back there.'

'Lines?'

'Telling the Afghan to leave, no matter how good his hand was. Telling Krishna that you'd kill him with his own gun.'

'Russian movies,' he said, frowning. 'You mean, you don't know dialogue from Russian movies? You'll love it. It's great material.'

We rode back to Colaba. I shook Oleg's hand, and left him outside a tourist hotel, on the strip.

Vanity hides in pride. I left Oleg standing by the side of the road, after he'd saved my life, telling myself that I didn't need anyone, not even a good man like him. But the truth was that I left him because I liked him, and knew that Karla would probably like him as much as I did, or more. It's a shame, my shame, to admit it, but I left that good man on the street because I was a little jealous of him, and Karla hadn't even met him.

CHAPTER SIXTY-ONE

I HAD TO FIND ABDULLAH. I had to know whatever he had or hadn't done with Concannon. I rode to the Nabila mosque, and Null Bazaar, and all the other places where Abdullah found comfort in the comradeship of hardcore criminals. I was angry. My fists were bleeding. I wasn't polite, even to people I liked.

'Where's Abdullah?' I asked, again and again, the engine of my bike growling.

Hard men who put their lives on the line demand respect, and there was some blowback.

'Fuck you, Lin. You wanna look down my gun? He might be hiding in there.'

'Fuck you. Where's Abdullah?'

I found him singing at an all-night festival of Sufi singers. They were doing a long chant of *Ali Munna*, and I knew it could go on for hours, the singers passing chillums in glowing baton circles.

I caught Abdullah's eye, and he stood at once, threading his bare feet delicately among the seated singers.

We walked outside to a dusty, gravel parking area, bordered by trees.

'*Salaam aleikum*,' he said, greeting me with a kiss on the cheek.

'*Wa aleikum salaam*. What the fuck, Abdullah? Did you kill someone with that Irishman, Concannon? Is that why you shot him twice, that day? To shut him up?'

'Come with me,' Abdullah said gravely, leading me by the arm.

We walked a few paces to a space beneath a wide arch of magnolia branches, dancing the occasional breeze in slow time. We sat on a row of large stones, left in the open space as barriers for parked cars.

The singers continued in the tent, a few metres away. A crow, out too late or too early, called from a branch above our heads.

Two bright lights strung on a tracery of wires showed the entrance to the singers' tent. It was an impromptu devotion, assembled from time to time in different places, wherever permission was given, and disassembled without a trace soon after dawn each time.

It was peaceful, and safe, because everyone believed that to disturb such pure devotion, once begun, would bring a curse on seven generations. It was a risk that no-one was willing to take, not even rival gangsters. Sometimes, it's the unborn generations that protect us.

'We took contracts from outside our own Company,' Abdullah began. 'It was Sanjay's decision. I think that he had political motives, but that is only my thought. The first job was the killing of a businessman.'

He stopped, and I gave him time. I'd ridden a long way, and it had been a hard day's nightmare.

'The Irishman was offering himself to every Company. Sanjay hired him, and sent me with him, to see that it went well.'

He stopped again.

'But it didn't go well,' I prompted.

'His wife and daughter were at home. They were not supposed to be there. They saw us, and could identify us, but I could not kill them.'

'Of course not.'

'But . . . Concannon killed them, and I let him kill them, and I listened to it, as he did it, and I am cursed by it.'

Abdullah, Abdullah, invincible Abdullah. I felt him slipping away from me, as love does, sometimes, when the bridge is too far, and the earth on the way to it becomes sand.

'What have you done, man?'

'He cut their throats,' he said.

'Oh, God.'

'It was in all the newspapers. You must have seen it.'

Husband strangled, wife and daughter killed, money stolen: I remembered the story. I remembered not liking the story.

'After that,' Abdullah said, 'I told Concannon that if I ever saw him again, I would kill him. I cut his connection to the Company, and Sanjay sent our contracts to the Cycle Killers, instead.'

'Why didn't you tell me? The guy put a contract out on *me*, for fuck's sake.'

'I was ashamed,' he said.

'*Ashamed?*'

Ashamed. I knew shame. And he was my brother, and brotherhood has no sky.

'You should've told me, Abdullah. We're brothers.'

'But, if you had shunned me, for my shameful acts?'

Fate makes you a judge, as often as you're judged. I was an escaped convict, doing black market business on the streets, and Abdullah lifted me to the bench, gavel in hand. I wanted to hit him with it.

'You should've told me.'

'I know,' he said, hanging his head.

'No more secrets,' I said. 'You and Didier, I swear, you love your secrets, both of you.'

'No more secrets,' he repeated.

'On your oath, as a soldier?'

'On my oath.'

'Good. Keep your eyes open. I visited Concannon tonight, and he'll either back off, or he'll come out of the cave biting.'

'You went without me?'

'I was okay. I had some help.'

'Did you beat him?' Abdullah asked, brightening again.

'It got messy. Keep your head up.'

'I am proud of you, Lin,' he said.

'That makes one of us,' I said. 'It shouldn't have happened, but he's a hard man to reason with.'

'Shall we go in, and join in the singing?' he suggested.

'Thanks, but no thanks. I've gotta get home. Karla might be there. See you soon, brother.'

I rode back toward the Island City, swinging through long, wide Marine Drive before heading back to the Amritsar hotel. The road was deserted. The sea wall was deserted. The houses on my left were sleeping, sending peace into the ocean.

Then I saw a man, playing the guitar. He was sitting under a streetlight in the partition on the centre of the boulevard.

It was Oleg. I pulled up beside him.

'What are you doing?'

'Playing the guitar,' he said happily.

'Why are you playing the guitar in the middle of the road?'

'The acoustics are perfect here,' he smiled, infuriatingly. 'The sea behind me, and the buildings in front. It's perfect. Do you play guitar? We should play here together. We could –'

I rode away and reached Nariman Point before I turned back, and drew up beside him again.

'You wanna get drunk?' I asked, the bike rumbling.

'With you?' he asked, suspiciously.

I rode away again and reached Nariman Point before I turned back, and drew up beside him again.

'Yes! I'd love to get drunk,' he said.

'Get on the bike, Oleg.'

'Can I drive?'

'Don't ever talk about my motorcycle like that again.'

'Okay,' he said, climbing up behind me, the guitar slung at his side. 'Just so long as we know where the boundaries are.'

'Hang on tight.'

'Are we going to fight someone, when we get drunk?'

'No.'

'Not even each other?'

'Get off the bike, Oleg.'

'No, no,' he said. 'It's just that I'll stay sober if we're going to fight each other, because you fight dirty.'

'Fuck you.'

'We Russians can't fight dirty. That's why we're such pushovers.'

'Oleg, if you say the word *Russian* once more, I'll throw you off in a curve.'

'What am I supposed to say? I'm Russian, after all.'

'Let's call them R-people.'

'Got it,' he said, holding on. 'We R-people are quick on the uptake.'

He was a good passenger, and it was fun, riding with him. I was in a good mood as we parked the bike and climbed the stairs to my rooms at the Amritsar hotel.

Just as we approached my door, Karla opened hers, going somewhere else.

She was in a sleeveless evening dress, and high sneakers. Her hair was twisted into a knot, and fixed with a swordfish rib-bone she'd bought at the fish market. She'd cleaned it, polished it, and fixed one of her jewelled rings to the wider end. It reflected the lights of the room behind her.

'Wow,' Oleg said, peering into the Bedouin tent.

'Karla, this is Oleg. He's a Russian writer, and a good man in a bad corner. Oleg, this is Karla.'

Karla looked me up and down, her head tilting like the woman in the glittering black burkha in the Taureg's house of arches. Something was wrong: more wrong than usual. She looked at Oleg. She smiled.

'Bad corners, huh?'

'Karla,' Oleg said, kissing her hand. 'What a lovely name. I have a special love, and I call her Karlesha. It's my love name for her. It's an honour to meet you. And if I flirt with you, your boyfriend says he will cut me.'

'Oh, he will, huh?' Karla smiled.

'You know what,' I said, 'Oleg and I came here tonight to get drunk, in my room. It's been a long night. A rough night. Would you like to join us?'

'Would I *like* to, or would I be *willing* to?'

'Karla.'

'It's a fair question,' Oleg said.

I looked at him.

'I'm only saying . . . '

'No, thanks,' Karla said, switching off the lights, slamming shut the door to her room and locking several locks. 'But, you know what, I've got an offer for *you*, Oleg.'

She turned to face him, all sixteen queens.

'What kind of an offer?' Oleg asked amiably.

'We need field agents, and you look right.'

'Field agents?'

'Let's open that bottle of oblivion, Oleg,' I suggested. 'And get drunk.'

'We've got a bureau, one door along from mine,' Karla said, leaning against the doorframe. 'And we need field agents with spike. Have you got spike, Oleg?'

'I can be spiky,' Oleg said. 'But what makes *you* think I've got the right stuff?'

She jerked her thumb at me.

'He wouldn't introduce you to me, if you didn't. Are you in?'

He looked at me.

'Will you cut me, if I accept?'

'Of course he won't,' Karla said.

He looked back at Karla.

'Great!' Oleg said. 'Fired and employed twice, in the same day. I knew I'd get rich in this city. When do I start?'

'Ten,' Karla said. 'Put on a nice shirt.'

Oleg smiled engagingly. Karla smiled back. I wanted to choke Oleg with a nice shirt.

'Okay,' I said. 'So, I'll see you soon.'

I went to kiss her, to hug her, to smell the ocean, to go home, but she held me back, her hands on my chest.

'Go inside, Oleg,' I said, throwing him the keys.

He opened the door, and gasped.

'Holy minimalism,' he said, alone with my decor. 'It's Solzhenitsyn in here, man!'

'What's going on, Karla?' I asked her, when we were alone with whatever was going on.

She looked at my face as if it was a maze, and she'd found her way out of it before. She stared at my lips, my forehead, and my eyes.

'I'm going away for a couple of weeks,' she said.

'Where?'

'Do you know that it's lovable and maddening at the same time, that I knew you'd ask me that?'

'Stop trying to put me off. Where are you going?'

'You don't want to know,' she said, burning queens.

'I *do* want to know. I wanna know where to break the door down, if you need me.'

She laughed. People laugh so often, when I'm being serious.

'I'm gonna spend a couple weeks with Kavita,' she said. 'Alone.'

'What the hell?' I said, speaking my think.

She cocked her head to the side again.

'Are you jealous, Shantaram?'

I wasn't. I think back, now, and I know I was more jealous of the Russian writer, because he was a pretty cool guy, than I was of Kavita.

But Kavita had spoken harm at me, and I suddenly realised that it still hurt me. Karla wasn't going to another lover, in my mind: she was going to someone who hated me.

I didn't tell Karla then, that night, what Kavita had said to me. I should've said something. I should've told her. But it had been a rough night.

'Madame Zhou paid a visit to the alley under this building, and warned me to stay away from Kavita. Do you really think it's safe to be going away with her?'

'What do you want from me?' she snapped, all fire and furious pride.

'What I want is to be the closest thing to you, Karla. It's a sin for you to use that against me. Stop playing games with me. Tell me to leave you alone, or tell me to love you, with everything I've got.'

She was stung. I hadn't seen it often: a reaction in her face or her body that she couldn't hide.

'I told you before about trusting me, and how it might get harder to do.'

'Karla, don't go.'

'I'm staying with Kavita,' she said, turning away from me. 'Don't wait up.'

She walked away. I watched her to the stairs, and then raced through my apartment to catch a glimpse of her as she walked to the taxi stand at Metro cinema.

Oleg came to stand beside me. She got in a taxi, and she was gone.

'You've got it bad, bro,' Oleg said sympathetically. 'Your vodka is shit, by the way, but your rum is okay. Drink up.'

'I gotta get clean, first,' I said. 'I'll leave the shower ready for you. Make yourself at home.'

He cast a glance around him at the sparse room, the wooden floors gleaming like the lid on a lacquered coffin.

'Okay,' he said.

I stood in the shower, turning it on in bursts, fits and starts. The water in our building was carried in trucks, and pumped upwards into gravity feed tanks on the roof. Everyone in the building shared those tanks.

Trying not to waste water, I shut the shower off from time to time, leaning against the wall until everything that had happened with Concannon came back so hard that I shuddered, retching, and turned on the healing water again.

In the world we created for ourselves, it's a lie to be a man, and a lie to be a woman. A woman is always more than any idea imposed on her, and a man is always more than any duty imposed on him. Men empathise, and women lead armies. Men raise infants, and women explore

627

the exosphere. We're not one thing or the other: we're very interesting versions of each other. And men, too, cry in the shower, sometimes.

It took me a while to scrub the emotion from my face. Afterwards, while Oleg showered, I cleaned my gun as meditation, and stashed it in a hidden shelf beside my bed.

'Your soap is shit,' Oleg said, drying himself off. 'I'll get you some R-soap. It will scrape the barnacles off you.'

'I'm relatively barnacle-free,' I said, offering him the bottle. 'And I like my soap.'

He offered me the bottle back, and I drank and offered it back, and he drank and offered it again, and I drank it back.

'That's my T-shirt,' I noticed, mid-swappery.

'I hope you don't mind,' he said. 'It's so nice to put on something clean. I lived in the last one through a geological age.'

'Keep it,' I said. 'I've got another one, where that one came from.'

'I saw that. And two pairs of jeans. You travel light, man. If I borrow a pair of yours, do you mind if I roll the bottoms up? I really like that look.'

'Roll them up to the Urals, Oleg. But turn down the smiling. If we get any drinkier than this, it'll start to freak me out.'

'Got it, man. Smiling less. We R-people are nothing if not adaptive. Do you have music?'

'I'm a writer,' I said, passing back the bottle. 'Of course I have music.'

I had a CD system, wired into aftermarket Bollywood speakers. I liked the way they blended everything I played into the same sound-ocean, the same whale of signals from some not entirely air-breathing place.

'Your system is shit,' he said.

'You're a critical motherfucker, Oleg.'

'Actually, I'm just making mental notes, you know, of things I get for you that are better than shit.'

'Whaddaya wanna hear, Oleg?'

'Got any Clash?'

I played *Combat Rock*, and he jumped up to grab his guitar.

'Cut to the last track, "Death Is a Star",' he said. 'I know how to play that. Let's play it together.'

We strummed Russian–Australian–Indian acoustic together,

jamming with the faraway Clash in a hotel room in Bombay. We played the song again and again until we got the timing just right, and laughed like kids when we did. And the strings reopened the cuts on my fingers, and blood from the fight with Concannon stained the body of my guitar.

We got too drunk to play, and we were just beginning to stop caring about that, or anything else, when I found a messenger in my room. He was dressed in the khaki uniform of a messenger, and was holding a message in his hand.

'Where did *you* come from?' I asked, swaying to keep him in focus.

'From outside, sir,' he said.

'Well, that's alright then. What can I do for you?'

'I have a message for you, sir.'

'I don't like messages.'

'But it's my job, sir.'

'You've got a point. How much do I owe you?'

I paid the messenger and sat down, looking at the message. I didn't want to read it. The English say no news is good news. The Germans say no news is no bad news. I'm with the Germans on that one. Something inside me, and I still don't know if it's the part that saves me or damns me, always says that I should tear the message up before reading it, no matter who sent it, and sometimes I do. But I had to read it, in case it had something to do with Karla. It didn't. It was from Gemini George.

Dear Lin, old mate. Scorp and me have gone jungle. We're searching for this guru, to lift the curse. Naveen gave us a good lead, and we're starting on the canals of Karnataka tomorrow. Fingers crossed. Love you, mate.

I thought it was a happy, hopeful letter, and I was glad. I didn't realise that it was a cry for help. I dropped the letter on my table, put good reggae music on my bad sound system, and we danced. Oleg danced for the fun of it, I think, but maybe the smiling Russian had demons of his own to release. I was thinking of the fight with Concannon, and I danced for absolution from victory: for defeating a foe, and regretting it.

The moon, our lonely sister, filters pain and harm from sunlight, and reflects it back to us safely, free of burn and blemish. We danced

629

in moonlight on the balcony that night, Oleg and I, and we sang and shouted and laughed, hardening ourselves to what we'd done in life, and what we'd lost. And the moon graced two fallen fools, on a fallen day, with sunlight purified by a mirror in the sky, made of stone.

PART ELEVEN

CHAPTER SIXTY-TWO

OLEG MOVED IN. He asked if he could sleep on my couch, and I agreed, which meant that I had to buy a couch. He went with me, and it took him a long time to make up my mind. The one he chose was in green leather and long enough to stretch out on, which he often did, soon after it was delivered.

When he wasn't a field agent, with spike, chasing down lost loves with Naveen and Didier, he was on the couch, his hands folded across his chest, and talking issues out of his own psychological steppes. The Taureg would've loved it.

'Did you say that you could change your dreams, the other day?' he asked me, stretched out on the couch, a week after he started at the bureau. 'Actually *in* the dream, while you're dreaming it?'

'Of course.'

'You mean, while you're dreaming, and completely asleep, you can alter the course of your dream?'

'Yes. Can't you?'

'No. I don't think many people can.'

'Let me put it this way, a nightmare is a dream I can't control, and a dream is a nightmare I can control.'

'Wow. How does it work?'

'I'm writing a story here, Oleg.'

'Oh, sorry,' he said, his bare feet tapping against one another at the other end of the couch. 'Go back to work. Utter silence from me.'

I was working on a new story. I'd thrown the happy story away. It didn't end well. I was sketching some paragraphs about Abdullah, and thinking about a couple of stories built around him. There were eagles of narrative in him, each tale a winged contradiction, but I'd never written anything about him.

That afternoon I felt compelled to capture him, to paint him with words, and the writing came fast. Paragraphs bloomed like hydrangeas on the pages of my journal.

Years after that sunny afternoon at the Amritsar hotel, a writer told me that it was bad luck for the living, to write about the living. I didn't know that then, and I was happy, in the pages I had on Abdullah: happy enough to forget about threats and felonies, enemies who hide in a smile, Kavita and Karla, and everything in the world, so long as nothing disturbed me, and I could keep writing.

'What's the story about?' Oleg asked.

I put the pen down.

'It's a murder mystery,' I said.

'What's it about?'

'It's about a writer, who kills someone for interrupting him while he's writing. You wanna know the mystery part?'

He swung his legs around, and sat with his forearms on his thighs.

'I love mysteries,' he said.

'The mystery is why it took the writer so long.'

'Sarcasm,' he said. 'You should read Lermontov. The Caucasus is notorious for its sarcasm.'

'You don't say?' I said, picking up the pen.

'Can you really change your dreams?'

The pen in my hand drifted toward him, hovering above my elbow on the desk. I was hoping that it would turn into a caduceus, and I could use it to make him go to sleep.

'I mean, how does that work? I'd love to change my dreams. I have *some* dreams, you know, that I'd really, really like to put on repeat.'

I closed the pen, closed the journal and got two cold beers, throwing one to him. I sat back in my chair, and raised my can in a toast.

'To mysteries,' I said.

'To mysteries!'

'Now, sit back, relax, and tell me what's up, Oleg.'

'Your Karla,' he said, taking a sip of beer. 'I know what you're feeling, because I have my Karlesha, back in Moscow.'

'Why aren't *you* back in Moscow?'

'I don't like Moscow,' he said, taking another sip. 'I'm a St Petersburg boy.'

'But you love the girl.'

'Yes. But she hates me.'

'She *hates* you?'

'Hates me.'

'How do you know?'

'She paid her father to have me killed.'

'She had to *pay* him? What is he, a banker?'

'No, he's a cop. A pretty big cop.'

'What happened?'

'It's a long story,' he sighed, looking toward the breeze of white curtains, fluttering on the sunlit balcony.

'Fuck you, Oleg. You killed my short story. You can fill the space with your long story.'

He laughed bitterly. One of our purest expressions, a thing of our human kind: the bitter laugh.

'I slept with her sister,' he said, staring at his beer.

'Okay. Not classy, but there are worse things that people do to people's sisters.'

'No, it's complicated. They're twins. Non-identical twins.'

'Where are you going with this, Oleg?'

There was a call from the hallway. It was Didier.

'Hello? Are you home, Lin?' he said, as he walked through the open door.

'Didier!' I said happily. 'Grab a seat, and have a beer. Oleg is venturing into territory beyond my couch, and you're just the man to guide the way.'

'Lin, I am afraid that I have many appointments, and –'

'My girlfriend in Moscow hates me,' Oleg said flatly, helplessly, 'because she's a non-identical twin, and I slept with her and her non-identical sister, at the same time.'

'Fascinating,' Didier said, settling himself into a chair. 'If it is not an indelicate question, Oleg, did they have the same . . . aroma?'

'Indelicate?' I mocked. 'You, Didier?'

'Funny you should say that,' Oleg muttered, searching Didier's face. 'They *did* have the same smell. Exactly the same smell. I mean, the same smell . . . everywhere.'

'That is indeed a rare phenomenon,' Didier mused. 'Exceedingly rare. Did you happen to notice the length of their ring fingers, compared to their index fingers?'

635

'Can we get to the part where her father tried to kill you?' I suggested, thinking that I had writing to do.

'Marvellous,' Didier said. 'Tried to kill you, eh?'

'Sure. See, it happened this way. I was in love with Elena, and nothing ever happened between me and her sister, Irina, until one night, when I was very drunk, totally *razbit*.'

'*Razbit*?' Didier asked.

'Smashed, man, I was totally smashed, and Irina sneaked into my bed, naked, while Elena was at the neighbour's place.'

'Wonderful,' Didier enthused.

'It was completely dark,' Oleg continued. 'Very dark. We had blackout blinds on the windows. She smelled like Elena. She felt like Elena.'

'Did she kiss you?' Didier asked, a master of sexual forensics.

'No. And she didn't speak.'

'Precisely. That would have given her away. She's a clever girl.'

'Elena didn't think so, when she came back, switched the light on, and found us making love.'

'No talking your way out of that one,' I said.

'She threw me out of my own apartment,' he said. 'I'm not sure that's even legal. I mean, I'm still paying the rent from here. And her father put up the threat of prison bars, between me and the woman I love.'

'I don't think Elena felt very loved, Oleg.'

'No,' he said. 'I mean *Irina*. When we made love, drunk and all as I was, it was the best thing that ever happened to me. She was a maniac, in all the right ways. I was mad for her. I still am.'

'Marvellous,' Didier smiled. 'But what happened?'

'I managed to get a message to Irina, asking her to run away with me. She agreed, and we planned to meet at midnight, at Paveletsky Terminal. But she told Elena our plans, and Elena came to see me, asking me not to take Irina away. I talked to her, but I refused. I met Irina at the station, and we were running away together, then she stopped me and asked me if I was really sure that it was *her* I loved, and not her twin.'

He paused, searching for the right way through his hedge of recollection.

'Yes?' Didier asked, stamping his foot a little. 'What happened?'

'We were standing together, in the shadows. She asked me how I could be so sure that it was really her and not Elena that I loved. And, you know that moment when a woman asks you for the truth? And you know, you really, clearly know that it's the last thing you should do?'

'Yeah,' we both agreed.

'I told the truth.'

'How bad?' I asked.

'I told her that I was absolutely *sure* that it was her I loved, because just to be completely certain, I had slept with Elena again, when she'd come to see me, two hours before. And it was nothing, with Elena. I hardly enjoyed it at all. So, I was certain that Irina was the one for me, and it wasn't just the fact that I was pretty drunk that night, and I kind of hallucinated how good she was.'

'Oh, shit.'

'*Merde*,' Didier agreed.

'She took a swing at me,' he said.

'I want to swing at you myself,' Didier said. 'It is a disgrace to tell any woman the unembellished truth.'

'You dug that grave yourself, Oleg,' I laughed. 'And neither one forgave you?'

'Their father put professional bad people on my case. I had to run, and run fast.'

'Tough break,' I said. 'Serves you right, for falling in love with a policeman's daughters.'

I turned to Didier, who was sitting back in his chair, his legs crossed, and his hand supporting his chin.

'Any advice?'

'Didier has a solution,' he declared. 'You must wear two of those T-shirts, that common people wear, under your shirt, for two weeks. You must not wash with soap, or hair products. Only water. You must not wear scent of any kind, and you must not brush against any person wearing scent. And you must not wash the shirts.'

'And then?' Oleg asked.

'And then you mail the T-shirts in two packages, one to each of the twins, with only two words on the back – *Leopold's, Bombay*.'

'And then?'

'And then you give copies of Irina's photograph to the waiters at Leopold's, and offer a reward to the first man who identifies her, and calls you.'

637

'What makes you think she'll come?' Oleg asked.

He had the same expression shining in his smile that the students on the mountain had, when they listened to Idriss.

'The scent,' Didier smiled back at him. 'If she is yours, the power of your scent will bring her. She will come to you, like a pheromone pilgrim. But only if she is yours, and you are hers.'

'Wow, Didier!' Oleg said, slapping his hands together. 'I'll start right away.'

He jumped up, pulled my second T-shirt from my wardrobe, and pulled it on over my other one, which he was wearing.

'Why a photograph of Irina, and not Elena?' I asked Didier. 'Or, why not photos of both?'

'The sex,' Didier frowned. 'Did you not pay attention? Irina is Elena, without inhibitions.'

'You got that right,' Oleg said, straightening his T-shirts.

'Exactly,' Didier said, sniffing Oleg to make sure he wasn't wearing scent. 'The sex you had with Irina was exceptional. Do I need to say more?'

He stood up, brushing at his sleeves.

'My work is done here,' he said, pausing at the door. 'Do physical sport, Oleg. Climb to high, dangerous places, jump off things, provoke a policeman, start a fight with a bully, and above all, flirt with women, but have sex with none of them, until you send the shirts. She must smell tiger on you, and wolf, and ape, and a man hungry for sex, and women hungry for him. *Bonne chance.*'

He swept out, flourishing his grey-blue scarf.

'Wow,' Oleg said.

'You know,' I said, 'how I asked you not to use the R-word all the time?'

'Yes . . . ' he said uncertainly.

'I'm adding *Wow* to the list.'

'There's a list?'

'There is now.'

'Shit, there's a list of things I can't say,' he grinned. 'You're making me homesick for Moscow, and I don't even like Moscow.'

He was right. A list of things not to say?

'You know what, fuck it. Say anything you want, Oleg.'

'You mean it?'

'Yeah.'

'Wow, I'm Russian again.'

'You know what,' I said. 'You wanted to ride my bike, right?'

'Can I?'

'Never gonna happen. But there's an old banger bike downstairs. I saw her neglected down there, where I park mine. She belonged to a waiter at Kayani's. I didn't like how he was treating her, so I bought her off him. I've been cleaning her up, the last couple of weeks.'

'*Kruto*,' Oleg said, finding his shoes.

'What was that?'

'That's me, not saying *Wow*. Kruto means fucking *cool*, man.'

'*Kruto?*'

'That's it. *Kruto*, man.'

'Can you ride?'

'Are you kidding?' he scoffed, tying his sneakers. 'We Russians can ride anything.'

'Okay. I've gotta make some rounds, and you can come with me if you like, seeing as you have the day off.'

'Great material for a story,' he said. 'Thank you.'

'Don't mess with my material, Oleg. Just ride, and observe, and wipe the breathy window of recollection clean afterwards, okay?'

'But what if I find a great character, someone I see you talking to, someone who's really, you know, amazingly good?'

I thought about it. He was a decent guy.

'I'll let you have one character,' I said.

'Great!'

'But not Half-Moon Auntie.'

'Oh. She sounds like a good one.'

'That's why you can't have her. Are you ready to ride, or not?'

'I'm ready for anything, man. That's my family motto.'

'Please, please, don't tell me about your Russian family.'

'Okay, okay, but you're missing a lot of great Russian characters, and I'd give them to you free.'

CHAPTER SIXTY-THREE

W E RODE TWO CIRCUITS OF THE SOUTH, touring the Island City at slow speeds. We rarely had to change gear, because we jumped every red light that could be jumped without a fine, and took every short cut unknown to man.

Oleg loved his visit to the black bank. He asked them if they had rooms to rent. And he loved Half-Moon Auntie. She liked Oleg, too: enough to take him through two lunar cycles.

I dragged him away at nine minutes and thirty seconds, the pair of us sliding away from Half-Moon Auntie in an escape that got slower, the faster we tried to run.

Night controlled the lights as we were completing a loop that took us near the President hotel, in Cuffe Parade. We heard the persistent blaring of a horn behind us.

I gestured with my right hand, giving the sign that it was okay to pass. The horn kept braying, so I slowed to a stop beneath a canopy of street-lit plane trees, still vivid green from the monsoon long gone.

There was a laneway beside me where I'd stopped. It was an escape route that a car couldn't follow, if I needed it. Oleg pulled up close behind me. A limousine stopped beside us. I put my hand on a knife.

The tinted window slid down and I saw Diva, with the two Diva girls.

'Hi, kid,' I said. 'How ya doin'?'

She got out of the car. The chauffeur scrambled to open the door for her but was too late, and she waved him away.

'Don't worry, Vinodbhai,' she said, smiling at him. 'I'm fine.'

He bowed, and glanced at the Diva girls quickly before lowering his eyes, as he waited beside the car.

It was significant that she'd added the honorific *bhai* to the end of his name. It was respectful, and probably the only other time he'd ever be addressed so respectfully, outside the circle of family and friends who knew the worth of the man inside the uniform.

It was superb, something beyond class, and I liked the young heiress for it.

'Lin,' she said, coming to hug me. 'I'm so happy to see you.'

It was the first time she'd hugged me. It was the first time she hadn't insulted me, in fact.

'*Kruto*,' I said. 'Someone happy to see me, for a change.'

'I just wanted to thank you,' she said, placing her hand flat against my chest. 'I never got to do it, after the fire, and getting back into Dad's company and all. And I've been thinking about thanking you, and wanting to let you know how grateful I am to you, and Naveen, and Didier, and Johnny Cigar, and Sita, and Aanu, the *real* Aanu, and Priti, and Srinivasan the *dudhwallah*, and —'

'You're freaking me out, Diva,' I said. 'Where's the tigress?'

She laughed. The Divas laughed, inside the air-conditioned limousine.

'Who's your friend?' Diva asked, giving Oleg the twice over.

'This is Oleg,' I said. 'He's a Russian writer, and a field agent for the Lost Love Bureau.'

'Diva Devnani,' Diva smiled, offering her hand. 'Very pleased to meet you.'

Oleg kissed her hand.

'Oleg Zaminovic,' he said. 'We think our great grandfather made up the name, but, hey, he made all of us as well, so we don't hold it against him.'

'I'm Charu,' one of the Divas said.

'I'm Pari,' the other said.

Oleg bowed gallantly from the seat of his motorcycle.

'Get in,' Charu said.

'Absolutely,' Pari said.

The door of the limousine opened silently, as if by an act of will.

'What a splendid idea,' Oleg said, looking at me hopefully.

'Great!' Diva said. 'It's all settled. I'll go on ahead into the slum with Lin on the bike, and Oleg will go with the girls.'

'Wait a minute,' I said. 'You're forgetting something here.'

'I'll be fine, Lin,' Diva said. 'I rode on the petrol tank of our servant's motorcycle from the age of three.'

641

'I'm talking about the motorcycle *he's* riding.'

Oleg looked into the limousine at the pretty girls, and their short dresses, much shorter on the back seat. He looked at me.

'You don't abandon a motorcycle, Oleg.'

'Remember Didier's advice?' he asked limply, pleading with me, guy to guy. 'You know what I mean, Lin. The smelly T-shirt thing. I think I should start tonight. What do . . . what do you think?'

He glanced back inside the limousine. They were undeniably pretty girls, and unambiguously interested in Oleg.

'Park her over there on the footpath, next to that gate,' I said. 'Give the watchman a hundred roops to watch her, until I can pick her up.'

'Great!' he said, bristling the bike up onto the footpath, and smothering the watchman's protest with a fair amount of money.

He sprinted back to the limousine, threw me the keys and ducked inside, pulling the door shut after him.

Diva was smiling at me. She was standing beside my bike. Night was a lizard crawling past us on the footpath. People recognised her, from time to time. Some of them stopped to look.

'What are you smiling about?' I asked her.

'I'm smiling,' she said, 'because you have no idea what a nice man you are.'

I frowned. People, friends, enemies were changing too fast around me, as if I was the last man to wake during an attack.

'Charu and Pari are single girls, with multiple minds,' she said.

'What the hell?'

'They think you're interesting, too,' she said. 'I haven't disabused them of the notion.'

'What?'

'They think you're interesting,' she said. 'That's all I'm saying.'

'Everybody's interesting.'

'You really do love Karla, don't you?' she asked, smiling again, not a tiger in sight.

'Why are we going to the slum, Diva?'

'There's a women's party. I'm the guest of honour, I'm honoured to say. I'd like you to come with me. Tell me that isn't the best offer you've had in the last twenty minutes.'

My turn to laugh. Maybe she really had changed. People do.

'Guest of honour, huh?'

'Let's go, Cisco,' she smiled, swinging a leg behind me over the bike.

We parked the bike outside and walked through lanes decorated with flowers. Long, thick garlands linked every house. Johnny's nephew, Eli, guided us with a torch in lamp-lit shadows. He paused at every spectacular bouquet, scanning the torch over the cordons of flowers, allowing us to admire every bloom. He was dressed in his finest clothes, suitable for devotion, as was everyone we passed in the lanes.

He finally led us to an open space, used in the slum for weddings and festival days. Plastic chairs had been arranged in a wide semicircle around a small stage. The space was becoming crowded.

Women gathered in a flame-lit garden of coloured dresses, their hair plaited with frangipani flowers, their talking laughter like birds at sunset.

Charu and Pari arrived with Oleg. Then Kavita joined the crowd, with Naveen and Karla a few steps behind.

Karla.

She saw me, and smiled. Those things inside, when the woman you love smiles at you: those spears of courage, that rain.

People called for Diva to speak. She found an open space, where all could see her short form, but her speech was even shorter.

'I want to thank you all, so very, very much,' she said in Hindi. 'I know, because you saved my life here, that we can do anything, together. And from now on, I'm with you all the way. I'm supporting fair slum resettlement in decent, safe, comfortable homes across the city. I pledge myself to that, and I'm doing it with all the resources I have.'

The women cheered, the men cheered, and the children leapt about as if the earth was too hot to tolerate more than a frantic skip. The band played furiously until no-one could hear properly.

A place had been set out for a meal, with a long, blue plastic sheet on the ground. Authentic banana leaves were arranged, side by side, for guests to receive food. I'd already eaten, but it was impolite to refuse, and bad luck.

We all squatted beside one another. Charu and Pari had to sit side-saddle, because their designer skirts were too short, but they didn't mind. Their eyes were as wide as if they were studying lions in Africa.

It was their first time on the wretched side of the line. They were repulsed, horrified, and terrified of germs in the food. But they were also fascinated: and a fascinated Indian is yours.

As Fate would have it, Kavita sat on my right, and Karla on my left.

Vegetable biryani was served, along with coconut paste, Bengali spices, Kashmiri refinements, tandoori-fired vegetables, cucumber and tomato yoghurt, yellow dhal, and wok-fried cauliflower, okra and carrot, offered by an endless line of people, smiling as they served us.

'Funny time for a party,' I said to Karla.

'If you knew anything about this,' Kavita said, leaning over to catch my eyes, or my soul, or something, 'you'd know that this is the time between shifts, and the only time that day workers and night workers can join in together.'

It was silly. I'd lived in that slum, and Kavita hadn't, and there wasn't much she could teach me about it.

'You really won't let this go, will you, Kavita?'

'Why should I, cowboy?'

'How about you pass me the pungent chutney, instead?' Karla said, playing peacemaker.

I passed it across, my eyes catching Karla's for a moment.

'Ran away, when Lisa died,' Kavita said. 'And running away now.'

'Okay, Kavita, just get it off your chest.'

'Is that a threat?' she asked, squinting spite at me.

'How can the truth be a threat? I'm just sick of the guilt games. I came to this city with my own crosses. I don't need you making new ones for me.'

'You killed her,' she said.

I didn't see it coming.

'Calm down, Kavita,' Karla said.

'I wasn't even here. I wasn't even in the same country. That was on *your* watch, Kavita.'

She flinched. She was hurt, and I didn't want to hurt her: I only wanted her to stop hurting me. Her eyes brimmed, like snow domes of the world inside, made of tears.

'I loved her,' she said, the domes bursting. 'You only used her, while you waited for Karla.'

'This is the ideal moment, with foresight, to stop this, and focus on the occasion,' Karla said at last. 'Stop this bickering, both of you, and

644

be gracious guests. We're not here for us. We're here for Diva, who suffered a lot as well.'

I pretended to eat, for a while, and Kavita pretended to stop. Neither one of us managed it.

'It should've been you who died on that bed, all alone,' Kavita spat at me, losing control.

'Stop this, Kavita,' Karla said.

'Nothing to say, Lin?'

'Stop it, Kavita,' I said.

'That all you got?'

I started to get up, but she pulled at my sleeve.

'You want to know what she said about *you*, while she was making love to me?'

I should've stopped. I didn't.

'You know, Kavita, you work at a newspaper that sells white-skin potions to a country full of brown-skinned people,' I said. 'You talk about the environment, and you take money from oil companies and coal companies for advertising. You lecture people who wear fur, and accept advertising from battery-fed chicken chains and hormone hamburgers. Your economists forgive bankers no matter what they do, your opinion pages shrink opinion, and your criticism is a flea on the elephant of intolerance. The women in your pages are dolls, while the men are sages. You cover up as many crimes as you report, and you've campaigned against innocent men just for ratings, and we both know it. Come down off your throne, Kavita, and leave me alone.'

She looked at me with a determination that revealed nothing, but maybe nothing was all she had, because she was silent.

I stood, excused myself, and walked back through the slum alone. Naveen caught up with me in a lane filled with small shops.

'Lin,' he said. 'Wait up.'

'How you doing with lost love?' I asked.

I touched a nerve without knowing it. He let the anger-face out of the cage.

'What's that supposed to mean?' he growled.

'You know what, Naveen, I like you. But this really isn't a good night to play sulky.'

I walked off alone, but when I reached my bike on the wide street

645

outside, where children were still playing, someone came up behind me quickly and quietly.

I spun around, grabbed a throat in one hand and had my knife in the other before I knew it was Karla.

'You got me there, Shantaram,' she said, as I released her.

'I always get you there.'

She didn't pull away from me.

'Sneaking up on people like that will buy you conniptions, girl,' I said, my hands in the small of her back.

'Conniptions? How American of you.'

'You have no idea how American I could get tonight.'

'Would that fix my conniptions?'

'Maybe not. Maybe I should put a bell on your bracelet.'

'Maybe you should,' she purred.

I kissed her, leaning against the bike, praying that she'd never leave me.

'Whoa,' she said, easing away. 'You're ready to invade Troy, and the ships haven't even landed.'

'Whatever that means,' I said, 'can you explain it horizontally?'

'*My* current place, or *your* current place?' She laughed.

'Any current place,' I said.

She laughed again.

'That didn't come out right,' I said quickly. 'We haven't been together since the mountain. Does that seem like a long time, to you? It seems like a really long time, to me.'

I might've been telling jokes. She laughed harder with every word I said. She actually pleaded with me to stop, because she was choking.

'You're driving me crazy, Karla. That thing you feel, when something makes you feel completely right? I only feel that, with you.'

She stopped laughing, and looked me up and down. I don't know what it is about me that makes people look me up and down, but I've had my share.

She kissed me. I kissed her. Rain, wave, and that place inside where we dance better than we dance: she kissed me.

She slapped me.

'Damn! What was that for?'

'Pull yourself together,' she said. 'I thought we had this talk. I told you. We're in this game together, or I'm in it alone. They're *your* options, not mine.'

'Fair enough. Agreed. What game?'

'I love you, Shantaram,' she said, slipping away. 'I need Kavita, at the moment. I've got a plan, and I can't tell you about it, remember? I need her, and I need you to rise above, and be the better man.'

Dogs barked, as she trotted back to the slum.

I didn't understand any of it except my part, and I wasn't really sure about my part. But at least I knew that I was back in Karlaville. I could still feel her slap, and her kiss.

CHAPTER SIXTY-FOUR

I DIDN'T SEE OLEG FOR TWO WEEKS AFTER THAT NIGHT. He found a new couch, for a while, and the Diva girls found a new plaything. I took a taxi, the day after he vanished, and collected the banger bike he'd left by the side of the road. I talked to the bike for a while and assured her, even though my heart belonged to another machine, that I'd protect her in future, especially from Russian writers. She carried me home without incident, her engine humming a song the whole way: a brave motorcycle, not ready to die.

I did my rounds day to night, helped decent people out with loans and collected money from indecent defaulters, swapped funny jokes and funnier insults, smacked a cheeky money changer on the ear from time to time and knelt in prayer with others, bribed cops and Company soldiers for blessings from below, dropped donations into churches and temples for blessings from above, fed beggars outside mosques, chased a brutal pimp from my collection area, and came third in a knife-throwing competition, which I'd entered to find out who was better at a throwing a knife than I was: always a handy thing to know. In one way and another, golden days became silvered nights.

A couple of weeks after Oleg's olfactory defection I was swinging back toward Leopold's one day, thinking of their veg curry rice and hungry enough to eat it, when a man ran onto the causeway, stopping me in traffic.

It was Stuart Vinson.

'Lin!' he shouted. 'I've been looking for you everywhere. Park the fucking noisy bike, man.'

'Steady on, Vinson,' I said, patting the gas tank of my bike. 'Language, man.'

He blinked at me, and at the bike.

'What?'

'Calm down. You're a one-man traffic jam.'

Cars were moving around us, and the Colaba police station wasn't far enough away.

'It's serious, Lin! Please, meet me at Leopold's. I'll go there right now.'

He scampered away through the traffic toward Leopold's, and I made the traffic scamper around me while I did an illegal turn, and parked the bike.

I found Vinson pestering Sweetie for a table. There was nothing at Didier's table but a *Reserved* sign. I handed the sign to Sweetie, and sat down. Vinson joined me.

He didn't look good. His surfer-healthy face was thinner than I'd seen it, and there were dark rings on the high cheekbones where optimism used to play.

'Looks like beer,' I said to Sweetie.

'You think you're the only customers I have to serve?' Sweetie asked himself, walking back to the kitchen.

'Do you wanna do this *before* the beer, or *after*?' I asked.

It seemed like a reasonable question, to me. I've seen both, and I know what it's like: the same story, told by different maniacs.

'She's disappeared,' he said.

'Okay, *before* the beer. Are you talking about Rannveig?'

'Yeah.'

'Disappeared . . . how?'

'She was there one minute, and gone the next. I've searched everywhere for her. I don't know what to do. I was, like, hoping she might've contacted you.'

'I haven't seen her,' I said. 'And I have no idea where she is. When did this happen?'

'Three days ago. I've been searching everywhere, but –'

'Three days? What the fuck, man? Why didn't you tell me before?'

'You're my last resort,' he said. 'I've tried everything, and everyone else.'

The last resort: the last person who might help you. I'd never thought of myself as that. I'd never been that. I was always one of the first called, when someone needed help.

The beer arrived. Vinson drank it fast, but it didn't help.

'Oh, my God! Where is she?' he wailed.

'Look, Vinson, you could ask Naveen for help. It's his job to find lost loves.'

'Can you call him for me?'

'I don't use the phone,' I said. 'But I can take you there, if you like.'

'Please,' he said. 'Anything. I'm so worried about her.'

We stood up to leave, my beer untouched. I left a tip for Sweetie. It wasn't sweet enough.

'Fuck you, Shantaram,' he said, replacing the *Reserved* sign on the table. 'Who's going to drink your beer? Tell me that?'

I delivered lost-love Vinson to the Lost Love Bureau, two doors along from my own, and left him with Naveen.

Things had been cooler between Naveen and me. I'd hurt him, somehow, I was sure of it, but I had no idea how. I brought Vinson to the office because I trusted Naveen, and I hoped he saw that.

He smiled vacantly at me as I walked back to my room, then he turned to Vinson, serious questions writing themselves on his face.

I ate a can of cold baked beans, drank a pint of milk and settled the emergency ration lunch with half a glass of rum. I left the door open, and sat in my favourite chair. It was a curved captain's chair, padded with faded, dark blue leather. It was the manager's chair. Jaswant Singh had inherited it from the previous manager, who'd inherited it from someone with damn good taste in writer's chairs. I'd bought it from Jaswant and replaced it for him with a shiny new manager's chair.

Jaswant loved his new chair, and had put coloured lights around it. I put my old chair in a corner, where I had a view of the balcony, and a clear line of sight into the hallway, the manager's desk and the stairs leading up to it. I did some of my best writing there.

I was doing some of my best writing, when Naveen tapped on the door.

'Got a minute?' he asked.

He was intelligent, brave and devoted. He was kind and honest. He was all the things we'd wish a son or a brother to be. But I was writing.

'How many a minute?'

'A couple.'

'Sure,' I said, putting my journal away. 'Come in, and sit down.'

He sat on the couch, and looked around. There wasn't much to see.

'You always leave your door open?'

'Only when I'm awake.'

'Your place is . . . ' he began, searching for a clue in a room that was packed for flight. 'It's kinda boot camp, if you know what I mean. I thought it would get warmer, you know, the longer you lived here. But . . . it didn't.'

'Karla calls it Fugitive Chic.'

'Does she like it?'

'No. What's on your mind, Naveen?'

'Diva,' he said, sighing the name, his head sagging.

'What about her?'

'She offered me a job,' he said, his face stretched and creased with distress. 'That's why I've been so touchy lately.'

'Not such a bad thing, a job.'

'You don't understand. She called me to a meeting. One of her people took me all the way up to the roof of her building, on Worli Seaface. She has offices there. I hadn't seen her for a while. She's . . . we've both been busy.'

He pressed his mouth shut on whatever it was that he'd been about to say. I waited, and then nudged him.

'Uh-huh.'

'She . . . she looked amazing. She cut her hair. It looks great. She was wearing red. There was wind, on the roof. I looked at her. For a second I let myself believe that she'd called me there to tell me that she . . . '

His head dropped, and he stared at his hands.

'But she called you there to offer you a job, instead.'

'Yeah.'

'For a lot of money?'

'Yeah. Too much, really.'

'Okay,' I said. 'She's trying to protect you. She's kinda stuck on you. The two of you went through some stuff together. She's worried, now that the Lost Love Bureau is putting you back on the street.'

'You really think so?'

'I think it's her way of saying that she cares about you. It's not a bad thing, it's a good thing.'

'Maybe you're right. She almost kissed me that night, remember?'

'She told you to shut up, and kiss her. Maybe you should do that.'

'You know,' he mused, 'the new Diva, man, she's taking some getting used to. I always knew what the old Diva was thinking, and what

651

she'd say. Happy, smiling Diva is impossible to read. It's like snow on the radar. It's like I have to fall in love with the same woman all over again.'

'You know, I read a book once, called *Women for Idiots*.'

'What did you find out?'

'I couldn't make head or tail of it. But it confirmed a point from my own messed-up experience, which is that you can't know what's in a woman's mind, until she tells you. And to do that, you have to ask her. One of these days, you've gotta ask that girl if it's a serious thing.'

'You think I should take the job?'

'Of course not. You worked for her father. Now, you're on your own. She'll respect a *no* more than a *yes*. She'll probably find another way to keep you close.'

He stood to leave, offering to wash his glass. I put it back on the table.

'You're a good man, Naveen,' I said. 'And she knows how good you are.'

He turned to leave, but spun around quickly, boxer-ballet.

'Hey, don't forget the race tonight.'

'What race?'

'You haven't heard? Charu and Pari went to the slum, and I challenged Benicia to race me. It's all set.'

'Benicia agreed?'

'She's into it.'

'Did you meet her?'

'Kind of. See you later.'

'Wait a minute. *Kind* of?'

He relaxed again, but avoided my eyes as he leaned against the door jamb.

'I set up a meeting with her, to buy jewellery,' he said. 'It's the only way to see her. She's not an easy girl to reach. She sat me down on a carpet, in this very old apartment. She rents it for her business. And she did the whole transaction in a niqab.'

'The full black cover, or just the black mask?'

'Just the mask. And those eyes, man, I swear.'

'Is she a Muslim?'

'No. I asked her that, and she said no. She just digs the niqab. It's not really a niqab. It's actually just sunglasses that cover her face, and only leave the eyes unshaded. She must've had them specially made. Those eyes, man, I swear.'

'A masked hero. Karla's gonna love her.'

'Those eyes, man,' he said again. 'I swear.'

'Settle down, Naveen. How did it go, with Benicia?'

'I did the deal, and bought a bunch of Rajasthani jewellery as a show of good faith, and then explained the situation to her. She agreed, but on one condition.'

'Ah, terms and conditions always apply.'

'I have to go on a date with her.'

'If you win, or if you lose?'

'Win, lose or draw.'

'Are you kidding?'

'No, I'm serious.'

'Damn, Naveen. Diva's not gonna see it in a rosy light that you're on a date with an enigma, who happens to ride a vintage 350cc motorcycle faster than anyone in Bombay.'

'Anyone but me,' Naveen said. 'I've been practising, Lin. I'm fast.'

'You better be fast, when Diva hears about the date.'

'It's a done deal,' he said.

'Well, Diva will definitely kick your ass for this, but you're racking up some legend points with Didier, kid. He's gonna go nuts when he hears about it.'

'He already knows. Everybody knows. Everyone . . . but Diva. I thought *you* knew.'

I didn't know. No-one had told me. Somehow, I was disconnected from a world of friendship I'd helped to build.

'Where's the race?'

'Air India building, Marine Drive, Pedder Road, and back again, three times.'

'Where are you turning on Pedder Road?'

'The last signal before Haji Ali.'

'When?'

'At midnight.'

'The cops are gonna love it.'

'The cops are helping us. They're maintaining traffic security, and we're so grateful for their cooperation, so to speak, that we paid them what they asked, which wasn't cheap. We had to bring them in. We needed their police radios to call the race. There's a lot of money on this.'

'Some of it mine,' I laughed.

'You know,' he said hesitantly, 'on the spur of the moment, with the race in my mind and all, I totally didn't think about what Diva would make of it, if I went out with Benicia on a date.'

'You can't blame this on the moment, Naveen.'

'But, if I was still with the old Diva, you know, who hit me in the balls every time I stood up, it couldn't have happened.'

'Bring new Diva along on the date. Benicia might like her. And Diva likes jewellery.'

'It's not that kind of date Benicia has in mind.'

'How do you know?'

'Those eyes,' he said. 'She did this . . . she was . . . you had to be there, but there's no mistake. It's more than a date she's got in mind.'

'And you agreed to that?'

'I told you, I was carried away.'

'Call off the bet.'

'I can't do that. Too many people have put too much money on the race. I've gotta give it all I've got.'

'Well, when you have the date with Benicia, tell her you're in love with another girl. Tell her then what you should've told her when she asked for a more-than-date, through her sunglasses niqab.'

'I feel shitty,' he said.

'Don't feel shitty. Win the race, and make it right.'

He hugged me so intensely that I was standing in a river, and water was rushing past me, chest high, just gently enough not to knock me off balance.

He dashed through the door.

'See you there!' he said, starting down the stairs.

'Wait!' I called, and he sprinted back to stand on the top step.

'That girl, Vinson's friend, Rannveig.'

'Yeah,' he said, standing on one foot, a deer waiting for velocity. 'I spoke to him before. He's with Didier, in the office.'

'She's a friend of *mine* as well. If you're trying to find her, go spiritual. That's where I'd start.'

'Okay, spiritual. Got it. Anything else?'

'No. Run.'

He jumped and bumped his way down the stairs.

For some reason, I wanted to close the door, lock the locks, clean my gun, sharpen my knives, write things, and get drunk enough to miss the race. In that moment, I didn't want to know anything else, about anyone else's love drama.

I stood up and walked toward the door, but Vinson beat me to it.

'Got a minute?'

'Fuck it, man, who hasn't got a minute? And who doesn't know that it'll take a lot longer than a minute? Everybody. So leave your self-deprecating passive aggression at the door, come in, park your carcass on Oleg's sofa, have a beer, and tell me what's on your mind, or what's on Oleg's mind, if you'd care to guess.'

'You're in a mood,' he said, sitting.

I threw him a beer.

'Nice couch,' he said. 'Who's Oleg?'

'What's on your mind, Vinson?'

He talked about her, that girl from the North Lands who carried the ice in her eyes wherever she went. He blamed himself for being overprotective, for making her feel like a prisoner, for withholding his affection, and for all the other wrong things.

'*You're* the prisoner, man,' I said.

'*I'm* the prisoner?'

'You're chained to what you do, Vinson. And she's a free bird.'

'What do you mean?'

'I don't want to talk about Rannveig unless she's here to join in the conversation,' I said. 'But I'll just say that I think she's a sensitive person, and what you're doing hurts something inside her. Her last boyfriend died at the business end of heroin, remember?'

'I don't take heroin.'

'You're a drug dealer, Vinson.'

'I've kept her away from it,' he said defensively. 'She doesn't know anything about what I do.'

'Well, knowing that girl the little that I do, I think it matters to her what you do. I don't know, Vinson, but I think it might come to a choice you'll have to make, between the money and the girl.'

'I can't, like, live the way that I do, you know, without the money I make. I live big, Lin, and I like it.'

'Live smaller.'

'But Rannveig —'

'Rannveig will love it, so long as you bring the maid. She likes your maid.'

'I'll have to find her, first.'

'You'll find her. Or she'll find you. She's a smart girl. She's stronger than she looks. She'll be alright.'

'Thanks, Lin,' he said, standing to leave.

'What for?'

'For not thinking I'm stupid to care so much. To love her so much. The cops think I'm crazy.'

'The cops think that anyone who walks into a police station voluntarily is crazy, and they've got a point.'

'Do you really think she'll come back to me?'

'She might come back to you, but not to what you do.'

He walked down the stairs slowly, shaking his worried head.

Faith is unconditional love, and love is unconditional faith. Vinson, Naveen and I were men in love, without the women we loved, and faith was a tree without shade. I hoped Vinson was lucky, and that Rannveig wanted to be found. I hoped that Diva would give Naveen the shelter of certainty. And I hoped that Karla's scheme, whatever it was, wouldn't cost us what we almost had.

CHAPTER SIXTY-FIVE

I ALMOST HAD THE DOOR CLOSED, but Didier pressed his hand against it from the other side, and pushed it open.

'I have a problem,' he said, throwing himself on the couch.

'I should charge this couch by the hour,' I said. 'It's busier than I am.'

'There is a special party, tonight.'

'Uh-huh.'

'A costume party.'

'I'm closing the door, Didier.'

'There were only two costumes left, at the best costumier, and I have put them both on hold, but I cannot choose.'

'What did they have?'

'A gladiator, and a ballerina.'

'I don't see the problem.'

'The *problem*? You do not see the problem? Didier is perfect for both roles, quite obviously, so it is impossible to decide between them.'

'I see.'

'Lin, what shall I do?'

'My advice,' I said, channelling the energy of Oleg's couch, 'is to wear the gladiator to the waist, and the ballerina from the waist down. You'll be a gladerina.'

'A gladerina,' he said, rushing to the door. 'I must try it on, immediately.'

He shuffled down the steps, and I shuffled to the door, finally succeeding in closing it for a while. And I should've been happy, but I wasn't. I didn't like closed doors, pretty much anywhere. I didn't like the closed doors in my dreams: the ones I pounded on, night after night.

I settled in my chair, but I couldn't write. I stared at the locked door for a minute too long, and I was all the way back there in a cage.

Every blow struck against a chained man, every injection to pacify rebellion, every electrocution of will is an insult to what we'll be, when we become what we're destined to be. Time is a membrane, a connective tissue, and it can be bruised. Time can't heal all wounds: Time *is* all wounds. Only love and forgiveness heal all wounds.

Hatred always leaves a stain on the veil. But sometimes the hatred isn't your own. Sometimes you're chained, and the hatred beaten into you is another man's, grown in a different heart, and it takes longer than a fading bruise to forget.

Even if we find a way, some day, to weave the strands of love and faith we find along the way, a blemish always remains on the skin of what can't be forgotten: the yesterday that stares back at you, when you look at a closed door.

For a while I was a lost son, drifting away from friends, drifting away from love, turning a key in memories of fear, anger, uprising, a prison riot, the chapel burning, guards in armour, men willing to die rather than put up with another day of it, just as I was ready to die, when I stood on the wall, and escaped.

Time, too, will die, just as we do, when the universe dies, and is born again. Time's a living thing, just as we are, with birth, longevity, and extinction. Time has a heartbeat, but it isn't ours, no matter how much of ourselves we sacrifice to it. We don't need Time. Time needs us. Even Time loves company.

I looked away from the door, and ran instead into fields of Karla, lakes of Karla, shorelines and trees of Karla, clouds of Karla, storms of Karla tearing everything apart, and when I got there, I wrote verses about Karla and Time, fighting it out with love at stake.

It didn't work. But I marked the page when I closed the journal, because some of the best writing comes from things that don't work yet.

I went to the balcony, and smoked one of Didier's joints.

The intersection below was relatively empty. The frantic insect cars had returned to their hives in hordes. It was time for my last round, and Naveen's race with Benicia wasn't long away, but I didn't want to move.

Karla, Didier, Naveen, Diva, Vinson, the Zodiac Georges, Kavita: I couldn't understand what was going on. There was so much change, so much uncertainty, so many times that I felt that I was on the wrong side of a wall I couldn't see.

I was lost in the mess of it all. I'd spent the evening giving advice to others, and I couldn't advise myself. I could only follow an instinct to make Karla choose, once and for all: life with me, somewhere else, or life in the Island City without me.

Whatever she was doing in Bombay, it didn't include me, and I felt that it should. I was ready to ride away alone, and wait for her somewhere else, if she wouldn't leave with me. I knew that she'd be at the race. I wanted to be there. I had to talk to her, even if it was just to say goodbye.

When your life has no plan but the straightest road out of town, and your heart has waited too long for the truth, or your soul has waited too long for a new song, Fate sometimes strikes the ground with a sacred staff, and fire stands in your way.

Cars rushed past me at killing speed. I saw Hussein men and Scorpion men, speeding in different directions. A rider was approaching me. His bike had very high handlebars. I recognised him from two blocks away. It was Ravi.

I put my bike on the side-stand, and waved him down.

'What's up?'

'Fire, at Khaderbhai's house,' he said quickly, as he drew alongside.

'The mansion?'

'Yeah, man.'

'Is Nazeer okay? And Tariq?'

'Nobody knows. They're trying to save the mosque. That's all I heard. Only bikes can get through. They say it's jammed up on Mohammed Ali Road. Stay off the streets tonight, Lin.'

Khaderbhai's mansion, burning.

I saw the boy in the emperor chair, his head cocked to the side, his long fingers supporting his forehead. I saw my Afghan friend, Nazeer, his grizzled face lit by dawn prayers.

And something was pulled from my chest, some inner thing that wasn't mine any more, and I felt the connection blur. I felt love slip away, draining from me, as if sorrow cut a vein. And I was afraid, for all of us.

659

Ravi rode off and I started my bike, swinging after him.

Sometimes, in those years, the call to die was as strong as the will to live. And sometimes I climbed the mast of fear on my heart, that boat on the sea, and opened my arms to the tempest, breaking the world.

CHAPTER SIXTY-SIX

Ravi was fast, but I was only a few beats behind him. We rode easily along the dragon spine of Mohammed Ali Road at first, but finally hit a wall of cars, trucks and buses, all of them with their engines turned off.

We had to use the footpaths, filled with people who couldn't walk on the blocked road. I was glad that Ravi was in front, as he nudged people out of the way with the wheel of his motorcycle. He negotiated the legs and arms and children's bobbing heads with fluid respect, harming no-one, but maintaining a walking pace. And he repeated only one word, as he rode.

Khaderbhai!

He shouted it again and again, as an incantation. And people moved out of the way each time they heard it.

The Company that Khaderbhai created had become the chrysalis of the Sanjay Company and the calyptra of the Vishnu Company, but when blood was in the fire, only Khaderbhai's name had the colour of instinct, and the power to part waves of hurrying people.

I was so afraid of losing contact with Ravi, and having my own wave of people to negotiate, that I rode too close to him and bumped his fender several times.

He sounded his horn calmly, to tell me to calm down, and then he went back to shouting that unforgotten name.

Khaderbhai!

We reached a corner close to the mosque, but a high wall of motorcycles, handcarts and bicycles blocked the way forward on the footpath. The tide of people surged away, branching off through gaps in the cars on the road.

Through the arches of the pavement awnings we could see smoke, flames and fire trucks. The road beside us was a solid building made of cars and buses.

We shoved our bikes into a doorway, used my chain to lock them together, and climbed the accidental wall of bicycles, baskets and carts, dodging under signs strung outside shops.

We tumbled down the steep metal fall, landing behind a police line, where the jam ended. There was a piece of rope, suspended by the police between the fender of an Ambassador car and the handle of a handcart. It was all that had stopped the flood of people. We lifted the rope and slipped around the shops at the base of the mosque, heading to Khaderbhai's mansion.

Fire trucks were training powerful hoses on the walls of the mosque, trying to stop the fire from spreading. The mosque seemed to be intact, but when we threaded our way through the black snakes of leaking fire hoses, we saw that Khaderbhai's mansion was finished.

A lone unit of firemen was trying to slow the fire, but most of the resources had been diverted to stopping the fire from taking the mosque, and becoming a wider catastrophe in the street.

Men from several mafia Companies were already there, standing across the narrow street, staring at the flames painting rage on their faces. They were Hussein Company men, mostly, but there were a few Vishnu men and gangsters from other Companies. There were about twenty of them. Abdullah was in the centre, his eyes savage with fire.

Firemen were holding the gangsters back, pleading with them to withdraw and let them do their job. Abdullah broke ranks. He brushed three firemen aside and knocked out another, who'd tried to stop him entering the building. He disappeared in the flames.

Company men looked at the firemen, wondering if they were going to fight. Firemen wear uniforms. As far as the Company men were concerned, anyone who wears a uniform works for the other side.

The firemen backed away, taking their colleagues with them. They were paid to save people, not fight them. The men who *were* paid to fight people, the police, rushed toward the retreating firemen.

Fighting the cops is a tricky business. Lots of cops like to fight, but they're sticklers for rules. No disfigurements, and no weapons: just fair, square, kick the shit out of each other. That pretty much covers it, except for two things. First, they have very long memories: longer than most criminals I've met, who are considerably more forgive-and-forget. And second, if things get out of hand, they can shoot you and get away with it.

The Company men put their weapons away, or threw them away, and stood in front of the burning building. The cops kicked in with everything they had, and the gangsters kicked back.

There's a moment of choice, of course, every second that you live. I watched the fight begin, with fairly even numbers, the Company men holding their own. I saw a new gang of cops running to help their friends. Ravi stepped away from me with another gangster, Tricky, and they broke into a run, throwing their lives at the fight. I could've stayed there. I could've watched it happen. I didn't. I dropped my knives behind a handcart, and ran into the mess of what none of us should be.

It was a short run. A cop hit me before I reached the line. He was good. He was quick. I heard the bell, and I didn't know which round. I followed instinct: duck and cover, then lead with a combination. I came out swinging, but the cop was already at my feet. Tall Tony, tall, skinny Tony, had floored him.

We reinforced the Company line. Cops came to help cops. People were grappling and stumbling. Cops were hitting cops. Company men were hitting friends.

I had a cop by the shirt, and I was twisting it close to me. I figured that if he couldn't hit me, he couldn't hit anyone else.

I was wrong, on both counts. He swung a fist over my elbows and connected with some part of my head that shut things down: the part that plays the Clash, in a room somewhere, with a Russian writer, a long way away.

I fell backwards, my hands knotting instinct in his shirt, and he came with me. Other cops came with him, pulling gangsters down into the maul. The front of the mansion had burned, and was starting to collapse. We fell into cindered wood and ashes.

I don't know how many people were on top of the cop who was on top of me: a tree of humanity had fallen. Incense burned my eyes, as if already lit for the dead, and filled the air around us as pieces of sandalwood smouldered.

Scorched pages from sacred texts burned in the rubble. I smelled hair burning, and too much sweat, from too many bodies, piled too high on top of me.

Bullets started firing from inside the mansion. I was suddenly glad to be covered by bodies.

'Bullets are exploding in the heat!' an officer said, in Marathi. 'They're going off at random. Hold your fire.'

The cops and Company men on top of me weren't taking any chances. They hunkered down, pressing into the only hunkering they had, which was me. I was rabbit-breathing, in tiny gasps. The bullets stopped, as the ghost magazines ran their course. Then the arch above our heads gave way, at last. The fallen mob hunkered down a little further.

Fragments of scripture broke from the false arch, and fell on us. I couldn't lift my arms. My hands were still locked in the cop's shirt. I couldn't see. I was breathing ash, in air, but glad to have any air at all.

And then it stopped. The cops and gangsters staggered and stumbled back, one by one. The cop on top of me was the last. He tried to crawl away, but I had his shirt. He kept lurching on his knees, not looking back at me, until I let go.

I got up, wiped my eyes, and looked at the burning house, the house, burning, where Khaderbhai had given me hours of instruction, hours of his life, to argue philosophy.

The arched courtyard was a shivering silhouette, drawn in red-yellow flames. The partitions of the mansion dropped away in sheets. The burning frame, just a star of wooden beams, was ablaze. And it was all gone. Gone.

I couldn't stand it. I couldn't accept it. The place I'd thought of as eternal, somehow, was gone in flame and ash.

I turned, and saw Abdullah. He was on one knee in the open space, near the mosque. He had the boy king, Tariq, in his arms. People were standing back, awed by their own reverence. Abdullah cradled the boy, but Tariq's head had already fallen toward the grave, and his strong young arms were seaweed in the ocean of time.

The fighting stopped. The cops established a new barricade a respectful distance away. People rushed through it to touch the dead boy's cloak.

'Nazeer?' I asked Abdullah, when I could push through the thorn of mourners. 'Did you see him, inside?'

'I took his body from this boy's,' Abdullah said, still kneeling, still crying. 'He is no more. I could not save his body. He was dead and burning, as I took Tariq.'

Abdullah was also a dying man, and we both knew it. He'd promised his life to Khaderbhai as a shield for the boy, and the boy was dead. The limp body was a tattered flag, draped on Abdullah's knee. If it took his last breath, Abdullah would make the men who killed Tariq and Nazeer see the same flag in their eyes, before they died.

'Are you sure he was dead?'

He looked at me, Iranian deserts drifting across his eyes.

'Alright, alright,' I said, too shocked to do anything but agree.

Nazeer was a pillar, a stone pillar: the man who tells you the story long after everyone else has died.

'He was already dead, when you found him?'

'Yes. His body was burned, on the back, but his sacrifice preserved the face and body of Tariq. They were shot, Lin. Both of them. And their guards are nowhere to be found.'

Mourners, mourning violently, shoved me aside to touch the fallen king. I scrambled through a quickly gathering crowd that no police rope could hold. People were coming from every stairway and narrow lane. I broke through to the main street and clambered over the collapsing wall of bicycles and handcarts to find Ravi, standing next to my bike.

'Glad to see you, man,' he said. 'I need my bike. There's gonna be hell tonight.'

If hell means fire and fury, he was right. Outrage breaks the dam of temper. The murder in the mansion, which also threatened a beloved mosque, would release waves of wolves, and we all knew it. The beautiful city, the tolerant Island City, wasn't safe any more.

I wondered where Karla was, and if she was safe.

I unlocked my chain, set our bikes free, and we jammed our way back to Colaba. Ravi split away from me at Metro Junction to meet his brothers in arms. I ran up the stairs at the Amritsar hotel, checking to see if Karla was there.

'You need a shower,' Jaswant said. 'And a change of clothes.'

My T-shirt was a mystery, ripped off in the fight. My vest was scorched and blackened. My bare arms and chest were covered in ash and scratches.

'Have you seen her?'

'She went to see the race.'

'Thanks.'

'Fuck you, baba,' he said, as I took the steps four at a time.

I had to find the place where Karla would watch a legendary race. My guess was that she'd be drawn to the most dangerous turn on the course: the place where Fate and Death might watch together, with a picnic hamper.

It wasn't easy to get there. The city was starting on lockdown, and I had to bribe cops at four checkpoints, just to keep my knives.

Inter-communal disharmony can cost lives in the thousands, any-where in India, even in a tolerant city like Bombay. The cops locked the streets down tight, while a mosque was near to flames, and Hindus were thought to blame.

By the time I reached the vantage point the race was already run, and the traffic cops were responding to reports of a riot in Null Bazaar. *A mob is coming from Dongri*, I heard police radios saying, again and again in Marathi.

I rode down to the Haji Ali juice centre. I thought that Naveen might celebrate or commiserate the race there, because it was one of the few public places still publicly open.

There were people on the streets as I rode, running toward the Hindu temple, and the Muslim shrine. They'd heard that parts of the predominantly Muslim area of Dongri were in flames.

I had to weave between them, stopping now and then for panicked people who ran directly in front of me on the road. I slithered to a stop at Haji Ali, pulling my bike up some distance from a long line of foreign motorcycles, parked in front. I glanced inside the seated section of the juice bar, and saw Naveen, sitting with Kavita Singh.

I looked back to the biker boy group. There was a slim girl in niqab sunglasses, a red leather jacket, white jeans and red sneakers: Benicia. She was sitting on her bike, a matt black vintage 350cc with clip-on handlebars. The word *Ishq*, meaning *Passionate Love*, was painted on the petrol tank.

There were about a dozen people, all of them dressed in coloured leathers, despite the heat. I didn't know any of them. A head turned toward me. It was Karla.

Karla smiled, but I didn't know what her eyes said to me. It was either *I'm so glad you're here*, or *Don't do anything stupid*. I walked the distance between us, and took her arm.

'I have to talk to you, Karla.'

The boy racers on Japanese motorcycles were looking me over. I was ashes, scratches, and burned-black marks.

'What happened?' she asked.

'Khader's house,' I said. 'It's gone. Nazeer and Tariq, both gone.'

A psychic thing, but a thing real enough to make her shudder, forked through her body, jerking her head back in distress. She fell into me and slung her arm around my waist as we walked back to my bike. She sat on the bike, her back to the group outside the juice bar.

'You look hurt,' she said. 'Are you okay?'

'It's nothing, I –'

'Were you there, at the fire?'

'Yeah, I –'

'*Lunatic!*' she snapped, simmering queens. 'Things aren't dangerous enough, without you have to go play with fire? Why am I taking all this trouble to keep you safe, when you take so much trouble to be unsafe?'

'But I –'

'Gimme a joint,' she said.

We smoked. I was listening to the cops, in the police post nearby, talking about locking the whole city down as Plan B, if the rioting spread beyond Crawford market, which wasn't far enough away from where we were.

I wanted to get her out of there. I wanted to take her home, dirty and all as I was. I wanted to take a shower and visit her in the Bedouin tent.

The biker boys were looking at us. They were hopped up on watermelon juice and someone else's victory. Young men, with girls to impress: body language, looking for an offence no one committed.

Fire, I was thinking. *It's gone. All of it. Nazeer, Nazeer, Nazeer, they shot you, and burned you, my brother.*

'He's dead, the boy?' Karla asked, grabbing a rope of detail, and pulling me from the fire.

'Yes. I saw him. He was dead, but untouched by the fire. Nazeer shielded his body. Abdullah brought Tariq's body out of the building, but he had to leave Nazeer inside.'

'May the universe comfort this young, returning soul,' she said.

'Comfort both their souls.'

'Both their souls,' she repeated.

'They were shot, Karla, and their guards have disappeared.'

'Are you sure?'

For a moment I looked at her as Abdullah had looked at me on the burning street, an extinct legacy in his arms.

'Okay,' she said. 'Okay.'

A biker boy approached us. I moved around the bike.

'Are you okay, Karla?' the biker boy asked. 'Is this guy bothering you?'

'No, Jack,' I said, unamiably. '*You're* bothering *me*. Back off.'

He was a nice kid, probably, but it was the wrong moment on the wrong night. And besides, I was talking to my girl.

'Who the fuck are you?'

'I'm the guy who's telling you to back off, Jack, while you can.'

'Go and sit down, Abhay,' Karla said, her back turned.

'Anything for you, Karla,' Abhay said, his shiny jacket creaking like stairs as he bowed. 'If you need me, I'm just over here.'

He backed away, glaring at me until he rejoined his friends.

'Nice kid,' I said.

'They're all nice kids,' she said. 'And they're all going to the party tonight.'

'What party?'

'The party that I uninvited you to.'

'Uninvited me?'

'You *were* invited, but I uninvited you.'

'Who invited me, before you uninvited me?'

She turned her head a little to the side.

'The hostess, if you must know.'

'What party are we talking about, again?'

'A special party, and believe it or not, I had to pull strings to cut you from the list. You should feel okay about that.'

'I don't feel okay about anything, right now.'

Another biker boy approached us behind Karla's back, staring at me. The new biker boy was upset about something. I put my hand up, with a hard face behind it, and he stopped.

'Don't.'

He backed away again.

'Take it easy, Lin,' Karla said, close enough to kiss.

'This is as easy as it gets, tonight.'

668

'They're friends. Not good friends, and not close friends, but useful friends.'

'Come with me, Karla.'

'I can't –' she began.

'You can.'

'I can't.'

'I *won*, Lin!' Naveen said, running up to hug me. 'What a race. That girl is phenomenal, but I won. Did you see it?'

'Great, Naveen,' I said. 'Tell your biker boys to calm down.'

'Oh, them?' He laughed. 'They're hot-headed, but they just like to ride, man.'

'Speaking of riding,' Karla said, 'I'm two-up with Benicia tonight.'

'You're . . . what?'

'Naveen is bringing Kavita to the costume party, and I'm on Benicia's back. I hope you're good with that?'

I was so bad with it, I wanted to pick up motorcycles and throw them at God.

'You know what,' Naveen said, watching Karla and me. 'I'll just be over there, when we're ready to roll.'

He backed away a few steps, and then jogged to meet his friends.

'If I have to get burned or beat up to talk to you, Karla,' I said, when we were alone, 'we probably need counselling.'

'Speak for yourself,' she said, leaning away from me. 'Counselling is for people too bored to tell the truth.'

'That's funny, coming from someone who won't tell me the truth right now.'

'I can't tell you all of the truth. I thought you understood that?'

'I don't understand anything. Are you really going with those people tonight?'

She glanced over her shoulder, and turned back to me again.

'This party is something different. Do you believe me, that I'm going to this party, and I uninvited you, because I love you?'

'What I mean is, you're going to a party, any party, no matter how important it is, after what happened tonight?'

She flared her lips for a second, showing her teeth, locked together. Her eyes opened wide. I knew the look. It wasn't threatening: it was biting back something that would hurt me. I didn't care.

'You knew them, Karla. We're talking about Nazeer. I don't know about you, but all I want to do right now is be with you.'

'It's hard, what happened to the boy –'

'And to Nazeer.'

'And to Nazeer. Sweet Nazeer.'

She stopped, memories of the burly Afghan rubbing at the edges of her resolution. Karla and I both lit the same lamp when we saw Nazeer's deeply lined face and his fierce, scowling smile, as he opened the door of the mansion.

She took a deep breath, smiled at me, and took my hand in hers.

'This party really is important, Lin. It will open a lot of secret doors, and it's gonna let me close a door that I probably shouldn't have opened in the first place.'

'What door?'

'It's too soon. Please, trust me. Please. Just trust me when I say that this party could give me a chance to walk away from all of this, and live with it, for a long time afterwards, without looking back.'

'Why is the party so important?'

'God! You won't leave it alone, will you? And you won't trust me.'

'You give me so little, Karla. And this is a bad night. I'm sorry. I guess I'm a little faith-challenged.'

She looked at me, maybe a little disappointed, maybe simply looking at the disappointment on my face.

'Alright,' she said. 'It's a fetish party.'

'And . . . so what?'

'It's the first of its kind in Bombay, and the veils will come down on a lot of the people there.'

'How many veils?'

'All of them, of course,' she said softly, her hand on my cheek. 'That's why I uninvited you.'

'What?'

'I like you the way you are. I love you the way you are. That's what this is all about, one way and another. I'm not about to compromise that by letting you loose in Babylon.'

'But *you're* going.'

'I'm not you, baby,' she said. 'And you're not me.'

'Come with me, Karla.'

'I have to go, Lin,' she said. 'I've got things I have to finish. Just trust me.'

'Everything's finished. Come with me.'

'I have to go,' she said, standing to leave, but I put fingers on her wrist where a bracelet might rest.

'In case you didn't hear it, the trumpet blew. The walls have fallen. It's —'

'A biblical reference,' she smiled. 'Tempting, Shantaram. More tempting than the damn party, but I gotta go.'

'I'm not kidding. It's not a time to party. It's a time to fortify, and defend. It's gonna get messy. Places are gonna burn. Streets will burn. We should get in some supplies, wait this out, and then find another town.'

She looked at me so lovingly that I was swimming in a river of honest affection, and had no idea how I'd left the shore.

'It's the things that make us one, that make us one worth having,' she said.

I was all out. She was too close. The lights from the hectic drive-in juice bar lit neon fire in her eyes, and I was burning, again.

'What does that mean?'

'Don't give up on me,' she whispered.

'But —'

'Don't you *dare* give up on me,' she said.

She kissed me. She kissed me so truly that she was already gone when I opened my eyes.

She ran to join the biker boys. They were revving their engines. She climbed up behind Benicia.

The Spanish racer girl pulled on a full-face helmet and shut the visor: a black curve of lights where her eyes had been. She took her privacy seriously, and you can't object to that. But Karla was on the back of her bike, and I wanted to object to that. Benicia leaned over to grip the low-slung handlebars, and Karla leaned in close to her.

Then she sat upright and look around, her eyes finding mine without searching. She smiled.

Don't give up on me.

She folded herself against Benicia's back.

Kavita got up behind Naveen. He made an artful loop in front of the juice bar, and pulled up beside me.

'Why aren't you coming, Lin?' he asked, as the other biker boys revved their engines.

671

There was a fire, I was thinking. *People died. Nazeer died. Parts of the city are locked down.* But he was happy. He was a winner. I couldn't take that away.

'Have fun, Naveen. I'll see you in a couple of days.'

'Sure thing.'

He started revving his engine.

'Behold, the Uninvited,' Kavita said, as Naveen prepared to leave. 'What thing, inside *you*, was too terrible to invite to a weekend party, Lin?'

Naveen thumped the gas and skidded off under clutch, and the biker boys followed him.

Karla threw her arms wide, as Benicia roared away.

Don't give up on me.

I was burned, scratched, beat up, covered in ashes, and alone with the dead in a city going into lockdown.

Don't you dare give up on me.

CHAPTER SIXTY-SEVEN

I RODE BACK TO THE AMRITSAR AND CLIMBED THE STAIRS, one at a time, my body heavier than will.

'You were right, Jaswant,' I said, as I passed his desk on my way to my room. 'I need a shower.'

'I told you so! And there's no hot water, now, and the whole city is going crazy, so serves you right, baba, and goodnight, sleep tight.'

I sat at my desk, opened my journal, and wrote what I felt and what I'd seen that night. Ash from my hand and arm smudged the pages. My left hand, pressing the journal flat, made fingerprints, perfectly arranged and deeply defined, while my right hand described the scene of the crime.

Black ink flames ran across the pages. Flames reflected in a policeman's eye, flame reflecting chrome-blue off a wall of bicycles, neon flames from motorcycle exhausts and steel boots, scraping rebel sparks from the righteous roundabout of revenge.

When I couldn't write any more I took a bottle and hit the shower prison style, with all my clothes on.

I drank some, and washed my dirty clothes, peeling them away one textured leaf at a time, and drank some more, and washed my dirtier body, my skin sour with the scents of fear, and her non-identical twin, violent fear.

They were shot. Killed. Burned. They're dead.

Clean and dried and naked, I closed the curtains, banning the day to come, locked all my locks, put weapons around the room wherever I thought I might need them, played music on my bad sound system, said a prayer of thanks for my bad sound system, and I paced.

When you do enough time in a cell, you learn to walk, because walking stills the voice inside, calling you to run.

673

Don't you dare give up on me.

I walked. I drank some more. The music got louder, or maybe it just sounded louder. I was riding a Bob Marley wave to a brighter shore, and I wanted to look at Karla's smile, and I realised that I didn't have a photograph of Karla.

I searched everything I had without success, and decided that a joint might help. The joint found lots of interesting stuff I didn't know I had, including a friendly cricket that didn't sing, which I relocated to the balcony, but there was no picture of Karla.

I was getting a little high, and the first thing I wrote in my journal, after the fruitless search, was a question.

Is Karla real?

I wrote a lot of other things. I recited poetry. *When, in disgrace with fortune and men's eyes*, I began, and I got to *like him with friends possessed*, when someone seemingly possessed started banging on the door.

I went on with my war dance for the dead, and the banging stopped, and the drumming in the music thumped me around the room, and I could write again.

I wrote pages of notes on Nazeer. Departed loved ones never leave the heart, but the living picture of them fades, paled in memory's river. I wanted to write Nazeer, before I couldn't. I wanted to write those eyes, so often like the eyes of an animal, a hunting animal, unknowable and capable of anything: those mountain eyes, born in sight of the planet's peak, that were so seldom lamps inside the cave of his tenderness.

I wrote the humour, hidden in ravines of his grimacing. I wrote the shadow that covered his face in any light, as if the ashen end was stamped on his face from the beginning.

I wrote his hands, those Komodo claws, the dark earth of early labour years branding them for life: Martian canals of lines and wrinkles on his knuckled fingers, some of them as deep as cuts from a knife.

I wrote Tariq. I wrote about the little beads of sweat that broke out on his lip whenever he was pretending to be someone else. I wrote the precision in his movements, as if his life was a tea ceremony that never ended.

And I wrote how handsome he was. There was a handsome man already growing in the awkward boy: a face that would make girls think about him at least twice, and a brave eye that would challenge every man he met.

I tried to write him, to keep him, to save him, and Nazeer, in words that might live.

I wrote until something ran out, or everything ran out, and I reached that place where words stop and thinking stops and there's only emotion, feeling, a lonely heartbeat sounding through colder depths of the ocean inside, and I slept, dreaming of Karla, pulling me from a house on fire, her kisses burning love on my skin.

PART TWELVE

CHAPTER SIXTY-EIGHT

I WOKE TO FIND THAT IT WASN'T KARLA'S KISSES burning my skin: I'd
fallen asleep with my face on a statue of Lord Shiva, and His trident
had carved a mark on my cheek. I hit the shower and washed up again,
determined to keep the door locked for a couple of days, and maybe
continue my wake for the dead. But when I dried off and looked in the
mirror, the trident mark was still there. It seemed as if it would last a
few days before fading. And I knew, staring at that folly, that if I got so
wasted that I branded my own face, when there were enemies who'd
happily scar it for me, it was time to stop getting wasted.

And with that sobering thought, it occurred to me that Karla
might've left her fetish party early, and could be stranded somewhere
in the Island City, because of the rioting. I dressed in battle gear, did a
pocket check, and walked into the entry hall. There was a barricade of
furniture against the door leading to the stairs. It was common practice in hotels during a police lockdown of the city, in those years, to
keep guests safe on one side of a barricade, and looters or rioters on
the other.

'The whole of South Bombay is locked down,' Jaswant said, reading
his newspaper. 'I was lucky to get this newspaper. And no, you can't
have it until I'm finished.'

'Where?'

'You can't have it anywhere. There's a line before you, baba.'

'I mean, where's the lockdown?'

'Everywhere.'

A lockdown meant that I couldn't travel anywhere in the city during
daylight: nobody could.

'For how long?'

'What the fuck do you care?'

679

'Fuck it, Jaswant. What's your hunch? One day, or four?'

'Given all the fires and rioting last night, I've got the bookies on three days,' he replied. 'And I repeat, what the fuck do you care?'

'Three days? I don't think I've got enough inspiration for three days.'

'Inspiration!' Jaswant said, putting down the newspaper and swinging his swanky new executive chair round to face me.

He threw a switch on his desk, and a panel slid open in the wall beside me. It was a secret cupboard filled with alcohol, cigarettes, snack foods, tiny cereal packets, cartons of milk, boxes of sugar cubes, pots of honey, tuna fish, baked beans, matches, candles, first aid kits, and indiscernible things pickled in jars.

He threw another switch, and a cascade of tiny coloured lights rotated around the cupboard.

'Hey,' he asked, peering at the trident on my face, illuminated by his coloured lights. 'Do you know you've got a Trishula mark on your face?'

'Let's not get too personal, Jaswant.'

He waved a hand at his cupboard of pleasures.

'Always happy to keep things on a business level, baba,' he said, raising his eyebrows in sequence. 'There's music, too.'

He threw another switch, and Bhangra dance music stomped out of speakers on his desk. The paperweight danced with the stapler on the glass-topped surface, jittering back and forth across Jaswant's reflected smile.

'We Sikhs have learned to adapt,' he shouted, over the music. 'You wanna survive World War Three, move into a Sikh neighbourhood.'

He let the song play to the end, and it was a pretty long song.

'I never get tired of that,' he sighed. 'Wanna hear it again?'

'No. Thanks. I wanna buy your booze, before Didier does.'

'Didier's not here.'

'I don't wanna take the risk.'

'That's . . . just about the smartest thing you ever said to me.'

'People don't lay smart on you, Jaswant, because your attitude is wrong.'

'Fuck attitude,' he said.

'The prosecution rests.'

'Attitude doesn't pay my rent.'

'Wrap up some rent for me, Jaswant.'

'Alright, alright, keep your wrinkly fucking shirt on, baba,' he said, joining me at the window and bagging the supplies I pointed out.

'Have you got any pre-rolled joints?' I asked.

'Sure, I've got fives, tens, fifteens —'

'I'll take them.'

'What *them*?'

'*All* of them.'

'*Chee, chee!* Didn't anyone ever teach you the art of business, man?'

'Gimme the stuff, Jaswant.'

'You don't even know what it costs, man.'

'How much does it cost, Jaswant?'

'A fucking bundle, man.'

'Done. Wrap it up.'

'There you go again. You've got to *fight* for the *price*, or it isn't really the *price*. You're cheating *me*, when you don't bargain me to the fair price, even if I come out in front. It's how it's done, man.'

'Tell me the *fair* price, Jaswant, and I'll pay *that*.'

'You're not getting me,' he said patiently, teaching an ape. 'The game, for both of us, is to *discover* the fair price. That's the only way to know what anything costs. If we don't *all* do that, we'll be fucked. It's spoilers like you who mess everything up, because you'll pay anything, for anything.'

'I pay what it costs, Jaswant.'

'Let me tell you something. You can't opt out of that system, man, no matter how hard you try. Bargaining is the bedrock of business. Didn't anyone ever teach you that?'

'I don't care what it costs.'

'*Everybody* cares what it costs.'

'I don't. If I can't afford it, I don't want it. If I want it, and I can afford it, I don't care what it costs in money. That's what money's for, isn't it?'

'Money's a river, man. Some of us go with the current, and some of us paddle to the shore.'

'Enough with the old Sikh sayings.'

'It's a new Sikh saying. I just made it up.'

'Wrap my stuff, Jaswant.'

Jaswant sighed.

'I like you,' he said. 'I'll never say that in public, because I'm not showy in public. Everybody knows that. But I like you, and I see some interesting qualities in you. I also see some errors in your spiritual thinking, and because I like you, I'd be happy to realign your chakras for you, so to speak.'

'You've made that speech before, haven't you?' I asked, taking my two sacks of essential stuff.

'A few times.'

'How did it go over?'

'I can sell a story, Lin. I once played Othello, in —'

'Nice doing business with you, Jaswant.'

'That's it!' he said. 'That's what I was trying to tell you before! I *like* you, see, but when you're *like* a child, and you're *not* a child, you take all the fun out of being an adult, see?'

Cue music. He punched the Bhangra music awake.

I stashed my supplies, ate two cans of cold tuna, sharpened my knives while the food settled, and then did push-ups and chin-ups until night gave me the chance to move across the city.

A full *bandobast*, or shutdown of the city, is impossible to negotiate by daylight. Anyone on High Street at high noon is a victim, or soon to be. The cops were scared. There weren't enough of them to stop the people, when the people went to war with one another, or to save the banks. The shutdown made everything much clearer for the cops: if you're on the street, you're meat.

'I'm going out, Jaswant,' I said, just before midnight.

'The fuck you are. That barricade stays.'

'I'll make a mess of it, if I pull it down,' I said, moving to the barricade.

'No way!' he said, coming around his desk to ease the barricade away from the door. 'This is an intricate defence. My Parsi friend could do it better, I wish he were here. But it's good enough to keep the zombies out.'

'Zombies?'

'This is how it starts, man,' he said anxiously. 'Everybody knows that.'

He nudged the artwork of chairs and benches away from the door, and opened it a slender crack.

'You'll need a code word,' he said.

'What for?'

'To get back in. So I'll know it's you.'

'How about, *Open the door*.'

'Something more personal, I was thinking.'

'If I make it back, and you don't open the door, I'll break it down.'

'How?'

'The hinges are on the outside, Jaswant.'

'Hinges!' he hissed. 'My Parsi friend would've thought of that. I'll bet *his* zombie barricade is flawless.'

'Just open the fucking door, Jaswant, when I come back.'

'Come back uninfected please,' he said, shoving the barricade against the door.

Night is Truth wearing a purple dress, and people dance differently there. The safest way to get around at night during a shutdown in Bombay, if you absolutely have to get around, is to ride on the back of a traffic cop's motorcycle.

I knew a good cop, who needed the money. Corruption is a tax imposed on any society that doesn't pay people enough to repel it themselves. His story, at roadblocks, was that I was a translator, a volunteer, who was warning tourists to stay off the streets at night.

And we did encounter a bewildered tourist, here and there, on the rounds: people with backpacks, not packed for barricaded hotels in a ghost city, and who were glad to see a cop, with a foreigner tagging along.

We drifted through most checkpoints on idle, answering questions with a shout and a wave, and I rode around the silent city behind a cop, with a gun, paying him by the hour to help me find Karla, on his rounds. I wanted to be at her side, or to know she was safe.

Legends are written in blood and fire, and the streets were red enough to write new ones. The traffic cop escorting me said that violent clashes had broken out near the Nabila mosque. Some had died, and many more had been wounded. The mosque was intact, with not a tile damaged. People called it a miracle, forgetting how many firemen had been injured to save the sacred space.

'It is a nicely impressive time,' Dominic the traffic cop said Indianly, calling over his shoulder as he rode just above stalling speed, on empty streets.

'Impressively scary, Dominic.'

'Exactly!' he laughed.

683

'Let's try the Mahesh hotel,' I suggested.

'This is a time to tell your grandchildren about,' Dominic said, veering toward the Mahesh, and staring through shadow curtains into every deserted laneway. 'A time when ghosts roamed freely, in Bombay.'

We didn't find Karla, but we found her car. When we drew alongside, we found Randall at the wheel, and Vinson in the back seat.

Randall hissed down the window. Vinson was hissing down a scotch.

'Hi, Randall. Where's Karla?'

'I don't know, sir. I haven't seen her since she left on the motorcycle, with Miss Benicia.'

'I found her!' Vinson said from the back seat, a little drunk.

I turned to face him.

'Where?'

'In an ashram!' he said happily.

'Karla, in an ashram? Not unless she's buying it.'

'Not Karla. *Rannveig*. Naveen found her. She's in an ashram, about a hundred miles from here. I'm gonna go there, as soon as all this calms down.'

I turned back to Randall.

'What's going on?'

'My instruction was to meet Miss Karla at the Amritsar hotel,' he said. 'But the *bandobast* came down so fast, and the police wouldn't allow me to move, and I wouldn't abandon the vehicle, so I got stuck here, sir.'

'And the passenger?'

'Mr Vinson dived into the car when a looter, trying to steal a car like this one, was shot at in this street, at two o'clock this afternoon, sir.'

'Lucky for me you opened the door, Randall,' Vinson said, opening the liquor cabinet.

'And you've been here ever since?'

'Yes, sir, waiting for an opportunity to rendezvous with Miss Karla, at the Amritsar hotel.'

'The Mahesh is only five hundred metres away, Randall,' I said. 'This isn't a night to be out. You'd be safer in there.'

'I will not abandon the vehicle, sir, unless my life is in the balance. I am perfectly comfortable. But, perhaps Mr Vinson would care to make a run for it.'

'No way, man,' Vinson slurred. 'I wanna be alive, to find my girl. She's in an *ashram*. That's, like, heavy shit, man.'

I looked at Dominic.

This will cost you, his look said, and fair enough. I was asking a lot.

'Make it a Press car,' he said, wagging his head. 'We'll get through.'

'Have you got a pen, and white paper?' I asked. 'Can you make a PRESS sign?'

They bickered about drawing the sign, as people do, even when very important things are at stake, but finally agreed on the draft.

Randall placed it on the dashboard, propped against the window by one of Karla's shoes.

Dominic cruised us through checkpoint after checkpoint. Randall saluted. Vinson drank, impersonating the press.

At the alley behind the Amritsar, I paid Dominic and thanked him for his help.

'You're a good guy, Lin,' he smiled, pocketing the money. 'If I thought you were a bad guy, I'd shoot you. See you in two hours. Don't worry. We'll find your girl. This is Bombay, yaar. Bombay always finds a way to love. Get some rest.'

He rode away, the thrum of the motorcycle reminding those behind shutters and doors that someone was there: a brave man, maintaining order.

CHAPTER SIXTY-NINE

WHEN DOMINIC LEFT, RANDALL SLIPPED AROUND THE CAR to open the door for Vinson. Before he could reach it there was a voice from the alleyway, and we both stopped.

'I warned you,' Madame Zhou said. 'I warned you to stay away from Kavita Singh.'

Her goons, the twins and the acid throwers, peeled off their skin of shadows. I was about to answer, but Randall stepped forward, standing beside me.

'Please,' he said, quietly.

'I got this, Randall,' I said, trying to watch five dangerous minds at the same time. 'Madame Zhou does a regular show in this alley, and somehow I always get a ticket.'

She laughed, but she was the only one.

'Please, allow me to speak,' Randall said softly. 'I've been waiting for this.'

He meant it. I allowed him.

'Permit me to present myself to you, Madame,' he said, addressing the veiled figure. 'I am Randall Soares, one of two men who stand here for the Woman. If any harm comes to the Woman, I will kill you, and all your pets. This is your last warning, Madame. Leave us alone, or die.'

He had guts. It was more than I'd have said, in his place, because I knew that Madame Zhou's specialty was second-hand revenge. I was hoping that Randall didn't have a family that could be traced through his name.

Randall had his hand in the pocket of his jacket. The acid throwers had their hands in their pockets. I had my hands on my knives. Madame Zhou moved backwards into the alleyway until shadows ate her again.

686

'Randall Soares,' she said, the last word a rattlesnake's hiss. 'Randall Soares.'

The pets backed into the shadows. The alley was silent.

'Get in touch with any Soares that you know,' I advised him. 'That woman is all grudge.'

'I have no family,' Randall said. 'I am an orphan, given up at birth, and never adopted from the orphanage that I left, at the age of sixteen. Madame Zhou cannot hurt a family I don't have.'

'You'd really kill them?'

'Wouldn't you, sir?'

'I'm hoping to stop it before it comes to that. Are you ex-army?'

'No, sir, Indian Navy Marines.'

'Marines, huh? For how long?'

'Six years, sir.'

'What happened?' Vinson called from the car.

'Bat's in the wrong belfry, sir,' Randall said, opening the door for him. 'A small fist, knocking on Hell's gate.'

'So fricking great to get out in the air,' Vinson said, stretching. 'I was in that car for *hours*. I gotta piss, man, like urgently.'

He made for the nearest wall.

'Get civilised, Vinson,' I said. 'Hold it in, until you get upstairs. There are motorcycles parked here.'

Randall put the car close to a wall in the arched alleyway, permitting traffic through the lane but allowing for a quick getaway.

'No-one will mess with it,' I said, as Randall locked the car. 'You can come upstairs, and stretch your legs.'

'Wonderful, sir.'

'Enough with the *sir* bullshit, Randall. My name is Lin, or Shantaram, if you prefer, but never *sir*. You might as well call me *boss*.'

'Thank you, Mr Shantaram,' he smiled, Goan sunsets gleaming in his eyes.

'Can I piss somewhere?' Vinson asked, riding waves on the footpath.

Randall and I shuffled Vinson up the stairs, and I banged on the door.

'Open up, Jaswant.'

'What's the password?' Jaswant called from the other side of the door.

'Open the fucking door, you motherfucker,' I said, supporting Vinson.

'Lin!' Jaswant said, from behind the door. 'What do you want?'

'What do I *want*, you landlord's excuse for a Punjabi? I want to strangle you with your turban, and stab you with your own *kirpan*.'

'Over my baptised ass,' he said. 'What do you *really* want?'

I looked at Randall, who seemed to be enjoying himself. I looked at Vinson, drooling off my arm. He was certainly enjoying himself. I looked at the locked door to my own hotel.

'I would like to come in please, Jaswant,' I said, as sweetly as possible with clenched teeth.

'No problem,' he said. 'Do you have any infected with you?'

'Open the fucking door, Jaswant.'

The barricade scraped and shuddered away from the door, and we scrambled inside. Jaswant shoved the sculpture back into place, turned quickly and pointed at Vinson, who was swirling drunk.

'He looks infected,' Jaswant said.

'I have *so* gotta piss,' Vinson said.

'Is he leaking fluids?' Jaswant said, stepping back a pace.

'He'll leak them on the floor, if you don't stop talking,' I said, trying to escape.

'Did you see any infected out there?' Jaswant asked.

'Enough with the zombies,' I said, leading Vinson to my room. 'This is Randall.'

'Hi, Randall. I'm Jaswant. How was it out there?'

'Quiet for now,' Randall said. 'But I'm completely with you on zombie vigilance. Prudence is the only wisdom, where the undead are concerned.'

'Exactly!' Jaswant said, returning to his chair. 'I keep telling them. Plagues. Chaos. Situations like this. It's always how it begins.'

'Jaswant,' I said, trying to keep Vinson vertical and open the door to my rooms, which was surprisingly difficult. 'I'm gonna need more supplies. As you can see, I've got guests.'

'You bet your foreigner ass you have,' he laughed.

I opened the door and found Didier in my room, with Oleg, Diva, and the Diva girls, Charu and Pari.

They were all in costume. Diva was in a leopard-print bodysuit. Didier had abandoned his gladiator torso, except for a leather mask, but kept the tutu and tights. Oleg was a Roman senator, in sandals, and a toga made from one of my sheets. Charu and Pari were cat people, complete with tiny ears and long tails. Charu was Persian grey, and Pari was night black.

'Lin!' Didier said from his place beside Diva on a mattress on the wooden floor. 'We were being fashionably late for the party, and we were stopped at a police roadblock before we got there, so we returned here, just as the whole city went into lockdown.'

'Hi, Lin,' Diva said. 'Do you mind that we're here?'

'Of course, not. Happy to see you. This is –'

'Randall, Miss Diva,' Randall said. 'And your beautiful face begs no introduction.'

'Wow,' Charu and Pari said.

'Hi, I'm Vinson,' Vinson said, 'and I found my girlfriend. She's in an ashram.'

'Wow,' Charu and Pari said.

'This is Charu,' Diva said. 'And this is Pari.'

'She's in an ashram,' Vinson said, shaking hands with Pari.

'Is she like, possessed?' Pari asked.

'Or dying of an incurable disease?' Charu offered.

'What?' Vinson asked, swaying as he tried to focus on them. 'You know, I really gotta pee.'

I steered him to the bathroom and shut the door.

'You look messed up, Shantaram,' Diva said, standing up and offering her arms. 'Gimme a hug, yaar.'

She hugged me, and sat down again next to Didier on the mattress. I looked at the mattress. It was familiar. I glanced through my bedroom door at my bed. The mattress was gone. The bare wooden bed was a coffin. My mattress was on the floor.

'I hope you do not object, Lin,' Didier said, drinking my zombie rations. 'Since we are all stuck here for the Devil knows how long, it seemed like the only viable solution, to move the mattress here.'

'Jaswant!' I called out to the manager. 'I have more guests. I'll take everything you've got!'

'That's not how it's *done*, baba,' he called back. 'You *know* that.'

'Jaswant, it's either me, or I'm sending Didier out there to negotiate.'

'Apology accepted,' he said. 'The stuff is yours.'

He brought cardboard boxes into the room, and cases of bottled water. He returned with a gas bottle and a two-burner stove.

He shoved my journals and notes to the side, and installed the stove, lighting it with a battery-powered sparker shaped like a pistol. He turned the gas high and low and high again, as if releasing fireflies from a bottle.

'Wow,' Charu and Pari said.

Jaswant bowed.

'Restaurants are closed,' he said, 'and there's no take-out, no deliveries, and nothing but what you cook yourselves, for who knows how long.'

'We're gonna need more to smoke,' I said, at the door to my room.

'That can be arranged, but it won't be cheap, with this lockdown.'

'I'll take it all.'

'There you go again. Haven't you learned anything? You're a menace to honest business.'

'Didier!'

'Apology accepted. I'll bring the stuff along later. It's in the tunnel.'

'The *tunnel*?'

'Yes.'

'There's a tunnel, underneath this hotel?'

'Of course there's a tunnel. That's why I bought it. Sikhs, surviving World War Three, remember?'

'Can I see it?'

His eyes narrowed.

'I'm afraid . . . that's above your pay grade,' he said.

'Fuck you, Jaswant.'

'Unless –'

'Fuck you, Jaswant.'

'Unless,' he persisted, 'the zombies break through, and it's our final option. If I had that phaser pistol, we'd be on easy street.'

'*Enough* with the zombies.'

'You're no fun at all,' he said, walking back to his desk. 'The stove is a rental. I've put it on your bill.'

I took a look at the barricade, thinking of Karla, waiting for the time to search again, and glanced back at the people in my room.

Oleg was going through the boxes. He pulled out some pots and pans.

'Very useful,' he said.

'If only we'd saved a servant,' Pari said.

Diva lost it, laughing so hard that she pulled her knees up to her chest and rolled herself into a very tight in-joke.

'No need for servants,' Oleg smiled. 'Have you ever tried Russian food? You'll go mad for it, I promise you.'

'Wow,' Charu and Pari said.

Oleg had sent the T-shirts to Moscow, one to each non-identical twin, and by Didier's rules he was free to get re-scented while he waited for Irina, his pheromone pilgrim, to respond.

The Diva girls liked him. Everybody liked him. Hell, I liked him. But all I could think of was Karla, out there, stuck in a building somewhere, with no security but her own.

'Can I help with the cooking?' Vinson chimed in as he drunk-shuffled out of the bathroom.

'Inadvisable, Mr Vinson,' Randall intoned. 'I suspect that Mr Oleg's culinary skills are a spectator sport, not a blood sport.'

'Who are you again?' Diva asked, leaning against Didier on the mattress.

'He's Randall,' Didier said. 'I told you about him. He's a mystery, explained in clever phrases.'

'I'm Randall, Miss Diva,' Randall said. 'And honoured to make your re-acquaintance.'

'Please, come and sit with us, Randall,' she said, patting the bed.

'May I respectfully request, Miss Diva, that Mr Vinson be permitted to join me? He seems to have been left in my charge, and I think he should gently recline.'

'Of course,' Diva said, patting the mattress. 'Put it here, Vinson.'

'Thank you so much,' Vinson said, as Randall eased him into a semi-slump on my mattress, one of my pillows behind his head. 'My girlfriend is in an ashram, you know. I'm afraid I got a little tight, tonight, and actually even yesternight, because she's in an ashram, you know, and that means, like, God is her *boyfriend* now or something, and how can I fight that? How can anyone fight God? And, like, if He's so powerful, why doesn't He get His own girl? It's got me beat. It really has.'

'It's got you bad, baby,' Diva said.

'It's got everybody bad, if you'll pardon me, Miss Diva,' Randall said. 'It's the fight or flight of affection.'

Diva reached across Didier to put her hand on Randall's arm.

'If I said I'd double what Karla is paying you, would you jump ship, Randall?'

'Working for Miss Karla is beyond price,' Randall smiled. 'It is a privilege, so, with respect, I will remain on board, and help Miss Karla man a lifeboat, if required.'

Diva sized him up, wandering through his smile.

'We're going to get to know one another considerably better,' she said, 'if we stay locked up here all night.'

'Every minute in your company is an honour, Miss Diva.'

I left that minute with them, honoured to be alone for a minute in my bedroom, but Diva quickly followed me, spun me around, and grabbed the lapels of my vest.

'Is there something between Randall and Karla?' she whispered.

'What?'

'If there is, I wouldn't poach on her territory. I like Karla.'

'Poach?'

'But if there isn't, I tell you, Lin, this guy is so hot. He's like *melting* fucking *hot*, yaar.'

Places in our beautiful Bombay are burning, I thought. *Places are gone. People are gone.*

'Right,' I said, staring at her, not understanding why she wasn't preparing for a lockdown of the city that could last for days, but glad to see a tiger-growl of the old Diva.

'So, it's cool, then?'

She was searching my eyes innocently.

'Yeah.'

'And there's absolutely nothing between Karla and Randall? Because, I mean, he's so hot, it's like pretty hard to believe, you know?'

Worlds aren't meant to change so quickly, so strangely, but they always do. I couldn't understand any of it. Karla riding with Benicia, Naveen riding with Kavita, Diva dancing with Randall, my room filled with people riding out the storm. I only had one rope in that storm: Karla, maybe stuck somewhere, waiting for me to come.

'You're cool, Diva. It's okay.'

She skipped from the bedroom, and I shut the door behind her, leaning against it without locking it. I didn't want them to hear the sound of the lock turning, and feel unwelcome. They were welcome to stay for a month, as far as I was concerned. I pushed against the door with my back, expecting someone to open it at any minute, but needing a minute to myself.

Kavita was right. Karla never moved from the altar inside, even while I lit candles of devotion with Lisa. Karla *was* the altar inside, from the first second that I saw her.

Is it a sin to give your love to someone, when you can't give your heart? Did we die inside, for a while, or did we keep love alive? Did she cut her wings, that dove, when she threw the window open? Was the happy life I thought we had, just the happy life I thought I had? Did I live a lie with Lisa, or lie a life?

Laughter rollicked in the rollicking room next door: a lifeboat, adrift on irresistibility. And for some peaceful minute of unwelcome truth, the door against my back was the wall of a confessional, and all my sins of omission and commission tumbled through my heart: Nazeer and Tariq, neglected friends burned and shot, and Lisa, neglected love lost forever. Remorse for my selfishness crawled across my skin. And I begged the dead to forgive me.

Laughter and stamping feet drummed through the door, tapping me on the back. I didn't know if it was absolution or penance. I decided to call it even, and began to clean up my bedroom, in case any of the survivors in the next room needed a place to sleep.

I folded sheets and a blanket on the wooden bed base, to provide as much comfort as possible for any weary sleeper. I tidied the room, put my books in one corner, and my guitar in the other, and wiped the floors over with a damp cloth.

And somewhere in that unexpected service to unexpected guests, somewhere in the peace and simplicity and necessity of it, the stream of regret became a river, and I let Kavita and Lisa go.

Wherever they'd been, wherever they were going, living or dead, I let them go. I remembered how they laughed, how I'd made both of them laugh. And I smiled, thinking of it, and that smile opened the grated window, and set them free.

CHAPTER SEVENTY

LIFE ON THE RUN STRINGS ITS OWN FENCES. The living room was full of peaceful friends, but it was also full of dangerous weapons. I'd placed each weapon carefully, from every corner and piece of furniture, and from the balcony to the front door, considering every contingency of attack. I hadn't considered that the room might be invaded by friends.

I went back into the room and picked up the notes and journals Jaswant had sacrificed for his stove.

'Guys, guys,' I said, interrupting them.

Everyone looked up. They were smiling.

'I was planning for uninvited guests, and instead, tonight, I've got invited guests.'

They cheered and clapped.

'No, wait, you're all welcome, of course, and thanks to Jaswant's foresight we've got plenty of food and water and other stuff to ride this out.'

They cheered and clapped.

'No, wait, the thing is, I was expecting *uninvited* guests, see, so I left a few weapons around.'

They blinked at me. They thought it was a joke, I guess, and were waiting for the punchline.

I reached above the almost empty bookshelf, and brought down a hatchet.

'Just go back to what you were doing,' I said, hatchet in hand. 'Relax. I'll go around picking up the weapons, because I don't want anyone to get accidentally hurt. Okay?'

They blinked at me again. Didier was wearing a mask, and even he was blinking.

'Wow,' Charu and Pari said.

I put the jungle-street weapon on my wooden bed and went back to the room, gathering up knives, a gun, two clubs and a nifty knuckle-duster. The last weapon was a set of Vikrant's throwing knives, which I'd hidden behind a corner balcony support, near where Diva was sitting.

'You're either tragically paranoid,' Diva said, 'or tragically right.'

'I don't have time to be paranoid,' I laughed. 'There are too many people out to get me.'

I kept the handgun in my vest pocket. I couldn't hide it in the apartment, because I couldn't trust any of them if they found it. *It's bad karma to let someone get killed with your gun*, Farid, dead Farid the Fixer, once said to me. *Right up there under killing someone with it yourself*.

Didier and Oleg had their own guns, if guns were needed. And there was a chance, if things got worse, that they might. Riots burn city blocks in Bombay, and other Indian cities. And around the fire in rings of blades and clubs are some of the people who lit the fire, waiting for prey to run.

I'd made a deal with Dominic to make another tour, in two hours. He needed to go home, eat, take a nap, and report again for duty. With the city in lockdown, every cop worked every shift.

I'd planned to forget the food, and go straight to the nap, but with my place full of people and my mattress on the floor, the night had unplanned itself.

I went back into the main room and looted Jaswant's supplies, heaped on the table beside the stove. I ate a banana off the bunch with one hand, and almonds with the other. I drank half a glass of honey from a pot. Then I cracked three eggs into a big glass, poured milk on it, threw in some turmeric powder, and drank it down.

The girls had been watching.

'Eeeuw,' Charu said.

She was a pretty girl. For a second, the vain part of me wanted to explain that I had to be on the road again, without any place to eat, and I didn't have time to cook. But I was in love, and vanity, that little shadow of pride, couldn't weaken me.

'You want one?' I asked, offering her the glass.

'Eeeuw,' Charu said.

'Is that like a magic trick, or something?' Pari asked.

'If it's tricks you like, Miss Pari,' Didier said. 'Look no further than Didier.'

'Wow. I want to see every single trick, Didier,' Charu said.

'Make it thrilling, Didier,' Pari added.

Things got back to unusual. Everybody said something essential, inessentially. I went back to my bedroom, racked my weapons into a roll, and stashed them on a window ledge, obscured by a dresser.

'You know, if this was a horror movie,' Oleg said, leaning in the doorway behind me, 'the hidden weapons would be a tension point.'

'Unless *you* knew,' I said, tucking the roll out of sight. 'Then *you'd* be the tension point.'

'Damn!' he said. 'Have you ever played *Dragon Quest*? They're mad for it in Moscow.'

'I'm taking off, Oleg,' I said, turning to face him.

'Wait a minute,' he said quickly, 'you're taking off? I thought nobody was taking off. Never split up. That's the first rule of crazy-time survival tactics.'

'Strange as these words are, I'm leaving you in charge.'

'In charge of what?'

'In charge of my room, while I'm gone.'

'Okay,' he said, considering. 'What do you want me to do with it?'

'Don't let anything happen to my journals. Make sure the rations hold out for everybody. And if Karla comes back before me, guard her.'

'Sure you want to take a risk on me?' he asked. 'I'm a tension point, now, because I know where the weapons are.'

'Cut it out, Oleg.'

'Sorry,' he smiled. 'But it's so much fun. Randall said that there were these creepy experiments in a lab near here, and one of the subjects escaped recently. It was in the newspaper. The girls are scared to death. I might get lucky tonight. Is that allowed, if it's on the couch?'

I looked at him, thinking about burning buildings, and burning friends.

'Is that look a *yes*, or a *no*?' he asked, smiling.

'Are you writing this, Oleg, what's happening tonight?'

'Hell, yeah. Memorising it all like a time-camera. Aren't you? It's a pretty unusual situation, and a pretty unusual mix of people. I mean —'

'Stay awake, Oleg. Buildings like this burn, when people burn things in Bombay. It's not a joke. That's why I haven't been drinking. It's why I haven't had a smoke. This is the shit, and I need you to stay straight while I'm gone.'

'Don't worry about the lifeboat while you're gone,' he smiled. 'They'll all be here, when you swim back.'

'You wrote that, just before, didn't you?'

'*Chert, da.* Thank you so much for this, Lin,' he said. 'I really appreciate it.'

'If Karla comes back before me, keep her here.'

'You're insulting me,' he said. 'You told me that already.'

'I mean, guard her above everything, and anyone. You get that, right?'

'I get that,' he grinned. 'This just gets better and better.'

I walked back into the room dressed for battle. Didier was playing rock-paper-scissors with Diva. Charu and Pari were trying to explain the rules to Vinson, who saw too many hands to make sense of it. Randall was keeping score with polite cheating. Everyone was laughing. I walked through to the entrance hall.

'Again, with the fucking barricade?' Jaswant complained.

'Open it, Jaswant.'

'It's a *bandobast*, idiot! It'll be dawn in a couple of hours, and then you'll be a sitting goose.'

'A duck. A sitting duck. Open up.'

'Don't you realise,' he asked patiently, 'that every time you *open* the barricade, you *weaken* the barricade?'

'Please, Jaswant.'

'If my Parsi friend was here, he would've devised a *moveable* barricade for contingencies like this, but –'

'Jaswant, open the barricade, and if you ask me for a code word when I come back, I'll get a jeweller to write it on your *kara*.'

'My fat Punjabi ass, you will,' he said, shifting his considerable belly to his considerable chest. 'And apology accepted.'

He eased the barricade away from the door, but as I was slipping through he stopped me.

'If Miss Karla comes back,' he said, 'she'll be safe, with me.'

'You just became a friend, Jaswant.'

'There's a security fee,' he said, as I squeezed through the gap in the door. 'For my services as a bodyguard. I'll just put it on your bill.'

I ran the steps in jumps, sliding along the wall, to find Dominic waiting impatiently for me in the alley underneath the hotel's arch.

'You took your time,' he said, as we rode away. 'You're hard enough to explain as it is, Shantaram, without having to explain why I'm late on my rounds.'

'Did you get any sleep?' I called over his shoulder.

'An hour. You?'

'I had company. What's the latest? How bad is it?'

'Very bad,' he said, images of the bike shooting forward and backward in streetlight windows as we passed. 'There were fires in Dongri, Malad, and Andheri. Hundreds have lost their homes and shops. VT station is packed with refugees, finding shelter or leaving the city.'

'Has there been any fighting?'

'Youth leaders from Hindu and Muslim communities have rallied their people. When a fire starts in a Hindu area, Hindu students arrive in trucks. They make a cordon of witnesses, so that no violence can begin. It's the same on the Muslim side. They don't want it to be like the last riots in Bombay.'

'How's that working out?'

'So far, the students are doing a pretty good job of keeping the peace. We should do a recruiting drive among them. We need kids like that in the police.'

'Who's starting the fires?'

'When a fire takes a street in Bombay,' he said, spitting on the road, 'a shopping mall or apartment block takes its place.'

Profiteers sometimes used communal tension as an opportunity to burn down streets of small shops standing in the way of their profit schemes. They hired thugs, tied orange headbands on their heads when they were burning Muslim shops, and green headbands when they burned Hindu streets.

Dominic wasn't being cynical about that truth: he was defeated by it. He was thirty years old, a father of three, two girls, ten and eight, and a four-year-old boy: he was an honest, hard-working man who risked his life day and night in the uniform that he wore, and he'd stopped believing in the system that dressed him in it, and gave him a gun to defend it.

He talked bitterly, as he rode, and I'd heard it before, many times, in slums, on the streets and in small shops. It was the voice of resentment at the double unfairness of a social inequity that preys upon the poor, while telling them that it's their karma to be deprived.

Dominic's family had been Hindus, in his grandfather's time. They'd converted to Christianity in the wave of conversions summoned by the elegant, ethically indelible speeches of Dr Ambedkar, India's first law minister and a champion of the Untouchables.

The family suffered after the conversion at first, but by the time that Dominic and his wife were making their own family, they were fully integrated into the Christian community, just as many others had become Buddhists or Muslims to slip the chain of caste.

They were the same people, the same neighbours, simply going to different places to connect with the Source. But each religion resented, and sometimes violently resisted, attrition from its own faith franchise, and conversions remained a fiercely contested issue.

We made his circuit of the city, from Navy Nagar to Worli Junction, through every route possible. Trucks of chanting Hindus and Muslims passed us, their banners rippling, orange for Hindus and green for Muslims.

Politicians and the rich defied the lockdown, riding in armed escorts on the empty roads, always passing at speed as if being chased. A few people dared to risk the streets, here and there. When we saw them, they saw us, and ran away. Apart from that, the city near dawn was empty.

There weren't any zombies, but the dogs and rats were plentiful, and hungry, without humans leaving refuse for them to eat. They took over many deserted streets, howling and squeaking for scraps.

Dominic was very careful. Indian people like dogs and rats. Indian people like just about everything. He stopped once, when there was a swarm of rats in front of us, blocking the way like sheep on a country road.

He revved the engine, flashed the high-beam headlight, and sounded the horn. The rats didn't move.

'Any ideas?' Dominic asked.

'You could fire your gun in the air to disperse them. Cops do that with people, when they stand on the road.'

'Not an option,' Dominic said.

A thin pariah dog approached, jittering, its thin legs jerking as it walked. The Indian street dog has been around for thousands of years, and this dog knew its way around. It stopped, and began a complicated growling, barking message.

The rats scurried, scrambled and slithered away, a thick grey pelt looking somewhere else for trash. The dog barked at us.

Get outta here, I think he said.

We rode on.

'Nice dog,' Dominic said over his shoulder.

'Yeah, and I'm glad he didn't have any friends. Thirty-five thousand people die of rabies every year in India.'

'You really think on the dark side,' he said, swinging the bike toward Worli Naka.

'I think on the survival side, Dominic.'

'You should let Jesus in your heart.'

'Jesus is in every heart, brother.'

'Are you serious?'

'Of course. I love that guy. Who doesn't?'

'A lot of people don't,' he laughed. 'Some people hate Jesus.'

'No. Brilliant mind, loving heart, significant penance: Jesus was the real deal. They might know *Christians* they don't like, but nobody hates Jesus.'

'Let's hope that nobody hates Him tonight,' he said, glancing in alleyways as we passed them.

We reached Worli Naka, a five-way junction under bright lights, with a football field of open space around a single cop, standing on the beat.

Dominic pulled up beside him, and turned off the engine.

'All alone, Mahan?' he asked in Marathi.

'Yes, sir. But, not now, sir. Because you are here your good self, sir. Who's the white guy?'

'He's a translator. A volunteer.'

'A volunteer?'

Mahan gave me the once-over, watching me carefully in case I made any funny moves, because only a crazy person would volunteer to be on the street.

'A volunteer? Is he mad?'

'Give me a fucking report, Mahan,' Dominic snapped.

'Sir! All is quiet, sir, since my shift commenced, at –'

There was a heavy double-thump, as a fully loaded truck crested a speed breaker. We turned and saw it approaching from the right.

700

The huge truck had a wooden tray at the back, with sides that reached chest-height on the men who were crammed into it. Orange banners were flashes of sun-coloured light as the truck passed beneath streetlamps.

The truck ran a second speed hump, and the singing men in the back bobbed up and down as the wheels bumped the hump, two waves passing through them from the first heads to the last men, jammed against the tailgate.

Ram! Ram! was the chant.

A horn sounded behind us and we turned to see another truck, approaching from the left. It was flying green banners.

Allah hu Akbar! was the chant.

We all glanced back at the orange truck, and then back to the green. It was clear that the trucks were going to pass one another pretty close to where we were standing, in the middle of the road.

'Okay,' Dominic said calmly, putting the motorcycle on the side-stand. 'Hail Mary, full of grace.'

'Narayani,' Mahan muttered, also praying to the feminine Divine.

I stood together with the cops. We looked left and right at the approaching trucks, which were slowing down to a crawling pace.

Mahan, the cop who'd manned the wide intersection alone, had a police radio and a bamboo stick. I looked at him, and he caught my eye.

'All is okay,' he said. 'Don't take tension. Sir is there with us.'

'And sir has us,' I said in Marathi.

'True!' Mahan replied in Marathi. 'Do you like country liquor?'

'Nobody does,' I laughed, and he laughed with me.

The drivers had decided to test their skill, passing one another as closely as they could. Truck-cabin helpers tilted mirrors and pulled banners upright. Others leaned over the sides, shouting instructions to the drivers, and banging the wooden panels.

The trucks, elephants on turtles, crawled turtle-slow toward one another, closer than anything but faith would tolerate. Not far from us the trucks paused and stopped beside one another, singers for singers. There were at least a hundred chanting men in the back of each truck. Their faith was frenzy. Their sweat baptised them. For a few bars, their chants enfolded and merged, the words echoing the words, and then becoming orange praising green, and green praising orange, singing one God.

I was tense, and ready for anything, but there was no anger in the trucks. The young students had no eyes but for their brothers, and devotion, and they chanted without pause.

They were on a mission. Fire brigade units had been prevented by mobs from responding to fires in Hindu and Muslim neighbourhoods. The young men in the trucks were citizen witnesses, putting their lives in harm's way to make sure that harm didn't stop civilian authorities from doing their jobs.

Their mission was sacred work, saving communities, and was beyond provocation. The trucks eased away from one another in frantic chanting, but without a single frown of violent intent.

As the trucks pulled away, driven on by chanting, she was there, Karla, standing alone on the far side of the intersection. She had hitched a ride on one of the trucks.

She was dressed in black jeans, a sleeveless black hot-rod shirt, and a thin red coat with a hood pulled over her black hair. Her carry bag was over her shoulder. Her ankle-strap shoes were clipped to the bag. She was barefoot.

I watched her wave the green banner truck away, and I ran.

'I'm so glad to see you!' she said, as I hugged her. 'I thought it would take me forever.'

'Take *what* forever?' I asked, holding her close.

'Finding *you*,' she said, streetlights on green queens. 'I thought you might be stuck somewhere with unsavoury types. I came to rescue you.'

'That's funny. I thought you were stuck somewhere with savoury types, and I came to rescue *you*. Kiss me.'

She kissed me, and leaned back, looking at me again.

'Have you been practising?'

'Everything is practice, Karla.'

'Fuck you, Shantaram. Holding my own lines against me. Shameful.'

'That's not all I'd like to hold against you.'

'I might hold you to that,' she laughed.

'No, really. I don't know what your plans are, or what you've gotta do, but until this all settles down, please come back with me, Karla. Just, you know, so you're sure *I'm* safe.'

She laughed again.

'You're on. Lead the way.'

'Come and meet Dominic. He's a friend, and he's been helping me.'

'Where's your bike?'

'It's a total lockdown,' I said. 'I'm double-up with Dominic. It's the only way I could get around and keep looking for you.'

'Are you really riding behind that traffic cop?'

She looked across the empty field of light at Mahan and Dominic.

'He's also our taxi home,' I said, 'if you don't mind riding three-up.'

'Long as I'm in the middle,' she said, taking my arm.

'How'd you hitch a ride on the truck?'

She stopped us in the deserted intersection before we reached Dominic. She grabbed the collars of my vest, and pulled me into another kiss.

When I came out of it she was a step away, and I was still leaning like there was a reason. The cops were whistling, singing and dancing.

I scooted back to them, and introduced her.

'A pleasure, Miss Karla,' Dominic said. 'We have searched in places very high for you, and very low.'

Discreet, in India, means not interrupting you to tell you something indiscreet.

'How nice, Dominic,' Karla sultried. 'I'd like to hear your report on those *low* places, whenever you're not saving the city.'

We rode three-up. Karla had her back against my chest. She clung to me, her arms clutching at my vest to hold on, pulling us close. She put her head back on my chest, and closed her eyes. I would've felt better about it, if she didn't have her legs around Dominic, and her feet on the tank of his motorcycle.

We passed through checkpoints as if charmed. Dominic only used one mantra to swerve around the police barricades. *Don't ask*, he said in Marathi, as he passed through roadblocks with me on the back and Karla's legs decorating the front.

None of the cops asked. None of them even blinked. *You gotta like cops*, a wise con once said to me. *They think like us, act like us, and fight like us. They're outlaws who sold out to rich people, but the outlaw is still in there.*

Dominic dropped us at the lane behind the hotel.

'Thanks, Dominic,' Karla said, placing her hand over her heart. 'Nice ride.'

I gave him all the cash I had in my pocket. It was mostly US dollars, but there was an emergency mix of other stuff I'd carried for contingencies. It was about twenty thousand dollars. That sum passed through my hands every other day, but it was a lot of money to a man who lived on fifty dollars a month. It was enough to buy a one-room house, which was his dream, because the cop saving the city during the lockdown, like too many of them, lived in threadbare barracks.

'This is too much,' he frowned, and I realised that I'd insulted him.

'It's all I've got in my pockets, Dominic,' I said, pressing him to take it. 'If I had more, I'd give it to you. I'm so happy, man. I owe you on this. Call me, if you ever need me, okay?'

'Thanks, Lin,' he said, stuffing the money into his shirt, his eyes wondering how fast he could rush home, after his duty rounds, to tell his wife.

He rode away, and Karla started into the arched lane, but I stopped her.

'Whoa,' I said, holding her elbow. 'Madame Zhou has a habit of popping out of these shadows.'

Karla glanced at the new day, painting muddy grey horizons around the buildings.

'I don't think she comes out in daylight,' Karla said, striding ahead. 'It's good for her skin.'

We climbed the stairs to the blocked door on our floor.

'What's the password?' Jaswant called out.

'Ridiculousness,' I shouted back.

'What are you, fucking *psychic*, man?' he replied, with no sign of the barricade moving. 'How can you know that?'

'Open the door, Jaswant. I've got an infected girl, here.'

'Infected?'

'Shift . . . the barricade . . . and open . . . the door!'

'Baba, you have absolutely no sense of play,' he said, shoving the artwork barricade aside.

He opened the door a crack, and Karla slipped through.

'You don't look infected at all, Miss Karla,' Jaswant gushed. 'You look radiant.'

'Thank you, Jaswant,' Karla said. 'Did you stock up, for this catastrophe, by any chance?'

'You know us Sikhs, ma'am,' Jaswant said, twirling the threads of his beard.

'A little more gap in the *door*, Jaswant,' I said, still trying to squeeze through.

He eased the structure aside, I grabbled through, and he shoved it back into place again.

'What do you have to report?' he asked me, clapping dust from his hands.

'Fuck you, Jaswant.'

'Wait a minute!' he said seriously. 'I want to know what's going on, out there. What's your sit-rep?'

'My *sit-rep*?' I said, trying to pass him and get to my room.

'Wait,' he said, blocking my path.

'What is it?'

'You haven't given your report! What's going on out there? You're the only one who's been outside for sixteen hours. How bad is it?'

He was earnest. He meant it. People had walked down public streets, after the anti-Sikh riots, with severed Sikh heads in their hands, strung by the hair like shopping bags. It was an Indian tragedy. It was a human tragedy.

'Alright, alright,' I said, playing along. 'The bad news, depending on how you look at it, is that I didn't see any zombies. Not one, anywhere, unless you count drunks, and politicians.'

'Oh,' he said, a little defeated.

'But the good news is that the city's infested with rivers of rats, and packs of ravenous dogs.'

'Okay,' he said, smacking his hands together. 'I'm gonna call my Parsi friend. He's been nagging me about a Rat Plague Plan for years. He'll be thrilled to hear this.'

We left him, dialling his Parsi friend.

'The bodyguard standby charge still applies,' he called to me, as he dialled. 'I was on standby, even though Miss Karla came back with you. I'll put it on your bill.'

The door to my room was unlocked. We heard strange noises coming from inside. I quietly opened it wide. From the doorway we saw Didier, speaking tongues to Charu on my mattress, while Oleg gambled his scent on Pari and my couch.

The strange noise we'd heard was Vinson, trying to play my guitar upside down. He was lying on his back, with his legs resting upright on the wall. No-one noticed us.

We walked in a step to look into my bedroom. Diva and Randall were stretched out on my wooden bed. They were kissing each other with their hands, as well as their lips.

I wanted to slap Randall away from a girl that I knew Naveen loved, but slapping Randall away was Diva's job, if slapping was required.

Karla pulled my vest.

'You are *not* riding out the apocalypse here,' she whispered, leading me away by the hand.

We walked back to the door of her room. My heart was beating. She put the key in the lock, then stopped, turned, and looked at me.

I never took Karla for granted. But the key was in a lock that opened the door to her Bedouin tent, and my heart was too flooded with hope to doubt. I was hoping that a citywide lockdown and the small satyricon in my rooms might be what it took to make her open the tent.

She smiled, opened the door, and gently pushed me inside. She lit secret lights, and put incense in the right places. She took the collars of my vest, while I was goggling at the banners of red and blue silk above my head, and walked me backwards to the foot of her bed.

She kissed me, and used the advantage to shove me back on the bed, leaving my feet dangling over the edge.

She pulled an ottoman to the foot of the bed, sat down, and began to unlace one of my boots. Her fingers fretted at the knots, then loosened the laces and pulled off one boot. It hit the floor with a boot-thud, and she started on the other. It thumped the floor a few seconds later.

She pulled my vest and T-shirt off, unbuckled my jeans, and dragged me naked.

'You know what your problem is?' she said, looking me over. 'You're harder than you need to be.'

'That's *your* fault,' I said, my hands behind my head, on Karla's pillows, in Karla's Bedouin tent.

'Who said it's a fault? It's just that sometimes, a girl likes to provoke.'

I was confused again, but that was okay. I was very happy to be looking up at haloes of silk above her head.

'You really came back for me?' I asked. 'You left the fetish party, and came looking for me?'

She was standing with her feet apart, her hands on her hips.

'I'd swim the Colaba Back Bay for you, baby,' she said, smiling at my confusion. 'I mean, I might ask Randall to come with me, because I'm not a great swimmer, but I'd come for you, baby.'

'Indians can't swim like Australians,' I said. 'Australia has more sharks.'

She unbuttoned her black shirt, and threw it aside.

'You know,' she said, slipping off her jeans, and stripping naked, 'it might be a lot easier for everybody, if I just keep you in sight from now on.'

She cocked her head to the side to study my reaction.

'I think we should never be apart again,' I said seriously. 'What do you think, Karla?'

'You'll know exactly what I think,' she said, creeping along my body to kiss me, 'in about sixteen minutes.'

King of everything, and a beggar at her banquet at the same time. Thrown at her, thrown at me, turning, moving, changing, touching, and sweating too-long-alone.

My hands against the wall, pushing shadows away. Her feet against my chest, speaking softly, soles and toes, while harsher tongues shouted everywhere else.

The world rolling off the bed. My back on the floor. Her knees on the carpet, the coloured tent behind her head, fan-blades whirling doves of smoke from sandalwood incense.

Karla leaning over me, pressing her forehead to mine, eye for eye, subliming me with connected light. Lost in her pleasure, forgetting my own, finding it again in her eyes, coming home: Karla's eyes, without fear or fences, coming home to me.

Arms entangled, fingers sewn together, legs in carnal coincidence we lay breath against breath, curled into one another like runaways, sleeping in a forest.

CHAPTER SEVENTY-ONE

KARLA AND I DIDN'T LEAVE HER TENT AGAIN, during the lock-down. On the first morning, I woke to see her walking toward me with coffee cups on a tray. I always woke before anybody, even in prison, especially in prison, and it was strange to wake with another consciousness already coffee-cool.

She was dressed in a kind of housecoat, but it was black, and completely sheer, and she was naked inside it. It was as if she was swimming in a shadow every time she moved, and I wanted to swim with her.

She set the tray down on a large street-drum she used as a night table, kissed me, and sat beside me on the bed.

'Let me tell you what's been going on,' she said, her hand on my knee.

'Going on now?' I hoped.

'Since the day I met Ranjit.'

'I see. *Not* now.'

'Not now. Do you know how Ranjit and I met?'

'At a dog fight?'

'You need this, Shantaram.'

'No, Karla, I don't. I just need you.'

'Yes, you do need me, and you do need this.'

'Why?'

'Why do you need me, or why do you need this?'

'I know why I need you – you're the other half of everything. Why do I need to go back to you and Ranjit?'

'The other half of everything,' she smiled. 'I like it. You need this talk because I've treated you bad, and I feel bad, even though I did the right thing, for you I mean, all the way along the line.'

'Okay, but –'

'I don't *like* feeling bad, especially about you, so that has to be squared up, somehow. And the only way is for you to know what I've been doing, so you completely understand.'

'I don't care what you've been doing.'

'You deserve to know.'

'I don't want to know. And I really don't care.'

She laughed, and ran her hand up to my chest.

'Sometimes, you're funnier than the truth.'

'And happier,' I added, kissing her, and swimming in the black shadow with her.

Some time later she brought new cups of coffee to the bedside, and started again.

'I wanted to get slum resettlement on the political agenda in Bombay.'

'This is really good coffee,' I said. 'Italian?'

'Of course, and stay on the subject.'

'Slum resettlement,' I said. 'I get it. I'm just not sure I *want* to get it.'

'Want to get what?'

'Karla, I love you. I honestly don't care what you've been —'

'Humane, well-compensated resettlement for slum dwellers,' she said. 'You get that, right?'

She was imitating me, and doing a pretty good job.

'I get that. I just —'

'Ranjit and I met in an elevator,' Karla said.

'Karla —'

'In a stuck elevator, to be precise.'

'That's a pretty good Ranjit metaphor. A stuck elevator.'

'The elevator got stuck between the seventh and eighth floors for an hour,' she said, crowding me into her memory.

'An hour?'

'Sixty long minutes. There was just the two of us, Ranjit and me.'

'Did he make a pass at you?'

'Of course. He flirted with me, and made a pass, and I slapped it away. So he made another pass, and I slapped it a lot harder, and then he sat on the floor and asked me what I wanted to achieve in life.'

I drank coffee, slapping Ranjit twice, in my mind.

'It was the first time in my life that anyone ever asked me that question,' she said.

'I've asked you that question. I've asked you more than once.'

'You asked me what I want to *do*,' she said, 'just like I ask *you* what you want to do. He asked me what I want to *achieve* in life. It's a different question.'

'It's the same question, in a different elevator.'

She laughed, and then shook her head.

'I'm not getting into that now, much as I'd love to kick your koans in the ass.'

'The ass kicks,' I said, straight-faced. 'When the burden is great.'

'I'm not doing this, Lin. I'm going to tell you what you need to know, and then I'll aphorism your ass so bad you'll think you're drunk on homemade wine.'

'Promise?'

'Go with me, here.'

'Okay, so you're locked in a marriage, sorry, an elevator, with Ranjit, and when he can't achieve *you*, he asks you what you want to achieve. What did you say?'

'I answered it without thinking. I said *I want to achieve decent resettlement for slum dwellers*.'

'What did he say?'

'He said *This is a fated connection. I'm going into politics, and I'll make your program a priority, if you'll marry me*.'

'He said this in the elevator?'

'He did.'

'And you accepted?'

'I did.'

'After an hour in an elevator?'

'Yeah,' she said, frowning.

She scanned my eyes, green queens prowling through my grey skies.

'Hold it a minute,' she demanded. 'You don't think a man would propose to me after an hour in a stuck elevator, is that it?'

'I didn't say —'

'My fastest proposal was five minutes flat,' she said.

'I didn't say —'

'I'd defy you to beat that, but I know you can't, and I wouldn't let you try.'

'No offence, but apart from you, what was his angle?'

'He said that he wanted to piss off his family, and there was no better way. He'd been looking for someone just like me.'

'Why did he want to piss off his family?'

'Ranjit had control of the money, his family estate, but he had brothers and sisters who were snapping at his crooked deals. They'd taken him to court three times, trying to get control of the money he was misappropriating. He'd been looking for a wife he could weaponise.'

'To antagonise them?'

'Exactly. He couldn't cut them off without a reason, and he knew they couldn't keep their mouths shut about his foreign wife, especially if his foreign wife couldn't keep her mouth shut about them.'

'You cooked this up in an hour? You fix his problems, and he fixes yours. Strangers on an elevator, huh?'

'Exactly. Each time I provoked one of them to insult me, he cut them off. I was his reverse pension plan.'

'You're pretty cute, even when you're trying not to be,' I smiled. 'How did you get them to dislike you so much?'

'They're a nasty bunch. They hate easy. And Ranjit told me all their dirty secrets. I took an honesty pill every time I saw them. It made them sick.'

'So, when you and Ranjit got all the way down to the ground floor, you married him?'

She was suddenly serious.

'After what I did to you, with Khaderbhai, I thought you'd never speak to me again. And I was right, kind of. We were apart for two years without a word.'

'I gave you space, because you married Ranjit.'

'I married Ranjit to give you space,' she said. 'And I spent two years helping him cut family ties, and pushing him up a political hill that he was ill-equipped in anything but ambition to climb.'

'So, you inappropriately alienated his family, so that he could misappropriate the family fortune, and in exchange he pushed your slum resettlement agenda? Am I getting this right?'

'Substantially. At least, that was the deal, if he'd stuck to it.'

'Karla, that's . . . kinda nuts, what you were doing with Ranjit.'

'And living with Lisa wasn't nuts, in its own way?'

'Not . . . every day.'

She laughed, and then looked away.

'At the last moment, Ranjit ditched the resettlement program, and pulled out of the race, because of a few scares the other side threw at him.'

'When did that happen?' I asked, thinking that his withdrawal from politics might've had something to do with Lisa's death.

'That day at his office when you came in growling for me, I'd just had it out with him. It was all over. Everything I'd worked for. He'd withdrawn his nomination. He was shaking and sweating. He quit, and you know I can't stand a quitter. I went and sat in the corner while he settled down, and I told him that if we ever found ourselves in the same room again, so long as we lived, we'd sit as far apart as possible.'

'Neither one of us knew he was so scared that day because he thought I knew he'd been with Lisa at the end.'

'I was so happy when you walked in.'

'As happy as I am now?' I asked, kissing her.

'Happier,' she purred. 'I was sitting in the corner, with everything I'd planned and worked for in ruins around me, and then you walked in. I was never more glad to see anyone in my life. I thought, *My hero.*'

'Let me get you something heroic to eat. I don't know about you, but I'm starved.'

'No, let me.'

She brought us a platter of dates, cheese and apples, and wine in long, red glasses with feet like a hawk's claws.

She talked about Kavita Singh, and how Ranjit's disappearance gave Karla one last hand to play, because she had a proxy vote on Ranjit's shares, which he couldn't rescind without resurfacing. Karla elevated Kavita to deputy editor, in exchange for a promise from Kavita to make slum resettlement a banner issue.

Working together, Karla and Kavita developed a citywide beautification program to nudge public consensus toward humane resettlement of slum dwellers, as a matter of civic pride. They played it out on newspaper pages still technically owned by Ranjit.

'The editor was a problem,' Karla said. 'We tried for weeks to get him on the team. He fought us to the fourth quarter on everything. But when he accepted an invitation to the fetish party, it was easy.'

'What was easy?'

'Compliance,' she said. 'Smoke a joint with me.'

'Why were you on Benicia's bike last night?'

712

'Does it hurt more that I was with Benicia, or that I was on her very pretty motorcycle?'

'It all hurts. I don't ever want to see you on any motorcycle but mine, unless you're riding it yourself.'

'Then you'll have to teach me to ride, renegade. You start with your legs wide, right?'

'Wide enough to hold on,' I smiled.

'Smoke a joint with me,' she said, lying back on the bed, her feet in my lap.

'Now?'

'Look, the city's in lockdown. We can't go anywhere. Jaswant has plenty of supplies. I've got a gun. Relax, and smoke a joint with me.'

'I'm pretty relaxed, but okay, if you think it's a good idea.'

'Some doors,' she said slowly, 'can only be opened with the grace of pure desire.'

Some time later she brought us fruit on a blue glass tray, and fed me with her fingers, piece by piece. Love is connection, and happiness is the connected self. She kissed my hands, her hair like wings fanned for the sun. And an instant blessed by a woman's love washed wounds away.

'Compliance,' Karla said, settling in beside me with a glass of wine.

'Compliance?'

'There's nothing like a fetish, to get a man's compliance point out in the open.'

'The chief editor?' I asked, still cocooned in the segue.

'Are you zoning out?' she asked. 'Of *course*, the editor.'

'How did you find out his fetish? Did he present a card, or something?'

'When the guests arrived, we'd already supplied every fetish in the book, with girls in masks, dressed by damnation. We paraded them past him, until one got a reaction. It didn't take long, actually.'

'Which one?'

'Dominatrix, in a fake-leather sari. It's a catalogue item.'

'Then what?'

'Then he got filmed, in a private booth, getting dominated.'

'You and Kavita filmed him?'

'Not just him. We also filmed a judge, a politician, a tycoon and a cop.'

'You set all this up?'

'Kavita and I had a woman on the inside.'

'Who was that?'

'The hostess.'

'Who was?'

'Diva,' she said.

'*Diva*, our Diva, who's next door, with Randall?'

'Our Diva, who left earlier, with Charu and Pari, while you were asleep,' she said. 'Some cars arrived to bring them home. Bodyguards were banging on the door. Jaswant thought the zombies were trying to break in. We pulled the barricade away and —'

'Wait a minute, I slept through all that?'

'Sure, soldier,' she purred. 'Diva said you looked cute.'

'Diva said *what*?'

'She wanted to talk to me, while Charu and Pari were getting ready to leave. It takes those girls a time to do anything. Diva came in here, and we sat on the bed.'

'While I was asleep?'

'Yeah. She was right, you're cuter asleep than awake. It's lucky I've got a weakness for awake.'

'How long was Diva here?'

'We smoked a joint,' Karla said.

'That long?'

'And drank a glass of wine.'

'While I was sleeping?'

'Yeah, she came in to tell me that Kavita had a new secret admirer, and she'd been acting a bit nuts.'

'Kavita *is* a bit nuts,' I said. 'She had a thing with Lisa, and it won't let her go. She's clever and capable, but she's been acting nuts with me, too. I think that's why Madame Zhou likes her — they're as crazy as each other.'

'Kavita did this whole thing with us, Lin,' Karla said. 'She was with us every step of the way.'

'And you put her next in line to run a major daily newspaper.'

'I won't let you talk her down,' she said. 'I won't let anyone talk her or any of my friends down. Just like I wouldn't let anyone talk you down.'

'Okay. Fair call. But it's my job to tell you when I sense a threat.'

'Your job?' She laughed.

'Yeah, and it's your job to warn me,' I smiled. 'So, Diva left with the girls?'

'The bodyguards escorted them away. They had some explaining to do, about staying out all night.'

'And I slept through all of this?'

'Sure did. We helped Jaswant put the barricade back, I showered, got back into bed, and you got very glad to see me. The girls said good-bye, by the way.'

I was feeling strange. I was always the first up, no matter how tired I was, and if someone in a room next door dropped a pen on the floor, I started awake from deep sleep. But somehow, I'd slept through a conversation on my own bed.

It was an unusual feeling, disorienting, all slow pulse rates and blurred edges, and negotiating it was like walking along the deck of a rolling ship. It took me a while to realise what it was: I was feeling peaceful.

Peace, Idriss once said, *is perfect forgiveness, and is the opposite of fear.*

'Are you with me, Shantaram?' Karla smiled, shaking me by the chin.

'I'm so with you, Karla.'

'Okay,' she laughed. 'Where were we?'

'You were telling me how you and Kavita put this together,' I said, holding her close.

'Kavita, Diva and me. Diva's the richest girl in Bombay right now, and when she threw a fetish party, the rich rowed up in limousines.'

'But Diva wasn't even there.'

'We set it up for her to be turned away at a roadblock, and pushed back into the city, with plausible deniability about anything that happened at the party.'

'To cover her assets.'

'To cover her assets,' Karla said, tapping me on the chest in agreement.

It was the first time she ever did it: the first time that little gesture born in who she was, when she was completely relaxed in love, made its way to my skin.

'So, you set up fetish games, and cameras?'

'We had seven targets, counting the editor, but only five of them turned up.'

715

'Targets?'

'Impediments to progress, that we wanted to make vessels of change.'

'And now the five are –'

'Vessels of change, and we'll get slum resettlement, and more attention to women's issues. Win—win, women style.'

I sat up on the bed. She offered me a towel, scented with ginger, and we wiped our faces and hands.

'If these guys are big shots, Karla, they're dangerous, by definition. That film's a bomb, and it'll keep ticking as long as it exists.'

'We've got intermediaries,' she said, leaning into my arm again.

'They'll need to be bulletproof.'

'They are,' she said. 'We've contracted the Cycle Killers to talk for us.'

'Now, that makes things much saner. The Cycle Killers?'

'I don't do anything face to face with anyone but them. They do all the negotiating with the other side.'

'How did that happen?'

'You really wanna know?'

'Of course I wanna know.'

'Well,' she said, sitting up and facing me, her legs lotus. 'Randall and I noticed the Cycle Killers following you, twice, and I sent Randall to find out what they wanted.'

'He fronted the Cycle Killers alone?'

'No doubt.'

'He's a keeper,' I smiled. 'I'm glad he's on board with you.'

'With *us*,' she corrected.

'What do you make of it, Randall and Diva? I know Naveen is crazy about her, and I thought she liked him.'

'It's a lockdown, Shantaram. What happens in a lockdown, stays in a lockdown. Best we keep out of it.'

'You're right, I guess. Go back to the Cycle Killers.'

'So, Randall found out that Abdullah had hired them to watch over you for a while, and he made a couple of friends.'

'And when you found out they were for hire, you hired them.'

'I did, and they were happy to do it.'

'Uh-huh.'

'Yeah, they're working on their image. They'd like to move into more public-minded areas than killing people for money.'

716

'Like *threatening* people for money.'

'Something like that,' she said. 'It's an upward image step, but I think they're serious. I think they wanna come in from the cold.'

'Uh-huh.'

'When I had the Cycle Killers to negotiate for us, I had a plan. I couldn't have done it without them, because I couldn't trust anyone else not to buckle under the pressure, and give us up. When Fate put them behind you, I got them behind me.'

'In front of you, actually.'

'Exactly. Ishmeet, the boss, is the man talking to the vessels of change.'

'I've met Ishmeet.'

'He's a true gentleman,' she said.

'Salt of the moon.'

'And Pankaj, his friend, who really likes you, by the way, is a riot. I invited him to the fetish party.'

'I bet you did. And did I have to be kept so deep in the dark, through this dark scheme?'

'I was protecting you,' she said. 'I was keeping you away from the fire.'

'Like a fool?'

'Like a soul mate,' she said. 'If the whole thing blew up, I wanted to make sure it didn't reach out to you. You're on the run too, remember?'

She was beautiful, in a new way. She was defending me, guarding me with a part of her soul.

She got up to light new incense, seven sticks, fireflies hovering in the coloured room, and put them in the mouths of clay dragons. I watched her moving around the bedroom, and my mind was fighting Time, trying to stop everything but *This*.

She sat down beside me again, taking my hand.

'If I'd told you that I wanted to move the whole city in the direction of humane slum resettlement,' she asked, 'would you have joined me in it, or would you have tried to stop me? Honestly?'

'I would've tried to get you to leave, and set up again somewhere else, with me.'

'That's why I protected you,' she said.

'That's why?'

'You would've helped me, because you love me, but your intention wouldn't have been pure, going in, and that would've made you vulnerable. And me, too, probably.'

I thought about it, not really understanding it, but a different question asked itself.

'Why did you do it, Karla?'

'You don't think the cause is important enough?'

She was teasing me.

'Why did you do it, Karla?'

It was her turn to think. She smiled, and went with honesty.

'To see if I could,' she said. 'I wanted to see if I could do it.'

'I think you can do anything, Karla. But we should've done it together.'

She laughed again.

'You're so loved,' she said. 'And I'm so glad to finally tell you.'

It was too much, it was every dream. Doubt, the thing that fights love, pushed me to the cliff, daring me to jump. I jumped.

'I love you so much, Karla, that I'm lost in it, and I always will be.'

Men don't like to be that honest about love: to put the gun in a woman's hand, and hold it against their own hearts, and say, *Here, this is how you kill me*. But it was okay. It was okay.

'I love you too, baby,' she said, all green queens. 'I always did, even when it looked like I didn't. I'm stuck on you, and you better get used to it, because we're inseparable from now on. You see that, right?'

'I see that,' I said, pulling her down to kiss me. 'You thought all this out pretty long and hard, didn't you?'

'You know me,' she purred. 'I do everything long and hard.'

PART
THIRTEEN

CHAPTER SEVENTY-TWO

I LET OLEG HAVE MY ROOMS FOR A WHILE. The rent was paid out for a year, and I was happy for him to have a home. Oleg was happier. He hugged me off the ground and kissed me. *It's a Russian thing*, he said.

Karla went everywhere with me, even on my black market rounds, and I went everywhere with Karla. We rode together, with Randall always following discreetly in the car.

My round of the money changers was dangerous, but some of what Karla did was almost as dangerous. Her round of art and business contacts was disturbing, but some of what I did was almost as disturbing.

People took a little while to get used to us as a double act, and they reacted in different ways. As it turned out, my friends in the Underworld took it better than her friends in the Overworld.

'You'll have tea with us, Miss Karla,' my black market dealers said to her at every stop. 'Please, have tea with us.'

'No entry,' her white market dealers said to me at every security desk. 'Passes required, beyond this point.'

Karla got me a security pass, and insisted that I sit by her side, everywhere. I got to attend meetings with powerful financial figures, in chambers and panelled rooms that all looked like the inside of the same coffin.

A business suit, Didier once said to me, *is nothing but a military uniform, stripped of its honour.* And it seemed that honour was a word rarely heard in those boardrooms and exclusive club lounges: when Karla spoke it, insisting that her proxy would only be used to support honourable causes, the same waves of distress always passed through the room, puffer-fish faces gasping, and coloured ties flashing in revolving chairs like weeds in a dissonant sea.

The artists were a different story, told by a tall, handsome sculptor, gathering fuel in vacant lots of millionaires.

The gallery had flourished. Scandal is always a seller's market. The scent of it, attached to works that fanatics had attacked, works that had been banned or threatened with bans, seared the sated senses of a wealthy clique of buyers. People with enough money not to queue anywhere waited for appointments, and paid in black market rupees. Taj, the sculptor, was managing the gallery, and making money faster than he could swing a mallet.

He was talking to a ledger of patrons when I walked in with Karla one day, a few weeks after the lockdown. Rosanna was at a desk, working phones.

Taj nodded to Karla, and continued his discourse to the patrons. We walked through to the back room. It had been transformed from motorcycle lights to red fluorescents, a dozen of them, strewn around the room.

We sat on a black silk couch. There were paintings leaning against the walls, a sleeve of one becoming a frame for the other. Anushka brought us chai and biscuits.

When she wasn't in character as a body-language artist, Anushka was a shy young woman, eager to please, and the gallery was a second home for her.

'What's happening, Anush?' Karla asked her, when she sat down on the carpet beside us.

'Same old same old,' she smiled.

'Three days ago you said that the new show of Marathi artists was ready,' Karla said. 'And I don't see it being prepped.'

'There's . . . there's been some argument.'

'Ar . . . gu . . . ment?' Karla said, growling syllables.

Taj walked in and sat down next to Anushka, folding his long legs under him elegantly.

'Sorry,' he said. 'I had to finish with those clients. Big sale. How are you, Karla?'

'I'm hearing about some argument,' she said, staring him down. 'And feeling argumentative.'

Taj looked away from her quickly.

'How are you, Lin?' he asked.

Every time I looked at Taj, I thought of the two mysterious days he'd

722

spent with Karla, somewhere outside Bombay: the days she'd never told me about, because I wouldn't ask her about them.

He was the kind of tall, dark, and handsome that makes the rest of us think jealous thoughts. It's not their fault, the handsome guys. I've known quite a few handsome guys who were great guys, and great friends, and we ugly guys loved them, but even then we were still a little jealous of them, because they were so damn good looking.

It's our fault, of course, not theirs, and it was my fault with Taj, but every time I looked at him, I wanted to interrogate him.

'I'm fine, Taj. How *you* doin'?'

'Oh . . . great,' he said uncertainly.

'Argue me, Taj,' Karla said, pulling his attention. 'What's the problem with the exhibition?'

'Can we get stoned first?' Taj asked, gesturing to Anushka, who rose immediately in search of psychic sustenance. 'I've had back-to-back buyers for the last four hours, and my head is just *spinning* numbers.'

'Where is it?' Karla asked him.

'Anushka's bringing it,' Taj said, pointing helplessly at the door.

'Not the dope,' Karla said. 'The Marathi artists exhibition. Where is it?'

'Still in storage,' Taj said, looking at the door, and calling Anushka with his mind.

'In storage?'

Anushka returned, smoking a very large joint, which she passed to Taj urgently. The sculptor held his hand out to Karla, pleading with her to wait while he smoked his way into a small cloud, and finally offered the joint to me.

'You know I don't smoke with Karla on the bike,' I said, not moving to take it. 'I've told you that before. Stop offering it to me.'

'*I'll* take it,' Karla said, swiping the joint from his hand. 'And I'll take that explanation, Taj.'

'Look,' Taj said, stoned enough to pretend well again. 'People feel that devoting an exhibition to one group of artists, from one language group, is not the direction they want to go.'

'People?'

'People here at the gallery,' Taj said. 'They *like* the Marathi artists exhibition, but they're just not *comfortable* with it.'

'You've been running a Bengali artists exhibition here for the last two weeks,' Karla said.

'That's a different context,' Taj struggled.

'Explain me the difference.'

'Well, I, that is . . . '

'I love this city, and I'm damn glad to live here,' Karla said, leaning toward him. 'We're on Marathi land, living in a Marathi city, by the grace of the Marathi people, who've given us a pretty fine place to live in. The exhibition is for them, Taj, not you.'

'It's so political,' Taj replied.

'No, it's not. All of these artists are good, and some of them are terrific,' she insisted. 'You said so yourself. I hand-picked them, with Lisa.'

'They're good, of course, but that's not really the point here.'

'The point for you, and me, and Rosanna, and Anushka,' she said, 'and all the others in the team who weren't born here in Bombay, is that it's simply the right and grateful thing to showcase talent from the city that sustains us.'

'Karla, you're asking too much,' Taj pleaded.

'I want this show, Taj,' Karla said. 'It was my last project with Lisa.'

'And I'd love to give it to you,' Taj moaned. 'But it's just impossible.'

'Where's the art?' Karla asked.

'I told you. It's still in the warehouse.'

'Send it to the Jehangir gallery,' she said.

'The whole exhibition?' he asked, stricken. 'There are some fine paintings in there, Karla, and if they were put on the market, in the right way, one at a time —'

'Send it to the Jehangir gallery,' she said. 'They've got the integrity to run it, and they deserve it more than you do.'

'But, Karla,' he pleaded.

'I think we're done here,' she said to me, standing up.

Taj unfolded his tall frame to stand in front of her.

'Please reconsider this, Karla,' he said.

He grabbed her arm.

I shoved him away.

'Stay back, Taj,' I said quietly.

'You're making a mistake, Karla,' he said. 'We're really moving into big money, here at the gallery.'

'I've *got* money,' Karla said. 'What I *want* is respect. I'm done here,

Taj. The gallery is yours, from now on. Be as apolitical as you like. I'm walking out. The exhibition insurance is on you, while you send the Marathi show to me, so make sure nothing happens before it reaches the Jehangir. Good luck, and goodbye.'

We rode away, switching to one of my rounds.

'You know he's gay, right?' Karla asked as we rode, her arm over my shoulder.

'I know *who's* gay?'

'Taj.'

'Taj is gay?'

'You didn't know, did you?'

'Unless people tell me, I almost never know.'

'And you were jealous, right?'

I thought about it for a kilometre or so.

'Are you saying you can't be attracted to a gay man?'

She thought about it, for a kilometre or so.

'Good point,' she said. 'But not *that* gay man.'

'But you went away with him for two days.'

'To a spa,' she said. 'To drink juices, and get myself recharged for the fight. Taj just came along for company, to work out gallery stuff.'

'And I couldn't have come along for company, to work out stuff?'

'I was protecting you from my schemes, remember?' she said, whispering into my ear. 'And anyway, Didier likes him.'

'Didier and the sculptor?'

'Taj has already done some nude studies of Didier. They're pretty good.'

'He's going to make a statue of Didier?'

'Yeah.'

'I'll never hear the end of this.'

'Oh, yeah. I promised we'd be there for the unveiling.'

'I might pass. I've already seen Didier unveiled.'

'He's doing Didier as Michelangelo's *David*, at forty-nine years old.'

'I'm definitely not going.'

I slowed the bike and stopped at the kerb of a wide, relatively empty boulevard. When you ride the Island City's streets for long enough, you get to feel them.

'What's up?' she asked.

'The traffic's not right,' I said, looking around.

'What's not right about it?'

'There isn't any. The cops are holding it back for some reason.'

A fleet of cars passed us at speed, lights flashing red as new blood. A second cavalcade followed, and a third. We watched them rush lines of light into the night until the street was quiet again, and the normal traffic resumed.

'They're heading to Bandra in a hurry,' I said, as I put the bike into gear, and rode away slowly. 'Cops and journalists. Must be something big.'

'Do you care?' she said, her arm around my shoulder.

'No,' I called back. 'Come and meet somebody cool. I have to drop some money off at a bank.'

Half-Moon Auntie excelled herself for Karla. At one point she sent me away, telling me that the next portion of her performance was for women only.

I slipped and slid away at slow speed on the fish-oil floor, resisting the impulse to glance back.

'Nice,' Karla said, when she joined me in the Colaba market. 'That's some serious yoga. Someone absolutely has to paint that woman.'

'Maybe one of your young painters?'

'Good idea,' she laughed. 'I think we're going to do some pretty interesting stuff together, Shantaram.'

'You got that right.'

A young prostitute, from the Regal Circle sex roundabout, was returning home through the market to her hut in the fishermen's slum. Her name was Circe, and she was a handful.

Her bing, if she hadn't made enough money, was to pester men to have sex with her until they did, or until they paid her to stop pestering.

'Hey, Shantaram,' she said. 'Fuck me long, double price.'

'Hi, Circe,' I said, trying to pass her, but she scampered into my path, her hands on her hips.

'Fuck me quick, fuck me long, you shit!'

'Bye, Circe,' I said, dodging away again, but she grabbed her yellow sari in her hands, and ran around to face me again.

'You fuck, or you pay,' she said, seizing my arm mid-pester, and trying to rub against me.

Karla shoved her in the chest with both hands, sending her reeling away.

'Stay back, Circe,' she growled in Hindi, her fists raised.

Circe brushed her sari into place and walked away, avoiding Karla's eyes.

'Oh, so that's how it's done,' I said.

'Cute girl,' Karla said. 'Ever since the fetish party, all I've met are people I would've added to the list.'

'I'll bet. I've finished my rounds. Where to next, Miss Karla?'

'Now, my love, we rise all the way to the bottom of the pork barrel.'

CHAPTER SEVENTY-THREE

WE RODE SOUTH TO THE TAJ MAHAL HOTEL, where Karla had a meeting with stockholders of Ranjit's media conglomerate.

Early evening was still gold in the eyes of the Sikh security team that greeted Karla at the hotel. She was wearing clear plastic sandals and a grey boilermaker suit she'd cut up, leaving wide, open shoulders, and roped in with a belt made of black plaited hemp. Her hair was styled by the wind, on the back of my motorcycle, and looked pretty good.

I was wearing black jeans, my denim vest and a Keith Richards T-shirt I'd bartered off Oleg, and looked not so pretty good for a business meeting. But I didn't care: they weren't dressed for my world, either.

The meeting was in the business clubrooms. We stepped into a tiny elevator. As the doors closed, I offered Karla my flask. She sipped it and passed it back as the elevator opened on a narrow corridor, leading to a treasure room of affluently understated decadence.

Leather chairs and couches, each one the price of a family car, were parked against wide mahogany panels, imported from faraway countries where mahogany trees are murdered for their flesh. Crystal glasses stung the eyes with glittering reflections, carpets surrendered like sponges, expensive paintings of expansive business leaders enriched the walls, and white-gloved waiters waited patiently on every unfulfilled need.

There were six businessmen in the room, all of them well dressed and well preserved. When we entered the clubroom they froze, staring at Karla.

'I am so very sorry for your loss, Karla-Madame,' one of the businessmen said.

'So very sorry, Madame,' others said.

I looked at Karla. She was reading their eyes and faces. Wherever it led, she didn't like it.

'Something happened to Ranjit,' she said.

'You don't know?'

'Know what?' Karla asked quietly.

'Ranjit has expired, Karla-Madame,' the businessman said. 'He was shot by someone, tonight, in Bandra. Just now. It is on the news.'

I realised that the red cavalcades of police cars and press cars we'd seen, rushing toward Bandra, were racing to the scene of Ranjit's shooting. Karla had the same idea. She looked at me.

'Are you okay?' I asked.

She nodded, her lips taut.

'If you will excuse me, gentlemen,' she said, her voice firm. 'I will ask you to adjourn this meeting for forty-eight hours, if that is suitable.'

'Of course, Karla-Madame.'

'Anything you say, Karla-Madame.'

'Take all the time you need, Karla-Madame.'

'So sorry for your loss.'

In the elevator she clung to me, her face in my chest, and cried. Then the elevator jammed to a halt, stuck between floors.

She stopped crying, wiped her eyes, and looked around with a widening smile.

'Hello, Ranjit,' she said. 'Come out and fight me like a ghost.'

The elevator started again, and began to descend.

'Goodbye, Ranjit,' I said.

On the street, beside the bike, I held her hand.

'What do you want to do?'

'If I could, if he's still there,' she said, 'I'd like to identify him. I don't want to do it in the morgue.'

I took her to Bandra, riding fast, Randall following behind. We pulled up at a press cordon, established near the dance bar where Ranjit's silver bullet had found him.

His body was still inside the nightclub. The police were waiting to remove the corpse of the famous tycoon, we heard, because one of the major television reporters hadn't arrived. Karla, Randall and I took up a position in the crowd with a view of the arc lights trained by local camera crews on the entrance to the nightclub.

I didn't feel good about it. I didn't want to see Ranjit's body being carried out on a gurney. And there were a lot of cops standing around.

I looked at Karla. She was blazing queens, scanning the scene, taking in the large broadcast vans, the arc lights, and the lines of cops.

'You sure you want to do this?'

'I have to do it,' she said. 'It's my last job for Ranjit's family. My way to make it up to them for playing Ranjit's game, I guess.'

Karla lurched forward through the press cordon. Cameras flashed. I was half a pace behind her, and Randall was at my side.

'Stand aside,' Randall said calmly in Marathi and Hindi, passing through the ranks of the cops and journalists. 'Please, show respect. Please, show respect.'

The press and the cops let Karla into the club, but stopped Randall and me at the door. We waited for ten long minutes until she came back to us. Her head was high, her eyes staring straight ahead, but she was resting on the arm of a senior officer.

'It is a terrible business, Madame,' the officer said. 'We have not completed our enquiries, but it seems that your husband was shot by a young man, who —'

'I can't discuss this now,' Karla said.

'Of course not, Madame,' the OIC said quickly.

'Please, excuse my rudeness,' Karla said, stopping him with a raised hand. 'I simply wanted you to attest that I have identified Ranjit's body. His family must be informed, quickly, and with my positive identification you can now perform that onerous task, isn't that so?'

'Yes, Madame.'

'Then, do you attest my identification, and will you inform Ranjit's family?'

'I attest it, Madame,' the officer said, saluting. 'And I will perform that duty.'

'Thank you, sir,' Karla said, shaking his hand. 'You no doubt have questions you would like to ask me. I'll visit your office at any time that you require me.'

'Yes, Madame. Please, take my card. And may I express my sorrow, for your loss.'

'Thank you again, sir,' Karla said.

When we left the cordon of cops to walk back to the bike, some photographers tried to take Karla's picture. Randall held them back, and paid them to stop shouting for the freedom of the press.

We rode back to the south, and she cried, her cheek pressed against my back. When we stopped at a traffic light, Randall jumped from the car and offered her tissues from a red ceramic box. Karla accepted them, before the signal changed. And I think that little, thoughtful act saved her, because she stopped crying after that, and simply clung to me, and never cried for Ranjit again.

CHAPTER SEVENTY-FOUR

I TOOK HER BACK TO THE AMRITSAR HOTEL, and the Bedouin tent. She let me undress her and put her to bed: one of a lover's treasures. And she slept through dawn and daylight, and violet evening, and woke under an exile moon.

She stretched, saw me, and looked around her.

'How long have I been out?'

'A day,' I said. 'It's nearly midnight. You missed tomorrow.'

She sat upright quickly, messing her hair perfect.

'Midnight?'

'Yeah.'

'Were you watching me, while I slept?'

'I was too busy. I wrote out a pretty eloquent statement for the cops, and signed it for you, and delivered it. They liked it. You don't have to go back.'

'You did all that?'

'How you feeling?' I smiled.

'I'm good,' she said, wriggling off the bed. 'I'm good. And I gotta pee.'

She came back showered, in a white silk robe, and I was trying to think of a way to let her talk about Ranjit, dead Ranjit, and what it felt like, seeing his body, when there was a knock on the door.

'That's Naveen's knock,' Karla said. 'You wanna let him in?'

'You know his knock?'

I opened the door and welcomed the young detective into the tent.

'What's up, kid?' I asked.

'I'm so sorry about Ranjit, Karla,' he said.

'Someone had to kill him,' Karla replied, lighting a small joint. 'I'm just glad it wasn't me. It's okay, Naveen. I slept it off, and I'm okay.'

'Good,' he said. 'Glad to see you're still punching.'

He stared at me, then at Karla, then at me again.

'What's up?' I asked.

'Sorry,' he said. 'Just getting my head around the two of you being together all the time.'

'Uh-huh.'

'There's a hotel pool, you know,' he said happily, 'on how long Oleg gets to keep your rooms. Oleg picked three —'

'Any other news, Naveen?' I asked, pulling on jeans.

'Oh, yeah,' he said. 'Dennis is ending his trance, tonight. There's gonna be a lot of people there. I thought . . . maybe . . . you need to get out in the air, Karla.'

Karla looked interested in seeing Dennis rise from his two-year sleep, but I wasn't sure if she was ready for distraction. I wasn't sure I was ready for it myself. I'd stayed up most of the night and day, watching over Karla and paying the cops to leave her alone. And the whole time I'd asked myself again and again the questions about Ranjit and Lisa, that only Ranjit, dead Ranjit, could answer.

'You wanna go out, or stay in, girl?'

'And miss a resurrection? I'll be ready in five,' she said.

'Okay, I'm in,' I said, pulling on a shirt. 'It's not every day someone rises from the dead.'

We walked down to the arch beneath the hotel and found Randall sitting in the back of the car. He was reading a copy of *Bury My Heart at Wounded Knee*, the interior lights a blue-white blush on his face.

Karla had given him the car, because he refused to stop following her while she rode with me, just in case she needed him. He'd accepted the gift, and transformed the capacious rear seats into a sleeping lounge, complete with a small refrigerator running on battery power, and a sound system that was better than mine.

He was barefoot, in black trousers and a white, open-necked shirt. His bronze, Goan eyes, faded by generations of sun and sea, were filled with happy light. He stepped from the car, and slipped into his sandals.

He was handsome, tall, smart and brave. As he came to greet Karla, smiling teeth at her like shells on a perfect shore, I could see why Diva liked him so much.

'How are you, Miss Karla?' Randall asked, taking her hand for a moment.

'I'm fine, Randall,' she said. 'Got a nip you can give me, from your well-stocked bar? I had a bad dream last night, and I'm thirsty.'

'Coming up,' Randall replied, opening the door of the car and fetching a small bottle of vodka.

'To the spirits of the departed,' Karla said, throwing it back in two gulps. 'Now, let's go raise the dead.'

'Would this be the rise of Dennis the Sleeping Baba, Miss Karla?'

'Indeed it is, Randall,' she replied wistfully. 'Instead of a wake, let's have an awake, shall we?'

'With unadulterated pleasure,' he smiled, sad for what she'd been through, but glad that she was up and out again. 'To the psychic resuscitation it is.'

'And not a death certificate too soon,' Naveen added.

I looked at the Indian–Irish detective, who was talking to Randall while he prepared the car, and wondered what thoughts roamed his mind: for three weeks, Randall had been dating the woman Naveen loved. I liked Randall, and I liked Naveen, almost as much as they seemed to like each other. Naveen hugged Randall, and Randall hugged Naveen. It looked genuine, and it was confusing: if things got ugly, I wouldn't know which one to hit.

'I'll leave my bike, and ride with Randall,' Naveen said, as Karla and I saddled up the bike.

We rode between satin banners of traffic to the Colaban hive of ancient housing, near Sassoon Dock. The night smell of dead and dying sea things followed us past the dock, and lingered to the colony of verandas where Dennis reposed.

There was a crowd on the street. Huge buses on the regular route ploughed fields of penitents, who moved aside in waves of heads and shoulders to let the metal whales swim through.

We worked our way to a place near the front with a view of the veranda where Dennis, it was expected, would emerge from his long self-induced coma.

People were holding candles and oil lamps. Some were holding bunches of incense. Others were chanting.

Dennis appeared, standing in the doorway of his rooms. He looked at the wide veranda for a moment as if it was a red-tiled river, and then looked up at the crowd of supplicants gathered on the street a few steps below.

'Hello, all and everyone, here and there,' he said. 'It is quiet in death. I have been there, and I can tell you that it is very quiet, unless someone kills your high.'

People shouted and cheered, calling out names for the Divine. Dennis took tentative steps. The crowd screamed and chanted. He walked across the balcony, down the steps, onto the road, and then collapsed in the centre of the crowd.

'Now, this is entertainment,' Karla said.

'You figure?' I asked, watching believers rain tears on Dennis, who was horizontal again.

'Oh, he'll get up again,' Karla replied, leaning against me. 'I think the show only just started.'

Dennis sat up suddenly, scattering the crowd awaiting his blessing.

'I have it,' he said. 'I know what I must do.'

'What is it?' several voices asked.

'The dead,' Dennis said, his deep voice clear in the hush. 'I must serve them. They, too, need ministry.'

'The dead, Dennis?' someone asked.

'Exclusively the dead,' he replied.

'But how to serve them?' another voice asked.

'First of all,' Dennis appealed to them, 'do you think I could smoke a very strong chillum? Being alive again is killing my high. Will someone prepare a chillum, please?'

Dozens attended to that, making the task more complex than required, until Billy Bhasu finally squatted beside the stricken monk of sleeping, and offered him a chillum.

Dennis smoked. People prayed. Someone rang temple bells. Someone else clanged finger cymbals, while a faint voice recited Sanskrit mantras.

'This guy is a movie,' Karla said.

She cocked her head over my shoulder to look at Randall, half a pace behind us.

'Are you clocking this, Randall?'

'Quite a spectacle, Miss Karla,' Randall said. 'Spontaneous canonisation.'

'You've got to give it to Dennis,' Naveen added. 'He's his own universe.'

Dennis struggled to his feet. A palanquin arrived, borne by sturdy young men threading their way through the crowd with shouts and grunts. It was the same bier that carried the dead to the burning ghats, but it had been modified to accommodate a chair, covered with silver imitation leather.

The young men put the palanquin on the ground, helped Dennis into the chair, then raised it to their shoulders and carried Dennis away on their long march to the Gateway of India monument.

Dennis smiled benevolently, blessing upturned faces with the chillum in his hand.

'I love this guy,' Karla said. 'Let's follow the parade.'

We rode beside and around the procession, winding through leafy streets to the Gateway monument. The crowd of people grew, as drummers and dancers and trumpet players left their homes to join the march. By the end of the procession there were more people who had no idea what it was all about than people who started the parade.

And by the time we rode to a vantage point, Dennis was in the centre of a frenzy that welcomed him home, whether they knew it or not, from years of silent penance.

A hundred metres away in the chambers of the Taj Mahal hotel, men who ruled the Overworld were networking: a pro-business government had been selected by them, and elected by the poor, and successful men were throwing nets into a new sea of commercial corruption.

Five hundred metres away, Vishnu, the head of the newly named 307 Company, after the number in the Indian penal code covering attempted murder, ruled the Underworld in a ruthless purge of Muslims from his gang. The only ones allowed to stay were the ones who told him about Pakistan, and everything else they knew about fallen Sanjay's schemes.

Abdullah vanished, after the fire, and no-one knew where he was, or what he was planning. The other Muslims from the original Company broke away, gathered again in the heart of the Muslim bazaars in Dongri, and opened closer ties with gun suppliers from Pakistan.

The riots had scarred the city, as they always do: calls for calm from leaders high and low couldn't still the rills of fear. Beyond the horror of communal violence itself, there was the cold realisation that such a thing can happen at all, even in a city as beautiful and loving as the Island City.

Karla clapped in time with the chanting. Randall and Naveen wagged their heads from side to side, going with the beat. And hundreds of the poor and the sick struggled and pressed through the thickening throng to touch the palanquin carrying Dennis, risen in glory.

Lights shone on the huge Gateway Monument, but from where we stood, the wide archway was just a slender thread: the eye of the needle that the camel of the British Raj couldn't pass through.

The sea beyond was a black mirror, scattering lights from hundreds of small boats in jagged waves: fingerprints of light pressed on a pane of the sea.

And desperate prayers echoed from the Trojan tower that the British left in the Island City: sounds that moved away, like every sound, eternally.

Every sound we utter goes on forever, continuing through space and time until long after we're gone. Our home, our Earth, transmits to the universe whatever we shout, or scream, or pray, or sing. The listening universe, that night, in that somehow sacred space, heard prayers and cries of pain, raised by hope.

'Let's ride,' Karla said, swinging onto the back of my bike.

We swung away from the Gateway area slowly, giving Randall and Naveen time. And the crowd chanted louder, cleansing the conflicted signals in the Island City's air, for a while, with the purity of their plea.

CHAPTER SEVENTY-FIVE

HAPPINESS ABHORS A VACUUM. Because I was so happy with Karla, the sadness in Naveen's eyes reached deeper into the pool of empathy than it might've done, if sadness was still a vacuum in my own heart, as well. The brave love in his affection seemed to have retreated, and I wanted to know if it was recovering, or defeated.

When we returned to the Amritsar hotel, I got a moment to pull Naveen's sleeve in the corridor behind Jaswant's desk.

'What's going on?' I asked him.

'Going on?'

'Randall is dating the woman you love, and you're huggin' him like a brother. I don't get it.'

He bristled, in the way that dangerous young animals bristle, more from reflex than rage.

'You know, Lin, there are things that are private, for a reason.'

'Fuck that, you Irish-Indian. What's going on?'

He relaxed, sure that I cared, and leaned against the wall.

'I can't do that world,' he said. 'I can't even *be* in that world, unless I'm asking uncomfortable questions, or helping to arrest someone.'

'What world?'

'*Her world*,' he said, as if they were his words for hell.

'You don't have to join her *world*, to be her *boyfriend*,' I said. 'Randall is dating her, and he lives in his car.'

'Is that supposed to make me feel good?'

'It's supposed to make you realise that when you went on that more-than-a-date with Benicia, you messed it up. You gotta make it right. You earn the love you feel, man.'

He hung his head as if it was the third round of a six-round fight he couldn't win. I felt bad. I didn't want to depress him: I wanted him to know that he was Randall, and then some. And I wanted to remind him that Diva knew it, too.

'Look, kid –'

'No,' he said. 'It's okay. I hear what you say, but I'm not fighting this, and I never will.'

'If you don't get it out in the open now, it'll come out with someone else, later on. And that'll be on you, because you can fix this now.'

He smiled, and stood up straight, his eyes on mine.

'You're a good friend, Lin,' he said. 'But you're shaking the wrong bush. I'm a free man, and Diva's a free woman, and that's the way it should be.'

'I said my piece,' I said, still saying my piece, 'but I don't see you quitting.'

'Every peace is made by somebody quitting,' he shrugged.

I looked at him, squinting the truth out of him.

'You practised that for Karla, didn't you?'

'Yeah,' he confessed, smiling. 'But it's true, in this case. I'm not going there, Lin, and I'd appreciate it if you don't go there again either, after this. I really mean it. And I've got nothing against Randall. He's a good guy. Better him than a bad guy.'

'You got it,' I said, sadder than he was, it seemed. 'Let's go see what Karla is doing.'

Karla was on the carpeted floor with Didier, doing a séance with a ouija board.

'Oh, no, I cannot continue,' Didier said, when we walked in. 'Your energy is so disruptive, Lin.'

'One of your finest qualities,' Karla said. 'Come sit here, Shantaram, and see if we can disrupt the spirits of the Amritsar hotel.'

'There's too many spirits in this town that I knew in person,' I said, smiling. 'And speaking of spirits, Didier, that box of wine you ordered is sitting on Jaswant's desk. You'd better get on it, before he taxes it. He loves red wine.'

Didier scrambled upright and hurled himself through the door.

'My wine!' he said, as he fled. 'Jaswant!'

Naveen walked out after him to help. I walked over to Karla, pushed her back on the carpet, lay down beside her, and kissed her.

'See how tricky I am?' I said, when our lips parted.

'I know exactly how tricky you are,' she laughed, 'because I'm trickier.'

Kisses without consequence or expectation: kisses as gifts, feeding her, feeding me with love.

There was a knock on the open door. It was Jaswant, and Jaswant wasn't a go-away guy.

'Yes, Jaswant?' I said, leaning away from Karla to look at him, framing the doorway.

'There are some people to see you,' he whispered. 'Hello, Miss Karla.'

'Hello, Jaswant,' she said. 'Have you lost weight? You look so fit.'

'Well, I try to keep –'

'What people, Jaswant?' I asked.

'People. To see you. Scary people. At least, the woman is scary.'

Madame Zhou, I thought. Karla and I were on our feet at the same time. I was reaching for weapons. Karla was putting on lipstick.

'Lipstick?'

'If you think I'll see that woman without lipstick,' she said, ruffling her hair in the mirror, 'you just don't get it.'

'You're so . . . right. I don't get it.'

'I have to *kill* her, before I kill her,' she said, turning to me. 'So, let's go kill her, twice.'

We slipped from her rooms to Jaswant's foyer, Karla beside me.

Acid. Karla. Acid. Karla.

I had my knife in my hand. Karla had a gun, and knew how to use it. We edged around the partition wall to see the desk area clearly, and saw two people standing in front of Jaswant's desk. Jaswant looked worried.

I edged around further. I couldn't see the man, but the woman was short, thirty and chunky. She was wearing a menacing stare and a blue hijab.

'It's okay,' I said to Karla, walking into view. 'We're old friends.'

'That's stretching it,' Blue Hijab said, still menacing Jaswant into his swanky chair.

'Identity approved,' Jaswant said. 'Please go through, Madame.'

She was with Ankit, the concierge of the hotel in Sri Lanka. He smiled and saluted, two fingers against his brow.

I waved back. Blue Hijab had her arms folded. She kept them folded as she scowled Jaswant deeper into his seat, then came to greet me. Ankit was a step behind.

'*Salaam aleikum*, soldier,' I said.

'*Wa aleikum salaam*,' she said, unfolding her arms to show the very small automatic pistol she had in her hand. 'We have unfinished business.'

'*Salaam aleikum*,' Karla said. 'And that's my boyfriend you're talking to with a gun in your hand.'

'*Wa aleikum salaam*,' Blue Hijab said, staring back at the queens. 'The gun is a gift. And it's still loaded.'

'Just like mine,' Karla smiled, and Blue Hijab smiled back.

'Blue Hijab,' I said, 'meet Karla. Karla, meet Blue Hijab.'

The women stared at one another, saying nothing.

'And this is Ankit,' I added.

'A distinct privilege to meet you, Miss Karla,' Ankit said.

'Hi, Ankit,' Karla said, her eyes on Blue Hijab.

'Ankit makes a drink that's gonna make Randall absinthe with envy. It's like a liquid portal between dimensions. You've gotta try it.'

'Always a pleasure to prepare the portal for you, sir.'

'You girls have got so much in common,' I said, and thought to say more, but Blue Hijab and Karla looked at me in exactly the same not very flattering way, and I unthought it.

'You marry them,' Blue Hijab said, 'hoping they'll change, and grow. And they marry us, hoping that we won't.'

'The connubial Catch 22,' Karla said, taking Blue Hijab by the arm and leading her back to the Bedouin tent. 'Come with me, you poor girl, and freshen up. You look very tired. How far have you come today?'

'Not so far, today, but twenty-one hours yesterday, and the day before that,' Blue Hijab said before her voice faded, and Karla shut the door.

Jaswant, Ankit and I were staring at the closed door.

'That's one very scary woman,' Jaswant said, wiping sweat from his neck. 'I thought Miss Karla was scary, no offence, baba, but I swear, if I'd seen that woman in the blue hijab coming up the stairs in time, I'd have been in the tunnel.'

'She's okay,' I said. 'She's more than okay, in fact. She's damn cool.'

'I noticed a liquor store not far from here on our arrival, sir,' Ankit said. 'Might I presume to buy the ingredients for your special cocktail, and prepare a portal or two for you, while we await the ladies?'

'Buy?' Jaswant said, throwing the switch and opening the panel to his survival store.

He threw the next switch, and the lights began to flash. His finger hovered over the third switch.

'You know, Jaswant —' I tried, but I was too late.

The stomp and shake jive music of Bhangra banged from the desk speakers.

I looked at Ankit as he inspected the goods in Jaswant's secret store. His grey hair had been cut to Cary Grant sleekness, and he'd grown a thin moustache. A thigh-length, navy blue tunic with high collars and matching serge trousers replaced his hotel service uniform.

He looked over Jaswant's goods with a scholarly eye: a debonair affair examining baubles in adultery's window.

'I think we can work with this,' he said.

Then the Bhangra got to Ankit, and he backed away from the coloured window and started to dance. He wasn't bad: good enough to get Jaswant out of the chair and dancing with him until the end of the song.

'Want to hear it again?' Jaswant puffed, his finger over the switch.

'Yes!' Ankit said.

'Business before pleasure,' I essayed.

'That's true,' Jaswant conceded, coming around to the secret window. 'Let me know what you want.'

'I need to do a little chemistry,' Ankit said. 'And I believe that you have all the right chemicals.'

'Alright,' I said. 'Let's get these drinks under way. We're in for the night. Karla and I have nowhere to go, and all the time in the world to get there. Do your stuff, Ankit.'

Bottles poured, lime juice filled a beaker, coconut dessicated, bitter chocolate was grated into powdered flakes, glasses appeared, and we three men were just about to test the first batch of Ankit's alchemy when Karla called out to me.

'Start without me, guys,' I said, putting my glass down.

'You're leaving the cocktail party before it starts?' Jaswant objected.

'Save my glass,' I said. 'If you hear gunplay while I'm in there, come and rescue me.'

CHAPTER SEVENTY-SIX

I FOUND BLUE HIJAB AND KARLA sitting cross-legged on the floor near the balcony, the carpets around them a pond of knotted meditations. There was a silver tray with rose and mint flavoured almonds, slivers of dark chocolate and chips of glazed ginger, beside half-drunk glasses of lime juice. Red and yellow lights flashing at the signals below blushed their faces softly in the darkened room. The slow overhead fan fretted incense smoke into scrolls, and a slow breeze reminded us that the night, outside, was vast.

'Sit here, Shantaram,' Karla said, pulling me down beside her. 'Blue Hijab has to go soon. But before she does, she's got some good news, and some not so good news.'

'How are you?' I asked. 'Are you okay?'

'I'm fine, *Alhamdulillah*. Do you want the *good* first, or the not so good?'

'Let's have the not so good,' I said.

'Madame Zhou is still alive,' Blue Hijab said. 'And still free.'

'And the good news?'

'Her acid throwers are finished, and the twins are dead.'

'Wait a minute,' I said. 'Can we back this up? How come you know about Madame Zhou? And how come you're here?'

'I didn't know about Madame Zhou,' she said. 'And I wasn't interested in her. I wanted the acid throwers. We've been hunting them for a year.'

'They burned someone you know,' I realised. 'I'm sorry to hear that.'

'She was a good fighter, and she's still a good comrade and a good friend. She was on leave in India, from the war. Somebody hired those two acid throwers, and they made her face into a mask. A protest mask, I suppose you could say.'

743

'Is she still alive?' Karla asked.

'She is.'

'Is there anything we can do?'

'I don't think so, Karla,' Blue Hijab said. 'Unless you'd like to help her punish the acid throwers, which she's doing now, as we speak. It will go on for some time, yet.'

'You caught the acid throwers?' Karla asked. 'Did anyone get burned?'

'We threw blankets on them, and kicked them until they shoved their acid bottles out from under the blankets, and then we dragged them away.'

'And the twins jumped in to help them,' I said, 'thinking you were a threat to Madame Zhou.'

'They did. We didn't realise they were protecting Madame Zhou. We didn't care. We wanted the acid throwers. Madame Zhou ran away, and we let her run. We stopped the twins, and grabbed the acid throwers.'

'You stopped the twins for good?'

'Yes.'

'What did you do with them?'

'We left them there. That's why I have to leave soon, *Inshallah*.'

'Whatever you need, it's yours,' I said. 'How did you think to tell me about this?'

'We took the acid throwers to a slum. Four brothers and twenty-four cousins of the girl they burned are all living there. And the girl is living there, with a lot of other people who love her. We questioned the acid throwers. We wanted a list of every girl they've ever burned.'

'Why?'

'So we could visit the families, later, one by one, and tell that them those men are dead, and will never do it to another girl. And then to visit every one of the clients who paid them to burn girls, and make them pay in cash for the hell they spat on them, and give the money to the girls they ordered burned, *Inshallah*.'

'Blue Hijab,' Karla said, 'I know we only just met, but I love you.'

She put her hand on Karla's wrist.

'When the acid throwers started talking,' she said, turning to me, 'we heard your name on their list. They told me they'd been following you for the Madame, that woman in black who ran away. I got the acid throwers to tell me where you live, and I came to warn you about the woman.'

It was a shock, a lot of shocks, and one of them was the thought of the acid throwers, being tortured to death by people they'd tortured. It was too much to think about.

'Thanks for the heads-up, Blue Hijab,' I said. 'You're leaving tonight. How can we help you?'

'I have everything I need for myself,' Blue Hijab said, 'but I must be far away from here, by morning. My problem is Ankit. I can't go on with him, because the sudden change in plans allows for only one of us to be smuggled at a time. I know he will insist on staying, and letting me go on, and that is what I have to do, but I'm afraid to leave him.'

'No-one will harm him if he stays here with us,' I said.

'No,' she said. 'I'm afraid to leave him, because he's so violent.'

I thought of the amiable night porter with the delicate anticipation of others' needs, the debonair moustache and the perfect cocktail, and I couldn't put it together.

'Ankit?'

'He's a very capable agent,' Blue Hijab said. 'One of the best, and most dangerous. Not many made it to grey hair in this war. But it's time for him to retire. His last assignment was almost three years as the night porter in a hotel, where every journalist enjoyed a drink, and liked to talk. But he's too well known now. That was his last assignment. I was supposed to take him to contacts in Delhi, where he can find a new life, but shooting the twins changed the plan.'

'Is he wanted?' I asked. 'Should we hide him?'

'No,' she frowned. 'Why would he be wanted?'

'Two dead twins come to mind.'

'My comrades and I shot the twins. He's not involved at all.'

'The twins were hard men to stop. You shot them with that little gun?'

'Of course not,' she said, taking the small automatic from the pocket of her skirt and holding it in her palm. 'I only shoot my husband with this gun. That's why he stole it from me.'

'But you had it in your hand when you said hello,' I smiled.

'For a different reason,' she said, her thoughts dreaming into the pistol in her hand.

'Can I see it?' Karla asked.

Blue Hijab passed the small pistol to her. Karla looked it over, finding the place in her palm where lines of intent meet the power of consequence. She allowed her eyes to drift slowly upward until they met mine.

'Nice,' she said, passing the gun back to Blue Hijab. 'Wanna see mine?'

'Of course,' Blue Hijab replied. 'But I want you to keep this pistol. I'm going to meet my Mehmu soon, *Inshallah*, and I know I won't need it this time, or ever again. We've been talking, and things are very good now, *Alhamdulillah*.'

'You want me to have it?' Karla asked, taking the small automatic back.

'Yes, I was planning to give it to Shantaram, but now that I met you, I think it should go to you. Do you accept my gift?'

'I do.'

'Good. Then I would like to see your gun.'

Karla had a matt black snub-nosed five-shot .38 revolver. She took it from beneath a flap of carpet beside her, flipped the chamber open, let the cartridges fall into her lap, and snapped the empty chamber back in place.

'No offence,' she said, handing the gun to Blue Hijab. 'Hair trigger.'

Blue Hijab examined the small, deadly weapon expertly, and handed it back. She felt the heft of her own gun again reassuringly, closing palm to fingers, while Karla reloaded the snub-nosed pistol.

For a few seconds they both looked up at me, guns in hand, their expressions thoughtful, but strangely blank at the same time. For me, it was a wall of womanness in their eyes, and I had no idea what was going on. I was just glad to be a witness; to see two wild, strong-minded women meet.

'Blue Hijab,' Karla said, after a while, 'please let me give you a gift in return.'

She pulled the long spike from the curl at the back of her head, shaking panther-paws of black hair free to prowl.

'For when you're *not* wearing a hijab,' she said, offering the hairpin. 'Be very careful. Only ever hold it by the jewel, as I am. Hair trigger.'

It was a blowpipe dart. There was a small ruby fixed into a brass collar at the blunt end.

Karla stood up quickly, skipped to her bedroom, and returned with a long, thin bottle in red glass. There was a Mayan design set into the screw cap.

'Curare,' she said. 'I won the dart and the bottle in a word game with an anthropologist.'

'You won this playing Scrabble?' Blue Hijab asked, holding the bottle in one hand and the dart in the other.

'Something like that,' Karla replied. 'You leave the dart soaking in the Curare overnight, once every full moon. And hey, wear it carefully, I scratched myself once and had wide-awake dreams for a couple of hours.'

'Wonderful,' Blue Hijab said. 'Is it so fast acting?'

'Jab it into a man's neck and he'll only follow you six or seven steps. Overcomes the disadvantage of high heels.'

'I love it,' Blue Hijab said. 'Can I really keep it?'

'You must.'

'Thank you,' Blue Hijab said shyly. 'I'm very pleased with your gift.'

'What do you and Mehmu fight about, when you're duelling at dawn?' Karla asked.

'The hijab,' Blue Hijab said, sighing memories of past fights.

'He thinks it's too orthodox?'

'No, Karla, he doesn't think it's cool enough. He's so much into fashion. He has twelve pairs of jeans, and fights for the poor in all of them. He wants me to take the hijab off, and look as cool as the others, who come from Europe, and have long blonde hair.'

'You do look cool,' Karla said. 'That's a great blue, by the way.'

'But not as cool as the other comrades,' she growled.

'The other comrades?'

Blue Hijab looked at me, then back at Karla.

'Shantaram didn't tell you anything about me, did he?'

'I don't know anything,' I said. 'I don't know what colour your flag is, and I didn't ask.'

'You don't have loyalty to a flag?' Blue Hijab asked, frowning.

'Not really,' I said. 'But very often to the person holding one.'

'Mehmu, Ankit and I are communists,' she said, turning to Karla again. 'We were with the Habash group. We trained with Palestinians from the PFLP in Libya, but we had to break away. They got too ... emotional, in what they were doing.'

'What's a Tamil girl from Sri Lanka doing in Libya, with

Palestinians?' Karla asked. 'If I can ask it without stepping into your garden.'

'Learning to defend our people.'

'Did it have to be you?' Karla said softly.

'Who will take up the guns, if we all lay them down?' Blue Hijab replied bitterly, trapped on a wheel designed by revenge to keep rage rotating.

'You and Mehmu really fight about the hijab?' Karla asked, changing the mood with a smile.

'All the time,' Blue Hijab smiled back, covering her girl-mouth with her soldier-hand. 'The first time I shot him, it was because he said that the hijab put ten pounds on me.'

'Walked into that one,' Karla laughed.

'You don't think it *does*, do you?'

'Your hijab has a slimming effect,' Karla said. 'And you have a lovely face.'

'You think so?'

'Wait a minute,' Karla said, springing up quickly and skipping to the bedroom.

'You're a lucky man,' Blue Hijab said.

'I know,' I smiled, my eyes waiting for Karla to come back. 'And so is Mehmu.'

'No,' Blue Hijab said. 'I mean, you're a lucky man because your name was the next on the acid throwers' list.'

I turned to face her, reading dark things in her eyes that she knew darkly.

Karla padded back to sit with us. She had a small blue velvet pouch with her, and she pressed it into Blue Hijab's hands.

'Lipstick, eye make-up, nail polish, hashish, chocolate, and a little book of poems by Seferis,' Karla said. 'For when you get wherever you get, and can close the door.'

'Thank you so much,' Blue Hijab said, blushing.

'We girls have gotta stick together,' Karla said. 'Who else is gonna save our men? Tell me about the second time you shot your husband.'

'The second time was because he said that one of the girls from the East German delegation insisted that he touch her long, silky hair, and that he liked it, and wanted me to take off the hijab and show my hair.'

'I might've shot *her*,' Karla smiled.

748

'I can't shoot her for suggesting it,' Blue Hijab said seriously, 'Mehmu is a handsome man. But I justifiably shot *him* for *doing* it.'

'Where did you shoot him?' Karla asked, hazardously.

'In the bicep. Men hate losing their big muscles for six months, and it doesn't do much permanent damage. You use the small-calibre pistol, press it against the inner side of the bicep, aim outwards, and let one go. All you need is a good wall on the other side to stop the bullet.'

'Have you thought of marriage counselling?' Karla asked thoughtfully.

'We've tried everything –'

'No, I mean, have you thought about *becoming* a marriage counsellor,' Karla said. 'I think you're a natural, and there's another office free, downstairs, in this building. We could link it to my business.'

'Which is what?' Blue Hijab asked. 'If I can ask it without stepping into your garden.'

'I'm a partner in a company called the Lost Love Bureau. We find lost loved ones, and reunite them with their families. Sometimes, finding is as strange as losing, and reunited lovers need counselling. It's a good fit, and you're welcome to fit in.'

'I like this idea,' Blue Hijab said shyly. 'I've been looking for a new window, one that isn't covered with newspapers. I'm . . . very tired, and so is Mehmu. When it's safe to return, I will visit with you and discuss it again, Karla, *Inshallah*.'

I was trying not to be noticed, and doing a good job. Their secret women's business was being acted out in front of me, and men don't get to see that, unless invited. Then they noticed me, and kind of uninvited me. Karla was smiling, but Blue Hijab was scowling, the poisoned dart in her hand.

'You, ah, you said you had a problem with Ankit?' I asked.

'The escape route is only for me, now that the plan has changed,' Blue Hijab said, softening a little, and turning to Karla. 'I can't take him with me. But I can't just abandon him. He's a good comrade. A good man.'

'I'll find him a job in the black market, if you like,' I suggested. 'He'll be okay, until you come back for him.'

'*I'll* hire him,' Karla said. 'He was the night porter of a large hotel for three years. Those talents are always needed.'

'Or, he could work in the black market, with me,' I repeated, defending my gutter.

749

'Or not,' Karla countered, smiling at me. 'Under any circumstances.'

'Either way he'll be okay with us,' I said. 'Don't worry.'

Blue Hijab fixed the jewelled hairpin into the cap of the long thin bottle, and screwed the deadly thorn shut. She slipped it into another invisible pocket in her skirt.

'I have to go,' she said, standing up a little unsteadily.

Karla and I rushed to help her but she held us away, her hands like anemones.

'I'm fine,' she said, 'I'm fine, *Alhamdulillah*.'

She straightened up, patted her skirts into place, and walked out with us to Jaswant's desk.

Ankit was nowhere in sight. Jaswant wasn't at the desk: he was eating snacks from his own survival stash. He turned to face me, crumbs in his beard, biscuits in his hands.

'Where's Ankit?' I asked him.

'Ankit?' he gasped, as if I was accusing him of eating him.

'The cocktail captain. Where is he?'

'Oh, him. Nice fella. A bit shy.'

He drifted off, shaking biscuits from his beard, and staring at the pattern they made on the floor.

'How many cocktails did you have, Jaswant?'

'Three,' he said, four fingers in the air.

'Hang up the *Closed* sign,' I said. 'You're on the chemical ride. Where's Ankit?'

'Randall came up here, had a couple of drinks, and took him downstairs to show him the car. Why?'

'Where's Naveen? And Didier?'

'Who?'

I turned to Blue Hijab and Karla.

'I can take you to Ankit on your way out,' I said.

'No,' she said quickly. 'I can't say goodbye. Too many times I said goodbye, and never got to say anything else. Is there another way out of this hotel?'

'Take your pick,' I said. 'There are several ways out.'

'I'll escort the lady myself,' Jaswant said, cocktailed enough not to be scared of Blue Hijab. 'I need to take a walk to get my head clear.'

'Would you like us to come with you, Blue Hijab?' Karla asked.

'No, please, it's better when I'm alone. I'm safer when I only have to fight for me, *Alhamdulillah*.'

'Until you join your husband,' Karla said. 'And then you'll be together, and maybe you'll do something happier, like marriage counselling. Have you got money?'

'All I need, *Alhamdulillah*,' she said. 'I will see you again, Karla, *Inshallah*.'

'*Inshallah*,' Karla smiled, hugging her.

Blue Hijab faced me, a smile glowering in a frown.

'I cried for my Mehmu and me, that day in the car,' she said. 'But I also cried for you. I'm sorry that the girl died while you were away, and I couldn't tell you. I liked you. I still do. And I'm happy for you. *Allah hafiz*.'

'*Allah hafiz*,' I replied. 'Take care, Jaswant, okay? Look sharp. You're three sheets to the wind, man.'

'No problem,' he smiled back. 'Security guaranteed. I'll put it on your bill.'

When we were alone, Karla sat behind Jaswant's desk. Her finger hovered over the third button.

'You wouldn't,' I said.

'You *so* know I would,' she laughed, throwing the switch.

Bhangra rumbled from the speakers, shoulder-shaking loud.

'Jaswant's gonna hear that, and charge me for it,' I shouted.

'I hope so,' she shouted back.

'Okay, you asked for it,' I said, pulling her up from Jaswant's chair. 'Time to dance, Karla.'

She eased up out of the chair, but leaned against me.

'You know bad girls don't dance,' she said. 'You don't wanna make me dance, Shantaram.'

'You don't *have* to dance,' I shouted over the music, dancing away from her a few steps. 'That's okay. That's fine. But *I'm* dancing, right over *here*, and you can *join* me, any time you get the *urge*.'

She smiled at me and watched for a while, but then she began to move, and she let it loose.

Her hands and arms were seaweed, surfing waves made by hips. She danced over to me and around me in circles of temptation, then the wave lapped against me, and she was all black cats and green fire.

Bad girls do dance, just like bad guys.

751

She was dreaming the music at me, and I was thinking that I definitely had to get this music from Jaswant, and maybe his sound system as well, when I danced into a postman, standing in the doorway.

Karla threw the switch and the music stopped, leaving us with the hissing echo of sudden silence.

'Letter, sir,' the postman said, offering me his clipboard to sign.

It was still night-dark, and wasn't far from dawn, but it was India.

'Okay,' I said. 'A letter for me, is it?'

'You are Mr Shantaram, and this is for Mr Shantaram,' he said patiently. 'So, yes, sir, this is for you.'

'Okay,' I said, signing for the letter. 'Kinda late to be on your rounds, isn't it?'

'Or, very early,' Karla said, standing next to me and leaning against my shoulder. 'What brings you out at this time of not-working, post-man-*ji*?'

'It is my penance, Madame,' the postman said, stowing the clipboard in his shoulder sack.

'Penance,' Karla smiled. 'The innocence of adults. What's your name, postman-*ji*?'

'Hitesh, Madame,' he said.

'A *Good Person*,' she said, translating the name.

'Unfortunately not, Madame,' he replied, handing me the letter.

I stuffed it into my pocket.

'Why are you doing penance, may I ask?' Karla asked.

'I became a drunkard, Madame.'

'But you're not a drunkard now.'

'No, Madame, I am not. But I was, and I neglected my duty.'

'How?'

'I was so drunk, sometimes,' he said, speaking quietly, 'that I hid a few sacks of letters, because I could not deliver them. The postal department made me enter a program, and after I completed it, they offered me my job back if I deliver all of the undelivered letters on my own time, and with an apology to the people I betrayed.'

'And that brings you here,' she said.

'Yes, Madame. I start with the hotels, because they are open at this hour. So, please accept my apology, Mr Shantaram, for delivering your letter so late.'

'Apology accepted, Hitesh,' we said, at the same time.

'Thank you. Good night and good morning to you,' he said, a sombre look pulling him down the stairs to his next appointment.

'India,' I said, shaking my head. 'I love you.'

'Aren't you going to read it?' Karla asked. 'A letter delivered by Fate, in the person of a reformed man?'

'You mean, aren't *you* going to read it, right?'

'Curiosity is its own reward,' she said.

'I don't want to read it.'

'Why not?'

'A letter is just Fate, nagging. I don't have great luck with letters.'

'Come on,' she said. 'You wrote *me* two letters, and they're the two best letters I ever got.'

'I don't mind *writing* them, now and then, but I don't like *getting* them. One of my ideas of hell is a world where you don't just get a letter every week or so, but you get one every minute, of every day, forever. It's the stuff of nightmares.'

She looked at me, and then at the corner of the letter, poking from my pocket, and back at me.

'*You* can read it, Karla, if you want to,' I said, giving her the letter. 'Please do. If there's anything I need to know, you'll tell me. If there's not, tear it up.'

'You don't even know who sent it,' she said, reading the envelope.

'I don't care who it's from. I have bad luck with letters. Just tell me if there's something I should know.'

She tapped the envelope against her cheek thoughtfully.

'It's already out of date, so I think I'll read this later,' she said, sliding it inside her shirt. 'After we find Ankit, and make sure he's okay.'

'Ankit's fine. He can take care of himself. He's a dangerous communist, trained by Palestinians in Libya. I'd rather go into your tent, and make sure everything's okay up here.'

'Let's go down there first,' she smiled, 'before we come up here.'

CHAPTER SEVENTY-SEVEN

WE WENT DOWN, THINKING OF UP, and heard Randall and Ankit laughing before we turned into the archway, behind the façade of the hotel.

When we reached the converted limousine, parked against the wall, we found Randall and Ankit stretched out in the back, Vinson sitting on the mattress between them, and Naveen in the driver's cabin with Didier.

'Nice,' Karla said, smiling wide. 'How you doin', guys?'

'Karla!' Didier shouted. 'You must come and join us!'

'Hi, Karla!' other voices called.

'What's the occasion?' Karla asked, leaning on the open rear door of the car.

'We are commiserating,' Didier said. 'We are all abandoned men, or tragically separated men, and you will enjoy our masculine misery immensely.'

'Abandoned?' Karla scoffed. '*Et tu*, Didier?'

'Taj broke it off with me, tonight,' he sobbed.

'Imagine,' Karla replied. 'Chiselled out of love by a sculptor.'

'Miss Diva broke it off with me, too,' Randall added.

'And with me,' Naveen said. 'Strictly friends, from now on, she told me.'

'I have never found love,' Ankit said. 'My search has not yet ended, but I have been alone in it for a very long time, and have my own bubbles of sorrow in the glass we raise.'

'Rannveig kicked me out of the ashram,' Vinson said. 'I found her, and I lost her again. She said I had to stay there with her for like another month. A whole month. My business would go to hell, man, if I did that. She didn't get it. She kicked me out. Lucky I found *these* guys.'

They were drinking Ankit's anaesthetic in cocktail glasses. Vinson was loading the bowl of a bong. The glass reservoir was shaped like a skull. A small mother-of-pearl snake emblem was swimming in it.

He offered it to me, but I deflected it to Karla.

'If I'm gonna do that, and try Ankit's famous cocktails,' she said, waving it away, 'I've gotta sit inside that car, guys.'

'Sit here between us, Karla,' Didier pleaded.

'Come on, Lin,' she asked me. 'Where do you want to sit?'

'I'm gonna wipe the bike down,' I said, knowing that she'd find the limousine full of masculine lament finer entertainment than I would. 'You go ahead, and I'll join you guys later.'

She kissed me. Naveen got out of the car and held the door for her. She crawled into the front seat beside Didier, but backwards. She propped a cushion against the dashboard and sat comfortably, looking into the back of the car, her legs crossed on the seat.

Naveen gave me a smile as he got in the car, and shut the door. Randall switched on some flashing Jaswant survival store lights, and passed Karla one of Ankit's cocktails. She raised the glass.

'Gentlemen!' She said. 'To the Lost Love Bureau!'

'The Lost Love Bureau!' they shouted.

On cue, Oleg strolled into the alley, his perpetual smile struggling a little. He brightened when he saw the party in the car.

'*Kruto!* So glad to see you, Lin.'

'Where have you been, man?'

'Those girls,' he said. 'Those Divas. They wrung me out like a wrestler's towel, man, then they threw me out. I'm feeling totally —'

'*Razbit?*' I offered.

'*Razbit,*' he repeated. 'What's the party about?'

'It's the annual meeting for lost lovers, and it started without you. Get in there, man.'

They shouted and hooted and dragged Oleg into the lounge in the back, where he lounged beside Randall, cocktail in hand.

Waiting for my love, I walked to my bike, parked near the best exit from the alleyway. I took cleaning rags from under the seat, and wiped her down tenderly.

While Karla roared and Didier shrieked with laughter, I talked to my bike and reassured her that she wasn't alone.

I was worried about Madame Zhou. I didn't know her well enough to know if she loved the twins, or loved anything at all. But she'd been inseparable from them for many years. She was already deranged, and prone to revenge. I wanted to know if she was angry and defeated, or just angry.

And the shadow that she seemed to prefer materialising from, every now and then, was the shadow in the archway under our hotel, where Karla was having so much fun.

Dawn was an hour away, and that sacred sun would sear the vampire, I hoped. I sat on the polished bike and smoked a joint, watching both entrances to the alley, and turning at every footstep, or sound of a vehicle.

Some thinking and worrying time later, the front door of the car laughed open. A tipsy Naveen shuffled out of the car, holding the door with exaggerated chivalry.

Karla stepped out quickly, and strolled to join me, doing very good languid.

Naveen called farewell, and the boys in the stretch-bed car shouted goodnight. Randall lowered the shutters on the windows of the car, preparing for daybreak.

'Do you mind if we sit here, until dawn is up and running?' I asked.

'Not at all,' she said, sitting beside me on the bike. 'You're on guard duty, aren't you?'

'Madame Zhou gives me the creeps. And she was attached to those twins.'

'She'll get hers,' she said. 'She already got some, from Blue Hijab. Karma's a hammer, not a feather.'

'I love you,' I said, watching dawn's pale shadows light her face, wanting to kiss her, but enjoying the thought of it so much that I didn't kiss her. 'How was it in the car?'

'Damn good,' she said. 'I've got so much stuff to work with, in the next aphorism contest. It was like an acupuncture map of male insecurity.'

'Give me one,' I said.

'No way,' she laughed. 'It's not refined yet.'

'Just one,' I begged.

'No.'

'Just one,' I double-begged.

'Okay, okay,' she surrendered. 'Here's one. Men are wishes wrapped in secrets, and women are secrets wrapped in wishes.'

'Damn nice.'

'You like it?'

'I do.'

'It was fun seeing the men unwrapped, so to speak. It was Didier, of course. None of them would've been so open, without him letting them do it.'

'Did you tell Ankit about Blue Hijab?'

'Yeah,' she smiled. 'I managed to slip it into the general consternation. He took it well.'

'Good.'

'And I offered him a job. He took that well, too.'

'Smart man. And fast work, on your part. What else do you do fast, Karla Madame?'

The morning was awake enough to leave the boys to themselves, and I wanted to go back to the tent. I took a step to walk us away, but Karla stopped me.

'Will you do something with me?' she asked.

'Now you're talking,' I smiled. 'That's just what I had in mind.'

'No,' she said. 'I mean, will you *go somewhere* with me?'

'Is it upstairs, to your tent?'

'After the tent.'

'Sure,' I laughed, just as laughter cackled from the men in the darkened limousine. 'But only if you stop stealing my characters.'

'Your characters?'

'Ankit, and Randall, and Naveen,' I smiled, knowing that she'd understand.

She laughed.

'*You're* one of *my* characters,' she said. 'And don't ever forget it.'

'Well, since you're writing it, where do I want to go with you?'

'To the mountain,' she said. 'To see Idriss.'

'Great,' I said. 'We can make a long weekend of it.'

'I was thinking longer than that,' she said.

'How much longer?'

'Until the rain starts,' she said softly. 'And maybe until it stops.'

Two months?

It wasn't a simple thing: not when your business is black.

There was a kid I knew, a young soldier named Jagat, who'd fallen through the cracks in Vishnu's purge: he was a Hindu who didn't agree

757

with throwing Muslims out simply because of their religion. Vishnu couldn't hurt him, because he was a Hindu, but he threw him out with the Muslims.

The kid was capable, still on talking terms with the 307 Company, and could keep the money changers in line if I stepped away.

It was possible to take a break, and possible that young Jagat, the Ronin cut off from his Company, could keep the business running for me.

It was also possible that I'd return from such a long break to the ruin of all I had, and the young Ronin dead, or gone.

'Sure,' I said. 'I'll go anywhere with you, Karla. I can get away that long, but can you?'

'I signed Ranjit's proxy shares over to his unfavourite sister,' she said, taking my arm as we walked back to the stairway. 'I gave Taj and the gallery committee my shares in the gallery. I signed over everything I might inherit from Ranjit, after probate, to his unfavourite brother. He was the one who bribed Ranjit's chauffeur to put the fake bomb in Ranjit's car. It seemed fitting.'

'Washing Ranjit's liquid assets out of your hair.'

'I kept some liquid,' she said, 'to rebaptise myself, from time to time.'

'You really want to stay on the mountain for a couple of months?'

'I do. I know it's not easy up there, and you've got your stuff going on here, but I want us to have some fresh air, and fresh ideas, for a while. I need to scrub the ghosts off, and make a clean start with you. Do you think you could do it? For me, and for us?'

I'm a city boy, who loves nature, but I like my city comforts. It wasn't a first choice to spend months with lots of other people in a close community, having cold showers and sleeping on a thin mattress on the ground. But she wanted it, and needed it. And the city was still tense, after the riots and the lockdown, and hadn't fully settled into its usual semi-strange. It was as good a time as any to be somewhere else.

'Alright,' I said, making her smile. 'Let's see what the mountain does to us.'

PART
FOURTEEN

CHAPTER SEVENTY-EIGHT

O N THE FOREST ROAD TO THE MOUNTAIN, soft leaves of new trees brushed our faces as we passed them, kissing away blue horizons with every curve in the road. Monkeys scattered to boulder perches, sitting in judgement. An omen of crows tried to worry us forward, swooping in phalanxes of feathered shields, and lizards scampered on crumbling trunks of fallen trees.

We were on the bike, Randall and the others behind us in the car. A wild tiger's roar from the preserve, far away, shook coloured birds from trees. They flew into the open road, a cloud parting in flight around us as we reached the mountain car park.

We parked the bike and car behind the snacks and cold drinks shop, paying the attendant well to watch over them. I also told him that I'd be back every two days to check on my bike, and wouldn't react happily if she were offended in any way while she was in his care. I didn't worry about the car. The car was big enough to take care of itself.

We had a crew with us: Randall, Vinson, Ankit and Didier. Naveen and Oleg wanted to come, but the two lost lovers were holding down the fort at the Lost Love Bureau. When we reached the first steep climb, Didier asked if there was an alternative route.

Karla was about to tell him, I think, but I cut her off. I knew how sceptical and belligerent Didier could be in the presence of sanctity. I wanted him to sweat his way into Idriss's camp on the summit, not stroll into it.

'Are you saying you can't *make* this climb?' I challenged.

'Certainly not!' Didier snapped. 'Show me the most difficult path. There is no mountain taller than Didier's determination.'

We set off with Karla in the lead, me following, then Didier, Randall, Vinson and Ankit. Didier climbed well, with my hand pulling from above, and Randall pushing him from below.

Vinson clambered his way past us, enjoying the climb. I was surprised to see Ankit only a few steps behind him, vanishing above us in the seaweed smother of grass, bushes and vines.

Karla laughed at one point in the climb, and I thought of Abdullah, complimenting her by telling her that she was as agile as an ape.

'Abdullah,' I called out to her.

'Exactly what I was thinking,' she laughed.

Then we both shut down, thinking of the tall, brave, violent friend we loved. He'd vanished again, just as he'd done before. I wondered when we'd see him, and if we were ready for what we'd find, when we did.

We reached the summit in silence, joining Vinson and Ankit, who were standing with their hands on their hips, looking at the mesa, the school for the sage, Idriss.

There were strands of flowers strung from a new temporary pagoda made of bamboo poles. A canvas sheet in orange, white and green, the tricolour of the Indian flag, repeated itself in waves of wind in the canopy.

The pagoda provided a wide area of shade in the centre of the courtyard, which had been covered with fine carpets. Four wide, comfortable cushions were arranged in a semicircle around a small, fist-high wooden stage.

Beyond the pagoda, students were busy preparing for a significant event.

'Is it always like this?' Randall asked.

'No,' I said. 'It must be some special occasion. I hope we're not intruding.'

'I hope they have a bar,' Didier said.

I caught Karla's eye.

'You're wondering who brought those carpets and bamboo poles up here, aren't you?' Karla asked me quietly, as our crew of city sinners took in the scene.

'Someone had to drag that beauty up here for big shots to sit on,' I smiled. 'Even on the easy path, that's either a lot of deference, or a lot of respect. I'm wondering which.'

Silvano came through the groups of people who were setting out decorations and preparing food on trays.

'*Come va, ragazzo pazzo?*' he asked me, as he approached. *How you doing, crazy guy?*

762

'*Ancora respirare*,' I replied. *Still breathing.*

He kissed Karla on both cheeks, and then hugged me.

'It's wonderful you're here today, Lin,' he said happily. 'I'm so happy to see you. Who are your friends?'

I introduced Silvano, and he greeted everyone, his smile devotion-bright.

'It's the Divine that brought you all here today, Lin,' Silvano said.

'Oh, yeah? I thought it was Karla's idea.'

'No, I mean that there is a great debate today. Great sages, from four districts, have challenged Idriss to a discourse.'

'A discourse on philosophy?' Karla asked. 'It's the first one in more than a year, isn't it?'

'Indeed,' Silvano answered. 'And today we will have all the big questions at once, and all the answers. It is a great challenge, by great holy men.'

'When does it start?' Karla asked, queens warming up for battle.

'It should be about an hour from now. We are still getting ready. There is plenty of time to get fresh, after your climb, and eat a snack, before the challenge begins.'

'Is the bar open yet?' Didier asked.

Silvano stared back at him, uncomprehending.

'Yes, sir,' Ankit said, rattling the backpack that he'd carried up the ragged slope.

'Thank God,' Didier sighed. 'Where is the bathroom?'

I left Karla with Didier and the others, took a pot of water into the forest, found a secluded space that didn't seem to mind too much, and washed myself.

As soon as Karla detached from me, after that long ride to the mountain, I began to hear the shriek of something breaking, somewhere. Climbing to the camp on the mesa with Karla, I realised that the shrieking I heard, and couldn't stop hearing, was the acid throwers, breaking on revenge.

From the moment that Blue Hijab told me about the capture, and torture, and death of the acid throwers, I'd been feeling that red tide of burning souls, lapping at my feet.

On the ride to the mountain with Karla holding me, I'd drifted in love, a leaf on a Sunday pond. But when we detached, and as we climbed, memories crawled deeper into the flinch of fear. The bruise

763

of the chain, worse than the bite: screams of surrender, always louder than screams of defiance.

At the summit, while everyone was getting ready for the great debate of wise thinkers, I went to the wise forest to clean myself, and to be alone, with memories of torture and submission.

I was hurting for Blue Hijab and her friend, the horribly burned comrade, and all the cousins and neighbours who were so outraged and angry that they did to the torturers what the torturers had done to them.

But every execution kills justice, because no life deserves to be killed. I survived the desert-inside of prison beatings, and stumbled on, because I forgave the men who tortured me. I learned that trick from tortured men, who felt it their duty to pass it on, when I was chained and beaten in my turn.

Let it go, those different wise men said. *Hating them, like they hate us, will ruin your mind, and that's the one thing they can't hit.*

'Are you good, baby?' Karla's voice called from behind the trees. 'The debate starts soon, and I'm gonna reserve seats for us.'

'I'm good,' I called back, not good, not even not-good-okay. 'I'm good.'

'Two minutes,' she called back. 'We can't miss this. It's made for us, Shantaram.'

I knew why Karla had brought us to the mountain and the fabled sage: she wanted to heal me. She wanted to save me. I was breaking inside, and she could see it. And maybe she was, too. Like Karla and every other soldier I knew, I joked and laughed about things that made other less wounded hearts weep, and I'd learned to harden myself against loss and death. I look back now, and the past is a slaughter: almost everyone I've ever loved is dead. And the only way to live with the constant cull of what you love is to take a little of that cold grave into yourself, every time.

When she left, I let my eyes drift into the maze of leaves that only trees understand. Hatred has its gravitational web, locking stray specks of confusion into spirals of violence. I had my own reasons to hate the acid throwers, if I wanted to hate them, and I wasn't immune to the tremble in the web. But it wasn't hatred that I tried to clean off myself, in that forest, on the mountain: it was a shame I didn't create, but didn't stop.

Sometimes, for some reason, I couldn't stop it, or I didn't stop it. Sometimes, for some reason, I was a part of something wrong, before I knew that I wasn't right any more.

In the forest, alone, I forgave what was done to me. In the kneeling place within my own faults I forgave them for what they did, and hoped that someone, somewhere, would forgive me. And the wind in lavish leaves said, *Surrender. One is all, and all is one. Surrender.*

CHAPTER SEVENTY-NINE

FAITH IS HONESTY INSIDE, a renegade priest once said to me. *So, fill up whenever you can, son*. Faithful students of the mystic teacher Idriss hoping that the exchange with his inquisitors would fill them with wisdom, gathered on the white-stone mesa in late-afternoon sunlight.

Some unfaithful observers gathered as well: a few followers of the great sages, who were hoping to see Idriss, the arrogantly humble thinker, tumble from a cliff of contumacy. Faith is also its own challenge, like sincerity, and purity draws swords in fearful hearts.

Didier, faithful to his own pleasures, found a hammock strung between trees, and wrestled with the alligator of knotted rope for a while, hoping to find a way to stay on it beneath a shady tree for the duration of the discourse.

Karla wouldn't let him.

'If you miss this,' she said, pulling his jacket, 'I won't be able to talk to you about it. So you can't miss it.'

She put our group together with a view of the questioning faces and the interrogated sage.

The spectators had made an arena of cushions, arranged around the pagoda close enough to hear every inflection or inference. Expectation, the ghost of reputation, moved through the crowd as students swapped stories about the legendary sages who'd challenged Idriss.

The holy men emerged from the largest cave, where they'd meditated together in preparation for the thought contest. They were senior gurus with their own followings, the youngest of them thirty-five, and the eldest perhaps seventy, a few years younger than Idriss.

They were dressed in identical white *dhoti* garments, wrapped luxuriously about their skin, and wore rudraksha beads in chains around their necks. The beads were reputed to have significant spiritual powers to detect positive and negative substances. As legend has it, rudraksha beads held over a pure substance rotate in a clockwise direction, and in an anticlockwise direction over negative substances, which is one of the reasons why no guru is far from a high-quality strand.

They also wore rings and amulets to maximise the power of friendly planets in their astrological charts, and minimise the harm of unfriendly spheres, far away, but never powerless.

The students had whispered that we were forbidden from speaking the names of the famous sages, because they wanted their challenge to Idriss to remain anonymous, out of modesty.

In my mind, as I saw them walk out to take their places on the large cushions, with students throwing rose petals in their path, I called them Grumpy, for the youngest one, Doubtful, for the next, Ambitious for the third, and Let Me See for the eldest in the group, who was the quickest to find his seat, and the first to reach for a lime juice and a piece of fresh papaya.

'How long will this take?' Vinson whispered.

'Okay,' Karla said, holding frustration at bay with very tight lips. 'Do you want to spend seven years studying philosophy, and theology, and cosmology, Vinson?'

'I'm gonna say *No*,' he replied, uncertainly.

'Do you wanna *sound* to Rannveig like you've done seven years of study?'

'I'm gonna say *Yes*.'

'Good, then be quiet, and listen. These challenges to Idriss only happen once a year or so, and this is my first. It's a chance to get all of it in one shot, and I'm gonna hear it, from start to finish.'

'Will there be an intermission?' Didier asked.

Idriss knelt at the feet of each sage, eldest to youngest, and took their blessings before he took the small stage, settled himself, and greeted the assembly.

'Let us smoke,' he suggested gently. 'Before we begin.'

Students brought a large hookah pipe into the pagoda, and gave a smoking hose to each of the sages. The longest hose reached to Idriss, who puffed the bowl alight.

'Now,' he said, when all had smoked, including Didier, who kept pace with the holy men on a finely tapered joint. 'Please, challenge me with your questions.'

The sages looked at Let Me See, offering him the first assail. The elderly sage smiled, drew a breath, and waded into the shallows to skip a semantic stone across the water.

'What is God?' Let Me See asked.

'God is the perfect expression of all the positive characteristics,' Idriss answered.

'Only the positive characteristics?'

'Exclusively.'

'Can God not do evil, then, or commit sin?' Let Me See asked.

'Of course not. Are you suggesting that God can commit suicide, or lie to an innocent heart?'

There was a conference among the holy men. I could see their problem. Gods in all ages, according to many sacred texts, kill human beings. Some gods torture human souls eternally, or permit it. Idriss's version of a God incapable of evil was difficult to reconcile with some of the great books of faith.

The conference broke up, with the baton still in Let Me See's hands.

'And what is life, great sage?' Let Me See asked.

'Life is an organic expression of the tendency toward complexity.'

'But are you saying that life was created by the Divine, or that it created itself?'

'Life on this planet began from the strangely improbable but perfectly natural cooperation of inorganic elements, in alkaline vents under the seas, leading to the first bacterial cells. That process is both self-creating, and Divine, at the same time.'

'You are speaking science, great sage?'

'Science is a spiritual language, and one of the most spiritual pursuits.'

'And what is Love, great sage?'

'Love is intimate connection.'

'I was speaking about the purest form of love, great sage,' Let Me See replied.

'As was I, great sage,' Idriss answered. 'A scientist applying her talents, trying to find a cure for a disease, is making an intimate connection, and is flooded with love. Walking a dog that trusts you through a meadow is an intimate connection. Opening your heart to the Divine, in prayer, is an intimate connection.'

Let Me See nodded, and chuckled.

'I yield the floor, temporarily, to my younger colleagues,' he said.

'How can we know,' Ambitious began, wiping sweat from his shaved head, 'that there is an external reality?'

'Indeed,' Doubtful added. 'Even if we allow *cogito ergo sum*, how can any of us know that the world beyond the mind that we *think* is real, isn't just a very vivid dream?'

'I invite anyone who does not believe in an external reality,' Idriss said, 'to accompany me to the edge of the ravine, not far from here, and then I invite you to jump into it. I will take the slow path, down the hill, and when I get to the bottom, I will continue the discussion about an external reality with any survivors.'

'A good point,' Let Me See, the eldest sage, said. 'I, for one, am a survivor, and I am staying right here.'

I'd heard all the questions at one time or another on the mountain, and I knew most of Idriss's answers by heart. His cosmology was conjectural, but his logic was elegant and consistent. His was an easy mind to remember.

'Free will,' Grumpy, the youngest of them, said. 'Where do you stand, Idriss?'

'Beyond the four physical forces, and matter, space and time, there are two great spiritual energies in the Universe,' Idriss said. 'The first of those energies is the Divine Source of all things, which is continuingly expressed since the birth of the Universe as a spiritual tendency field, something like a magnetic field of darker energy. The second invisible energy is Will, wherever it arises in the Universe.'

'What is the purpose of this tendency field?' Grumpy asked.

'Its purpose is indeterminable, at this point in our awareness. But, as with energy, we know what it *does*, and how to use it, even though we don't know what it is.'

'But what is its value, sage?' Grumpy asked.

'Its value is inestimable,' Idriss smiled. 'The connection between the spiritual tendency field, and our human Will, is the purpose of life at our level.'

Idriss waved for a new hookah pipe, and Silvano brought it to the pagoda. The Italian acolyte had left his rifle outside the arena, but still moved his elbow as he bent to place the pipe, as if expecting the invisible weapon to fall from its sling.

'Okay,' Vinson said, whispering to Karla. 'Like, I didn't get *any* of that.'

'You're kidding, Stuart, right?'

'Like, *nada*, man,' Vinson whispered. 'I hope the whole show's not as brainiac as that part. How much did *you* follow?'

Karla looked at him compassionately. One of the things she loved most in the world, maybe the thing she *did* love most in the world, was a foreign language to him.

'Why don't you let me dial it down from ten for you,' Karla suggested, her hand on his arm, 'and give you the T-shirt version? Till you get on your feet.'

'Wow,' Vinson whispered back. 'Would you really do that?'

Karla smiled at him, then looked at me.

'Can you believe how cool this is?' she asked.

'Oh, yeah,' I smiled back.

'I told you we had to come up here.'

Idriss and the other sages emptied the burning inspiration from the bowl, and turned again to burning questions.

'How so, master-*ji*?' Doubtful asked quickly. 'How can the connection to this tendency field, or to the Divine, explain the meaning of life?'

'The question is invalid,' Idriss said softly, being kind to a colleague who was also pursuing a truth worthy of penance. 'Meaning is not an attribute of life. Meaning is an attribute of will. *Purpose* is an attribute of life.'

The sages conferred again, leaning toward Let Me See, who was facing Idriss directly. They shoved angels from the head of a pin, one by one, deciding which portion of the tiny dome would give them best purchase.

Idriss sighed, looking out at the faces of the students, dressed in white, a magnolia circle of fascination. The tallest trees braved the departing sun, shielding the holy men with shade.

'So —' Vinson began to ask.

'Meaning of life, wrong question,' Karla said. 'Purpose of life, right question.'

'Wow,' Vinson said. 'So, that's, like, *two* questions.'

The sages drew apart. Doubtful cleared his throat.

'Are you speaking of connecting with the Divine, or with other living creatures?'

'Every true connection, honest and free, no matter where it occurs, with a flower or a saint, is a connection to the Divine, because every sincere connection automatically connects the connectors to the spiritual tendency field.'

'But how can one know that one is connected?' Doubtful asked doubtfully.

Idriss frowned, lowering his eyes, unable to suppress the sadness he saw waving from a lonely shore of Doubtful's devotion. He looked up again, smiling at Doubtful kindly.

'The tendency field affirms it,' Idriss said.

'How?'

'Sincere penance, such as kindness, or compassion, connects us to the tendency field,' Idriss said. 'The tendency field always responds, sometimes with a message from a dragonfly, sometimes with the granting of a fervent wish, and sometimes with the kindness of a stranger.'

The sages conferred again.

Vinson used the break in the discourse to throw his arm around my shoulder and pull me into his confusion. He leaned us in to whisper to Karla, but she didn't let him start.

'The force is always with you, if you give up force,' Karla said.

'Oh.'

The sages coughed their way back into the debate politely.

'You seek to wrap meaning up in a conundrum of intention,' Grumpy replied. 'But are we really free in what we decide, or are we determined by Divine knowledge of all that we do?'

'Are we *victims* of God?' Idriss laughed. 'Is that what you're suggesting? Then why give us free will? To torment us? Is that what you really want me to believe? Our will exists to ask questions of God, not just beg for answers.'

'I want to know what *you* believe, Master Idriss.'

'What I *believe*, great sage, or what I *know*?'

'What you fervently believe,' Grumpy replied.

'Very well. I believe that the Source that birthed our Universe came with us into this reality as a spiritual tendency field. I believe that Will, our human will, is in a constant state of superposition, interacting with, and not interacting with the spiritual tendency field, like the photons of light from which it's made.'

The sages conferred again, and Vinson almost asked what was going on.

'The force is actually *you*,' Karla whispered in summary, 'if you're humble enough for it.'

'You are basing very much of what you say on the possibility of choice, master-*ji*,' Ambitious said. 'But many of the choices we make are trivial.'

'There is no such thing as a trivial choice,' Idriss said. 'That is why so many powerful people try to influence all of our choices. If it were a trivial thing, they would not bother.'

'You know the things of which I speak, master-*ji*,' Ambitious said, a little irritated. 'There are a thousand trivial choices that we make every day. Choice cannot be such an important factor, as you suggest, when so much of it is of trifling importance, or made without spiritual thinking.'

'I repeat,' Idriss smiled patiently, 'there is no such thing as a trivial choice. Every choice is significant, no matter how unconsciously made. The choices we make, every time we make them, collapse the superposition that we call human life into one reality or another, and one perception or another, and that decision has minute or great but nonetheless eternal effects on the timeline.'

'You call that power?' Ambitious challenged.

'This is energy,' Idriss corrected. 'Spiritual energy, sufficient to alter Time, which is no small thing. Time was the lord of all living things, for billions of years, until Will arose to greet him.'

Let Me See called the sages to confer. He was enjoying himself, even at the expense of his colleagues, or perhaps especially at the expense of his colleagues. It was impossible to tell if his tactical conclaves were designed to confound Idriss, or his fellow sages.

Vinson looked at Karla, and was about to speak.

'Cover your karmic ass,' Karla synopsised, 'everything you do affects the timeline, dude.'

I kissed her quickly. I know it was a holy assembly of holy thinkers, but I was betting that they'd forgive me.

'This is the second-best best date ever,' she said, as the sages sat up straight, three intellectual corner-men leaning away from Grumpy, the youngest sage, with fresh energy for the challenge.

'This is digressive,' Grumpy began. 'I have found your technique, master-*ji*. You *divert* from questions, through semantic tricks. Let us get down to sacred texts and instructions. If the human soul is an expression of our humanity, as you seem to suggest, is it essential to do one's duty in life, as the sacred texts instruct us?'

'Indeed,' Ambitious added, hoping to trap Idriss in a snare of caste. 'Can any of us escape the wheel of karma, and our Divinely appointed duties?'

'If there is a Divine Source of all things, our rational and logical duty is to that Divine Source,' Idriss replied. 'Our only other duty is to the humanity that we share, and the planet that sustains us. Everything beyond that is a personal preference.'

'Are we not born with a karmic duty?' Ambitious pressed.

'*Humanity* is born with a karmic duty. Human beings are born with a personal karmic *mission*, playing their individual part in the common karmic duty,' Idriss said.

The sages looked at one another, ashamed, perhaps, that they'd tried to trap Idriss in the quicksand of religion, while he kept lifting himself free on a branch of faith.

'Does a personal God speak to you?' Let Me See asked, tangling his long grey beard with knotted fingers, bruised on the inside from years of counting red amber meditation beads in cycles of one hundred and eight.

'Such a lovely question,' Idriss laughed gently. 'I presume that you mean a God that cares about me, personally, and that I can communicate with, personally, while that God, who dreamt the universe into creation, is busily connecting with every consciousness like mine, wherever it arises. Is that correct?'

'Precisely,' the elderly guru said.

Idriss laughed to himself.

'What's the question?' Vinson asked.

'Does God walk the talk?' Karla whispered quickly, smiling encouragement at Vinson.

'I get it,' Vinson whispered back happily. 'Like, does God pick up the phone?'

'I see the Divine in every minute that I live,' Idriss answered. 'And I receive constant affirmations. It is a language uncommon, of course. It is a spiritual language of coincidence and connection. I think you know, great sage, of what I speak?'

'I do, Idriss,' he replied, chuckling. 'I do. Can you give an example?'

'Every peaceful encounter with nature,' Idriss said, 'is a natural conversation with the Divine, which is why it is advisable to live as near to nature as you can.'

'A fine example, great sage,' Let Me See replied.

'Extending your heart to put the light of affection in the eyes of a new friend, is a conversation with the Divine,' Idriss said. 'Honest meditation is the same conversation.'

'You were imprecise, before, Idriss,' he said. 'Tell us, succinctly, what the meaning and purpose of life is.'

'There are two questions in your challenge, as I said before,' Idriss said. 'And only one of them is a valid question.'

'We have touched on this, and I still do not understand,' Grumpy pouted.

'Without a fully conscious Will to ask about the meaning of anything,' Idriss answered patiently, 'the question is not just meaningless, but impossible.'

'But surely, master-*ji*, this human Will that you champion cannot be *meaning* in and of itself?' Doubtful asked, frowning hard.

'I repeat, the question *What is the meaning of Life?* is an invalid question. Meaning is a property that emerges when a fully sentient Will exists to collapse the superposition state of possibilities, by making freely willed choices, and asking freely willed questions.'

There was a pause, and I was glad, because I knew that if Vinson disturbed her concentration at that moment, Karla might shoot him, after the debate.

'Asking the question *is* the meaning,' I whispered to him.

'Thanks,' Karla whispered, leaning against me.

'Meaning is an attribute of Will,' Idriss continued. 'The valid question is what is the *purpose* of Life?'

'Very well,' Let Me See said, chuckling, 'what is the purpose of life?'

'The purpose of life is to express the set of positive characteristics to the most sophisticated degree that you can, by connecting with pure intention to others, and our planet, and to the Divine Source of all things.'

'How do you define these positive characteristics, master-*ji*?' Doubtful asked. 'In which sacred texts can we find them?'

'The set of positive characteristics is found everywhere, in every place where people live humanely with one another. Life, consciousness, freedom, love, justice, fairness, honesty, mercy, affinity, courage, generosity, compassion, forgiveness, empathy and many beautiful others. They are always the same, everywhere that kind hearts survive to preserve them.'

'But what specific sacred texts do you refer to in your analysis, master-*ji*?'

'Our common humanity is the sacred text of the peaceful human heart,' Idriss said. 'And we have only just begun to write it.'

'And how does the expression of these positive characteristics lead us to purpose?' Ambitious challenged.

'We humans are born with the capacity to accumulate non-evolutionary knowledge, and the capacity to shape our behaviour as animals,' Idriss said, reaching for a glass of water. 'Which are very difficult things for other animals to do, but are very easy for us, thanks to the Divine.'

'Can you be specific about this non-evolutionary knowledge, master-*ji*?' Doubtful asked. 'This is a term I am not familiar with.'

'Things that we know, that we don't *have* to know, in order to survive. Extra knowledge, about everything.'

'We *know* things,' Ambitious said. 'That is hardly a revelation. And we can shape our behaviour. Where do you see purpose in this, master-*ji*?'

'Without either one of those things,' Idriss continued, 'we could not claim to have a destiny. But with *both* of them in place, the *fact* of our destiny is undeniable.'

'How, master-*ji*?'

'We are not apes forever. We can change ourselves. We are changing, all the time. We will discover most of the laws of everything, and we will control our evolution. That is destiny controlling DNA, rather than DNA controlling destiny, as it did forever, until now.'

'Can you define destiny?' Ambitious demanded.

'Destiny is the treasure we find in the awareness of death.'

'Oh, yes!' Karla shouted. 'Sorry!'

'Perhaps it is time,' Idriss suggested, 'that we take a break, and refresh ourselves for the challenge.'

The students rose to escort the sages to their cave. The sages walked away, frowning their thoughts.

Idriss looked around as Silvano offered his arm. He found Karla's eyes, and smiled at us.

'Glad you're here, Karla,' he said, as he walked back to his cave with Silvano. 'So nice to see you two together.'

'You know,' Vinson said when we were alone. 'I think I'm getting the hang of this. You're on to something with the T-shirts, Karla. You're keeping notes, Randall, right?'

'Meticulous notes, Mr Vinson.'

'I'd like to see those later, if it's okay.'

'Me too,' Karla said.

'Me three,' I agreed.

'I'm so happy we have that settled,' Didier said. 'Now, will someone please open the bar. My soul may be improved, but mind is screaming for mercy.'

CHAPTER EIGHTY

DOUBTFUL HAD A QUESTION, after the contest resumed, but Idriss raised a soft hand of insistence, silencing everyone, and pushed on to the horizon of his thought.

'So far as I can see,' he said quietly, his raised hand like a trident made from pure patience, 'we are the only species with the capacity to be more than we are, perhaps even more than we dream we are, and the potential to get wherever it is that we choose to go.'

He stopped for a moment.

'Why do we let the few push the many to compete and consume and fight?' Idriss said. 'When will we demand peace, as passionately as we demand freedom?'

Sudden tears fell into his upturned palms, resting in his lap.

'Forgive me,' he said, rubbing his eyes with the heels of his hands.

'Great sage,' Let Me See said, crying sympathy with him. 'We are all drawn here today by the power of love. Let us remain happy in our spiritual endeavours.'

Idriss laughed, clearing his eyes of moonstone tears.

'That is a semantic error, great teacher,' he said, composed again. 'Love has no power, because it can only be freely given.'

'Very well then,' Let Me See smiled, 'what is Power?'

'Power influences or directs people or processes,' Idriss said. 'Power is a measure of control, and is always connected to authority. Power is fear, submitting to greed. There is no fear and there is no greed in love, just as there is no authority or control, which is why it is beyond illusions of power.'

'But what about the power of healing?' Grumpy asked. 'Do you deny that?'

'That is the *energy* of healing, master-*ji*. Every healer knows that there is no power in it, but that the energy is abundant. Energy is the process. Power is the attempt to influence, direct or control the process.'

'Even the power of prayer, master-*ji*?' Ambitious asked. 'Is there no such thing?'

'There is the spiritual *energy* of prayer,' Idriss replied, 'just as there is the spiritual energy of love, and both are reservoirs of grace, but there is no power. Energy is the process, and power is the attempt to control the process.'

Vinson was wriggling to speak.

'Power bad, energy good,' he whispered to Karla. 'Absolute power corrupts.'

'Very good, Stuart,' Karla whispered happily.

'Let us smoke again for a while,' Idriss said to the sages.

'Very good, Idriss,' Didier whispered more happily, and the assembly relaxed, while the sages and my French friend sated themselves.

'Shall I continue?' Idriss asked, when the sages were high enough to get down to metaphysics again.

'Certainly,' the sages replied.

'The fact that we are *what* we are,' Idriss said, as if the discourse had never paused, 'asking all the right questions, no matter how many centuries it takes us to get to the truth, is destiny itself. Destiny, too, like life, is an emergent phenomenon.'

Vinson leaned in to whisper a question, but Karla beat him to it.

'Energy plus direction equals destiny,' she said quickly, focusing on the debate.

'But destiny?' Doubtful said, his shaved head glistening with sweat in the warm evening. 'Can you explain that again?'

'Our human destiny is a *fact*, not a supposition,' Idriss said. 'Destiny is the ability to focus spiritual energy, in the form of will, to change the future course of our lives. We are all doing this, to a greater or lesser extent, in all our lives, and in the collective life of our species. We are living directed lives already, and it is up to us to realise it, and to direct them more positively.'

'But realise it *how*?' Let Me See asked.

'Express the set of positive characteristics to the best of your ability,' Idriss replied. 'That is the realisation of the soul, expressed in human kindness and courage.'

'Why?' Ambitious asked. 'Why should anyone ever bother to do good or positive things? Why not simply work for self-benefit? Since you are so much a man of science, isn't that evolutionary?'

'Not at all,' Idriss smiled, answering a question he'd faced hundreds of times before. 'Everywhere that some people look, they see a savage world, competing to the death. But there is also magnificent cooperation in the world, from ants in colonies, to trees in colonies, to human beings in colonies. Adaptability is exquisite cooperation. Cooperation *is* evolution.'

'But surely the fittest survive,' Ambitious pressed. 'And the fittest rule. Do you mean to overturn the natural order of things?'

'The natural order of things is cooperation,' Idriss countered. 'Molecules do not *compete* to form organic molecules, they *cooperate* to form them. And we, great sages, are very large collections of very cooperative organic molecules, thanks to the Divine. When they stop cooperating, we are in trouble.'

'Since you like to take this discourse back to first principles,' Let Me See observed, 'can I ask if you are suggesting that there is a different moral order, beyond that found in the sacred texts?'

It was a trick question. I knew that Karla was itching to answer it, because we'd discussed it several times.

'The sacred texts are there for us to know what we can *become*,' Idriss said. 'Until we get there, in our tragically long cultural evolution, until we get to a place that is worthy of such beautiful revelations, our common humanity is a very useful guiding star to the essential truth in all of them.'

'Are you brushing the sacred texts aside?' Let Me See asked.

'You speak those words, not I. My advice, for what little it is worth, is simply that the sacred texts are like sacred places. Just as we should be clean when we enter sacred places, so should we be clean when we enter sacred texts. And the best way to present a clean soul to the great revelations of the Divine, is to be a clean human being in your dealings with others, and the world that sustains us.'

The sages conferred again, and Idriss took the opportunity to call for a new hookah pipe, puffing it alight for the sages contentedly.

'Good heart, good faith?' Vinson suggested during the pause.

'You're really getting this,' Karla said quietly.

Randall was taking notes in his journal. Ankit was helping him, whispering the end of a half-remembered line from time to time.

'How do you like it, guys?' I whispered.

'It's like jumping up in a parachute,' Randall replied. 'Instead of down.'

'We could use this teacher of yours in the Party,' Ankit said admiringly.

'There's a party?' Didier asked, brightening.

'The Communist Party,' Ankit whispered back drily. 'But a small party might be arranged for you later tonight by the fire, Mr Didier, if you desire it.'

'Superb,' Didier enthused. 'Oh, God, the holy men are talking again.'

'I confess, great sage,' Let Me See said modestly, 'that you have lost me in the jungle of your imaginative ideas.'

'Yes,' Doubtful added. 'I am also lagging behind, because your discourse on spiritual matters does not employ the usual spiritual language, Master Idriss.'

'Everything is a spiritual language, noble thinker, but simply on a higher or a lower frequency of connection,' Idriss replied. 'This discourse that we share is but one of many.'

'How can there be more than one spiritual language?' Doubtful asked.

'If there is a God, and a spiritual language that connects us to God, then by definition it is the only language of purpose, simply expressed in different ways.'

'Even in negative ways?' Grumpy asked, waking to the theme.

'Wouldn't you prefer to concentrate on the higher spiritual language, as we have done so far, and not on the lower?' Idriss lamented.

'Do you not *have* examples, then?' Ambitious asked.

'Much of the human world is an example,' Idriss said, his face sombre.

'Then it should not be a problem for you to provide spiritual languages other than our own,' Ambitious retorted.

Idriss settled into a patient understanding of the younger man, and took a forgiving breath.

'Very well,' he said, 'let us walk in the dark, for a while.'

He sipped at his lime juice, and began his answer to the challenge.

'Exploitation is the spiritual language of profit,' Idriss began sadly.

The students, who'd heard Idriss riff before, were already beginning to nod their heads in time to his ontological poetry.

'Oppression is the spiritual language of tyranny,' Idriss said.

The students began to mumble, wakening to Idriss's chant.

'Hypocrisy is the spiritual language of greed,' Idriss continued. 'Ruthlessness is the spiritual language of power, and bigotry is the spiritual language of fear.'

'Are you taking notes, Randall?' I asked, as Idriss took a breath.

'Aye aye, sir,' he replied.

'Violence is the spiritual language of hate,' Idriss said, 'and arrogance is the spiritual language of vanity.'

'Idriss!' several students called out.

'Wait!' Idriss requested, his gentle hands parting the waters of interjection. 'We are gathered here in the quest for understanding. Please, dear students and guests, do not call out in the presence of these great sages, even though I have encouraged you to call out freely in our discussions.'

'Your wish, master-*ji*!' Ankit called out in an unexpectedly commanding tone, his finger to his lips as he scanned the crowd, and all was silent again.

'May I ask you to travel with me on a path of higher spiritual languages, great sages?' Idriss asked.

'Certainly,' Let Me See said.

'With what examples, master-*ji*?' Doubtful asked.

'I invite *you* to give them to *me*, great sage,' Idriss replied. 'Because I would love to see what happy birds fly from your mind.'

'This is another trick,' Ambitious interjected. 'You have prepared your responses in advance, have you not?'

'Of course,' Idriss laughed softly. 'And memorised them. Haven't you?'

'Once again I remind you, master-*ji*, that *you* are the answer on this occasion, and *we* are the question,' Ambitious said, retiring behind a reputation-barricade.

'Good,' Idriss said, his back straight. 'Are you ready for my response?'

'We are ready, great sage,' Let Me See replied.

'Emotion is the spiritual language of music,' Idriss said, 'and sensualism is the spiritual language of dance.'

Idriss paused, waiting for comment, and then continued.

'Birds are the spiritual language of the sky,' Idriss said. 'And trees are the spiritual language of the earth.'

He paused again, as if listening.

'I think I died,' Karla whispered, 'and went to Smartass Heaven.'

'Generosity is the spiritual language of love, humility is the spiritual language of honour, and devotion is the spiritual language of faith.'

Many of the students had seen Idriss face the fire before. And loving him as they did, they were joining with him innocently: not willing him to win, but willing him toward truth, no matter who uttered it in the séance.

'Truth is the spiritual language of trust, and irony is the spiritual language of coincidence.'

Students swayed in place, obeying the silence.

'Humour is the spiritual language of freedom,' Idriss said, 'and sacrifice is the spiritual language of penance.'

He stopped again, struggling with vanity, knowing that he could go on for a long time with the same poem. He looked at the students, his face lashing itself with a blush, and he smiled his way back.

'Everything is spiritual, and everything is expressed in its own spiritual language. The connection to the Source can never be broken, only disturbed.'

The students shouted and applauded, then silenced themselves, proud and penitent at the same time.

'If you do not mind,' Idriss suggested, 'I would appreciate another break, of an hour, perhaps, if it is agreeable.'

Students rose on instinct, guiding the sages back to their cave.

'I don't know about you,' I said to Karla, glad of the break, 'but I need something unholy.'

'My thought exactly,' she said. 'And I don't mind if I drink it or smoke it. My nerves are in my mouth.'

'You wanted to be out there, didn't you?'

'That was some serious smartass shit,' she said, her happy eyes gleaming.

Idriss was clever and charismatic, but he'd faced inquisitions many times. He knew where the solid ground was, and the philosophical sand. I'd brought questions to teachers before, many of them, and I found that sometimes cleverness covered a lack of principle, and charisma cloaked ambition. I liked the teacher, but he was a saint already in the eyes of his students, and that worried me a little, because every pedestal is taller than the man who sits on it.

The sages returned, and the discourse continued for three inter-rogative hours, until the sages ran out of questions. Then they knelt at Idriss's feet, asking for a blessing in return for the one they'd given him at the start of the contest.

'I do love our games, Idriss,' Let Me See remarked, the last to part. 'I am always grateful to the Divine that we are free to be generous with our ideas, and all the new ones to come, may we be so blessed.'

The sages left along the easier path, with rose petals protecting their feet. And they were thoughtful, perhaps, if not less doubtful, ambitious and grumpy.

Idriss retired to bathe and pray. We helped to pull the temporary pagoda down, and gathered up the carpets and trays.

Karla took over the kitchen as a volunteer, and cooked vegetarian pulao, cauliflower and potato pieces in coconut-cream gravy, green beans and peas in coriander and spinach sauce, carrot and pumpkin pieces foil-roasted in the fire, and basmati rice scented with almond milk.

Watching Karla operate large pots and woks of rice and vegetables on six gas jets at the same time, her mastery of taste and colour sizzling in hurricanes of steam, I was mesmerised, marvelling at it like an owl, until she pulled me in to wash the dishes.

We worked in the kitchen shelter with three young women from the community of students. They chatted with Karla about music, fashion and movies, while preparing food for twenty-eight devoted people. They regarded cooking for Idriss and the others on the mountain as a sacred duty, and they put their love in the food that their teacher would taste.

When not cooking, praying or studying, the devotees liked to eat, and not a crumb of Karla's fragrant preparations remained when the feast ended. She didn't eat much herself, but raised her glass to the many compliments, offering a toast at the sated end.

'That's it for me, for another year,' she said. 'To cooking once a year!'

'To cooking once a year!' devotees who cooked every day shouted.

When all was stacked in gleaming towers, and most of the devotees left the camp or went to sleep, the mountain sinners sat around the fire: Karla, Didier, Vinson, Randall, Ankit and me.

Didier suggested a suggestive game, where anyone who inadvert-ently said a suggestive word in the conversation had to take a drink.

His theory was that the one who was most obsessed with sex would get drunk the fastest, and then we'd all know.

I already knew that it was Didier, who was also, as it happens, almost immune to alcohol. Karla knew it, too, and redirected the conversation.

'How about *this*, guys,' she suggested, standing to leave. 'Why don't you tell each other the true story of why you're sitting here, and not sitting somewhere else, with the love of your life?'

'Rannveig's in an ashram,' Vinson began without help. 'And it's my fault. I love her so much that I think I made her, like, *holy*, you know? And I don't think there's a reverse exorcism for that.'

'I know exactly what you mean,' Randall averred. 'But I wish I didn't.'

Karla and I said goodnight. I grabbed one of the rolls of carpet, a canvas sheet, a coil of rope, and my backpack of essential supplies. Karla carried two blankets and her own bag of indispensables. We walked by torchlight to the knoll, scaring ourselves with leaping shadows when the path turned suddenly.

'You almost shot that shadow, didn't you?' I asked, tucked in beside her on the narrow path, the torch in her hand throwing circles of coherence on the dark canvas of night's forest.

'You're the one who reached for a knife,' she said, cuddling close.

I used the rope to set up a fairly decent shelter. *With the right rope*, the president of a trucker's union once said to me, *and enough of it, a trucker can do just about anything*.

In my trucker's tent we talked, and kissed, and went through every argument and reply we'd heard in the discourse.

'You guys are so completely not getting it,' Karla said sleepily, when we'd run through the valley of ideas together.

'Us *guys*?'

'You guys.'

'Not getting what?'

'The truth,' she said.

'What truth?'

'The big truth.'

'About what?'

'That's the point, exactly,' Karla said, her eyes green mirrors.

'The point about what?'

'You men are obsessed with the truth,' Karla said. 'But the truth isn't such a big deal. The truth is just inhibition, after three drinks.'

'I don't need a drink,' I smiled, 'to be disinhibited with you.'

We kissed and loved and kept talking, and arguing, working our way back to the end of the beginning until we slept, as a half-moon proclaimed the sky with fuzzy brilliance.

I woke suddenly, aware that we weren't alone. I lifted my head slowly and saw Idriss, with his back turned. He was standing at the edge of the knoll a few metres away, and staring at the silver cup of the moon.

I glanced at Karla. She was still sleeping beside me, wearing my T-shirt like a nightdress.

'I am glad that you see me,' Idriss said, not turning around.

'I'm always glad to see *you*, Idriss,' I whispered. 'I'd stand up, but I'm not dressed for it.'

He chuckled, leaning on his staff to look at the stars.

'I am very happy that you and Karla are here,' he said. 'And I want you to understand that you're welcome to stay, for as long as it pleases you to remain.'

'Thank you,' I said.

Karla woke beside me, and saw Idriss.

'Idriss,' she said, sitting up. 'Please, sit and be comfortable.'

'I am always comfortable, Karla, wherever I am,' he said cheerfully, still not turning to face us. 'And, I suspect that this is true for both of you as well, isn't it?'

'Can we offer you something?' Karla asked, rubbing her eyes awake. 'Some water or juice?'

'In offering something to me with those words,' Idriss said, 'I am nourished already.'

'We'll get dressed, and join you,' I suggested. 'I can make you a cup of tea by the fire.'

'I will leave, in a minute or two,' he replied. 'But there is something that I must tell you both, and my mind will not allow me to ignore it, so I must apologise for the intrusion.'

'We're the intruders,' Karla said.

He laughed again.

'Did you wish that you were beside me today, Karla,' he said, 'when I was facing the inquisitors?'

'I did, Idriss,' she laughed. 'Pencil me in, next time.'

'Done,' he replied, already leaving us in his mind. 'Are you two ready to receive my instruction?'

'Yes,' Karla whispered uncertainly.

'You must renounce violence, both of you, and do whatever it takes to live peacefully.'

'It's hard to be non-violent in a violent world, Idriss,' Karla said.

'Violence, tyranny, oppression, injustice, these are all mountains on the topography of life's journey,' Idriss said. 'Life is an encounter with those mountains. The safest way to pass beyond the mountain is to walk around it. But if you choose that path it becomes the whole of your life, because walking around becomes a circle that never stops, and one of those mountains becomes your destiny. The only way onwards, to something else beyond the circle, and to see clearly enough to avoid new mountains, is to climb the mountain and cross it from the peak. But the thing about a mountain is that no part of the climb is less dangerous than the part you just completed.'

'Which means?' I asked.

'I worry about you both,' he said. 'I worry about you often. The view from the top, after the dangerous climb, is something you can't have if you take the safer path within the circle, but it has great risks. And you must rely on each other and help each other more than ever before. You are already climbing through the mountain shadow, both of you.'

'Have you climbed all your mountains, Idriss?' Karla asked.

'I was married once,' he said softly and slowly. 'A long time ago. And my wife, may her soul know happiness, was a constant companion in the spiritual search, as you are for one another. I would be nothing, without all the many things we learned together. And now I climb through the mountain shadow alone.'

'You're never alone, Idriss,' Karla said. 'Everyone who knows you carries you inside.'

He laughed softly.

'You remind me of her, Karla. And you remind me of myself, Lin, in another life. I was not always the peaceful man you know. Never give up on the love you feel for one another. Never stop searching for peace, within yourselves.'

He turned silently, and walked back toward the camp.

Night noises returned, and a bell tolled at a railway signal somewhere far away. Karla was silent, staring at the leaf shadows where Idriss had vanished.

'We've got some stuff to work out, you and me, if we're gonna get this right,' she said, looking back at me, her eyes green moonlight. 'And I want to get this right, for once, with you.'

'I thought we already had it pretty right.'

'We just got started,' she smiled, stretching sleepily, and snuggling in beside me. 'Couple of months up here, like this, we'll work all the kinks in just right.'

She pulled away from me suddenly, and fetched around among her things until she found the letter she'd been holding for me.

'This is the right time for a mountain shadow letter, if ever there was,' she said, giving me the letter and cuddling in beside me again.

She yawned, gorgeously, closed her eyes, and slept. I opened the single-page letter. It was from Gemini George. I read it by the light of the torch.

Hey, mate, Gemini here, letting you know that me and Scorpio haven't found the guru that cursed him yet, but we're still on the trail. We was in Karnataka, on a mountain, then Bengal, and somewhere in between I got sick, mate, and I'm not feeling too good, but I can't let Scorpio down, so we'll keep on searching. I just wanted someone who cares about me to know that I don't have no regrets, if I don't come back, because I love my life, and I love my friend Scorpio.

Yours sincerely,
Gemini

I put the letter away, and held Karla close until she slept deeply in my arms, but it took me a while to find sleep.

I was thinking of the men sitting together by the fire, Ankit and Vinson, Didier and Randall, separated from love but finding it again in shared stories, thrown into the fire one wooden tribute at a time.

I thought of Abdullah, who never lost his faith in anything, but was almost always alone. I saw Vikram in a dark lane of memory, as alone in death as he was in the half-life of addiction.

I thought of Naveen, knowing that he was in love with Diva Devnani, but that he was staring at her through a wall of thorns called polite society.

787

I thought of Ahmed, of the House of Style, who told me once, during a very close shave, that he'd loved the same young woman passionately all his life, though both his family and hers had torn them apart, and he hadn't seen her since he was nineteen years old.

I thought of Idriss, alone, and Khaderbhai alone, and Tariq alone, and Nazeer alone, and Kavita, alone without Lisa, and all the others who were living and dying alone, but always in love, or believing in love.

The wonder isn't that love finds us, as strange and fated and mystical as that is. The wonder is that even when we never find it, even when love waits in the wings of dream too long, even when love doesn't knock on the door, or leave messages, or put flowers in our hands, so many of us never stop believing in love.

Lovers, too happy loving, don't need to believe. Lives unloved that never stop believing are saints of affection, keeping love itself alive in gardens of faith.

I looked at Karla, breathing into my chest. She flinched in the corner of a dream. I soothed her until her breathing was my personal music of peace again.

And I thanked whatever Fate or stars or mistakes or good deeds gave me that beautiful peace, when she was with me. And I slept, at last, and the half-moon, a silver chalice, showered stars on our dreams of the mountain shadow.

CHAPTER EIGHTY-ONE

THE MOUNTAIN MADE ITS OWN PLACE IN TIME, marked by rituals and sunsets, meals and meditations, fires, penance, prayers and laughter. One by one our crew of friends left the teacher's mesa, and finally only Karla and I remained with Idriss, Silvano and a few students.

And she'd been right to ask for the time away from the city: simplified living, strangely enough, added new complexities to our relationship, and the splinters of city life were slowly blunted on the handle of understanding. We talked for hours every day and night, visiting the past while the present escaped us.

'He saved me,' Karla said one day, weeks into the stay, when the conversation drifted into the Khaderbhai years.

'You met him on the plane, when you were on the run.'

'I did. I was a mess. I'd killed a man, a rapist, my rapist, and even though I knew I'd do it again if I had to, I was a mess. I made it to the airport, and I bought a ticket, and got on the plane, but I fell apart in the air, five miles above the earth. Khaderbhai was sitting beside me. He had a return ticket to Bombay, and I had a one-way ticket. He talked to me, and when the plane landed he brought me here, to the mountain. And I went to work for him the next day.'

'You loved him,' I said, because I'd loved him.

'Yes. I didn't like him, and I told him that, and I didn't agree with his way of doing things, but I loved him.'

'For better or worse, he was a force in the city, and in all of our lives.'

'He used me,' she said. 'And I let him. And I used people that he asked me to use. I used you, for him. But I don't feel anything but . . . love . . . for him, when I think of him. Is it the same for you?'

'It is.'

'I still feel him sometimes, standing beside me, when things get bad.'

'Me, too,' I said. 'Me, too.'

Karla and I enjoyed the time on the holy mountain, but we still liked to stay in touch with the unholy city. A newspaper made its way up the mountain once a week, and occasional visitors brought news of friends and foes, but our best updates came from the young Ronin, Jagat, who was running my bing for me while I was on the mountain.

Jagat met us in the car park beneath the caves, every two weeks. The news that he brought from the city always made us feel good about the steep climb back to the peak.

Politicians and other fanatics, Jagat reported, were doing their best to ensure that cooperation was impossible, especially among friends. In some areas, plastic barricades had begun to segregate neighbours and neighbourhoods, sometimes on nothing more than food preferences, breaking the shell of tolerance.

In streets and slums and working places across the city, people of every inclination got along well, and did good work. But in political party offices, those elected to represent the people put up fences between the people wherever friendship threatened political war. And people rallied blindly on both sides of the line, forgetting that barricades only ever separate armies of the poor.

Vishnu completed his purge, and the fully Hindu 307 Company was blessed by holy men, in Vishnu's new mansion on Carmichael Road, not far from the art gallery that Karla had abandoned to Taj, but much deeper in the deep-pocket belt of Bombay's elite.

A lavish housewarming party warmed the frosty noses of local snobs, Jagat said, and some of the movie star guests remained regular visitors to Vishnu's excess.

'Vishnu put up the money for a really big Hindi picture,' Jagat said. 'They're shooting it in Bulgaria, or Australia. One of those foreign places. His photo was in all the papers, at the big shot party, when they announced the new movie.'

'And nobody moved to arrest him for killing the Afghan guards, killing Nazeer and Tariq, and starting the fire that ate Khaderbhai's house, and a portion of the city?'

'No witnesses, baba-dude. Charges dropped. The Assistant

Commissioner was at the party to announce the new movie. The hero of the movie is a rough and ready cop, based on the Assistant Commissioner dude himself, and how tough he was on crime and criminals, and how many of them he killed in encounters. And Vishnu is paying for it. I don't get it, man. It's like robbing your own bank, somehow.'

'I hear you,' I said.

'Funny guys,' Karla laughed. 'How many bodyguards did Vishnu have with him?'

'Four, I think,' Jagat said. 'About the same as the Assistant Commissioner.'

'Why the bodyguard question?' I asked her.

'It's the *Inverse Fair Law*. The more bodyguards, the less integrity.'

'And the Cycle Killers have totally changed their image,' Jagat replied, shaking his head. 'They got a complete new look.'

'*Recycled* Killers,' Karla said. 'How's the new look?'

'Well, I guess you can say it's better than the old look. They wear white slacks, and peppermint-coloured shirts.'

'All of them?'

'Yeah. They're heroes, now.'

'Heroes?' I doubted.

'I'm not kidding. People love those guys. Even my girlfriend bought me a peppermint shirt.'

'Cycle Killers in Jeeps, huh?'

'In Jeeps, with chrome bicycles attached on the roll bars.'

'And they don't kill people any more?'

'No. They're called *No Problem* now.'

'No Problem?' Karla asked, intrigued.

'Yeah.'

'That's like calling yourself *Okay*,' I said. 'Everybody says *no problem* every three minutes, in India. People say *no problem* even when there is a problem.'

'Exactly,' Jagat replied. 'It's brilliant. No problem too big, or too small. No Problem.'

'You're kidding me, Jagat.'

'No way, baba-dude,' he insisted. 'I swear. And it's working. People are asking them to negotiate for the release of kidnap victims, and such. They got a kidnapped millionaire free last week, and the only fingers he had left were on his left hand. Those fingers were on the line, too, until No Problem got on the case. People are asking them to fix building and construction problems that have tied up crores of rupees for years, man. They're working shit out, for anyone who pays them.'

'Nice,' Karla said.

'Uh-huh,' I said, not easy with what I'd heard.

Back Street, Main Street and Wall Street are the three big streets in every city, and none of them play well together on the shallower edges of tangled banks.

The streets are apart, and false distinctions keep them apart, because whenever they intersect eyes find love, and minds see injustice, and the truth sets them free. Power, in any street, has a lot to lose from free minds and hearts, because power is the opposite of freedom. As one of the powerless, I prefer the Back Street guys to stay out of Main Street, the cops to fund their own movies, and the Wall Street guys to stay out of everything, until all the streets become One Street.

I had to pull my thoughts away: I knew that every hour Jagat spent with us added traffic to his ride back to the city. Karla, thinking with me perhaps, brought me back.

'Have you been checking on Didier for us?' Karla asked the young Ronin.

'*Jarur*,' the young street soldier said, spitting. 'He still hangs out at Leopold's, and he's fine.

'Hey, those Zodiac guys,' he said, 'the millionaires, they're back in town.'

'Where?'

'The Mahesh, man,' he said. 'I can't check on anyone inside that place. Not born with the right barcode to get past that scanner, you know.'

'If you find anything out, let me know.'

'Sure. Hey, you know why people looked after those two foreigners so much when they lived on the street?' he asked thoughtfully.

'They're very nice guys?' I suggested.

'Apart from that,' he said, his foot making a pattern of swirls in the dust at our feet.

'Please, tell us,' Karla urged, always drawn to the sun inside.

'They were called the *Zodiac* Georges,' he said. 'That's why. In India, I mean, it's like a really big deal, you know? It's like calling yourself Karma, or something. Everywhere they went, they carried the Zodiac with them, in their names. When you fed them, you fed the Zodiac. When you offered them a safe place, you offered safety to the Zodiac. When you protected them from bullies, you protected the Zodiac from negative energies. And making offerings to the planets that guide us and mess us up is, like, really important. There's a lotta people out there, baba-dude, who miss the chance to offer something to the Zodiac guys, now that they're so rich they don't need it.'

India. Time measured in coincidence, and the logic of contradiction. Jagat pushed me off a perch of equilibrium I thought I'd claimed in India. But that shock happened almost every day, and shook the branch every time. The world I was living in, and not born into, rained strange flowers from every tree that gave me shelter.

'That's a lovely story, Jagat,' Karla said.

'It is?' he asked, shyness hiding in a frown.

'Yes. Thank you for sharing it.'

Jagat, whose name means *The World*, blushed and looked away, instinctively reaching for the handle of the knife in his belt.

'Hey, listen, man,' he said, turning back to me, his scarred young face telling the same stories every time someone looked at him. 'I don't feel right, taking all the money from your operation.'

'You're doing all the work,' I said. 'Why shouldn't you take all the money? I'm the one who's in your debt, for keeping it running. I owe you significant on this, Jagat-dude.'

'Fuck you, man,' he laughed. 'I'm putting twenty-five per cent aside for you, every week, whether you like it or not, okay?'

'Cool, *jawan*,' I said, using the Hindi word for *soldier*. 'I accept.'

'When you get back from this spooky place full of tigers and holy men, there'll be something there for you.'

'When I get back to your spooky place full of businessmen and cops,' I said. 'I'll be damn glad to get it.'

'Let's ride with Jagat to the highway and back,' Karla suggested.

'Good idea. Want some company, Jagat, or you wanna go fast?'

'Let's glide all the way down, baba-dude.'

'*Kruto!*' Karla said.

'What's this? Has Oleg been teaching you Russian?' I asked, taking my bike off the stand.

'*Sprosite yego*,' she laughed.

'Which means?'

'Ask him.'

'I will,' I said, and she laughed harder.

A motorcycle is jealous metal. A motorcycle that loves you always knows when you even think about another motorcycle. And when she knows, she won't start. And because I'd looked at Jagat's bike, my bike didn't start for me, even after three kicks.

Jagat thumped his bike into slow staccato motorcycle music, the 350cc single-piston engine like a drum that gets you from place to place, so long as you let it play its own tune.

I tried the kick-starter again, but all I got was a derisory cough.

Karla leaned over, hugging the tank of my bike, her arms around one of the handlebars.

'A trip down the mountain and back again will be so good for you, baby,' she said to the bike. 'Let's go for a ride.'

I kicked, and she started, jamming the throttle for a second, showing off.

We rode with Jagat, coasting downhill side by side on the deserted forest road, to the beginning of the fiercely determined highway. We waved him away, and turned back.

We rode through an evening forest, shifting from daytime daring to nighttime cunning. Birds were returning to roosts, insects were rising from slumber and bats as wide as eagles were waking for the feast.

We rode the long road to the caves as slowly as the bike would allow. We rode through soft wind in shadows, hiding and revealing the sky. The young night was clear. The first stars woke, rubbing their eyes. A leaf-fire somewhere sent earth perfumes into the air. And we were two happy fugitives, together and free.

CHAPTER EIGHTY-TWO

W E REACHED THE SUMMIT CAR PARK, happy and free, and found Concannon waiting for us. He was sitting on the trunk of the red Pontiac Laurentian, and wearing a white shirt. I wanted it to match the car.

'Hold on, baby,' I said to Karla, sloping the bike to a stop.

I spun the bike around, and sped down the hill a few hundred metres before stopping again.

'What are you doing?'

'There's a hollow tree just through there,' I said. 'Wait for me.'

'Hide?' she asked, as if I'd asked her to give blood to Madame Zhou.

'Just wait. Until I get back.'

'Are you crazy?'

'That's Concannon, back there.'

'*That's* Concannon?' she said, intrigued by intriguing people.

'Wait here, Karla,' I said. 'I'll be back soon.'

'I repeat, are you crazy? I'm the one with the gun, remember? And I'm a better shot. And I thought you said we were in this together, never apart.'

It was a tough call. When your enemy is ruthless, losing begins where mercy ends. But she was brave, and probably be the last woman standing in any fight.

'Alright,' I said reluctantly. 'But don't take any chances with this guy. He talks as good as he fights.'

'Now I *have* to meet him,' she said. 'Let's make an entrance, Shantaram.'

We rode back to the car park, and I slugged the bike onto the side-stand. Karla and I walked away while the bike was still breathing, the steps between Concannon and me shrinking at a motivated clip. I ran the last step hard, and hit him on the jump.

795

'What the fuck?' he said, holding the side of his head.

He rolled off the back of the car, and danced around me, feigning a few jabs. I rolled with him, but he covered up, breaking away fast.

He was dancing me away from Karla. He might've had friends somewhere. I stepped back slowly until I was beside her.

'What are you doing up here, Concannon? Where are your goons?'

'I came here alone, boyo,' he said. 'Which is more than I can say for you.'

He grinned at Karla, waving a hand.

'Hello,' he said.

Karla slid the gun from her bag, and pointed it at him.

'If you're carrying a gun,' she said, 'throw it away.'

'I never carry a gun, miss,' Concannon replied.

'Good, because I always do. If you make a move, I'll hit you twice before you get halfway.'

'Understood,' he grinned.

'It's not very smart, coming up here,' she said. 'There are tigers in this forest. That's a good way to get rid of a body.'

'If I thought I could bend my knee,' Concannon grinned, 'without your boyfriend kickin' me in the undefended head, I'd do it, Miss Karla. It's an honour. Concannon's the name.'

'My boyfriend got pretty upset,' she said, 'when I burned your letter, and I wouldn't tell him what it said. I've been waiting for this chance, and I'm glad you gave it to me. Say it out loud, now, in front of him, if you've got the guts.'

'Well, so it's the *letter* that's got you so upset, is it? No, no, I'll decline your invitation to repeat my indecent proposals in front of this convict. I don't think that would be wise.'

'Like I thought,' she smiled. 'You wrote it, but you haven't got the guts to say it.'

'Did you not enjoy my little innuendos, then?' Concannon asked. 'I thought they were quite inventive, myself.'

'Shut up,' I said.

'You see what I have to deal with?' Concannon appealed to Karla.

'Shut up,' Karla replied. 'Right now, you're dealing with both of us. And not doing so good. What do you want here?'

'I came to tell your boyfriend somethin',' Concannon said. 'If I sit up there on the car, like I was before, will you not let me speak?'

796

'I'd prefer you in the trunk, Concannon,' I said. 'With the car going over the cliff.'

Concannon smiled, and shook his head.

'Hostility is ageing, you know,' he said. 'It adds *years* to your face. Can I sit peacefully on the fuckin' car and talk to you like a fellow Christian, or can't I?'

'Sit,' Karla said. 'Christian hands where I can see them.'

Concannon sat on the trunk of the car, his feet resting on the bumper.

'This would be a good time to talk your way out of this,' Karla said.

Concannon laughed, looking Karla up and down, and then looked at me, blue eyes still bright in the faint light of the car park.

'I didn't have nothin' to do with Lisa,' he said quickly. 'I never touched her. I only met her the once, well, the twice, I suppose you could say, but I liked her. She was a sweet thing. I'd never do anything like that. I only said it to get a rise out of you. I never touched her. And I never would've. It's not my way.'

I wanted to stop him. I wanted to lift the curse that someone had put on me with the mention of his name. It was bad: everything connected to him was bad.

'Keep talking,' Karla said.

'If I'd known what a sick thing Ranjit was, I'd have stopped him,' Concannon said. 'I swear it. I would've killed him myself, if I'd known what he was.'

His head was down. His guard was down. I wanted to run at him, and push him backwards through whatever malevolent window he'd jemmied open. But Karla wanted to know everything.

'Keep talking,' Karla continued. 'Tell us everything you know.'

'I didn't find out until later,' Concannon said. 'If I'd known before, there wouldn't have been any later.'

'We got that. Go on,' Karla said.

'I met that maniac, Ranjit, through the drugs. The high and mighty don't hesitate to come callin' on my kind, when they need drugs. When he told me he was buying stuff to put Lisa to sleep, that night, I wanted to come along.'

'Ranjit wanted the stuff, so he could put her to sleep?' Karla asked, too gently, it seemed to me.

'He did. Rohypnol tablets, he bought. I thought it was just a

797

prank. He told me they were friends, and they were havin' a private party.'

'But why did you tag along with him?'

'To torment your boyfriend,' Concannon said, pointing at me. 'That's why I sent the dirty little letter to you, and put my filthy mind in yours for a while, to torment this berserk convict motherfucker.'

'Shut up,' we both said.

'Well, you're a fine pair of holy hooligans. A perfect match.'

'Why were you there, Concannon?' Karla asked, the mention of his name pulling his blue eyes to her.

'I told you,' he smiled. 'I knew that if Lin, here, knew that I'd been in his home with his girl, while he was away, he'd be wilder than a stallion.'

'Why did you want him wild?'

'I did it to hurt him, because I knew that it would hurt that Iranian.'

'Abdullah?' Karla asked.

I hadn't told her. I couldn't betray the glory that Abdullah was, by speaking the truth of what he'd allowed himself to become that night, with Concannon.

'We killed a few people together,' Concannon replied casually. 'No big deal. But he went native on me, and it became a war between us. Your boyfriend here was just collateral damage.'

'Okay, that's enough for me,' I said.

'Have you ever tried anger management?' Concannon asked.

'Go away, Concannon. I just ran out of shut-up.'

'Before you go, if we let you go,' Karla said. 'Tell us what you know about Ranjit.'

I couldn't understand it. I didn't care about Ranjit, and I didn't want Lisa's name to slither from Concannon's serpent lips again, ever. Knowing what Concannon was capable of inflicting, knowing that his pedigree was approved by the Taureg, I wanted him unconscious or gone.

'Don't play games with us, Concannon,' I said. 'If you've got something to tell us, spit it out.'

'I ran across Ranjit at a party, in Goa. He was wearing a wig, as a disguise, but I knew it was him right away. Seein' as how he was a millionaire on the run and all, I thought he must have some money stashed away, so I got him wasted on cocaine and heroin, and persuaded him to take me back to his digs.'

'Ranjit had a house in Goa?' Karla asked.

'He was rentin' it, I think. A fine big place it was, though. A grand place. And all the while, I'm edgin' him toward the safe, wantin' him to open it for me, when he suddenly opens it himself, and says *Would you like to see a movie?*'

Karla put her hand on my arm gently.

'What kind of movie?'

'Sex tapes, it was,' Concannon laughed. 'Although it was very one-sided sex. The girls were all drugged senseless, you see. He wore a shower cap, and rubber gloves, leaving no trace of his sinfulness. He cleaned them and dressed them again, when he was done with them, and left them on his couch with a cosy blanket over their knees, so they woke up, and never even knew it happened.'

'Ranjit did that?'

'Yes, that he did,' Concannon said. 'You didn't know?'

I just got back another *shut up*, but Karla squeezed my arm.

'Did he tell you why he did it?'

'He said his wife was frigid, if you'll pardon me for his words, and she never had sex with him, so he used those sleepin' girls, like, to pretend that he was having sex with her. With *you*, that is.'

Karla squeezed my arm.

'You're saying that's what happened to Lisa?'

'I think,' he said, allowing his eyes to drift. 'I think he drugged her with the Rohypnol, in a drink, but gave her too much. My stuff was pure, you see. I think she died, poor thing, before he used her.'

'Who were the other girls?'

'That, I don't know.' Concannon shrugged. 'I only recognised one of them, and that's because her face is in the papers, sometimes. But . . . I can tell you one thing. They all looked like you, and he dressed them all in a black wig, when he had his way with them.'

'I've had enough of this,' I said.

'Don't be tellin' me to shut up again, boyo,' Concannon said to me. 'I didn't come here to cause trouble. I'm sick of trouble, though I never thought I'd hear meself say it. I'm retired.'

'This is a good place to make it permanent.'

'You're a wicked lad,' Concannon said, smiling. 'With wicked thoughts, in your wicked mind.'

'What did you do, when Ranjit showed you the movies?' Karla asked.

799

'Well, I knocked him about quite a bit, of course, and left him sense-less. I couldn't kill him, though I wanted to, because too many people had seen me with him. Then I took all the money from the safe, and I also took that tape of him with the girl from the papers.'

'What did you do with it?'

'Now, that's the funny part,' Concannon said, folding his arms, his feet poised on the bumper.

'*Funny?*' I said. 'You think any of this is funny?'

'Hands where I can see them,' Karla said, and Concannon lounged backwards on his hands. 'Funny how?'

'There's this young fool who buys cocaine from me now and then. He's not big, but he's got a very bad temper. His own family put a restraining order on him. He wants to be a movie star, so he deals a little stuff to the real movie stars, and gets the odd part. The girl in Ranjit's sick film is an actress, and he's her bad-tempered boyfriend.'

'Did you give him the film?' Karla asked, her eyes gleaming.

'I did, when he came to buy stuff,' Concannon replied, grinning happily. 'Ranjit used to sneak back into town, from time to time, and he always bought stuff from me. I told the violent lad that Ranjit would be ghostin' around, in disguise, at a nightclub he liked in Bandra.'

'So you told the kid where Ranjit would be.'

'Not only that. I gave the young savage a present. Gift-wrapped it meself. There was the movie, Ranjit's appointment at the nightclub, and an untraceable gun, full of untraceable bullets. Human nature took care of the rest.'

Karla squeezed my arm.

'You came up here, to tell us that you set up my ex-husband?' Karla asked.

'I came up here to warn your boyfriend,' Concannon said, straight-ening up.

'And you're gonna take a warning home again, Concannon.'

'There you go again,' he said, happily exasperated. 'You are the hard-est man in this whole city of screechin' heathens to befriend. I know executioners who are more fun than you. I'm tryin' to tell you, I'm a changed man.'

'I don't see a change,' I said. 'You're still breathing.'

'There's those wicked thoughts again.'

'Listen,' he said calmly, 'I've done with all that. I'm a businessman now, and legitimately so. The fact that I bear you no grudge for our last encounter should testify to that.'

'You just never learn, do you?'

'But I *did* learn,' he insisted. 'That's what I'm tryin' to say. After that fight we had, I thought about everything. I mean, everything. I got hurt, you see. My shoulder hasn't healed well, and it doesn't work the way it should. My timing's off, and I'll never again fight the way I did. See, I never before let anyone get close enough to best me, and it shook me up. My Road to Damascus experience was in a warehouse in Bombay, and it was an Australian convict who knocked me off my horse. I've changed. I'm a businessman, now.'

'What kind of business?' Karla asked, relaxing her grip on my arm.

'I've put all my money into a venture with Dennis.'

'The Sleeping Baba?'

'The same. One fine day, I got to thinkin' about that proverb, you know, that if you sit quietly by a river for long enough, the bodies of your enemies will float by.'

I wanted Concannon to float by, on the Ganges.

'And it occurred to me, in another Road to Damascus moment, that the river isn't made of water, it's made of stainless steel. It's the under-taker's table, you see? So, Dennis and me, we bought an undertaking business, and now we're undertakers. Already, since we started, one of my enemies floated by on the preparation table. A fine drunken laugh I had that night, dressin' him up nicely for the drop.'

'Dennis went for this?' I asked.

'We're a natural fit. I know what dead *looks* like, and he knows what dead *feels* like. I've never seen a man more tender with a body. He calls them sleepers, and he talks to them like they're just asleep. It's very kind. Very tender. But I keep a baseball bat handy, in case one of them ever talks back.'

Concannon stopped, clapped his hands together, then put the swol-len knuckles into a knotted pyramid of prayer.

'I know it's hard to think that a menace to the living and the dead, like me, can give the whole thing up, but it's the truth. I've changed, and the proof of it is that I've come up here, riskin' your temper, to tell you two things. The first, I've already told you, which is all that I know about Ranjit, and that sweet girl.'

'And the second thing?' Karla asked for me.

801

'The second thing is that the 307 Company have hired some out-of-town *goondas* to kill that Iranian, Abdullah, tonight. And since Abdullah's hiding out up here, that puts you two in the firing line.'

'When will they come?' I asked.

Concannon checked his watch, and grinned the reply.

'In about three hours,' he said. 'You'd have had longer, if you weren't so bloody obstreperous, and I could've cleared me mind without interruption.'

For all I knew, Concannon was setting us up. I didn't like it.

'Why are you telling us this?' Karla asked.

'I'm tyin' up loose ends, miss,' Concannon smiled. 'I never had nothin' against your man. I tried to recruit the stubborn fool, and I wouldn't have done that, if I hadn't taken a shine to 'im. I treated him poorly, when it was Abdullah that I hated, because he turned on me, and threatened my life.'

'Stop talking about Abdullah,' I said.

'But I don't hate him any more,' he persisted. 'He did nothin' wrong, even if he is an Iranian . . . person. It was *me* that did wrong, and I admit it freely. Anyway, the Iranian will likely meet his end, tonight. And now I found a place where I feel at home, and in one way or another, I know I'll find peace, as other people kill my enemies and send them to me. I'll be with my own kind, so to speak. I don't know if you understand.'

'We understand,' Karla said, although I didn't.

'Do you believe me, when I say that I have no quarrel with either of you, and that I wish you no harm?'

'No,' I said. 'Goodbye, Concannon.'

'They say he's a writer,' Concannon winked at Karla. 'They must be teenie weenie little books that he writes.'

'He's the big book,' Karla gave back. 'I'm the big character. Thank you, Concannon, for the heads-up. What's your first name, by the way?'

'Fergus,' I said before he did, and he laughed, jumping from the car with his arms wide.

'You *do* like me! I *knew* it! Will you stab me, if I give you a hug?'

'Yes. Don't come back.'

He let his arms fall slowly, smiled at Karla, and walked a few steps backwards to his car.

'There's no use in callin' the police,' he said at the car. 'There's a lot of money been paid to keep this mountain dark tonight, until the Iranian is dead, once and for all.'

He started the car, locked the wheel, hit the gas and spun around beside us, his arm resting on the open window.

'Would you like some dynamite?' he asked. 'I've a box full in the back, and no purpose for it at all, now.'

'Maybe next time,' Karla smiled, waving him away.

The twinned tail-lights on either side of the car were bats, swooping into the first curve. She turned to me quickly, waking the queens.

'We haven't seen Abdullah up here, so he must be at Khaled's. We've gotta warn him.'

'Agreed, and then Silvano and the students. This might spill up the hill to Idriss.'

She braced herself for the run to Khaled's mansion, but I held her back.

'Can we talk about something, before we talk to Khaled?'

'Sure,' she said, relaxing from a run almost started. 'What's up?'

'You know how we said we'll always be together?'

She looked at me, hands on hips.

'I'm not hiding in a hollow tree, Shantaram,' she said, the squint in her smile scanning me.

'I don't mean that. I'm trying to explain something.'

'Now?'

'If things get rough tonight, don't separate from me. Stick to my side, or my back. Lock your elbow in mine, if you have to. If we're back to back, you shoot, and I'll cut. But let's be one thing, because if we're not, I'll go nuts worrying about you.'

She laughed, and hugged me, so I guess some part of it must've been right.

'Let's go,' she said, getting ready for the run to Khaled's.

'Wait,' I said.

'Again?'

'*Maybe next time?*' I said, repeating her final words to Concannon.

'What?'

'You said *Maybe next time* to Concannon, when he offered us dynamite.'

'*Now?* You're bringing this up *now?*'

'Concannon isn't a *next-time* guy. He's a *one-time* guy, and half a planet is almost far enough away.'

803

'You don't believe in redemption?'

She was adorable, when she teased, but we were talking about Concannon, and there were killers coming to the mountain to kill our friend.

'I don't believe Concannon,' I replied. 'The *overtaking* version, or the *undertaking* version. I don't believe anything he says. This could be a trap.'

'Good,' she shouted, sprinting up the path. 'Coming?'

CHAPTER EIGHTY-THREE

W E HEARD MUSIC AND CHANTING, hundreds of voices in harmony, as we turned the last bend on the tree-lined path to Khaled's mansion. It was lit like a prison, with spotlights fixed to trees.

'His flock must've grown,' Karla said quietly, as we stopped together on the path before the steps, looking at the floodlit veranda. 'That's quite a chorus.'

The trees around us, bleached of leaves by spotlights, were startled skeletons with their hands in the air. The chanting was intense, the singers drunk on devotion.

Khaled walked out through the wide doorway and onto the veranda, his hands on his hips.

He was a shadow figure, black against the lights that were slow-burning our eyes. He had two shadow figures with him.

He raised his hand, and the devoted chanting stopped. Insects sang the silence again.

'*Salaam aleikum,*' he said.

'*Wa aleikum salaam,*' Karla and I both said.

Very loud, very big dogs started barking somewhere. It was a sound that makes you think of sharp teeth, and running away. Karla slipped her elbow through mine. The barking was ferocious. Khaled raised his hand again, and the barking stopped.

'Sorry, wrong tape,' he said, handing a remote control to a shadow figure. 'What are you doing here, Lin?'

'We came to see Abdullah,' Karla said.

'What are you doing here, Lin?'

'Like *she* said,' I replied. 'Where is he?'

'Abdullah has cleansed himself for death, and is at prayer,' Khaled replied. 'No-one can disturb him. Not even me. He is alone with Allah.'

'They're coming for him,' I said.

'We know,' Khaled said. 'There are no students here. The ashram has been closed for some time. We are —'

The chanting started again. After a few frenzies it stopped, mid-mantra.

'Stop playing with the remote, Jabalah!' Khaled shouted over his shoulder.

Insects and frogs welcomed the silence again.

'We are ready for war,' Khaled said.

'Now, where have I read that before?' Karla said.

Khaled held up his hand imperially.

'I am the one who spread the rumour that Abdullah is here. I am the one who provoked this attack, out of the city. This is a trap, Lin, and you are standing in it.'

Dogs barked again.

'Jabalah!' Khaled shouted, and tape stopped.

Khaled walked down the silence, to join us on the path. He'd lost half the weight he'd gained, and had been training again. He looked fit, strong, confident and dangerous. It seemed that he'd learned to love himself.

He took my hands in his, leaning close between us, but he spoke to Karla in whispers.

'Hello, Karla,' he said, embracing me. 'I cannot greet you, directly, in front of my men, because you are a woman, in the company of a man who is not your family.'

He hugged me close to him, whispering into my ear for the sake of his men, but speaking to her.

'My commiserations, on the loss of your husband. You must leave this place, now. There will be war tonight.'

He pulled away, but I held his arm.

'You knew about this, and you didn't warn us?'

'You are warned *now*, Lin, and you should take that as a blessing. You *must* leave. My men are nervous. Let's not have any accidents.'

'*Allah hafiz*, Khaled,' Karla said, dragging me away.

'Tell Abdullah . . . tell him we're here, on the mountain, if he needs us,' I said.

'I'll tell him, but I can only speak to him when the fighting begins,' Khaled answered sadly. 'Peace be with you both tonight.'

He waved, because we were at the end of the path, and it was too far away for him to speak his mind. We waved back, and we jogged to the start of the long climb up the mountain.

I stopped her. It was dark, but reflections glittered in her eyes.

'Can I tell you something?'

'*Again?*' She laughed.

'It might get bad tonight,' I said. 'If you want to get far away, I'll take you anywhere you want to go.'

'Let's go warn Idriss first,' she smiled, starting on the path.

I chased her all the way up the slope, and we were puffing hard when we rushed onto the mesa, bright with students, talking late by the fire.

We found Silvano, and pushed him to a meeting with Idriss, in the big cave.

'Killers,' Idriss said, when the story told itself.

'And pretty good at it,' I said. 'We've gotta get away from here, Idriss. At least for tonight.'

'Of course. We must take the students to safety. I'll give the instruction at once.'

'I will stay and protect this place,' Silvano said.

'You must not,' Idriss said. 'You must come with us.'

'I must disobey,' Silvano replied.

'You must come with us,' Idriss repeated.

'It's just good sense, Silvano,' I agreed. 'If someone from down there tries to escape up here, and others start chasing him, nobody will be safe.'

'I must stay, master-*ji*,' Silvano said. 'And you must go.'

'It is possible to be too brave, Silvano,' Idriss said. 'Just as it is possible to be too loyal.'

'All of your writings are here, master-*ji*,' Silvano said. 'More than fifty boxes of them, most of them unpacked for study. We cannot gather them together in the time we have. I will stay, and guard your work.'

I admired his dedication, but it seemed like too big a risk, to me: too high a price for the written word. Then Karla spoke.

'We'll stay with you, Silvano,' she said.

'Karla,' I began, but she smiled true love at me, and, well, what can you do?

'Looks like you've got company, Silvano,' I sighed.

807

'It is settled, then,' Idriss said. 'Come with me, now, and gather the students together with their valuables, as quickly as possible. We will walk the slow path to the Kali temple, where the highway begins. Send a message to us there, when all is quiet again in our sanctuary.'

'Idriss,' I said. 'I feel bad that this has found its way up here. I'm sorry.'

'Taking responsibility for the decisions and actions of others is a sin against Karma,' Idriss said. 'Equal, in gravity, to avoiding responsibility for your own decisions and actions. You did not cause this. It is not your karmic burden. Be safe tonight. You are blessed, all of you.'

He placed his hand on our heads, one by one, chanting mantras of protection.

The students tipped their personal belongings into shawls, tied them into bundles, and assembled at the entrance to the slow path downhill, the torches and lanterns in their hands whirling like fireflies.

Idriss joined them, turning to wave to us, and led the way, the long staff in his right hand.

Another student, named Vijay, had decided to stay with us. He was thin, tall, and dressed in white pyjama-style cotton shirt and pants. He was barefoot, and carrying a bamboo pole that reached to his shoulder.

His young face was expressionless, as he watched his teacher depart. He turned his fine features on me, eyes lit with India.

'Are you fine?' he asked.

I looked at his bamboo stick, remembering the men I'd fought in the last year, from Scorpions to Concannon, and thinking that it might be a good idea to tie a knife to the end of that stick.

'I'm fine,' I said. 'I've got a spare knife, if you want to tie it to that stick.'

He stood back, began to whirl the stick around, jumped while he whirled, and brought the stick down a toe away from my boot.

'Or . . . maybe not,' I said.

'Shall we split up, and take different vantage points?' Silvano asked.

'No!' Karla and I said, together.

'Anyone who comes up here, comes onto our ground,' I said. 'We find a position with cover, with an escape route, where we can see the top of the climbing path. If anyone comes into the open space, we can scare them away with gunfire, and noise.'

'And if it becomes a fight?'

'We kill them,' Karla said, 'before they kill us. You're a dead shot, Silvano, and I'm not bad. We're okay.'

'Or,' I suggested, 'we could escape, regroup, and wait it out. There are plenty of places to hide, and they can't stay on this mountain forever.'

'I say we fight,' the student with the stick said.

'I say we decide to run or to fight, when we have to decide,' I said.

'I agree that we should have a good place of cover,' Silvano mused. 'The cave nearest to the path is the best place to see them coming.'

'No exit strategy,' I said. 'I always like a way out.'

'There *is* a way out,' Silvano said. 'Let me show you.'

There was a curtain at the far end of the cave. I'd seen it, but had always thought that it hung there to cover the bare cave wall.

Silvano pushed it aside, and led us by torchlight along a narrow channel that had formed or been carved between the first cave and the last.

We emerged from the passageway into Idriss's cave, close to the ragged edge of the jungle: only a few steps from cover.

'I like it,' Karla said. 'I'd buy it, and live here, if I could.'

'Me, too,' I agreed. 'Let's get set up in the first cave. We don't have long.'

'I don't know about you,' Silvano said, rubbing his belly, 'but I'm hungry.'

We brought cold food, water, blankets and torches to the cave. I ate the plate of food Karla passed to me before I knew what it was. But when hunger was satisfied, fear started nagging.

Karla, sitting beside me, and killers on the way: my instincts were shouting to get the hell out of hell. But she was calm, and resolute. She'd finished her food, and was cleaning her gun. She was humming. And I guess, when I look back at it, she always had enough guts for both of us.

'Where are the boxes of Idriss's writings?' I asked, looking away to Silvano.

'In the main cave,' Silvano replied, finishing his food.

'Then let's keep any action away from there. A stray bullet could start a fire.'

'Agreed.'

Vijay took Karla's plate and stacked it with the others, outside the cave.

'I know this forest,' Silvano said, standing and stretching. 'I will make a search of the area, with Vijay. And I need to visit the bathroom.'

He walked out to join Vijay quickly, and they passed from sight, moving to the right. The point where the path led onto the mesa was to our left.

So many feet had moved across the ridge that only wild grasses grew here and there. There was no moon yet, but it was a clear night, and we had a good view of the flattened space, fifty metres away.

My heart was beating fast. I slowed it down, willing it calm, but thoughts of Karla hurt or captured pulled the heartbeat back again. She looked at me, and she knew how afraid I was for her.

'*Make a big noise, and run and hide?*' she said, her mouth a beautiful sneer. 'That's your strategy?'

'Karla —'

'*Chee, chee!* Can you keep that one to yourself at the next meeting?'

'*I say we fight*, the guy with the bamboo stick says,' I laughed. 'That's a better strategy? I just don't think it's worth fighting for.'

'A writer who doesn't think written wisdom is worth fighting for?'

'No. I've escaped through windows, because the cops were chasing me, and I had to leave everything behind. It's all gone, that work, but I'm still here, and I'm still writing. No life is worth the written word.'

'How so?'

Karla didn't ask *How so* unless it was a challenge.

'It's not because the texts are sacred that life is important. It's because life is sacred that the texts are important.'

She grinned happy queens at me.

'That's my guy. Let's get ready.'

We piled boxes and sacks in the entrance to the cave, and stretched out with a view of the open ridge. She held my hand.

'I wouldn't be anywhere else on this planet, right now,' she said.

I couldn't reply, because we heard the first shot.

The further you are from a gunshot, the feebler the fear. The blast that deafens you, close to your ear, is a click of the fingers from far away. We heard the first shots, sounding like handclaps, and then it became volleys of applause.

Silvano and Vijay scampered back to the cave, squatting down beside us.

'There's an army down there,' Silvano said, listening to the spatters of gunfire.

'Two armies,' I said. 'And let's hope they stay there.'

The fusillades finally subsided. There was silence, and then single shots snapped, one after another, a few steps apart. There were quite a lot of them.

We waited in the dark, listening hard to every broken twig or shuffle of wind. Minutes passed in threatening silence, and then we heard noises, grunting and moaning, coming from the steep path.

Silvano and Vijay were up and running before I could caution them. Karla made to leave as well, but I held her down beside me.

A man appeared at the summit of the path, crawling on hands and knees. Silvano was a shadow, standing to his right, aiming the rifle at his head. The man staggered to his feet. He had a pistol in his hand.

Vijay swung his stick, disarming the man, but the pistol fired, and a bullet hit the wall of the cave not far from where we hunkered down.

'Good call, Shantaram,' Karla said. 'That bullet had my name on it, if I was standing there.'

The man hovered on wavering legs for a second and then fell, face flat to the ground. Vijay turned him over as Karla and I arrived.

The man was dead.

'You better check there wasn't a tail wagging on this one, Silvano,' I said.

'You know him?'

'His name's DaSilva.'

'Which side was he on?'

'The wrong side,' I said. 'Right to the end.'

Silvano and Vijay trotted away down the path to check for stragglers.

Staring at the body, I knew that I couldn't let it be found in the camp where Idriss taught. There was no choice. I had to move it. Karla had moved two bodies in her life: two that I knew about. I've moved three: one in prison, one in a friend's house, and the dead gangster who hated me, DaSilva. He was the hardest of them for both of us.

'We can't leave him here for the cops to find,' I said.

'You're right,' she replied. 'This is the kind of scandal that kills cleverness.'

'Not gonna be easy. That's a steep climb, with a dead body.'

'Yeah,' she said, looking around, her hands on her hips.

We wrapped him in a student's sari, and tied him securely. We fastened ropes for us to hold, at both ends.

We were just finished, when Silvano and Vijay arrived. Vijay's eyes were oysters of dread.

'A ghost?'

He was trembling, pointing at DaSilva's wrapped body.

'I hope so,' I said. 'We're taking him down to the house. There's no need for the cops to know he was up here.'

'Thank you,' Silvano said quickly. 'Let us help you.'

'We got this,' Karla said. 'They're our friends down there. They know us, but they don't know you, and they might start shooting if they see you. It'll be safer if we do this without you. Stay here and guard those books.'

'Okay,' Silvano smiled, doubtfully. 'Okay. If you insist.'

'*Presto*,' Karla said, tugging on the dead man's rope. 'This ghost has a way to go yet.'

CHAPTER EIGHTY-FOUR

W E DRAGGED DASILVA'S BODY TO THE RIDGE, and started down the path. I went first, taking most of the weight, while Karla held on as best she could from above.

I felt ashamed that I hadn't protected her from that sad and criminal thing we had to do: more ashamed, in fact, than I was of doing the sad and criminal thing. I thought of Karla's hands, and the rough rope shredding her skin, and scratches and grazes wounding her feet with every second step.

'Stop!' she said when we were just past halfway.

'What is it?'

She took a few deep breaths, and shook the tension from her arms and shoulders.

'Okay, this,' she puffed, one hand wiping hair from her forehead, the other holding a dead man, 'is officially the best date ever. Now, let's get this corpse down this fucking hill.'

At the base of the mountain, I carried DaSilva's body on my back along the path to Khaled's mansion. The path was still lit, and the door of the mansion was open. It seemed deserted.

We climbed the stairs together, and walked into the vestibule. I slipped DaSilva's body to the floor, and we began to untie him.

'What are you doing?' Khaled asked, from behind me.

I spun round to face him. He had a gun in his hand.

'*Salaam aleikum*, Khaled,' Karla said, and she had a gun in her hand.

'*Wa aleikum salaam*,' he responded. 'What are you doing?'

'Where's Abdullah?' I asked.

'He's dead.'

'Ah, no, no,' I said. 'Please, no.'

'May Allah take his soul,' Karla said.

'Are you sure he's dead?' I asked, choking the words. 'Where is he?'

'There were four other dead men on top of him, when I found him. One of them was Vishnu. I knew that arrogant thug would come here in person, to gloat. Now he's dead, and my Company will take everything he had.'

'Where's Abdullah's body?'

'With the bodies of my dead men,' Khaled said. 'In the dining room. And I ask you, for the last time, what are you doing here?'

'This miscreant wandered too far,' I said, pulling the cover back to reveal DaSilva's face. 'We're wandering him back. Is he one of yours, or theirs?'

'He's the man we used to set up the trap,' Khaled said. 'I shot him myself, after he served his purpose, but he got away.'

'He got back,' Karla said. 'Can we leave him here, Khaled? We want to keep Idriss out of this.'

'Leave him. My men will be back, soon, with the trucks. I'll put this one with the bodies we're throwing into the sewer tomorrow.'

'I don't want to see Abdullah's body, Khaled,' I said. 'Do you swear to me that he's dead?'

'*Wallah!*' he replied.

'*I* want to see him,' Karla said to me. 'But you don't have to come.'

Everywhere together, never apart: but sometimes the two of you is something that only one of you must do.

'I'll come,' I said, feeling sick already. 'I'll come.'

Khaled led us through a drawing room to the main dining room. Four bodies were lying on the table neatly, like pavement dwellers sleeping together on the street.

I saw Abdullah at once, his long black hair trailing over the edge of the table. I wanted to turn away. I wanted to run. That beautiful face, that lion heart, that fire in the sky: I couldn't bear to see it emptied, and cold.

But Karla went to him, put her head on his chest, and wept. I had to move. I drifted along the table, dead men's heads a breeze against my fingers, and took Abdullah's hand.

The face was stern, and I was comforted to see it. He was wearing white, and it showed blood everywhere. A clear line crossed his brow, where his white cap had been, but his proud face, all eyebrows, nose and beard like a king of Sumer, was speckled and blotched everywhere else.

He'd been shot, and stabbed, but his reddened face was unmarked.

It hurt inside like a cramp to see his time stopped. My own threads of time vibrated within me, one strand of the harmony silenced.

It hurt to see no breath, no life, no love. It was hard to stare at a man still there, and already suffered for, and already missing.

She was right, to make us cry. *If you don't say goodbye*, an Irish poet once said to me, *you never say goodbye*. And it took a long time to cry goodbye.

Finally I let the dead hand fall, and let the myth of the man fall with it. Each one that leaves us, leaves an unfillable space. She came back with me to the veranda in control again, but grieving, and knowing that there was an empty cave inside both of us: a cave that would draw us again and again to sorrow, and remember.

Khaled was waiting for us.

'You should hurry,' he said. 'My Company is very jumpy tonight.'

'Your Company?'

'The Khaled Company, Lin,' Khaled replied, frowning. 'This night, we took Vishnu's life, and now we take everything that Vishnu had. This night, the Khaled Company is born. That was the plan. Abdullah's plan, in fact, to use himself as the bait.'

'You know what, Khaled –' I started to end it with him, but I stopped, because just then a man stepped out of a shadow.

'*Salaam aleikum*, Shantaram,' the Taureg said.

'*Wa aleikum salaam*, Taureg,' I said, standing closer to Karla.

'The Taureg has been freelancing for me,' Khaled said. 'He set all of this up. And now he's back home, in the Khaled Company.'

'You set this up, Taureg?'

'I did. And I kept you out of it, by sending you after the Irishman,' the Taureg said. 'Because you shook my hand.'

'Goodbye, Khaled,' I said.

'*Allah hafiz*,' Karla said, taking my arm on the steps, because we were both unsteady on our feet.

'*Khuda hafiz*,' Khaled replied. 'Until we meet again.'

When we reached the base of the mountain, Karla stopped me.

'Do you have the keys to *State of Grace*?'

'I always have the keys to my bike,' I said. 'You wanna ride?'

'Oh, yeah, let's ride,' she said. 'I'm so messed up that only freedom can save me.'

We rode to the temple, where Idriss and the students were

sheltering for the night, and told them that the danger was over. Idriss sent a fit, young student to tell Silvano the news. We took a blessing from the sage, and left.

We rode the last hours before dawn, going nowhere the long way, the bike chattering machine talk on empty boulevards, with signals on both sides flashing green, because nobody in Bombay stopped, at that hour, for red.

We parked the bike at the entrance to the slower, softer path to the mountain. I chained the bike to a young tree, so she wouldn't be afraid, and we walked the long, gentle, winding path to the mesa.

Karla clung to me. I put an arm around her waist, supporting her, and making her steps a little lighter.

'Abdullah,' she said softly, a few times.

Abdullah.

I remembered when she said it to make us laugh, on the steep climb. I remembered when Abdullah was a friend I could laugh with, and tease. We cried together as we walked.

We reached the camp, and found students there, already bringing things back to function and faith.

'Okay, this is too busy,' Karla said, leaning against my shoulder. 'Let's hit the grassy knoll.'

We headed for our makeshift tent on the knoll. I set her down there, unresisting, falling back onto a cushion as if into a dream, and within a minute she was asleep.

We had a large water bottle in our kit of supplies. I soaked a towel, and cleaned the cuts and grazes that I'd already imagined, and then found, on her hands and feet.

She moaned, from time to time, when cloth and water sent streaks into her sleeping mind, but didn't wake.

When the wounds on her hands and feet were clean, I rubbed them with turmeric oil. It was the medicine that everyone on the mountain used for cuts and scratches.

When I finished massaging oil into her scraped and cut feet, she curled onto her side, and went deeper into that annihilating sleep.

Abdullah. Abdullah.

I took water into the forest, emptied myself, cleaned myself, scrubbed myself, and returned to find her sitting up, staring at our patch of sky.

'Are you okay?' I asked.

'I'm okay,' she said. 'Where were you?'

'Cleaning up.'

'After you cleaned the cuts on my hands and feet.'

'I'm a sanitary guy.'

I settled in beside her, and she settled in beside me.

'He's gone,' she said, her face against my chest.

'He's gone,' I echoed.

Day raised the blue banner, and sounds of life shuddered from sleep: a shout, a laugh, bird cry brazen in the light, and doves trembling stories of love.

She slept again, and I was calm with her, in the peace that only sleeping love creates, while thoughts of Abdullah, bullet wounds in the mind, kept bleeding.

He was self-discipline, he was kindness unto blood for a friend, and he was ruthless enough to shame his own honour, which I was, too, in my own way.

I slept, at last, riding a wave of consolation in words, words Idriss spoke, running through my mind again and again, sheep counting sheep.

The mystery of love is what we will become, the phrase repeated. *The mystery of love is what we will become*. And the susurrus of syllables became the first gentle rain of the new monsoon, as we woke the next morning.

Still wounded by the night we returned to the camp as heavy rain filled the sky with seas, purified in ascension and pouring from tree-shoulders, shaken in the wind.

Rivulets played, making their own way through prior plans, and birds huddled on branches, not risking freedom's flight. Plants that had been thin apostrophes became paragraphs, and vines that had slumbered like snakes in winter writhed insolent in vivid new green. Baptised by the sky, the world was born again, and hope washed a year's dust and blood from the mountain.

PART
FIFTEEN

CHAPTER EIGHTY-FIVE

AT THE END OF THAT FIRST WEEK OF RAIN, after watching Silvano dance with students in a rare, sunny shower, and even Idriss shake a step or two, leaning on his long staff, Karla and I made our way down the mountain for the last time.

We didn't know that the steep path we took would vanish, in a year or so, erased by nature. We didn't know that the mesa, and the caves, too, would be overgrown not long after Idriss and his students dismantled their camp and left for Varanasi.

We didn't know that it was the last time we'd ever see him. We were bubbling stories about him all the way down to the highway, unaware that he was already a ghost of philosophy, continuing in us through memories and ideas alone. We didn't know that Idriss was already as lost to us in time as Abdullah.

We raced a black cloud all the way back to the birth of the peninsula, at Metro, and parked the bike under the arch beneath the Amritsar hotel, just as a new storm hit.

The tempest came at us from both sides of the archway, and we clung together, laughing as torrents scourged us. When the storm passed, we wiped the bike down together, Karla talking to her all the while like a psychic mechanic.

We climbed the stairs to the lobby, and found it changed, after our weeks on the mountain. There was a glass refrigerator door, where Jaswant's secret cabinet had been. He still had his swanky chair, but a swanky new glass and synthetic laminate counter replaced the wooden reception desk.

Jaswant himself was in a swanky suit, complete with a tie.

'What the hell, Jaswant?' I said.

'You've got to embrace *change*, man,' Jaswant said. 'Hello, Miss Karla. How *lovely* to see you again.'

821

'Nice suit, Jaswant,' she replied.

'Thank you, Miss Karla. Do you think it fits okay?'

'Very slimming. Come, say hi. But be careful, I'm dripping wet.'

I was still frowning old doubt on the new desk.

'What's the matter?' he asked.

'Your reception desk looks like an airline counter.'

'So?'

'An airline counter is something you go to because you *have* to, not because you *want* to.'

'You can visit the old desk, any time you want. Oleg bought it. It's in your rooms.'

'Oleg! Damn, he's good. He beat me to it.'

'The new desk's okay, Jaswant,' Karla said. 'Put a plant on the top shelf, and a nice big shell beside it, and maybe a blown-glass paperweight on the second shelf. It'll soften things. I've got a shell you can borrow, if you like, and a paperweight that has a dandelion in it.'

'Really? I'd love that.'

'There's no rum in here,' I said, wiping condensation off the glass door of his new refrigerated cabinet. 'And no cheese.'

'There's a new menu,' Jaswant said, flipping a laminated card on the laminated airline counter.

I didn't look at it.

'I liked the old menu.'

'We didn't *have* an old menu,' Jaswant frowned.

'Exactly.'

'The Lost Love Bureau is bringing a lot of people through the door now, and I have to present the right corporate image. You've got to get with the times, Lin.'

'I prefer it when the times get with me.'

'Heads-up, Jaswant,' Karla said. 'I've been thinking of making some changes to my rooms.'

'Changes?' Jaswant asked, commerce tightening his new tie.

Karla dismantled the Bedouin tent over the next few days, and we painted her rooms red, with black trim on the doors and doorways. Jaswant couldn't complain, because he'd sold us the paint.

She cut pictures from science magazines, and had them mounted in Bollywood-gold frames. She framed a feather, and a leaf, and a page from a book of poems that she found floating in the breeze in a quiet street:

The Begging Rain

Afterwards
when I am not with you
and you are alone enough
to count the nails in your heart,
studded like a treasure house door,
when you arrange your silence
in the vase of an hour,
memories of our hands,
and a spike of laughter
colouring of my eyes,
when you sit within the swell
of heartbeat,
the purple tide of daydream
lapping at the shores of love,
and your skin sings, perfume-pierced,
surrender to this thought of me:
as mimosas long for monsoon,
I long for you,
as crimson cactus flowers long for Moon
I long for you,
and in my afterwards,
when I am not with you,
my head turns to the window of life
and begs for rain.

She put up large pictures of Petra Kelly and Ida Lupino, two of her heroes, in black baroque frames. She took her balcony plants inside, and filled every corner with them, leaving a few outside to rotate in sunlight.

I think she tried to recreate the mountain forest in a hotel suite, and she did a good job. No matter where you sat in the main room you were looking at plants, or touched by them.

And she installed a long, thin, stylised sculpture of a Trojan soldier, sculpted by Taj. I tried to put a plant in front of it, but she wouldn't let me.

'Really? It's because of this guy that you left the gallery.'

'He's a good sculptor,' Karla said, arranging the doomed soldier, 'even if he's not a terrific guy.'

I used it as a hat stand. I had to buy a hat, but it was worth it. And little by little, things settled down to the semblance of peace that's good enough, when you know enough about bad enough.

Oleg's green rooms, as my rooms became to match the couch, were popular. Karla and I went to a few of his parties, and had a good time. We laughed our way through several more parties, listening to the crazy conversations being shouted next door, transmitted through our wall in high infidelity.

The young Russian had given up on Irina, the girl he called his Karlesha, and as the pictures he'd given to the waiters at Leopold's faded and wrinkled, he stopped asking them if they'd seen her.

'Why do you call Irina *Karlesha*,' I asked him once.

'I was in love with another girl named Irina,' he replied, his perpetual smile fading in the half-light of reflection. 'She was my first love. It was the first time I ever really fell down, inside, with love for a girl. We were both sixteen, and it was over within a year, but I still felt unfaithful to her, the first Irina, by using the name. Karlesha was a pet name that my father used for his sister, my aunt, and I always liked it.'

'So . . . you didn't feel unfaithful to Elena by going with Irina, but you felt unfaithful to your childhood sweetheart, by using the same name?'

'You can only be unfaithful to someone you love,' he said, frowning at my ignorance. 'And I was never in love with Elena. I was in love with Irina, and I'm in love with Karlesha.'

'And the girls who come and go in your green room?'

'I've given up hope that I will see Karlesha again,' he replied, looking away. 'Didier's T-shirt strategy didn't work. Maybe it's just not meant to be.'

'Do you think love might spark with one of these girls?'

'No,' he answered quickly, brightening again. 'I'm Russian. We R-people love very hard and very deeply. It's why our writing and our music is so mad with passion.'

He worked madly and passionately with Naveen, and they became an intuitive team. Didier worked with them on a case that drew publicity, when they reunited lost lovers and uncovered a slavery ring at the same time, leading to arrests and the break-up of the gang.

The dangerous, debonair Frenchman devoted more time and seriousness to the Lost Love Bureau after that, and when he wasn't holding court at Leopold's, he was always with the young detectives, working on a *shockingly urgent* case.

Vinson sold his drug racket to a competitor, and went back to the ashram with Rannveig. He sent a letter to Karla, after a few weeks of penitent floor scrubbing, saying that he didn't really connect with the holy men at the ashram, but he got on well with the gardeners who grew their marijuana for them. He was happy, and he was working on a new business plan, with Rannveig.

The Khaled Company didn't fund any movies, and when a cop was killed in the south the truce between the police gang and the mafia gang was broken. Lightning Dilip worked triple shifts, as the prisoner count grew.

A journalist was beaten on her doorstep for telling the truth, and a politician was beaten in his home for not telling a lie. Skirmishes between the police and the Khaled Company at court hearings were commonplace, and sometimes turned into riots. The Company blamed every prosecution on religious bias, and the cops blamed every punch on criminal intent.

Khaled's crown was slipping, and Abdullah wasn't there to set it straight. The mystic-turned-mafia-don was losing control: his unnecessary violence was an insult to dishonest lawlessness, and everyone on Back Street wanted him to stop.

We couldn't stop Khaled, but we did stop Lightning Dilip. Karla said that she had a birthday present for me, and she wanted to give it to me early.

'I don't celebrate –'

'Your birthday, I know. You wanna know what the present is, or not?'

'Okay.'

'The cop that we got on the fetish tapes,' Karla said. 'It's Lightning Dilip.'

Karma's a hammer, not a feather, I remembered Karla saying.

'Very interesting.'

'Wanna know what his fetish was?'

'No.'

'It involved a lot of sandwich wrap,' Karla said.

'Please, stop.'

'Leaving only his insubordinates and his mouth exposed.'

'Okay, enough.'

'And in one part, the girl had to swat his privates with a flyswatter.'

'Karla.'

'A plastic one, of course, and then —'

I put my fingers in my ears and said la-la-la-la-la-la-la-la-la-la until she stopped. It was childish, and beneath us both, and it worked.

'Okay. Seeing as how it's your birthday present, and we can make him do anything that we want,' Karla asked, a wicked smile shining from insurgency, 'what do you want to do with the Lightning Dilip film?'

'I'm guessing you've already thought it through.'

'I was thinking he should retire,' Karla said. 'Citing his remorse, for having mistreated prisoners. Demoted, disgraced, and without a pension.'

'Nice.'

'Lightning Dilip has been digging his own grave for years, one kick at a time,' Karla said. 'I think he's about ready to fall into it.'

'When?'

'I'll ask No Problem to deliver the message tomorrow, with a deadline for him to resign in twenty-four hours, or we go public. Sound right to you?'

'No problem,' I smiled, glad to be rid of him, and wondering who the next Lightning Dilip would be, and how much more we'd have to pay.

'I was also thinking he should retire to a village somewhere, far away,' Karla mused. 'The one he came from might be nice. I'm pretty sure the people who watched him grow up will know what to do with him when he comes back.'

'They'll do it in an isolated spot, if they know him well.'

CHAPTER EIGHTY-SIX

G EMINI GEORGE WAS IN A SPECIALLY EQUIPPED ROOM on the penthouse floor of the Mahesh hotel, watched over by Scorpio George and a prestige of doctors. The hotel had provided specialists through international contacts, and Scorpio hired medical expertise from the best hospitals in India.

It seemed that it might be too late for Gemini, whose thin body failed and faded day by day, but he always greeted each new expert with a joke, and a smile.

Scorpio made us suffer to see Gemini, because no-one else stayed still long enough to suffer listening to him.

'I've been off my food,' Scorpio said, as we stood outside the door to Gemini's room. 'And I've got a blister on my foot from pacing up and down, worrying about Gemini. And I deserve it, because it's all my fault.'

'It's okay,' Karla said, taking his hand. 'No-one blames you, Scorpio.'

'But it *is* my fault. If I hadn't been searching for that holy man, Gemini wouldn't have got dengue fever, and we'd be okay, like before.'

'No-one loves Gemini more than you do,' Karla replied, as she opened the door. 'He knows that.'

Gemini was in a fully adjustable hospital bed, with tubes coming from too many places. A new plastic tent covered his bed. There were two nurses attending to him, checking data on machines arranged around the left side of the bed.

He smiled at us as we approached. He looked bad. His thin body was the colour of a cut persimmon, and his face revealed the skull beneath the smile.

'Hello, Karla,' he said cheerily, although the sound of his voice was weak. 'Hello, Lin, mate. So glad you've come.'

'Damn good to see you again, man,' I said, waving at him through the plastic tent.

'How about a game?' Karla purred. 'Unless you think those meds you're on stole your edge.'

'Can't play cards yet, although I'd love to. I'm in this plastic tent for a few weeks, you see, and they daren't take it off. My immune system's down, they say. I think the machines are just for show. They're keeping me alive with rubber bands and kindness. Me organs are shuttin' down, one by one, like people leaving a train, you know?'

'Are you in pain, Gemini?' Karla asked.

He smiled, very slowly: sunlight burning shadows from a meadow.

'I'm right as rain, love,' he said. 'They've got me on a drip. That's when you know you're dyin', innit? When all the best drugs are suddenly legal, and you can have as much as you want. It's the upside of the downside, so to speak.'

'I'd still like to play a few hands,' Karla smiled, 'while we're all on the upside.'

'Like I said, it's my immune system that's up the spout. That's why I got this tent. It's actually *you* that could hurt *me*. Funny, innit?'

'Gemini George, a quitter?' Karla teased. 'Of *course* you can play cards with us. We'll deal you a hand, and I'll hold the cards up for you without looking. You trust me, don't you?'

Karla never cheated at any game, and Gemini knew it.

'You'll have to clear it with *them* first,' Gemini said, nodding at the nurses. 'They've got me on a pretty tight rein.'

'Why don't we start?' Karla replied, winking at the nurses. 'And if they get worried, we'll stop. Where are the cards?'

'In the top drawer of the cabinet, just beside you.'

I opened the drawer. There was a deck of cards, a cheap watch, a small bell from a charm bracelet, a war medal that might've been his father's, a cross on a chain, and a wallet worn thin with patient penury.

Karla pulled three chairs close to the bed. I gave her the cards, and she shuffled them, spilling out hands on the spare chair. She held Gemini's hand up to the plastic shield.

The nurses checked the hand as closely as Gemini did.

'We'll call your cards one-to-five, your left to your right,' Karla said. 'Anything you want to throw, call it by number. When you have your hand, call it by number, and I'll rearrange it for you, okay?'

'Got it,' Gemini said. 'I sit pat.'

One of the nurses made a noise, clicking her tongue against her teeth. Gemini turned to her. Both nurses were shaking their heads. Gemini turned back again.

'On second thoughts,' he said, 'throw one and four, and give me two cards, please, Karla.'

The nurses nodded. Karla withdrew the unwanted cards, dealt two more into his hand, and showed them to him. They must've been good cards, because Gemini and the nurses poker-faced us.

'I bet fifty,' Gemini said. 'Fight it out and stretch it out for me, Karla. I've got nowhere else to be, but in this game.'

'I'll see your fifty, and raise you a hundred,' Karla said, 'if you've got the stomach tubes for it.'

'I'm out,' I said, throwing in my cards, and leaving the duel to Karla and Gemini.

'I'm so ready for this,' Gemini laughed, and coughed. 'Do your worst.'

'I only play to win, Gemini. You know that.'

'You remember that night,' Gemini said, his smile a sunset in the valley of yesterday. 'The housewarming party we threw, me and Scorpio? Remember that night?'

'Great party,' I said.

'Good fun,' Karla added.

'That was a great party. The best ever. That was the time of my life.'

'You'll pull through,' Karla said. 'There's plenty of pavement left in you, Gemini. Money time. Put up or shut up, street guy.'

We did the best we could for Gemini, and with a little help from his nurses he managed to cheat, for old times' sake, every time we played.

We visited often, but at the end of every visit, away from Gemini's room, we argued with Scorpio that his Zodiac twin should be in a hospital. Every time, Scorpio refused. Love has its own logic, just as it has its own foolishness.

In another room of life and death, across the city, Farzad, the young forger, responded to treatment. As the blood clot on his brain dissolved, he recovered his speech and movement.

A tremor that twitched his left eye closed, from time to time, reminded him that making cheeky remarks to vicious men ends viciously. The mysterious disappearance of Lightning Dilip reminded him, with a happier smile, that no-one escapes karma.

The three families shared the treasure, leaving a portion in a collective account to pay for the redecoration of their combined homes. They retained the domed space as the common area it had been, but took down the scaffolding, one freshly painted or remodelled section at a time, revealing the small basilica that it had become in the search.

Karla liked the scatter of catwalks, reaching three floors above us, and she liked the happy mix of Parsis, Hindus and Muslims even more.

While I went through paperwork with Arshan, once a week, bringing the illegal documents I'd created for him into line with his newly legal ones, Karla worked on the scaffolding with the families, paintbrush or power drill in hand.

She was a river, not a stone, and every day was another curve in tomorrow's plain. She was pulled from a family she loved, and that loved her, she thought, until they took the word of a man, a friend and neighbour, who raped her. Years later, when she killed the rapist and went on the run, she severed every connection to her own life.

She was runaway tough, a dancing cat, a green witch, and safe from everything but herself, like me.

She used the money she'd made on the stock market to hire people, new friends and not-quite strangers, giving them office space she'd rented in the Amritsar hotel. She was gathering a new family around her, as so many in the old family she'd found in Bombay left the Island City, or died, or were dying, like Gemini George.

I didn't know how much of the gathering she did at the Amritsar hotel was considered, and how much was unconscious instinct. But when she worked with the three families in the treasure-hunters' palace, she settled quickly and happily into their routine, and I saw the hunger for it, in both of us: the desire that had matured into need.

The word *family* is derived from the word *famulus*, meaning a servant, and in its early usage, *familia*, it literally meant the servants of a household. In its essence, the longing for family, and the ravenousness that the loss of family creates in us, isn't just for belonging: it's for the grace that abides in serving those we love.

CHAPTER EIGHTY-SEVEN

I T WAS A SEASON OF CHANGE, and the Island City seemed to be sprucing itself up for a parade that hadn't been called. Road dividers wore gleaming new coats, painted by men who risked their lives at every stroke. Shops redecorated, and shoppers redecorated with them. New signs announced old privilege on every corner. And beloved mould, nature's comment on our plans, was scraped from buildings and painted over.

'Why don't you like the new makeover?' a friend who owned a restaurant asked me, staring up at his freshly painted enterprise from the pavement.

'I liked the *old* makeover. Your paint job is dandy, but I liked the one made by the last four monsoons.'

'Why?'

'I like things that don't resist nature.'

'You've gotta keep up with the times, man,' he said, holding his breath as he entered his renovated restaurant, because it was impossible to breathe and stay conscious at the same time, so close to the drying paint.

Fashion is the business end of art, and even Ahmed's House of Style finally succumbed to the tyranny of assimilation. His hand-painted sign was corporatised into the stigmata of avarice, a logo. Straight razors and angry bristle brushes were gone, replaced by a selection of hair-care chemicals that signs assured us hadn't been tested on baby rabbits, and wouldn't blind or kill the people who used them.

Even the aftershave, *Ambrosia de Ahmed*, had vanished, but I was lucky enough to arrive in time to save the mirror, starred with pictures of Ahmed's free haircuts, each one like the death photo of an outlaw, murdered by justice.

'Not the mirror!' I said, stopping small men with big hammers from smashing it off the wall.

'*Salaam aleikum*, Lin,' Ahmed said. 'The whole place is being renovated, for Ahmed's New House of Style.'

'*Wa aleikum salaam*. Not the mirror!'

I had my back to the mirror, my arms wide to stop the hammers. Karla was standing beside Ahmed, her arms folded, a cheeky smile playing in the garden of her eyes.

'The mirror has to go, Lin,' Ahmed said. 'It doesn't fit with the new look.'

'This mirror goes with *every* look,' I protested.

'Not with *this* look,' Ahmed said, sliding a brochure from a pile, and handing it to me.

I looked the picture over, and handed it back.

'It looks like a place to eat sushi,' I said. 'People can't argue politics and insult each other in a place like that, Ahmed, even with the mirror.'

'New policy,' he said. 'No insults. No politics, religion or sex.'

'Are you mad, Ahmed? Censorship, in a barber shop?'

I looked at Karla, and she was having a pretty good time.

'Come on,' I pleaded. 'There has to be at least *one* place where nobody kisses anybody on the ass.'

Ahmed gave me a stern look.

It wasn't his own stern look: it was the stern look on a handsome face beneath a pompadour haircut, in a catalogue of cuts and styles for the New House of Style.

I flipped through the pictures, knowing that Ahmed was probably proud of it, because he'd illegally included photos of movie stars and prominent businessmen to give the collection currency.

I didn't want to hurt his feelings, but for me the catalogue was the wrong set of victims.

'You can't break the mirror, Ahmed.'

'Will you sell it to me, exactly as it is?' Karla asked.

'Are you serious?'

'Yes, Ahmed. Is it for sale?'

'It would take me some time, to clean off the pictures,' he said thoughtfully.

'I'd like it *with* the pictures, if you don't mind, Ahmed. It's perfect as it is.'

I love you, Karla, I thought.

'Very well, Miss Karla. Would, say, a thousand rupees, including transport and installation, be acceptable to you?'

'It would,' Karla smiled, handing him the money. 'I've got a free wall in my place, and I've been trying to think what to put on it. If your men can remove it carefully, and set it up for me again at the Amritsar hotel today, I'd be much obliged.'

'Done,' Ahmed said, signalling the hammer-men to stand down. 'I'll walk you out.'

On the street, Ahmed looked left and right to make sure that no-one could hear, and leaned close.

'I will still do *house calls*,' he whispered. 'Strictly off the books, of course, and top secret. I don't want people thinking I'm not whole-hearted, in the *New* House of Style.'

'Now, *that's* good news,' I said.

'So,' Karla whispered, 'if we were to gather a group of argumenta-tive, very insulting men at our place, you'd be happy to come by and create Ahmed's *Old* House of Style?'

'You've already got the mirror,' Ahmed smiled. 'And I will really miss the dangerous discussions, in the New House of Style.'

'Done,' Karla said, shaking hands with him.

Ahmed looked at me, frowned, and straightened my collar so that it stood up at the back of my neck.

'When are you going to buy a jacket with sleeves in it, Lin?'

'When you start selling them at the New House of Style,' I said. '*Allah hafiz.*'

'*Salaam, salaam,*' he laughed.

We rode away, and then Karla told me that the mirror was my second birthday present, reminding me, again, that it was my birthday, which I'd happily forgotten.

'Please don't tell anyone else,' I called over my shoulder.

'I know,' she called back. 'You like celebrating other people's birth-days, and forgetting your own. Your secret's safe with me.'

'I love you, Karla. I was thinking that, just before. And thanks, for the mirror. You really got me there.'

'I always get you there.'

We had more time to get one another, and ride and share a drink and eat meals together, because I sold my money-change operation to

Jagat, for the twenty-five per cent he was already giving me. He managed the racket better than I did, and earned more money, respect and discipline from the shopkeeper changers. The fact that a year or so before he ran my bing he'd cut the little finger off a thief who stole from him added a certain sting to his slap.

I couldn't visit Half-Moon Auntie in the fish market again, because Karla recruited her.

'You want me to run your books?' Half-Moon Auntie asked.

'Who knows more about keeping people's money safe than you do, Half-Moon Auntie?' Karla said, facing pointed quarters of the moon.

'That's true,' Half-Moon Auntie replied, considering. 'But it could be a big job.'

'Not that big,' Karla said. 'We only keep one set of books.'

'I am accustomed to my regular visitors,' Half-Moon Auntie said, leaning forward and beginning an orbital drift toward half-moon.

'What you do behind your closed door is your business,' Karla said. 'What you do when the door is open is *our* business. If you're interested, I have a friend, named Randall, who has a limousine. It's parked below my building, most of the time.'

'A limousine,' Half-Moon Auntie said thoughtfully.

'With blackout windows, and a long mattress in the back.'

'I will consider it,' Half-Moon Auntie replied, lifting one foot effortlessly behind her head.

And a few days later she considered her way into an apartment office, under our rooms at the Amritsar hotel, where Karla had rented the whole floor.

Half-Moon Auntie's office was next to two others, already painted and furnished. One room bore the title *Blue Hijab Marriage Counselling Services*. The Muslim communist, or communist Muslim, had reunited with Mehmu earlier than expected, and she'd called Karla, asking if the offer of a partnership was still open.

'She's not here, yet,' I said, when the brass sign was attached to the door.

'She will be,' Karla smiled. '*Inshallah.*'

'What's the third office for?'

'Surprises,' she purred. 'You have no idea what surprises I have in store for you, Shantaram.'

'Can you surprise me with dinner? I'm starving.'

We were having dinner in the front garden of a Colaba Back Bay bistro, when we heard shouting from the street, a few steps away.

A car had stopped beside a man walking on the road. The men in the car were shouting for money he owed them. Two of the men got out of the car.

As we looked at the commotion, I saw that the man was Kesh, the Memory Man. He had his hands over his head as the two thugs began to hit him.

Karla and I got up from the table and joined Kesh. We made enough noise for them to get back in the car, and drive away.

Karla helped Kesh to sit with us, at the table.

'A glass of water, please!' she called to the waiter. 'Are you alright, Kesh?'

'I'm okay, Miss Karla,' he said, rubbing a knot of bad debt on the top of his head. 'I'll go, now.'

He stood to leave, but we pulled him back into his chair.

'Have dinner with us, Kesh,' Karla said. 'You can test your memory against ours. You're pretty good, but my money's on us.'

'I really shouldn't –'

'You really should,' I said, waving the waiter to our table.

Kesh looked at the menu carefully, closed it and made his choices.

'The zucchini, black olive and crushed artichoke paste risotto,' the waiter repeated. 'The iceberg, seasoned with cracked pepper, ginger and pistachio sauce, and a tiramisu.'

'You're incorrect,' Kesh said. 'The cracked pepper, ginger and pistachio sauce is with the rocket salad, which is number seventy-seven on your menu. The iceberg is with lemon-garlic, chilli pepper and walnut-avocado sauce, which is number seventy-six on your menu.'

The waiter opened his mouth to reply, but his mental scan of the menu confirmed Kesh's correction, and he walked away, shaking his head.

'What's the problem, Kesh?' I asked.

'I owe money,' he said, smiling from the side of his disillusion. 'The Memory Man business isn't what it used to be. People are using phones for everything, now. Pretty soon, the whole world will be able to communicate with anyone, so long as they're not actually there.'

'You know what?' I suggested, as the food arrived. 'Grab a taxi, and come to the Amritsar hotel after this. We'll be there ahead of you, on the bike.'

'What have you got in mind?' Karla squinted at me, lashes like lace.

'Surprises,' I tried to purr. 'You have no idea what surprises I have in store for *you*, Karla.'

Didier was certainly surprised when I brought Kesh into his office, next to Karla's at the Amritsar.

'I do not see the . . . *requirement* for his services,' Didier said, sitting professionally at his desk beside Naveen's.

'Kesh is the best Memory Man in the south, Didier,' Naveen observed, sitting professionally at his own desk. 'What did you have in mind, Lin?'

'You know how you said that people always freeze up when you record their witness statements? They see the recorder and they freeze up?'

'Yeah.'

'Kesh can be your recorder. He remembers every conversation he hears. He can be your human recorder, and people will talk naturally in front of him.'

'I like it,' Karla laughed.

'You do?' Didier doubted.

'I'll hire him right now if you don't, Didier.'

'Hired,' Didier said. 'We have an interview with a millionaire and his wife, tomorrow morning at ten. Their daughter has gone missing. You can attend. But your mode of dress must be more . . . *executive* . . . in appearance.'

'See you guys later,' I said, pulling Kesh with us from their office.

In the corridor outside I gave him some money. He tried to stop me.

'You have to clear all your debts tonight, Kesh,' I said. 'We don't want those guys showing up around here. And you're going straight tomorrow morning, remember? Go around and pay everyone off. Get clean, and be here at nine. Be the first one here, and the last to leave. You'll do fine.'

He started to cry. I stepped back a pace, and let Karla take over. She hugged him, and he calmed down quickly.

'You know what Didier said, about dressing like an executive?' I said.

'Yes. I'll try to —'

'To hell with that. Dress like you are. Act like you are. People will talk to you, just like *I'm* talking to you, and you'll be good at this. If Didier hassles you, tell him I ordered you not to dress like a slave.'

'He's right, Kesh,' Karla said. 'Just be yourself, and everything will be fine.'

'Okay,' I said. 'Go and pay those debts tonight, man. Get yourself clear.'

He took each downward step on the stairway as if it was a new level of consideration, pausing before taking the next pondered step. His head bobbed out of sight around the curved staircase.

I watched him out of sight thoughtfully, and then turned to see Karla smiling at me.

'I love you, Shantaram,' she said, kissing me.

Some time later, Kesh solved two cases within two weeks, and became the star of the Lost Love Bureau. His attention to detail, and retention of detail, proved decisive in solving cases, and no interview proceeded without him.

Half-Moon Auntie and her intrepid clerk did the accounts for the bureau, and safeguarded sums of money for clients from time to time. She was an astute businesswoman, and spent long hours redesigning the business plan, saving money and hours for everyone else.

Her private sessions in Randall's limousine kept her lunar-starved visitors content. *A talent is how you use it*, she said to me once, using her talents to illustrate the point.

Vinson and Rannveig returned from the ashram bleached of pride, but we didn't see them often, because they were busy with their plans to open a coffee shop, and the necessary renovations.

When we did manage to catch them mid-renovation for a few minutes, Karla took Rannveig's arm, leading her to girl talk, and leaving me with Vinson in the unfinished coffee shop.

'It's . . . like, you know that *wave*, that perfect wave, that just keeps on going, and won't let you fall?' Vinson said.

'No, but I ride a motorcycle, and that's like surfing civilisation.'

'You know that totally, like, forever wave?'

'I have a gas tank. I know how far forever is.'

'No, I mean, it's like that tendency field jelly that Idriss was talking about.'

'Uh-huh.'

'I'm, like, surfing the superposition, you know, between equally surfable waves. Rannveig and Idriss, they really opened my mind up so much, man. Sometimes, I feel like I'm so full of ideas they're falling out of my head.'

'I'm glad you're happy, Vinson. And it's great, the coffee bar thing. Really happy, for you and Rannveig. Well, guess I'd better be getting along. We —'

'This coffee thing is amazing,' he said, gesturing toward large sacks, arranged against a wall. 'I mean, like, if I just explain the difference between Colombian and Ghanaian blends to you, it'll blow your mind wide open.'

'Thanks for the warning. But you know, Karla will be along any minute, so I doubt we'll have time to get into a big story like that.'

'If she comes back, I'll start it again,' he said unhelpfully.

'How's Rannveig?' I asked helpfully.

'You know that wave, man, the perfect wave that, like, won't let you fall?'

'So glad you're happy. Where do you think Karla and Rannveig got to?'

'Just *smell* these fresh beans up close once,' Vinson said, opening a sack. 'They're so good, you'll never drink another cup of coffee again.'

'Is that your slogan?'

'No, man, our slogan is our *name*, man. *Love & Faith*, that's the name of the place, and that's the slogan.'

There was an innocence in Vinson that Rannveig had lost, when her boyfriend had died from the same drugs Vinson unthinkingly sold. And the innocence she found again, in his willingness to change, was the tender truth in the name they'd chosen for their business, *Love & Faith*.

'Smell my beans,' he insisted.

'Ah . . . I'm good.'

'Smell them!' Vinson said urgently, dragging a dead body of beans toward me.

'I'm not smelling your beans, Vinson, no matter how Colombian they are. Stop dragging that carcass.'

He shoved the bag against the wall again, just as Karla and Rannveig came back to join us.

'He won't smell my beans,' Vinson complained.

'He won't?' Karla scoffed. 'The Lin I know is a bean fanatic.'

'Stuart made a special blend,' Rannveig said proudly. 'I think it's the best coffee I ever tasted.'

'I've got it in the other room,' Vinson said, ready to leave. 'You can smell it, if you like.'

'I'm good,' I said quickly. 'I can smell it from here.'

'I told you, my Easter Bunny,' Vinson said, hugging Rannveig. 'People will smell our coffee from the street outside, and they'll be, like, *hypnotised* or something.'

'Good luck, guys,' I said, drawing Karla out of the renovated shop.

'Opening is at full moon,' Rannveig said, mid-hug. 'Don't forget.'

On the street, we climbed onto the bike, but Karla stopped me before I could start the engine.

'What did you feel from Vinson?' she asked, her arm on my shoulder.

'Waves of beans,' I said. 'What did you feel from Rannveig?'

'Did he tell you what they're calling the place?'

'Yeah. *Love & Faith*. Why?'

'Far as I can see,' Karla said, 'he's the love, and she's the faith.'

A car pulled up beside us, blocking the way. It was a hearse, in fact, with Dennis, the Not-Sleeping Baba, at the wheel. Concannon was in the passenger seat. Billy Bhasu and Jamal, the One Man Show, were sitting in the back, beside a shop window mannequin laid out in what looked like a clear plastic coffin.

Concannon had his elbow on the window.

'Wanted,' he said, grinning at Karla. 'Dead or alive.'

'Move,' I said.

'Hello, Karla,' Dennis said. 'So nice to meet you, awake. Did we meet, when I was on the other side?'

'Hi, Dennis,' she laughed, her arm around my shoulder. 'You were certainly high, the first time I saw you. What the hell are you doing?'

'We are testing the movements of Sleepers, while they are transported in a sleeping chamber,' he said patiently. 'I have attached sensitive strips to the mannequin. They will indicate bruises, of varying degree. That will help us to determine the most comfortable inner cushioning of the sleeping chambers we will have made for them.'

'You're making your own coffins?' Karla asked.

'Indeed,' he said, passing a chillum to Concannon. 'We must do it. Current sleeping chambers force the Sleepers to have their legs pressed together. Our sleeping chambers will have a wider stance. It's very important for the comfort of Sleepers.'

'I see,' Karla smiled.

'They will have the softest silk lining, padded with feathers,' Dennis continued, his hands on the steering wheel. 'And they will be made of glass, so that the Sleepers can have plants, small animals and insects roaming about in the earth, all around them, to keep them company while they sleep.'

'Nice,' Karla smiled.

'May I present Billy Bhasu and Jamal, the One Man Show?' Dennis said. 'Boys, this is Karla-Madame.'

Billy Bhasu waved a smile at Karla, while Jamal wagged his head, jangling chained gods.

I couldn't help myself.

'One Man Show,' I said, nodding at Jamal.

'One Man Show,' he repeated.

I looked at Karla, and she understood.

'One Man Show,' she said, smiling at him.

'One Man Show,' Jamal replied on cue, smiling back.

I looked at Concannon, wanting him to leave, but he was talking, instead.

'The dead can dance, you know,' he said conversationally.

I moved my eyes to Dennis, at the wheel of the hearse.

'Are you sure you should be driving, Dennis?' I asked, trying to shut Concannon down.

'I must drive,' Dennis intoned, his rumbling voice echoing in the hearse. 'Concannon is not stoned enough to drive a hearse.'

'The dead can dance,' Concannon repeated, smiling happily. 'They really can, you know.'

'You don't say,' Karla said, leaning against me.

'I do say,' Concannon grinned. 'I've learned a lot on this job. It's been a real education. I usually walked away, you see, while they were still twitchin', and never looked back.'

'Concannon,' Dennis said. 'You're killing my high, man.'

'I'm only havin' a conversation, Dennis. Just because we're undertakers, doesn't mean we can't be sociable.'

'True,' Dennis said. 'But how do you expect me to test-drive this new hearse, if I'm not high?'

'I'm only sayin', like,' Concannon persisted. 'They wriggle around, dead bodies, long after they're gone, shakin' about on the table all of a sudden like. One body we had, yesterday, danced better than I do. But

I was never the one for dancin', truth be told, when there was fightin' or kissin' to be had.'

'Light the next chillum,' Dennis said, putting the hearse into gear. 'If you don't care for *my* high, listen to the mannequin. He's screaming for it.'

They pulled away, the slogan of their company streaming past us slowly on the long windows of the hearse: *Peace In Rest*.

'Now, that's an interesting team.'

'A marriage made in Limbo,' I said. 'But the mannequin seemed like a nice guy.'

CHAPTER EIGHTY-EIGHT

DIVA DEVNANI CALLED US TO A MEETING at her corporate office. It was on the Worli Seaface, a long slow smile of buildings beaming at the sea from a wide, curved boulevard. Diva's building was like the upper deck of an ocean liner, with tall, rounded windows in full sail, and a continuous balcony serving as the rail.

When the elevator doors closed, I offered Karla my flask. She took a swig, and handed it back. The elevator operator glanced at me. I offered him the flask, and he took a swig, dripping the rum into his mouth without touching it to his lips. He passed it back, wagging his head.

'God bless everyone,' he said.

'Speaking for everyone,' Karla said, 'God bless you back.'

The doors opened onto a marble and glass prairie, with several very pretty girls in very tight skirts grazing at desks of distraction.

While Karla spoke to the receptionist, I wandered among the glass and steel desks, glancing over shoulders. The girls were listening to music on their headphones, playing video games and reading magazines.

One of the girls looked up at me mid-flip in her magazine. She turned down the volume on her headset.

'Can I help you?' she threatened, her eyes fierce.

'I'll . . . you know . . . I'll just be over there,' I said, backing away.

The receptionist took us to an alcove with a view of the door to Diva's office, where we sat in plush chairs. There was a side table, with business newspapers and magazines, soda water in a glass jug, and some peanuts, offered in a bronze cast of a human hand.

The palm of peanuts drew my eye as we sat down. I pointed at it, trying to figure out the message.

'This is what we're gonna pay you?' I whispered to Karla. 'Or maybe, this is what happened to the last guy who asked for a raise?'

'*Beggars can't be choosers,*' Karla said.

'Damn good,' I smiled, my eyes applauding.

A tall, pretty girl appeared at our side.

'Can I get you a cup of coffee?' the girl asked.

'Maybe later, with Diva,' Karla said. 'Thanks.'

The girl left, and I turned to Karla.

'It's pretty weird, out there in reception.'

'It's still a marble tile or two short of weird.'

'No, I mean the girls. They're not doing anything.'

'What do you mean, they're not doing anything?'

'It's a jive of inactivity.'

'So? Maybe it's a slow day.'

'Karla, come on. There are seven very pretty girls out there, and not one of them is doing anything. It's kinda weird.'

'It's kinda weird that you counted them,' she smiled.

'I –'

The door to Diva's office opened. It was exactly one minute before our meeting. A grasp of businessmen filed out, wearing similar suits and identical stares of ambition, fed.

'Punctuality is the time of thieves,' Karla said, glancing at the clock, and standing.

Diva came to the door of the office, her hands on her hips.

'Come in,' she said, kissing Karla on both cheeks. 'I've missed you both so much. Thanks for coming.'

She flopped into an immense chair, behind the curve of a black grand piano that she'd shortened, and converted into a desk.

A photograph of her father in a silver frame rested on the piano-desk. Flowers trailed over the picture, spilling yellow against lacquered black. Incense burned in a tray shaped like a peacock's tail.

It was a big room, but there were only two chairs facing her desk. All those blank-eyed businessmen had stood, during the meeting with Diva. *Tough girl*, I thought, *and who can blame her?*

'That was something,' she said. 'Can I get you guys a drink? God knows, *I* need one.'

She pressed a button on a console, and the door opened a second later. A very pretty girl walked across the large room, stalking the

843

slippery floor on hysterical heels. She stopped at the desk with a flourish of her short skirt, long legs stiff.

'Martini,' Diva said, 'I want you to meet Miss Karla and Mr Shantaram.'

Karla waved hello. I stood, put my right hand over my chest, and inclined my head. It's the most polite way to greet any woman in India, because many women don't like to shake hands. Martini inclined her head at me, and I sat down again.

'I'll have a Manhattan,' Diva said. 'What about you, Karla?'

'Two jiggers of vodka over two cubes, please.'

'A lime soda, for me.'

Martini spun on a fifty-calibre heel, and stalked away slowly, a giraffe in a glass zoo.

'I suppose you're wondering why I called you here,' Diva said, giving me a different wondering, because I wasn't.

'I'm wondering,' Karla said, 'but not about that. You'll get to the point when it's sharp enough, right? How are you, Diva? It's been weeks.'

'I'm good,' she smiled, straightening up in the chair that looked like half a bed for her small frame. 'I'm tired, but I've been working on that. I sold everything today. Just about everything. That was the last, in a very long line of meetings I've had, yesterday and today.'

'Sold everything *how*?' Karla asked.

'All the men who actually *run* the companies, in my portfolios, have tranches of shares as bonuses. I told them that if I sold my portfolio in one hit, their shares would be worthless. But if they gave the shares back to me, they could take the companies and run them with their own boards, and give themselves sweaty-palm bonuses, without spending a dollar, and I would resign.'

'Smart move,' Karla said. 'As principal shareholder, you have an annual general meeting to use against them. But you skip the day-to-day. It's like getting drunk without the hangover.'

'Precisely,' Diva said, as Martini arrived with the drinks.

'Have you got a joint?' Diva asked.

'Yes,' Karla and Martini said at the same time, turning their heads instantly to look at one another.

It looked tense, to me. But silent struggles between beautiful women are feminal magician's tricks, faster and subtler than male eyes

844

and instincts can follow. I couldn't be sure what was going on, so I smiled at everybody.

Karla took a slender joint from her case, and passed it to Diva. Martini glowered, all legs and no pockets, and whirled away, the frills of her skirt like a creature designed by a reef.

'Thanks, Karla,' Diva said. 'I'm a free woman, as of this minute. If the sun was down, I'd be drinking champagne. I can drink cocktails all day, but when I start on champagne my IQ drops twenty points, and that's a stupidity I'm keeping in reserve, for later tonight. Meanwhile, to freedom for women!'

'Freedom for women!' Karla toasted.

Diva was silent for a while. Karla brought her back.

'How bad was it?'

'They all wanted control,' Diva said, turning her drink in her hands. 'They couldn't bear to see it, a woman in control, when they'd all happily licked a man's boot.'

'They let you know?' Karla asked.

'I saw it in their eyes, at every meeting. And the whispering always came back to me, from men who betrayed men. Power, in my hands, was a declaration of war to them. These parasites that my father let infest the companies, these men who looked the other way when black money almost ruined us, they started getting nasty. Even threatening. You know what I mean, Karla?'

'Men like that you crush, or you leave behind,' Karla said. 'You could've crushed them, Diva, because your father left you the power to do it. Why are you walking away?'

'My dad was into energy stocks in a big way. That's all we've got left, while the construction business pays off debts, and those stocks are still paying well. I wouldn't have made those bets on oil and coal, but he did, and he locked me onto a wheel that thousands of people are running on. I can't just turn it off.'

'So you're still in the game?' Karla asked.

'I'm stepping out, but I told the new managers that for every year they get cleaner, and better at what they do, they get a tranche of their shares back.'

'What are your plans?' I asked.

'I kept one company, and quarantined it from the sale. I kept the combined modelling agency and bridal boutique, the one I told you about. I added a wedding advice service, and I've renamed it. I'm going to run it.'

'Ah,' I said, 'so the girls you've got here are models, waiting for assignments.'

'You could say that,' Diva replied, turning to Karla. 'I know it's a while since we talked about this, Karla, but I was hoping you're still interested. I'd love to have your ideas in this. What do you think?'

'I liked it when it was just an idea,' she said. 'And I'm happy to see you make it real. Count us in, for as long as we're here in town. Let's talk about it next week, over dinner at our place, okay?'

'Yeah,' Diva said vaguely, her eyes drifting to the garlanded photograph of her father.

We let her have some time, both of us content to wait until her trance ended.

'You know why I insisted that everyone call me Diva?' she asked after a while, still staring at the photograph. 'I was in the bathroom, at a party, and I heard what my own friends called me, behind my back. *Trivia Divya*, they said. Trivia Divya. And you know what? They were right. I was. I was trivial. So I changed my name to Diva, that night, and made everybody call me that. But this is the first time that I've felt untrivial, if there's such a word.'

'*Essential* is the word, Diva,' Karla said.

The young heiress turned her face to Karla's and smiled, laughing softly.

'It's all good,' she said, standing from her chair with a stretch and a yawn.

We stood with her, and she walked us to the tall doors of her office.

'So glad you're free,' Karla said, hugging her as we left. 'Fly high, baby bird.'

We roamed free on the bike, at slow speed, thinking different thoughts. I was thinking of the poor little rich girl, who'd lived in a slum and given away a fortune. Karla was thinking something else.

'They're all very classy ex-callgirls,' she said over my shoulder.

'What?'

'They're all ex-callgirls.'

'Who?'

'The pretty girls back at the office, who were doing nothing, very prettily. They're all ex-callgirls. Dominatrices, actually. Experts in fetish. Diva hired them for the fetish party, but after the party, offered them jobs. They all came. They're not modelling for Diva. They're running the marriage and wedding agency.'

'They should do fine,' I said. 'Why didn't you tell me, when I brought it up?'

'Stop the bike,' she said, leaning away from me.

I pulled into the exit lane, near a bus stop.

'Are you seriously asking me,' she asked, her breath on my neck, 'why I didn't tell you that we were going to a carnival of ex-callgirls?'

'Well . . .'

I swung back into the traffic and rode for a while, but then stopped again, because Oleg was sitting in the middle of the road divider, playing the guitar. We pulled up beside him.

'What are you doing, Olezhka?' Karla asked, smiling a handful of queens.

'Playing guitar, Karla,' he grinned back, Russianly.

'See you round, Oleg,' I said, revving the engine.

Karla pressed a finger gently on my shoulder, and the engine cooled down.

'Why here?' Karla asked.

'The acoustics are perfect,' he said, smiling, deliberately. 'The sea behind me, and the buildings —'

'What are you playing?' Karla asked.

'It's a song called "Let the Day Begin", by The Call. This guy, Michael Been, he's like a saint of rock and roll. I love him. Can I play it for you?'

'See you round, Olezhka,' I said, revving again.

'Why don't you hop on board,' Karla said.

'Really?' Oleg and I said at the same time.

'We'll drop you at home,' she said. 'We're on our way to Dongri.'

Oleg climbed up behind Karla. We rode with her legs wrapped around me on the petrol tank. She was leaning against Oleg, who had his guitar strung on his back.

We cruised past a group of traffic cops, waiting at a crossing to bring down a zebra or two in the jungle street.

'*Vicaru naka*,' I said in Marathi. *Don't ask.*

847

CHAPTER EIGHTY-NINE

KARLA HADN'T VISITED THE PERFUME BAZAAR IN DONGRI, or anywhere in the area, since the fire at Khaderbhai's mansion. But she mixed her own perfume, and needed her special fragrances. When she finally felt ready to face a page she'd turned without reading, we became a thread in the tightly woven carpet of traffic to visit her favourite shop, just off Mohammed Ali Road.

Great Ali, one of three cousin-brothers named Ali in his family, the others being Sad Ali and Considerate Ali, welcomed us into his shop, settling us on cushions.

'I'll pour some tea, Karla Madame,' Considerate Ali said.

'It has been so long,' Sad Ali said. 'We've missed you.'

'I have your private selection ready for you, Karla Madame,' Great Ali said.

We drank tea, while Karla examined her special essences and listened to a story about a rare perfume, carried from a rare corner of the rarefied world.

As we were leaving, the large elderly merchant, dressed in white, asked if he could inhale Karla's own perfume, but once. Karla obliged, extending the frond of her slender wrist, the palm of her hand falling like a leaf in the rain.

The perfume traders all inhaled several times professionally, and then shook their heads doubtfully.

'One of these days,' Great Ali said, as we left, 'I will discover the secret of your bouquet.'

'Never say die,' Karla replied.

We walked the street again, on the way back to the bike, Karla's small vials of precious scents and oils jingling softly in a black velvet bag. After a few steps, we saw two men we knew well from the old days of the Khaderbhai Company. They crossed to the footpath near us.

Salar and Azim were street guys, who'd spent years on the lowest tier of Company condescension. While favoured sons died, they survived there in the shallows long enough to find higher positions in the new Khaled Company, desperate to replace its fallen soldiers.

They wore new Company clothes, and fidgeted with their new gold chains and bracelets, still finding the right place to carry the burden of obedience.

They'd known Karla since before my time with the Company, and liked her. They told her a scary-funny gangster story, because they knew she'd like it. She did, and responded with a scary-funny bad-girl story. They laughed, throwing their heads back, their gold necklaces catching the evening light.

'So long, guys,' I said. '*Allah hafiz.*'

'Where you going?' Salar asked.

'Back to the bike, on Mohammed Ali Road.'

'We'll walk with you. There's a short cut, through here. We'll show you.'

'We're going *this* way,' I said. 'Might do some more shopping. *Allah hafiz.*'

'*Khuda hafiz,*' Azim replied, waving goodbye.

I didn't want to walk anywhere with Khaled Company men, or any soldiers, from any Company. I didn't want to reminisce. I didn't even want to remember.

For the thousandth time, I thought about leaving the Island City with Karla, and setting up somewhere else on a remote beach. You can't escape the Company in the city. The Company *is* the city. You can only escape the Company in a place where there's nothing left to own.

We walked through thin crowds, and we were about to cross the cobbled entrance to a side alley, when screams ripped silken peace, and people ran panicked from the entrance to the alleyway.

I glanced at Karla, wanting to be somewhere else. We both knew, or suspected, that Salar and Azim must be involved. We'd known them for years, but Company street wars weren't my problem any more, and I was ready to leave.

Karla wasn't: she urged me forward, and we edged closer to look. A man came staggering out of the alley and stumbled into me. It was

Salar. He was bloody, all over. He'd been stabbed several times in the chest and stomach. He collapsed against me, and I held him in my arms.

I glanced past him and saw Azim, face down, and pulsing the last of his blood into the stones of the alley.

'I'll get a cab,' Karla said, darting away.

Salar lifted his hand, with effort, and tugged at his gold neck-chain until it broke.

'For my sister,' he said, pressing it against me.

I put the chain in my pocket, and took a firm grip around his waist.

'I can't let you lie down, brother,' I said. 'I wish I could, but I'll never get you up again in one piece, if I do. Karla's got a taxi coming. Hold on, man.'

'I'm done for, Lin. Leave me. *Y'Allah*, the pain!'

'I don't know how, but they missed your lungs, Salar. You're still breathing air. You're gonna make it, man. Just hold on.'

Karla arrived in two minutes, swinging the door of the taxi open. We bundled Salar into the back with me, while Karla gave instructions from the front seat.

I don't know how much she paid the taxi driver, but he didn't blink at the blood, and got us to GT Hospital in record time, driving against the flow of traffic.

At the hospital entrance, orderlies and nurses put Salar on a gurney, and wheeled him inside. I started to go with them into the hospital, but Karla stopped me.

'You can't go anywhere looking like that, my love,' she said.

The shirt and T-shirt under my cut-off vest were smothered in blood. I took the vest off, but it only made the splash of blood across my T-shirt look worse.

'To hell with it. We've gotta stay with Salar until the Company gets here. The guys who did this might try again, and we can't call the cops to help.'

'Just a minute,' Karla said.

She stopped a lawyer, walking toward us briskly, his white court-collar stiff with presumptions and his client papers bunched against his arm to prevent escape.

'I'll give you ten thousand rupees for your jacket,' Karla said, waving a fan of notes.

The lawyer looked at the money, squinted at her, and started emptying the pockets of his one-thousand-rupee jacket. Karla dressed me with crossed lapels, and a turned-up collar. She cleaned the smudges off, licking her fingers and wiping them over my face.

'Let's go see how Salar is doing,' she said, leading me into the hospital.

We waited in a corridor, near the operating theatre. Black and white tiles, begging for a pattern unsquared, met grey-green walls showing low-tide marks from the hypnotic mops of tired cleaners. Function is servant or master, and wherever it rules, suffering sits in corridors purged of consideration.

'Are you okay, kid?'

'I'm good,' she smiled. 'You?'

'I'm —'

Four young Khaled Company gangsters clamped along the corridor, pushing attitude. Their leader, Faaz-Shah, was a hothead, and for some reason it got hotter when he saw me.

'What the fuck are you doing here?' he demanded, stopping a few paces away.

I stood up in front of Karla, my hand on a knife. She knew most of the older gangsters in the Company, but not many of the young volcanoes.

'*Salaam aleikum*,' I said.

Faaz-Shah hesitated, looking for something he couldn't find in my eyes. I'd fought beside two of his older brothers, in battles with other gangs. And I'd fought beside Khaled, their new leader. I'd never fought beside Faaz-Shah.

'*Wa aleikum salaam*,' he said more softly. 'What happened to Salar? Why are you here?'

'Why weren't *you* here?' I asked. 'How did you hear about it?'

'We have people in the hospital,' he said. 'We have people everywhere.'

'Not in the alley, where Azim and Salar got knifed.'

'Azim?'

'He was gone, bled-out, when I saw him.'

'Where was this?'

They were hard young gangsters, the kind who always find a bad mood, no matter how hard you try to hide it, and they were angry.

I was safe, because I was the guy who simply did the right thing, and sooner or later they'd know that. But none of them were safe, if they got angry enough to get mouthy with Karla.

'Karla,' I said, smiling her with me, 'can you please find out if there's some tea, somewhere?'

'Be a pleasure,' she said, smiling back mystery as she walked past the young gangsters.

'It was the first open gully, on Mohammed Ali,' I said, when Karla left. 'Coming from the perfume bazaar, heading back to the city. I met them, just before it happened.'

'You what?'

'We were in the bazaar, and we ran across Salar and Azim. We talked, and we kept walking. They took a short cut, through the alleys. By the time we walked around to the open gully, it was all over. Salar fell into my arms. Someone was waiting for them.'

I opened the black jacket, showing the blood, and closed it again. They were abashed, as gangsters are, when they realise that they're in a debt of honour.

'We got him here in a taxi,' I said, sitting down. 'We've been waiting, to see if he's okay, after surgery. You can join us, if you like. Karla's bringing tea.'

'We've got things to do,' Faaz-Shah said.

'We've also been waiting for someone from the Company to sit with Salar. He's not safe here. Leave a man with him, Faaz-Shah.'

'I need every man I've got. And you're here. You're still loyal to the Company, aren't you?'

'Which Company is it now?'

He laughed, and then stopped hard on a different thought.

'I really do need all my men tonight. He's family, you know.'

'Salar?'

'Yes. He's an uncle of mine. His family's on the way. I'd appreciate it, if you'd stay until they get here.'

'Done. And keep this for him,' I said, pulling the chain from my pocket. 'He wants it to go to his sister, if he doesn't make it.'

'I'll give it to her.'

He accepted the chain gingerly, as if he expected it to move in his hand, and then scrunched it into a pocket. He looked at me, his eyes floating on reluctant shores.

'I owe you on this, Lin,' he said.

'You don't.'

'I do,' he said, clenching his teeth.

'Okay then, transfer the debt to Miss Karla. If you ever hear any-thing that might harm her, warn her about it, or me, and we'll be square. Okay?'

'Okay,' he said. '*Khuda hafiz.*'

'*Allah hafiz,*' I replied, watching them stamp out, shields of revenge in their eyes.

I was glad to be out. I was glad to be *carrying* the wounded, instead of wounding them, I guess, just as Concannon was glad to be burying them, instead of killing them. In that grey-green silence, the smell of disinfectant, bleached linen and bitter medicine was suddenly too medical, and my heart was beating fast.

For a few seconds, emotions running on habit had stamped out into the night with Faaz-Shah and the others, riding to war before we knew it was declared. All that fight and fear rushed back into me, as if I'd already fought a battle. And then I realised that I didn't have to fight it. Not this time. Not ever again.

CHAPTER NINETY

I LOOKED UP FROM BRUTAL THOUGHTS AND SAW KARLA, walking toward me slowly down the long hospital corridor. She had a man with her. He was a cleaner, dressed in the working clothes of a *peon*, or someone who does menial work. Karla's face was brilliant with light, her smile a secret, waiting to be told.

She sat the man next to me.

'You absolutely have to meet this man, and hear his story,' Karla said. 'Dev, meet Shantaram. Shantaram, meet Dev.'

'*Namaste*,' I said. 'Pleased to meet you.'

'Please tell him, Dev,' Karla said, smiling at me.

'But it is not a very entertaining story, and it is sad. Perhaps another time.'

He started to rise from the seat, but we eased him down gently again.

'Please, Dev,' Karla urged. 'Just tell him, as you told it to me.'

'But I could lose my job,' he said uncertainly, 'if I don't return to my duties.'

'Good,' Karla said. 'Because, when we leave here, you're coming with us.'

He looked at me. I smiled back.

'Whatever she says,' I said.

'I can't do that,' he said. 'I have a shift to finish.'

'First the story, please, Dev,' Karla said. 'Then we'll finish at the start.'

'Well, as I was telling you while we were waiting for the chai,' he began, looking at his hands. 'My name is Dev, and I am a sadhu.'

His head was shaved, and he wore no amulets or bracelets. Beyond his uniform, he was stripped clean. He was a very simple, lean man, with a cap on his head and bare feet.

His face was stronger than the man, though, and his eyes, when he raised them, still burned fires on beaches.

Shiva sadhus cover themselves with ashes from the crematoria, talk to ghosts, and summon demons, even if only in their own minds. The body language was submissive, but the face was indomitable.

'I had long dreadlocks once,' he mused. 'They're antennae, you know, for people who smoke. I never went without a smoke, with my dreads. Now, with shaved head, no stranger will share a glass of water with me.'

'Why did you shave them off, Dev?' I asked.

'I shamed myself,' he said. 'I was at the peak of my powers. Lord Shiva walked step by step with me. Snakes could not bite me. I slept with them, in the forest. Leopards visited me, waking me with kisses. Scorpions lived in my hair, but never stung me. No man could look into the eyes of my penance without flinching.'

He stopped, and looked at me, his eyes still roaming with the wild, and the dead.

'It's greed, you know,' he said. 'Greed is the key. Follow the greed to the sin. I was greedy for more power. I cursed a man, a foreigner, who challenged me on the street. I cursed him, told him that his riches would bring him ruin, and when I did that, every one of my powers drained from me like rain on a window.'

The hairs on my arms were standing up, and I looked at Karla, sitting on the other side of the holy-man-cleaner. She nodded.

'Were there two foreigners that day?' I asked.

'Yes. One of them was very kind. An Englishman. The other was very rude, but I regret what I did. I regret any harm I may have caused him. I regret my betrayal of my own penance. I tried to find the man, but I couldn't, although I searched everywhere, and I couldn't lift my own curse.'

'Dev,' Karla said. 'We know this man. We know the man you cursed. We can take you there, to meet him.'

The shaven sadhu crumpled, taking short breaths, and then slowly sat upright again.

'Is it true?'

'Yes, Dev,' Karla said.

'Are you okay, Dev?' I asked, a hand on his thin shoulder.

'Yes, yes,' he said. 'Maa! Maa!'

'Do you want to lie down for a while?' I asked.

'No, I'm fine. I'm fine. I'm ... I ... lost my way, and I started drinking alcohol. I wasn't used to it. I'd never had it in my life. I did bad things. Then a great saint stopped me, in the street, and took me to his Kali temple.'

He looked up quickly, as if breaking the surface for air.

'Do you really know this man I cursed?' he asked, his voice trembling.

'We do,' I said.

'And will he see me? Will he allow me to lift the curse?'

'I think he will,' Karla said, smiling.

'They say Maa Kali is terrifying,' he said to me, his hand on my arm. 'But only to hypocrites. If your heart is innocent, She cannot help but love you. She's the Mother of the universe, and we are Her children. How could She not love us, if we make a place of innocence for Her inside ourselves?'

He was silent, breathing hard for a moment before he calmed himself, a hand on his heart.

'Are you sure you're quite well, Dev?' Karla asked.

'I am,' he said. 'Thanks to Maa, I'm well. It's just a bit of a shock.'

'How did you come to be here, Dev?' I asked.

'I shaved my head, and I came to this place, doing the most humble job I could find, serving the helpless and afraid. And now my question has been answered, because you found me here, to bring me to this man. Please, take this.'

He handed me a laminated card that was blank on one side, and had a design on the other. I slipped it into my vest pocket.

'What is it, Dev?' Karla asked.

'It's a yantra,' he replied. 'If you look at it with a truthful heart, it will clear the negative from your mind, so that you can make wise, caring choices.'

'We're waiting for news of our friend,' I said. 'Can we get anything for you, Dev?'

'I'm very fine,' he said, sitting back against the bench. 'Am I really resigning from my job?'

'It would seem so, Dev,' Karla said.

Salar's relatives arrived, escorted by two Company men, and the news came through that Salar was going to live.

We took Dev, the penitent holy man, to the penthouse floor of the Mahesh hotel. We watched Scorpio fall to his knees, and the sadhu fall with him, and we turned and went back to the elevator.

'You know,' she said, as we waited. 'This might be just the thing to give Gemini's immune system a jolt.'

'It just might,' I said, as the elevator pinged.

'I know where we're going,' Karla said, passing the flask back to me on the way down.

'You think you're so smart,' I said, pulling the lawyer's black jacket around my blood-stained shirt.

'We're going to get your bike,' she said. 'She's still on Mohammed Ali Road, and you care more about *her* than you do about getting cleaned up.'

She was so smart, and reminded me from time to time on the ride back to the Amritsar hotel. My happily rescued bike hummed machine mantras all the way home.

When we tumbled into her rooms, Karla freshened up, and left the bathroom for me.

I emptied my pockets onto the wide porcelain bench beneath the mirror. The money in my pockets was stained with blood. My keys were red, and the coins I spilled on the bench were discoloured, as if having been in a wishing fountain too long.

I put the knives and scabbards on the bench, dropped the lawyer's suit jacket on the floor, and let the bloody shirt slide off my just as bloody T-shirt.

As I tossed it away, I noticed the card that Dev had given me. I picked it up, and placed it on the bench. I looked into the mirror for the first time, meeting myself like a stranger in a meadow.

I looked away from my own stare, and tried to forget what I couldn't stop thinking.

The T-shirt was a gift from Karla. One of her artist protégées had made it, copying the knife-work of an artist known for biting the canvas that feeds him.

There were slashes, rips and tears all over the front. Karla liked it, I think, because she liked the artist who made it. I liked it, because it was incomplete, and unique.

I pulled it off carefully, hoping to soak the blood from it, but when I looked into the mirror, I let it fall into the sink.

The T-shirt had left a mark in blood on my chest. It was a triangle, upside down, with star-shapes around it. I looked at the card that Dev had given me. It was almost the same design.

India.

I let the card fall from my fingers, and stared into what I'd let myself become. I looked at the design on my chest. I asked the question we all ask sooner or later, if we stay in India long enough.

What do you want from me, India? What do you want from me, India? What do you want from me?

My heart was breaking on a wheel of coincidence, each foolish accident more significant than the next. *If you look at it with a truthful heart*, the sadhu said when he gave me the card. *Wise, caring choices.*

I escaped from a prison, where I had no choice, and cut my life down to a single choice, everywhere, with everyone but Karla: stay, or go.

What do you want from me, India?

What did the blood-design mean? If it was a message, written in another man's blood, was it a warning? Or was it one of those affirmations that Idriss talked about? Was I going mad, asking the question, and searching for a significance that couldn't exist?

I stumbled into the shower, watching red water run into the drain. The water ran clean at last, and I turned it off, but leaned against the wall, my palms flat against the tiles, my head down.

Was it a message? I heard myself asking without asking. *A message in blood on my chest?*

My knives clattered off the bench onto the tiled floor, startling me. I stepped out of the shower to pick up the knives, and slipped on the wet floor. Clutching at the knives as I steadied myself, I cut the inside of my hand.

I put the knives down, and cut myself again. I hadn't cut myself with those knives in a year of practice. Blood ran into the basin, spilling onto the card I'd dropped. I scooped the card out of the basin, and dried it off.

I ran my hand under the cold tap, and used a towel to press the cuts closed. I cleaned my knives and put them away safely. And I stared at the card, and into the mirror, for quite a while.

I found Karla on the balcony, a thin blue robe over her shoulders. I wanted to see her like that every day, for the rest of my life, but I had to go out. I had something to do.

'We gotta go out again,' I said. 'I've got something I have to do.'

'A mystery! Hey, speaking of, is that a bandage on your hand?'

'It's nothing,' I said. 'Are you up for another ride? The sun will be up soon.'

'I'll be ready before you are,' she said, slipping off the robe. 'I hope you haven't got anything scary in mind.'

'No.'

'It's just finding Dev for Scorpio and Gemini, by taking Salar to the hospital, by being in the perfume bazaar, I think we've used up our quota of karmic coincidence, Shantaram. We shouldn't push our luck.'

'Nothing scary, I promise,' I said. 'Unsettling, maybe. But not scary.'

By the time we reached the shrine at Haji Ali, pearl banners announced the Sun, the sky-king, waking devotion. Early pilgrims, pleaders and penitents were on the path to the shrine. Beggars with no arms or legs, arranged in a ring by their attendants, chanted the names of Allah, as passers-by put coins or notes in their circle of necessity.

Children visiting the shrine for the first time wore their best clothes: the boys in sweating suits, copied from movie stars, the girls with their hair pulled fiercely into decorated traps at the back of their heads.

I stopped us, halfway to the shrine, halfway to the sleeping saint.

'This is it,' I said.

'You're not going to pray today?'

'Not . . . today,' I said, looking left and right at the people passing by.

'So, what *are* you going to do?'

There was a pause in the flow of people, and we were alone for a few seconds. I pulled my knives from their scabbards and threw them into the sea, one at a time.

Karla watched the knives whirl through the air. It was the best whirling I ever did, it seemed to me, before they whirled into vanishing sea.

We stood for a while, watching the waves.

'What happened, Shantaram?'

'I'm not sure.'

I handed her the card with the yantra design that Dev had given to me.

'When I took my shirt off, that design was on my chest. It was almost exactly the same, painted on me in Salar's blood.'

'You think it's a sign?' she asked. 'Is that it?'

859

'I don't know. I . . . I was asking myself that same question, and then I cut my hand on my knife. I just . . . I think I'm done with this. It's weird. I'm not the religious type.'

'But you are the spiritual type.'

'I'm not. I'm really not, Karla.'

'You are, and you just don't know it. That's one of the things I love most about you.'

We were silent again for a while, listening to the waves: the sound that wind makes, surfing through trees.

'If you think I'm throwing my *gun* in there,' she said, breaking the silence, 'you're crazy.'

'Keep your gun,' I laughed. 'Me, I'm done. If I can't fix it with my hands, from now on, then I probably deserve what's coming. And anyway, you've got a gun, and we're always together.'

She wanted the long way home, even though we were stamp-foot tired, and she got it.

When we'd ridden long enough with her new understanding of a slightly different me, we returned to the Amritsar, and showered off the last dust of doubt. I found her smoking a joint on the same balcony we'd left, an hour before, in the same blue robe.

'You could've hit a fish on the head with one of those knives,' she said. 'When you threw them in the sea.'

'Fish are like you, baby. They're pretty quick.'

'What you did before, with the knives. Did you mean it?'

'I mean to try.'

'Then I'm in it with you,' she said, kissing my face. 'All the way.'

'Even if it takes us out of Bombay?'

'Especially if it takes us out of Bombay.'

She drew the curtains to hide the day, and slipped off her robe to try out the mirror from Ahmed's Old House of Style. They both looked good. She put some funk on her music system and funked at me, all mermaid arms and hips. I held her. She put her hands around my neck, and swayed in front of me.

'Let's go a little nuts,' she said. 'I think we deserve it.'

CHAPTER NINETY-ONE

LOVE AND FAITH, LIKE HOPE AND JUSTICE, are constellations in the infinity of truth. And they always pull a crowd. So many excited coffee devotees crowded into the Love & Faith café on its opening night that Rannveig called and told us to come a little later, because love and faith alone couldn't guarantee a place.

We found Didier at Leo's, happily insulted by two waiters at the same time, and giving the service that he got. Leopold's was sit-down jumping. People laughed at anything and shouted at nothing with happy determination. It looked like fun, but we had somewhere to go.

'Just one drink,' Didier pleaded. 'Love & Faith has no alcohol. Have you ever heard of such a thing?'

'One drink,' Karla said, sitting beside him. 'And not a mood-fluctuation more.'

'Waiter!' Didier called.

'You think you're the only customer who ever got thirsty in this place?' Sweetie asked, flicking a rag at the table.

'Bring alcohol, you fool!' Didier snapped. 'I have a curfew.'

'And I have a life,' Sweetie said, slouching away.

'Gotta give you credit, Didier,' I said. 'You got things back to normal. I've never seen Sweetie surlier.'

'What is credit,' Didier preened, 'but something you have to give back, with interest.'

'Lin's unarmed, Didier, and naked to the world,' Karla said. 'He threw his knives into the sea this morning.'

'The sea will throw them back again,' Didier said. 'The sea can't get over it that we crawled onto the land. Mark my words, Lin. The sea is a jealous woman, without the charming personality.'

A man approached our table carrying a parcel. It was Vikrant, the

861

knife-maker, and for a second I felt a twinge of guilt that his superbly made instruments, my knives, were on the bottom of a shallow sea.

'Hi, Karla,' he said. 'I've been looking for you, Lin. Your sword is finished.'

He unwrapped the calico parcel, revealing Khaderbhai's sword. It had been repaired with gold rivets, and they'd been moulded into the eyes of two dragons, meeting at the tail.

It was beautiful work, but it was a painful thing to remember the sword. I'd forgotten it, in the year of mountains and burning mansions, and it shamed me to know that I had.

'I rest my case,' Didier said. 'The sea is a jealous woman. Didier is never wrong.'

'You can take the boy from the sword,' Karla said, 'but you can't take the sword from the boy.'

'It's beautiful work,' I said. 'How much do I owe you, Vikrant?'

'That was a true labour of love,' he said, moving away. 'It's on me. Don't kill anyone with it. Bye, Karla.'

'Bye, Vikrant.'

The drinks arrived, and we were about to toast, but I stopped us with a raised hand.

'Take a look at that girl over there,' I said.

'Lin, it is hardly gallant to remark on another woman, when a woman is in your —'

'Just take a good look at her, Didier.'

'Do you think it's her?' Karla asked.

'Oh, yeah.'

'Who?' Didier demanded.

'Karlesha,' Karla said. 'It's Oleg's Karlesha.'

'Is it really!'

The girl was tall and looked a little like Karla, with black hair and pale green eyes. She was wearing skin-tight black jeans, a black motor-cycle shirt and cowboy boots.

'Karlesha,' Karla muttered. 'Not bad style.'

'Sweetie,' I called, and the waiter shuffled over to me. 'Have you still got that picture Oleg gave you?'

He scraped through his pockets petulantly, and produced a wrinkled photo. We held it up against the face of the girl, sitting five tables away.

'Call Oleg, and get your reward,' I said. 'That's the girl he's been waiting for, over there.'

He goggled at the photograph for a while, looked at the girl, and scurried away to the phone.

'Are we about done?' I asked.

'You don't want to stay, and see Oleg and Karlesha reunited?' Karla teased.

'I'm tired of being Fate's unwilling accomplice,' I said.

'I *must* see the reunion,' Didier said. 'And I will not move from this spot until I have witnessed it with my own eyes.'

'Okay,' I said, ready to leave.

A man approached our table. He was short, thin, dark-skinned and confident.

'Excuse me,' he said, 'are you the one they call Shantaram?'

'Who wants to know?' Didier snapped.

'My name is Tateef, and I have something to discuss with Mr Shantaram.'

'Discuss away,' Karla said, waving a hand at me.

'I hear you are a man who will do anything for money,' Tateef said.

'That's a mighty offensive thing to say, Tateef,' Karla said, smiling.

'It certainly is,' Didier agreed. 'How much money?'

I held up my hand to stop the auction.

'We've got an appointment, Tateef,' I said. 'Come back at three, tomorrow. We'll talk.'

'Thank you,' he said. 'Goodnight to all.'

He slipped between the tables, and out into the street.

'You don't even know what he has in mind, this, this, *Tateef*,' Didier warned.

'I liked the look of him. Didn't you?'

'*I* did,' Karla said. 'And I think we're gonna see him again.'

'Certainly not,' Didier puffed. 'Did you not see his shoes?'

'Of course,' I said. 'Military half-boot, white on the sides with salt, and on the edges of his jacket. My guess is that he's spent a lot of time at sea, recently.'

'I mean the *style*, Lin,' Didier sighed. 'They were hideous. I have seen *taxidermy* with more style.'

'Bye, Didier,' Karla said, standing. 'See you at the opening.'

Karla and I rode beside the crowded night causeway, and found a bigger crowd a few blocks away at the opening of the Love & Faith coffee shop, spilling onto the footpath and a splash of the road. We parked the bike outside, and sat there for a while.

The sign over the door, showing symbols from all faiths and written in Hindi, Marathi and English, was lit with a circle of white magnolia lights.

A crimson halo of frangipani lights framed the street window, showing customers inside drinking espresso, while Vinson and Rannveig worked the Italian coffee machine, steam rising industrially.

There were three empty stools in the curved counter of fifteen. Rannveig had reserved them for us, but I wasn't ready, yet, to go into that corner of affection they'd created.

My thoughts were of a girl from Norway, seen in a locket one hour, and seen standing in Fate's shadow an hour later. I looked at her, smiling in love and faith's window, already in her own forever. Vinson exchanged a quick glance with her, smiled quickly, and talked happily to a customer.

I didn't want to go inside. There was a purity in the thing they'd become together that I didn't want to disturb.

'I'm staying here, for a minute,' I said, standing beside the bike. 'You can go ahead. I'll be there in a minute.'

'Always together,' Karla said, sitting on the bike again, and lighting a joint.

Didier joined us, a calming hand against his breathless chest.

'What happened?' Karla asked.

Didier held a hand out to stop her, regaining his breath.

'Is . . . is . . . is my place still reserved, inside?' Didier gasped.

'Front and centre,' I said. 'What happened, with Oleg and Karlesha?'

'Oleg ran inside,' Didier replied, his heart slowing to medicated levels again, 'and he just picked her up, like a sack of onions, and walked out with her into the night.'

'You didn't follow them?' Karla asked, laughing.

'Of course,' Didier said. 'Didier is a detective of the Lost Love Bureau, after all.'

'Where did they go?' I asked.

'He disappeared,' Didier hissed, 'in Randall's limousine. He is exasperating, that Randall.'

'In the nicest possible ways,' Karla said.

'Are you not going inside?' Didier asked, looking at the crowd laughing in the new café.

'We're gonna sit here for a while,' Karla said. 'Go ahead, Didier. Class the joint up.'

'Then it is Didier who must raise the flag for love and faith,' he said, draping his scarf over his shoulder. 'We live in the age of opening your mouth as wide as you can. Watch me, as I scream and shout for us.'

He straightened his jacket, crossed the footpath and embraced his way inside. He sat beside a young businessman, stumbling into the handsome victim as he sat. The businessman liked it, and began talking brightly.

We sat down and we watched the bustling, successful opening for a while in silence, and then Karla leaned against me.

'I like bike-talk,' she said. 'Even when we're side by side.'

'So do I.'

'You wanna know who Kavita Singh's new silent partner is?' she asked softly.

'Will it scare me?'

'Probably,' she replied.

'Good. Tell me.'

'Madame Zhou,' Karla said.

'How did *that* happen?'

'Madame Zhou wanted to blackmail her former clients, and make a comeback as a power broker in Bombay. Fate, with a little help, brought her to Kavita. Zhou has a book, with a record of every customer she ever had, and every sexual preference. I'd like to read it, actually, when they're done with it.'

'Why did Zhou come to Kavita for help?'

'I put the idea in her head.'

'How?'

'You want all the answers, don't you?'

'I want all the everything, when it comes to you,' I laughed.

'I knew about the book, and I knew she was weakened, without the Palace, but still ambitious. I also knew the name of her most loyal patron. He's a businessman, and I bought his business. In exchange, he suggested that the ideal person to broker the blackmail ring was Kavita Singh. That's when Madame Zhou started getting interested in Kavita.'

'And when the twins were killed, she went to Kavita for help.'

'Just as I'd hoped she would. Vices live in habits, and habits make people predictable.'

'What does Kavita get out of it?'

'Apart from the sex?'

'Please, Karla, don't —'

'I'm kidding. I told Kavita, six weeks ago, that it was Madame Zhou who killed her boyfriend. Her fiancée, actually. He objected to Madame Zhou's bribery of officials, in his area. He was getting a following. She killed him for it.'

'How did *you* know who did it?'

'Do you really wanna know?'

'Well, I . . . '

'It was Lisa.'

'Okay, Lisa? How did *she* know?'

'She was working for Madame Zhou at the time, at the Palace of Happy. It was before I got her out of there.'

'And burned the place down.'

'And burned the place down. Lisa couldn't tell Kavita what she knew, so she told me.'

'Why couldn't Lisa tell Kavita?'

'You know how Lisa was. She couldn't talk to anyone she was having sex with.'

'I'm beginning to think you knew her better than I did.'

'No,' she said, smiling softly. 'But we did have an understanding about you.'

'She said something to me about that. How she met you at Kayani's, and talked about us.'

She laughed gently.

'You really wanna know what happened?'

'Again, with the really wanna know?' I smiled.

'I kept tabs on you, from the moment you walked away from me. At first, I was happy for you, because you seemed to be happy with Lisa. But I knew Lisa, and I knew she'd mess it up.'

'Wait a minute. You were checking on me, for two years?'

'Of course. I love you.'

So clear, so light: trust in a human eye.

'How does this . . . ' I began, recollecting myself, 'connect to your little understanding with Lisa?'

She smiled, sadly.

'I heard that Lisa was back to her wicked ways, and was
around on you, a lot, and that you didn't know about it.'

'I didn't ask about it.'

'I know that,' she said. 'But everyone was talking about it. Eve
except you.'

'It doesn't matter. It didn't matter.'

'It wasn't right, because you're better than that, and you des
better than that. So, I walked up behind her one day, at her favou
dress shop, and tapped her on the shoulder.'

'And what did you say to her?'

'I told her to tell you exactly what she was doing, and let you deci
if you wanted to stay, or to stop slutting around.'

'Slutting around? That's pretty harsh.'

'Harsh? There wasn't a man or a woman safe at that art gallery,
including the customers. I could have cared less, except that she was
doing it to you.'

'And you made some kind of agreement with her?'

'Not then. I gave her a chance. I loved her. You know how easy it was
to love her, when you were looking at her. But she didn't change. So I
sat down with her at Kayani's and told her that I love you, and I didn't
want her to hurt you any more.'

'What did she say?'

'She agreed to let you go. She wasn't in love with you, but she was
deep in like with you. She said she wanted to do it a piece at a time,
and not just disappear in a cold break.'

'You broke us up, Lisa and me?' I asked, disturbed by a gust of truth.
'Is that what happened?'

'Not exactly,' she sighed. 'I can see her face, when I found her, on
the bed. I remember what I said to her. If you don't tell the truth, and
you keep on hurting him, I'll stop you.'

'And you meant it? Even though you loved her?'

'Every dinner you went to with Lisa in that last year,' she said quietly,
'you were dining with her lovers, husband and wife both, sometimes,
and you were the only one at the table who didn't know it. I'm sorry.'

'She was out a lot, and I never asked her. I was away a lot, and I
couldn't tell her where I'd been, or what I'd been smuggling. She was
in trouble, and I didn't realise it.'

trouble. When she agreed to stop
...ani's, she made a pass at me.'

...eautiful, crazy and popular.'

...ght you were naïve. But you're not. You're
...bout you. I love being trusted. Trust is the
...neant so much to me that you didn't give up
...o me that we did it apart on trust, than if we'd
...ou know what I mean?'
...ve're in it together from now on, Karla.'
...om now on,' she repeated, leaning against me.
...ched out for me, all that time?'
...u never left the city, as you said you might.'
...Not while you were still here.'
...us people were laughing and joking on the footpath
...& Faith. I scanned the street for threats, taking in every
..., drug dealer and racketeer working the edges of the herd.
...y: illicitly quiet.
...ever told anyone what Lisa said, that Madame Zhou ordered
...ng?'
...ept the secret to myself, until the time was right. Now Kavita
...s, and she'll keep Madame Zhou close, until she has the book.
...n she'll introduce Madame Zhou to her little friend, karma.'
Madame Zhou and Kavita? It seemed to me like a double-headed coin,
...xed to hurt someone no matter how it landed.

'Let me get this straight: Madame Zhou doesn't know that Kavita is
the fiancée of a guy she killed, what, four years ago?'

'That's right. Kavita Singh isn't her real name. She was in London,
freelancing, when her boyfriend was killed. She came back, used a
byline name, and worked for Ranjit. She always hoped to find out what
happened to her boyfriend one day, working as a journalist. I waited
until Kavita was strong enough to confront and defeat Madame Zhou,
and get away with it. I built her up, and gave her power. And then, the
day she was waiting for came knocking, and I told her.'

'So, Kavita's watching Madame Zhou, who's using her to shake
down people in the book to get back the power she lost, and when
Kavita gets the book, she'll get rid of Madame Zhou?'

'That's it. Chess, played by dangerous women.'

'How long till Kavita gets that book?'

'Not long.'

'Will Kavita use the book, once she gets it?'

'Oh, yeah,' Karla laughed. 'Making ocean-going vessels of

'I don't know which one of them is scarier, Kavita or M
Zhou.'

'I told you that you misjudged Kavita,' she said.

'I don't judge anyone. I want a world without stones, or people
throw them at.'

'I know that,' she laughed.

'What's so funny?'

'Something Didier said, about you.'

'What?'

'Lin has a good heart, which is inexcusable.'

'Thank you, I think.'

'You wanna know who's got the third office, downstairs?'

'This is certainly a night for revelations. You're enjoying this, aren't
you?'

'Absolutely,' she said. 'You wanna know who's behind door number
three, or don't ya?'

'Of course I do. I wanna see the *tunnel*, which I still haven't seen.'

'You won't sign the non-disclosure agreement.'

'Every time you sign a legal document, Fate takes a day off.'

'It's Johnny Cigar,' she said.

'In room number three?'

'Yeah.'

'When will you stop stealing my characters? You've got half a novel
at the Amritsar, and I haven't even written it yet.'

'Johnny's starting a real estate business,' she said, ignoring me ador-
ably. 'He's specialising in slum relocation.'

'Here comes the neighbourhood.'

'I financed him,' she said. 'With the last of Ranjit's baptism money.'

I thought for a while about the multiplying ménage at the Amritsar
hotel.

'Even with Karlesha back,' I said, 'Oleg's not leaving, is he?'

'I hope not,' she smiled. 'And so do you. You like that guy.'

'I do like him. And I'd like him better one degree less chirpy.'

869

't?'

'...r Diva. One way or another, that girl
...nd close.'

'...t to hope for something I wasn't
...will never give up on Diva. No
...And if you put an Indian and
...get a guy who can't give up on

...ith gathered on the footpath, holding up
...ny exchanging them.

...out?'

...r the T-shirt version of what Idriss was saying? The one
...gave Vinson?'

...eah.'

'Vinson and Rannveig used Randall's notes, from what Idriss said,
and they put his quotes on T-shirts. They're giving them away as open-
ing-night gifts.'

A young man, not far from us, was holding a T-shirt up to read it. I
read it with him, over his shoulder.

A heart
filled with greed, pride or hateful feelings
is not free.

When I heard Idriss say it, on the mountain, I agreed with it, and I
was glad to see it preserved and living, somehow, in the world, even
just on a T-shirt. And I also had to admit that I'd found shares of greed
and pride inside myself, and too often.

But I wasn't alone any more. As Rannveig said, I'd reconnected.

'What do you think?' Karla asked me, watching people swap quota-
tions from Idriss on their free T-shirts.

'Teachers, like writers, never die while people still quote them.'

'I love you, Shantaram,' she said, cuddling in beside me.

I looked at the happy, laughing group, crammed into the narrow
coffee shop. The people we'd lost, in our Island City years, would fill
the same space.

Too many, too many dead who were still alive, whenever I thought

of them. And almost all of them were lives that humil
would've saved. Vikram, Nazeer, Tariq, Sanjay, Vishnu, a
names chanted at me, always ending in Abdullah, my brot
my brother.

Karla relaxed against me, her foot tapping to the music co
Love & Faith. I tipped her face to the light until she was the l
kissed her, and we were one.

Truth is the freedom of the soul. We're very young, in this y
universe, and we often fail, and dishonour ourselves, even if onl
the caves of the mind. We fight, when we should dance. We compet
cheat and punish innocent nature.

But that isn't what we are, it's simply what we do in the world that
we made for ourselves, and we can freely change what we do, and the
world we made, every second that we live.

In all the things that really matter, we are one. Love and faith,
trust and empathy, family and friendship, sunsets and songs of awe:
in every wish born in our humanity we are one. Our humankind, at
this moment in our destiny, is a child blowing on a dandelion, without
thought or understanding. But the wonder in the child is the wonder
in us, and there's no limit to the good we can do when human hearts
connect. It's the truth of us. It's the story of us. It's the meaning of the
word God: we are one. We are one. We are one.

ity or generosity
d all the other
her, Abdullah,

ning from
ght, and

oung
 in